**THERE ARE TEN MEASURES OF BEAUTY
IN ALL THE WORLD,
THE SAGES SAY ...**

AND NINE OF THESE ARE IN JERUSALEM

One of those rare novels that captures the reader's heart like a love affair, THE TENTH MEASURE is a novel of Ancient Judea, of an indomitable people, and of a valiant and unforgettable woman's passionate struggle to be free.

BRENDA LESLEY SEGAL

THE TENTH MEASURE

BERKLEY BOOKS, NEW YORK

This Berkley book contains the complete
text of the original hardcover edition.
It has been completely reset in a type face
designed for easy reading, and was printed
from new film.

THE TENTH MEASURE

A Berkley Book / published by arrangement with
St. Martin's Press

PRINTING HISTORY
St. Martin's edition published 1980
Berkley edition / July 1981

ISBN: 0-425-05095-5

A BERKLEY BOOK® TM 757,375
Berkley Books are published by Berkley Publishing Corporation,
200 Madison Avenue, New York, New York 10016.
PRINTED IN THE UNITED STATES OF AMERICA

FOR DANNY AND ALIZA,
whom I love beyond measure.

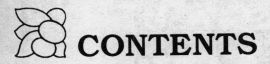

CONTENTS

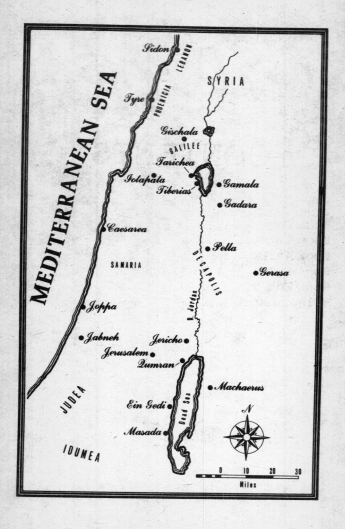

*There are ten measures of beauty in all the world,
the sages say,
and nine of these are in Jerusalem.*

BOOK ONE

IT WAS late in the afternoon when the travelers arrived at Beit Harsom, the house of the Jew, Samuel, in the city of Caesarea. The sun hung red in the sky, like a ripe fruit ready to drop into the sea in that sudden, glorious descent to night which is all there is of twilight in the land of Judea, and a lazy, golden stillness had fallen over the busy port.

The streets were quiet. There seemed to be only the sound of the litter as it wound through the sleeping marketplace, the occasional clop, clop, clop of a Roman soldier's horse, and now and again, mingling with the rush of surf nearby, the echo of the cheering spectators in the great stone amphitheater.

As he passed the swine shops, now shuttered, and the booths with their assortment of amulets, charms, and household gods, Shammai ben Harsom, priest of the Temple, member of the great Sanhedrin, descendant of innumerable priests and princes of Israel, made no attempt to conceal his disdain. The marble statues adorning the neatly laid-out streets, their stone limbs now flushed with pink, did not delight him, nor did the magnificent colossi guarding the harbor, which dazzled the eyes of voyagers far out at sea. Even the classic white temples and graceful palaces that had been visible as far back as the inland hills of Samaria failed to impress the proud Jerusalemite. Passing a synagogue covered with graffiti, the priest wondered, as he always did, and now with even greater concern, why his brother chose to live here and not in the City of David.

His antipathy to Caesarea's distinctly pagan atmosphere was not shared by the young man who stood beside him in the courtyard of the fine villa, for the air was wonderfully spiced with the scent of flowers and sea, the breeze was warm, and the city gave promise of a variety of amusements and adventures. Arching his back a bit so that the sun might fall full upon his face, Josef ben Matthias took a deep breath. As his nostrils filled with the sweet-salt wind, he wondered with some

3

humor how it was that the Lord let his priests freeze in the winter of holy Jerusalem, when here, in what must surely be as strong an outpost of Hellenic culture and Roman power as there was outside of Greece and Rome, it was sweet as summer.

"Ungodly, that's what it is," Shammai muttered, as though divining Josef's thoughts, which in fact he was not. He was still incensed by the defaced synagogue. "An abomination. An utter abomination! Images of stone, men fighting in the arena like beasts, every kind of filth served up . . . Mark my words, we are doomed for allowing Caesarea to exist. I don't care how it serves the Roman purpose. I tell you, no good can come of it. It is a defilement of our sacred soil. Why you live here is beyond me," he went on, upbraiding his brother as the door opened and the man embraced him in welcome.

"So you say every winter," Samuel ben Harsom replied with a smile.

"I would not be here now but for a matter of some importance—"

"Yes, yes. Of course, of course!"

"And to see a little of my family, whom you insist on keeping in this—this—"

"Ungodly place," Samuel finished mildly with a hint of a smile. He turned to Josef and clasped his hand. "This must be the son of Matthias. I have heard wonderful things about you, young man. They say you could recite all the books of the Bible by the time you were fourteen. Well, never mind, we won't ask you to do that for us now, although I trust you will prove an inspiration to my two youngest sons." He suddenly grinned. "On the other hand, my daughter might just prove to be your match. Welcome! Welcome to Beit Harsom," he went on before the astonished Josef could reply.

"Where is Devorah?" Shammai demanded as his brother ushered them past a large, sparkling fountain.

"Inside. We were all sleeping. The whole city is asleep. Come, Devorah makes herself ready for you. The Almighty forbid you report back to Jerusalem that my wife is not more beautiful than ever." He winked at Josef. "Come, come inside where it is cool. Ezra"—he beckoned to a servant—"tell Batya to prepare food for our guests. And see that basins of water and clean linen are brought forth so they may refresh themselves. Make sure the attendants are also cared for. Where are the children? Ah, Shimon . . ." He gestured to a boy who had come silently into the room and now stood yawning in a corner. "Where are the others, Shimon? Where is Joshua? And Benjamin and Alexandra?... Wake them. Tell them we have guests."

"Lexa and Beni are not here," the boy said sullenly. "They've been gone since morning. But I know where they are. On the docks. Talking to sailors."

To his great disappointment, whatever Shimon might have hoped for as a result of this disclosure was not forthcoming; his father was too busy at the moment to do more than wave him away, saying absently, "Yes, yes, well, go and find them. Tell them Uncle Shammai has come from Jerusalem."

Disgusted, the boy began to amble from the room. Suddenly, he heard the priest exclaim sternly, "Docks? Sailors!"

Shimon grinned and eagerly ran from the house, righteously intent on delivering his younger brother and odious sister to the punishment they deserved for going off without him again.

Caesarea was awakening for a last lazy hour of business. The potters were back at their wheels; storekeepers stood at the entrances to their shops issuing invitations to the strolling legionaries; even the whores were out of bed, if not for long. Murmuring to each other as they held lengths of transparent fabric up to the rosy light or bent to sniff some perfumer's vial, they cast sidelong glances at the passing soldiers.

The city was a busy place. Along the Royal Road, from Damascus by way of Scythopolis, caravans loaded with gold and valuable spices wound their way daily to the seacoast town. To the great harbor built by Herod—an artificial basin as large as the famed Piraeus—came ships from every part of the world, their holds crammed full with fabric and jewels, copper from Cyprus, pottery from Samos, wheat from Syria. Phoenician sailors sporting blue tattoos, with monkeys or exotic pet birds perched on their shoulders, mingled on the docks with bearded merchants wearing the fringed shawl of the Israelite; Roman centurions, their red cloaks spread across the backs of their horses, rode past Syrian mercenaries on foot. For every woman with painted eyes and rouged lips who wore the scant, gauzy gown of Caesar's court, another passed dressed in plain linen and heavily veiled. Here and there in the market or on the breakwater, with its towers and vaulted warehouses and quays, the black skin of a Nabatean could be seen, or the desert headdress of some nomad chief, for if there was anything at all to be bought or sold, sooner or later it would find its way to Caesarea.

It was more than that the city was beautiful—the very model of a classic Greek city, with its theater, games, and statues copied from works of great renown, and its various temples to diverse gods—or that it had great commercial importance, possessing the finest harbor along the coast. Caesarea was the official seat of the Roman governor of the imperial provinces of Judea and Samaria, and while the nation of Israel might continue to look to Jerusalem as its spiritual center, Judea's capital was actually no longer David's City, but this sophisticated Greco-Roman metropolis. In the great white palace of the procurator, as Caesar's military governor was called, resided the ultimate and absolute power of life and death over every Judean.

The girl was sitting on a sack of Syrian wheat, her legs open, and one dark braid undone. She was eating something, but that did not keep her from conversing animatedly with one of the dockhands in the sailor's own vulgar patois. She grinned at something the man said, her large, strangely light eyes growing even bigger with delight.

Shimon screwed up his face in disgust. He had known Alexandra would be on the breakwater, Beni as usual by her side, chatting away with the workers like any common child of the street; but the sight of his sister now did not much please him. She and Beni were always on the docks—or running crazily among the stalls of the marketplace, or sneaking off to the sea, where they nimbly scrambled up the rocks on the beach more quickly than their older and somewhat heavier brother, who was invariably left behind. Shimon had made up his mind to forgive Beni for the secrets and adventures not shared with him; the boy was obviously too young to realize that for all her deftness at games and her ability to move around in the ocean like a fish, Alexandra was only a girl, and a rather hateful one at that. She thought she was so smart, learning all the lessons he, Shimon, was supposed to know, and forever correcting his Greek. That was bad enough, but she didn't behave at all the way a girl should. She showed no interest in the house, failed to express proper admiration for her three brothers' accomplishments, and ran around without the slightest degree of modesty or shame. Why, look at her now, lolling about in such an unseemly manner, lifting her chin in that cheeky way she had, and crossing her legs like a tailor, with no thought to what might show! She was past twelve, a full year into maidenhood (mother had made such a fuss), and still trying to pretend she was a boy! Well, she was as skinny as one. Which was a good thing, Shimon thought suddenly, or one of the sailors might get dangerous ideas. Shimon frowned. He loathed Alexandra; but she was, after all, his sister. It was time to announce his presence.

He did so by pushing her over the bale of goods on which she was perched, meanwhile grabbing the honey roll in her hand. "You know you're not allowed to eat this stuff," he said, popping the confection into his mouth. "It's unclean."

"It's not pork, stupid. It's only cake."

"Doesn't matter," he mumbled, mouth full. He licked his fingers. "How do you know who made it? It could have been an offering to one of their gods. Did you get it from a Greek?"

"No, a rabbi gave it to me. He got it from a Greek."

"You are as ugly as your tongue."

"And you are as stupid as your face. By the time you learn just one Book of Torah, the Messiah will have come and died of old age."

"Maybe," he replied, smiling slowly. "But there is one prayer I have learned to say quite well—and every morning, too. I'm sure you know the one I mean." Gazing earnestly heavenward, Shimon recited piously, "'Thank you, Lord, for not having made me a woman.'" And with that the coward turned and ran—as well he might, for no words spoken by anyone in any tongue could anger Alexandra bat Harsom so much as those.

She flew after him, Beni at her heels, the three children knocking into peddlers, sailors, and anyone else unfortunate enough to be in their path. Catching him finally in the courtyard of Beit Harsom, Alexandra jumped on Shimon's back and with a triumphant laugh grabbed hold of his hair.

"Now you've got him, Lexa!" Beni cried. A year younger, the boy might have passed for her twin. They were close partners, and he cheered now as Alexandra wrapped her long legs around Shimon's thick middle and, slapping him on the back, demanded, "Give us a ride, donkey!"

More like an angry bull, Shimon tossed the slender girl to the ground. She was on her feet in a second, kicked him in the shin, and laughing merrily, ran into the house with Shimon howling in pursuit and Beni, as always, close behind.

"Alexandra!"

She skidded to a stop, looked up, still full of glee, and froze. Her eyes widened, and the laugh that had been forming in her throat became a gasp. It was not her mother's commanding tone that so arrested her, but the presence of the young man by the beautiful Devorah's side. Years later when she thought of Josef, Alexandra would always see him as she had that first moment in Beit Harsom, turning to her in surprise, the classic profile becoming the face of a Greek statue come to life.

He was beautiful.

He was, she thought, the most beautiful man she had ever seen.

She stood there, motionless, unable to do anything but stare at him.

He smiled.

But her mother was not amused.

"Alexandra! How dare you come running in like that! And you, Shimon! Benjamin! Out! All of you! Don't let me catch sight of any of you until you are properly attired and can manage to conduct yourselves with a reasonable degree of composure."

Shimon had taken off even before his mother finished speaking, but Alexandra remained motionless, hardly hearing Devorah's imperious commands. Suddenly she became aware of Beni tugging at her arm and, looking away from the still-smiling, dark-eyed man, saw her mother take a step forward. Her senses returned. Another quick look at the stranger, and she dashed from the place as quickly as she had entered it.

She did not go far, however. Pressed against the wall, she could hear Devorah apologizing as the servants rushed to attend their young mistress. Alexandra pulled away from them impatiently; she wanted to hear the man speak. But when he did his voice was too low for her to make out any words. Reluctantly she allowed Batya and the others to bustle her off, but she continued to think about the young man and to wonder who he was while the women bathed and dressed her.

"How dreadful," Devorah murmured, masking her patrician outrage with a show of pretty confusion. "What must you think!

I am sure I would not blame you in the least for believing the worst of the children. And what must you think of me?"

"That you are indeed, as I had heard, the loveliest woman in Judea," Josef replied quickly. "Forgive my boldness—I mean no disrespect—but I have been schooled to speak only truth."

Devorah smiled. She was of an old family, directly descended from King David through the all-important maternal chain, with roots that went as deep into the past as those of the olive trees that terraced the Judean hills. Her hair was red, that fiery hue said to be the mark of the true nobility. Her eyes were green and almond-shaped, and her skin, despite Judea's fierce sun, a flawless cream. A tiny woman with a great and natural arrogance, as renowned for her wit as she was for her beauty, she looked as if she were made of glass. But the delicacy of her wrists belied an iron will; and while the thin nostrils revealed a certain tension common among the offspring of generations of marriage within a few select families, those who knew her did not doubt the strength and determination of this seemingly fragile woman.

"Is that what you shall say, then, when you return to Jerusalem?" she asked, eyebrows arched.

"But I thought you knew. I shall not be going back to the Holy City. I am to sail for Rome. That is why I am here."

"Rome! How wonderful! But why?"

"To rescue Ben Ishabi and the others," the priest Shammai said, joining them. He shook his head. "To think of it . . . Temple priests, honored men, rotting away in a Roman prison on a trumped-up charge so ridiculous no one can even remember what it is! Abomination!"

"But that matter is at least two years old," Devorah wondered. "They may all be dead by now. They are none of them young men."

"They are alive," Shammai replied, "albeit barely. Word has reached Jerusalem that while they have eaten nothing but fruits and nuts all this time in order not to transgress the dietary laws of our faith, our imprisoned priests have been kept alive by the grace of the Almighty."

"And so you have decided to give the Almighty a hand?" Devorah asked Josef in such charming fashion that he could not take the slightest offense.

"Josef has persuaded us that he can win their release," Shammai answered for him. "The High Priest has consented to the venture, and I have assured him the House of Harsom will provide passage on the next ship setting sail for Rome."

"Of course," Samuel ben Harsom said now, entering the room. "If this young man stands willing to risk his neck in such noble cause, I can do no less than give whatever aid is required."

Josef lowered his head in a modest gesture of thanks.

"I must tell you, though," Samuel went on, "that it will be some weeks before any ships will venture out upon the winter sea. You are welcome, of course, to remain with us until such time."

"It will be an honor and a pleasure to reside in the House of Harsom," Josef said, looking straight into the green eyes of Samuel ben Harsom's wife.

"And I am sure we shall enjoy your company," Devorah replied graciously, taking her husband's arm. "Come, gentlemen! You must be famished after your journey. The roadside inns are too terrible, are they not? And I want to hear all the gossip. Is it true, Shammai, that the Sanhedrin debated three days over the perfume allowance one of the daughters of the House of Gorion is entitled to receive?"

A dark woman with piercing black eyes brought forth the new, saffron-colored tunic. For once Alexandra did not protest but stood docilely as the servant arranged the fine linen folds on her slim body.

"Hagar," she demanded breathlessly, "who is he?"

A flicker of amusement seemed to light the dark eyes momentarily. "For one as smart as you pretend to be, it should be easy enough to recognize your own kin."

"My what?"

"Surely you have not forgotten your uncle the priest."

"Uncle Shammai?" She made a face. "Is he here? No, no," she went on impatiently. "The one with mother. The young man. He has curly black hair and wonderful dark eyes—and he is beardless, like the Roman centurions."

Hagar shrugged. "A guest. From Jerusalem." She began to braid the girl's hair.

"From Jerusalem..." There had been talk of a suitable betrothal for the daughter of the wealthy and respected Samuel ben Harsom. Devorah, herself a Jerusalemite, was adamant that a match be made with a family from the Holy City. And now there was this stranger . . .

The girl's heart took a sudden leap forward.

Hagar handed her a mirror of polished brass, and for perhaps the first time in her young life Alexandra began to study herself with real interest. Enormous round eyes of clear gray fringed with thick black lashes stared solemnly back at her. They were strange, light eyes, almost colorless, seeming to take on the hue of things around them, so that at the moment they appeared golden, reflecting the color of the saffron gown. Her gaze beneath the slender, winged brows was unusually direct; the servants called her "little owl."

She had her mother's nose and lips, the sensuous curve of her mouth prophetic of a part of her nature still dormant. She would be taller than Devorah, small-boned but long-limbed, with the same high cheekbones and deceivingly delicate appearance. Her hair was dark, like her father's.

"Am I pretty, Hagar?" She was curious, but the question had been posed in a strangely detached manner, as though it were academic and did not personally involve her.

The woman cast a brief glance at the boyish figure and small, solemn face. "No," she said flatly. "But you have . . . something," she added in a softer voice.

"Will I be pretty one day, then?"

"No. You will never be pretty." Black eyes met gray within the circle of the mirror. "You will be beautiful."

They were all seated at the great white marble table when Alexandra made her appearance, newly shy and wondering if she would ever get used to things dangling from her ears. Samuel ben Harsom looked up as she entered the room, and smiled, extending his hand to her. Devorah also looked up and, taking note of the saffron-colored gown, the smoothly braided hair, and the delicate filigree earrings that Alexandra had hitherto regarded with such disdain, gave a quick little nod of approval. The girl let out her breath and started to perch on her father's lap. A second look from her mother made her think better of that, so she drew forward a stool to sit beside him.

Pleased with his daughter's appearance and sudden show of decorous behavior, Samuel rewarded her with a small amount of honeyed wine, meanwhile nodding in his wife's direction as if to say, "There, you see! Alexandra is not such a wild little bird after all."

Shimon had also looked up, forgetting for the moment the large chunk of walnut cake that had so far captured all his interest. Narrowing his green eyes, he studied his sister for any visible defects, then, laughing silently, pointed to her arm. In the courtyard tussle she had fallen and cut herself on a clay shard. An ugly red gash ran now from wrist to elbow. Alexandra quickly pressed her arm against her side and picked up the goblet of wine with her left hand, silently vowing to murder her brother when she could.

"I've brought you that jellied wine you are so partial to, Devorah," Shammai was saying.

"Ah," the woman said wistfully, "but it is never same as in Jerusalem."

"Nothing is as it is in Jerusalem," the priest agreed pointedly.

"I find the wine here to be excellent," Samuel said. "The merchant, Lukas, is an interesting fellow. His mother was a daughter of Israel, but his father was Greek—one of the Syrian cohorts, I believe."

"A bastard?" Shammai reached for a fig.

"I suppose so. Anyway, he has joined the Christians, as they now call themselves. There are quite a few of them in Caesarea. You know, the ones who believe that rabbi from the Galilee was the Messiah."

"The *meshokim?* Heretics?"

"No, their sect is composed of more than just Jews—as they now refer to those of their own Christ's race. There are a number of Greeks who have adopted their ways, and even, Lukas tells me, some legionaries, although the soldiers take great pains to keep their new faith secret. The wife of the centurion is one, Lukas said. But the centurion himself has not left his old gods."

The priest sniffed disdainfully. "Gods and goddesses! Worshipping bulls and birds and women!"

"And flags," Alexandra said cheerfully. "The soldiers make offerings to their own standards, don't they, father?"

Her uncle made a disgusted sound. He turned again to his brother. "You say your winemaker's mother was an Israelite?"

"Yes, a slave. Her father was forced to sell her in order to pay Caesar's tax."

The priest shook his head. "Abomination," he muttered.

"The selling of the daughter?" Devorah wanted to know, smiling slightly. "Or the tax?"

"It is just such refuse," Shammai went on, ignoring her, "who go off into the hills following any fool they see, shouting to one and all that the Messiah has come. From the Galilee alone there must be at least as many 'Messengers of the Lord'— blessed be the name of the One True God—as fingers on each hand. And all of them stinking of fish and onions. The world's gone mad. Devorah, this cake is delicious."

"You shall have to do better than that, brother. I do not think I appreciate your vehemence regarding the worship of women. Or do you suppose, like Adam, you are grown from a lump of mud?"

Alexandra grinned.

"It is unkind to call those who are unfortunate 'refuse,'" Joshua, Samuel ben Harsom's eldest son, said suddenly.

Surprised, Alexandra turned to look at her brother.

"Our people are desperate for something to alleviate the pain of their existence, their poverty and oppression. Fathers forced to sell their children into slavery . . . the offspring of violent, unwelcome alliances, without legal name or rights . . . the sick, the hungry . . . If they turn to false prophets, is it not because their own priests and leaders have failed them?"

Alexandra blinked. Was this truly Joshua speaking?

"They fail themselves," their uncle stated. "There is comfort for those of whom you speak. There is guidance. There is the Way. It is all in Torah, the written word of the Lord. They have only to look."

"What if they cannot read?"

"There is not a town in all Judea," the priest said, "not a village from Dan to Beersheba, without its school. The Law states quite clearly that all male Israelites shall begin their studies by the age of three. If they do not, it is because they are lazy. Or stupid."

"Or too busy working for their bread."

"No doubt," was the tart reply. "Your precious peasants are too busy as well, I suppose, to make pilgrimage to the Holy City, also prescribed by the Law."

"And when they do, you laugh at them," Joshua said quietly. "Calling them ignorant Galileans, sneering at those who are not of the priestly class of Kohanim, or Levites, but merely *am ha' eretz*, 'the people of the land.' People of the land," he repeated. "It ought to be a badge of honor, not a mark of shame. You mock all they hold dear—the Book of Esther, the teachings of Hillel . . ."

The priest's eyes turned cold. He was a Sadducee, member of the highest order of the twenty-four classes of priests, also called Zadokites, and ostensibly descended from the High Priest who had served under David the King. Like other "sons of Zadok," he believed in the "reasonable views of the ancient fathers as embodied in the written law called the Torah, and in fact thought well of many of the teachings of the Greek philosophers. But he rejected utterly the spreading popular belief in angels, the new apocalyptic ideas, and the concept that a full afterlife would follow the death of the mortal body, as the rabbis, or "teachers," now called Pharisees, had begun to claim.

"There is but one Law, Joshua," the priest said. "I know you have become of Pharisaic persuasion and will be leaving soon for Jerusalem to take up residence with Rabbi Johanan ben Zakkai. Your father knows what I think of this, and I shall not now be drawn into the debate you obviously desire—we shall speak later, you and I. All I will say now is that there is one Law for all the children of Israel. One written Law. One Book."

"Your pardon," Josef ben Matthias murmured, a faint smile playing upon his lips. "Not one Book, but five."

The tension was broken. Everyone laughed appreciatively. Even the priest smiled. "We picked the right one, eh, Samuel, to send to Rome? If he charms Nero as well as he has the daughters of Israel, we may have some hope."

Alexandra turned to look at the young man in question. She had barely taken her eyes from him since coming to the table, but for the moment the exchange between her uncle and eldest brother had captured her interest. She had not much feeling for Joshua one way or the other, although he was not unkind to her; it was just that he was so immersed in the world of Torah—a world from which her sex excluded her—that she hardly knew him. She had noted his conversion to the Pharisees with typical curiosity and had listened with academic interest to his eager explanations of the teachings of the sage, Hillel, and his disciple, Johanan ben Zakkai. But in the end Alexandra had no use for any of Joshua's newfound beliefs, particularly those regarding angels or messiahs, which she considered merely additional instruments of a male world that did its best to restrict her.

The fact was that she thought Joshua a fool to turn from the adventurous world that was his birthright and give it all over to Shimon, who was next in line and, in Alexandra's opinion, hardly worthy. What a surprise to see Joshua stand up to Uncle Shammai, who, like Shimon, was not one of her favorite people. What a wonder that Josef ben Matthias could be so cheerful after traveling all the way from Jerusalem with the dour old priest. Josef was smiling now—the loveliest, most beautiful smile any man might possess. His teeth were so straight and white, even all around, and with not a space between them. His eyes were wonderfully dark and intense, glowing with the fire of—what was it Homer had written?—the fire of something or other. Anyway, they were beautiful eyes. A man with eyes like that would never turn his back on a fortune in land and ships just to sit all day in some rabbi's house disputing minute points of the Law and interpretations of Scripture. Now, if her mother found him favorable . . .

But she did. See how she leaned across the table toward him, chin in hand, her face like a pale flower on a graceful stem. Devorah awed her daughter. To Alexandra, she was like a star alone and brilliant in some midnight sky. How easily she could make worthless an object another found dear. How precious was her praise, bestowed so quickly on the boys and directed so sparingly toward her only daughter. Would she find Josef acceptable as a prospective son? Alexandra's hands clenched on her lap. She must. She must.

"Perhaps," Samuel was saying to the young man, "while in Rome you may learn the outcome of our dispute with Caesarea's Greek citizens. They have demanded the right to take over the city," he explained, "claiming Herod built it for them since it is filled with temples and statues forbidden to those of our faith. They accuse the city council—which we control—of sending all their money to Jerusalem, and they resent our refusal to allocate funds for gladiatorial combat. Three years ago the procurator sent delegations from both sides to present their arguments before Caesar. And still no decision." He sighed. "It would be well to have the dispute resolved. Animosity grows, and many homes as well as synagogues have been attacked."

"But surely the procurator will take steps against such harassment," his brother exclaimed, visibly upset. "The legions are garrisoned in Caesarea. If they cannot keep order—"

"I think it is Rome's dearest delight to see us at each other's throats," Devorah said calmly. "Idumeans, Syrians, Samaritans, Judeans... so long as we fight among ourselves, they remain strong."

"But why do you stay here?" Shammai asked. "If there should be a gentile uprising..."

Samuel merely smiled. "As you are often quick to say, dear brother, one must trust in the protection of the Lord. Even," he added wickedly, "in Jerusalem."

The priest raised his eyebrows. "Jerusalem?"

"I have heard that those of our class fear for their lives even as they stand in the Temple courtyard, lest they brush unwittingly against the knife of the Sicarii."

The priest was silent a moment. Then he sighed and nodded grimly. "The Zealots are determined to have a war with Rome, to 'liberate Judea from the foreign oppressor.' And they have declared those of us who do not agree with them to be as much their mortal enemies as Caesar's soldiers. Well, what can you expect? Galileans, most of them. Scum of the earth. Yes, those whom you defend so nobly, Joshua. Every thief and murderer in Judea now declares himself a patriot, and we—we who do our best to keep these troublemakers from the salt mines, the galley, and the arena, stripping ourselves of money and honor so that the procurator and his red-cloaked baboons should remain happy—we, now, are 'traitors'!"

"Who are these Sicarii?" Devorah asked.

"A dangerous offspring of the Zealot faction," her husband explained. "The legionaries have so named them for the short knife, the *sica*, that they conceal beneath their cloaks."

"Daggermen," Alexandra whispered, catching Beni's eyes. He nodded back solemnly.

"Hotheads!" the priest exclaimed. "Bunch of young fools get muddied by some centurion's shying horse, and next thing they are running around calling for war." He sighed. "So you get a little dirty. So you pay a tax here and another there. So what? Was it better under Herod? Or Hyrcanus, that murderer? I grant you, none of the procurators has been, shall we say, the best of men—and this last one seems the worst of the lot. But Gessius Florus will not be here forever. No doubt his successor will be more reasonable."

"How can you say that?" Joshua cried. "Each man sent by Rome has been worse than the one before! As for Gessius Florus, everyone knows not a boy or girl is safe from his sick desires!"

Shammai cleared his throat. "That may be. But you don't go to war with a whole nation over the trifling misdemeanors of one man. Especially when the nation we are talking about is Rome."

"Trifling misdemeanors! We are legally robbed of what is ours, forced to pay taxes that have crippled the entire nation, subject to every evil any of Caesar's governors take into their heads—"

"We are allowed to worship our God!"

"Allowed!" Joshua was incensed. "It is our right!"

"Bear in mind," his uncle said firmly, "that Rome does not interfere with the Temple service. Nor do the soldiers bring their standards into Jerusalem, or the procurators make any attempt to confiscate the priestly tithe."

"But they do not hesitate to dispose of those priests they find 'troublesome,'" the young man shot back. "And the sacred robe and vestments of the High Priest are held under lock and key so that you must go to the procurator and beg for them when they are needed. Just as now Josef must make supplication to Nero, who by all accounts is even worse than Gessius Florus! Oh, uncle, can't you see what an affront it is to the Almighty for His people to be ruled by such tyrants? And if we suffer, how much more must He, seeing what we have become?"

There was silence. Then Samuel ben Harsom, who had been staring thoughtfully at his son throughout this new debate, said lightly, "You amaze me, Joshua. You are born a Sadducee, you profess to be a Pharisee—and now here you are, talking like a Zealot."

"That is not so unusual these days," Josef ben Matthias confessed. "I too am of the priestly class, and I too have found most worthy the philosophy of the good Hillel. But even Hillel, who was the mildest of men, they say, might chafe at the Roman bit we are forced to endure."

Shammai raised his eyebrows. "You are for an insurrection, Josef?"

"No," the young man replied smoothly. "Because I do not think it would be successful. But I cannot pretend we serve generous masters, or those inclined to our welfare."

Samuel nodded. "Still, you must not think, Josef, that all Rome abounds with scoundrels. I have a great admiration for many things Roman—their Senate, for example. It has always struck me how unable we are to set up a stable and continuous government for ourselves. We seem always to depend upon the enthusiasm of the moment, the excitement of a crisis, or the expectation of some inspired savior—a Messiah—to unite us. I had hoped that Rome would impart a sense of order to our troubled and fragmented land. And with order, perhaps . . . peace."

His brother nodded. "For once we are agreed. Look at Herod," he demanded of those present. "A monster. A madman. And yet . . . sixty-nine years of peace, prosperity, and civic order under his rule."

"Peace!" Joshua exclaimed. "Prosperity! Order! I am talking about something more precious than that! Freedom! What good is your stable government if it turns men into slaves!"

"Listen to me, nephew," his uncle said, turning on him angrily. "You are very righteous, but you don't know what you are talking about. If you did, you would pray day and night for good government, because without it men would swallow each other alive."

"Do you never wonder," Josef ben Matthias asked, absently running his finger around the rim of a silver goblet, "why our ancestors did not try to retain their independence when Pompey first invaded our land? Their resources were far superior to what we have today, they faced a fraction of the Roman army, yet they offered no resistance."

"Because they had sense!" Shammai exclaimed. "Greece with all her glorious past takes orders from Caesar. The Macedonians with their dreams of Philip and Alexander are loyal to Rome. The Gauls, the Germans, nations by the thousands . . . What, shall we alone refuse to serve the masters of the world?"

"Yes," Joshua said. "If no other, then we."

"Where are the men, then? Where are the weapons? Where is the fleet to sweep the seas? Where are the funds to pay for it? What, do you think you are taking on a bunch of Egyptians, or some nomad tribe of the south?"

"The Lord is with us."

"The Lord is with Rome," the priest said in disgust. "Without the help of the Almighty how could so vast an empire have ever been built?"

Joshua lowered his head. His ears, Alexandra thought, were very red.

"And what of the Temple? The Sanctuary?" Shammai was relentless. "Do you imagine anything would be left standing when you were done playing soldier? Do you think when the Romans had won—as indeed they would—they would be kind to us, they would forgive us? Listen, Joshua, listen. . . ." He wagged his finger at the silent young man. "While the vessel is in harbor the wise man keeps his eye on an approaching storm. He does not sail off without a thought into the midst of a hurricane. Those on whom disaster falls out of the blue are entitled to a little pity. But a man who would plunge into destruction with his eyes open is worthy only of contempt."

Joshua did not answer. Instead he looked at his father; but Samuel only said sadly, "We are not alone, my son. There is not a country without its quarter of Israelites. If Judea declares war, the streets of every city in the world will run with our people's blood."

Joshua bowed his head again; but to Alexandra it seemed that her brother's lips were set in a very determined line. Shortly afterwards he excused himself and left the table. Impulsively she touched his hand as he brushed past her.

Devorah noticed the gesture and quietly began to study her daughter. The girl's cheeks were pink with excitement and wine, her large gray eyes unusually bright. The combination, Devorah thought, was not unattractive.

Girls Alexandra's age were already accepting their *mohar*, or dowry gift. At thirteen, Devorah had been wed to a man more than fifteen years her senior. But while Alexandra was now capable of bearing a child, Devorah mused, she was still little more than one herself. And if ever a girl had little taste for those womanly duties and traits extolled by the world, it was her own daughter. Samuel, of course, spoiled her. True, she was exceptionally clever, and Devorah, herself the product of one of Israel's great houses, which had encouraged the education of its female members to a most sophisticated degree, saw nothing amiss in indulging Alexandra's hunger for learning. But Alexandra must know her place in the world. And she must learn to be as competent in the affairs of the house as she was in mathematics and the writings of the Greek philosophers.

Devorah allowed a small sigh to escape her. Of late it seemed that she and Alexandra were always at odds. *And yet*, the mother thought defensively, *all that I do is out of love and a knowledge of the realities a woman must face*. If, for example, the girl would only learn to carry herself with a semblance of maidenly modesty. But she simply did not know the meaning, much less the value, of a downcast eye. Her gaze was disconcerting, one that men might misinterpret as being bold. It was better, Devorah knew, that a man not be able to take his full measure of a woman.

"I fear Joshua will be disappointed," Josef ben Matthias remarked, "to discover that Rabbi ben Zakkai does not favor a rebellion against Rome or war of any kind."

"But I thought the Zealots were followers of the Pharisees," Samuel said.

"The Zealot faction may be one with the Pharisees as to their spiritual concepts, but not all Pharisees listen to the revolutionary call of the Zealots. Ben Zakkai and his followers have disassociated themselves from any and all political movements, and concern themselves solely with man's understanding of Torah."

"It is hard to think of Joshua all grown up and going off to Jerusalem," Devorah said with a sigh. "I suppose Alexandra will be next to leave us. She is well into her thirteenth year, and a match must be made for her."

Great gray eyes turned to the woman. The child was sitting quite still, but the linen folds of the saffron-colored gown moved noticeably with the beating of her heart.

"There is a son in the family of my betrothed," Josef ben Matthias said casually, "whom you might consider. A bright, handsome fellow. The family is of the House of Anan, all of them, as you know, high priests of the Temple. You can be sure the boy has a good future, and I am certain the family would welcome the alliance."

"But how interesting!" Devorah exclaimed. "They are the very ones we had in mind—" And she went on to speak with Josef of the House of Anan, both of them laughing now at various pieces of gossip concerning the family.

But Alexandra was no longer listening. She sat still as stone, the honeyed wine turning bitter in her mouth.

He was betrothed.

That was as good as married.

The House of Anan could drown in the sea for all she cared.

She looked up; and though Shimon made no sound the others could hear, she knew he was laughing at her. She stared fiercely back, inventing a variety of tortures that she proceeded to inflict upon him with her eyes.

"Alexandra is quite clever, you know," Devorah was saying. "Her Greek is flawless, and she speaks the tongue of Caesar as well as a Roman."

"Perhaps, then, you will be my instructor," Josef said, turning to the girl with another of his captivating smiles. It was the first time he had addressed her. "Such knowledge would be useful on my journey, especially if those among whom I sojourn do not realize I comprehend their speech. Will you teach me?"

Shimon could not contain himself any longer, knowing full well the choice invectives and Latin slang his sister had learned from the soldiers. He let out a wild whoop of laughter.

It was too much. Jumping up from the table, Alexandra flung the contents of her goblet straight in Shimon's face and ran from the room and out of the house.

It was night when Hagar came at last to fetch her, treading silently across the sand. She stopped a short distance from the girl, standing beside her like a strange black bird at water's edge.

"How did you know where to find me?"

"Where else would you go?" The woman's dark eyes traveled out across the sea, their diamond brightness seeming now to soften. "Sooner or later we come to the Great Mother."

Alexandra turned to look at her. Hagar was a proselyte, a slave once, from the island called Crete. She had converted to the faith of her master long ago, and as an Israelite, had been entitled to receive her freedom after seven years' bondage. She had chosen to stay on with the family, however, a servant in the House of Harsom for as long as Alexandra had memory— a solitary creature who kept apart from the other members of the household, with dark eyes that seemed to see everything.

Once, Alexandra had caught the woman kneeling before a small, carved idol with outsized breasts and a tiny waist. Although the girl had made no sound, Hagar sensed her presence like an animal suddenly alert to danger. Her back straightened; the strange mumbling stopped, and when she turned, her eyes were guarded. Alexandra met her stare in that typically curious yet detached way she had and finally turned away, leaving the woman to her gods, and the incident a thing between them to be left unspoken.

"What is your real name?" the girl asked suddenly. "Hagar" had been as close as Samuel ben Harsom could come to pronouncing the woman's Cretan name.

"What is yours?"

She was taken aback. "Mine?"

"'Alexandra' is Greek. You are a Jew."

"There was a great queen of Judea named Salome Alexandra," the girl replied defensively.

Hagar shrugged. "It is of little importance. The Good Goddess knows our true names."

"You must not say that," Alexandra said sternly. "It is—it is an abomination. There is but one God. The Lord our God."

"Lord of men," Hagar said flatly.

"Of us all."

"Of men," she repeated.

Alexandra stared at her.

"Come. We must go back. It is not safe to walk the streets at night. The soldiers are always drunk."

"Not yet . . ."

"Are you afraid your father will beat you? I do not think he will. He never does. But for sure you will be punished. And rightly so."

She shrugged. "I don't care." Her heart beat faster. "Is mother very angry?"

"She is not pleased. She cannot think who would want you for a wife."

"Good." She would dress in boy's clothes and be a sailor and see all the places there were to see and learn all the tongues people spoke so she could know what they thought. . . . "I'm never getting married anyway. There isn't a man in this world I'd marry."

"Not even the Jerusalemite?"

She was silent. The image of a finely chiseled face and cap of jet-black curls rose before her. She could see in the night the dark eyes that had glowed with such intensity, the white teeth, the cleft chin, the slim, smoothly muscled figure of the young man. She shrugged. "What's so wonderful about him?"

"For me, nothing." The woman paused. "The servants from Jerusalem say he has much love of learning but that he is of a reckless nature. He was born to priesthood. His mother is of the royal house of the Hasmoneans. But he will not serve the Temple. He left the priests, the servants say, to live in the desert with some crazy holy men who eat no meat and take no wives."

"Do you mean Essenes?"

She shrugged. "In any case he did not stay with them, as you can see."

"He said he had become a Pharisee," Alexandra mused, recalling the conversation at the table. "Oh!" she exclaimed suddenly, desperately. "I knew he was interesting!"

"Dangerous, you mean," Hagar said.

"Why do you say that?" Alexandra asked, surprised.

But Hagar only shook her head. "All young men are hungry. But this one . . . Give him the chance, and he will chew people up and spit out their bones."

But Alexandra was not listening. A thousand stars were swimming in the sea like schools of silver fish. Something was stretching inside her, warming, ripening. . . .

She looked out across the water, and in it she saw the moon shimmering, like the face of a pale and lovely woman.

"The world is hard," Hagar was saying softly, her voice one with the whispering surf. "A woman knows much pain and loneliness. The Good Goddess understands. . . . She listens to the secrets of the heart. . . ."

Alexandra stared at the moon floating in the sea, and her heart flew across the water to the woman's face she saw there and whispered to it . . .

"Give him to me. Make him mine."

It was many weeks before Samuel ben Harsom's ship, the *Judea*, set out to sea, and in that time Josef ben Matthias made himself a welcome member of the House of Harsom. The handsome young Jerusalemite was easy to like, with his quick wit and easy smile, his store of tales both droll and learned, his thoroughly ingratiating manner. Despite Hagar's suspicions—founded, it seemed, on nothing more than primal instinct that time would or would not prove correct—there appeared to be no reason why everyone in the family should not grow as fond of Josef as they did. And perhaps if he had a knack of being all things to all men—and to all women—who could say now if this was a cultivated talent or something that simply occurred in the eyes of the beholder?

Samuel ben Harsom, for example, saw only an eager young adventurer who might have been himself at twenty-six, excited by the world across the sea, restless to cross the borders of experience. Joshua saw a fellow scholar and student, pursuing knowledge no matter where the search led, from the school of

the Sadducees to the philosophy of the Pharisees, even to living
with the sect called Essenes in their community near the Dead
Sea. Shimon, who did not make friends easily, found Josef a
sympathetic and understanding soul; for the Jerusalemite was
also a second son and seemed to know what special attention
and respect Shimon craved. Josef did not ignore even the
youngest children; he skipped stones across the water with Beni
and went swimming with the boy and his sister in a sheltered
spot behind a cove of rocks.

It was difficult for Josef to think of the girl as more than
a child despite the small breasts that pushed against her wet
shift. She was a wild little thing. He could not help but wonder
why Samuel ben Harsom, who seemed so wise in all other
matters, permitted his daughter to behave with such abandon,
or how Devorah, who was the very model of grace, could be
the mother of this coltish girl. He had of course laughed away
Alexandra's display of temper at the table that first night. It
was only natural, he had said, that the girl should be excitable,
living in a city inhabited by garrisons of soldiers and great
numbers of hostile Greeks. As soon as she was married and
settled in Jerusalem, he had added diplomatically, the natural
grace and sweetness she no doubt possessed by virtue of being
Devorah's daughter, would blossom forth.

He was himself betrothed to a girl hardly older. Roxana
was a quiet little thing with a rather sallow complexion, but
she was the daughter of a high priest of the House of Boethus,
and, what was most important, Josef's father wanted the
match. It was difficult enough for him to please the venerable
Matthias of Jerusalem, Josef often thought, whereas his older
brother had but to smile to make the man dance. If marrying
Roxana would make his father happy, it was a small enough
thing for Josef to do. He found himself wondering, however,
why no mention had ever been made of this girl, Alexandra.
There was no doubt of the family's position within the priestly
class, which was further enhanced by Devorah's royal heritage,
nor of their wealth, nor of the fact that the House of Harsom
had always enjoyed the best of relations with all the procurators
as well as with Herod's descendants. Why, then, had this girl
been withheld?

They were not Jerusalemites. That, and Samuel ben Harsom's extensive, friendly dealings with the gentile world,
would be enough to put his father off, Josef mused wryly.
Spoons of ivory and plates of gold and silver notwithstanding,

this family would not measure up to that of a poor Temple scribe. Not as far as Matthias of Jerusalem was concerned. Not even for his second son.

For himself, Josef did not question for a moment his host's affinity for Caesarea and the world outside Judea. Knowing the glories of Jerusalem, he also knew its restrictions and what he suspected to be a provincial frame of mind. How eagerly he had accepted this mission to Rome; indeed, it was he who had pressed for it. The Temple was not for him; the life of a desert ascetic was definitely not to his liking; and while he found himself at ease with the philosophy of the Pharisees, he was not about to spend the rest of his life at some rabbi's knee in hopes of sitting in the Sanhedrin one day with a following of his own. Going to Rome now was his last chance, his only chance for... what?

He turned his attention to the boy and girl playing on the beach, not daring to formulate his thoughts any further. Absently he watched the girl climbing the rocks that stretched out to sea, her body poised at the very tip like a ship's figurehead. Then she was scrambling back, challenging her brother to a race across the wet sand. Still lost in thought, he watched her running toward him, and suddenly something jolted him into taking real notice, but he could not say what it was. The look in her eyes as she ran... her wet, dark hair flying behind, pieces of it sticking to her face as she turned with a laugh to measure her lead . . . There was something . . . unholy . . . about it, Josef thought with some shock. Still, he smiled as she came close.

Seeing him before her, she stopped in mid-flight, flushed and suddenly confused.

He smiled again, inwardly pleased that his presence could so affect her animal spirits as to make her realize the impropriety of her behavior. He took a step toward her.

This only added to her confusion. Without a word she turned and ran away, as she had that first day.

She is going to earn many a beating from the man who becomes her husband, Josef thought; and he felt sorry for her, although again he could not say why.

"It is not seemly," Shammai complained. "She is too bold, Devorah. A certain amount of arrogance is becoming and befitting in a princess of Judea—but Alexandra's is misplaced.

With servants and slaves she is mild and too fond, and with those who rightly demand from her humility and modesty she is proud. Too proud."

Devorah sighed. "She is what Samuel wishes her to be."

"He does her no service. I grant you, she is clever and of a prodigious learning for one so young—and a female at that. Now, don't stiffen up on me, Devorah. I mean only that she asks too many questions, she challenges, she—" He shook his head. "I cannot think where it will lead or what good it will do."

"Have we become as gentiles, brother?" Devorah asked coldly. "We have always taken pride that our sons and daughters love learning. In the great houses of Israel, women have always been educated. I myself—"

"I know, I know." He sighed. "But Alexandra . . . You must do more to educate her in the ways of a woman, Devorah," he said finally. "You prescribe a life of misery for her if you do not."

"She will find her way," Samuel said later, when his wife approached him. He was unpreturbed. "Or make her own."

"She is my daughter!" Devorah exclaimed. "Not a traveler seeking a road through life! There is no 'way' for her to find or make, as you put it—only that which has been beaten into a path by those who have gone before her." She sighed. "I know I seem to be harder with her than with the others. But I love her, Samuel. As close as you are to her, you will never know Alexandra as well as I do, nor feel for her as I can. I know what she is—and I know what the world is. I want her to be happy. I want her to be safe. There are things a woman must learn. . . ."

"Let her have her childhood," he said gently. "Let her run free. Soon enough she will have a household of her own—and," he added with a smile, "a daughter over whom to fret."

"She won't be ready. She—"

"Alexandra will be all right. She has a strong will, but she is not stupid. She will survive," he said cheerfully. "Even marriage."

She sat in a corner of the courtyard nearly hidden in the shadows. Josef and Joshua were wrestling, stripped to the waist, their bodies wet with the effort of their struggle. Constant exposure to the mild days and seaside sun of Caesarea had deepened Josef's skin to a rich, ruddy brown. His teeth were very white as, grinning, he circled his adversary, searching for the hold that would pin the indomitable Joshua to the ground; for what the young scholar lacked in skill he made up in determination and a natural strength inherited from his father. Across the courtyard, Shimon and Beni cheered the friendly opponents on, calling out warnings and encouragement indiscriminately, Shimon following the pair as they moved slowly around the fountain, Beni perched on top of an overturned basket. Both boys were more interested in the prowess displayed than in the question of who might win this contest, but it was very important to Alexandra that Josef be the victor. And when at last he found his opening and neatly flipped the surprised Joshua to the ground, she let out her breath, relieved at this vindication of her judgment.

"You see, Joshua? That is how it is done." He stood grinning above the dazed boy, hands on hips, legs spread apart. His body was like amber, and his back glistened with sweat. "When you come to Jerusalem we will go together to the gymnasium."

"Show me once more," Joshua panted.

Josef laughed. "I wonder, do you think such activity befits a scholar of the Lord?" he teased, putting out his hand to help Joshua up. "I should think you would be more interested in wrestling with the prophets."

"Time enough for that. Besides, the children of Israel must be more than scholars. We are the warriors of the Lord. Have you forgotten? That is the meaning of the name *Hebrew*."

The Jerusalemite raised an eyebrow. "I am no teacher of martial arts, Joshua, nor do I have much love for them." He grinned again, showing those white, perfect teeth. "But I can tell you one thing I have learned. No victory is ever gained through this"—he put his hand on the muscle of Joshua's arm—"so much as it is through this"—and here he tapped his own head. "Remember that."

Samuel ben Harsom suddenly appeared, striding through the courtyard waving a rolled parchment. "Josef! Good news! I have just come from the captain of the *Judea*. You are to sail two days from now."

The young man's eyes sparkled.

"I confess I am loath to have you leave us," Samuel said, putting his hand on Josef's shoulder. "I have come to think of you as another son. I know Devorah will miss your tales of Jerusalem. I think we shall all miss you," he added, as his own boys came forward now. "But I know how eagerly you look forward to this voyage."

"I look forward to acquitting myself of the duty with which I am entrusted," Josef answered quickly and earnestly. "It is my hope to persuade Caesar—"

"Yes, yes, of course. I do not doubt your devotion to your mission. I have, however, taken it upon myself to write certain letters of introduction to various associates that will stand you in good stead—should your duties permit, of course."

Josef bowed his head in thanks. "If there is any advice you care to—"

"No more than we have already discussed. I think you will do very well in Rome. It is clever of you to go beardless. I have always found it prudent to adopt as much as possible the manners of those among whom I travel. It puts people at their ease and helps to win their confidence. It is also good sometimes for one of our race to be, shall we say, anonymous. The world, after all, is not Jerusalem."

I hope not, Josef was thinking. His heart was beating rapidly now with excitement.

"But if the outward man appears changed, the inner man must remain faithful to Torah. It is his surest safety, Josef. The grace of the Lord is our truest shield."

"My father has said the same."

"I am sure of it. Come, let us go inside. There are some matters of business that you might perhaps see to— Alexandra, what are you doing hiding in that corner there? Come here, girl. You are so quiet.... You are feeling well, I hope?" He drew her close. "Come, we must prepare a farewell banquet for Josef. He will be leaving us shortly." And without waiting for a reply, he continued to converse with the young man, one arm around his silent daughter, the three of them moving together out of the sun into the cool darkness of the great house.

TWO

Spring was in the Galilee, the hundred hills fragrant with laurel and jasmine, blooming with tulips and poppies; while in the plain along the harp-shaped Lake Kinneret—the Sea of Galilee—the Greek anemone, or "wind flower," grew in colorful profusion. It was the time of Shavuot, the Feast of Weeks, and the roads leading to Jerusalem were crowded with farmers returning from the Temple, the best of their produce offered up there in thanksgiving on Yom Ha-Bikkurim, the Day of the First Fruits. No one had better reason than they to rejoice in the Lord's bounty, for the Galilee was rich, fertile land. Wheat fields stretched from the plains of Esdraelon to the first bare rocks of the Carmel, while between the shoulders of the mountain were olive groves banked by oaks and sycamores, maple and myrtle and walnut trees. Apricots and figs grew here, pistachios and almonds and pomegranates, and the vine in such profusion that it was said to be easier to bring up a legion of grapes in the Galilee than to raise a child. The towns and villages surrounding the Kinneret were hives of activity, with many fisheries and timber mills; they were famous for their pickled and smoked goods and for the oil pressed from their plentiful olives. Above the wheat- and barley-cloaked valleys, the pastures were filled with flocks, and the narrow, high-banked hill roads brimmed with sheep and cattle.

Producing in abundance the fruit and fish and dairy products that sustained all Judea, the Galilee had been praised since earliest times for its beauty and great fertility. This admiration, however, did not extend to the Galileans themselves. Scorned by Jerusalem's aristocracy for the Amorite blood that made them a tall, fair people with eyes the blue-green color of their lake, they were also distrusted by the rabbis, who suspected them of being not nearly strict enough in their observance of the Law, and looked down upon by other Judeans as backward

provincials who spoke with such thick country accents that,
it was joked, one never knew if a Galilean was asking for wine
(*hamar*), lamb (*immar*), or an ass (*hamor*).

It was true that for the most part they were unschooled and
unmannered, with little or no claim to the "pure" blood of
Jerusalem's nobility. But the Galileans were also courageous
and hardy, as even their enemies were quick to admit, and they
were known to be fierce and fearless fighters. Their resistance
to foreign occupation was legendary and had won them a reputation as "troublemakers" in both Judean and Roman circles.
It was hardly surprising that the Galilee should be the home
of the Zealots, spawning as it had in every generation men
who refused to admit any king but God.

The breach between Jerusalem, which having learned to
survive through accommodation, tolerated Caesar, and the
Galilee, where men, unable or unwilling to curry favor, had
little defense against the moods of Rome, was as deep and
bitter as the animosity between the great house of Judea and
the *am ha'eretz*. For while rich Sadducee families grew yet
more wealthy from their holdings and, in particular, from the
priestly tithe untouched by Rome, the poor farmer or fisherman
was taxed by the Temple and by Caesar. If he protested this
or any other inequity, he was labeled a "Zealot." And all
Zealots had been proclaimed outlaws.

The persecution of Zealots by the succession of Roman
procurators had been abetted by many Judean nobles who, like
the priest Shammai, feared the consequences of insurrection.
Bands of revolutionaries—among them the dread Sicarii, or
Daggermen—had been forced from their homes and had taken
to the hills, living in the caves there, preying upon caravans
of wealthy travelers.

It was therefore with some concern that Samuel ben Harsom
scanned the stony terraces and wooded hills lining the road
that led to the village of Bersabe. It was madness, he thought,
to have allowed Alexandra to accompany him on this journey
to the Galilee. Nearly two years had passed since Josef ben
Matthias had sailed away from Beit Harsom to Rome; and the
gawky child who had once run pell-mell into the villa was now
a slender creature who moved with a dancer's grace. No longer
could Samuel permit his Lexa to walk alone in Caesarea or
stroll unattended on the beach or breakwater. She had in fact
been accosted by two Syrians, soldiers of the Roman cohorts,
one afternoon as she was hurrying home from a forbidden

swim. Fortunately the men had done no more than make in-
nuendos before they were stopped by the centurion Jocundus,
who then escorted Alexandra home.

"My daughter is very willful," Samuel had admitted to the
Roman after making proper thanks. "She has been warned
about going out alone. With the city home to so many soldiers . . . I fear, centurion, yours is a profession that intensifies
those violent instincts which are man's by nature."

"They were Syrians, not Romans," the centurion had said
quickly. He had hesitated. "I should not say it, but these auxiliaries are the worst bunch I've ever run into. A meaner, dirtier
lot you will not find." He had hesitated again, then said, "There
is bound to be trouble. It hangs in the air like the wind from
the desert—the *sharev*, I think you call it." His eyes had seemed
to say more as he stared at Samuel. Then, abruptly, he had
turned to Alexandra, who was eating her dinner as though
nothing unusual had occurred that day. "You had best obey
your father," he'd said, not unkindly. "It is not safe for a young
woman to be out alone in Caesarea. Particularly," he had added
with another meaningful glance at Samuel, "one of your race."

She had barely looked up. "I will not give up my freedom."

"Freedom is one thing," her father had said sternly. "Foolishness is another."

She had sighed.

She was like a bird forever wanting to fly away, Samuel
thought now as he looked at the girl riding so proudly beside
him, her gray eyes full of the bright spring sky. Always talking
of sailing off to the Indies or the far-off land of the yellow-
skins. Always clamoring for "adventure."

"Let me come with you to Bersabe," she had begged.
"Mother says it is a scandal how long you have postponed my
wedding, and that the House of Anan will not allow the betrothal to be prolonged further. Oh, father, I have to leave you
soon, and I know I will hate living in Jerusalem! Let me come
with you to the Galilee this last time!"

He had hesitated, wanting to take her with him, yet not
unaware of the danger. The roads were never safe, particularly
in the Galilee, where the Sicarii made no distinction between
their own race and any other. Only last month they had murdered a priest on his way to Jericho and taken his son for
ransom. There were other outlaws one might encounter—or
Samaritans, always hostile—or stray companies of soldiers.

But in the end she had prevailed, and after their holiday

pilgrimage to the Temple and a brief visit with the House of Anan, they had set off for the north.

Samuel looked at his daughter again. She was in high spirits. As soon as they left the City gates, she had refused to ride in the litter, instead mounting a fine horse (which Samuel had purchased for her), to Shimon's annoyance and the shock of the small retinue of servants. She was, Samuel thought with a smile, as indifferent to the effects of her behavior as she was oblivious to the dangers of the road, or indeed to her own emerging beauty. The girl was but a morning star's distance from the woman, trembling in the last midnight moments of childhood, a little afraid, perhaps, of the day to come.

It was as if she did not believe or wish to believe what was happening to her. She knew she could not outrun Beni any longer, and Shimon refused to wrestle, no matter how she provoked him. And sometimes she had strange, funny feelings, feelings that made her restless, as when she thought about Josef ben Matthias before falling asleep at night. Or when she thought about the soldiers who had tried to make her go with them. (What would they have done with her?)

There were other intriguing things to consider. Jerusalem abounded with tales of the Sicarii. Alexandra's cousin Micala whispered that a caravan from the House of Kathas had been stopped by the bandits, and the priest's daughter stolen away. She was kept for a full month, Micala reported solemnly, and made to do the humblest of tasks, and—Alexandra's cousin had giggled—who knew what else? The girl was returned upon payment of an enormous ransom and, after being examined by the authorities, declared "untouched." But, Micala shrugged, the House of Kathas could find a bloody wedding sheet for the whore of Babylon. Moreover, she confided, the girl was often seen now with her eyes turned wistfully to the hills outside the City. Imagine! Micala said. The daughter of a priest turned into a servant!

Instinctively Alexandra looked now to the rocky, densely wooded hills rising on either side of the road. Any number of men could be hiding behind those trees, outlaws who made their home in the woods and knew every stone and leaf of the place. It was said they never bothered the farmers or common folk who traveled the many roads that crossed Judea, and in particular the Galilee; but no sooner did a group of legionaries appear, or a priestly caravan, or some royal litter from the court of Rome's puppet king Agrippa, than the Sicarii were upon them, their terrible war cry echoing through the hills.

"Keep your eyes open at all times, Samuel," the priest Ananias had warned as they took their leave. "I am sending one of my servants with you. He is from the Galilee and knows every possible place of ambush. You must heed his warnings. The Lord be with you until we are all together for the festivities joining our two families."

Alexandra smiled, forgetting the Sicarii now. It had been quite clever of her—if she said so herself—to drop that little remark to her future sister-in-law regarding the irregularity of her menses. Nothing could stop a wedding faster than a bride who might not be able to bear children. Alexandra's smile widened into a grin. It was a double evil to tell a lie in Jerusalem, but she'd stood on one foot and had asked her father later to sacrifice a white dove in her behalf. She'd always hated the idea of sacrifice—all those poor, dumb creatures getting their throats cut—but she would do anything to postpone this marriage.

It was nearly two years since Josef ben Matthias had sailed away; thanks to his efforts, those for whom he made the journey had long been released, but he still remained at the court of Caesar. Many reports came back to Judea telling how favorably the young Jerusalemite had impressed the Romans, how indeed he had captivated them, and particularly the empress Poppea. Well, but it was good, Alexandra thought, that Josef should remain where he could do the most for his people's welfare. Besides, he would not remain in Rome forever. And while he was away, his own marriage could not proceed. Meanwhile she must hold off the House of Anan—and her mother—until Josef returned to Judea. If there were only some way to persuade her father to make a journey to Rome . . .

She was too engrossed in daydreams to take notice of the scene ahead. The servant from Jerusalem was urging them toward a certain suddenly isolated spot where they might rest the horses. Samuel, however, was suspicious of the suggestion; and while the two argued back and forth, Samuel's worst fears were realized. It happened very quickly: a terrible warlike cry, and then a group of men on horseback swooping down from the nearby hills, making a ring around the startled party before any of them could move to protect themselves. Only two of the Zealot outlaws alighted and came forward: one, a burly, red-haired fellow; the other, a tall young man with broad shoulders and hair the color of gold.

"Where are you going?" the redhead demanded brusquely.

"Bersabe," was the calm reply.

The man looked Samuel over carefully, taking note of his fine but plainly tailored garments. "You do not live there." It was a statement, not a question.

"My home is in Caesarea. I have come to the Galilee for the celebration of the spring harvest, to join with friends in the feast of Hag Hakatzir."

"Friends? In Bersabe? Who might you know in such a small village?"

"The family of Avram ben Zevulon."

"You are friend to Avram?" the man asked, surprised.

"Since we were boys." He did not mention the fact that Avram's father had been a slave freed by Samuel's own father.

The outlaw frowned. "Have I not seen you in Jerusalem?"

"We come now from the Holy City. But I told you, we live in Caesarea."

"Caesarea." He spat. "The place is a Roman brothel. It is a city of abomination."

"So many say," Samuel agreed, thinking with nervous humor of his brother.

"I suppose you made a visit to the Temple. How much money did you give the priests?"

Samuel spread his hands. "Would any man here not part with a shekel for the House of the Lord?"

"I would think you had more than just a shekel, friend," an amused voice said. The tall young man took a step forward now and cast a sidelong glance at Alexandra, who had come to stand near her father. His gaze rested a moment on the amethyst clasp at her waist. Then, slowly, he raised his eyes to her face.

The girl felt her cheeks go hot. Her chin came up. "Are you Jews?" she demanded.

The question caught them all by surprise. "Can't you rich folk recognize your poorer brothers?" the redhead asked angrily. "Do you think we all travel with fine litters and servants?"

"I do not question the meanness of your appearance," she replied coldly, "but the poverty of your spirit. Indeed we recognize our brothers, for they greet us with *shalom*, and not with rude questions and," she added, looking straight at the tall young man with golden hair, "insolent eyes."

Samuel signaled her to be still, but Alexandra was not looking at her father.

The bandit grinned and took a step closer to her. "'A woman of valor,'" he said admiringly. "'What is her worth? Far above rubies...'" He stretched out his hand and with one finger touched the amethyst buckle.

She slapped his hand away. There was a flurry of movement in the background, but she was oblivious to it, as was the blond Galilean. They stared at each other, their eyes locked angrily, as though for this single, suspended moment no one else existed. She saw now that his eyes were a very deep blue. He had a strong, handsome face, the nose short and straight, lips cleanly chiseled above a firm chin. His skin was the color of bronze, and his hair was darkly gold. She knew she ought to be afraid of him, and in truth she was a little, but she was also determined not to let him see her fear. Suddenly, just when she thought she could not hold her gaze steady another moment, the anger left his eyes, and he laughed.

"Sadducee nobility!" The redhead spat again. "They might as well be Romans." He pulled a dagger from his belt. "Good riddance to them!"

"Joav!" The blond one gestured for him to be still.

"What harm have we done you?" Samuel asked wonderingly. "Are we not your brothers, as you say? Do we not suffer like you beneath the Roman yoke? And if our position is greater than yours, so too is our suffering, for we are treated poorly not only by Caesar's soldiers but also by men such as yourselves." He sighed. "What can I say? Our possessions offend you, yet you want them for yourselves. Take them. Your need is greater than our own."

Joav seemed confused by this. He looked to his companion for guidance.

"We do not seek these things for ourselves," the tall young man said quickly. "It is not our desire to be rich. We want only to be free men and to rid our land of the Roman. Your gold will be turned into steel."

Samuel nodded. "I have heard this."

"Also, there are men who cannot pay what Caesar demands. Without help they would be forced to sell themselves and their families into bondage."

Samuel nodded again. "Yes, the taxes are intolerable."

"But you tolerate them."

Samuel shook his head. "Only the hope that men may live

in peace. No sum is too great if it will insure that, and the safety of all we hold dear."

This roused Joav again. "Sadducees! They claim to care about the Torah, but all they care for is their own comfort. The words of the prophets are nothing to them. They copy the Greeks and read the writings of the gentiles. I know them well. They say they are sons of Zadok, David's priest, descended from Aaron, brother to Moses—but I say they are dirty sons of Rome!"

His speech seemed to set the others afire, and now they dismounted and set about appropriating whatever they deemed of value or interest. Shimon, who had stood pale and silent throughout, was relieved of his sword; but no one touched Samuel or Alexandra or made any move to rob the trembling servants. Some of the Zealots, however, tried to persuade members of the retinue to join their band, aided by the servant from the House of Anan, who was one of their number. But as none of the attendants was a slave and all had great affection for their employer, they shook their heads, confused by the suggestion.

The tall young man who appeared to be the outlaws' leader did not join in the looting. Leaning lazily against a tree in a manner Alexandra found most infuriating, he said pleasantly, "Don't look so troubled, friends. Think how much better your journey will be now that my comrades have relieved you of your heavy burdens. And consider that you have not lost anything of real value, but rather exchanged your goods for knowledge—a lesson in politics, if you will. And truly it is written," he said with a smile, "'How much better to get wisdom than gold, and understanding before silver.'"

"It is also written," the gray-eyed girl said tartly, "'Of what use is money in the hands of a fool? To buy wisdom when he has no sense?'"

His body seemed to roll off the tree toward her.

"Do not harm her," Samuel said hastily. "Take what you want, but let her be. She is only a child."

The Zealot looked up in surprise, as though he disagreed with Samuel's judgment. Then he looked back at Alexandra. "Then it is time," he said softly, "that she grew up." But he did not move.

The bandits, having completed their inventory and acquisition of goods and horses, were making ready to move off.

"There is a small leather pouch," Samuel said in a low tone.

"Its contents were meant as dowry money for my friend Avram's daughter. He is not a rich man, as you no doubt know. I promised . . ."

Again the young man looked surprised. He hesitated, looking back at his busy friends, then turned again to Samuel and gave a quick little nod.

The one called Joav came up to Alexandra now. Grinning, he put his hand on the amethyst set on her belt, drawing her to him as he did. She raised her fist, but before she could strike, Samuel said quietly, "Give him what he wants, Alexandra. Do not add to the man's sins by making him a murderer as well as a thief."

The burly Zealot stepped back, his face red with anger.

Obeying her father, Alexandra undid the clasp and placed the jewel in the man's hand. He stood there, seemingly at a loss. Suddenly, in a quick, catlike manner, the tall young man moved forward and, grabbing the pin from his comrade's open palm, angrily pushed him to his horse. Once again the dark blue eyes met Alexandra's stare. He threw the amethyst at her feet and without a word turned and jumped on his horse, signaling the men to leave.

Shimon found his voice. "You are brave enough now," he called after the departing band. "But what will you do against Rome and the might of Caesar?"

The one with golden hair turned back, his horse rearing up on its hind legs as he answered Shimon. "Caesar be damned! Judea is ours!"

"The legionaries will kill you!"

But the young Galilean only laughed. "What is death?" he shouted. "It is nothing. Freedom is all that matters! None but the Lord shall be our King!"

They watched him ride away up into the hills, lost finally in the dust of horses' hooves.

The rest of the journey was uneventful; Alexandra found it quite pleasant. "Liberated" from her horse, she ran happily through the flower-covered hills, gathering great bunches of anemones and daisies, which she gave to all present.

"You are crazy, Lexa," Shimon said. He was in a terrible humor. "By the Lord's own grace we have just escaped certain death, and you go running around like a field girl!"

She stuck a flower behind his ear. "Don't be cross. Bersabe

is only a short distance from here, father says. We are sure to arrive before nightfall." She laughed. "Anyway, you can use the exercise."

"Don't flip your gown like that. It is not modest. Father, look at her! Isn't it bad enough that we must walk all this way without her playing the fool?"

Alexandra laughed and began pelting him with flowers.

"All right, then," Shimon said, brushing a daisy from his hair. "If that's how you want it." And he took out after her, forgetting his fear and fatigue as they ran across the lush fields and up a hill sweet with laurel and the scent of new grass. He finally caught her by an oak, and laughing, they rested together against the tree.

"You are crazy," Shimon panted, shaking his head. "Why do you act like this? It is not seemly for a girl."

"Oh, Shimon, don't spoil it," she said breathlessly. "Look how beautiful everything is!"

He followed her glance and saw now the village of Bersabe below them, with its tidy rows of fields and houses, and in the distance beyond, the blue Kinneret dotted with the sails of fishing boats.

Alexandra stretched her arms up to the sky, feeling the blood like rich green sap rushing through her body, tingling in her fingertips.

"You could have gotten us all killed," Shimon said in a low voice. "You think you are so clever. But you don't know how a man could hurt you if he wanted."

"What do you mean?"

"Oh . . . never mind. But you go too far. Your husband won't let you get away with things the way father does."

"I'm never getting married."

"Yes, you are. You are betrothed to Ananus."

"I may be betrothed, but I won't marry him. I won't, I tell you. Something will happen, you'll see. Besides he's so stupid. He's even more stupid than you."

"How do you know? You've only seen him once, and no words passed between you."

"I know. I can tell. Anyway, all men are stupid." All but one, she thought. And he was in Rome.

"What will you do if you don't get married?" The idea shocked him. "What else is there for you?"

She did not answer. There was no point in telling Shimon she had long ago made up her mind to marry Josef ben Matthias.

How that would be accomplished, however, she was still not sure.

"If you don't like your betrothed, you could always marry one of the Sicarii." Shimon grinned. "I fancy that big blond Zealot looked hard enough at you. Yes, he'd be just the one, all right. He wouldn't take your nonsense. He'd beat some sense into you, and quick enough."

"He'd have to catch me first." She made a face. "Zealots! Sicarii! It is you who are crazy, Shimon."

He laughed, happy that he had finally provoked her.

Bersabe was not a large village, but it was a thriving one, thanks in part to Samuel ben Harsom, who kept a keen ear to his tenant farmers' needs. Avram came running now with his family to greet their party. While the men disappeared into the house, Alexandra remained outside with Avram's daughter Mary, a modest creature, willing and pretty in her own plump way, just like her sisters. The two older girls were married now, their futures insured by the dowry money bestowed by Samuel ben Harsom. There was a fourth daughter, younger than the rest, and a mute; and while some considered this affliction no disadvantage for a wife, the girl had one blue eye and one brown one, which had so far forestalled any match.

For once Alexandra did not have to rack her brains searching for a topic of conversation she could share with the country girl. "They were huge!" she exclaimed animatedly. "Goliaths! I've never seen such big men! And this one horrible one had red hair and mean little eyes, and for a moment I was sure he was going to kill us! Oh, he was so close! But I had a plan, you see. I thought I'd catch hold of his knife— Why do you make your eyes big? Do you think for a moment I was afraid? Well, even if I was—a little—I'd never let them know it! A Sadducee does not cringe before Sicarii! At least this one doesn't. Anyway, as I was saying— What are you looking at, Mary? Don't you want to hear what happened?" Annoyed, she turned around and, catching sight of two horsemen who had ridden into the area, gasped, "There they are! The bandits from the road! I must warn my father!" She started to run to the house, but Mary held her back.

"Don't be afraid," the girl said. "They will not harm us."

Alexandra stopped in amazement. "They are Sicarii! Daggermen! Murderers!"

"Oh, no! You only think so because you are rich and"—she hesitated—"friendly with the Romans."

"What are you saying?"

"Don't be angry with me. But it is true."

"What is true?"

Mary took a deep breath. "You live in an ungodly city—a city of the *Kittim*—so I suppose you cannot know any better. We do not hate the Zealots," she said suddenly. "They are our friends." And with that she went to the well to draw water.

Alexandra followed her. She could hardly believe what she had just heard. Especially from Mary. "How can you be friends with thieves and outlaws?"

"It is only Rome and the court of Agrippa who call them outlaws. Besides, they do not take anything from us. Only from those who have more than they need." She turned red. "Oh, Alexandra, I'm sorry!"

"That's all right." What was true was true. Certainly no one of the House of Harsom was poverty-stricken. She frowned. "But my father is a good man, Mary. Why, we have traveled all this way only to bring your dowry money, which, I may add, your Zealot friends took for themselves."

"Oh, I'm sure if they knew what it was for they would return it. Perhaps that is why they are here now. Anyway, I don't mind if they have it."

Alexandra was utterly amazed. "I suppose you wouldn't mind either if they had killed us," she finally blurted.

Mary lowered her head. "They do not like Sadducees."

"Well, fine! Because I don't like *them!* And we will see how well you like them when they bring the wrath of Rome on us all!" She was about to launch into a stern lecture that would have gladdened the heart of her uncle in Jerusalem, when something soft brushed against her leg. Jumping back nervously, she saw a baby lamb and, immediately forgetting Zealots, Sicarii, and the wrath of Rome, swept the little creature up in her arms. "Oohh . . . he's so soft. . . . Isn't he dear?"

"He was born four days ago," the girl said, relieved to see Alexandra smiling again. "You had best put him down. When they are small like that, once you pet them they follow you everywhere. You will never be able to lose him now."

"I don't care. He's lovely." There was something she had wanted to ask Mary. "You say I live in the city of the *Kittim*. What do you mean by that? Where did you hear such a word?"

"There are Essenes living with us in the village. The Holy Ones have joined the Zealots."

"I thought they did not believe in making war."

"They are against killing. But they prepare now for a great battle against the ungodly—the Sons of Darkness, they call them. The *Kittim*."

"The Essenes want a war against Rome?"

But Mary was no longer listening. Following her gaze, Alexandra now saw the tall young man with golden hair who had captured the girl's attention. He was speaking to a fellow with him—not, Alexandra was glad to see, the horrible redhead who had wanted to slit their throats. As the young Galilean sent his companion to the rear of the house, Alexandra found herself studying him despite herself, recalling the features she had seen at close range earlier in the day.

He was very tall, very broad-shouldered, but narrow through the waist and hips. He seemed hard to her, very strong, as though carved of rock or gold. His skin under the dust of the road was burned to bronze, and his hair was the color of the afternoon sun. He had dark, deep-set eyes that she knew were not black or brown but an intense shade of blue. She remembered how he had stared at her.

They were rude eyes, she thought, reddening as she recalled the slow, deliberate way he'd looked her over. And he had an insolent grin. Some might find him attractive, his smile appealing, though Alexandra could not imagine why. Still . . . there was something in the way he moved, a kind of easy grace . . .

Once, in the streets of Caesarea, she had watched a lion being led to the arena. There was something about this golden-haired Galilean that reminded her of the cat. It made her feel funny to think of it.

She shook her head as though to clear it, impatient with herself. What foolishness to waste thoughts on a common bandit! Certainly the maidens of the Galilee might kick each other's shins running to fetch water for such a creature, but not Alexandra bat Harsom! As though in confirmation of this opinion, she caught sight of Mary, totally enraptured by the sight of the young man, staring after him with what Alexandra always thought of as her "dumb cow's eyes." Alexandra expected the girl to utter a long *moo-oo* in his direction any minute. She had to laugh.

"Mary, you nitwit, what are you looking at?"

Mary sighed. "Oh, Alexandra, isn't he beautiful?"

Alexandra pretended to look all around. "Beautiful?" she echoed with mock ignorance. "Who? Ah! The little lamb! Yes, I told you he was a sweet creature. I did not realize you had grown so fond of him. Remind me to send you a dozen more when you are wed."

"No! Oh, Alexandra, you are really too mean!"

"I? Mean? I just said I would give you a present—"

"Sshh! He's coming this way!"

The girl was really an idiot, Alexandra decided. She pinched her hard to bring her to her senses, but Mary didn't seem to mind, so enthralled was she by the approaching figure. Disgusted, Alexandra put down the lamb and made to leave. But as she did, she felt a strong hand on her arm.

"Well, Gray Eyes, and are you no friendlier than before?"

"No more than you have learned any manners since we last met."

He let go of her arm and grinned, unperturbed by this show of disdain. Turning to the astonished Mary, he said in a courteous voice, "Would you be so kind as to find your brother, Aaron, and tell him I am come to see him?"

She hesitated, obviously wanting to stay, but a gentle smile from the Zealot nudged her into obedience. With a sigh and a last backward glance, she went off.

Alexandra tossed her head. "I would not have guessed you were capable of such soft speech."

"I have only respect for the good people who work the land."

"A fine one you are to say that, being what you are!"

"And what am I?" He moved toward her, smiling.

She took a step back. "You are a Zealot. You are one of the Sicarii."

"Oh? One and the same?" He took another step forward, and she two back. "Are you sure you know what a Zealot is? Or a—pardon, what was the other?"

"You are a bandit! A thief and a murderer! Yes, you are all murderers—and you rob people too! And—and you defy everyone, even the high priests! You want us to go to war and—Oh!" There was suddenly no place for her to go. The well was at her back, and it was lucky she hadn't fallen in.

"And who told you this? Your Roman friends?" The lids of his eyes lowered dangerously. Blue, deep as the sea far from shore, they seemed to take on a light, to gleam suddenly, as when the sun strikes upon water.

"I have no Roman friends. Everyone knows what you are. Your own brothers cry out against you."

"I have no brothers if they be those who bear the Roman yoke like sheep. I have no brothers if they be priests who eat the fat of the poor man's lamb, who grow rich on the Israelite's labor. I have no countrymen if they be those who bow to Caesar and kiss the feet of men who defile the land of God and degrade His people." He was very close to her now. The well post was at her back. There was no way for her to run, although she wished—and yet did not—to move away. As in their earlier meeting, she felt the power that came off him like something that touched her skin. She could not put a word to it, but it was a power, a force that drew one in. He seemed to move within a circle of light. . . .

"Yes," he was saying, easy again, the smile returning to his lips, "I suppose I am one of those the Romans call Sicarii."

He was so close to her now that she could feel the short knife beneath his cloak. Her eyes widened, but she raised her chin and said, trying to put some careless courage into her voice, "Shall you kill me, then?"

He grinned. "I don't think so. It is the custom in these parts to throw little fish back into the Galilee."

And then . . . she would remember his face coming down to hers, his dark blue eyes with that shot of light in them. . . . And then it was as if the sea had opened up for her and she was drowning in a golden dream, a green-gold haze, with honey feelings in her, all around her. . . . She was drowning in a strangely sunlit night.

It was the first time a man had kissed her as he would a woman, not a child. When he drew away at last, she stood quite still and dumb.

He grinned again. "Good-bye, Gray Eyes." And he was gone.

"So now you love him too." Mary had returned and stood smiling at the silent girl. Alexandra turned to her and gave her a good slap. Mary howled in pain, her eyes wide with confusion.

"You are so stupid, Mary, it is a wonder you walk on two feet and not four. What did you see, anyway?"

"N-n-nothing! Nothing! Only you staring after him, and—and—nothing!" She seemed genuinely bewildered.

"Oh, Mary, I'm sorry." She began to kiss and pet her.

"Truly I am. I have a wicked temper, and those men gave me such a fright on the road. There, I'm sorry. Say you don't mind. Please. Look, I shall give you this clasp. See how lovely the amethyst is. Oh, stop crying! Please! Why do you cry now? If you don't stop, I swear you will not have the clasp. There. That's better. Good. Are we still friends?"

"Yes," she sniffed, wiping her nose on her sleeve. "I guess so."

Alexandra sighed. The girl was such a ninny.

"The Law cannot be against a man defending himself," Avram was saying. "There would be none of us left to obey it if that were the case. I know the commandment says, 'Thou shalt not kill,' but—"

"The Covenant endures because of the righteous, not the vindictive," Samuel declared. "It rests upon the shoulders of the just, not upon the strength of armies."

"You would rely, then, solely upon the protection of the Lord?"

"In all things."

"Well and good, Samuel ben Harsom," the grizzled farmer replied. "But let us remember that the Lord helps those who first help themselves."

"In the Book of the Maccabee," Shimon broke in, eager to be part of the discussion, "it is written how a group of our people hid in a cave in their attempt to escape the soldiers of Antiochus and allowed themselves to be burned alive there rather than desecrate the Sabbath by doing battle. 'They did not defend themselves nor even block up their hiding place,'" he recited, casting a sidelong glance at Alexandra, who was duly impressed for once, "'saying, "Heaven and earth will testify in our behalf, that we have been destroyed against all justice."'"

"'But when the Maccabees heard this they mourned greatly,'" Avram's son, Aaron, continued in a firm voice, "'saying, "If all of us do as our brothers have done and do not fight for our lives and our laws, the heathen will soon destroy us all." And they said, "If any man attack us in battle even on the Sabbath day, let us oppose him, that we may not all die as our brothers did."'"

Samuel said nothing. He broke off a piece of bread and rolled it between his fingers until it became a ball of dough.

"The Law is the law," he said finally. "The sons of Matthias transgressed. They did so in a spirit of righteous conviction, but the fact remains, they transgressed."

"But they fought for the Law!" Avram exclaimed.

Samuel shook his head. "You do not fight for the Law by breaking the Law."

"It is easy for you to say," Aaron said now in a rather sullen tone. "You sit in your high place, protected by wealth. No one is pushing you into a cave where you must fight or die. No one comes into your house as though it were his own and puts his feet upon your table and causes your mother and sisters to hide themselves for fear of being evilly used. No ring of *Kittim* surrounds you and exposes your private parts, to laugh at you and call you 'mutilated' and 'half a man.'"

Shimon reddened. "We live in a gentile city, Aaron. I know what it is to bear their insults. The Greek whores walk with their heads high, loudly proclaiming how much better it is to be a harlot than a Jew."

"Why don't you kill them, then? Why don't you fight?"

"Aaron!"

"No, father, I will not be still!" He stopped, though, and caught his breath. "I did not mean to be insolent," he apologized, "but my heart is full. I am choking on this thing."

"It is all right," Samuel said gently. "I would rather sit with a man who is honest in his feelings though we disagree. Besides, my own son Joshua is of the same mind as you, Aaron. I can only hope the rabbis in Jerusalem have turned the fire of his spirit toward Torah and that the teachings of the gentle Hillel have placed some restraint upon his 'flaming' convictions." He smiled. "I am glad to see there is little truth in the talk of Galileans being unlearned. Your memory of the Book of the Maccabee is quite impressive, Aaron."

The boy lowered his eyes. "It . . . it is of special significance to many of us here."

"The rabbi of Bersabe must be quite a man, or you quite a scholar. 'A wise son maketh a glad father,' eh, Avram?"

But Avram was staring at his son.

"I . . . I did not learn it from the rabbi. I . . . I learned it from . . . from friends."

Avram's face had turned pale, the skin becoming like a parchment mask. "You said you would not go with them!"

The boy lowered his eyes again. "I have not taken the oath. But I can't help it if I believe they are right."

"Aaron," his father pleaded. "You are my only son. Their way leads to death—"

"All ways lead to death," the boy snapped, throwing his head back to face his father squarely. "Death is nothing. Freedom is all. Only the Lord shall be our king."

Alexandra's eyes widened.

"You have indeed become one of them," Avram mourned.

"Yes, father, in my heart. But I gave you my word. I will not leave until I have your permission—and your blessing."

"Never!" Avram thundered, bringing his fist down upon the table with such force that his wife and daughters came running in from the kitchen to see what had occurred.

Aaron was silent, his lips set in a thin line.

"You want to join the Zealots?" Samuel asked softly, in a bewildered voice. "You wish to ride with the Sicarii?"

"Yes." His voice was firm.

"But they are murderers! They kill their own people as easily as they do Romans."

"Traitors! They kill those who have betrayed us, who have sold us to Caesar!"

"They are thieves," Samuel protested.

Aaron looked steadily at the man. "Will you give your gold to raise an army against Rome? Will you contribute horses and weapons?"

Samuel shook his head. "War would only mean disaster and destruction for us all."

The boy smiled wryly. "Well, then . . ."

"I am not with you completely, Samuel," Avram said slowly. "I want the *Kittim* gone from our land. And the Zealots—even those who are called Sicarii—are not all you make them out to be. They are not the enemies of the people, of the *am ha'eretz*. You see how they gave back the dowry money. They do not take from us. But"—he turned again to his son—"I want you to stay away from them. There is a price on every man's head of the lot—and particularly your friend Eleazar. I too am fond of him. But he is the nephew of Menahem, leader of the Sicarii—"

"He is the grandson of the Galilean," Aaron said proudly.

"Yes, and it is death to be caught by the soldiers in his company. Aaron, please . . . you are my only son. . . ."

Aaron lowered his eyes again and said nothing.

$$\bullet \quad \bullet \quad \bullet$$

There were fires lit that night, and the young people danced around them, slowly at first, then faster and faster as the drums beat louder. Alexandra stood apart, watching the people of the village celebrate the spring harvest, seeing Mary walk off into the shadows with the young man who would soon be her husband, taking note of the band of young men around Aaron—Shimon among them—all of them engrossed in what seemed to be urgent conversation; and above all, dreaming...dreaming of a prince with dark hair like clusters of grapes upon his brow, with dark eyes that burned like the fire in the night.... She dreamed of Josef, and in her fancy saw him lead her to the well and kiss her there while the others danced....

"Who is the Galilean?" she asked later as they were returning to Caesarea.

Samuel's eyes were on the road. "Who?"

"The Galilean. Aaron said—"

"The Galilean? That must be Judah of Gamala."

"Who is Judah of Gamala?"

"Not now, Alexandra. I must mind what is before us. Have you forgotten our meeting with the Sicarii?"

"But they have already taken all our possessions." *And a kiss as well*, she thought, reddening slightly at the memory. "I do not think they will bother us again. Please, father, tell me about Judah of Gamala."

"He was a rebel," Shimon said, drawing his horse closer. "It was he who first organized the Zealots. Aaron told me all about him."

"What did he say? Tell me, Shimon, please!"

"What is it to you?" he teased, secretly thrilled that for once he knew something she did not. "Or are you planning to ride up into the hills and join the revolutionaries?"

"If I rode up into the hills it would be only to take back what was stolen from us," she retorted. "Which, I might add, you did little to preserve. And if I ever join a band of Zealots, it will be to run through cowards like you!"

His face flushed. "I don't blame you for saying that. You're right, Lexa. I behaved badly. You could have been hurt—you and father—and I did nothing to protect you. Aaron's right," he said suddenly, angrily. "We are all so used to stepping aside for the Romans, swallowing their insults, bowing to their commands, letting them do as they like, that we have forgotten how to be men."

Samuel turned to his son. "Prudence is not unmanly, Shimon. There are times when the wisest action is to take no action."

"I did not act out of wisdom or prudence, father," Shimon said bitterly. "I acted out of fear."

Samuel stared at the grim young man a moment; then, turning to his daughter, who was also staring at her brother, he said, "Now, what was it you were asking, Alexandra?"

"I—I wanted to know about Judah, called 'the Galilean,'" she stammered, hardly able to draw her eyes away from Shimon.

"I will tell you what I know. Perhaps Shimon can add to the tale. Long ago, you recall, in the days of the Maccabee, Judea was ruled by Antiochus Epiphanes, who dared proclaim himself 'God.' Antiochus wished to make our country a Greek state, and he forbade our people under pain of death to worship the God of Israel or follow the faith of Moses. It was then that the priest Matthias, father of Judah the Maccabee, stole from the Temple and, returning to Modin, the village of his own fathers, gathered the people in revolt."

"But what has this to do with Judah of Gamala?" Alexandra asked.

"When Matthias fled Jerusalem, the High Priest, Hezekiah, also disappeared. Many believed he had been murdered by Antiochus. But others said he was alive, living in a cave deep in the hills of the Galilee, where secretly he did all that was required of his office but had been forbidden."

"He did more than that!" Shimon exclaimed. "Aaron told me how he and his sons fought alongside the Maccabee."

"So it is said," Samuel agreed. "But there was a break in the families after the defeat of Antiochus, when the brothers of the Maccabee took the crown of Judea and began to call themselves Hasmoneans."

"They also took upon themselves the office of High Priest," Shimon reminded him, "although the uniting of priesthood with kingship has always been forbidden."

"What did the real High Priest, Hezekiah, say to this?" Alexandra wanted to know.

"No doubt he protested. In any event, he disappeared."

"He was murdered," Shimon declared. "The Hasmoneans

killed him and everyone in his family but for two sons who managed to escape."

"Was Judah of Gamala one of these sons?" Alexandra asked.

"Many generations would pass before the birth of the Galilean," Samuel replied. "The sons of Hezekiah would disappear among the towns and villages of the Galilee, the glory of Greece would fade, and while the Hasmoneans used up Judea's strength in senseless civil wars, Rome would take control. And a new Hezekiah would appear, calling upon the people to resist the rule of Caesar."

"Was he descended from the High Priest who had fled the Temple to fight alongside the Maccabee?" Alexandra asked.

"So it is said," her father replied. "He was a Pharisee rabbi— a warrior rabbi as, perhaps, his great-grandfather had been a warrior priest. Hezekiah's band did their best to disturb the *Pax Romana*, as the Zealots do today, raiding caravans, attacking small detachments. There was little anyone could do to stop them, but Herod finally managed to track down the renegades and to execute them rather brutally."

"But what has all this to do with Judah of Gamala?" Alexandra asked again.

"Hezekiah's infant son managed to survive Herod's massacre," Shimon explained. "When he was grown to manhood he continued the resistance, fighting not only Rome but also the false princes and priests of the House of Herod. Aaron says Judah of Gamala was a tall, broad-shouldered man, fearless, with a soft way of speaking that drew all to his will. The people called him 'the Galilean.' He was greatly loved."

Samuel nodded. "Unfortunately he met the same end as his father. He was captured and hanged by the procurator."

"He had three sons," Shimon went on excitedly. "Two were crucified, but the third son, Menahem, managed to escape capture. It is he who leads the Sicarii."

"The Sicarius we met on the road, Aaron's friend—I think his name is Eleazar—he is nephew to this Menahem, is he not?" Alexandra asked, knitting her brows.

"Yes, and the grandson of Judah the Galilean."

"If so," Samuel remarked, "then he is the last of a line that for more than a hundred years has refused to acknowledge a foreign king, even in death." He fell silent now, musing over the events he had related and the remarkable clan that for so many generations had stood so firmly for freedom.

Remembering the tall young man with golden hair who had spoken with such conviction at the well, Alexandra too was still. There had been that curious shot of light in his eyes, and when he took her in his arms . . .

Startled, she looked about; she felt embarrassed, as though she had been exposed in some intimate way. Angry with herself for harboring thoughts of a man who, though he might be an uncommon thief, was still, after all, a bandit, she determined to dismiss the Zealot completely from her mind. Which, in fact, she did for a very long time.

Shimon saw them first. He pointed to the men camped beside the road. "Father . . . look."

Taking note of the urgency in his son's voice, Samuel quickly followed his gaze. "I believe they are Essenes," he said, relaxing. "They will do us no harm. Strange . . . to see them here. I did not think they ever left their desert home."

Alexandra leaned forward on the small donkey she had been given, stretching her neck that she might catch a glimpse of the "Holy Ones."

There were three of them, two in their middle years, the third a boy of fifteen or so. They were dressed in the simplest of linen, but all in white; and though travel was harsh even on the excellent roads laid down by the Romans, they were remarkably free of dust and dirt. They appeared to be unhampered by possessions of any sort, nor was there any sign of weapons either on their persons or in the camp. As Samuel and his party approached them, an elderly man with hair and beard as white as his garments suddenly emerged from the trees. He had a small hatchet or paddle that he carefully wiped on the grass before depositing it in a knapsack on the ground.

"*Shalom*," Samuel said. "Peace to you."

The Essenes nodded. "And to you and yours," one of the men replied.

"Will you travel with us? The roads abound with many dangers. These hills are home to the Sicarii—and you are alone and unprotected."

"Our safety lies with the Lord. Besides, it is the Sicarii we seek. Do not be alarmed," he added quickly, seeing their concern. "There is no reason for you to be fearful."

"I thought—your white attire—you were of the community of the Holy Ones." Samuel gestured at the knife he saw suspended from the man's leather belt. "But I know now I was mistaken. No Essene would have upon him any weapon other than the burying tool for his body's waste. And no Essene would seek the company of thieves and killers."

"You seem to have some knowledge of our ways." The white-haired man stepped forward. "Yes, we are from Qumran. There are many of us now among the people of the land."

"For what reason," Samuel asked, "have the Apostles of Peace ventured forth?"

"We have not come to speak of peace but of war."

"War with Rome?"

"The War of the Sons of Light against the Sons of Darkness."

Samuel was silent, the astonishment in his eyes giving way to bewilderment and then despair.

"Do not be troubled," the Essene said softly. "You fear that which you do not know, which is the way of men. But I will tell you now of the mystery to come and the End of Days that draws near." He came closer and said, "On the day when the *Kittim* fall, a day appointed from ancient times, the land of Israel shall be returned to the righteous, and all wickedness shall be banished, as darkness is banished by light. The spirit of knowledge shall fill the world, and folly shall no longer exist."

Samuel sighed. "And how many will die?" he asked. "How many will suffer?"

The elder nodded. "There will be terrible carnage."

"Can this be the will of the Lord?"

From the God of Knowledge comes all that is and all that shall be. Before they ever existed, He established their whole design, and when they come into being, it is in accord with His will."

Samuel said nothing. He thought of Avram's son, Aaron; the Sicarii on the road; his own son Joshua. . . . And now the Essenes, the Holy Ones, venerated as the men closest to understanding and embodying the perfection of God's will . . .

It was inevitable, he thought suddenly. War was inevitable.

Alexandra came forward with the waterskin, offering it to the men beside the road, but they drew back from her as if she were diseased. Confused, she stood there with the bag and cup.

"They won't go near you because you're a woman," Shimon whispered.

The girl reddened, anger filling her body with heat.

Suddenly the white-haired Essene came up to her. He touched her hand, and she felt her shame and fury leave her, as when a cool wind touches sunburnt flesh.

"You have the eyes of morning light," he murmured, wondering. He raised his hand to her face, touching a long, bony finger to her cheek. His own eyes were like a dark well that seemed to go back to a place before time and a time before place. "You seek the Light that springs from Knowledge," he said, "but you will only find it through your heart." He took the cup from her hand and nodded for her to pour a libation, to which he touched his lips. "Trust in the deeds of God," he said in a soft voice, returning the cup to her. "He will direct your steps to the way." He smiled, and she felt bathed in a sweet warmth. "May the Lord bless you with all good, Daughter of Light. May He preserve you from all evil."

Beni was waiting anxiously at the villa. He was recovering from the "spotted sickness," for which reason he had missed the journey to Jerusalem and Bersabe. He seemed pale, which might have been ascribed to his recent illness; but in fact the boy's nervousness stemmed from something else.

"The procurator was here," Beni whispered to Alexandra.

"What did he want?"

"I don't know. He acted funny."

"Did he come with the soldiers?"

"No, he came alone. Lexa...he walked straight into mother's chamber. She was not expecting him—I am sure of that because she looked so surprised to see him. I know, because I followed him into her room. He wanted me to leave, but she hugged me to her and would not let me go."

"What did he say?"

"He said she had the eyes of a cat. And mother said if that were so then he had the eyes of a dog, because the one chases the other."

Alexandra smiled.

"Then he said other things to her, funny things. I didn't understand it all, but it made mother very angry. She said the procurator must leave because she might be ill with the same malady that her son—she meant me—had suffered. Gessius Florus asked what that was, and when mother said I'd had the spotted sickness he left in a great hurry." The boy laughed, remembering the man's hasty retreat. Then he grew serious. "She was scared, Lexa. Mother was frightened. I could see it in her eyes. And she held me to her so tightly I could scarcely breathe. And she was shaking. I've never seen her like that, have you?"

Alexandra shook her head and stared thoughtfully at the door to the chamber that the Roman procurator had dared to enter, and where her father had quickly gone to his wife.

While not a frequent visitor, Gessius Florus was no stranger to Beit Harsom. Treasure brought up from the holds of Samuel ben Harsom's ships—a length of prized China silk or goblet carved of onyx—sometimes won remission of a poor man's prison sentence, and a dinner in the Roman's honor was an appropriate time to discuss pardon for one accused of some trumped-up misdemeanor.

What treasure did the procurator seek now? Alexandra wondered.

Samuel held his wife close. "He will not touch you. I swear it. I will go to him—"

"No! Samuel, no!" Devorah pulled away, her green eyes piercing his. "You must not, or say one word of what has passed here. Promise me you will not. . . ."

"Devorah, I would be less than a man if I—"

"You will be less than a man if you confront him. You will be dead. Or worse. Lost in the catacombs of his prison . . . dispatched to the salt mines . . . Who knows what charge Florus would bring against you? Have you not heard the talk of his torture chamber? They say he wields the whip himself, that he enjoys it! Samuel! I beg you . . . let it pass. Let it pass. . . ."

THREE

The tall young Zealot who so disturbed Alexandra had ridden away from Bersabe alone, leaving his companion to enjoy the harvest celebration and the attentions of family and friends. Eleazar ben Ya'ir had no family to detain him, and he never stayed in any town or village longer than was necessary. The hills were Eleazar's home, had been since he was twelve and orphaned by the legion, his mother raped and killed, his father nailed to the cross. But even before that time, in happier, earlier years, he was always to be found in the open land of the Galilee, running free across the rich plain—on foot or on the back of a borrowed horse—climbing to the highest, deepest cave, or lying in the limbs of the taberinth at night, listening to the wind calling to the stars through the leaves of the ancient oak. He was quick to learn, the rabbis said, but restless in the quiet of the schoolroom, and impatient with dictated curriculum. He was uneasy in the great Temple in Jerusalem the time his father took him there; and though he would not say it, he had not found the Almighty in the Temple, and never would. For him, the Lord was in the hills, in the land he loved; and while he hated the Romans who had defiled his country with their temples and standards and crosses of death, he would never stop loving the God that he knew in the wind and the stars and the taberinth.

He must have been loved in turn by the Lord—or so it was thought of those as fair as he; moreover, in all his forays against Rome or the mercenaries who protected Agrippa—grandson of Herod, and Judea's titular monarch—he had never received a wound or scar, which was considered another sign of the Lord's favor. Like David, he was made in the beauty of legendary kings, taller than most men, with the strong, broad shoulders of his grandfather Judah, and a certain sinuous yet masculine grace. His hands were large, the hands of a farmer or fisherman like his own father. But the darkly golden hair and deep-set eyes were identical to those of his ancestor the High Priest Hezekiah, who, two centuries before, had left the Temple in Jerusalem to fight alongside the Maccabee.

A sudden rustling of leaves caused him to draw up his horse, one hand on the hilt of the knife stuck through his belt. Then he saw Miriam running toward him and smiled. He waved and waited until she had come up to him.

"Eleazar! Oh, Eleazar, I'm so glad you are back! I thought—I was afraid—"

He shook his head, still smiling. "You are always worrying about me. I'm the one who is supposed to take care of you, remember? Didn't Joav tell you I had gone into Bersabe?"

"Yes, but—"

"Little cousin," he teased, "you are worse than a mother."

She hung her head, abashed.

"Come on," he said, laughing, and pulled her up behind him.

Hesitantly, she put her arms around his waist, glad that he could not see her face, uncomfortably aware of the sudden rapid beating of her heart. She was a tall girl with long, blond braids and the blue-green eyes that were said to be a Galilean's only jewels. More than a few in camp would have liked to marry the fair, soft-spoken Miriam, but she would not leave her uncle and cousin, preferring to tend to them like the daughter and sister neither had. The truth was that she had always been in love with Eleazar. He could not know how he had wounded her by saying "mother" and not "wife." She sighed and laid her cheek against his back.

"Is uncle well? Has the falling sickness come upon him again?"

"Not since the night you and the others rode out." She raised her head. "He is in wonderful spirits. We have been visited by three Essenes, one of whom seems to be very important to their sect. The others call him Righteous Teacher. Menahem says that in the midst of the falling sickness he heard the voice of the Lord telling him these men would come to him. He is very excited. I hope he does not . . . you know . . ." She shuddered, recalling the man writhing on the ground, foaming at the mouth in one of his epileptic seizures. "I know it is a holy thing, that the Lord speaks to him then . . . but it frightens me. It seems so terrible."

"God is sometimes terrible," Eleazar answered.

"I suppose so. Still, I hope the Lord has said all that He wants to say for now. It frightens me," she said again.

They had reached the camp of the Zealots. Eleazar dismounted with the ease of a natural athlete. Smiling, he lifted Miriam to the ground and brushed a leaf from her pale hair.

Joav came up to him now. "Why didn't you take me to Bersabe instead of Baruch?" he demanded.

"I thought you'd have your stomachful of Judean nobility." He grinned and slapped his comrade on the back.

"We should have finished them off on the road," Joav growled. "Let a Sadducee live, and he'll have the legion on you before you turn around."

"There, you see? Just thinking about them makes you turn color. You look like an angry grape."

Miriam laughed. The ginger-haired outlaw had indeed become quite purple in the face.

"Why didn't you let me kill them?" Joav insisted.

"The girl too?"

He was shocked. "Are you mad? I don't kill women."

"Why not?" Eleazar asked easily. "She was a Sadducee. Why stop with her father and brother?" The smile left his face. "When you ride with me," he said evenly, "do not speak of killing unless you have soldiers in mind. Save your sword for the *Kittim*, Joav. I don't murder civilians. And I won't kill Jews."

"They are not Jews," Joav said, following him. "They are Greeks, or as good as, Greeks and Romans. They don't even speak the language of Israel among themselves. And they look down on us. They hate us. They hate us as much as—"

"As we hate them," Eleazar finished quietly.

"Why not? Who has more right? And you— When your grandfather—blessed be his memory—when he raised the people against Rome, did they, did the rich and the mighty of holy Jerusalem care? What was a tax to them? They would not forfeit their children or their own freedom to pay it. They would bow and call Caesar god just so they might live in their grand villas. They wanted no part of Judah of Gamala. They begged the authorities to do away with him. They were glad when he was killed, when his sons were crucified. Our war is with these priests and princes of Judea as much as it is with Rome. They, too, are the ungodly. They are the *Kittim*."

Eleazar's jaw tightened. "We don't have a chance," he said in a low voice, "unless we are all in this together. We can't fight inside and outside at the same time. We are a small enough force—even taken together—against the legions of Rome."

"The Lord is on our side," Joav said confidently.

"Then you had better pray He takes it upon Himself to unite us, my friend. Otherwise," he said again, "we haven't a chance."

"Well . . ." Joav was uneasy. He had never before heard one of their number express doubt. "The Essenes are with us now. That should count for something."

Eleazar shrugged. "The Holy Ones have been sending members of their sect out for some time now. It is hardly a secret that they are against the presence of Rome. It was they who first called Caesar's men *Kittim*."

"But this is something more."

"You had better see Menahem. He asked to be told when you returned to camp."

"It is important, then?"

"Go to your uncle. He will tell you."

The leader of the Sicarii was in high humor and embraced his nephew with hearty affection. His eyes were feverishly bright, and his red beard seemed like a thing alive, like the curling flames of a fire. He was a big man, no taller than Eleazar but massively built, so that he seemed twice the size of the young man. Those closest to him, men who had been with him since earliest times, referred to him with fearful affection as the Red Bull. Many a legionary had felt the bull's charge; few had lived to tell of it.

"They have come to me, Eleazar," Menahem cried, his deep voice vibrating with excitement. "To me! The time is near," he went on in a rush. "The great battle at the End of Days . . . the War of the Sons of Light against the Sons of Darkness. The leader of the battle has at last been revealed to them. Their prophesies have led them here." He spread his arms wide. "It is in their sacred writings . . . 'The name of the Messiah is . . . Menahem'! I am ready, Eleazar," he said, dropping his arms, his voice becoming a whisper. "The warrior of the Lord is ready. I will lead our people to the freedom so long denied us, and then to the true destiny of the Chosen—to greatness!"

Eleazar grinned. "Let's start with the first, uncle. Freedom seems hard enough to attain."

"You must have faith, Eleazar." Menahem frowned. "You must not make light of this. I speak to you now of the will of the Lord, our God."

"I know it is God's will that men should not make slaves of other men," Eleazar replied. "And I know there is no one better than you, uncle, to lead us in this great battle."

Menahem smiled now. "And there is no one I would rather have beside me than the son of my beloved sister, Rachel— you, who have been like my own son these many years. And even before.... You were always my son, Eleazar. Mine, and your grandfather's. Your father, may he rest in peace, was not one of us. He was a good man, but he hadn't a warrior's heart. Even after the death of the Galilean, after my brothers were crucified...he still could not bring himself to join us." His face darkened, then grew sad. He sighed. "Well, but he was good to your mother. And she loved him. How she loved her fisherman, the man called Ya'ir." Menahem nodded to himself. Once more his mood changed, his features contorting with anger, his voice becoming hard and bitter. "But his innocence did not save him the day the soldiers came. They passed my sister among themselves...and they nailed her gentle fisherman to a cross. He was still alive when we rode back into the village. Do you remember, Eleazar? I had taken you hunting in the hills. You were only twelve, not yet a *bacchur*, but I wanted to see if you had the heart of a warrior. I feared you were like your father. Well, but I soon found out what you were made of! Not in the hills hunting game but in the village below, fighting Romans!" The Red Bull's eyes sparkled. "They were no match for us, were they? A dozen soldiers against one man and a boy! And they were no match for us!" He threw his arms around his nephew, embracing him, tears welling up in his eyes. "When it was over you came back to me. Twelve years old and a *bacchur*—a warrior, an outlaw, and an orphan all in one day." Shaking his head at the memory, Menahem released the young man but continued to pat him on the back. "And here you have been ever since. My right hand. My son." Suddenly, his features grew stern. His hand dropped. "But you are lax, Eleazar. You are lax."

Accustomed though he was to the frequent, swift changes of emotion that more and more seemed to characterize his uncle, Eleazar took a step back, surprised at this sudden severity and puzzled as to Menahem's meaning.

"You pray wherever you stand," the Zealot accused, "instead of facing Jerusalem. Don't deny it. I have seen you. And you are late many a morning to offer your prayers to the Lord."

Certain Menahem was joking, Eleazar grinned. "Well, uncle, there is hardly room in one family for two messiahs. I will let you be my passkey to the Lord's favor."

The Red Bull's arm shot out, the suddenness of the blow nearly knocking down the startled young man. "And His wrath," Menahem thundered. "I will tolerate no laxity in your devotion to the Law. You do not seem to realize what it means to have the Essenes join us, to have the Holy Ones with us. For a long time I have heard the voice of the Lord telling me . . . telling me . . ." His voice trailed off. "Come," he said suddenly, once more putting his hand on his nephew's shoulder. "You shall meet the men from Qumran. Yes, I want you to meet them. Eleazar . . . the time is near!"

The white-haired Essene leaned back against the wall of the cave. It was not as he had thought it would be. Something was wrong, but he could not say what it was that disturbed him. He closed his eyes, focusing on the spot of light he saw within his self-imposed darkness, letting his body float free in his mind's night. His breathing deepened, then grew light, almost imperceptible. His eyes opened and, from a point outside his body, took in the area of the firelit cave, the awed Zealots in one corner, his two companions beside him, and himself, seated cross-legged on the damp earth. For a moment he hovered over himself and then returned within, spirit harbored once more inside the mortal framework of flesh and bone. But no answer had come to him, only a growing doubt.

Had he misread the prophecies? *From the seed of Hezekiah . . . from the loins of the Galilee . . . the leader of the Righteous, armed in strength and beauty and the Lord's love . . . the Warrior of the Lord will lead the Sons of Light in the great battle at the End of Days. . . .*

Nathaniel placed his hand before his eyes.

. . . The name of the Messiah is . . . Menahem. . . .

No. It was not Menahem. The man fulfilled the bloodline of the prophecies, and yet . . . And yet . . . no. It could not be Menahem.

"Are you well, teacher? Has the journey been too hard?"

Nathaniel let his hand fall. "Thank you, Jonatan," he said quietly. "I am not ill, only . . . troubled."

The boy knit his brows. "Have we come to the wrong place?"

"No. That which we seek is here, I am sure of it. Only . . ." He sighed. "Perhaps you are right. I am tired after all, and there is so much noise. . . . It is not quiet like the desert. Like Qumran."

As if to illustrate the Essene's complaint, the Sicarii leader now returned, the clatter and thud of sword and boot accompanying his great, booming voice. "Holy Ones," Menahem announced, "this is my nephew." With undisguised pride he put his hand on the shoulder of the tall young man beside him. "Eleazar. My sister Rachel's son."

Nathaniel felt a sharp chill cross the back of his neck. He leaned forward slightly. "Judah of Gamala had a daughter?"

"My sister, yes. She was killed by the *Kittim*." Menahem's eyes flashed, his hatred feeding once more at the fires of memory. "The boy's father was crucified."

The Essene nodded sympathetically. But his breath had quickened, and his dark eyes went now to the young man who had been standing quietly, respectful but at ease throughout this exchange, and who met the penetrating stare of the Righteous Teacher with an even, steady gaze. The light from the fire seemed to cast a glow upon the young Galilean's head and shoulders, haloing the darkly blond hair with a kind of misty flame. Then, inexplicably, Nathaniel had a sudden vision of the young female he had encountered on the road. The girl's strange, light eyes seemed transposed onto the features of the young man before him. Then the vision faded and vanished. *Their paths are intertwined*, the Essene thought with some surprise, but how and why was not to be considered now. There were more important matters.

With no trace of fatigue, like a young man, Nathaniel rose effortlessly to his feet, continuing to study the nephew of Menahem with such intensity that the leader of the Sicarii also turned to look at Eleazar and then back again at the Essene.

"You are without mother and father," Nathaniel said at last. "You must feel quite alone."

"No man is alone," Eleazar replied, "so long as he believes in the Lord."

"Still . . . your parents killed so cruelly . . . You must hate the Romans greatly."

"I hate what they do to our people."

Nathaniel nodded slightly. A light was beginning to glow

in his dark eyes. There would be more questions later. There must be time for him to talk alone with this young man, grandson of Judah of Gamala. There was much to learn about him, and much to teach. But for now, Nathaniel was content. He had come, after all, to the right place.

"The son of Ananias is here," Joav said. "The party was spotted on the road. They have not been followed."

"Good. Are all the men with him?" Eleazar asked. "Are they all right?"

"All seems to be well. Menahem has said you may carry out the exchange with your Sadducee friend."

Eleazar shook his head ruefully. "You call him that, Joav? Hasn't he proved to you by now that he is one of us? He could have betrayed us many times. Why are you still suspicious?"

"He is the son of the High Priest."

"He is my friend. We share the same name and the same cause. Don't forget, it was Eleazar ben Ananias who first thought of the ransom exchange. Come on, let's go and meet him on the road."

"No need for that. He is here." As he spoke, a half-dozen riders entered the camp, five of them Sicarii, and one the son of the High Priest of the Temple in Jerusalem. Laughing, the men dismounted, calling greetings to their comrades, who now came up to welcome them. The trick had worked again.

It was a simple enough maneuver, owing its success to the premise that the men Rome sent to Judea were more interested in filling their pockets than in catching Zealots. It had begun during the governorship of Albinus, whom the High Priest, Ananias, had taken great pains to cultivate. Unaware that his own son, commander of the Temple guards, held Zealot sympathies, Ananias responded immediately when the young man was "kidnapped" by Menahem, who threatened to kill him unless ten Sicarii captured by Albinus were released.

The High Priest had finally persuaded Albinus to yield; henceforth, the Sicarii regularly ransomed their men by kidnapping one or another of Ananias's dependents. The practice continued when Gessius Florus succeeded Albinus as procurator, with the new governor amusedly declaring that he did not give a damn who stole what from whom in Judea, so long as he received his share.

The two Eleazars embraced, the one tall and blond, the

other dark and with the aquiline nose of his Babylonian forebears.

"How goes it in the Holy City?" the Galilean asked with a grin. "Any more murders committed by the Sicarii?"

"Two each day, by my reckoning. One of the sons of the House of Phiabi was stabbed by his slave-mistress. The family dragged the body into the street and set up the lamentation that he was slain by Zealots for defending the Law." He laughed ruefully. "I fear every pickpocket and murderer in Jerusalem goes free while the blame for their crimes is placed squarely on your uncle."

"Amazing, isn't it," Eleazar said good-naturedly, "how he gets around?—and with only two legs to carry him!"

The priest's son laughed. "It makes me think I might write my name in the blood of a few high-placed traitors and let you take the credit. After all, it would not be a lie to say, 'Eleazar did this,' would it?"

"I doubt you would achieve the confusion you desire. Menahem the Sicarius is famous throughout Judea. But who knows the name of Eleazar ben Ya'ir?"

"They will, my brother," the son of Ananias replied. "And soon. When we gather the people together against Rome, I shall command the forces of Jerusalem, and you will be general of the Galilee."

"The people might not follow me. You forget, they look to my uncle."

"They look to you, Eleazar." It always amazed him how unaware the Galilean was of his own power. "The people follow your uncle because of what he stands for and who he is. They respect him, and they fear him, but they love you. It is you," he repeated, "whom they love."

Eleazar shook his head, uneasy. "You don't know Menahem. You don't know how generous he can be. He is different with you, cold and suspicious because you are a Jerusalemite and a prince."

"I know. He hates my father."

"He hates all the priests. He believes the bloodline of our ancestor Hezekiah supersedes those who now serve in the Temple. He believes—" He hesitated. "He believes, by virtue of descent—that he is the rightful High Priest."

"And he is probably right," the High Priest's son said calmly. "But there are others with the blood of Aaron in their veins. You, for instance."

"I? My father was a fisherman."

"Your mother was the daughter of Judah the Galilean."

"I do not care if she was the daughter of Moses. I would as soon be a tanner or a cutter of trees as spend my days in the Temple. The place stinks."

"Incense and blood. The Lord's chief delight."

"I do not think so, Eleazar ben Ananias. I think the Lord loves honest prayer more than the stench of perfume and slaughtered animals—or He is no God of mine." He grimaced. "That charnal house! How can you stand it?"

"You miss the whole point." The Jerusalemite was amused. "The splendor, the glory, all those treasures—all of it leading up to a tiny, curtained room, the Holy of Holies, around which and to which all this magnificence has been built. And behind the curtain, inside the room—nothing. Absolutely nothing."

Eleazar ben Ya'ir shrugged. "I am not learned in these matters. I leave the Temple and its significance to you—and welcome to it."

"Well, I am only Captain of the Guards, not a priest. I leave that to my father and brothers—and as you say, welcome to it!"

They laughed together.

"But speaking of learning," the son of Ananias said, "where is the tutor I left with you? Your five companions have been returned, but I have yet to see my cousin. Where is the beauteous Tabitha? Her husband, the priest Nicodemus, is, as you may imagine, quite anxious to have her beside him again. I am sure," he added drily, "that she is as anxious to return to him."

The outlaw grinned. "Surely."

"You did not mind, I hope, learning the language of Rome from a woman?"

"The important thing is that I am able to read the enemy's dispatches. It eliminates torturing couriers."

"That bothers you."

"I don't like seeing us behave as they do, as the *Kittim* do. Tell me, how did 'the beauteous Tabitha' learn the language of the Romans?"

"She is a clever woman," her cousin said with a smile.

"Assuredly," the young man replied with a certain private respect.

The Jerusalemite cast a sidelong glance at the handsome Galilean. "You had best be careful, Eleazar. My cousin can be quite possessive and demanding, especially if she considers you to be in her debt."

Eleazar ben Ya'ir grinned. "Don't worry. She's been paid in full."

"How so?"

"The learning was two-sided, my friend. She taught me a few things, and"—he cleared his throat—"I did the same for her."

"Well, she doesn't seem any the worse for it," the Jerusalemite murmured as an angry young woman stormed up to him. "Tabitha. Dear cousin. You look wonderful. Country air agrees with you."

"You promised me a month," she said angrily. "You said it would take at least that long to arrange the exchange. You owe me a week."

"Dear Tabitha. The rigors of hill life have not dimmed your graciousness and charm." He spread his hands. "I'm sorry. It was easier than I thought."

"Well for you to say! You don't have to go back to an old man who—" She stopped. "Never mind." She sighed. "And we were just beginning to get on . . . so well . . . together." She looked wistfully at the tall Galilean.

Eleazar ben Ya'ir bowed his head slightly and cleared his throat. "You have been most cooperative, madam. It gives us heart—here in the hills—to know that we have friends in quarters where we would least suspect."

"Mmmnn." She looked up at him and sighed again. "I suppose it is too dangerous for you to come to Jerusalem. . . . I mean, it would be a pity not to continue your . . . education."

The Zealot grinned. "I would be a coward indeed not to match your courage."

She smiled, content. Later, however, as she rode beside her cousin, headed home to Jerusalem and the arms of her loving if aged husband, the Judean noblewoman sighed again. "What a pity," she mused. "If only he were of priestly blood—or at least a Jerusalemite."

Ben Ananias looked at her with unconcealed amusement. "I gather you refer to your Galilean captor." He laughed. "The fact is, my dear Tabitha, Eleazar ben Ya'ir—by all that is holy to us—should be commanding the Temple guard, not I. While your ancestors and mine were scratching out a living in the Delta quarter of Alexandria, his were offering sacrifice upon the altar of Solomon's Temple."

"But he is a Galilean!"

"Spoken like a true Jerusalemite." He laughed again but then grew sober. "There are more true kings and priests in the Galilee, cousin, than sit in the royal palace or the Temple. Farmers, fishermen, workers of wood . . . For too long now, the arena has served as their court, and the cross their throne."

"How depressing you are," she replied. "Really, I did not know you were so melancholy." She raised an eyebrow. "I suppose you will now tell me the Messiah will arise out of the *am ha'eretz* to assume the crown of David." She wagged her finger at him. "You have been listening to slave tales, cousin— or talking to Pharisees."

"Why did you agree to be a hostage, Tabitha?" he asked suddenly. "Why did you want to be part of this?"

She shrugged delicately. "For the adventure. The excitement. Men are not the only ones to need such things."

"You think that is why—"

"Surely you do not really mean to aid those whose rise to power would mean the end of all we know and enjoy. That big redbeard is a madman! I had time enough to hear the talk in camp. His followers call him the True High Priest. Lucky for us they haven't a chance to succeed in what they wish to do. Can you imagine that peasant rabble in Jerusalem? Horrendous . . ." She looked at him, angered by his silence. "What do you suppose would become of your family if they took over? Have you any idea how greatly these people hate your father? No, my dear, you cannot tell me you have involved yourself with the Zealots because you share their cause."

"Why, then?" he asked quietly.

She laughed. "Because it is amusing."

The son of the High Priest said nothing. It was better to let the woman believe as she did. But she had touched upon a tender spot. He was not unaware of the animosity directed toward his father. Menahem had promised, however, that the High Priest would suffer no harm at the hands of the Sicarii; he had pledged this. Eleazar ben Ya'ir had also given his word that his friend's father and brothers would never be a target of violence.

What a pity, the Jerusalemite thought suddenly, that the Zealot could not get to know the priest in the same way that he wished Eleazar ben Ananias to view Menahem. Ananias was set in his ways, but the old man was no fool, the son thought. He knew very well what and who was behind this constant kidnapping and exchange of hostages. He had even remarked to his secretary, seeing the man laden with work, that he might perhaps enjoy a vacation in the country as a respite, adding with a sidelong glance at his youngest son, "It seems easy enough to arrange."

Ben Ananias suppressed a laugh. The old man was certainly no one's fool. He frowned. But in a way he was—to believe that Rome could be controlled, kept content, and most of all, that Rome could maintain order in Judea. The people were like a mass of twigs and straw, the slightest spark serving to set all aflame. Practical arguments in favor of peace were useless against a resentment that had been building up for generations. Nor were matters helped by the behavior of the procurator—especially Gessius Florus. When Cestius Gallus, the governor of Syria, had come to Jerusalem at Passover time, thousands had gathered around him to beg for relief from Florus's tyranny. The man in question had stood beside Gallus and laughed. "You know the Jews," he'd said, waving their complaints aside.

"He has managed to convince Gallus of the inconsequence of the talk against him," Ananias had remarked later, "but he is worried." The High Priest had looked straight into his son's eyes. "You may get your war after all, Eleazar, and sooner than you think. The procurator is thinking of helping you to it. The acts of one man tend to be diminished by the proportions of full-scale revolt. My son, if you love your country as I know you do, tell your friends. . . . Don't play into his hands."

But the priest's warning had only served to excite Menahem further. "The time is near," he kept saying. "The time is near. . . ."

FOUR

"I tell you, there's going to be trouble," Shimon declared. "The Greek builds his swine shop closer and closer to the synagogue. Soon he will be right on top of us. It's bad enough having to enter the house of worship through an alley—but the smell! And the taunts of that man and his pig-eating gang of—"

"Enough, Shimon. I know how you feel," Samuel said. "We are all unhappy about the turn of events. But you and your friends must not cause any trouble."

"Trouble! There has been nothing but trouble for us ever since Nero handed Caesarea over to the Greeks! You and your friends have been removed from the city council, and the new authorities permit every act of vandalism and harassment against our people to pass unpunished. Meanwhile, they have refused us the right of assembly, and there is talk they are going to prosecute the elders of the synagogue for 'maintaining an unlicensed club'!"

"As you say, it is only talk."

Exasperated, Shimon turned away.

"Father has spoken to the procurator," Alexandra said, coming forward. "Haven't you, father?"

Samuel nodded. "Florus has been given eight silver talents to halt the building of the swine shop. He promises full cooperation."

"And does nothing," Shimon finished. "Just as he promised he'd persuade the man to sell the property to you and did nothing about that. Well, if he won't put a stop to what's going on, there are those of us who will!"

"Shimon, listen to me. You must not start a fight. The Roman cohorts are Greeks and Samaritans. You would find yourself facing them as well as the citizens of Caesarea. I know how you feel," Samuel repeated, "but the only things to be gained by the kind of confrontation you want are broken bones and heads. Yours, and those of your friends, I fear." He paused. "I wish it were otherwise. It is not. So hold your temper in check, my son, and let others devise more subtle and effective means to gain our end."

"Like buying the procurator?"

"Yes."

"How can you put your faith in Gessius Florus?"

"I have not found him to be unreasonable in the past."

"He will take your money with one hand and stab you in the back with the other."

"We shall see." Samuel rose. "I have some accounts to look over. Shimon . . . you will not do anything foolish, will you?"

"No. I will not do anything . . . foolish." But when Samuel had gone from the room, Shimon turned to his sister with an outburst of emotion. "What's happened to him? He never used to be like this. Doesn't he understand what's happening?"

"I heard him talking to mother about sending us all to Jerusalem."

"Running away isn't the answer. Anyway, I don't want to live in Jerusalem. This is my home. Why should we leave? Or give up all that is ours?"

"Good for you, Shimon!"

He flushed with pleasure. "Well, something has got to be done. If we let things go on as they are, we'll end up with no rights at all. Anyone in the city—not just the Romans—will feel free to walk into a Jew's house and do as he likes. Greeks, Samaritans . . ." He stood up and cleared his throat. "I'm going out for a walk."

"Let me come with you."

"No." He paused. "There is to be a meeting," he said in a low tone.

"You promised father you wouldn't get into trouble."

"I said I wouldn't do anything foolish. Anyway, we're not going to start trouble. But we're going to be ready for it when it comes."

"Let me come with you," she said again.

"You can't, Alexandra. You're—"

She held up her hand. "Don't say it." She sighed. "Oh, how I wish I were a man!"

"I, too," he said solemnly. "You have spirit, sister. I would not mind having you at my side in the days ahead."

"Oh, Shimon!" She ran to her brother and hugged him.

"Be careful."

"Don't worry. Where's Beni?"

"He's with the tutor. He was found doing handstands on the rim of the fountain when he was supposed to be studying, so now he must sit and learn."

"Well, see that he stays where he is. Remember, if anyone asks, I've gone for a walk."

An hour or so after Shimon left the villa the noise of a fracas became clearly audible within the walls of Beit Harsom. Nervously, Batya, a servant in the house, went about closing the shutters as Alexandra and Beni went rushing into the room where Samuel sat calmly perusing his ledgers.

"Father! We were on the roof! We can see it! They are fighting in the streets, soldiers and everything!"

"It's the synagogue!" Alexandra exclaimed without thinking. "Shimon said there would be trouble."

"Shimon?" Samuel looked up and frowned. "Where is Shimon?"

"He went out earlier," Batya said, "without a bite to eat. That's not like him."

Samuel looked at the woman and then at his daughter and son. Suddenly, without a word to any of them, he made for the door.

"Master!" Batya cried. "You mustn't go out there!"

But he was already gone.

Samuel's mind was a jumble of thoughts as he headed toward the sounds of battle emanating from the street where the synagogue was located. What had started in that small alley, however, had quickly spilled into the adjoining streets, and Greeks and Jews were going at each other in a fury. Legionaries had been called into the area, but their attempts to stop the fighting were half-hearted at best, the soldiers clearly enjoying what was taking place. Frustrated in his attempts to push through the mob, Samuel found himself backed into a doorway and standing next to the servant Hagar, who had been out marketing; she had taken refuge there and was now calmly waiting for the whole affair—like a sudden rainstorm—to end. She had lost her market basket but was firmly holding two large onions, one in each hand.

"Hagar! What is it? What's happened?"

"Some fools turned a jar over in the passage to the place

of worship. They sacrificed a bird on the jar and said it was
to rid the city of the leprosy."

"Leprosy?"

"They call Jews lepers."

Samuel sighed. "Have you seen Shimon?"

She shook her head.

"I must find him. If the soldiers arrest anyone it will not
be the Greeks."

"I saw the centurion Jocundus. He dashed the jar that the
bird was killed on against the wall." She shrugged. "It does
not matter. They will fight until they tire of it. And then they
will begin again."

"I must find Shimon," he said once more, and seeing the
mob before him suddenly part, rushed out into the breach and
was quickly lost to the woman's sight.

The street was filled with brawling men and even some
women wielding straw brooms for weapons. Buckets of water
were tossed indiscriminately from windows. Samuel caught
sight of two legionaries leaning against a building, grinning
while three Greeks pummeled a Jew. He was about to go to
the soldiers when he saw them straighten and hurriedly pull
the gang off as their commanding officer barked an order at
them.

"Centurion! Centurion!" Samuel waved frantically at the
Roman.

Jocundus saw the man and tried to guide his horse through
the crowd to "Go home!" he cried.

"My son Samuel. . . . Shimon. . . . Have you seen him? Is
he—"

The horse reared, and as it came down, the centurion swung
at the battling men before him. "Break it up!" he shouted. "Go
home! By the gods, you will know Roman steel in another
moment! Break it up, I say!" He raised his head. "Samuel! Go
back to the villa. I will find Shimon!"

Devorah was waiting with Alexandra and Beni when he
returned. "I could not find him," he said.

"Perhaps—perhaps Shimon did not go to the synagogue,"
Alexandra stammered. "There is a young woman he has spoken
of—the daughter of John the tax collector—perhaps he went
to see her."

It was this man, John, who finally told them where Shimon
was. Seeing the synagogue invaded by the Greeks, who did

not waste a moment in tearing it apart, the young man and several of his companions had managed to seize the Law book and certain other items before they could be destroyed. They had fled with these to Narbata, a Jewish community some seven miles from Caesarea.

"We were determined to appeal once more to Florus," the tax collector said. "After all, there is the business of the eight talents. He owes us something—if only a guarantee for the safe return of our sons."

Samuel nodded grimly. "I will go with you."

Devorah opened her mouth to protest, but her husband silenced her gently. "There is nothing to fear," he said. "We are innocent in this matter."

But Gessius Florus received the delegation angrily, allowing no one the opportunity to bring up the matter of the silver talents. Instead, he straightaway accused the men of inciting a riot and conspiring in the subsequent theft of items belonging to the city, and declared they must all be put in prison.

The servant Ezra brought back the news of Samuel's arrest. Alexandra gasped with indignation, and Beni's lip trembled, but Devorah listened with stoic calm. "Has bond been set?" she asked. "What ransom does Florus demand?"

The servant lowered his eyes. "The procurator said you alone can best determine your husband's worth."

Devorah betrayed no emotion at this. She said nothing.

The following day, in the afternoon, in that hour when most of Caesarea's citizens and all of the household of Beit Harsom slept or rested, Devorah slipped out of the villa and made her way to the Praetorium. She was pale and tense when she returned from the governor's palace, curtly ordering Hagar to prepare her bath, and avoiding Alexandra's questioning look. But when she was cleansed to her own satisfaction and freshly robed, she caught her daughter to her and kissed the girl.

"You must be wed soon," she whispered. "You will be safe in Jerusalem."

"I am not afraid," Alexandra said, not understanding the look in her mother's eyes.

"I know," Devorah said. "I know." She kissed her again. "But you must not stay in Caesarea. You will be safe in Jerusalem," she repeated.

That night, Samuel ben Harsom was returned to his family. "You see," he said, "I told you there was nothing to fear. Truth is the honest man's sword and shield. We must never lose faith in the Lord, blessed be His Name."

"Yes," Devorah said. "Blessed be His Name."

The days that followed Samuel's release from prison saw an uneasy calm descend upon Caesarea and the House of Harsom. Sporadic incidents of street fighting continued; and though harassment of the Jewish populace went unpunished, as Shimon had predicted, these acts of violence and vandalism appeared to be the spontaneous work of hooligans rather than any organized effort by the city as a whole. Beit Harsom enjoyed a noticeable immunity from attack, since the family of Samuel ben Harsom had, for whatever reason, been returned to the procurator's favor. Despite this, Devorah seemed more highstrung than ever, often taking long walks by the sea with Hagar and an escort of one of the procurator's personal guards. She claimed the walks gave her relief from the now frequent headaches she suffered, but Alexandra, who was never permitted to accompany her mother on these outings, noted that she generally returned more ill than when she had gone out. As though to allay her family's concern over her behavior, Devorah openly fretted over the fact that there had been no word from Joshua in many weeks.

Meanwhile, the priest Shammai wrote from Jerusalem to say that Gessius Florus had demanded that seventeen silver talents be removed from the Temple's treasury and sent to him at once, claiming the sum was merely a loan to Caesar that he had been ordered to forward. "Evidently," the priest had added wryly, "the mighty Roman Empire has fallen on hard times."

"But the Temple treasury has always been inviolate!" Alexandra exclaimed when her father read the news. "Surely Caesar—"

"Don't be a fool," said Shimon, who had been allowed to return home. "What is a handful of silver to Nero? The money is for Florus."

Alexandra looked at her father. "What will the priests do?"

It was her mother who answered. "What do you think, child?" Devorah's voice was dry, emotionless, and—Alexandra thought—odd. "They will give it to him, of course." She laughed suddenly. "Anything . . . to keep the peace."

• • •

It was Samuel ben Harsom's custom to walk in the evening, often with the Christian wine merchant Lukas. All through his life, Samuel had been most comfortable in the presence of men who toiled hard and honestly for their bread: the sailors on his ships, his tenant farmers, even his own servants. It was not surprising, therefore, that the same democratic tendencies could be found in his children, most particularly in Alexandra, who, as the priest Shammai had noted disapprovingly, seemed happier sitting on a footstool in the kitchen listening to servants' tales than in the company of other young women of her class. She had been allowed to join her father and his Christian friend this evening. Samuel felt sorry for the girl, confined as she was to the villa, albeit for her own protection.

"I have sent word of my willingness that Alexandra be wed to young Ananus as soon as possible," he told Lukas. "Your mother is right," he said gently to the girl as she turned her large eyes to him. "You must go to Jerusalem. There is no life for you here, much as I wish to keep you with me. You have said yourself that you are confined to the house like a prisoner." He sighed. "I think perhaps you must all go to Jerusalem."

"Shimon won't leave," she reminded him.

"But why, Samuel?" Lukas asked. "Why should your son wish to remain in what must be a most unpleasant place for a young man of his spirit?"

"That is precisely why. Shimon and his friends are bent on confrontation despite the fact that they are outnumbered and, as you well know, with no hope of the soldiers remaining impartial in any clash between the Greeks and ourselves. I ought to have sent the boy straightaway to Jerusalem from Narbata. I must have been mad to let him return here."

Lukas shook his head sorrowfully. "All this fighting for control of a city . . . when all belongs to God. Where we live on earth matters so little. It is the Kingdom of Heaven toward which we ought to direct our thoughts, for we will dwell there forever when our brief lives here are done."

As he spoke, a soldier stumbled forth in the darkness, laughing drunkenly. A moment later, a woman emerged from the alley out of which the man had come. She smoothed her garments, touched a hand to her hair, and sauntered toward Samuel and Lukas. The expression in the men's eyes told her she found no favor with them. Seeing now the figure of the young girl with them, she raised an eyebrow, shrugged, and haughtily brushed past.

A sudden sound of laughter caused Samuel to tense, alerted. The woman had halted.

"Wasting your time, darling," one of a pair of men lounging against a wall declared. "Jews don't have fun. Why, just look at them. Ever see a more solemn, self-righteous, pickle-faced bunch?"

The whore laughed. "Don't I know?" She tossed her head angrily. "Thinking they're better than everyone else! The way they put on airs and set themselves apart! . . . They don't eat the same foods as ordinary folk or offer sacrifice to any of the gods—Why, they don't even pray to something anyone can see!"

"What I hear," the other man offered, "is that once every seven days they drink the blood of a Greek babe."

The woman gasped. "Do they, now? I thought it was the Christians did that."

"Well, they're like Jews, aren't they?" the first man asked. "I tell you, it's good for us the soldiers know who this city belongs to. They never needed Caesar to tell them that. They know what's right." He raised his voice deliberately. "But Nero's put it in writing, the gods bless him for that. Jews have no legal rights in Caesarea, and if they're as smart as they pretend to be they'll pack up and get out while we're still in a good humor." Laughing loudly at this, he put his arm around the woman, and the three moved off. "They never go to the games," he was saying as they disappeared into the darkness. "Line up ten Jews, and I will give you a gold piece—if I had any, darling—if just one knows the name of Lucillius the charioteer. I tell you, they don't deserve to live among real people."

Samuel relaxed. He looked at his daughter. Her light eyes were aglow with cold fire, but she uttered not a word. Finally she said, "Is that why they hate us? Because we don't cheer the gladiators? How stupid!"

Samuel had to smile. "I think their animosity goes deeper than that."

"I suppose," she replied thoughtfully. Then, angrily, "Drinking the blood of a child! What awful lies! Why, the Law works only to make people better to one another than they might otherwise be."

"The world does not suffer goodness gladly," Lukas said. "He who would teach the children of earth how to be the children of heaven cried tears of blood for this frailty."

Samuel patted the man's shoulder. "I am afraid, my friend,

that, as the rabbis say, we are living in a time when every Jew must suffer a readiness to be crucified. Come," he said abruptly, taking his daughter's hand. "We must return to the villa. There is much to do. I have made up my mind. You must all go to Jerusalem. It will be a good tonic for your mother. She is so pale and tense.... The mountain air will restore her to good spirits. Yes, and she will be happy to be near Joshua and all her old friends, as well as helping you, my girl, settle into married life. Yes," he continued cheerfully, "Jerusalem is the place. You will all be safe there."

"No, Samuel," Lukas said suddenly. "I agree it would be wise to send your family away from Caesarea, but ... do not go to Jerusalem. Not to Jerusalem."

"What are you saying?"

"The city is doomed. The Christ foretold its destruction, and there are portents that the end is near. During the Passover, for instance, at midnight, the East Gate of the Temple Sanctuary was seen to swing open of its own accord. This, a gate of solid bronze fastened with iron bars, and so heavy that twenty strong men are required to shut it. Soon after, many persons saw, at sunset, chariots speeding across the sky through the clouds, and heavenly regiments encircling the city."

Samuel laughed. "If I were the sort to believe in omens, Lukas, I could, I am sure, find many interpretations for the things you describe. You have seen for yourself the wall that surrounds Jerusalem, its towers and its fortress. Besides, even Rome respects our sovereignty there."

Lukas shook his head. "The city is doomed," he repeated.

"Say no more," Samuel said, giving his daughter a worried look.

But Alexandra's eyes were far away—in Rome, in fact, where Josef ben Matthias was even now. If her father was set on sending her away, perhaps he could be persuaded that the only truly safe place was the court of Caesar. It would be awfully difficult to convince him, but perhaps with Lukas's help ...

She was so engrossed in these thoughts that she hardly noticed the figure of the centurion Jocundus until they were practically upon him. With a start she realized they had come to the home of the wine merchant and that the Roman had obviously been waiting to see Lukas. The centurion appeared embarrassed to have been found there but finally admitted that his wife was a Christian.

"The longer I am away from her," Jocundus confessed, "the dearer she seems to me. Perhaps . . . if I were to learn more about the one she calls the Christ . . . we would somehow be together, if only in our hearts. As I have told you before, Lukas, I am not about to become a follower. I simply wish to know more than I do now. I would not listen when Julia, my wife, tried to tell me. . . ." He stopped, cleared his throat.

Lukas nodded with understanding. "Of course. Your Caesar has declared my religion to be a crime against Rome."

"Well, we are far from Rome now. Wait for me, will you, Lukas? Let me walk these people home. Then we shall talk."

"It is kind of you to accompany us, centurion," Samuel said as they moved off toward Beit Harsom, "but there is no need. I seem to be under the protection of providence. May the Almighty be forever blessed."

"You are well known," the Roman replied, "and despite your race, well liked. Also, your . . . family . . . is under the procurator's protection. But there are those who would not hesitate to slit any man's throat to steal his purse. Particularly in Caesarea."

Samuel sighed. "It would have been better for Florus to remain here and keep order than to go riding off to Samaria as he has. I know you do your best, but—"

"Gessius Florus is not in Samaria," the centurion blurted. "The procurator is in Jerusalem." He hesitated. "I have received orders to send additional troops to him." He avoided Samuel's questioning look. "I fear there has been trouble."

The centurion would say nothing more that night, but Alexandra remembered his remark some days later when she came upon her father standing by the window staring at something—or perhaps nothing; she was not sure which. Across the room, his head bowed, was a man she recognized as a servant from the household of her uncle, the priest Shammai. Alexandra hesitated: "Father?"

She had spoken softly, but Samuel looked around, startled. Seeing his daughter, he sighed. "Alexandra . . ."

"Is something wrong?" She looked at the messenger from Jerusalem. "Is uncle—"

"What? No." He looked at her with what she thought was a strange expression. He suddenly seemed to have grown quite old. "Where is your mother?"

"Resting. I think she is unwell again. She is not herself of late," she added, hoping he would explain Devorah's strange behavior.

He passed his hand before his eyes. "I must go to her." He brushed by the puzzled girl and left the room.

Alexandra stared after him a moment, then turned to the servant. "What is it? What's happened?"

The man was at a loss for words.

"It's all right, you can tell me. I shall find out anyway. When did you arrive?" she asked suddenly. "I didn't hear anyone enter the courtyard."

"Just a short bit ago." He seemed grateful that she had asked him something he could answer easily.

"You must be hungry," she said matter-of-factly. "Come, I'll take you to Batya."

"Thank you, miss."

She did not leave him alone with the servants, however, but sat across from him while he ate the food Batya gave him, resting her chin on her hands and staring at him with her large, mirrorlike eyes. "Now," she said, "what has happened?"

He gulped down the piece of cheese he had put into his mouth. "You had better ask your father, miss."

She stared thoughtfully at him, pursing her lips slightly. "Why won't you tell me? Has it something to do with me?" Then she put her hands down and grasped the edge of the table. "It's the wedding, isn't it? That's what it is! Is it off? Yes? Tell me! It is!" she cried before he could answer. "I know it is! Batya! Hagar!" She jumped up and began dancing around the room. "The wedding is off! I won't have to marry what's-his-face!" She laughed joyously, hugged Batya, then rushed back to the messenger, who was still seated at the kitchen table, mouth agape. "Here, have some wine. Batya! Get him some more wine. Tell me, what happened?" she cried merrily. "Has young Ananus up and died on us?"

"Not him, miss," the man blurted. "Your brother."

Batya gasped.

Alexandra stared at him. "My brother? Joshua? Joshua is dead?"

He nodded fearfully.

"How? Was he sick? What happened?"

"Alexandra!" Beni came running into the room.

"Beni—Joshua is dead."

"I know. I heard father telling mother just now. It was the

soldiers. There was terrible fighting in Jerusalem." He glanced quickly around the room. "Hagar, you had better attend to mother. You are to mix that potion to make her sleep."

The woman nodded and quickly left the room.

Alexandra turned again to the messenger.

"All right," she said firmly. "I want to know everything. Everything."

"Please, miss. If I tell you, you will grow angry, you will— I was a slave in the House of Gorion, and the mistress there— Please, miss—"

Her eyes widened in amazement. "What are you talking about? Do you think I would punish a messenger for bringing bad news? What do you think we are here?" She leaned forward. "But if you don't tell me what I want to know, I swear I *will* have you beaten. So talk!"

The man swallowed hard. Batya made a face at him as if to say, "Not to worry, there is nothing to fear"; and, reassured, the man began to relate the events that had taken place in Jerusalem.

When it became known to the populace, Florus's demand for money from the Temple treasury had been greeted with outrage, despite the acquiescence of the priests. In the marketplace, in the midst of escalating angry talk, someone suddenly grabbed up a beggar's basket and, taking it around, began to plead for pennies to feed "poor, starving Caesar." Others took up the joke, the basket going from hand to hand from one end of the busy Upper Market to the other as laughing Jerusalemites begged alms for Rome. The atmosphere of levity had reached proportions befitting a street carnival when the procurator rode into the city. It did not take long for Florus to realize what was going on, particularly when many souls made brave by the anonymity of the crowd began to shout a variety of unflattering remarks in his direction. For a stunned moment, the procurator and his men sat frozen; but even as the priests and nobles came rushing up to apologize for the tumult and insults, Florus issued an order the tight-lipped legionaries were glad to hear: "Sack the marketplace. Kill everyone who blocks your path."

"It was terrible," the messenger said. "Terrible. People jammed the alleys trying to escape. Women . . . children . . . they got all tangled up and fell over one another as they fled.

People were crushed to death. And the soldiers kept after them, trampling them under their horses, clubbing and stabbing away. It was terrible . . . terrible. . . .

"Afterwards, many were dragged before the procurator— men of the highest houses, some of them crying out that they held the rank of knight, bestowed by Caesar. But it didn't matter. They were whipped and then crucified. Thousands died. The hills outside the city were crowded with crosses. Thousands . . ." he repeated, shaking his head at the memory.

"Joshua . . . was he—"

"No, miss. That happened later, when the other soldiers were brought in. The priests said we must show the procurator we wished for peace, and so the people went forth at their bidding to greet the legionaries and shame them with a show of friendship."

Alexandra frowned.

"But something went wrong, and the soldiers attacked the people who had gone out to welcome them into the city. They charged into Jerusalem with their swords drawn—"

"How vile of them!" Beni cried.

"It was vile to counsel the people to crawl after those murderers," Alexandra said in a low voice. "Why must we always be the ones to do the giving?"

"Your uncle was among those who spoke for it. He heaped ashes on his head and tore his robe—"

"Yes, I'm sure he did. He's very good at those things. What happened then?"

"Well . . ." The man leaned forward. His eyes took on an unmistakable gleam. "You see, there were Zealots who had come to Jerusalem after what happened in the Upper Market— Sicarii. . . . And there were lots of folks who kept the same beliefs, but to themselves, if you know what I mean."

"Joshua made no secret of his feelings," Beni said. "He wanted to fight Rome. Remember, Lexa, how he said so to us?"

"He was not alone, young master. Even the nephew of Rabbi ben Zakkai turned out to be a Zealot all along. And there were others like him, even the youngest son of the High Priest! Well, they got their fight—although for some, like your brother, it was their last. But your brother, he was right at the front of it, alongside the Sicarii, helping to rally the people—"

"You mean you fought back?" Alexandra asked, excited.

"Yes, miss, we did! We just swung round and faced those

legionaries—and the Lord, He was with us because He knew it was His city and His Temple we were defending, and not just ourselves. The Lord was with us, and we stopped those soldiers! Some of us climbed up on the roofs—and we tossed stones at them and anything else we could put our hands to!" He paused, taking a deep breath. "It was good to see them run for once. To see them run from us!"

"Joshua was killed in this fighting?"

"Mortally wounded. During the night . . . he left this world. But I know he is in a far better one now."

Alexandra was taken aback by this statement. Then she remembered that talk of life after death was common among servants and slaves, even in Sadducee households. And then, Joshua too had spoken of—what was it?—the "immortality of the soul" . . .

"I wish I'd been there," Beni was saying eagerly. "I wish I'd been with Joshua in Jerusalem."

"So that your mother would know sorrow twice?" Samuel ben Harsom stood in the archway of the room, his face as well as his voice a grave reproach to the boy.

"Joshua died nobly," Alexandra said. "He died a hero's death."

"What does it matter?" Samuel said bitterly. "Dead is dead."

Alexandra regarded her father thoughtfully. She rarely disagreed with him, and she did not wish to add to his unhappiness now. And yet . . . and yet . . .

Slowly, Alexandra shook her head. "It matters," she said firmly. "I don't know why. But it does."

FIVE

Jerusalem was in an uproar. A veritable cacophony of wailing mixed with cries for justice and revenge filled the streets of the Holy City. Hardly a family had remained untouched by Florus's savage attack; there seemed to be a constant procession of mourners on their way to the Mount of Olives, where bodies were traditionally buried. Angrily, men tore down the crosses that had covered the hills outside the city, venting their remaining fury on the sticks of wood, piling these instruments of death one atop the other and setting all aflame.

In the courtyard of the Gymnasium a great crowd had gathered, calling upon the priests and nobles—in particular, Agrippa II, recently returned from Alexandria—to redress their wrongs. From the moment the young king set foot within the Hasmonean Palace, which overlooked the exercise court where the multitude was gathered, he had been bombarded with tales of atrocities committed by the procurator and his legionaries. But while Agrippa was profuse in his sympathy, he was evasive about taking action; despite his honorific titles, he had less real power than the procurator. Rome allowed him to name the High Priest and had bestowed upon him the domains of Chalcis, Trachonitus, Gaulanitus, and Tiberias, along with a number of villages and expanses of rich Galilean farmland. But the whole of Judea had been withheld from him, Nero, like Claudius before him, being convinced that the troublesome region needed tighter control than a client king could exert.

It was not that Agrippa was considered weak, even though he was known to be greatly influenced by his sister, the princess Berenice, with whom it was rumored that he enjoyed an incestuous relationship. The fact was, he was despised by the people of Judea almost as much as was the procurator. The Judeans did not even consider him Jewish, despite his Hasmonean blood through his grandmother Miriamne. For them he would always be, like his father before him, a son of Herod—Herod the Idumean, who was himself the product of a Nabatean mother. No amount of diligent observance of the Law in their presence or intercession with Rome on their behalf ever seemed to persuade the people of Judea—least of all the Jerusalemites—to forget that fact. Even so, they had come to him now. At last, they had come to him.

"You have an opportunity to win the hearts of the people," the High Priest, Ananias, counseled.

"Accusing the governor of Judea before Caesar is not a thing to be done lightly," Agrippa replied. "Even to win the hearts of the people."

"Agreed," the priest said quickly. "But we cannot simply let the matter rest. The people are determined to take their cause to Rome. The Sicarii are among them now—here, in Jerusalem—and even those who were once considered the mildest of men now loudly proclaim Zealot sympathies. On the other hand, you say that Cestius has received a report from the procurator in which he declares that we were the ones to start the fighting. If the governor of Syria—and more, if Caesar—receives no word to the contrary from someone reliable, such as yourself, then the real aggressor, Gessius Florus, will be vindicated. We can only guess what measures of discipline against us will be enacted by Rome. But measures will be taken. And that, my king, will lead to war."

Agrippa was silent.

"You will lose everything," the priest said softly. "And for what? Judea does not want war. Listen—" He gestured toward the balcony, where the angry shouts of the crowd below came up to them. "It is Gessius Florus the people cry out against, not Rome."

"The procurator *is* Rome," Agrippa snapped. "He is Caesar's hand, appointed by the emperor to represent him in Judea."

"But if he does not serve Caesar well . . ." A tall woman had come into the room. She accepted the priest's bow with a slight nod and moved quietly to stand a little behind the king.

"If we do nothing," Ananias continued, "if no balm is poured on their wound, the people, like dogs, will lick and bite at it until they make themselves mad. To stand by and wait until their fury reaches a point where it can no longer be checked may be dangerous. Even, my king, for you."

Agrippa looked at the priest and then at his sister.

"I have always thought," the princess Berenice murmured, "that the people of Judea would be happier in their service to Rome if they were given a real king of their own and not a succession of petty freedmen who have been stealing from Caesar for so long as they have set about ravishing Judea." She walked to the opening that led onto the balcony, leaning back against the wall so that she could easily view the mob in the Gymnasium courtyard but could not be seen in turn. "Yes," she said softly, "they would be happier with a king of their own. A king with the blood of the Hasmoneans in his veins. A king who understands them as well as he understands the power of Rome, and who is unquestionably loyal to Caesar." She turned back to her brother, her lips curving in a small smile. "You have demonstrated your agility many times in the Xystus," she said, referring to the exercise ground below. "But what you must do now is walk the length of a slender silken cord. I wonder, dear brother . . . can you do that, do you think?"

The crowd that awaited Agrippa was unruly and angry. Sicarii were scattered among the mob, their daggers concealed beneath rough, homespun cloaks. For the moment Jerusalem was theirs as much as anyone's; it was their appearance that had turned the tide against Gessius Florus and his soldiers. Whatever the priests and nobles may have thought of the "army from the hills," they kept silent now, not only out of fear that the short knife might suddenly flash in their direction, but because the City as a whole now seemed firmly one with the Zealots.

Flanked on either side by the first of the many orders of Temple priests in their ceremonial garments, Agrippa made his entrance, handsome, regal, attired in costly robes with golden threads and silken embroidery of Tyrian purple. As he took a position on the polished flagstone steps leading to the Gymnasium—itself a symbol of the hated Hellenism of Judea's aristocracy—the restless onlookers became still with awe. Their cries subsided to a murmur, then to a whisper, and finally to silence. They listened quietly as Agrippa began to speak, detailing the usual horrors of war and listing the awesome numbers of people and nations content to exist under Roman rule.

Along with the priests, they nodded their agreement as he warned of the threat to their beloved Temple. And even the most hardened Sicarii added their tears to his as Agrippa reminded them of the blessings of peace. But when, buoyed by the earnest attention of the crowd and by what appeared to be eager assent to every point he made, Agrippa proceeded to counsel goodwill toward Rome, and from there went on to urge "patient submission that would shame the procurator," one man, at least, decided he'd had enough.

He was a figure of less than imposing height, with no particular feature to distinguish him from the others in the courtyard. He was not one of the Sicarii, not even a professed Zealot. But hearing himself rebuked for not paying Caesar's tribute—which, Agrippa suddenly admonished, was long overdue—this particular Jerusalemite replied by disgustedly letting loose with a healthy wad of saliva.

"The little bastard," he muttered, surprising the Zealot Joav, who was standing next to him. "What does he care? All that fine talk. He has it all right." He jerked his head up toward the balcony of the Hasmonean palace behind the Gymnasium, where a solitary woman could be observed watching the proceedings below. "Him and his whore of a sister."

Before Joav could reply, another man, nodding vigorously, said, "Rome destroys us bit by bit, day by day. I don't care what the priests say. Could war be more terrible?"

And a third said, "They took away my brother's daughter to serve the procurator's lust and left her later to wander the streets. Now, poor thing, she sits in a corner all day long and will not speak to anyone."

Others began to speak now, telling of their sufferings under the soldiers. Their voices, hushed at first, grew louder and angrier until at last the man who had spat at the king raised his fist and, standing on tiptoe so there would be no mistaking his identity, shouted to Agrippa and the priests, "You lie! All of you! You do not care for us, and you do not care about the Temple! You care only for yourselves!"

The crowd roared its agreement. They shouted that Agrippa served Rome, that he was not one of them, that he slept with his sister. Once more all of Herod's crimes were recalled and added to the accusations hurled against the young king. Stones began to fly through the air, the crowd surging closer to the steps of the Gymnasium like a tidal wave that would soon engulf the figures standing there. The woman on the palace balcony had disappeared. The king and the priests made a hurried exit.

From the window of a fine villa in the section of Jerusalem called the Upper Town, home of the city's gentry and priests, another woman watched the proceedings in the Xystus.

"The king looks wonderful," she reported. "I don't remember him ever looking quite so attractive. Gold agrees with him, but that is always so with dark-complexioned people. Certainly Berenice wears enough of it. Well, three husbands have heaped her jewel chest full, not to mention Agrippa's generous gifts. What a fond brother that one is," she added slyly. "But she is so attractive—if one likes large women. I can assure you," she continued, "that henna color does not represent the true state of her hair. I have it on the best authority from—Oh, there she is! She's standing on the palace balcony. You can just see her from here." Tabitha turned to the man lying in her bed. "Don't you want to have a look?"

"What? Sorry . . . I was thinking of something. . . ."

She turned from the window and went to him. "Extraordinary," she said, looking at his outstretched form. "You are really quite perfect, you know." She ran her finger down the length of his body. "Really . . . perfect. If only we were not bound by so many ridiculous dictates," she said suddenly with a sigh. "If I were a Greek or a Roman, I would commission a statue of you, and when you were away—up in those hills of yours—I would make love to your image." She laughed. "What do you think of that?"

"I think you are blasphemous," he said mildly.

"Of course I am blasphemous. I am a woman. Perhaps . . . seed of Lilith." She bent her head and in mock ferocity nipped his shoulder with her teeth.

He twisted his hand in her hair, pulling her head back. "Is that supposed to frighten me?"

She smiled. "Does anything frighten you, Eleazar ben Ya'ir? Anything at all?"

"More things than you can know of," he said softly, drawing her down to him.

"Your uncle?"

"Menahem?" He let go of her, surprised. "Why should I fear him?"

"Why not? Everyone else does."

He did not answer but stared past her thoughtfully, frowning slightly.

She began to caress him. "Tell me," she whispered, "if I found a sculptor to fashion your image, would you model for my artist?"

"No."

"Why not?"

"You are the daughter of a priest, and you ask me that?"

She laughed. "I am the widow of a priest as well. Poor Nicodemus. . . . He had not counted on Florus being so unreasonable. And to think, he really died for your sins. No, Eleazar, don't go! Don't be angry with me! It's true I never loved him, but of course I'm sorry that he's dead and died so horribly. Don't go, please . . ."

He was buckling on the wide leather belt he wore. He stuck the short knife inside the belt.

"Eleazar," she said, standing before him, blocking his path. "Please . . . I do not care about what happened. . . . All those people killed. Look at me. See how I grieve." She had let her robe fall open, and now she allowed it to slip down, past her bare shoulders and arms, until the cloth lay like a pedestal around her feet, "You see?" she whispered. "No adornments."

He looked at her briefly. "Mourning becomes you," he said, and left.

Outside the villa, he took a deep breath of air; but the sweet-spicy odor of Jerusalem did not please him, just as the sultry perfume of the woman had not stirred him for more than a moment. He would be glad when they were out of the city and back in the Galilee, with its honest green scent—no incense but the smell of open land and the things that grew there.

Joav was waiting for him. "There is a meeting," he said. "We had best hurry. Menahem has been looking for you. He will not be pleased to see you come late."

Eleazar said nothing. Ever since the appearance of the Essenes and their Righteous Teacher, his uncle had become distant and strange. Several times, Eleazar had caught the Sicarii chief staring at him with an odd expression, the meaning of which he could not fathom. He only knew it made him uneasy.

"Why do you consort with those people?" Joav jerked his head back toward the villa of the widow Tabitha. "They are not our kind."

Eleazar grinned now. "You ought to be glad then, Joav." He made a gesture the other could not mistake. "Score one for our side."

But Joav did not smile. "What about Miriam?"

He stopped, surprised.

"Why don't you marry her?"

"Miriam? She is like a sister to me."

"She loves you."

"And I love her." He looked deeply into Joav's eyes, adding gently, "But not as you do, my friend."

The Zealot was silent.

"Why don't you marry her yourself?"

"She loves you," Joav said again, and walked away.

Eleazar stared after him a moment. Then he shook his head and smiled ruefully.

Eleazar ben Ananias, captain of the Temple guard, and a known Zealot sympathizer since the fight with Florus, came up to him. He hesitated, seeing his friend standing there so pensively. "What are you thinking about?" he asked.

The Galilean turned to him and gave a short laugh. "I was thinking of the school I attended before I came to live with Menahem. One day," he said, walking beside the Jerusalemite, "the rabbi said to me, 'Eleazar ben Ya'ir, how many legs are there on a cockroach?'"

"And how did you answer?"

Eleazar grinned. "I said, 'Rabbi, I wish I had your problems.'"

"Now!" Menahem pounded his fist into his open palm. "The time is now! The people are with us—you saw how they turned against Agrippa; they no longer believe the priests—and the Lord is with us! Judea shall be returned to the children of Israel! We will drive the *Kittim* from our land!"

Men nodded and murmured in agreement. Some cheered the Zealot leader. Sicarii and Jerusalemites, they had gathered together to hear the son of Judah the Galilean make his call to war.

"We must begin with Jerusalem. The Holy City and the Temple must be liberated from the ungodly and given back to the faithful!"

Again there was a murmur of agreement. What was the land of Israel without Jerusalem? Besides, Florus had left but a single cohort garrisoned in the City of David, and that at the request of the priests who wanted to demonstrate their fidelity to Rome. The soldiers, however, had not ventured forth from the fortress Antonia, aware of the feelings against them.

"I know we have the majority of the people in Jerusalem on our side," ben Ananias said, "but those who counsel against revolt have not lied about one thing. The soldiers stationed in Judea may be outnumbered, but they are trained in the skills of war, whereas most of us are not. And they are armed. We need weapons. We cannot fight all of Caesar's legions by throwing stones at them from rooftops."

One of Menahem's men drew the short dagger from his belt. "This friend of mine has not done too badly," he said.

"True enough," Eleazar ben Ya'ir agreed, grinning at the man. "Now all we need is a hundred more of you, Baruch, and a hundred more of your friend."

When the laughter had died down, a voice drawled, "I know where there are knives and swords and arrows enough for ten thousand men. That is, if they have the courage to go after them."

"Why, it's you!" Joav exclaimed, recognizing the speaker as the fellow who had spat at the king. "Who are you, anyway?"

"I am the son of Pampras the mason, who was in turn the son of Pampras the mason. My name," he added, "is Pampras. And I am a mason in the city of Jerusalem. I am a man who likes to live in peace and to set my stones neatly, one on top of the other. This my father taught me, as his father once instructed him. There isn't a palace or fortress in Jerusalem that does not bear the work of Pampras the mason."

"A *chev'raman*," Menahem said, smiling broadly. He went to the man he had just called comrade, who was a slight fellow, but with broad shoulders and well-muscled arms. Putting his own huge paw on the mason's shoulders, he added, "It is you who should live in a palace, for you are the salt of the earth. You are the one the Lord loves."

The little man raised his eyebrows and shrugged slightly. "All I know is, I see how they live and how we live. All right, some are lucky, and some are born to it. I do not argue with the priestly tithe. That is set forth in the Law of Moses. So if you are a Levite or Ha-Kohan, I say good luck to you. I do not quarrel with that. But to tell us—who bear the burden of Jerusalem and of Rome as well—that we must sit quietly and let men come and use us as they will, or others will come and use us as they will—I ask you, does that make sense? I am better with stones than with words, but I ask you, is this to be borne?"

"Your words are as true as the work of your hands," Menahem said, his eyes shining.

Pampras gave a nod of thanks. He was not in the least intimidated by the Red Bull. "And to be counseled by seed of Herod . . . Who asked him? Claiming to be King of Judea when there isn't a drop of David's blood in him. And the Hasmoneans as well. My family's worked for them all, and not one of them—not any of Herod's brats, and none of the Maccabee issue either—none of them, I tell you, has a fart's claim to the crown."

Menahem tried to interrupt, but the mason had warmed to the subject. "You know the Hasmonean villa near the Gymnasium? Look closely at the cornerstone on the right as you face it. See what has been scratched in the stone there. 'To hell with Shimon's palace, says Pampras.' That's what's written there. My grandfather's grandfather did that. Yes, he did. And I say, to hell with all of them—kings, queens, and the soldiers of Rome. To hell with them!"

When the cheering had died down and the mason was back on his feet again—Menahem having raised him up in a huge bear hug—it was the son of the High Priest who asked, "Was it Shimon, then, the brother of the Maccabee, who perhaps hid away a store of weapons?"

"Not that I know of. No," said Pampras. "It was Herod himself. You're right about there being a secret store of arms. You're smart like your father, aren't you? Yes, that's it. You guessed it. There's weapons—and gold, too, for all I know. There's everything you could want. Everything you can think of. But it takes a brave man to get it. And more than likely you'd be killed trying."

"You doubt our courage?" Joav growled.

"It's not the heart of a lion you'll need, redhead. It's the feet of a goat."

"What palace holds these things?" Menahem asked. "Where is it located?"

"It's more than a palace," Pampras said. "It's a city. A secret, fortressed city sitting atop a mountain in the desert wilderness. It is called the Masada."

There was silence. Then one of the men said, "That's not such a secret. I know about the Masada. There's a garrison of

Roman soldiers sitting there too. Gold and weapons . . . If there were any to begin with, do you think there'd be any left by now?"

"The Masada," ben Ananias murmured thoughtfully. "Yes . . . it was garrisoned by Alexander Jannaeus of the Hasmonean line. . . . He wanted to protect the southern border against the Nabateans. I know Herod's son Archelaus occupied the fortress following his father's death . . . but I was not aware that Herod had built the place up. A city, you say?"

Pampras nodded. "Palaces, warehouses, swimming pools . . . a real pretty place, according to my grandfather. Of course, there were a few lost their lives fixing it up for the king and his family—it's not so easy building steps in the side of a mountain. . . ."

"You said there were weapons enough for ten thousand men," Eleazar ben Ya'ir said. "Why do you say so? And what makes you think—if the *Kittim* are there, and before that, Archelaus—that anything of value remains?"

"Because they're scared, all of them," another man answered. "I too know of the Masada. My wife's family lives in Ein Gedi, nearby. The soldiers come there sometimes. They hate the place. They say it is haunted, that the spirit of Herod has put a curse on it."

"I do not think there would be gold and treasures there," Eleazar ben Ya'ir muttered to his uncle, "but if so many weapons were stored, there is a chance some of the cache remains."

"Everything is there," Pampras said, overhearing this. "The Romans don't know where to look, and they are too frightened of their ghosts to do much exploring. Besides, they could take what they wanted, and there'd still be plenty left. Herod didn't do things by halves."

"You know your way around this Masada?" Menahem asked.

"As well as if I'd been there myself. My grandfather—may he rest in peace—told a hundred stories about that place. . . . I can see it before my eyes now. . . . The palace of three tiers, the water cisterns cut into solid rock to catch the winter rains— they had a Nabatean engineer for that—even Roman-type baths with hot and cold rooms."

"It makes sense," the son of the High Priest said to Eleazar ban Ya'ir. "Herod was afraid of Cleopatra as well as of the people he governed. And he loved to build. You know all that he accomplished in Judea, despite his cruelty—the city of Caesarea, the Temple here in Jerusalem, the royal residence in Tiberias.... He may very well have commissioned a private kingdom for himself, hidden away in a place nearly inaccessible, a place where he might take his family, and a small army as well, if he found himself threatened...."

"What about the Roman garrison? If the place is as inaccessible as you say—a city on top of a mountain—how do we get to it?" Eleazar ben Ya'ir wanted to know. "Say there are weapons stored there," he went on. "Say even that this is a fairly inhabitable place, a place we could use ourselves—how do we get up there without the Romans picking us off one by one?"

"Dead of night?"

"Even so, they would spot our horses many kilometers away. We'd have to go on foot from Ein Gedi."

"You talk as if you'd already made up your mind to go," the son of the High Priest said.

The Galilean grinned. "Want to come?"

"There is work for me here in Jerusalem. I am determined to persuade my father and the other priests to refuse to perform the ritual sacrifice on Caesar's behalf. I have the backing I need now. If Rome has achieved her great power through the favor of the Lord, as they keep telling us, then it is time that Caesar's empire lost some points. Evidently, theft, rape, murder, and the enslavement of whole nations are not enough to make the Almighty angry. Perhaps missing out on the daily slaughter of a bullock and two lambs will do the trick. At least, it might in the eyes of our people. Besides, it's stupid to pray for the well-being of our enemy."

"That's not why you're doing it."

"No," he admitted. "I'm calling sides."

"Eleazar!" Menahem beckoned his nephew. "Listen to this. The mason says there are two paths leading up to the Masada. The one the *Kittim* guard is from the west. The mason says it ends in a large palace where they are most likely quartered. There are towers there, and they can see all who approach, even very far away. All around the mountain there are no other dwellings, and the stillness is such that the slightest sound can easily be heard at the top of the plateau. There is another way, however, coming from the east." He turned back to Pampras. "How did you say it was named?"

"My grandfather called it the Snake Path. It is as deadly as its name—nearly twice as steep as the western approach, and dangerously narrow. But if you could climb it, the Snake would put you at the Romans' back. The path is unguarded, I am sure. I wager the legionaries do not even know it exists—it is not easily seen. But it is dangerous," he said again. "My grandfather said many a poor slave fell to his death there. And now, after so many years, it could well be overgrown or crumbled away, either all or in part."

But Eleazar ben Ya'ir was not listening to this warning. His eyes had taken on that shot of light that turned them blue as the waters of the Galilee. He turned to his uncle. "Let me have this," he said, his voice low with excitement.

Menahem did not answer.

"It is too risky," the son of Ananias protested. "You don't even know if it is worth it."

Menahem was studying his nephew, who seemed now to be bathed in a kind of golden light, his features all aglow. Menahem's eyes narrowed. Then he nodded. "Yes," he said slowly. "You shall try it."

Eleazar grinned. "I'll bring you Herod's crown, uncle. See if I won't."

"Or be killed in the attempt," ben Ananias muttered angrily, recalling the mason's warning.

Menahem said nothing. He had turned away, his expression distant, unfathomable.

The land was like nothing he knew, the rocky wilderness giving way to stretches of sand upon which loomed great cave-dotted cliffs of tawny limestone and marl. The sun beat mercilessly upon his head; there were no oak or olive trees to cut the glare, no soft wind wafted by some palm. There was nothing; only the starved soil and the golden rocks and the white-eyed sky stretching on and on.

They had ridden seven hours without water, three with hardly a twig or leaf in sight, when suddenly, over the edge of a precipice, the small band of Sicarii caught sight of a river of green some four hundred feet below. Reeds and bush, trees and grass were scattered another three hundred or so feet down to a stretch of gardens, small fields of wheat, and orchards by the beach of the blue Dead Sea. They could hear the rush of Ein Gedi's life-giving waterfall and eagerly galloped to the oasis, with its busy village and terrace grottos and pools. Flowers grew in Ein Gedi—here, at the back of a broad desert—

and nuts and dates in abundance. Like Jericho, Ein Gedi was famous for palms and balsam; and for this it was sometimes called Hazazon-tamar, the Place of the Palm. The people tended goats and sheep, even as they did in the Galilee. But it was not the same, Eleazar ben Ya'ir thought; and he found himself intrigued by this new environment. Still, despite the comforts of the village, he was impatient to leave it and to get on with the business at hand. Moreover, he longed to return to the stillness and terrible splendor of the desert, which had stirred some deep part of his being.

There were no soldiers at this time in Ein Gedi, as his scouts had already ascertained, although the legionaries came often to the oasis and now and again established small garrisons there. From the villagers Eleazar learned the number of Romans on the Masada and, leaving the others in his group to refresh themselves, went with Joav and one of the villagers to deliver fresh meat to the soldiers. This gave him an opportunity to study the western ascent and satisfy himself as to the impossibility of staging a surprise attack from that quarter. There was a well-fortified tower at the narrowest point of the path, close to the top of the plateau, and the guard there would have little difficulty spotting any who approached. Eleazar also discovered one of the "tricks" of the mountain: the air was so pure, and the stillness so complete, that the soldiers above and the men below were able to converse easily in perfectly natural tones, with more than a thousand feet of distance between them!

The next day he returned by way of the land alongside the Dead Sea, to the east of the Masada. At first his eyes found nothing; then, finally, he saw what appeared to be a narrow path leading up to the very top of the plateau, twisting up and sometimes back upon itself like a snake wound around the rock, just as Pampras the mason had described it. In daylight it was formidable. At night it could well be a killing route. The men must climb single file, at times pressed close against the mountain with barely space for a footprint. There would be places where the path was broken and a man would have to leap across an abyss hundreds of feet above solid earth. There was the danger of falling stones, of the path crumbling away underfoot, and not least, of the soldiers hearing the climbers and picking them off with their arrows or lances or rock-missiles before they could even reach the top of the plateau. If they managed to surmount all these obstacles and get to the summit unscathed, they must then take the Roman garrison by surprise and overcome a group of professional soldiers twice their number.

Pampras was wrong.

They would need the feet of a goat *and* the heart of a lion.

And the blessing of the Almighty, Eleazar ben Ya'ir thought.

Returning to Ein Gedi, he gathered his men together and laid it all out before them, frankly admitting the difficulties and danger. But they heard only the excitement under his words and saw the light in his eyes and were not intimidated, vowing they would follow him.

"All right, then," he said, restless now to get on with it. "That night and the next night, the moon is at its brightest. That is in our favor."

"But won't the Romans see us, then, if it is light?" one of the men wondered.

"Well, they won't be looking for us, not the way we're coming. We need the moon to help us pick our way. Believe me, *chev'ra*, the soldiers are the least of it. But you will soon see that for yourselves." He hesitated. "When you see the Masada and the path of the Snake, you may feel it is too much. . . ."

"The Lord is with us, Eleazar." It was Baruch who spoke now.

"Let us hope so. But if, when you see the Masada, you think perhaps the Lord may not be altogether on our side"— he grinned—"I, for one, will give you no argument." He became serious again. "The decision to come with me or stay behind is your own. Those who ride with me must do so with a free heart, and because they believe our cause is just."

"What will you do if we decide against it?" another of the men wondered. "Would you go alone?"

"Not while I draw breath!" Joav exclaimed. "I am with you," he said to Eleazar.

"And I," said Pampras, the mason from Jerusalem. "I've waited long enough to see this place. My grandfather was always boasting of the steps he constructed at the northern end. Hidden steps they were, he said, cut solid into rock, linking three levels of the prettiest palace a king could want. He said the pillars were topped with gold, and painted below to look like marble, though they were only stone. No, now I'm here, I'm going up." He took a deep breath. "If it please the Lord."

"Tonight, then," Eleazar said, thinking that if something went wrong there would be yet another night of good moonlight.

It rose like a great ship in a sea of sand, ghostly looking and formidable, bathed in the cool light of moon and stars. An isolated mountain surrounded by a vast void, cut off from the Judean wilderness range by deep canyons; a rocky island in the arid desert, impregnable to armies and raiders. And they, a small band of daring Zealots—how could they hope to make this imposing tower of rock their own?

And yet the mountain beckoned; they knew it would be theirs. As a man knows a woman is meant for him, so the Masada seemed to Eleazar ben Ya'ir and his men.

The flat summit, the shape of a rhomboid, lay almost fourteen hundred feet above the ground whereon they stood. They could see the pale, moonlit outline of the Snake Path, winding and twisting all the way to the top. Despite the natural illumination of the bright night, they would have to go slowly, with infinite care. The climb would take hours.

Beside them lay the Dead Sea, which the Greeks had named Lake Asphaltitus, and which they knew as Yam Hamelach, Sea of Salt—and behind that, the dark mountains of Moab. Silence all around, not even the stirring of some small desert creature; for nothing living could be found near these sulfurous waters.

Eleazar stared up, and even as he gazed upon it, he knew the Masada was his, that he had come to something already destined as part of his life. He turned back to the others to see if their spirits had faltered. But they, like him, were caught up in the mystery of the place—its grandeur, and their desire to take the mountain. He did not even have to ask.

"We are with you," Joav said, his voice hushed lest it carry to the *Kittim* above. "To the death."

Eleazar's eyes showed his thanks. He looked again at the men who had ventured forth with him this night, each of his own accord; and a bond was made then and sealed among them, one unspoken but as deep as their Zealot oath.

"All right, then," Eleazar whispered. "Follow me."

A few at a time, they made a rush for the base of the mountain and the start of the Snake Path. Ten men behind their captain, Eleazar ben Ya'ir, inched their way up the mountain.

There were places where the path was wide enough for them to walk with ease; then, suddenly, it eroded away into nothing, and Eleazar had to stop and find a foothold in the mountainside or clear away an obstructing rock. When one slipped, the others held fast to him, pulling him up. They used their knives when they could, sticking them into the side of the mountain as a sort of hold on safety. More than one prayer was uttered that night, and more than one man learned the feeling of raw fear sticking in his belly.

"Don't look down," the plucky Pampras whispered. The air was so still and pure that his voice seemed as loud as if he had spoken normally. They stopped and waited, listening for soldiers who might have heard the man speak. Nothing. They proceeded.

A group of legionaries was gathered around a fire casting lots to pass the night when the Zealots attacked. The men of Judea had moved swiftly, silently, across the top of the mountain, taking shelter in the shadows of the structures there, crossing to the side of the plateau where the soldiers were concentrated, so sure of their safety that they did not bother to patrol or keep an eye on any but the western approach. There was no reason for them to fear attack: Judea had not declared itself at war with Rome; the people of Ein Gedi were friendly enough, earning a few extra denarii by accommodating the soldiers with food and wine and an occasional whore. The Essenes in the nearby community of Qumran were peaceable, albeit strange in their ways, and the only ones pledged to kill every legionary in Judea were the Sicarii, who kept to the Galilee, far to the north.

No, the garrison at Masada was neither a large nor an especially alert one, and the soldiers there were more likely than any others in Judea to bemoan their assignment. Theirs was a boring, tedious job in a hostile environment of searing sun and chilling winter rains. So the men grumbled about the weather and the wine and gambled far into the night, and some of them used one another as women while they kept watch from the tower of the western palace. They were hardly prepared for the group that swept upon them—out of nowhere, it seemed—like avenging angels or the ghosts they so feared.

With horrible, warlike cries that terrorized the Romans, Eleazar ben Ya'ir and his comrades quickly slew the detachment and threw their bodies over the side of the mountain. Some of the Zealots simultaneously raided the palace that served as barracks, killing the sleeping soldiers before they could move to protect themselves. The tower lookout had been slain first, silently, so as not to alert the others.

The Roman garrison exterminated, the Zealots took flaming torches in hand and began to explore. Still caught in the excitement of conquest, they turned breathlessly to claim their prize, but when their attention focused on the place itself, they suddenly realized with awe that they had won something far greater than most of them had imagined. It was as Pampras had said; before them, on this mountaintop, lay a city complete, a place such as poor men dream of. Silently, the band of Zealots moved among the moonlit buildings and palace courtyards, touching their hands to columns that seemed to be made of purest marble, lowering their torches to wonder at the intricate designs of colorful mosaic floors, listening to their voices echo in the great rock cisterns that stored the winter rain. Finally, they came to a vast rectangular complex of long structures in the northern section of the summit.

The storehouses were built in two blocks separated by an alley. In the southern complex they discovered row upon row of clay storage jars containing oil, wine, flour, olives, lentils, nuts, dried fruits, pressed dates—every manner of food that it was possible to preserve, and of a quantity sufficient to sustain a sizable community for some time. One of the men put his finger to some wine and then raised the finger to his lips. A grin split his face. "It's good!" he exclaimed. "Wine fit for a king!"

"It was meant for a king," Pampras said, taking the vessel from him and swallowing some of the liquid. He wiped his mouth with the back of his hand and passed the wine to Joav. "This was Herod's. Everything you see here. All of it."

"But it's as fresh as if it had been put here yesterday," another Zealot wondered, biting into a fig. If Herod the King had indeed laid in these provisions, they were little short of a hundred years old!

Pampras nodded. "It's the air," he said. "Nothing rots or perishes of mold. It's the air," he said again.

Eleazar ben Ya'ir was not listening. He was seeking the weapons Herod had stored for his protection. Impatiently he strode the length of the long, narrow halls of storerooms, searching for the arms; but there were none. Leaving the com-

plex of rooms, he crossed the road that ran from east to west
and entered the smaller block of storehouses.

The grandfather of Pampras the mason had not lied. There
were enough weapons stored here to outfit at least ten thousand
men: arms and furnishings of cast iron, brass, and tin, along
with knives, swords, lances, bows, and a vast quantity of
arrows. Eleazar stared wordlessly at the array. It was as if he
could see before his eyes a great army approaching, could hear
the sounds—not of a single hit-and-run guerrilla attack, but of
a battle where thousands of men were pitted against one another. Suddenly, he heard men rushing into the place; and he
turned, startled, only to realize they were his own men, laughing and exulting over the things before them. They had climbed
the Snake Path, vanquished a Roman garrison, and drunk
Herod's wine. And now there was this treasure. Excitedly,
they tried on breastplates, laid claim to this dagger or that
lance, brandished swords and shields in playful joust.

Eleazar did not join in their merriment. Almost absently,
his hand had gone out to a bow, a beautiful thing of fine,
polished wood, expertly made by some ancient, loving crafts-
man. His hand closed around it, and he carried it outside with
him, leaving the others in the armory to rejoice over their find.

It was almost morning. There were stars in the sky, but the
light was more gray than black. The buildings were misty and
faintly pink; they seemed delicate somehow, despite their grandeur. Only now could he see how beautiful they were.

He walked to the northern tip of the summit. A large wall
seemed to seal any approach to the palace there, but at its
eastern end he found a narrow passageway and a set of broad
steps. Moments later he found himself on a terrace, a large
semicircular porch commanding a breathtaking view of the
area. In the distance he could see the palm trees of Ein Gedi,
and to the east, the steely surface of the Dead Sea, and behind
that the lavender mountains of Moab. The stars were gone
now. He raised his eyes to the morning sky, letting himself
be blinded by the rising sun.

"Lord," he whispered, "may it be for good. What we have
done tonight, and what we will do in the days ahead . . . only
let it be for good, and in accordance with Thy will."

SIX

"They've done it now," Shammai ben Harsom told his brother. "They've stopped Caesar's sacrifice, and we will all pay heavily when Nero hears of it. The fools! Thinking they can challenge Rome and get away with it!"

Samuel listened but said nothing. His brother had arrived in Caesarea with a delegation of Jerusalem notables come to ask Florus's aid in stopping the insurrectionists.

"What could we do?" Shammai spread his hands in helpless anger. "They would have torn us apart had we not given in. You cannot believe the state of affairs in Jerusalem. Sicarii strutting openly on every corner. . . . Their leader, this Menahem fellow, walks around with a train of followers as if he were already crowned king of Judea. God forbid. I tell you, the world is falling apart." The man sat down heavily. "If Caesar gets wind of this—" He sighed. "But that is not what I most fear. . . . I fear the wrath of our God, Samuel. Abolishing the foreign sacrifice is more an insult to Caesar. It is courting disaster from the Almighty. Never, in all our long history, have we refused anyone who would make an offering to the Lord. It is irreligious—it is an abomination!—to bar anyone, whatever his race, from sacrifice or worship. Even the Pharisees agree on this point. Rabbi ben Zakkai told the mob as much."

"And they would not listen to him?"

"Listen to him!" The priest snorted. "Why should they listen to him? The man's own nephew is a Zealot organizer! Ben Zakkai is not the only one to look like a fool. It was the High Priest's youngest son, the captain of the Temple guards, who brought forth the proposal. How is that for being stabbed in the back? Poor Ananias. For once my heart went out to him."

Samuel sat quietly. His eyes were far away. "It is inevitable," he said, almost to himself. "War is inevitable."

"It is not inevitable! What's wrong with you, Samuel? I know how you feel about Joshua's death, but think at least of the other children. Shimon, Benjamin, the girl . . . do you want to bequeath them nothing but blood and ashes? Do you want to see them sold to the highest bidder? That is, if they survive a war that you do not seem to care a fig to prevent?"

"Of course I care. I pray we may see our land at peace."

"Well, then." The priest rose. "You will come with us to Florus. Despite your recent unfortunate—but mercifully brief—imprisonment, your relations with the procurator are still a little better than most."

"What do you expect Florus to do? It's clear by now he would like nothing better than to have Rome and Judea at odds."

"He has more to gain by playing along with us. If he will bring his soldiers to Jerusalem and rid us once and for all of these revolutionaries—now is the time for it; they are massed together in the city like a swarm of bees in a hive—if Florus will do this, we can assure him of full cooperation in the future and a grateful gift from the Temple treasury."

Samuel stared at him in disbelief. "You would ask Gessius Florus to march on Jerusalem? After he has massacred thousands of your citizens?" He stopped, stared a moment at the priest, then passed a hand before his eyes. "I cannot believe you would conceive of this," he said finally, in as calm a voice as he could muster. "You speak of bloodshed, devastation. . . . What do you suppose will occur when the legionaries go against an unarmed peasant mob?"

"Exactly! We will be rid of these Galilean murderers and their followers forever! That's what they are, Samuel. Murderers. It was the Zealots who killed Joshua—by filling his head with their nonsense! By making him believe he could fight Rome—fight a system so organized, so powerful, that it controls the world."

Samuel shook his head. "You are cruel, Shammai, cruel."

"I am an old man. I have no time for niceties. What I have is a healthy respect for survival. And that is what we are talking about, Samuel. Not the end of a bunch of troublemakers, but the survival of a people, their nation, and their God."

His brother said nothing, and the silence grew, punctuated only by the soft drip of the water clock, until finally Shammai asked, "Well? Are you with us?"

"No."

"Samuel—"

"No! I would go to Florus—I would go to Nero—and ask for peace between Rome and Judea. I would ask for this gladly. I would beg for it. But what you propose—no, Shammai, I will not go with you. And I beg you to reconsider the wisdom—the righteousness—of your appeal."

The priest turned to leave. "You are not yourself, Samuel. I shall ascribe your attitude to the grief and confusion you feel over the demise of your firstborn son. I always said you were strange," he could not help adding, "and now I know I am right. In any case, I suggest you pack up your family and belongings—before the civil authorities here make good their threat to seize all Jewish property—and move to Jerusalem. As for the Zealots, Agrippa has already promised to send three thousand horsemen against the insurgents. Together with Florus's soldiers, we shall make short work of those madmen."

"Perhaps not."

Shammai turned back, an eyebrow raised.

"Earlier," Samuel explained, "you compared the rebels to a mass of bees swarming about the city. It might be well to remember, my brother, that bees may sting."

The procurator greeted the delegation from Jerusalem warmly, affectionately, as if the time he had spent in their city had been a pleasant holiday and not a scene of rampage and crucifixion. Sympathetically he listened as priests and highborn Jerusalemites came forward to accuse the Zealots of treason against Rome and to bemoan their own helplessness against the militant faction.

"They are only a foolish minority," Shammai said. "But they must be checked now."

"I agree," the procurator said affably. "I suggest you do so immediately."

"But—"

"Dear friends, this is a matter between you and your kind. I couldn't possibly step in. It would only be interpreted as, oh, an oppressive measure on the part of the occupying force against your people's freedom of expression." Gessius Florus smiled. He was pleased with the way he had phrased that. "I would like to help you . . . but you do see my predicament, don't you?"

"Agrippa does not share your view," one of the delegation

said, stepping forward. "He has offered a large number of cavalry."

"Yes, well, Agrippa does not represent Rome." Gessius Florus did not doubt for a moment that the Jew king, as he always referred to Agrippa, would like a chance to impress Caesar with his ability to control the area, at the same time gathering the gratitude of Judea's elite. He was welcome to it. Florus had had quite enough of this dirty little province and its hotheaded inhabitants. He would be delighted to be recalled to Rome; and whether that came about because the area erupted into total war or because it was handed over to a puppet king mattered little to him. He was totally bored with the country. It would be better for everyone if the Jews fought each other into oblivion, or if Rome once and for all set her boot squarely on this irritating eastern pest.

Three thousand horsemen from the Greco-Arab kingdom of Agrippa II were galloping toward Jerusalem. They entered the walled city with no difficulty, the insurgents having fortressed themselves in the area of the Temple, in what was called the Lower City. For nearly a week, the rebels and the king's men traded missiles and insults but rarely engaged in hand-to-hand fighting. Agrippa's commanders were keeping their soldiers under tight control. The king did not desire to ravage Jerusalem, but to preserve it both for Rome and for himself. The Zealots, on the other hand, would gladly have gone at the foe, but only a small number were sufficiently armed. Every time they did venture from their position of safety, they were overwhelmed by the greater number of armed, well-trained soldiers and always forced back into a defensive posture. So they held off, hanging on, waiting and hoping for help from outside the city. Two of Menahem's men had managed to slip out of Jerusalem. A few kilometers from Jericho, they came upon the band of men returning from Masada and quickly told them of the presence of Agrippa's troops.

"The soldiers, the priests, and those who love Rome are together in the Upper City. We are holding onto the Temple, but we cannot fight our way out or drive them back. There are thousands of them."

"Are they stationed outside the walls as well?" Eleazar ben Ya'ir asked.

"No. They are not letting anyone leave the city, but from

the way they are placed I would say they expect no attack from the hills."

Eleazar was silent, his brows knit in thought.

"How long has the fighting been going on?" Joav wanted to know.

"Six days," the Sicarius answered. "We can't hold on much longer, and they know it. They're toying with us, waiting to starve us out. If they gave it a real go, we'd be done for sure. Luckily for us, the Sadducees who brought the soldiers to Jerusalem still care about the Temple. It's what keeps them from attacking."

"Two days," Eleazar said suddenly. "Can you hold on for two days more?"

Joav looked quizzically at him. "Shabbat is three days hence," he said slowly, thinking that perhaps the Galilean had it in mind to use that to their advantage.

"But the Feast of Wood-Carrying comes in two," Pampras the mason said. "I know because my cousins in Jaffa are to visit us then."

Eleazar nodded. "The Feast of Wood-Carrying it is. When everyone brings wood to the Temple altar so that the fire shall be forever kept alight." He smiled grimly. "Perhaps we can kindle a fire of our own—with bundles of steel instead of twigs." He leaned forward on his horse. "Can you get back to my uncle?" he asked the Sicarii who had ridden from Jerusalem. "All right, then. You tell him—and the son of Ananias too—that they have got to hold out until the Feast of Wood-Carrying and then offer a truce for the faithful to observe the holiday. Agrippa's men will honor this—the king still calls himself a Jew—but they may try to slip in some of their own. So if any coming to the Temple seem suspicious, ask them where they are from. If they answer anything but this—'The land that is ours'—hold them aside." Eleazar now turned to his own group. "All right. We don't have much time. We'll fan out and cover different areas. Might as well find out now who's with us. Now. Here is what we will do and where we'll meet. . . ."

On the eighth day of fighting between the Zealots and the soldiers, a truce was called by the rebels, and the Temple doors opened to admit the pilgrims who would pour in for the ceremonial rekindling of the altar fire. As the sun rose over the

Judean hills, crowds of people could be seen streaming through the city—men, women, children from every part of Judea, and all of them carrying bundles of twigs that they would offer to the priests. Ananias himself would preside at the ritual. The High Priest had returned to the Temple, walking steadily at the head of a line of Temple officials who believed that the truce and the Temple rendered them, at least for this one day, inviolate.

Darius, commander of Agrippa's cavalry, had tried to dissuade the old man from returning to the rebel stronghold, but Ananias had been adamant.

"The ceremony of the altar fire shall be performed as it has always been," the High Priest said firmly. "It was the Zealots who requested this truce, and we must honor their fidelity to our faith despite our mutual hatred. Besides, my son is among them. We differ politically, but he would never allow any violence to take place within the Temple—or any harm to come to me. Of that I am certain."

"At least let me send some of my men in with you."

"There is no need. No one, not even the Sicarii, would violate the Sanctuary."

And so he had gone to the Temple, seemingly oblivious to the Zealots who crowded to see him, Menahem's men staring with undisguised hatred at the Kohanim and Levites who made up the priestly hierarchy. But no one made a move to stop Ananias and his priests. No one said a word. In silence, the High Priest and his retinue marched through the grim crowd of rebels, entered the Temple, and made their way to the Sanctuary within.

From a balcony of the Hasmonean palace, Darius watched the proud old man make his way through the streets of Jerusalem. He saw the stream of people—a never-ending stream, it seemed—entering the city, walking solemnly to the Temple with their bundles of twigs. The Greek shook his head in disbelief and, turning to one of his aides, said, "What a strange people! Here we are in the midst of a battle, and suddenly everything must stop so they can go and make their holy bonfire. I've seen everything now."

But he had not seen everything. He had not seen, for example, that the bundle a small girl dropped, and which was courteously returned to the child by one of his soldiers, contained a dagger. Or that an old man's offering, unwrapped, proved to contain swords intermixed with the kindling sticks.

From bundles and shawls and cloaks and carts, lances, bows, arrows, shields, and swords fell until the outer chambers of the Temple resembled an armory more than a house of worship.

The pile of weapons grew, and so too did the force of fighting men as the pilgrims threw off their pious postures, took up the arms they had brought with them, and stood beside Menahem and the son of the High Priest. It was not long before Eleazar ben Ya'ir revealed himself to his uncle and, grinning, received the Red Bull's embrace. For a moment the recent strangeness between them was gone, and they were as they had once been to each other.

Then Menahem raised a great sword in the air. "Now!" he cried, and a thousand men rushed from the Temple at the surprised and confused soldiers. People came out of the shops and houses where they had hidden themselves during the past week and joined the fight, spurred by the courage of the rebels and eager to have their city back. In a short time the king's troops were overwhelmed, beaten back, and driven out of the Upper City. The mob then rushed into the vacated area and in a triumphant frenzy set fire to Agrippa's palace and many villas belonging to the wealthy Sadducees.

It was an army of peasants and workers that Menahem led, and he shouted now that this day would be a victory for the poor as well as a blow struck for a free Judea. Running to the building that housed the city's records and moneylenders' bonds, he set it afire. The crowd cheered as their debts went up in smoke, and once again the word passed from the lips of the Sicarii to the other Zealots and then to the Jerusalemites: "The name of the Messiah is Menahem!" His name was shouted over and over until the sound was like the beating of a drum: "Menahem! Menahem! Menahem!"

With the nerve center of the city up in flames, the rebels split into two groups. The two Eleazars gave chase to Agrippa's men, who had fled to the Upper Palace, while Menahem led his Sicarii against the Romans garrisoned in the fortress Antonia.

This token force left by Gessius Florus had stayed out of the fighting. They were all too aware of the feeling against them and had, moreover, received no orders from the procurator to join Agrippa's men. Therefore, when they saw themselves about to be besieged, their commander—the centurion Jocundus—sent his officers to Menahem, saying he would surrender so long as the lives of his men were guaranteed. Menahem stared at the fortress Antonia, his eyes narrowing. Then, tight-lipped, he nodded and sent several of his own men forward to promise the soldiers safety on their oath. On this, Jocundus marched his legionaries down.

One by one, the Romans laid down their shields and swords; they were about to march away when Menahem suddenly gave a great and terrible cry, lifting his sword high in the air. As if on signal, the Sicarii rushed at the soldiers and began to cut them down. "Oath! Oath!" Jocundus cried, and his men took up the call: "Oath! Oath!" It was all they said. Not one fought back or begged for mercy. They simply repeated the word until there were fewer and fewer of them to say it, and finally only one.

"Oath," Jocundus said, standing alone in the midst of his murdered men. He looked straight into Menahem's eyes.

But the Red Bull hardly saw the man before him. All he could see was the mutilated corpse of his dead father, his brothers suspended from wooden crosses, their shoulders striped from the whip. He saw the body of his beautiful, beloved sister... and with that roar that was as terrifying in its anguish as in its triumphant revenge, he raised his sword again and smote the last of the "*Kittim*."

The majority of Agrippa's troops had managed to flee Jerusalem, but many, together with those leading citizens who had brought the soldiers into the city, had taken refuge in the Upper Palace. Darius, the commander from Trachonitis, lined the breastworks and towers with his men, and from this position they were able to hold off those who attempted to assail the walls.

"We can wait now and starve them out," Eleazar ben Ya'ir told the son of Ananias. "As they would have done to you."

The Jerusalemite looked away. "My brother is in there." His voice was strained. "He led the delegation to Agrippa. Darius is his friend."

The Galilean put his hand on the other's shoulder. "These are bad times," he said softly. "Once your brother and your father realize it is the will of the people that Judea be free, they will stand beside you."

The son of the High Priest took a deep breath. "What we need," he said thoughtfully, "is a battering ram such as the

Romans have. Nothing can withstand that. The Ram always wins."

"Is that all? Why didn't you say so earlier?"

Ben Ananias laughed even as the two friends took quick cover from a barrage of stones and arrows. "Don't tell me you brought one back from that mountain of yours."

"No. But I've got a man who could probably build one out of nothing but spit and sweat—or come up with something better."

"Yes," Pampras said. "I know the construction of the palace. I ought to. My family—"

"Yes, yes," Eleazar ben Ya'ir said quickly. "But we must take it now. Any snake paths we can use?"

"Not this time." The mason studied the structure awhile. Finally he pointed. "You see that tower there? Well, it seems to me . . . if you could transfer its weight to something else and then set the support on fire, the whole thing would collapse."

The two Eleazars looked at each other. They nodded:

So, starting at a distance, the rebels dug a mine as far as the tower, transferred the weight of the tower to wooden props, set the props on fire, and withdrew. As Pampras had predicted, when the supports were burnt through, the tower suddenly collapsed, knocking in a section of wall in the process. But Darius had detected the Zealots' stratagem in good time; and even as the men outside the palace worked feverishly to construct their "war engine," his own men had set to building a second barrier. While the tired and dirty rebels stared, dismayed, at this new wall, the defenders of the palace made their escape.

Ben Ananias was secretly relieved. He was sure his brother and the other Jerusalemites had taken to the sewers that led under the city's wall to the hills outside Jerusalem; but he said nothing. Despite the unsatisfactory conclusion to their grueling effort, he turned to the Galilean beside him and smiled. "Beware of Greeks. They have tricky minds."

Eleazar did not answer. They were walking through the deserted palace, having finally determined that the place had been abandoned. Zealots and rebel Jerusalemites, furious that the foe had escaped, were tearing the place apart. The Galilean frowned, but he was powerless to stop the looting and vandalism that now went on.

"Let them be," the son of Ananias said. "They need to do this. They deserve it."

"Our war is with Rome."

"For Menahem ben Judah and his followers it has gone beyond that. It is the righteous against the unrighteous. The godly against the ungodly. The Sons of Light against the Sons of Darkness."

Eleazar ben Ya'ir picked up a piece of torn embroidered linen and wiped his soot-smeared face with it. "I wish the Essenes had stayed away," he said grimly. "Everything is different now." He looked around. "Well, there's little for me to do here. I'd better see if my uncle needs any help." He made a vague gesture; he suddenly felt very tired. "See if you can keep them from burning the place down, will you? I have no love for it, but a wind has come up, and the fire might get out of control."

The priests were gathered in the Sanctuary. During the fighting that had taken place outside the Temple, which they could plainly hear, they had not left the inner chambers of the great house of worship or strayed from their daily ritual. Even now, Ananias calmly went about the Ceremony of Wood-Gathering, his resolute mien bolstering the courage of those with him. "They will not harm us," he said, "so long as we remain here in the Temple and perform the duties ordained for us by the Lord."

"The Sicarii have not stopped at killing priests before," he was reminded, "even in the Temple courtyard."

"Outside the Temple," Ananias said. "Not within the walls of God's House. They would not dare."

But even as the High Priest chanted his invocations, Menahem and his men burst into the Court of the Levites. The priests had no more chance than the Roman soldiers who had been tricked into laying down their swords. Where bullocks and lambs had been sacrificed, now human blood spilled onto the floor and ran into the gutters especially constructed beneath the altar of God. And as they fell, the priests cursed their murderers and cried out against them for the blasphemy their swords had wrought.

Ananias, dying, managed to raise himself up. He pointed a trembling finger at Menahem. "You think you have taken the Temple back into the hands of the righteous," he said. "But you have destroyed that which even Rome could not. For it is written that the Temple of the Lord shall stand and no man shall pull it down until such time as His children raise their swords against one another." He had gripped the altar for support, but now his hand slid out from him, and he fell to the floor again. "You have profaned the House of the Lord our God," the High Priest gasped, taking his last breath. "And now . . . surely . . . you have begun its destruction."

The place was still. The Sicarii looked around in fear as if suddenly realizing what horror they had wrought. But the light in Menahem's eyes did not dim. He was in a kind of crazed glory, and he raised up his hands, a sword still in one huge fist, threw back his head, and cried, "Now is the beginning of the end of Belial's days! This hath been a place of abomination and a city of iniquity. . . . But the Lord hath cleared a path for the Children of Righteousness! He hath made His will known. . . . He hath taken His Temple and placed it in our hands, and given His City back to those who love Him! The Temple is ours! Jerusalem is ours! Judea will be ours!"

The fright caused by the High Priest's dying words was blown away by this speech, and the Sicarii raised their swords in the air and began to chant their leader's name. "Menahem! Menahem! The name of the Messiah is Menahem!"

Eleazar ben Ya'ir walked slowly among the bodies of the Roman soldiers. A wind had arisen, and the sound of it was like the voices of the corpses whispering, "Oath . . . oath . . ."

"Their weapons are all in a pile," Joav wondered. "They must have surrendered." He was confused. "There doesn't even look to have been a fight."

Eleazar did not reply. Images, pictures of things far and near, were swirling around in his head. He saw Menahem stopping a legionary who would have ridden his horse over a fallen boy. He saw his uncle rushing into a home set afire by Caesar's soldiers, coming out with a babe in his arms, holding the child tenderly as a mother might—and then returning to the burning house only to emerge again with an old man whom he carried as tenderly as he had the baby. He saw Menahem's face aglow as he led the men in the songs of the Lord and as he prayed to the Almighty. And he saw the man writhing piteously and frightfully when his seizures came upon him, afterwards looking so faint and weak despite his great strength.

Eleazar saw his uncle's eyes beaming at him with affection and then staring strangely at him, especially when he saw Eleazar together with the Righteous Teacher of the Essenes. He had questioned Eleazar closely, wanting to know what the old man had said to him. Lately, the Sicarii leader did not share his thoughts with his nephew as he once had. Menahem had become cold and distant and—there was no other word for it—strange. . . .

"Eleazar!"

He turned quickly, his hand instinctively reaching for his sword.

"You had better come to the Temple," Baruch gasped. The man had been running hard. "It's Menahem." He shook his head and gulped, trying to catch his breath. "He's killed the priests in the Sanctuary. . . . He . . . it's like some kind of madness has come over him. No, it's not the falling sickness. It's . . . he says he's the High Priest, that he was ordained by the Lord in one of his visions. You've got to get him out of there. Some of the priests got away. . . . I hadn't the heart to kill those old men . . . not there, anyway, not in the Holy Sanctuary. . . . If the Jerusalemites get wind of this before we—The son of Ananias swore he would kill any who harmed his father."

But Eleazar had already taken off for the Temple. Inside the Sanctuary, he stopped, stunned.

Menahem ben Judah, having declared himself the rightful High Priest of Israel, had put on the robes of that office, the blood of Ananias still staining the embroidered linen like some new scarlet design. The robe lay open on the Zealot's massive chest, revealing the Roman breastplate and the sword that hung from a wide leather belt around his hips. Slowly, his eyes burning with who knew what mad, private dreams, the leader of the Sicarii was advancing upon the Holy of Holies, the sacred chamber wherein the Spirit of the Lord dwelt. This was the most sacred spot in the Temple, in all Judea, accessible to no one—not even the kings of old—but the anointed High Priest, who might enter the holy cubicle at only one time in the entire year, on the Day of Atonement. Yet now Menahem approached it.

It was as though everyone in the room were under a spell. Some of the men, like Eleazar, seemed stunned, shocked by the enormity of the events that had taken place and by the circumstances of the moment. But many were in agreement with what was happening, sharing their leader's delirium. Had not the priests denied them participation in the rites of Judaism? Hadn't the rabbis cursed them, saying the *am ha'eretz* were irreligious and did not love the Law? They had taken only what was theirs. Menahem was one of them; he was truly their High Priest.

Eleazar stared at his uncle, frozen by what he saw. He did not realize his trembling fingers had touched his sword until he felt another hand upon his own.

"If you kill him, you will be forever accursed," Joav said in a low voice. "You must shed no blood in this place."

"He must be stopped," Eleazar whispered hoarsely. "We must stop him, or we will *all* be accursed."

"Then I will do it. For me, the stain does not matter."

A force greater than theirs, however, halted the sacrilege of the Sicarii leader. As Menahem put forth his hand to touch the curtain of the Holy of Holies, he was struck by the falling sickness, and with a great roar like that of a wounded animal, he fell to the floor, foaming at the mouth in an epileptic fit.

As Eleazar ben Ya'ir rushed to his uncle, Eleazar ben Ananias burst into the room with an angry mob behind him. For a moment the two Eleazars looked at each other, the one in bewilderment and shame, the other in mad fury. And then the place erupted in battle, sacrilege added to sacrilege as Jew killed Jew in the Temple of the Lord.

Eleazar ben Ya'ir would not remember later how he got outside; he did not know how Joav had pulled him to safety and, together with others who were sickened by what had taken place and unwilling to commit further carnage, found horses to quit the city. The men rode from Jerusalem in a wild gallop behind ben Ya'ir, who kept urging his horse to greater speed, not even knowing the direction in which he was headed. After a time, horse and rider exhausted, he pulled the animal up. Turning around, he saw that about thirty men had come with him. They had also pulled up and were waiting for his orders. Jerusalem was no longer visible. No one seemed to be giving chase.

Joav said but a single word. "Where?"

To the north lay the Galilee, with its green hills, its blue water, and the people and families of most of them. Yet even as that thought crossed his mind, the image of the Masada, that mountain in the midst of the desert wilderness, rose before his eyes.

"Do we go home, then?" Joav asked.

Eleazar turned his horse away from the north, toward the arid land where prophets had walked and lions roamed and there were few shadows to hide a man from himself.

"Yes," he said. "We're going home."

SEVEN

She awoke, restless, trying to recall the dream she'd had of Josef. Alexandra often dreamed of him; but these were self-made dreams, fantasies invented before sleep. This one had come of itself. All she could remember of it was that she had been sitting on the bench and Josef was in the water. He had waded out of the water and come up to her. . . .

What was the rest of it? Why couldn't she see what happened next?

She sat up and brushed her hair off her neck, holding it in a lump atop her head, as if she thought some morning breeze might cool her sticky back. But there was no wind. Morning had dawned hot as noon. For the past week, Caesarea had been in the grip of the still, dry heat of the *hamsin*, which struck the coastal region in late summer. It was as if the desert had settled over the area. Nothing moved—not a leaf, not a grain of sand, not a man if he could help it. And yet, despite the lethargy caused by the unnatural, heavy, hot air, tempers were unusually quick, and violence often flared. Murders committed during *hamsin* were many, and generally pardoned.

Alexandra walked to the edge of the roof and looked across at the tops of Caesarea's houses. The roof was a favored sleeping place for the inhabitants of the Mideastern world, particularly in summer. It was the coolest spot; and there were few adobes, no matter how humble, that did not have at the very least a pallet there, if not, as was the case with grander villas, a "guest room" or "summer house." A set of steps led down to the courtyards of the villas or sometimes outside to the street. In Caesarea as in Jerusalem, where space was at a premium, buildings were set so close together that it was possible to walk from one end of the city to the other without once descending to the street, by making one's way along the "Road of Roofs."

It was very early, hardly past the sun's rising; she could

113

see others who had spent the night under the stars awakening now and going below to begin their day. She heard Beni yawn and turned to him.

"Whew," he said. "It's hot."

She nodded. "I'm going for a swim."

"You mean to the sea?"

"Of course to the sea." She laughed and pointed below. "You don't expect me to dive into the fountain, do you?"

He sat up. "You can't, Lexa. I mean, it's Shabbat."

"I don't care."

His eyes opened wide.

"I'll be back before anyone knows I've gone. Just be quiet about it, will you?"

He shook his head. "If you're going, then so am I."

"You can't, Beni. It doesn't matter if I break the Sabbath"—she shrugged amusedly—"I'm only a woman. But you mustn't. Besides, mother might call for you. She always wants you near when she's ill."

"Not when she has one of her headaches. All she wants then is to lie in a dark, quiet room. I think she'll be abed all day." He looked up at the fiery sun. "Especially with *hamsin* still upon us." He got up. "I'm coming with you."

"Beni—"

"You can't go alone. You know what father has said. Don't worry about Shabbat. I'm not being irreligious," he explained. "We are commanded to keep the Sabbath, but we are commanded first to 'save those who are in danger.' If you are bound to go, then I must protect you."

She smiled. "All right." Her brother was small and slight and so full of tricks the family called him "the monkey." She could not imagine him a bodyguard, but she would not have hurt his pride for anything.

Nobody seemed to mind the pair making their way from housetop to housetop except the wife of Manasseh ben Aaron, whose stairs they descended finally in their run to the sea. Laughing while the woman upbraided them for using others' property as if it were their own, they ran to the beach and continued running until they were a considerable distance from the city. It was so early there were only birds walking the sand, and these scattered and flew as Alexandra and Beni raced to their favorite cove of rocks, falling happily into the water there. They swam for some while, proud of their ability to do so, for swimming was an unusual talent at that time. The Romans and the royalty had their baths and pools; but swimming in the ocean was not a common practice.

Leaving the comfort of the sea, they returned to the sheltered rocks and threw themselves down on the sand.

"That was lovely," Alexandra said breathlessly. "I wonder why the sailors will not swim. None of them know how. Father said so, and I asked, and it's true. Isn't it funny?"

Beni did not reply to this.

"I'm hungry," he said, his stomach echoing that thought.

She laughed. "Me too."

"Let's go back."

"Not yet."

"They may not have missed us. Besides, I want my breakfast."

"Just a little longer."

He was nervous now. "No, we had better go back."

"Go ahead, then. I'll come in a little while."

"I can't leave you alone."

"I'll be all right. No one can see me here. Besides . . . look." She pulled her wet shift away from her body. "You can see right through. I can't go back like this, not even on the roofs. Go on. Don't worry. I'll run and catch up to you."

He hesitated; but his stomach was making loud calls for help, and in the end he agreed to start without her.

Beni was no sooner gone, however, than she fell asleep, lulled by the sea and wearied from her swim. She wanted to sleep, to dream, hoping for the vision of Josef to return; but strange sounds intermixed with the soft crashing of waves on the shore, and she awoke with a start, her heart pounding with a strange sense of fear. Then, realizing where she was and thinking of the consequences that awaited her at the villa (they had most likely discovered her disappearance by now), she got up with a sigh and began to amble homewards. The sounds she had heard in her sleep—a murmur as of a great multitude— seemed to come back, to grow louder and more distinct as she neared the breakwater. Suddenly she heard what sounded like people screaming and crying. She ran to the dock and saw there a crowd converging on the quay.

The Greeks of Caesarea were driving groups of Jews through the streets, laughing at them, cursing them while they rained blows upon them. Without thinking, Alexandra moved toward the crowd. Then she saw Manasseh ben Aaron, his face a mask of terror and bewilderment, trying to shield his wife and children from the mob that was pushing them forward. The woman was holding a child. Alexandra saw the baby slip from her grasp, fall beneath the feet of the crowd. She heard the woman scream—or was it her own voice crying out in horror?

She turned away, stumbled over a barrel, and fell behind it. It was then that she heard the sobbing girl. Cautiously now, she looked around the barrel and saw the daughter of John the tax collector being dragged down by a gang of men. They fell on her, and her cries became stifled and then lost in the laughter of the men. Alexandra crawled away, her one thought to get back to the villa.

She ran right into the mob, slipping in and out among the hands that reached for her, managing to get to the house of the unfortunate Manasseh without being caught. The place had been set afire, but she climbed the stairs to the roof and from there made her way to Beit Harsom. Breathlessly, she descended the steps that led into the courtyard.

Everything was still, the only sound that of the fountain splashing upon itself. A man's body rested against the stone pool, his head face down in the water. She went to him, pulled him out of the water; and the servant Ezra fell back upon the paved stones, his eyes open and bulging. Slowly, she entered the villa.

Everything had been smashed, torn, broken, covered with blood and excrement. Samuel ben Harsom lay face down across the great marble table where he had played host to priests and procurators alike. His blood stained the floor like spilled wine. Shimon lay a few steps away, one hand still clutching a sword, the other upon his stomach as though to hold in the guts that spilled forth.

She made her way through the other rooms. The servants were all dead or gone. Devorah was sprawled across her bed, her cold fingers touching a small ebon chest that had held her jewels. The box was open, empty. Alexandra pulled her mother's robe down over her thighs and left the room, looking for Beni.

She walked slowly through the despoiled villa as in a trance, moving in a vacuum, surrounded by silence. She felt a rushing in her ears like the sound inside a seashell but heard nothing else—or could hear nothing else—so that she saw the men as from a distance, like statues, without sound. She had no idea how many of them there were because they seemed like one animal to her, one animal with a hundred legs and arms and contorted mouths. Their mouths were open, and yet she could not hear what they were calling. They seemed to move toward her, and yet she saw them without movement, now far from her, now near. Her eyes blinked, and they advanced. Another blink, and the thing was nearer, an ugly animal of many faces. Her eyes closed, opened, saw the ceiling of the villa now, the faces in a circle looking down at her. It was like being under water.

Suddenly sound and movement rushed together like the crashing of a great wave tossing her to shore. She could hear the men now. They were laughing, saying rude things to her. She felt their hands moving over her, grabbing her legs and arms, touching her body, pulling her hair. They ripped her clothes, and one, behind, held her breasts in his hands, burying his face in her shoulder. She felt his spittle on her neck; and, as if she had been soaked in a chilling rain, she began to shudder, to shake as with a terrible illness. Her teeth began to knock together, the sweat breaking out on her skin as she trembled with this strange cold. With an unnatural burst of strength, like one possessed, she lunged out of their hands and began to vomit. Again and yet again she threw up on the floor and on the men around her, panting and retching until there was nothing left inside to bring up. Still her body shuddered, her belly heaved, and she gagged on air now, making horrible sounds that echoed in the silent house. The men had gone. Why they had not killed her she would never know. But if some act of God had saved her, then she would wonder all her life why the Lord had not put forth His hand for the others of her family.

She was alone now. Alive. Cold, shaking, utterly bewildered that she still lived, still existed, she began to cry. She could hear the mob outside, but no more came in. There was only the sound of her weeping as she lay there. Finally, exhausted, she put her face down on the cold marble floor and fell asleep in the midst of her own tears and filth.

She woke up coughing. Torches had been thrown into the villa, and fires had begun throughout the place. She dragged herself to her knees, pulling the rags of her shift around her. It was dark now, night; but the fires lit her way. She started up the stairs, looking for Beni. The villa was beginning to fill with smoke. The roof was all in flames. Still she would have gone up had someone not pulled her back. She spun around, putting out her hand for some weapon she might strike with. It was the woman Hagar. Her face was like a demon's in this light. "Come," she commanded. "We must leave this place."

"Greek. Have you come to look for gold? Get out!"

For answer, the servant caught the girl to her and threw a cloak about her. Alexandra was so weak she could hardly stand, and the woman's arms were like iron. Yet when Hagar tried to lead her out of the villa, she struggled against her, crying out that she must find her brother Benjamin.

"Dead!" Hagar shouted. "They are all dead! As we will be if we do not leave now!"

As she spoke, the roof of the villa seemed to burst and fall on them. Still, they managed to escape.

The streets were full of people dancing, singing, locked in intimate embrace. Some were dressed in stolen finery, arrayed in mad, improbable combinations of costume. The fires of burning shops and houses lit the night like day.

Hagar gathered the cloak tight around Alexandra. From her robe she pulled out a goatskin. "Drink!"

Alexandra shook her head, dazed.

She forced the skin to the girl's mouth and poured the wine into her. Alexandra gasped, started to gag, and pushed her away. The wine ran from her mouth, staining the cloak. Again Hagar forced her to drink. "Finish!" she hissed. "You must stink of wine tonight so they will think you are one of them."

A boy danced by, his head draped in a self-arranged turban of purple silk, and with many necklaces on his dirty tunic. He grabbed the wineskin from Alexandra and drank deeply.

"Give us a kiss, sister," he cried. "We are kings tonight! A city of kings! All the stinking Jews are gone!" He pulled out a *talith*, the fringed prayer shawl that Samuel ben Harsom and his sons had worn when they prayed to the God of Abraham, and blew his nose in it.

Laughing loudly, Hagar put her arms around Alexandra and the boy and hugged them both. "Caesarea is ours," she echoed. "Why shouldn't we say we are kings? We are descended from kings, not from lepers, eh?" She nudged the boy in the ribs.

He laughed and threw his arms around Alexandra's neck.

"Whoops! Whoa, my prince." Hagar pushed him away. "If you wish to court my daughter, come and say so tomorrow. Jews or no Jews, we are a good Greek family, and my little girl is no night's merriment."

He laughed again. "Don't worry, old woman. I have had my fill of love today. Those we did not kill were driven to the docks to be sold as slaves. Some of the goods got a little shopworn, you might say."

They both laughed loudly at this.

Alexandra started to fall. Hagar caught the girl to her. "Oh," she said, "I think this one has had enough tonight! I promised her she might see the fun, but you can see it is too much for my little darling. I had better get her home."

The two made their way through the drunken, reveling crowds, Hagar holding the Jewish girl upright, half carrying, half dragging her along, scolding her all the while that she was a bad girl to have drunk so much wine, much to the amusement of those who paid any attention to them.

Finally they were away from the noisy streets, in a small room, meagerly furnished but clean and, Alexandra thought thankfully, quiet. Hagar led her to a narrow pallet. Alexandra sank upon it, exhausted; but Hagar would not let her be. Bringing forth water and cloth, she began to clean the girl's face and body. As she brought the cloth to Alexandra's breasts, the girl shrank away, her body tense. Hagar stopped and looked at her. Suddenly her hands moved to the girl's loins, and when Alexandra cried out at her prodding fingers, she merely smiled.

"You are still a maiden," she grunted, satisfied. "Your God has been kind to you."

"Shut up," Alexandra said weakly, and promptly went to sleep.

BOOK TWO

JOSEF BEN MATTHIAS walked through the dark streets of Jerusalem with the air of a man for whom night holds no terror. In ordinary times—in the best of times—one was careful when venturing out after dark; for the City of David, despite its holy character, was not without its thieves and assailants. But there was a heightened tension in the air now, an eerie apprehension of things to come. It was as if the ghosts of the betrayed legionaries and the priests slain in the Temple had cast their shadow over Jerusalem. The followers of Menahem ben Judah had been killed or routed, and the son of Ananias driven away when his vengeful fury would not be checked. Still, the city was full of Zealots. Small groups of men clustered ominously on street corners even at this hour, more often than not with small daggers stuck in their belts. When they looked up, their eyes showed three points of white—the mark, it was said, of dangerous men. Their hostile glances did not bother Josef; he continued past them unperturbed, not even deigning to look behind, as some might, to see if he was being followed. He knew he had nothing to fear.

It had always been this way with him. How many streets, how many nights, had he walked alone, unafraid? . . . Jerusalem . . . Caesarea . . . Rome. . . . At night he came alive.

Rome.

That was a city. There were nights and streets and people enough to interest any man.

Rome.

It was all he had dreamed a place might be. And how good it had been to be, in the best sense, anonymous there. No family on his back, no priests to point him away from anything. For the first time in his life he had been able to see and do whatever he had a mind to. And that, he thought, smiling a little, was considerable. The theater, the Circus, the games, the brothels, the food stalls... nothing had gone untouched, untasted; nothing that was in his power to know had been left unknown.

And he had been lucky. Oh, so lucky! If he were not what he was, he would have to say the gods favored him. Imagine a chance exchange of wit with a fellow in a trinket shop leading to a meeting with Caesar. For the stranger buying jewelry had been none other than the great comic actor Aliterus, renowned throughout Rome, and a friend to Nero and Poppea. Aliterus had revealed to Josef that he was born a Jew but had little knowledge of the customs to which they both were heir. Nothing would do but that the handsome Jerusalemite must be a guest in the actor's villa; to repay this hospitality, Josef would tell Aliterus all there was to know of Judea and the God of Israel. These discussions often took place in the most irreligious atmosphere; but Josef did not complain. Through his host, he met all the actors, mimes, poets, pimps, and whores of Rome, a collection of artists and rascals that never ceased to excite and fascinate him.

And then Aliterus had introduced him to the empress Poppea. There was little doubt the lady liked him, even without her proclaiming publicly that the "Judean prince" was quite as charming as had been reported. His future in Rome assured, Josef had plunged enthusiastically into the intrigues and amusements of Nero's court; and if he moved with equal ease between the palace and the gutter, he was not the exception but the rule of the day.

This was a time when the daughters of senators and the wife of Caesar vied with each other for a night with a Nubian gladiator who might well die at dawn. Their husbands meanwhile frequented the many male, female, or child brothels in the city, playing, as was said, the groom one night and the bride the next. These excesses were applauded by Caesar, who pardoned any sin so long as it was not boring. No one, in fact, Josef thought now as his footsteps echoed down the narrow passageway of the quiet Upper Market, loved prowling around at night so much as Nero. The emperor would take to the alleys at a time when honest men slept, always followed at a discreet distance by an escort of senior officers who made sure Caesar met no danger. How politely they turned their backs while Divine Nero went about his favorite sport of rape. He also liked to break into shops on these outings, afterwards opening a market at the palace with the stolen goods. At one such auction, Poppea purchased from her husband a carved onyx box set with "black" opals, which she subsequently presented to Josef. The box was in turn stolen from him—by a Circassian dancer, Josef believed, who had displayed a variety of talents together with an unusually agile body. It was just as well, he thought now. The box had been carved with figures of men and women. The depictions were chaste enough, but the Law of Moses forbade the rendering of any images, and there was no way he could have kept the item upon his return to Jerusalem.

The truth was, he had not much desire to come back. He had disposed of his mission fairly early, winning the release of the imprisoned priests by besting the tribune Nicanor in a wrestling match (Nero loved the sport). But he had stayed on with the excuse of attending to business matters for certain parties such as Samuel ben Harsom. In return for this work, he took commissions that enabled him to get along nicely, and he foresaw a comfortable life for himself in the Imperial City. Certainly he moved in the right circles. He valued his friendship with Nicanor, with Titus, son of the general Vespasian, and with other young Roman nobles. He was proud that this elite, aristocratic group considered him one of their own.

"By all the gods," Nicanor had sworn, "I find it hard to believe you are a Jew. You wrestle like an athlete, your speech is as witty as any satirist's, and you look—according to our divine empress, whose word cannot be doubted—like young Dionysus or some other god. No, you cannot be a Jew."

"You will offend him by this," Titus protested. "What he means, Josephus, is—well—" the young man broke off, laughing apologetically. "I hardly know how to say it myself without falling into Nicanor's fault."

Josef had smiled at them. It was a curious, slightly sad, slightly mocking smile. "I understand," he said. "And I thank you, Titus, for your kind regard." He sighed. "I only wish the people of Judea might come to know such as you, for they now believe that all Romans are as swinish as the cohorts that serve you." Smiling broadly now at their startled expressions, he added, "What bothers me, Nicanor, is that you have failed to mention the one attribute regarding which I am most anxious to know your opinion. Or have our nights in Rome's mansions of pleasure revealed my lesser qualities?"

The Roman grinned. "I would say greater, Josephus, not lesser. Whatever your religion took from you at birth, the remnant more than equals that of a whole man."

A whole man, Josef thought wryly. There were times when he wondered if the sum of the whole was not as fragmented as broken glass. There were pieces of himself in Rome, and pieces in Jerusalem, and pieces, yes, in the wilderness of Judea. A stark midnight landscape suddenly flashed behind his eyes. For a moment he saw a boy and a man dressed in animal skins moving against the moon. A jackal howled. . . . He blinked, and the image, thankfully, was gone.

No, Josef thought, his step quickening now, he would have preferred to remain in Rome. He did not approve of all that went on there and was not blind to the emperor's criminal mentality; but the place suited him. He had come back because there was, finally, no choice; but in his heart he cursed the rebels who had given him cause to leave.

He had been with the empress when news of Judea's revolt was brought to the palace. Infuriated by the massacre at Caesarea, Zealot bands had crossed the borders, sacked Syrian villages, and set fire to the Greco-Arab communities in the Decapolis, east of Judea. With righteous vengeance, they tore into the old Philistine cities of Gaza and Ascalon, the port of Ptolemais on the ancient Phoenician coast, and Sebaste, the capital of Samaria. The Syrians responded by striking at the Jewish minorities in their cities; and in Scythopolis, Tyre, Hippos, the Gadara, thousands were killed in fear and revenge for the attacks made by the Judean guerrillas. In Alexandria, where there had been constant strife between the natives and the Jewish colony ever since Alexander had given the "children of Israel" permission to reside in the city with the same rights as the Greeks, terrible riots sprang up. The governor of the Egyptian city was Tiberius Alexander, a Romanized Jew who twenty years earlier had been procurator of Judea. He sent two Roman legions, together with two thousand Greek soldiers from Libya, into the Delta ghetto. Word came to Jerusalem— and to Rome—that fifty thousand corpses clogged the streets of the Jewish quarter, filling the air for days with the stench of unburied bodies.

"What do you think of all this?" Poppea had asked Josef upon hearing of the massacre.

The Jerusalemite had listened to the messenger's report without a word or change of expression. He had risen, however, from the couch upon which he had been reclining, and was standing with his back to the empress of Rome. He turned to her now with that slight half-smile. "I think," he said, "that I am glad I am in Rome and not in Alexandria."

Meanwhile, Cestius Gallus, governor of Syria, had decided to act. He set out from Antioch at the head of the Twelfth Legion, along with two thousand picked men from each of the other three legions stationed in Syria. The various client kings, including Agrippa, sent even more soldiers to swell his army. A combined force of some thirty thousand men marched down the coast of Judea and then eastward to Jerusalem, ravaging the cities and villages along the way.

"Jerusalem!" Aliterus wailed. "The Temple! Titus! Josef! Do something!" He struck a theatrical pose. "I refuse to allow the sacred structures of my heritage to be destroyed." He turned to Josef. "They are sacred, aren't they? I mean, you are sure there isn't another city or building more important to us? Very well, then," he continued in a ringing voice, resuming the obligatory dramatic stance. "Jerusalem must be spared. The Temple of Solomon shall be inviolate."

"No, no, you've got it wrong," Josef said. "Solomon's Temple was destroyed by Nebuchadnezzar. This one was built by Herod."

"Is it as good as the first?"

"Much better, from all accounts."

"You never know. Workmanship is not what it once was."

"Gallus must bring order into the area," Titus broke in. "There can be no question about that. There is nothing but chaos and confusion throughout Judea and the neighboring territory. If the governor of Syria cannot put a stop to the rampaging and murders—on both sides—Caesar will be forced to show his hand. Why, he has only just closed the doors of the Temple of Janus to signify that the whole Roman world is at peace, and ordered coins to be struck in celebration of this." The Roman frowned. "Judea makes a travesty of the very idea of peace. No, Gallus must maintain order. Still," he said, putting his hand on the Judean's shoulder, "like Aliterus,

I too hope Jerusalem will be spared. I would not wish misfortune to befall your family, Josephus."

"I do not think it will. Jerusalem has no desire for war. These terrorists are from the Galilee. Cestius Gallus will find, I think, that Jerusalem is anxious to cooperate, and that the majority of Judeans wish nothing more than to be rid of the troublemakers among us."

He was wrong.

Cestius Gallus was encamped six miles from Jerusalem when the rebels fell on his men. The Roman governor had burned to the ground the Galilee stronghold of Zebulon, looted and burnt Joppa after slaughtering the inhabitants, and treated in similar fashion the toparchy of Narbatene, Sepphoris, Lydda, and the villages about these Judean cities. With this in mind, the insurgents found little merit in sitting in Jerusalem waiting for the Roman torch. Taking the initiative, they fell upon his soldiers, drove a wedge into their ranks, and, charging through the gap, inflicted heavy casualties. Had not the cavalry made a detour and come to the aid of the broken line, the whole of Gallus's army would have been in great danger. As it was, the Romans lost more than five hundred men, while the force from Jerusalem had only twenty-two dead.

The Judean fighters were a disorganized army. They were accustomed only to riots and guerrilla raids—the hit-and-run tactics of the Sicarii. Striking in the open, swooping down from the hills on an encamped unit, and taking that unit by surprise was their best shot. None of the rebels who fought with so much passion and conviction was a soldier in the real sense of the word. Jews had always been exempt from service in the legions, not only because their religion prohibited activity on the Sabbath, but because as legionaries they would be obliged to take part in many festivals and sacrifices honoring the gods of Rome. The various Caesars had long recognized that a military draft of the stiff-necked children of Israel would mean more trouble than it was worth and had wisely let the Jews alone. This policy worked now to Gallus's advantage, for the Judeans were no match for the onslaught of his highly organized war machine. While the rebels were still congratulating themselves on their success, Gallus regrouped, routed them, and beat them back to Jerusalem. It was the fledgling army's first bitter taste of the military discipline that had enabled Rome to conquer the world.

"We have no training in the arts of war," Josef had explained. "Judea has not had an effective fighting force since the days of the Maccabee—and we were not facing Rome then. There isn't a man in Jerusalem—none that I know and respect—who does not realize this." He raised his hand, beckoning the slave to pour more oil on his shoulders. The slave complied, rubbing and kneading the muscles of Josef's back with strong, skilled hands. Josef turned his head slightly, smiling reassuringly at Titus, who was stretched out on a neighboring slab. "They will come to terms with Gallus, you will see. An accommodation will be made. It would be too foolish not to. There is so little glory in extinction."

Gallus had taken the northern part of the city and was encamped in front of Herod's palace. The rebels had retreated into the Inner City and once again made the Temple their fortress. For five days the Romans kept up their attack but made no progress. On the sixth day, Gallus decided to assault the Temple from the north. The rebels stationed on the roof of the colonnade repeatedly drove his men back, but they were overwhelmed at last and forced to withdraw.

"What we do is this," Nicanor had explained. "The front rank rests their shields against the wall to be breached, and on these the second row of men rests theirs, and so on. The soldiers call it 'the tortoise.' Now, you see, under this protective shell they are quite free to work at undermining the wall in whatever manner is best."

"Fire?" Josef had asked.

"Generally speaking." The tribune paused, then with a raised eyebrow, "I ought not to instruct you so, my dear Judean. We may very well find ourselves one day on opposite sides of a wall that must be defended by one of us and taken by the other."

"I doubt it. Gallus will put things right soon enough. Besides, I have little taste for military excursions."

"Then why these questions?"

"Just curious. I like to know how things work—particularly things that work well."

For some reason unknown to history, Cestius Gallus withdrew. He could have taken the Temple; he could have captured Jerusalem. Certainly, he had the men and means to do so. But he did not. Perhaps he feared a prolonged siege with the coming of the winter rains, and the risk of being cut off from his home base in Syria. Perhaps the sight of the Temple gate struck some hitherto unknown fear into his heart. For whatever reason, he suddenly called off his men and retired from the city.

This sudden change of events seemed like an act of God to the rebels. They were convinced more than ever that the Lord was with them, and so it seemed to others who had, until now, hesitated to align themselves with the Zealot faction. Jubilant, the rebels followed Gallus, making hit-and-run attacks on the rear of his army. Lightly armed, quick on their feet, the Judeans managed to inflict heavy casualties on the retreating soldiers, who were encumbered by their heavy arms and afraid to break rank lest their whole line collapse. After a couple of days of this, Gallus ordered the mules and baggage animals killed in order to speed up the flight. Then he picked out four hundred soldiers, and while they camped for the night, he slipped away with most of his men, leaving the four hundred to deceive the Judeans into thinking his whole army was still there. The trick was discovered the next day, and the four hundred legionaries killed; but meanwhile, Gallus had gotten away.

Collecting all the equipment left behind, the rebel Judeans had joyously marched back to Jerusalem, singing hymns of victory and praise to the Lord God of Israel.

The fools, Josef thought now, his pace quickening in anger. Didn't they realize it was not the end, but the beginning? Rome had been insulted, not defeated.

The news of Gallus's loss had arrived simultaneously with a letter from Josef's father. There was no way now he could remain with honor in Rome. He had returned as quickly as he could to Jerusalem.

•   •   •

At the top of the gate leading to the courtyard of the villa was a carved figure of the new moon. A similar gate had stood in Caesarea. This one was not locked, and Josef ben Matthias let himself in, pausing a moment to inhale the scent of jasmine in the small garden. Then he proceeded to the entrance of the house of the priest, Shammai ben Harsom. The place was in some disarray. Despite the evening hour, servants rushed from room to room with various possessions, which they then passed on to other servants who were busily packing bundles meant for travel. Many prominent Jerusalemites had already fled, and the entire Christian community had gone to settle in the Greco-Arab city of Pella. A provisional government had been formed in Jerusalem, and while it contained many Zealot leaders, the majority were moderates like Josef, who, while making their preparations for war, still sought among themselves a way to avert it. It was no longer prudent, however, to advocate peace openly, as Josef had learned upon returning to his father's house. The venerable Matthias had become something of a Zealot himself, and his pleasure in Josef's return more than made up for the young man's reluctance—which Josef was careful to keep hidden—to come back to Judea. "You see?" Matthias went about saying. "You see? I told you he would come back!"

Shammai ben Harsom waved the young man in. The priest was half reclining, a robe covering the bottom part of his body. He looked wan.

"It is good of you to come to see me, Josef. We have not had much opportunity to talk since your return to Judea."

"Not by my will, sir. I had no sooner gotten back to my father's house than I was plunged into the council's deliberations."

"Of course. You have become an important political figure. The reports of your successes in Rome, and of the high esteem in which you are held there, together with your background and obvious intelligence, put you immediately in line for a position of command. The council would have been mad not to grab you up. You have done well for yourself, my boy." He sighed. "Perhaps too well. There is something to be said these days for obscurity."

Josef smiled. "When I was your student, you taught me, 'Love work, hate tyranny—and don't become too well known to the authorities.'"

"Exactly." He sighed again. "In those days, I meant the

procurator. But now . . ." He broke off sadly.

"I understand you have not been well," Josef said.

"The pains get worse," the priest admitted. "There is nothing to be done." He gave a short laugh. "Never mind. It is my imminent death, after all, that allows me to live. Our rebel leaders would do away with me in a minute if they did not think I would die any day now."

"I doubt you will fulfill that expectation," Josef said with an appreciative smile. "There is no better survivor than you."

"Tenacity is a family trait. And good fortune—if a Sadducee priest is permitted to use that term. I was halfway between Caesarea and Jerusalem when all the trouble started. Had I remained a day longer with my brother I would surely have been killed along with all the rest. Had I been here, I would no doubt have suffered the fate of Ananias."

Josef was about to reply when he sensed someone entering the room. He looked up briefly and saw a young woman approaching. He started to resume his conversation with the priest, stopped, and then looked up at the girl again. She was slender, with the graceful walk and figure of a dancer, but her bearing was not that of a servant or slave. She had dark hair that fell smoothly past her shoulders, and straight, winged brows beneath which two large, unusually light eyes stared into his. She had a provocative mouth. And a very direct way of looking at one, he thought, suddenly realizing that while he had been studying her, she had been doing the same to him.

The priest turned around. "Alexandra . . ." He gestured for her to come forward. "My brother's child," he said to Josef by way of introduction.

Josef nodded politely.

"You recall your stay in Caesarea? Samuel . . . Devorah . . ."

"Ah! Yes, of course," he said vaguely.

"Poor child. She is all that is left. The rest were wiped out. Wiped out," he repeated.

"So I heard." Josef spread his hands. "What can one say? We have all borne losses."

"I know, I know. That little girl your father had it in mind for you to marry . . . killed in the market, wasn't she? Yes. . . . Terrible, terrible, what these days have brought us. Well, I said it would lead to this. I warned them, do you remember? I warned them. But that is the way it goes. No one

listens to an old man. Never mind, soon enough they won't
have even the old man to listen to." He held up his hand before
Josef could protest. "I am so stiff with pain that I sometimes
wonder why I even bother hanging on to life."

"Then why do you?" the girl asked.

Instead of being angered by this impudent remark, he turned
to her with a smile. "Because, as we both know, my child,
life is all there is. Go. Bring us some wine."

Obedient, she left the room, feeling a pair of dark eyes
burning into her back as she departed. Trembling, she set the
pitcher and goblets on a tray and returned to the men.

"It would be better not to accept their offer," her uncle was
saying. "Why don't you come with us to Tiberias?"

"It would break my father's heart if I aligned myself with
Agrippa. Anyway, it is beyond choice now." A wry smile
crossed his face. "Our Zealot generals would probably kill me
if I refused to join them."

"You could slip away...."

He shook his head. "My father will not leave Jerusalem.
If I disappeared, they might take their revenge on him."

"Aghh . . . what a state of affairs. . . ." The priest shook
his head, disgusted.

"My father is quite proud that I have been chosen for a
command."

"I know." Privately, the priest thought Matthias was taking
his Hasmonean ancestry too seriously, for the gentleman
seemed determined to prove that if he had not fathered the
Messiah, he had, like the Matthias of old, sired a Maccabee.
"If you were my son," Shammai said testily, "I would have
told you to stay in Rome. Oh, I have no doubt your skills will
serve Judea well. I just wonder if *you* would not be better
served elsewhere. I cannot see any good," he repeated, "coming
from any of this."

"If you will allow me . . . I think you are wrong. If we can
keep moderates such as ourselves in controlling positions, there
is a chance we can bring this war to a quick conclusion. The
Zealots will not even consider bargaining for terms. It's all or
nothing for them. Well, we can't have the 'all,' as far as I can
see. But there is no reason why we must deliberately court
extinction. As you said, life is everything. Somehow, we're
in this war. It doesn't mean we can't get out with our lives.
We just have to find the way to do it."

"That is what I mean, Josef—you are wasted here. The people don't want men of sense. They want madmen in love with suicide. There are those who would call you a traitor for speaking as you just did."

"They can call me anything they like. But I will not see our people—our heritage, our history—crushed to death, and that dust blown away. Survival may be a limited victory, but in that sense I am in this war with all my heart to win."

The priest nodded. "Then you go to the Galilee?"

"Yes. The council has made me governor of the entire area."

"A fine present they have given you," Shammai said sarcastically.

"Not at all. The Galileans are eager to fight."

"Indeed. The question is, with whom? Be careful they don't turn around and slit your throat along the way."

Josef smiled. He looked up and caught Alexandra's eye. (Had she imagined it, or had his fingers deliberately brushed hers when he took the wine goblet from her hand?)

"You cannot believe how I look forward to Tiberias," Shammai was saying now. "The hot pools . . . there is sorcery in that water. Wonderful sorcery. Of course, Agrippa's court is not the Sanhedrin—but there is a scarcity of Pharisees there, thank the Lord. Ben Zakkai and his bunch believe wisdom to be solely contained in the ability to answer one question with another. His wit is as feeble as his philosophy."

Josef's eyes held Alexandra's. His lips seemed to curl in a faint half-smile, as though they two shared a secret. "You will accompany your uncle to Tiberias?" he asked her.

"Of course," Shammai said before she could answer. "Where else should she go? That is another reason I keep myself alive. I must find a husband for her. Samuel had her betrothed to a son of the House of Anan, but the boy was killed in the September fighting." He looked at his niece. For a moment the sharp eyes softened. "We are all that is left, she and I. The great House of Harsom. An old man and a girl."

"But in Rome—"

"Yes, there is a distant cousin there. A fool of little worth, as you may have gathered. And there may still be kin in Alexandria. We are related, you know, to Philo."

"Then there are ties with Tiberius Alexander?" Josef asked, wondering at the great sphere of wealth, learning, and power encompassed by this family.

Shammai ben Harsom nodded. "Along the way. But when he renounced his faith, we cast him out from us. Political reality is one thing," the priest said sternly. "Renouncing the One God is without excuse and merits no pardon." He winced suddenly and pressed his hand to his stomach. "So I am left," he said, recovering his composure, "to make a match for this child. The trouble is, every time I line up someone decent, the fellow gets done in. It is a dangerous business to be a Sadducee these days. No respect for the upper class," he added drily.

"Perhaps a court . . ."

"Exactly. Who knows? There is always Agrippa. The king has never taken a wife."

"Berenice would never allow it. The princess is, shall we say, most jealous of her brother's affections."

Shammai raised his eyebrows knowingly. "Can you believe it?"

But Josef ben Matthias was staring at Alexandra again. "It seems to me there was talk another time of a betrothal—" His eyes widened. "Of course! Alexandra!" He laughed. "Is it really you?"

"Have I changed so much?" she asked, smiling.

"You were a child when I left Judea, and now . . ." He did not finish the sentence but looked appreciatively at her.

Her uncle sighed. "She looks more like her mother every day. The hair is different . . . and the eyes . . . but I look at her and I see Devorah. Go," he said suddenly but not unkindly to the girl. "Leave us now. I love you, child. But it is too much. It is too much."

Her eyes met Josef ben Matthias's for a moment. Then she bent and kissed her uncle and left.

He seemed to know she would be in the garden. He took her hands in his. "Good-bye, Alexandra bat Harsom."

"When do you leave for the north?"

"Tomorrow. They are waiting for me in Jotapata."

"I pray you will be safe," she whispered.

He smiled, revealing those straight white teeth she remembered so well. "I will get along," he said cheerfully. "I always do. I am only sorry," he added in a low voice, bending his head toward hers, "that we have had so little time—none, in fact—to renew our friendship. Why has your uncle kept you hidden? And how did you manage to escape Caesarea?"

"I was hidden by a servant. A friend of my father's, a Christian—one Lukas by name—also helped to keep me safe. It was he who arranged to bring me here. I have not been in Jerusalem long, and since my arrival, I have hardly been allowed to leave the house."

"That may be for the best. The way things are . . . Zealots roaming the city . . ."

They both fell quiet. Her heart was beating so hard that she wondered if he could hear it. The scent of jasmine was in the air, and the perfume of roses. She put out her hand and touched a flower. The roses had been brought from Jericho and planted here by her father's mother, called Avigael—which was, in fact, Alexandra's Hebrew name.

The stillness was broken suddenly by the sound of silver trumpets and the voices of the Levites calling the faithful to evening prayer. The priests' song rose in the night like a bird taking wing, flying from the roses of Jericho to the gates of the Temple and back. The silver trumpets sounded, and then all was still again.

Alexandra's eyes had followed the sound. She remained looking toward the distance. "There are ten measures of beauty in all the world," she recited softly. "And nine of these are in Jerusalem." She looked at Josef. "I've always wondered . . . where do you suppose the tenth is?"

"Well, not in the Galilee," he said with a laugh, thinking of the journey before him. He broke off the rose and gave it to her. "Anyway, I would say the question is not where, but what. What is the tenth measure? I must confess I've never been able to figure out the first nine."

She smiled at this.

"You must leave Jerusalem as soon as possible," he said suddenly. "The atmosphere in the city is . . . unstable. Go to Tiberias with your uncle and stay close to the royal family."

"But they are traitors! Agrippa has pledged his support to Rome!"

He was amused by her outburst. "Do you mean to tell me I have been standing here in the dark with a Zealot after all?"

She lowered her eyes, confused.

He put his hand under her chin and tipped her head back. "Trust me," he said. "Go to Tiberias."

"Why not Jotapata?" she whispered.

He dropped his hand, surprised.

She could feel the intensity of his gaze as he sought to see her in the darkness. She felt more than saw the curious half-smile that had returned to his face.

"Tiberias," he repeated softly. "There you will be safe."

TWO

Jotapata stood on the side of a hill, surrounded by a formidable turreted wall. On its east, west, and southern sides, steep, ragged precipices fell away into what looked like bottomless ravines. On the northern side, however, the town extended up the slope of the hill toward its summit. There, Josef decided, studying the city thoughtfully, was the approach. Jotapata could only be taken—possibly—from the north. . . .

An impatient cough drew him from his reverie. He turned with an apologetic smile to the man on horseback beside him. "You must be tired, Saul, and hungry. Riding all day as we have . . ."

"Hungry?" The Galilean looked surprised. "No, I . . . I mean, I'm just anxious to . . ." He reddened and looked away angrily. The Jerusalemite was mocking him, no doubt. As if any man of the Galilee could not outride a soft Sadducee prince.

"You are anxious. Yes, I can see that. Well, we have much to do here, Saul ben Levi, and delay will not help our cause. But then, neither will action without thought." He pointed to the city in the distance. "There lies Jotapata. But you know that already, don't you? Yes, well, the reason I have been standing here so long is that I have been trying to imagine what I would do if I were sent by Rome and not Jerusalem."

The man stared at him.

"What would you do, Saul ben Levi? If you were Caesar's soldier, would you try to take Jotapata?"

Saul laughed now. "Jotapata is as strong as Jerusalem. You can see for yourself. The wall . . . the mountain . . . and every man there a fighter pledged to freedom or death. The Romans would be fools to try."

"They would be fools not to. Jotapata is the key to the entire area. If they take Jotapata, the Galilee will be theirs."

• • •

They did not remain long in the city. Satisified with its for-
tifications and with the attitude of Jotapata's citizens, Josef left
for Sepphoris with the wary Saul ben Levi at his side.

The Galilean had been appointed by the council to assist
Josef. It was thought that the people of the north would be
more cooperative if they had one of their own serving in the
echelons of power—under a Jerusalemite, of course, who was
not given to Zealot excesses or fanaticism. The priest Shammai
was of the opinion that the governance of the Galilee would
go better in the hands of someone like Saul ben Levi, who had
proved himself a fighter and a man of some solidity. But
Shammai had to concede that it was best to have the area under
the command of one who would not question orders from
Jerusalem. Josef ben Matthias seemed such a man. He was not
yet thirty, but he had demonstrated his competence, and he
also had a thorough if academic knowledge of Roman military
practices. "If he could win Nero," it was said, "then perhaps
he can control the rebels of the Galilee."

The appointment of the young man only recently returned
from Rome came as a blow to Saul. He had expected that the
command would fall to him and had been privately assured of
this by certain council members after the defeat of Cestius
Gallus. But that was the way it was with Jerusalemites, Saul
ben Levi thought bitterly. They said one thing while they plotted another. But why, of all men, had they chosen this one?
he wondered. The son of Matthias had never even been in
battle; he had been off in Rome while the rest of them were
fighting at home. The man had never served as a Temple priest,
although he had been trained as one, had never held a sword,
had never sat in the Sanhedrin. . . . Who was this young puppy?
Saul looked upon Josef with ill-concealed disdain. The young
"general" was certainly not an imposing figure. He was no
taller or bigger than the average man, though handsome, Saul
supposed, in a way pleasing to women. No doubt the Jerusalemite pleased them well with his fine manners and honeyed
voice. Saul ben Levi did not like men with honeyed voices.
He did not like men who smiled as much as this one did. And
it was a mocking smile. Several times the Jerusalemite had
asked Saul to repeat himself, requesting politely enough, but

only, Saul was sure, in order to make fun of the Galilean's country accent.

"I want you to round up seventy men," Josef said when they were settled in Sepphoris. "Not fighters. Elderly men, well known, respected. The leading citizens of Gamala, Gischala, Bersabe, Selame, Tarichea . . ."

"What should I tell them?"

"Tell them? Tell them I wish to see them."

Saul's jaw tightened. "Men of the Galilee do not come like sheep when a horn is blown. We may not be as learned as some, but we are free men here."

Josef looked up from the chart he was studying. "I see," he said. "Very well. Be so kind as to find the seventy I requested and make known to them my desire to solicit their advice and goodwill." Saul was still suspicious, so he added, "I intend to put them in charge. They may rule themselves."

"Rule themselves?"

"Yes. I have no intention of wasting my time listening to dowry disputes and petty land claims. I'll let my Galilean Sanhedrin take care of such matters, and I'll appoint magistrates in all the towns as well. They can spare me the task of dealing with local quarrels—and if I know our people, there should be enough of those to keep them off my back while I attend to matters of greater urgency."

"Such as?"

It was Josef's turn to look surprised. "Raising an army, of course. And training it."

The Galilean's mouth opened. This puppy was going to teach them how to fight? This smooth-voiced, slender prince who'd spent his life reading books or charming women with his smile and fine ways, this—this Sadducee was going to lead the warriors of the hills in battle? Saul lowered his head like a bull about to charge. "We know how to fight," he said gruffly.

"Do you?" Josef replied pleasantly. "Then you are familiar with the various ways of passing on signals? . . . And I suppose all the men hereabouts know how to sound the advance and the retreat. . . . They know how to make flank attacks and encircling movements, the means by which one unit relieves another one in difficulty? . . ." He paused, looking at Saul with raised eyebrows.

Saul did not reply, but his eyes showed new respect.

"It is not courage that has enabled Rome to conquer the world," Josef said patiently. "The Roman soldier knows the meaning of discipline—discipline and obedience. And make no mistake, his determination is as unshakable as your own."

"You don't know what you are talking about. You were not here when Cestius Gallus came with his legions. Those Roman soldiers of yours didn't waste time walking when they saw we meant business. They turned tail and ran. They ran, I tell you."

"The four hundred Gallus left to cover his retreat—four hundred against a thousand—did they also run?"

Saul fell silent again. No, those men had stood their ground and fought to the last one of them. Not one had surrendered or asked for mercy.

"That is the sort Rome will send against us now," Josef said. "And you had better hope we are ready to face them."

"But we are fighting for that which is dear to us. What do they care for Judea except that it is something their Caesar wishes to possess? We are fighting for the sacred right of freedom, for the land the Lord God of Israel promised His people as theirs alone. That must count for something in the final balance. I know," he said firmly, "that the Lord is with us."

Josef sighed. "Then let us perform the Lord's will and not depend on the Almighty to do for us what we must do for ourselves. Don't fight me, Saul," he said suddenly. "I did not ask for this position. In fact, it was my suggestion that the Galilee be given to you. And I would be happy to serve you, even as the council has appointed you to be my aide. But I am here as your commander and as governor of the Galilee—and the legions of Rome will soon be here as well. We must each do our best. I know you doubt my loyalty as well as my ability. The latter must speak for itself. But of the first quality, I will tell you this: I have pledged myself to the council and to my father—whose love and regard I cherish more than my own life—and I pray to the Lord that I may fulfill the duty that politics and providence have assigned." He put his hand on the other's arm. "Help me to do this, Saul ben Levi. Help me to help our people. Be my captain. Be my friend."

The Galilean bowed his head, ashamed now of the animosity he had displayed. "It is true," he said finally. "I was angry that the council made you commander of the Galilee. You are not one of us," he said bluntly. "And I have heard that you are uncommonly friendly with our enemy. In Jerusalem, it was said that you tarried in Rome for your own pleasure." His voice softened. "But perhaps it was the Lord's will that you remained there for as long as you did. You know the ways of those we must fight, and now you will teach these things to us."

Josef was about to reply, but Saul went on. "The men of the Galilee are known to be good fighters," the sturdy captain said. "We are strong here, and we fear no one but the Lord. But it is as you have said. We must be more than fighters. You must make us into an army."

"Gladly!" Josef cried.

Saul nodded. "I will help you." His eyes went deep into Josef, trying to cut through the smiling veneer to the real stuff of the man. "But if you betray us," the Galilean said, "I will kill you."

Josef's "Seventy" were chosen and duly appointed, an act that gave him the support not only of the area's leading citizens but of the grateful populace as well. This done, the Jerusalemite turned his attention to determining and then fortifying the most defensible positions in the Galilee. He raised a force of more than one hundred thousand men, equipped this army with weapons that he and Saul managed to round up from every conceivable place, and instituted a system by which his soldiers were regularly supplied with the rations they required. Josef made it clear to those who toiled in the fields that the food and wool they provided were being repaid with precious security. "You are soldiers, too," he told the farmers and fishermen who found themselves tithed.

Saul listened and watched, and as the days passed, his eyes began to glow with admiration. His young general seemed to be everywhere at once, now supervising the building of a stronghold at Selame, now offering final judgment in a murder trial at Tarichea, now calming the fears of the peasant woman whose only son had been conscripted for Josef's legion. From place to place, from duty to duty, Josef ben Matthias moved with a speed that his retinue of bodyguards and captains could scarcely match, and with an energy that seemed at times more than mortal man could possess. But somehow, as fast as he moved and as long as he worked, Saul stayed with him. Where the Jerusalemite went, the Galilean followed. And when Josef came at last to whatever chamber would be his refuge for the night, Saul was there waiting, having seen first that the place was clean, warm, equipped with writing materials, and safe from any adversaries or assassins.

They were back in Jotapata this night, having come to inspect the store of grains. Once he had determined that the walled town was the strongest and most easily defensible place, Josef wanted to make sure it was equipped to handle those who would seek refuge there when Rome's legions swept across the countryside.

He threw himself down on the narrow pallet that would be his bed and lay there unmoving, a hand flung back across his eyes. Saul thought he was asleep and was about to cover him with a blanket when he heard Josef sigh. "Time," the young man murmured. "There is not enough time. . . ." He rubbed his eyes. "Saul?"

The man came forward.

"Do you know how many years a legionary trains? Do you know what campaigns some of them have fought? Britain . . . Thrace . . . the Gauls. . . . And what have we got? A mob that knows the dietary laws of *kashrut* but still can't tell the difference between the decurions and the centurions I've appointed." He laughed wryly. "As if it mattered. They only listen to whoever comes from their own village—or, most likely, to themselves. Everyone's a general. Two hundred Galileans do not make a front and rear guard or four smaller fighting units. No, Saul. Two hundred Galileans make two hundred generals or two hundred tribunes or two hundred cavalry lieutenants. All those officers . . . and not one good private. . . ." Didn't the man ever laugh? "Well, I wish you could tell me how to get through to them. An army must have officers, and the officers must be obeyed."

"The Lord made all men equal."

Josef opened his eyes and stared at the ceiling. He knew he must not laugh, but he was so tired that he just might. "It isn't a matter of class or pride," he started to say with forced calm. "Ah, what's the use?" With a groan of fatigue, he turned over on his stomach and closed his eyes again.

Once more Saul thought the man was asleep. He was preparing to go from the room when Josef said suddenly, "The one from Gischala . . . John. . . . What is he up to?"

"He is rebuilding the walls of his city, as you ordered."

"Hmmn. At a fine profit to himself, no doubt. He sells us oil at eight times its value—I can just imagine what he is charging the good citizens of Gischala for labor."

"But he has supplied oil despite the shortage, even going across the border to obtain it. He takes great risks and—you are wrong—without any profit to himself."

Josef opened one eye and looked at the man, but he said nothing. John of Gischala had indeed marked up his ware eight hundred percent; one half of that was going into Josef's pocket. There was no need, however, to enlighten Saul. Instead Josef asked, "You are from Jotapata, are you not? Why are you here with me at this hour? Why don't you go home to your family? Surely they have seen little of you these past months."

It was the closest Saul had ever come to a smile. "You are in my house now."

Josef sat up. "What? Your house?" He shook his head. "I do not know anymore what day it is or where I am. . . . You must make my apologies to your family. Have you a wife? Never mind, I shall meet them all tomorrow. Yes, we must make a dinner tomorrow, and I shall meet all your relatives and friends. Will it be difficult to arrange? I leave everything to you."

"It will be a great honor for us, dining with the governor of the Galilee."

"Good. You see to it then." He could not suppress a yawn. "I hope I have not taken your bed, Saul, but if so you must find another, for I fear I cannot move another step today." He fell back and closed his eyes. "Not . . . another . . . step. . . ."

They were sturdy, solid people, like Saul—who, Josef had come to realize, was more than just another fervent peasant fighter. Saul ben Levi was not wealthy by the standards of Israel's great houses, but he was more comfortable than many, and he enjoyed, moreover, the respect of his townspeople— most of whom seemed to turn up for dinner the next night. If Josef found this company less than scintillating, he did not show it. Faced with a suspicious audience whose affection he was determined to win, Josef turned on his considerable charm like a generous host plying his guests with wine. The result was much the same.

Knowing instinctively that this gathering would be no place for subtle wit or courtly flattery, Josef presented himself as the most earnest, honest, god-fearing, patriotic fellow one could hope to meet. He was humble and yet stirringly passionate in his determination to liberate Judeans from the "ungodly foreigners" who had dominated their lives. He spoke frequently of "the Lord's will" and sprinkled his speech with the idioms of the region, which his quick ear and nimble tongue had already picked up. He was a success. As once a Roman tribune had found it hard to believe that Josef was a Jew, so now these Galileans slapped him on the back and called him brother.

While the meal itself offered no culinary surprises, the ingredients were exceedingly fresh and sweet, and Josef, who prided himself on his discerning taste, took public note of this. He had not had such good fare in Jerusalem, he declared, or even at the court of Caesar—where, he added quickly, he had been careful to partake only of such food as was not abhorrent to the Lord and the Law of Moses.

"What fragrant soup this is," he exclaimed before his hosts' curiosity as to his diet in Rome led to questions that would be better left unanswered. "These dumplings are quite wonderful. I am sure the manna of our ancestors could not have been better."

The company beamed at this, and before he knew what was happening they had pushed forward a young woman to acknowledge his compliment. She was quite shy and stood there with her head bowed, twisting her skirt in her hands, with two bright pink spots on her cheeks. She was fair, and though her hair was pulled back and hidden beneath a square of linen, soft blond tendrils curled at her temples, fine as silk. The wispy strands added to her air of vulnerability. When she dared at last to look up at him, he saw that her eyes were as blue as a baby's, with an expression that was at once childlike and maidenly in its sweet helplessness. But if the face of this lovely creature bespoke tender innocence, her body was quite another matter. The simple linen robe could not hide those full breasts and rounded hips. Pregnancy, age, and those dumplings would take their toll, but at this moment the girl was perfect: soft, ripe, obviously the most delicious thing at dinner, and as succulent a piece of flesh as Josef had ever seen. He cleared his throat.

He had been self-conscious and careful in his attitude towards the women of the Galilee, particularly tonight. He'd had no difficulty winning the elderly ones with what they took to be a kind of shy boyishness, at the same time impressing the younger ones with his solemn courtesy. No one, he thought, could accuse him of being anything but correct. The fact was, there had been little in the north to tempt him to display the charm for which he had been duly appreciated in Rome and

Jerusalem. Ordinarily that would not have stopped him from flirting, if only to amuse himself. But tempers were hot and quick in the Galilee, and while the rabbis might accuse the people here of a certain academic laxity, no one could doubt their strictness concerning their women's virtue.

Her name was Adinah.

"Truly it is said," Josef recited gravely, sounding like one of the grandfathers in the room, "'Many daughters have done valiantly, but thou excellest them all. Grace is deceitful and beauty is vain but a woman that feareth the Lord, she shall be praised.'"

She blinked, confused.

"'A woman of valor—she looketh to the ways of her household and eateth not the bread of idleness,'" Josef went on. He was getting a little confused himself. He had never seen a female who looked so soft. How he would like to lay his head upon those two sweet pillows. . . . He cleared his throat again. "Your husband is a fortunate man. To enjoy the blessing of your dumplings—I mean, such fine cooking—"

"Adinah is without a husband," Saul said. His eyes were bright with amusement. The girl's beauty was legendary in Jotapata, and Saul enjoyed seeing the Jerusalemite react as many a Galilean lad did upon first seeing her.

"How can that be?" Josef wondered.

"She has neither parents nor dowry."

Josef nodded. "Ah," he said.

"She is my wife's cousin," Saul went on. "I am willing to provide a marriage settlement—a modest one; I am not a wealthy man—provided one of good family comes forward."

"You mean no one—"

"We do not know who the girl's mother was," Saul said in a low voice. "There are those—as you may imagine—who would like to possess her, but I cannot in good conscience give her to someone who might ill use her. Naturally no respectable family wants an alliance with a penniless orphan who may not even be of our own race."

Josef nodded solemnly. With no proof of her mother's identity, Adinah's status was indeed questionable. It would not have mattered if her father had been Agrippa II; a Jew was a Jew by virtue of having a Jewish mother. Josef felt sorry for the girl (she was a beauty), but he did not allow his pity to show.

• • •

She brought him supper the following night. When he saw that it was she who had come to his chamber, he put aside his maps and charts and asked her to remain awhile and cheer his meal. She murmured her assent, her eyes downcast; but Josef thought she was perhaps not as shy as she appeared to be. He did not miss the fact that she and not some other had come to his room.

"Her father was brother to my wife's mother," Saul had told him. "He was a restless sort who went to make his fortune in Jerusalem. He had a pretty talent for carving things. . . . Well, the city must have swallowed him up, because we heard nothing thereafter. Whenever one of us made a pilgrimage we could never find him or any who knew of him. Years later, though, he turned up again in Jotapata with a baby girl, no money, and no wife. He claimed he'd married a woman of Tyre who was murdered by a band of Samaritans while traveling to Jerusalem to make a vow at the Temple. He said his wife had been the daughter of a rich merchant who had also been killed by the bandits. It was never proved. I do not wish to speak ill of my wife's family, but they know how to tell a story, and this fellow was no exception. He died soon after his return and left Adinah to our care. I tried to find out what I could, but no one seemed to know anything about a merchant of Tyre and his daughter, both slain by Samaritans. Adinah remembers nothing prior to her being brought here."

She was an orphan. And while the Law stated quite clearly that orphans must be cared for, it did not say one had to marry them. Even in the Galilee, where many a household was full of the blond, blue-eyed grandchildren of some long-ago-proselytized Amorite woman, Adinah was something of a problem. She was too beautiful for the women to pity and the men to ignore. Her virtue, however, was unquestioned.

Her white skin seemed faintly gold in the light cast by the oil lamps. She stood a short distance away from him, like a little girl pleased to have been asked to a party but not quite sure what to do there.

"Come and sit by me," Josef said. "I am sure you must be as tired as I—and look how I have caused you this extra work." He indicated the food she had brought him.

"Oh, no," she said quickly. "I was glad to—I mean, it is a great honor to have you with us." She had a small, breathless voice.

"An honor, eh? You mean to say I have found someone at last who does not hate a poor Jerusalemite?"

She was astonished. "Hate? You? But you are governor of all the Galilee! Saul says you are working so hard to save us from the Roman soldiers—and even if you were not the governor, how could anyone hate—I mean, you are—you are—" She broke off, lowering her eyes.

Josef allowed a sigh to escape him. "I fear there are those here who think I wish to work not for our people but against them," he said sadly. "It is a hard thing to be with those who mistrust you just because you were not raised among them. You cannot know what it feels like to be . . . an outsider."

She looked up. "I . . . I understand how you feel. But do not think that all hate you or mistrust you. I . . . I don't."

He smiled. "Then I am content."

She lowered her eyes again. "And I . . . I do not mind that you are from Jerusalem. Perhaps you could tell me about the Holy City. I have always thought . . . I would like one day to live there."

"Yes, I can see you there. Dressed in finest linen—or perhaps a veil of Persian silk shot through with threads of gold. . . . You'd like that, wouldn't you? Yes, I can see you in Jerusalem. At the Temple, in the Court of Women, standing next to the daughters of the Houses of Phiabi and Gorion . . . with a necklace of blue stones around your throat. Blue, to match your eyes. . . ."

"I should like that," she breathed. "You do not think I am too countrified?"

He laughed softly. "Dear girl . . . Adinah . . . beauty goes anywhere. Jerusalem, Rome . . ." He had pushed back the linen covering her head. Her blond hair was like a halo. "Did you know," he said, "in Rome, all the women want hair like yours? They lie on the roofs of their villas with their tresses loose and spread out, hoping the sun will turn them blond, like their Gaulish slaves."

But she was more interested in Jerusalem. "Do the women of the great houses of Israel wear many necklaces? Do they also wish to have yellow hair?"

"No, they all fancy themselves Berenice, with hennaed locks."

She frowned.

"When you are married and your husband makes his pilgrimages, no doubt he will take you with him. Then you will see for yourself all the things in Jerusalem. I wish it were I who might . . . show you . . . what you wish to see. . . ."

She looked at him shrewdly. "More than one has asked Saul for my hand."

"I do not doubt it. He has not agreed to a betrothal?"

"I have not agreed to one." She shrugged. "They were of little consequence. The poorest of the poor. They thought to take advantage—" She broke off and was silent.

"There are honest men in Jotapata, men of consequence and with some means. Last night, I saw the way they looked at you. . . ."

"Yes," she said almost to herself, seeming to smile. "They all want me." Then, in a louder voice, "Their families are against me. You see, no one knows who my mother was."

He brushed that aside. "Such information could be obtained if one went about it seriously."

She stared at him. "Do you mean it?"

"It would be difficult now, with everything as it is. The records office was set afire by the Sicarii, but there are files in the Temple offices. When a child is born," he explained, "the parent sends notice to the priests in order that sacrifice may be made to the Almighty. The child's name and the names of the parents are inscribed in the priests' ledgers." He wondered why Saul had not taken this avenue of inquiry.

The blue eyes appealed to him. "Could you—would you—"

He nodded. "I must send certain dispatches to Jerusalem. I will include a letter on your behalf. I must tell you, though, not to expect an answer forthwith. Everything," he repeated, "was in the greatest confusion when I left, what with the preparations for war and new priests taking the place of those slain by . . . Menahem ben Judah." He caught himself just in time. He had been about to say "slain by the Zealots" when he remembered that everyone was ostensibly a Zealot now, including himself. "It will take time, but I am sure the information you seek can be found." Or forged, he thought.

"Then I could be—No one could—" Her eyes were shining. Her full breasts rose and fell with excitement. Then, suddenly, she was a little girl again. "You would really do this for me?" she asked in that soft, breathless voice.

"Of course. I am your governor, Adinah," he said gravely. "The welfare and happiness of every man, woman, and child in the Galilee is my primary—my only—concern. I know you find it hard to believe but"—he took a step closer, took her hands in his—"you are as important to me as the defense of Jotapata."

She bent her head and kissed his hands, then brought them to her bosom and held them there a moment while she bestowed upon him a look of purest admiration.

Josef swallowed. He checked the desire to spread his fingers wide and grab hold of the soft mounds on either side of the valley in which they were held captive. She let go of his hands, but before he could make a move toward her she was at the door.

"Adinah!" he called.

She turned back, a shy or mischievous smile curving her lips. In this light it might have been either.

"Tell me," he said. "Saul ben Levi is your guardian. How is it he has given the choice of a husband to you?"

"He loves me," she said demurely.

A faint smile played on Josef's face. "As a daughter, of course."

She smiled too. A dimple appeared. "Of course."

He stared at the door long after she'd gone, lost in thought. That look of sweet helplessness . . . A man would be forever damned to betray such trust. She was so innocent. And yet . . .

The slight, one-sided smile returned. Adinah was not totally guileless. The child's head had somehow surmised that the woman's body might be an instrument of disaster or triumph. Adinah was not unaware of her weapons.

Well, we are all whores of one kind or another, Josef thought. Everyone and everything had its price. Even God.

But was there more, he wondered, to Saul's concern for the girl—more, that is, than was natural to a guardian? Josef grinned. Stern, righteous Saul. The people's protector. Devoted father and husband. Covetous? Well, why not? Josef had long ago learned that things were not always as they seemed. Jerusalem, Rome, the Galilee—wherever there were men there was folly, and wherever there were women there was trickery. Man controlled. Woman manipulated. Speaking of which, there had been some plotting, it seemed, in Jerusalem. His thoughts went to the message his father had sent:

"The priest Shammai has suggested an alliance between our houses," Matthias had written. "He proposes that the daughter of Samuel ben Harsom become your wife. I am not greatly averse to the marriage, although this girl is not a Jerusalemite, but I await your consent before proceeding with arrangements for the betrothal. I am aware of your friendship with the family and have considered that you may have private knowledge of them which you might now share with me. Despite their noble line (the mother was of the House of David) the father—as you know—chose to indulge in commerce. By all accounts, however, he was a respected and righteous man who might well have been High Priest, like his father before him. They are a curious family, Josef, which is why I await your consent. Their holdings, however, are considerable."

Considerable indeed. Josef wanted to laugh. How like his father to make the wealth of the House of Harsom an afterthought. Why, even with the losses of war, there was still property in the Galilee, ships, ventures in Rome and Egypt. . . . Josef frowned. Someone ought to be looking after this sizable empire. Someone ought to be taking charge.

Restless now, he went to the window and leaned out, looking at the town below. Saul's house was high on the mountainside against which Jotapata had been built, and the city seemed to fall away like a child's tumbled blocks. ·

It was night; all was still. A Nero prowling the streets would find little to interest him here. Josef sighed, unmoved by the starry beauty of the sky and the peaceful quiet of the sleeping town. There were those who took delight in hills and flowering trees, but Josef liked cities—big cities, crowded, noisy, packed with people and all the things people make and buy and do. The song of the nightingale did not please him half so much as the music of the marketplace. And country women, though oftimes generous and enthusiastic, were rather tasteless compared to the women of the city, with their spicy knowledge and subtle talents. The women of Rome, for instance—their perfumes, their gossamer gowns, their telling glances . . . It had been no sin to love in Rome. Ten measures of beauty in the world? There were ten hundred in Rome.

"Ten measures of beauty" . . . The girl had said that in the priest's garden. There had been the smell of roses and jasmine. . . . What was her name?

In a year's time—provided they were not all killed—she would become his wife, and all her father's property would be his. He might still be the second son of Matthias, but he would be a very rich son—richer than any member of his family, despite their sanctified background, had ever been.

· · · ·

"We have word from Josef," the priest Shammai told his niece. "He expresses willingness to abide by his father's desire in the matter of your betrothal."

"That is all?" Alexandra asked. "Nothing more?"

"Well, he is naturally honored to align himself with the House of Harsom, and so forth. It's a good match. I don't know why it did not occur to me sooner. I have always thought highly of that boy. And of course, his ancestry is unquestionably pure. Yes, I shall be well pleased to see this marriage take place—if I live that long. It was clever of you to suggest it. I really don't know why I did not think of it myself."

"But didn't he say anything more?" she broke in impatiently. "I mean, about me?"

"What? You? Yes, of course. He hopes you are in good health." He was rummaging through a small ivory box. They were in the garden. Despite the sun, the priest lay wrapped in woolen blankets, suffering from the chill that never seemed to leave him although winter was long past. It was months since the traveling chests had been unpacked and the things of the house returned to their normal places. There would be no journey to Tiberias. Shammai was too ill to travel, and notwithstanding the changed character of Jerusalem, which had taken on a certain Zealot austerity, he was determined that he should die in his beloved city.

"My memory fails," the priest murmured, evidently not having found what he had been seeking. He leaned back and closed his eyes, the box still in his lap. After a moment, he opened his eyes and looked seriously at his niece. "You realize, Alexandra, there is a great deal involved in this marriage. You are all that is left, and providing no one in Alexandria or Rome comes forward, you will bring to your husband the fortune of the House of Harsom. Now, I have locked away certain important documents, which, when the time comes, I shall be content to give Josef. I thought the key was in this box. . . . Never mind, I know where it is. We shall see to it later. I want you to be aware of their existence so that in the event of my . . . leaving . . . before I can attend to it myself, you will turn the records over to your husband."

She started to say something, then decided against it.

"The villa in Caesarea and certain enterprises are of course lost," her uncle went on. "You are quite sure everything was destroyed?"

"The house burned to the ground. Hagar could find nothing.

Mother's jewels . . . father's records . . . there was nothing left. Nothing."

"Civil records? The authorities, for tax purposes—"

"I do not imagine the Greeks of Caesarea would honor a request for information regarding the estate of Samuel ben Harsom."

He glanced quizzically at her. She seemed angry. No doubt her memories of the massacre were upsetting. Or was there something more? She was a restless creature. He had thought the betrothal to Josef would please her, but even now, she moved about the garden like a walled-in animal. He sighed and thought—as others had before him—that it would be better for all concerned when this girl was married and settled within her husband's authority.

"Anyway," she was saying, "father did not report everything. Not in Caesarea, that is. He was not above lessening his taxes to Caesar, but he would never deny Jerusalem and the Temple their due or hold back the correct priestly tithe. In short, uncle, the records are here. In the Temple offices."

He pushed himself to a sitting position. "Of course! Good girl!"

"Let me go and search them out," she asked eagerly. "Father always let me see his ledgers. He said I did the sums quicker than his managers. I know what to look for. Let me go for them."

"No, no, Alexandra, it is impossible. The Temple . . . no, no. It is not permitted."

"The council has made it their business to know everyone's affairs. Those robbers will confiscate our property just as the Greeks of Caesarea did. Only now they will say it is for the war effort—to 'free Judea.' And all the while they will be dividing everything up among themselves. We must make our own investigation, our own accounting. Now."

"Yes, yes, I shall send a message—"

"They mustn't know what it's about! Someone must be there. . . . One of us."

He nodded. "Yes. Yes, you are right. As soon as I am well . . ."

"Uncle . . ." She sighed. "You have not moved from your bed or this garden since . . ." She sighed again and turned away. "You have not left the villa for months," she continued softly. "You can scarcely stand."

He blinked. Had it been so long? No, it was only last week

that Josef had come to visit and . . . No, he had not come. It was a message they'd had from him. "Alexandra . . ."

"Give me the authority," she begged, kneeling beside him. "Let me seek what is mine."

"Yours?" He frowned. "Nothing is yours. You are a woman. It would have been your brothers' inheritance, apart from the portion set aside for your dowry. Now it will go to your husband, as you are all that is left— unless, of course, any male relatives outside Judea put forth a claim."

"Claim? It's mine, I tell you! Mine! I am the daughter of Samuel ben Harsom!"

"Yes, yes, you are Samuel's daughter." He tried to calm her. "That is the trouble. You are not his son. I don't know why I am talking to you like this," he said suddenly, peevishly. "It is not your concern."

She was already pale with anger, but her eyes widened at this.

"Alexandra," he said quickly, "it was a good suggestion. You are a clever girl. And you are right, someone must see to it that the council does not take advantage of us. But even with a note of authority from me, you could have no access to the records in question. Have you forgotten? You cannot enter the Temple Sanctuary. You are forbidden to go past the Women's Court."

"I could dress as one of your male servants."

"Abomination! A woman is forbidden to dress as a man. It is an abomination!" He raised his finger in warning. In the time she had been with him, he had come to recognize his niece's strong will. "If you attempt such a disguise, I will denounce you. I warn you. There is nothing more sacred to me than the Law and the sanctity of the Temple. I will not allow you to defile yourself and the Lord's own House."

She said nothing, but her eyes went through him like cold steel.

"Get out!" he exploded, furious with her, and with himself for being so helpless and infirm. "Go and do whatever it is a woman does! You will be getting married soon—prepare yourself for that. Embroider bed linens. Why don't you go and embroider some nice bed linens? I'm sure Josef would appreciate that." His eyes brightened. "Yes . . . Josef. Josef will see to things. Of course. He'll take care of everything. Why, he'll have the council hopping—he won't let them get away with anything. You can be sure of that. Not Josef."

Some of the tension went out of her body. Yes...Josef would not let anyone take away her inheritance. He would protect her and her property. And after the war they would go back to Caesarea and take what belonged to her family....

Shammai ben Harsom, seeing her assuaged, smiled now. He had grown fond of his niece, although he frequently berated her for not attending to what he called "women's tasks." He was, as his brother had once been, proud of her intelligence and quickness to learn. During his illness she had replaced the Sanhedrin, spending hours conversing with him on Pythagorean theory and the philosophy of the Stoics, as well as on the Law of Moses. She had a prodigious memory and knew many psalms, which she would recite in her pleasing voice when he found it difficult to sleep. Sometimes she read to him from Homer; he would either pretend not to know what she was about or would loudly state, "Let us hear again the foolishness of the gentiles that we may compare it to the wisdom of our Lawgiver. Thus may we praise the Almighty for bestowing upon us men of sense and not tellers of blasphemous tales." Then he would close his eyes and listen contentedly while she told of the wrath of Achilles and the wanderings of Odysseus.

Alexandra had been most pleasantly surprised to find this literature among her uncle's belongings; but she had come to realize that his stern manner and righteous rhetoric masked what would have been, unchecked, a libertine heart. He was not, after all, much different from her father or herself. But while their curiosity, their questioning nature and passion for knowledge, was directed toward the world of man, Shammai's was immersed in the world of the Law. It was as if the priest could not trust himself to be himself, Alexandra thought, realizing now that all the years her uncle had railed against heathen works of art he had secretly admired them. He would never admit this; the priest Shammai was not given to confession, apology, or even the simple admission of a mistake. Alexandra knew, however, that there was one thing he did regret, something that caused him almost as much pain as the disease eating away his life. Those last bitter words between himself and Samuel could never be recalled, would never be redressed. There had been no chance for reconciliation.

So she returned his smile now, putting aside her anger at what she felt to be his demeaning attitude toward women.

He nodded, relieved. "You must understand," he said. "It is my duty to tell you the truth. It would not do for you to be actively involved in matters of business. You would appear too bold, too . . . I don't know what. I do know, however, that Matthias would not approve—and I want nothing to jeopardize this match."

She raised an eyebrow. "I did not know that a member of the House of Harsom worried about the approval of others."

"It is true that Josef's family does not have our, shall we say, resources. But theirs is an old, distinguished line. Matthias guards his stock carefully. It is his only wealth."

"Mother was of the House of David—"

"But your father—may he rest in peace—was a man of commerce and was known to have extensive dealings with gentiles. And you are not a Jerusalemite. This tends to sully our standing somewhat."

She was silent a moment. "All right," she said finally. "It shall be as you wish. I will be quiet, modest"—she made a face—"detestably docile." At least until the wedding, she thought. "In other words, I shall do my best to appear stupid. Whatever you think will please Josef's father."

"It will please Josef as well." *Poor boy*, Shammai thought. *First the Galilee, then Alexandra.* "I shall send a message to Josef regarding your inheritance and the matters that we have discussed."

She brightened. "Good! Tell him—"

"Alexandra!"

She bit her lip.

"You must learn to trust to the wisdom of men. Mine, and that of your husband-to-be."

"Yes, uncle." She nearly choked on the words.

"And do yourself a favor," he added with a sigh. "After you are wed, let Josef do the thinking. Men do not love women who are too clever."

THREE

He was going over the defenses for the tenth—the hundredth—time when Saul came into the room and without a word set a heavy leather sack squarely in the middle of his charts. It was followed by others, some of them containing jewels as well as gold and silver. Josef looked up calmly.

"Yes?" he asked politely.

"These were found among your possessions," Saul replied in a tight, angry voice. "There are more—"

"The wooden chest. Why didn't you bring that along as well? Too heavy?"

"Not so heavy as the weight of your deceit. I am beginning to think John is right to denounce you."

"John of Gischala? What is that robber up to now?"

"He is in Tiberias—"

"Yes, I know," Josef broke in impatiently. "He wrote to me of his desire to take the hot baths. He said he had been ill—"

"There is nothing wrong with him—as you shall soon discover. He is in Tiberias to rouse the people against you. He says you betray us, that you work for your own ends." Saul leaned closer. "He says you will sell us out to your Roman friends and that even now you are in Agrippa's employ."

Josef sighed. The people of Tiberias had revolted against Agrippa and driven the king from the city. At the same time, some young men in Josef's army had waylaid Agrippa's chief minister, robbed him of his baggage, and brought the loot to Josef. When they received no share of the gold they had appropriated, they went about denouncing the young governor as a traitor, declaring that he meant to return the money to the king. Evidently their story, combined with the accusations of John of Gischala, had prompted Saul to make an investigation of his own.

"I know what you are thinking," Josef said. He waved aside the leather sacks. "But I had no intention of returning this money to Agrippa or of lining my own pockets with it."

"Then why—"

"What would you have me do with it, man? Share it out with the bandits who took it? When will you people learn that the days and the ways of the Sicarii are finished? We are a government now. We are an army. That gold must go for our defense. And it is in my possession because it is safe with me. In case you didn't know, there is more than one who has his eyes on these spoils—including John of Gischala."

Saul was silent a moment. "You had better talk to the people," he said at last. "If you cannot persuade them of your honesty, you may find yourself removed from office—and not by means of a diplomatic courier from Jerusalem."

"All right, then, let us go to Tiberias. I am willing to defend myself, although no defense is necessary. We will take a small guard only. We can ill afford a civil war now."

"You had better do some talking here in Jotapata, or you may find yourself going to Tiberias without even a small guard."

"Fine," Josef agreed, grimly resigned to what he privately considered a waste of his time.

It was not long before a large crowd had assembled, eager to confront the Jerusalemite with the rumors they had heard. Josef repeated his declaration that he had been holding monies for use in their best interests, adding that it was not he but John of Gischala who was guilty of profiteering. "The thief hates me because I will not pay the exorbitant sums he demands for the oil and grain we need if we are to survive a siege," Josef said. "You say that I am of a noble family. Yet it does not seem to bother any of you that John of Gischala, born a poor and humble man, has now become as wealthy as the High Priest. How, I ask you? At whose expense?"

But they were not altogether appeased. Galilean resentment against Jerusalem exploded now. "You are a Sadducee," men cried out. "Sadducees bow to Rome. They care nothing for the *am ha'eretz*. How, then, can you be concerned for our good? We are nothing to you."

Josef was not one to miss the way the wind was blowing. Seeing that their mistrust was more regional than rational, he held up his hand to silence them and said sadly, "It is clear to me now that you hate me because I am from Jerusalem, and born into the priestly class." He spread his hands in apology. "Was this of my doing? I am what I am even as you are what you are, and this because it is God's will that one should be born here and another there. But although you hate me because I am one thing, I do not hate you because you are another. In the time I have spent among you I have learned what greatness lies in the hearts of the people of the Galilee—and especially here in Jotapata. Truly, you are the Lions of Judah. And whatever else the rabbis in Jerusalem say, not one can say that the Galileans are not a fair and a just people. It is these qualities— your courage, your honesty, your fairness—that have guided me in all my decisions as your governor. I had hoped that I might somehow become one of you—truly a Galilean. In fact," he added almost offhandedly, "I had looked forward to making a woman of the Galilee my wife."

A murmur went up at this. The bachelor status of the young, handsome governor had been a subject of some discussion, particularly among those with eligible daughters.

"Yes," Josef continued, "there is among you a poor orphan girl whose virtue is as heralded as her beauty. But because her ancestry is suspect, no one of worth will share with her the holy bonds of matrimony. I am, as you have shouted at me, a Sadducee. I am a Jerusalemite. And I will bring to my wife the seed of the Hasmoneans." He paused, letting his words sink in. "I will marry this orphan of the Galilee, this daughter of the *am ha'eretz*. I ask the one you call Adinah to be my wife."

Above the gasps of surprise and astonishment, he heard Saul stammer, "But—but her mother—"

Josef turned to his aide with what might have been a cruel smile. "You needn't worry about that, my friend. I have sent to the offices of the Temple for records that will prove Adinah is of Hebrew descent. I expect there will be no difficulty in obtaining the necessary information. And you needn't worry about the dowry. Your blessing is fortune enough."

With Jotapata under control, Josef set out for Tiberias with a guard of men now fiercely loyal. The diplomatic skill he had displayed in one part of the Galilee did not fail him in another; he was victorious in his confrontation with John. However, there were others who distrusted the Jerusalemite, and Josef found it necessary time and again to defend himself against detractors and assassins. But when he could not talk himself out of a situation, there was always the sword of Saul ben Levi to back him up.

This constant political intrigue might well have continued until he was either killed or removed from office by the council had it not been for the arrival of an outside force of decisive importance. Caesar's men had returned to Judea, determined now to subjugate this stubborn people once and for all. The Roman army had crossed the Hellespont, traveled the length of Asia Minor, come down into Syria, and established head-quarters at Antioch. There, the world-famous Fifth and Tenth Legions were joined by the Fifteenth, from Alexandria, cohorts from Syria and Caesarea, and a large contingent of auxiliaries contributed by Agrippa, the kings of Emesa and Commagene, and the Nabatean monarch. A force of sixty thousand fighting men marched to Tyre, and down the coast to Ptolemais in Phoenician Syria, and finally eastward into Galilee. It was a sight to behold.

First came the light-armed auxiliaries, in oriental dress, many of them archers—a vanguard to forestall surprise attacks and to scout the area. Next came the heavy-armed Romans, some mounted and some on foot, with their helmets, cuirasses, spears, and shields shining in the sun. After them came the contingent that would lay out the camp, and the engineers who would level roads and eliminate or circumvent any topograph-ical obstructions that might impede the army's progress. The personal belongings of the commander and his officers fol-lowed in carriages guarded by a cavalry escort, behind which rode the general, magnificently armed, a long red cloak falling over his left shoulder and over the back of his great horse. A special guard consisting of spearmen and warriors who had distinguished themselves in battle accompanied the com-mander.

Each legion had its own cavalry, and these troops rode next, every man with a long sword hanging at his right side, a spear or pike in his hand, a quiver of darts beside him, and a shield angled across his horse's flank. Then came the mules carrying the battering rams and catapults; and the standards enclosing the Eagle, that great, gold image carried high and proud. The imperial symbol was followed by trumpeters, and in their wake marched the main body of the army, the infantry. Solid, stub-born, superbly disciplined, they were the core of Roman strength, these common soldiers who had given Caesar his empire. Shoulder to shoulder they had walked from one end of the world to the other, six men abreast, with their centurions to maintain the formation; each man in helmet and cuirass, a dagger at his left side, a long sword at his right, a javelin in one hand, his left arm thrust through the strap of an oblong shield; each man carrying three days' rations on his back, along with a pick, a chain, an ax, and other pieces of equipment.

Still the procession was not done. Straggling noisily behind came the servants of the legions, leading baggage mules and other pack animals. And finally, at the rear, marched the bulk of the auxiliaries—Greeks, Syrians, Nabateans, and other mercenaries—with a final rear guard of infantry and cavalry for further protection.

Professionals. No amateur army of farmers and fishermen, no mob of impassioned patriots or gang of religious fanatics. These were professional soldiers, fighting not by instinct or out of desperation, but according to the order, discipline, and engineering of the best military minds of the day. They had come to Judea not in vindictive anger but in a mood of just and necessary retribution, determined to subdue the rebellious province and reintegrate it within the orderly structure of their domain. The fact that their "peaceful" world consisted mainly of nations that had not willingly joined the Roman Empire but had been conquered and enslaved did not seem to bother these proponents of "order." A poll of the men marching across Judea might well have revealed the opinion that the world would be better off without the Jews, who, like the Christian sect they had spawned, were nothing but troublemakers, and hardly worthy foes like the Thracians and even the Gauls.

In time, the harsh climate of the land and the stubborn, suicidal resistance of its people would tear at the Roman temper, bringing forth a rage and hatred that was content with nothing less than total destruction. But for the moment, the generals and kings still thought in terms of punishment, not extinction.

Nero was on a theatrical tour of Greece when the first reports of the Jewish revolt arrived. The emperor was twenty-nine. He had already succeeded in having his mother assassinated, had murdered his rich aunt by making her doctors administer a lethal cathartic, and had ordered the philosopher Seneca, who had been his tutor, to commit suicide. He had raped the Vestal

Virgin (and, publicly, numerous girls and boys), possibly
started the great fire of Rome, and begun a violent persecution
of the Christians, whom he blamed for the conflagration. For
all this, he had been proclaimed divine and had heard the heads
of conquered nations, themselves descendants of many kings,
call themselves Nero's slaves. But none of these impressive
accomplishments was as important to him as this tour, for
Caesar's true love was the stage. He had of course performed
before audiences in Rome (who were not allowed to leave the
theater during his recitals, no matter how pressing the reason),
but, declaring that the Greeks alone were worthy of his genius,
he had sailed off to take part in the musical contests traditionally
sponsored by various cities in Greece. While a contestant at
Acte, he received word of the trouble in Judea. It is said that
he deputed an officer in his retinue to "defeat the Jews" and
then went on with his singing.

The general whom Nero had ordered to defeat the Jews was
Vespasian, a man of noble Sabine stock, but hardly one of
exquisite refinement. A soldier all his life, he had served well
in Thrace, crushed the German rebellion, and helped to add
Britain to Claudius's domain. He had briefly held a consulship
and served as governor in Africa. Bluff and unpretentious, he
showed obvious distaste for Nero's imperial Rome, and he in
turn was looked down on by the members of Caesar's court
for his "old-fashioned" morality and simple tastes. The legionaries, however, were fiercely loyal to him; their love for
the Old Farmer kept him safe from Nero's wrath. After he had
particularly offended Caesar by committing the gross error of
falling asleep during a royal performance, he had been forced
to retire to a small town to wait for the imperial rage to die
down. Called back to assume military command, he was clearly
eager to leave the perils of the court for the relatively simple
dangers of the battlefield. He was fifty-seven when, in the
spring of the year 67, he left for Judea: a strong, fit warrior
ready and able to withstand whatever grueling marches, rough
battles, or long sieges proved necessary to maintain the honor
of the Eagle. Joining him, with the legion from Alexandria,
was his eldest son, Titus.

Whatever else they thought of Josef ben Matthias, the inhabitants of the Galilee might well have thanked him for the walls
he had made them build around their cities. As Vespasian's

troops moved across the land, burning towns and villages in their path, slaughtering those who resisted, appropriating anything they desired for their use or pleasure, the Galileans fled to what seemed the impregnable bastions of Sepphoris, Tiberias, Gischala, and Jotapata. Josef knew that even these places, fortified as they had been, were no match for the Roman war machine. But at least a stand could be made; and if his Judean militia fought hard and well, perhaps Vespasian would be impressed by their valor and an honorable surrender could be concluded. Meanwhile, the boot of the legionary trod across the north of Judea, and the flowers of the Galilee were trampled beneath it.

Gadara was the first city to share the fate of the ravaged hamlets. All the inhabitants except small children were put to the sword. The message went out that the massacre was in memory of the way the Judeans had treated Cestius Gallus.

"What do you think they will do to avenge Gessius Florus?" Saul had asked. "We merely drove away the Syrian governor, but the Sicarii murdered the procurator."

"I don't know," Josef replied grimly. "I must inform Jerusalem of the situation. If they want us to fight, then they must send additional men."

"Of course we must fight! After what they've done to Gadara, in addition to all the rest— You'd better let me go to the council. You're right, we will need more men."

"No," Josef said hastily. "I need you here, Saul." His letter to Jerusalem included more than an appraisal of events and a call for forces. What he had in fact said was that if the council was ready to sue for terms, they should write back at once, or else send more men. Besides, it might prove uncomfortable were Saul ben Levi to learn in the course of his visit to Jerusalem that Josef was, regarding the matter of betrothals, "twice blessed." "We must return to Jotapata. I am convinced Vespasian means to take it. In any case," he added, "the city is our best refuge."

"But we leave the others unprotected."

"No, Vespasian will follow us. He knows I command the bulk of the army—his spies keep him well informed—and Jotapata, as I have told you, is the key."

His reasoning was correct. Infantry and cavalry had already been sent ahead to level the stony mountain track. After four days' work a broad highway had been opened, and the legions resumed their march. Josef managed to slip into the city before it was surrounded, and his appearance awakened new courage in the people, many of whom were eager to confront the enemy.

It was dusk when Vespasian and his entire force arrived before Jotapata. The Roman immediately saw what Josef had long ago discerned and led his army to the north of the town, conspicuously pitching camp in rising ground about three quarters of a mile from the city's walls.

Adinah's excitement at Josef's return had made her forget her fear of the foreign army. But as the line of horses, mules, wagons, and armored men appeared, bathed in the red glow of the sinking sun like monsters bloodied by the victims they had already devoured, she was stricken with terror. Mindful of nothing but her own need for reassurance, she ran about looking for Josef, whom she had come to think of as a heavenly benefactor. She found him on the parapet, staring thoughtfully at the encamped legions in the distance.

"Are they coming?" she asked fearfully.

"Not till morning. They are putting a line of men around the city to block any attempts at escape. Look, do you see how they have begun?" He slipped his arm around her waist. "Two lines of infantry . . . a third of cavalry . . ." He turned, hearing her gasp, and took her in his arms. She clung to him for a moment, then suddenly, shyly pulled back. But he caught her to him again, burying his face against her neck.

"No," she whispered. "Josef . . . no. . . ." But even as she protested, her eyes closed, her breaths deepened, quickening. He continued as if he had not heard her, his hands moving down her body, caressing her hips and thighs. His mouth brushed her throat, found her breast. . . .

"No. . . . No!" She pushed herself away from him. "We . . . we are betrothed, but we may not. . . . It is forbidden . . . until the wedding, Josef. We cannot. . . . It is forbidden."

"Adinah . . ."

"We cannot. You will think ill of me."

"How could I think ill of the sweetest, gentlest creature . . . she who will become my wife. . . ." He took her in his arms again, holding her head against his shoulder. "You are my wife," he said. "I make you now my wife."

"You cannot. . . ."

"I can. I was trained for the priesthood, and I am of the high priestly class. I have only to say the words. And I have said them, Adinah. I have just now said them."

She looked up at him. "In truth?"

"Look out there." He turned her around so that she faced the Roman camp. "Tonight they sleep. Tomorrow they will be here."

"Josef . . ."

"Who among us can say what tomorrow will bring? Who among us dares to speak for the will of the Lord?"

"Josef . . ."

"Tomorrow. This very time tomorrow. Who can say if either of us will be here, alive in Jotapata? . . ."

"Oh, Josef!"

"But we have tonight, Adinah. The Lord has given us tonight." He drew her against him. She sighed. His hands, gripping her shoulders, slipped down her arms, found their way to her breasts. "I have made you my wife," he whispered. "Now you must make me your husband. Now, Adinah. Now."

"They have been holding out for twenty-nine days," the priest Shammai said. "If they are still alive. Josef has managed to get another courier through the Roman lines. He says the enemy has built earthworks against the wall. To counter this, the Jotapatans have managed to raise the wall some thirty feet. The masons work under the protections of stretched oxhides, against which the Roman arrows are of little avail. He's a clever boy, our Josef."

"Clever enough to beat the Romans, uncle?"

"We must pray so, Alexandra. If Vespasian cannot enter Jotapata by force, then he will blockade the town until starvation makes the people surrender. Josef writes that provisions are ample but the water supply is inadequate. As it is summer now, there is little hope of rain. He has already begun to ration the contents of the cisterns."

"Why doesn't the council send out their troops? They could create a diversion to draw the Romans away from Jotapata."

"Exactly what Josef has requested."

"Well, then?"

"The Galileans have long boasted of their prowess. Now they are put to the test. Besides, if we send our men there, who will protect Jerusalem?"

"But it doesn't make sense—"

"Alexandra, please. You are a woman and cannot understand these things. All you can see is that your betrothed is in danger, and naturally you wish to save him—"

"I see that if the northern army is wiped out in Jotapata, we will face Vespasian alone."

"We will in any case. Do you imagine the Galileans would come to our aid?"

"But they have! Did they not follow the Sicarii to save the City from Agrippa's soldiers?"

"And you know what happened then. They did not come to save Jerusalem but to take it for themselves. Do not talk to me of Galileans. I only hope Josef has the good sense to slip out of Jotapata while he can. Now, then. . . . As you know, your future father-in-law has paid me a visit. We are agreed that if I should pass away before your marriage to Josef, you will live in the house of Matthias until such time as your wedding takes place. In the event that Josef does not make it out of Jotapata and I am not here to arrange your future, Matthias will assume guardianship and see that you are wed to one of Josef's cousins. It is all right; they are of the priestly line," he added hastily.

"You talk as if Josef were already killed, and you dead as well."

"We must consider the possibility of the first and the inevitability of the second. I have had dreams of late. . . . Sometimes I cannot be sure if I am awake or not, they are so real. Last night, I saw Samuel. . . . Well, then," he said, drawing himself out of his reverie. "It's settled. You know what is expected of you."

"No, it is not settled. I will not live in the house of Matthias, and I will certainly not marry some unknown clod. I don't like any of that family. They are all as cold as can be. No wonder Josef stayed so long in Rome."

Shammai chuckled. He did not particularly care for Matthias either.

"If you feel like dying, you go right ahead, uncle. By all means don't let me stop you. But I am going to stay right here. I will not live with Matthias," she repeated.

"The council will take the house from you, Alexandra. They talk even now of appropriating it for the use of their 'generals.'"

"Then I'll run away. Yes, maybe I ought to do that now." The idea was beginning to appeal to her. "If I could get to Jotapata . . . Why not? If someone could sneak out, then someone can also sneak in."

"Don't be foolish—"

"I'm tired of always being shut up behind walls! First father, now you. . . . Josef's father will be even worse. I know he will. Oh, how I'd like to be out on the road, living in the real world!"

"The world is cruel," he said sharply. "Men are animals. You saw—at Caesarea—what people can do to one another. You are young and quick and clever, but that is not enough."

"I am protected by the Lord."

"What arrogance! Do you presume the God of Israel has nothing better to do than look after a snip of a girl, even one with your sacred heritage?"

"It is true, uncle. An Essene told me long ago that I would be safe from evil."

The priest rolled his eyes heavenward. "An Essene. I am dying, and she talks of Essenes. Next we shall have the wit and wisdom of Johanan ben Zakkai."

"I did not mean to anger you or to sound arrogant," she said, thinking meanwhile that the spirit he now displayed might just serve to keep him alive. "Besides, I have a plan. I thought I could disguise myself—"

"Wonderful. An unprotected peasant girl alone on the road would be even less immune to danger."

"No one need know I am female."

"Even better," he said sarcastically. "You invoke the protection of the Lord for a senseless, perilous journey—which you propose to undertake in male dress, thereby breaking the Lord's Law. What next, niece? Will you brandish a sword alongside your betrothed? Or do you hope to personally rescue Josef from the Roman army? Alexandra . . . life is not the stories you have read, full of heroes and miracles and glorious conclusions. We are beasts but for the Law that makes us men— and the authority that makes us fear to break the Law." He sank back, exhausted by this debate; but he was not yet done. "Something . . . neither of us wishes to discuss. . . . But I must ask you to think of . . . what happened to your father and mother, your brothers. . . . Have you forgotten Caesarea?"

She turned away. "I have not forgotten."

"Then promise me you will remain in Jerusalem, with Matthias if necessary, until Josef returns. You are all that is left, Alexandra. You are of the House of Harsom and the line of David. You must live . . . bring forth sons. . . . Promise you will do as I ask. I am a dying man. Promise. . . ."

"I promise, uncle."

He sighed and was still. Suddenly his eyes opened, and he looked straight at her. "Liar," he said.

Nearly forty days had passed since the siege of Jotapata began, and still the town held out. Japha, ten miles away, moved to heroism by its example, attempted to revolt against the Roman occupiers but was quickly chastened by the detachment sent to subdue it. South of Galilee, the Samaritans, whose territory was already garrisoned by Rome, assembled on their sacred Mount Gerizim and talked revolt. In Jerusalem, men counted the days, awaiting reports from scouts and spies and the occasional messenger Josef managed to slip out. And in Jotapata, thirsty, exhausted, wounded, or mourning for those killed in valiant, desperate sorties outside the safety of their wall, the people held out, perhaps as surprised as anyone that they did, but realizing that they owed their lives not only to their courage but to the ingenuity of their commander.

Josef knew Jotapata would inevitably fall. The city could hold out for a long time, but not forever. He had seen how the Romans, from the heights above the north wall, watched the despairing townspeople congregate at the cisterns for their daily ration of water. He had come up with the idea of having the people dip clothes in the little water there was and hang them around the battlements, wet and dripping, for the Romans to see. Vespasian, believing therefore that there was in fact no shortage, had given up the idea of making Jotapata surrender through hunger and thirst. He regrouped his men, built platforms and towers on his earthworks, and moved up the battering ram. In desperation, Josef and Saul led their toughest fighters in savage sallies against the Romans, scattering their guards as they galloped into camp, tearing down tents, cutting and slashing and setting afire everything they could. They fought the old way, the Sicarii way: lightning-quick guerrilla attacks, hit-and-run. Fast and light-armed, driven by the passion of their fury and despair, the Jews became a dangerous force again.

It was nearly July. The land was burned brown; it would not turn green again until the time of the winter rains. It had also been ravaged by the invaders, the hillocks nearby torn up to supply material for the earthworks, and the heights around the town stripped of their trees for the platforms that were placed on the earthworks against the approachable section of

Jotapata's wall. Along with the timber and earth, the attackers had gathered mountains of stones to be discharged from the projectile throwers along with firebrands and lances.

It was indeed a strange, alien landscape that Saul ben Levi saw as he rode back into Jotapata after a raid on the Roman camp. This was where he had been born, had grown to manhood—but it no longer looked like home. It no longer looked like anything, he thought grimly. So war touched more than men; how obscenely it defiled the land.

Josef ben Matthias, riding beside him, was not concerned with the environmental changes Vespasian's troops had effected. He did not miss the trees that had once stood on the hills or worry how long it would be before the disrupted earth was fertile again. All he knew was that he was hot and tired and smelled like a horse. In his room he wasted no time unbuckling his sword belt, letting it drop with a clatter to the floor. Seeing a jug of water, he pulled off his tunic and began to wash.

"But that is your day's allowance," Saul protested. "You will have nothing left to drink."

"I'd rather be clean." He shook his head as the man handed him a cloth to dry himself. "No, it's cooler this way. I thought the Galilee was supposed to be pleasant in summer."

"They have cut down all the trees. It is a sin to do that. The Law forbids us to despoil the land—even in war, even in the country of the enemy."

"Yes, I know. Well, it is not the only sin Rome has committed, and I daresay not the worst."

"I don't know," Saul said slowly. The changed landscape troubled him. He was as shocked by the mutilated earth as he might have been upon seeing an ugly corpse. "What they do to the people is bad enough. But what they do to the land— to *Eretz Israel*—I don't know. It seems to me that is a sin against the Almighty Himself." He cleared his throat. He was ashamed of himself for voicing his thoughts so openly and cast a quick sidelong glance to see if the Jerusalemite might be laughing at him.

But Josef was thinking of something else. "Lucky for us that group came out of the hills when they did," the young commander said now. "We might not have made it back if they had not caused that diversion. I didn't think Vespasian would use any of his cavalry. He has been happy so far to let the Nabateans and Syrians take us on. I've never heard such a cry as those men let out when they rode toward us. Who were they?"

"Sicarii. It was the Sicarii cry you heard."

"Sicarii!"

"The one with the golden hair and beard—"

"Yes, yes! A big man. What a fighter! Who is he? Can you get word to him? Will he join us? We could coordinate our attacks—"

Saul shook his head. "The grandson of Judah the Galilean rides alone. He and his followers live in the desert atop a mountain called the Masada. They are outlawed by the council, but even if they were not they would not join an organized force. But they are there, so the people say, whenever they are needed. The messengers you send out—none of them would get through to Jerusalem or back without the help of Eleazar ben Ya'ir."

"Who? Is that his name? You are sure he will not join us? Perhaps if I could talk to him— What a fighter!" he exclaimed again.

"You fought well yourself," Saul remarked. The Jerusalem-ite had surprised him; he had been like a demon, slashing away from the back of his horse, his dark eyes bright with some unholy—no, Saul corrected himself—it was a God-inspired fire.

Josef smiled, his white teeth meeting in an animal grin, the spark Saul had seen earlier momentarily returning to his eyes. "It was exciting," he admitted. "I did not imagine it would be like that. I have always found the idea of force distasteful. But it wasn't. The heat, the blood, the noise, the stink of it . . . amazing. . . . I did not mind any of it. Now, thinking about it, I could puke. But out there . . . everything goes so fast. It was exciting," he said again.

Saul stared at him.

"Do you think I killed anyone?" he asked casually. "Yes, I am sure I did. There was one . . ." He broke off, came out of himself. "Do you know why Vespasian keeps his own men back?" he said in an entirely different voice. "He is saving them for his assault against us. It will come soon. He has moved up the battering ram. It won't be long before we hear it driving against the wall, over and over until the stone crumbles."

"It is a strong, thick wall."

"There isn't a wall built by man that has ever withstood the ram," Josef said with certainty. "Unless... if we could some-how cushion the blows...We could perhaps lower bags of chaff....Yes, and if they move the ram to another part of the wall, we can just move the bags of chaff...." His eyes were bright again.

Saul was staring at him, studying him. "You could leave," he blurted out finally. "You could slip out, make your way back to Jerusalem. Yet you stay."

"Return to Jerusalem..." He had turned away so the Gal-ilean could not see his face. There was an edge to his voice. "I don't think so."

"If the council would only send troops—"

"They won't. They have made it quite clear that I—we—are on our own." He reached for the water jug but, seeing it was empty, put it down disgustedly.

Saul rose to leave. "I will get you water."

Josef turned to him, an eyebrow raised in amusement. "What? Break the rules? You?"

"I break no rules. I will give you of my own ration."

"Saul—"

"And if you need still more you shall have my wife's, and after that, my children's."

At that moment Adinah appeared. Saul frowned. The girl had been spending an inordinate amount of time with Josef. They were betrothed, true, but it was not seemly for the maiden to be in the man's company as much as she was.

"What do you want?" he asked her gruffly.

She opened her mouth, but before she could answer Josef said quickly, "It's all right. I sent for her. I thought one of the messengers from Jerusalem had gotten through and brought her birth record." He went over to the man and clapped him on the shoulder. "Get some rest. And let your wife know you are not dead or wounded. Every time we ride out, she sets up a wail that would strike terror into any man's heart. You must speak to her. She must be an example of courage for the women even as you are for the men. Or else lock her up when we ride. Understand?"

Saul nodded grimly.

"And do not bring me your portion of water—or anyone else's. I will not accept it. That is an order." With a smile and a shove he had Saul out the door and the door closed before Saul could reply. He turned to Adinah. She was staring at his naked chest. He smiled, and she quickly averted her eyes.

"Aren't you hot?" he asked pleasantly. "The air is stifling. What a country God has chosen for us! Unbearable in summer, too damp in winter . . ." He went over to her and began to untie the cord around her waist.

"It is knotted twice," she said shyly in her small, soft voice.

"That's all right. I'm very good at these things. There, you see? Undone." He brushed her fair hair with his lips. "If I had been Alexander, I would not have used a sword. . . . I could have untied the Gordian knot with one hand held behind me. These things need a little thought, that's all." He pulled back to look at her. "You have no idea what I'm talking about, do you? Never mind. Women were made for better things than talk." Her robe was on the floor now. He guided her to his bed. What soft skin she had. She was so incredibly soft. A little lazy, but that was all right; one couldn't rush into things— although that was probably what he was going to do right now. He was too excited for preliminaries. His every sense seemed heightened, aroused in a way he had never known—and he prided himself on being a sensually acute man. No wonder there were those who lived for war. First to fight, and then . . .

He took her with the same demon energy he had shown in the raid against the Romans, wondering all the while if she would ever seem as wonderful to him again.

The head was of iron in the likeness of a ram; the body was a great beam of wood the size of a ship's mast. Suspended by cables from another beam in order to give it increased momentum, worked by a crew who drew it back and then let it swing forward again with one gigantic united heave, the huge machine butted against the wall of Jotapata. Again and again, under the protective cover of archers, slingers, and catapults, iron met stone. The ominous crash echoed in the mountain heights, merging with the gasps of the besieged as they listened to the steady, ceaseless sound.

The bags of chaff had worked for a while, cushioning the blows until the Romans attached scythes to long poles and cut them down. The attackers had mounted the ram on their earthwork platform so that it came into contact with the fortification laid in at the start of the siege. The wall so recently built was beginning to give way.

Night had fallen; still the sound of the battering ram went on, while arrows and javelins and stones sailed over the wall and newly killed men fell atop those already dead. It was the stones that did the most damage. Rome had perfected the art of war. The force of one of their quick-loaders or spear-throwers was enough to run a single lance through a row of men. The huge stones hurled by their engines carried away battlements, knocked off towers, threw men from the ramparts— one, struck in the head, had his skull flung like a pebble more than a hundred yards. Throughout the night there came the thud of bodies falling; the shriek of a woman; the groan of a man; the rushing sound and final crash of a catapulted stone; and the constant drumming of the battering ram as it drove again and again against the weakened wall.

Suddenly another sound cut through the darkness. From the distance came the cry of the Sicarii, and the hills were dotted with the light from their torches, which came nearer and nearer like stars falling out of the sky. Like avenging angels, they charged the ranks of the Tenth Legion, breaking through the Roman lines, tossing their torches at the catapult engines, the hurdles, and the platforms. Inspired by their example, the Jotapatans ran out of the city and began to set fire to what they could. Surprised and beaten back by flames, the Romans raced to rescue their equipment. The Sicarii disappeared into the hills again, and Josef's army returned safely to Jotapata, their spirits renewed by the sight of frantic Romans fighting fires instead of people.

But the victory was short-lived. While the Fifth Legion set about extinguishing the flames and the routed Tenth pulled itself together, the other units took control of the battering ram, continuing the machine's destructive work. With the coming of dawn the wall crumbled, and both sides prepared for battle.

Having ordered the women shut in the houses and the bravest men stationed at the breach of the wall, Josef awaited the coming of Vespasian. In the last moments of darkness a silence fell over the city and the surrounding area. It was, Josef thought, as quiet as it must have been the moment before God created the world. Then . . . Roman trumpets heralded the day, a fearsome battle cry burst from the throats of ten thousand legionaries, and a cloud of arrows blotted out the rising sun. Rank upon rank, their oblong shields locked together above their heads in the *testudo*, or tortoise formation, the enemy began their assault. Desperately, the Galileans drove at them, pressed them back; but no matter how many they killed still more advanced, thousands upon thousands.

When they saw they could not keep the Romans from the wall, the people poured pots of boiling oil down on them and watched, horrified, as men leaped into the air, falling from the wooden bridges to the ground, where they lay writhing and screaming as the scalding liquid oozed under their armor and ate through their skin. When the oil ran out, the Jotapatans dumped boiled fenugreek, a flowering herb, on the wooden gangways the legionaries were still trying to cross. The soldiers staggered like drunkards on the slimy stuff, clutching at each other as they lost their footing. Some fell on their backs on the gangplanks and brought their companions down upon themselves, while others tumbled off in a clattering mass of metal and flailing limbs.

Vespasian called off his troops; the assault had failed.

Day after day, it went on. Meanwhile, Vespasian had his soldiers construct three siege towers sheeted with iron, and these were eventually moved up on the earthworks. On the forty-seventh day of the siege the Roman platforms overtopped the wall. From the towers it would have been easy enough for the legionaries to rain carefully aimed spears, stones, and arrows down upon the already decimated population. But there was little left to snipe at. The fighting men still alive in Jotapata were few and spent with fatigue. A gray, heavily misted dawn lighted quiet, empty streets; even the sentries had sunk, exhausted, into a stupor from which many of them would never awaken. Noiselessly, Vespasian's son Titus stole into the city with a few men and disposed of the sleeping sentries. The signal was given, and more legionaries followed. Bands of soldiers began to roam the foggy streets, their movements hidden by the dense mountain vapor. Unchallenged, they walked into houses, rousing people at swordpoint. Confused, half-asleep, the Jotapatans did not realize the town had been taken until the massacre actually began.

There was a cave leading deep into the mountain against which Jotapata was built. It was not visible, for the entrance was hidden at the bottom of a wide pit. Soldiers searching for those who had attempted to escape to the sewers and various underground vaults had peered down into the pit, but seeing only a thorny ravine, they had gone away.

There were approximately forty people in the cave, which had been stocked—evidently in anticipation of this time—with enough supplies to last many days. The fugitives had listened fearfully as the legionaries called to one another from above. Even after the foreign voices died away they stayed inside, hushed and wary. For three days they remained so, waiting for Jotapata to be empty of its enemies. But the Romans did not leave. There had been a general slaughter of the population the first day; small pockets of resistance were instantly overwhelmed and exterminated; twelve hundred prisoners were herded into the cages thoughtfully provided for them. Vespasian ordered the city demolished; and the soldiers, remembering the boiling oil, the fenugreek, and their own dead, were not remiss in carrying out the task. There was little left of the forty thousand citizens who had once made Jotapata a flourishing town. Still the legionaries combed the hills and mountain caves searching for any who might have escaped Roman justice. In particular, they sought the man they considered most responsible for their long ordeal: the commander of the town, the one called Josef ben Matthias.

Evening came, the dark beauty of the mountain night disrupted by soldiers' bonfires, by the harsh laughter and curses of men as they gambled away the loot they had stolen, the women they had taken. Camp servants, themselves slaves, poked at the caged prisoners with sticks, taunting and jeering at the helpless captives. In the general's quarters, Vespasian and his son Titus discussed the Judean campaign with their officers and deliberated their next move.

Meanwhile, a figure emerged from the hidden cave and carefully made his way up out of the pit. He slipped into the town, a slim shadow moving among the houses, darting in and out of alleys like a nimble cat. He saw the piles of unburied corpses, the prison cages, the "soldiers' brothels," but none of this bothered him so much as the fact that there was not one avenue of escape. Every sentry post was guarded, and the guards there were alert. Despite appearances, Vespasian's army was still on the job. Josef returned to the cave.

About a hundred yards from the entrance he was met by Adinah. "What are you doing out here?" he asked, astonished to see her. "Have you any idea what would happen to you if you were caught? You must stay in the cave."

"I wanted to be with you. I was afraid." She put her arms around his waist and leaned her head against his chest.

He let himself out of her embrace. "You must go back. . . ."

"Not yet," she whispered. "It's been so long since . . . Perhaps you do not love me any longer."

"Love?" He wanted to laugh. Love . . . at a time like this.

"It's true," she said, frightened by his tone. "You don't love me, do you?"

"Adinah . . ." He took her in his arms. "If I did not care for you, would I be so concerned now? It is very dangerous to be here. The soldiers might come by—"

"Oh!" She clung to him more tightly than before.

"Sshh! Be quiet. . . . All right." He looked around, saw a spot where they would be safe, and led her to it. "Do the others know you are out here?"

"I don't think so. Most are asleep. Saul and some of the men are talking." She paused. "They say we must kill ourselves before the Romans find us. Oh, Josef, I don't want to die!"

"Sshh! You're not going to die. No one is going to die."

"But Saul says the soldiers will do terrible things to us and then they will kill us. Will they, Josef?"

"If we were Titus's prisoners we would not be abused."

"Saul says—oh, I don't want to think about it! Hold me, Josef! Hold me tight."

He complied, but his thoughts were elsewhere. "Tell me everything Saul said."

"I can't—I don't want to think about it."

"Tell me, Adinah. I must know."

"He says you must be the first—to fall on your own sword. You are our general, our commander. He says you must be the first to do it. Then we must follow—not out of fear of what the Romans will do to us, nor for the glory, but as a deed done for the Lord."

"The *Kiddush ha-Shem*," he whispered. The ultimate act of faith.

"I don't want to die," she said again.

Nor I, he thought, grimly certain now of what his comrades-in-hiding were about.

"Tell me again about Jerusalem."

"Not now. Adinah, do you remember the words I said when they first brought you forward to me?"

"Yes . . . no . . . I—"

"I quoted a verse from the Bible. It begins, 'A woman of valor, what is her worth?' A woman of valor. . . . I thought that the first moment I saw you, without knowing your history and how you must have suffered among these people who call themselves your friends."

"It is true.... They always made me feel I was not good enough...."

"Not good enough! There isn't a woman in Jotapata with your beauty, your sweetness, your courage...."

"Courage?"

"Was it not brave to come out here to look for me?"

"I never thought..."

"You are brave, Adinah. You have courage. You are a woman of valor."

"Well...I don't cry the way some of the women do. Saul's wife never stops."

"There is not a woman here—or in all the Galilee—who can compare with you. That is why I chose you—only you—to be my wife."

"But you won't let me tell the others—"

"Because it must be done properly—for your sake—with the veil and canopy and the High Priest."

"The High Priest!"

"You deserve no less," he said solemnly. "I had thought that when the siege was over we would go to Jerusalem, be married there.... But now...it seems it is not only Vespasian who has other plans for us."

"What can we do?"

"I don't know. If Saul and the others are bent on suicide, you can be sure they will kill those who do not want to comply—and consider it a favor to them."

She gasped,

"There is no escape for me. But you...you could be saved."

"I?"

"You must not return to the cave. You must find Titus. For the sake of our past friendship he will spare you, I know."

"But you—"

"My place is here. Saul is right."

"But you will die!"

"If that is the will of the Lord. At least I will know that you are safe." He took her face in his hands. "One last kiss.... Then we must part forever. I will show you how you must slip unnoticed to the officers' quarters, and I will tell you what you must say. Remember, Titus is my friend. He would not harm me no matter what the circumstances, and he will not harm what is dear to me. Kiss me now, Adinah. Let me know your warmth and beauty one last time. . . ."

He watched her until she disappeared in the darkness and then turned back to the cave. It was a gamble, but he had nothing to lose. As soon as she mentioned his name, the soldiers would extract from her the location of the cave. He hoped she would volunteer the information. It would be a pity if the girl was tortured—and a waste of precious time. Now he must deal with Saul and the others, stall them at least until morning. He sighed. Even now he would rather face Vespasian than a band of zealous Jews bent on self-destruction in the name of that which was sacred to them.

"There is no escape route open," Josef told them. "There are sentries at every point. Even the sewers are guarded. Nor have they given up their search. I overheard some soldiers talking amongst themselves. They have orders to find and bring in the officers of our army. They seem to know my name," he added innocently.

"You ought not to have gone alone," Saul said. "It was a risk—"

"—I gladly take. I am your general, have you forgotten?" He held up his hand before anyone could reply. "Listen to me, all of you. I have been thinking, all the way back here. . . . I have searched my mind—and my heart—as diligently as I have searched our surroundings—and there is no hope for us. No way out but one." He paused, staring at each of the men in turn. "You know what our ancestors have done in situations like this. The Hasidim of the days of the Maccabee, and before that, the martyrs of old— There is only one thing left to us. It came to me as I returned here to you—like a vision or commandment from the Almighty. The *Kiddush ha-Shem*."

A murmur went around, but Josef continued as if he had not heard them. "As a member of the high priestly class and a descendant of the Hasmoneans—and as your commander— I invoke the sacred principle that is the final act of faith and the greatest expression of courage."

"But isn't suicide a sin?" one of the men asked timidly.

"Yes, greatly so—when it is done to escape one's troubles or for vainglory. But the pure deed, that which is done in the name of the Lord and solely for the triumph and everlasting glory of the Creator—that is an act blessed by Abraham and all the prophets."

"Truly, the Lord has made His will known," Saul ben Levi said. "While you were gone we discussed such an action. It seemed to us, too, that the only path was that which led to the Lord. Now I know we are right and that we need not fear you will not lead us to this end as nobly as you have led our defense."

"Let us spend the night in prayer. When morning comes we shall, in the ancient way, choose lots, so that each in turn will offer his throat to the other until there is only one of us left to sacrifice himself by his own hand."

All through the night men prayed, huddled with their wives, speaking in whispers to them, kissing the children, who slept unaware of what morning would bring. Josef sat apart, alone, his face composed and grave, as befit a commander and priest. But unlike the others, who were contemplating the past, going over the deeds of their lives that would make them fit or unworthy to be blessed after death, praying for the courage to become martyrs to God, Josef was calculating the future. One thing he had learned from the Pharisee rabbis was their method of reasoning: To every question there were at least two answers, and for each answer there were two possibilities, and for each possibility at least two explanations. It could go on and on, but it did teach one to keep an open mind. So to every plan of action there must be an alternative—and substitutes for the alternative, which could possibly fail. What if Adinah did not make it to Titus? Or supposing Titus—

Sounds outside the cave drew his attention. The others with him paused and looked up, listening.

"Nothing," Josef said, his heart quickening. "An animal or bird rustling the leaves, looking for breakfast." He pointed to the cave's entrance, where a shaft of light had fallen across the ground. "See, it is morning."

Morning. Was it morning so soon? Too soon. He needed time.

"Let us have a final service," he said to the people. "There are more than ten men present to be witness to the Lord. I have, as you know, been trained as a priest, although I chose not to serve in the Temple. But now I shall hold service here as if this humble cave were the Lord's own House. And then, when all the prescribed prayers have been said, we shall offer final sacrifice to the Creator—not a lamb or a bullock or precious incense, but ourselves."

Some of the women started to cry. Saul hushed them. "Be quiet, all of you. I think I hear something outside."

"Nothing," Josef said. "Only the wind. It is the voice of the Lord—"

"I tell you I hear something!" Grabbing his sword, the man rushed out.

"Wait!" Josef cried, and ran after him.

The pit was ringed with Roman soldiers, their shields like a metal chain or fence. Adinah came scrambling down the side of the ravine. "Josef! I have come with Nicanor! He says you shall not be hurt—Titus has made oath upon it!" Her face was flushed and happy as she ran to him.

But Saul had turned white as chalk. "Whore!" he cried; and as the girl ran past him, he raised his sword and cut her down. Then he turned to Josef, his eyes red with fury and tears. "You—" he began, but before he could say another word a score of arrows pierced his body, and he fell dead beside the girl he had murdered.

"Josephus. Josephus, son of Matthias."

Josef looked up. The face of the Roman tribune as he peered down into the pit was haloed by the sun behind him. Nicanor looked like an angel descended from heaven.

"I have come," the Roman said solemnly, "to offer you safe conduct to my commander, Flavius Vespasian, empowered to act for Caesar in the province of Judea. You are now prisoner of Rome. You have my word and that of my general that no harm shall befall you prior to sentencing by Caesar for your treasonous activity." Nicanor put out his hand to help the Judean up out of the pit. He smiled.

"The will of the Lord be done," Josef said as he took the proffered hand.

FOUR

Cassius Basilides surveyed the field with a practiced, professional eye. He held a perfumed cloth to his face as he gingerly stepped over and around the scattered bodies. Behind him trailed the old woman and Niko with the cart. Both had covered the lower halves of their faces with scarves and then wrapped the scarves around their throats. A wind had come up from the sea, and the fabric fluttered behind them like wings. Like earthbound birds attending the dead, the trio moved across the now quiet battlefield.

Corpses floated on the Sea of Galilee; they clogged the shallow end, turning the water a strange copper color. Hundreds had been cut down on the beach, hundreds more washed back from capsized boats they had taken to in numbers far greater than such small fishing vessels could hold.

Basilides kept his eyes fixed on the ground. The smell of death and the sight of torn flesh did not bother him as they once had. Death was not pleasant, but it was part of the job. Besides, he felt lucky. This was his name day, and there had been certain fortuitous omens. There was, for example, the white dove's feather he had found lying at his feet, as if to say the gods had something good in store. It was about time some luck came his way. Working for Icelus Liberalis, who was considered the first slave merchant of Rome, with the patronage of Caesar himself, had not netted Basilides his own business as quickly as he had thought it would. True, he had learned the trade—and the tastes of important clients; but just when it seemed he might be able to open his own establishment, Liberalis had packed him off to Judea. Nero, it seemed, needed slaves for his new project: the construction of a canal that would cut across the Isthmus of Corinth. "We have a guaranteed contract for six thousand and an option for an additional four thousand," Liberalis had said. "Of course, all prisoners belong to Caesar, but it will be our job to see that they arrive in one piece at the sites assigned. Along the way, of course, keep an eye out for any promising individuals to be sent directly to the emperor for his pleasure. He has specifically requested twins, although he did not specify male or female. Try to get a pair of each. I know, I know. It won't be easy—but see what you can do. I trust your taste as I do my own. That is why I am allowing you the honor of this mission. If you prove yourself, I will, upon your return, help you set up your own establishment—as I know you have been eager to do. After all, this war with the Jews should provide more than enough business for all of us."

"The honor of this mission . . ." The old fart. He knew what a miserable province this was. How nice, while he, Liberalis, was eating berries and cream back in civilized Rome, to have someone else cutting his feet on stones or burning them in hot sand, doing all the dirty work for him. Well, perhaps Basilides might do some good for himself while he was at it. It was hard for an independent agent to get started, though. After Caesar's quota was met, the generals took their share, and then a certain number of women had to be set aside for the soldiers. There was really very little chance for an honest man to turn a profit without paying some officer or legionary a percentage. But sometimes, on the field of war, there might be one or two alive and overlooked. Clean them up, give them a little food, fix their wounds or cover the scars with paint, and maybe a man could make a living for himself.

"Master." The old woman was pulling at his sleeve. She pointed to the body of a woman, then bent down and pushed the corpse aside. Triumphantly, she held up the infant whose muffled cry she had heard. "It is a boy, master."

"It will cost too much to keep it until it can be sold."

"Nothing, it will cost nothing, master."

"Well . . . if it lives . . ."

The old woman stuck the child inside her robe, close to her breast, and they moved on.

A soldier was crouched over a pile of bodies, busily searching the garments of the dead. One man's tunic yielded a small leather purse. The soldier opened it quickly, pulled out a coin, bit it, put the coin in the purse, wiped the purse on its owner's body, and then stuffed it in his own belt. Seeing Basilides, he quickly straightened and drew out his sword. "Who are you?" he demanded brusquely. "What are you doing here?"

"My name is Cassius Basilides. I am a merchant of men in the service of Rome, with full rights to Judea and its suburbs. I have papers assuring me freedom of movement and acquisition in the emperor's interests."

"You've come to the wrong place. Prisoners have been taken to the stadium—"

"I've been there. I thought—" He cleared his throat. "You know how it is," he said in the tone of a fellow conspirator. "Caesar gets his, Vespasian gets his—even the little Jew-king and the black one from the desert get something for themselves." His eyes went to the purse in the soldier's belt. "In these times, a man must look out for himself, do a little business on his own, eh?"

The legionary looked at him a moment, then pointed to a group of bodies a few yards away. "I heard something there. Might be one alive."

Basilides nodded his thanks and hurried to the spot the soldier had indicated. He heard a moan, barely audible. The sound came from a young man who was severely wounded and hardly breathing.

"It's his leg," Niko said, examining the Judean. "He's pulled out the lance himself—look, he's still holding onto it. But the blood still flows. Here now," he said mildly as the fellow tried to strike him with the bloodied lance. The huge man took the weapon away as easily as he might have taken a toy from a child. Then he unwound the muffler from his neck, wrapped and knotted it tightly around the young man's thigh, and lifted him up for Basilides to see. The slave merchant nodded, and his servant put the now unconscious boy into the cart.

The shore of the lake was to yield even more. Basilides, certain now that the gods were smiling upon him, discovered another child, a boy of six or seven who had suffered a blow that left him still dazed and mute. There was also a woman who had, it seemed, given birth during the battle. Her dead baby lay nearby, crushed by some object or person. Niko lifted her into the cart, and the old woman took the infant she had saved earlier and laid it against the woman's breast. The child began to suck. The woman gasped, opening her eyes as she felt the baby's mouth on her. One arm was broken, but she managed to raise the other and put it around the child, holding it firmly to her. Then her eyes closed again.

The old woman looked at Basilides. "You see, master? It will cost nothing."

He did not reply. He had covered his nose and mouth with the perfumed cloth and was looking away across the littered shore. He thought he had seen something move; but all was still. It was the wind, no doubt, stirring a rag or lifting some corpse's hair. Still he stared across the open expanse, tensed in anticipation of he knew not what. Then he saw it: an arm raised up, pushing out from a pile of bodies; then another arm; and suddenly there was a creature, bloody and covered with sand, sitting up in the midst of the dead.

He hurried over. "A girl," he said, crouching down. "It's a girl, I think."

The dazed female stared at him, speechless, uncomprehending.

He pulled back as her eyes met his. "By the gods," he breathed. "The gray eyes of Athene." He put his hand to the bloodstained tunic. The fabric was not torn. There was no wound at all that he could see. "It's others' blood . . . from those that fell on you. . . ." He motioned for Niko to come, then turned back to the gray-eyed girl. "The soldiers must have thought you were dead, or you'd be in the stadium now, and sold with the rest."

She stared at him. There was no sign that she heard or understood.

"Not that you'd bring much of a price, from the look of you. Still, you're alive and all of a piece. Maybe once you're cleaned up . . ." He nodded at Niko, and the man picked the girl up and threw her into the cart with the others.

The legionary approached now and peered into the wagon. "Eh? What have you got? Two females?"

"More dead than alive," Basilides said quickly. "I doubt either will last until nightfall. Hardly worth my time. Still, a poor man must make a living."

The soldier looked at Basilides and then inside the cart again. That was a young girl the giant had tossed in. He'd thought it was a lad at first, the way she was dressed. She lay as still as one dead, but from the even sound of her breathing he could tell she was unhurt. He was about to roll her over in order to get a better look when the voice of the slave merchant stopped him.

"Why not wait until I get her cleaned up a bit," Basilides suggested smoothly. "Surely you have had your fill of blood and dirt. Come later to my residence—unless you wish to divide the spoils of the field now." His eyes went to the leather purse in the man's belt. "Equally, of course."

The soldier put his hand to his belt. He studied the portly Roman and the other man, who now took a step forward. He pursed his lips, then shrugged. "There's plenty in the stadium—and better than what you have there. A soldier gets his piece—as is due and only right, seeing we're the ones who do all the work. Keep what you have. I don't have to settle for them that's more dead than alive. But make no mistake. If I wanted what you have I'd take it, with or without your leave. The men of the Tenth need not say please." With that, he turned and walked away.

Basilides let out his breath. Gesturing to Niko and the old woman to follow, he climbed into the seat of the cart, and the wagon rolled away.

. . . Dark walls, and the smell of blood. . . . Rocking, rocking. . . .Was she in a boat again? No . . . it was something else. A wagon of some kind . . . wooden walls . . . the sides of a cart. But the blood . . . there was blood. And bodies. Bodies . . .

They were taking her away to be buried. They were going to bury her. . . .

"I'm not dead," she gasped, struggling to sit up. "I'm not dead!" She managed to pull herself up on her elbows, tried to reach over the side of the cart, but fell back as the wagon went over a rock. She heard a moan as the cart lurched forward and, rolling over on her side, saw the woman with the baby at her breast, the child curled up in a corner, and the wounded young man. She touched him. "Are you alive?" she whispered.

He opened his eyes, grimaced in pain, and then closed his eyes again. There was a cloth tied around his leg. It was red and wet.

The child in the corner stared at her without emotion. His eyes were all pupil, like two black stones.

Mother and babe were asleep. Or dead. Alexandra could not tell which.

She closed her eyes. It was beginning to come back to her now. . . . The journey to the Galilee to find Josef after the death of her uncle. . . . Tarichea. Panic in the city as word came of the legions' approach. Everybody fleeing to the shores of the lake . . .

The boats were too full. Too many people. And the wind died away. The water was so smooth. . . .

They could see the soldiers lining the beach on both sides, all around. The arrows came from the shore and from boats the Romans used to give chase. Arrows from every side. Flaming missiles. Poeple screaming. Boats capsizing. . . .

Desperate, she dove into the water, swimming beneath the surface, breaking for air only when she felt her lungs would burst, then quickly diving below again. Bodies of men and women floated down like dolls; she swam past them in the murky silence.

It was chaos ashore. People fell atop one another as they ran from the soldiers. There was noplace to go; they were cut down as they ran toward the water, or grabbed and killed as they swam to shore. But as once some unseen hand had led her through the mob in Caesarea, so now she slipped through the clutches of death.

She fell exhausted upon the beach. Before she could drag herself to her feet she was buried beneath new victims of the legionaries' onslaught. She clawed her way out from under but had no sooner escaped and taken a step than she was knocked down from behind, something striking her head. Much time passed before she opened her eyes and was conscious again.

It was late in the day; she knew that because there was a red haze and the sand was cool. The battle was over. She could see the soldiers going about seeking the spoils of their victory. She could hear faint moans and pleas for mercy. She lay very still. Two soldiers were talking nearby. They moved closer to her. Then a third pair of boots joined them, and she heard a new voice say, "They are to be taken to the stadium. You two, get that bunch over there and move them off before they make any more trouble." All the boots moved away.

She waited a bit, inched her way back to the bodies that had first fallen on her, and burrowed alongside them. Her neck and head throbbed; all she could think was that the pain must not show. No pulsing vein—nothing to reveal she was not dead.

Caesar's men were going about the field of battle, rounding up survivors, bestowing a final sword thrust to the mortally wounded or those they suspected of playing dead. All the while she lay there half-covered by corpses, trying to breathe as lightly as she could, trying not to think about what was going on around her. She must not cry. She must not tremble. She must not move. She forced herself to think of other things— the alphabet, first in Hebrew, then in Greek. Mathematics—

she made herself do sums, calculating impossible figures, improbable equations.

It grew dark; it was night. The shore of the Sea of Galilee in the town of Tarichea was quiet now, empty, it seemed, of any living soul. Alexandra lifted her head cautiously. She could see nothing but piles of bodies. She heard nothing but the water lapping gently on the shore. She tried to move out from her shelter, but her limbs were numb; all she could do was roll over on her back. Her head ached horribly; and the sand was cold and damp. Yet as she lay there, trembling with fear and exhaustion, she was struck by the beauty of the dark sky. Like bright yet gentle eyes the stars looked down, innocent, upon the gory beach.

Ten measures of beauty in all the world. . . . And nine are in Jerusalem. . . .

Ten. Only ten? What were they? Grace, for one. Harmony of color . . .

Incongruously, forgetting now that she was lying on a beach that had become a graveyard, she began to list in her mind the points of beauty according to the rules of esthetics set forth by the Greeks. But try as she might, she could not come up with ten. Always, one measure eluded her. Time passed; she lay there thinking, forgetting the peril of her situation, staring hypnotized at the stars. Somehow, she fell asleep.

It was morning when she awoke, confused and dazed. She was so stiff and cold she could barely move. Weakly, she managed to sit up. That was when the man had come over to her. She could not remember what he said. Then someone—another man—had picked her up and deposited her in this wooden wagon. Where were they taking her? Who were they? They were not soldiers. . . .

She ought to try to get away from them, to get out of this cart and run away. Run? Where? Besides, she was so weak she was not sure she could even stand. And her head hurt.

She closed her eyes.

"The Jew's wound has festered. I think he will die. The fever has already begun."

"The others?"

"The mother thinks the babe is her own. Milk flows strong in her breasts now."

"Good."

"The child plays, eats. He is obedient, but he does not talk."

"So long as he does not cry. If he does, or grows mischievous, beat him. Not hard, just so he understands what is expected of him. I am not a cruel man. It is a kindness to train him early. A slave's life depends upon the pleasure of those who own him. For himself he is nothing."

"Yes, master."

"Anything else?"

"The girl was only weak from hunger and fatigue. She is unharmed. She is a virgin," the woman added.

Basilides looked up. "You are sure?"

"Yes, master."

"A virgin. Well, that is something. What does she look like? I can't recall. Never mind. Clean her up and bring her to me."

"Yes, master."

She was standing on tiptoe, trying to look out the window. The room was dark but for the slice of light that fell through the small, barred opening. She could hear voices outside. Men's voices, speaking the tongue of Rome. Soldiers.

"What are you up to now? Trying to crawl through the window, are you?"

Alexandra turned to the woman. "Any fool can see it is too high—and too small to pass through," she said coldly. "Even without bars."

"Any fool, eh? What does that make you?"

They stared at each other in mutual hatred. It was the old woman who had examined Alexandra, ordering the giant Niko to hold her down while she felt her limbs, her belly and breasts, forced her mouth open to inspect her teeth, went through her hair looking for lice. The girl had fought like an animal until they had her stripped and spread-eagled; she had writhed helplessly under the big man's hands as the woman made a quick, more intimate examination of her body. The woman had looked up at Niko in surprise. "She has not been used," she said. At that moment Alexandra had pulled her legs back and placed a kick on the crone's chest that sent her halfway across the room. The man had raised his hand to cuff her, but the old woman's voice stopped him. "Never mind," she had gasped, raising herself slowly from the floor and nodding calmly at Alexandra. "I will allow you that. Once . . . I did the same."

But the girl did not appreciate kindness. Later, the woman had brought food to the small group. Alexandra reached eagerly for the bowl but drew back when she saw the contents. "What is it?" she wanted to know.

"What is it?" the woman exclaimed. "Food! Eat, girl."

Alexandra swallowed. It was close to two days since her stomach had held food. The bowl was warm in her hands; the sweet steam rising from it nearly made her swoon. She put it away from her. "You must tell me what this is," she said again.

"Milk broth. There's marrow in it for strength. And a bit of meat, too. It is a mark of the kindness of your master Basilides."

"I have no master," Alexandra said. "And I cannot eat this."

The woman's thin mouth grew even thinner. "Cannot, eh? Shall I bring you a menu, my fine lady? Perhaps you'd like some watery gruel with a bit of piss in it for taste. Or a cup of water and a crust of bread. Or nothing!" Snatching up the bowl, she left.

Alexandra looked around. The others in the room were staring at her. The nursing mother had quickly finished her portion, but not so fast as the child in the corner, who still wore a white mustache. The wounded young man had not protested when Niko dribbled liquid between his lips.

"'Thou shalt not boil a calf in the milk of its mother,'" Alexandra said. "Nor in the marrow either, I suppose." She sat down abruptly. She was feeling quite giddy and faint. No one else said anything.

It was a long time before the old woman returned. She placed a bowl in front of the girl sitting cross-legged on the floor. The girl just stared at it.

"Eat," the woman commanded.

"I cannot," Alexandra said faintly. The bowl was swimming in the haze of spots before her eyes. "It is unclean," she said politely.

"The others do not seem to share your fine feelings."

"The Law excuses them. They are ill, you see, or too young to be held accountable. I am neither."

"You are a fool, Jew."

"I am a Jew, fool."

The woman took an angry step forward. She stopped, however, and looked at the girl. "You are nothing," she said flatly. "Whatever you were before today is wiped away; it is a word written in sand. You are the property of my master Basilides.

You are a slave. Learn this now, and learn it quickly. For yourself you are nothing." She took up the bowl and left.

It was again many hours before she returned. The girl was curled up against the wall, her eyes closed. Her arms were cold as stone when the woman felt them, but she jumped at the touch, and her eyes opened. Gray and grave, they seemed filled with the mist of a faraway morning.

"Nuts and berries," the girl whispered. "The old men . . . the priests . . . lived on nuts and berries until Josef rescued them. And he will come for me. He will come, you shall see. . . . Jotapata . . . I must get to Jotapata. . . . He will come, you'll see. . . ."

"Jotapata? What are you mumbling about? There is no one in Jotapata who will buy you. The city has fallen. Everyone in it was killed or taken by the soldiers. No one escaped."

"What are you saying? Josef . . . Josef. . . ."

"I don't know who your Josef might be, but I can tell you this—he is dead now, or a slave like yourself. Probably dead." She shrugged. "Jotapata held out too long for the legionaries to show mercy."

Alexandra stared at her. Suddenly, with a small cry, she struck the bowl from the woman's hand, knocking it against the wall. The clay shattered as it hit the stone, its contents splattering and spilling to the ground. Alexandra watched the small river of thin, milky broth as it crept along the floor. It seemed to her it was her life, her hopes and dreams, her own blood and marrow that had spilled, disappearing into the cracks of the earth—right before her eyes.

"You go too far," the woman began; but something in the girl's eyes stopped her once more from doing violence to her.

"Get out," Alexandra whispered. "And get me something to eat. Anything."

"Nothing," the woman hissed. "I will get you nothing!"

"Then let me die, and answer to your master for it."

The woman's eyes widened. She laughed drily. "You learn fast, my girl, don't you? Very well. I'll keep you alive. But you may wish one day that I had let you die!" She spat. "Slave."

But the girl fared better than most. She was, after all, a piece of goods to be handled with some care. Unblemished, untouched, young, and possessed of formidable spirit, she would bring a high price. Basilides vowed an offering to the goddess Fortune commensurate with the selling price of his "birthday gift" and ordered his servants to see that no harm came to her. He had been well pleased when she was brought before him. Looking her over as critically and impersonally as a farmer judging a plough horse, he had noted the characteristics of a thoroughbred: the fine bone structure, the graceful posture, the slender hands that had obviously never known a day's work. This was no fisherman's daughter. There was something in the girl's bearing—an arrogance so natural that she would not realize others found her too proud. Perhaps he ought not sell her. He could keep her, bring her back to Rome, set her up as a hetaera, one of that special group of cultured, beautiful women who serviced kings and senators.

But Icelus Liberalis would be curious...resentful, no doubt. And Liberalis had the favor of Nero. They would take her away, and he, Basilides, would have nothing. No, he must dispose of her here, in Judea.

"Coan dress," he said, turning her around by the shoulders. "Yes, I think that will be nice. We shall present our Venus risen from the sea—almost—draped in this." He took a length of gauzy stuff in his hands. "From the island of Cos to you, my little princess." Smiling, he held up the delicate fabric; it was transparent as air. "Now, now, don't look so horrified. It isn't everyone I would give this to. My customers like unpackaged goods. They like to stick their fingers into things. By the gods, every time Liberalis—may his bowels dry up on him—gets his hands on a virgin—which isn't often these days unless you find yourself with an unattractive six-year-old—she is no longer one by the time his patrons finish examining her. Senators have long fingers. It must come from dipping into so many pots. Well, never mind, there are no senators about, more's the pity—I could fetch a handsome price for you. But there are one or two high-ranking officers I have in mind. . . . And there is young Titus, a handsome, healthy lad, and no doubt lonely on this long campaign. Here, let's see what you look like in this. Now stop trying to get away—" He sighed. "Don't make me beat you. I can do it so there will be no mark, but I don't like violence. I am not a cruel man." He motioned to the old woman. "Undress her."

"Gentle master," Alexandra said quickly.

He looked up, surprised. She had addressed him in Latin.

"Hear me a moment," she went on. "We are both after the same thing. You want to make a great deal of money from the sale of my person. I wish to obtain a comfortable position for myself."

His mouth fell open. "By the gods! A female of sense. Go on. . . ."

"You know that I am still a maiden. And I am, as you may have guessed, of noble blood." She gestured at the flimsy fabric he held. "In Coan dress I will look like a dancing girl from Gades, and while we both know there is a market for such exotica, it is nothing to compare with the price you may ask for a genuine princess of Judea." She paused, taking note of the excitement in his eyes. "Give me a tunic of plain white linen," she pleaded. "I swear to you I will wear it as the robe of a queen, and none will deny you the price of one."

He studied her shrewdly. "Who are you? Never mind, you don't fool me. I know you Jews are crazy when it comes to showing a bit of flesh. You have, none of you, the slightest feel for beauty. However, it is clear you are a girl of some refinement. And I am not an insensitive man. Very well. It shall be as you have said." He ordered the old woman to fetch the garment she had requested. "Yes," he said, looking over his captive once more. "The linen is more suitable. It shall not be Venus but Diana. Or perhaps, with those gray eyes, Athene." He looked at her closely. "I would say you have no knowledge of whom I speak, but somehow I think you do."

They remained in the Galilee for some weeks while Basilides attended to the business of fulfilling Liberalis's contract. During this time, Alexandra suffered nothing worse than confinement with its attendant boredom and anxiety, and the old woman's taunts and lewd suggestions concerning her future.

She stared coldly at the hag now. "Why have I been taken from the others? Why am I kept apart?"

"Miss your one-legged friend, do you?"

"You cut off Benjamin's leg?"

"Had to if he was to live."

"But he will need me now! Let me go to him! He will want someone to talk to."

"Talk to, eh? Yes, I daresay you two have done your share of talking. And what else would you be up to besides talk if I did not separate you?"

"What do you mean? He was ill—"

"Not too ill to touch your hair, to caress you. I have eyes. I see what goes on."

"He was in a fever. He doesn't even know who I am. He calls me Sara."

"And what do you call him?"

"His name is Benjamin." ("I told you I'd get us through," the boy had murmured in his delirium. He had held her hand so tightly. "You know your Benjamin would not fail you. . . . Sara, my love. . . . My love . . .") "I had a brother named Benjamin."

"And what games did you play with him? I have heard tell how close you Jews are within your families. Even the king and his sister, eh? Well, I guess you were not as close as that. Don't know what I'm talking about, do you?" For some reason this angered her. "Well, let me tell you this, girl—there's just one thing that separates you from the other garbage around here, and that's the fact that you haven't been served up for dinner yet. And it's my job to keep you that way. You're staying away from One Leg. You may not believe it, but I'm doing you a favor. In our world—a slave's world—it is not good to become attached. All right, come on. We're getting out of here."

"Where are we going?"

"What do you care? It is all the same to you."

"Please. I'd like to know."

The woman shrugged. "There is little left for Vespasian here in the north. Gamala has fallen, Gischala has been taken, and Gadara is occupied. My master says the generals are returning to Caesarea to plan their move against Jerusalem."

"Then we go—"

"To Caesarea, praise the gods. It is the only worthwhile place in Judea. Wait until you see it. You may thank the gods you have been given the opportunity to visit such a city."

She could smell the sea again. For a moment everything else was forgotten—the events that had driven her from her home, the battle at Tarichea, the death of Josef, her own captivity. All she knew was that she was close to the sea again; by day she would breathe fresh salt air, and at night she would be lulled by the seashell sound that had comforted her as a child. She strained her neck, eager to get a glimpse of the blue expanse; and Basilides smiled, thinking her excitement was caused by the white towers and spires in the distance ahead.

"It is a pretty sight," the slave merchant agreed. "I did not suppose there was anything so fine in the province. Of course, it cannot compare with the Imperial City, which, since the fire, Divine Nero rebuilds lavishly. Still, Caesarea has some style. Splendid theater and arena—you know about that, don't you, Niko? Yes, my friend, in your day you must have been quite a gladiator, eh? Well, be thankful you are not lying now with a lance in your heart. A bit more to the side, judging from the scar, and you would have been done for. Come now, give those horses some speed! Let us pretend we are charioteers and before us lies all victory, honor, and wealth! To Caesarea!"

The busy, bustling city had put him in good humor. Basilides was so cordial that Alexandra quite forgot she was not free to do as she wished but was in fact his property. The reality of her situation was soon made clear, however, after the slave dealer spent an evening consuming a large quantity of wine. It was deep into the night when the shadow of the man fell across her body. She sat up, shielding her eyes from the flickering candle that Basilides held close to her face.

"Disrobe."

"I—"

"No talk. Do as you are told."

"Has someone come—to buy me?"

He laughed softly. "At this hour? Come, come, do not waste my time."

She inched backward against the wall. "I am a virgin. You said yourself it would bring a better price."

"And so it will."

"But—"

"Don't you Jews know anything? Well, you shall by morning, girl. And I promise you will still be a virgin." He laughed again and reached for her now, but she eluded him, getting up on her knees like a cat ready to spring.

"If you touch me, if you use me in any way, you will be forever accursed."

Startled, the man drew back. "What nonsense is this?"

He could not see how she trembled; he only heard her voice, distant and cold as the eyes so eerily bright in the darkness.

"My family was killed by the Greeks of Caesarea. Yet I survived unharmed, untouched. At Tarichea, you saw. . . . I lived where others died. My life is in the hands of one beyond the power of men."

"Your God?" He sneered drunkenly.

"My God . . . and yours."

He stared at her. She seemed different now, changed in this light, no longer an insignificant wisp of a girl, but a forboding animal with pale cat-eyes and tensed body. "Who are you?" he whispered.

"I am all that is, all that was, and all that shall ever be. No man can lift the veil that covers me."

He staggered backward. "Neit," he said hoarsely. "Goddess of retribution. Goddess of revenge."

Whatever, she thought. Her voice grew stronger. "You saved me from the soldiers, Basilides. That is in your favor. Bring no curse upon yourself now. I swear you shall profit from this."

He stood there a moment longer, then bowed his head and disappeared.

She let out her breath and sank limply to the floor. Listening for a sign of his return, she wrapped herself in the dirty blanket she had been given and leaned back against the wall, hugging her knees to her chest. She stayed like that, wakeful and watching, until dawn; but Basilides did not return, nor did he attempt to approach her again in the nights to come.

There was, however, another girl in the household who did not escape the slave dealer's attention. She was a pale, slight creature who looked as though she hardly possessed the stamina to carry buckets of slops or endure the other heavy tasks assigned her, much less bear the weight of her master's body as she was nightly called to do. She seemed resigned to her fate and rarely spoke, never mentioning any other life or family she had known. She would often stare at Alexandra with a searching look that Alexandra found annoying and yet intriguing. One day, the other girl stopped, and pretending to retrieve the broom she had deliberately let fall, she scratched something quickly in the earth. After she had gone, Alexandra studied the drawing, then erased it with her foot. It was the outline of a fish.

Later, when they were alone together, Alexandra said, "You are a Christian, aren't you?"

The girl's eyes lit up. "And you? Do you follow the Master?"

"I?" Alexandra was shocked by the suggestion. "Certainly not. I am—" She stopped. She was determined not to reveal her identity to anyone here. "I stayed with a Christian family once. Here, in Caesarea."

"I am from Caesarea," the girl said. "My father was a gatekeeper at the theater. He was killed over a gambling debt. He never had any schooling," she went on, "but he could recite long pieces of the plays he'd seen. Sometimes, when he had a drink or two, he would do a whole play. All the parts, every one. And singing too. How we would laugh."

And she had thought the girl was a mute because she never spoke! "How . . . how you must have loved him," Alexandra said lamely, startled by this sudden flow of words.

"I think kindly of him now, for the Master's words have filled my heart with love. But for a long time I hated him. He beat me, you see, and gave me to his friends when he could not pay his wages. My name is Lilah," she said with a shy smile. "What is yours?"

Alexandra opened her mouth, then closed it. "I have no name," she said at last, turning away. "A slave does not need a name."

"There are no slaves in the eyes of Christ. We are all His children."

"How dare you—" She turned angrily, but the sudden fear in the girl's eyes stopped her. "Look," she said as calmly as she could. "I told you I spent some time among Christians, so I know a little of what it is all about. And I know that your rabbis teach love and kindness and many good things in addition to all the fanciful stuff. But I am in no mood to hear about love and kindness, nor about your Savior. He may be your Messiah, but he is not mine." He hesitated. Lilah was silent, her eyes sad, withdrawn. Alexandra sighed. She touched the girl's shoulder. "Call me . . . Lexa," she said. "If you like."

It was the first time she'd ever had a real friend her own age, and female too. How strange to come upon her this way.

"But we would never have met otherwise," Lilah said.

"Why not? All sorts of people came into our house—Romans, Greeks, Christians—even men of the desert. My father had business dealings with an Ishmaelite, a prince of Arabia—

I forget which tribe, they have so many. This one was wonderful to see with his robes and white headdress. He brought me a nose ring once, but my father would not let me wear it. You know how fathers are."

There was an uncomfortable silence. "You see?" Lilah said at last. "We are of different worlds."

Alexandra sighed. "Well, we are in the same one now. At least they don't put chains on you."

"Because I am nothing. But you will make the master rich."

Alexandra smiled. "Which master do you mean?" she teased. "Basilides or your Nazarene?"

"You must not say that, even for fun," Lilah said firmly.

"Why not? The way you go on and on about your Son of God. . . . Don't you know how blasphemous you are? My uncle could have told you."

"But Jesus was the Son of God."

"God is bodiless, Lilah. Faceless, nameless, without image. Or issue. Like . . . music. Not any music that we make here, but music like the . . . the stars make when they sing to the sea. . . ."

"Is that what your uncle taught?"

"My uncle was a priest. Priests don't teach. They officiate. They burn incense and light candles and say solemn things while they cut up a lot of poor animals—and they get very rich for doing all of this. Rabbis, on the other hand, are generally poor but very, very wise. They do the teaching. That's what *rabbi* means: 'teacher.' But I don't much agree with all that they say, any more than I care for your Christian stories. I used to think it was because I am a Sadducee. But now I think it is because I am a woman. I don't know. I guess I just see things in my own way."

They were asleep when the old woman came into the room. She pulled Alexandra's blanket off, peered closely at the startled girl, then went over to Lilah and kicked her. "Get up," she said. "He wants you."

"Again?" Alexandra asked. "She only now came from him."

"Oh-ho! And what are you, her mother, to worry so? Be glad it isn't you. Or perhaps you'd like to take your friend's place?"

Lilah got up, yawning. Wordlessly, she shuffled from the room.

Alexandra watched her go, then turned to the old woman but said nothing. There was nothing to say.

The old woman sat down on her haunches, surprisingly spry, and rested her arms on her knees.

"What do you want?" Alexandra asked guardedly. "Why don't you leave? I don't need your company."

"You still don't know you're a slave, do you? The way you talk, you think you're free."

"I know the feel of chains; you've seen to that."

"Not I. My master gives the orders. He simply wishes to make sure we have the pleasure of your company until such time as you leave us for another."

Alexandra did not answer her. The sounds of her present master's mating were clearly audible through the wall that separated the rooms. She grimaced as the man's grunts grew louder.

"Don't like the sound, eh?" The old woman missed nothing. "Well, you'd better get used to it. No one will be buying you for kitchen work, girl. At least, not at first."

Alexandra turned away.

"Don't like the sound of my talk, either, I see. Too bad. I could tell you a few things might make it go easier for you. Tricks is what a slave needs to keep alive. And a woman is a slave, bought or not."

Basilides was grunting steadily now, the rhythm rising in an arc. Alexandra stared at the wall; images danced across it: a girl dragged down on the docks by a gang of laughing men . . . her mother sprawled naked across a bloody bed . . . soldiers at Tarichea pulling women away from children who clung to them, or from the bodies of men they clung to. . . .

She shook her head as if to clear it. *I have seen too much*, she thought, unaware that she had whispered the words aloud.

"What? Seen it, have you? Is that it? Well, then, you know the ways of love."

Alexandra looked at the woman. "That's not love," she said disgustedly.

"Oh-ho! Listen to the princess! Not love, is it?" She jerked her head toward the wall. "What is it, then?"

"I don't know," the girl said fiercely. "All I know is this— no one is going to use me like a piece of meat! No one!"

The woman was quiet for a moment; then she said, "But that's what they do, girl. Whether you are bought for money or not."

"You only say that because you have been treated badly."

"And you know better, I suppose."

"I know that men—and women—can be cruel. But that isn't all there is to life." She looked at the woman, curious now. "Haven't you ever been happy?"

There was silence. Then: "When I had my babies. Didn't matter the pain of making them, birthing them. . . . Holding them was enough." She paused. "It's bad, though, when children come. You tell yourself, 'Don't love them. Don't love them too much. Then, when they take them from you, it won't hurt.' But it hurts. It is kinder to lose them right away. My last . . . they let me keep her until the blood cycle began. I tried to hide it from them, but they saw her little breasts. . . . Before that I used to pray she would be late becoming a woman, because I would lose her once she did. But she was quick, as I had been. Nine summers I had her, and then they took her away and sold her. Do not ask me to have pity or affection for you or"—she jerked her head toward the wall—"or that one in there. I have no fondness in me, and to tell the truth, I don't like you. You are too proud. You pretend you are not a slave when that is all you are. But for now you are my daughter, and if you listen I will tell you what a woman needs to know. How, for instance, to keep from getting with child, and what things please a man."

Out of curiosity, Alexandra listened. Little of it made sense to her, and she was glad when the old woman finally went away. Always, when she dreamed of Josef, her fantasies centered on and ended with a kiss. What followed then between a man and a woman—a husband and a wife—was a dark blank to her. The thing the soldiers did to women, what she had seen in Caesarea, that was something else, something bound up in violence and war. Whatever Basilides did to Lilah and would have done to Alexandra if she had not frightened him off was not—could not be—anything that Josef would have done. She was certain of that. And yet . . .

She waited for Lilah to return. Lilah had been with so many men. They were the same age, but it was true what Lilah had said. They were of such different worlds.

"What is it like?" Alexandra asked the sleepy girl. "Does it hurt?"

"Sometimes. When they do things."

"Like what?"

Lilah shook her head vaguely. "Things." She wiped her

arms and neck with a cloth, then passed the rag between her legs. "Mostly I don't feel anything. Not anymore. I pray to Christ, and I think of the Kingdom of Heaven that awaits me when I die. I don't mind what any of them do to me now. They can only touch my body. They can't touch my soul."

"Oh, Lilah," Alexandra said disgustedly.

"If I did not have my faith, if I did not believe the Christ loves me and that a better world than this awaits me, I . . . I don't know what I'd do." She stole a look at Alexandra. "Sometimes in your sleep you cry out. I see how you try to look out the window, how you test your chains. I know you must despair. But you never weep. If you do not believe in the world to come, what is it that keeps you strong?"

"Revenge! Escape! All those people out there walking the streets of Caesarea, living in houses that don't belong to them— I'd run every one of them through if I could!" She gestured toward the door. "And that old hag would be the first to go."

"Oh, Lexa, it is wrong to hate! No matter what is done to us, we must show love."

"You are an idiot, Lilah. You think hatred is a sin. Maybe it is. But I know it is a sin to allow others to commit evil, to be a willing victim of infamy. Your body is the work of God as much as that soul you are forever talking about. Yet you do not even seem to care how it is defiled and abused."

"The body is nothing."

"It is the soul's house, isn't it? Even if it is, according to you, only a temporary abode."

Lilah was getting confused. "I . . . I do not wish to argue with you, Lexa. You are my friend. But it would be better," she said softly, "if you believed."

"It would be better if I were out of here," Alexandra said grimly. "Have you ever tried to run away?"

"Oh, no! They brand you when you are caught."

"When? If. If you are caught."

"Aren't you afraid?"

She shook her head. "Once, I was afraid of only two things. The first was my mother's temper. She was awfully quick, and you never knew where the blow would land. Well, she is dead now. And the other thing I feared was not . . . well, not becoming the wife of . . . of a certain person. Well, now he is dead too."

"Aren't you afraid of what they might do to you?"

"Who? Men? If you must know, I'm curious. Once, a long

time ago, a man kissed me. I didn't like the man, but I liked the kiss. It made me feel . . . But I won't be treated contemptuously," she said suddenly. "And I won't be abused. No one is going to beat me or pass me around."

"But that is the way it is."

"It isn't! I know it isn't, Lilah. My mother and father loved one another. I know that. And as for me, I know what I want."

"What? What do you want?"

"I want a man who will talk to me as he would talk to a man, but who will touch me as he would touch a woman—a woman he cares for."

Lilah stared at her in astonishment.

"None of that matters now, I suppose," Alexandra said, yawning. She wrapped the blanket tightly around her body, curling up on her side. "All that matters is getting out of here."

"I think it will be soon. I heard the master say someone was coming to look at you. Maybe tomorrow." She blew out the candle.

Alexandra bolted upright. "Who is it? Do you know? Young? Old?"

"From what the master said, I think it must be a Roman of some importance."

Licinius Mucianus, commander of the Syrian legions, raised an eyebrow. "A girl? I thought you said someone special, Basilides."

"She is, my lord! Of noble blood—and a virgin."

"A virgin? Is she ugly, then?"

"You shall judge that for yourself, noble master."

"Hmnn. That means she is not. All right, let's take a look at her. I warn you, though, if I am presented with nothing but bosom and hips I shall be deeply disappointed in your judgment."

Basilides signaled the old woman to bring Alexandra forward. He turned back to the Roman with a smile and a bow. "Excellency, your patronage is as holy to me as the benevolence of the gods. To disappoint you would be a breach of faith— a blasphemy upon my heart. I would rather remain forever here, in Judea—the gods forbid—than return to Rome were it known I had failed to please the great Mucianus."

The Roman was not listening. His eyes were on the girl who had been led into the room. She was slim, straight-backed, with small, high breasts and a long, slender waist. She moved well, not in the voluptuous, overtly feminine manner that he disliked, but as a dancer might walk, graceful and proud. She stopped in front of him, and he saw that her skin was fresh and smooth; her confinement had bestowed upon her the aristocratic pallor that the ladies of Caesar's court and the highborn of Judea considered so desirable. Mucianus nodded approvingly. He rubbed her lashes with his thumb to see if they owed their dark color to paint, brushed back her hair to see if her ears were small, then looked deeply into her eyes, trying to determine their exact hue. Startled, he realized—as another once had—that the girl was studying him as intently as he was examining her. Her gaze disconcerted him, and he walked around her, perusing her buttocks now. There was not much to see through the heavy folds of the plain linen garment the slave wore. He frowned.

"Is she scarred?"

"Without a blemish, my lord."

"Then why have you covered her body?"

Basilides cleared his throat. "You know how it is, excellency. Put a virgin in Choan dress, and she'll start crying, and then her face gets all swollen and red. Besides, this one is something special, not for any eyes that might chance upon her, but for special eyes only." He spread his hands. "Who wants what all have seen and touched?"

Mucianus gestured at the linen robe. "Off."

Alexandra stared at him.

"Off, off," Basilides babbled. "You are not deaf, girl. Remove your robe."

Her fingers trembling, she undid the clasp at her shoulder but hesitated, not letting the garment fall. Impatient now, Mucianus pulled the robe from her body. Her head fell forward as the air hit her flesh; bravado gone, a crimson flush staining her pale skin.

She had been bathed and perfumed for the occasion, all bodily hair removed except for the "patch of Venus," as it was called, and that too had been scented in the manner of the Romans. "This will warm your blood," the old woman had said, grinning as she rubbed the sweet oil into the shivering girl's loins and her tingling, waxed armpits. Alexandra stole a look at the woman and saw her grinning now, smirking at her humiliation.

Slowly, Alexandra bat Harsom raised her head, relaxed her

shoulders, straightened her back. The Roman villa of Licinius Mucianus boasted an exquisite collection of sculpture; now the man stood silently admiring the human poetry of the young, perfect body before him. Alexandra saw the look in his eyes. She realized that he found her pleasing and in that second ceased to be embarrassed. *Now, this*, she thought in that curiously detached way of hers, *is interesting*.

"You see," Basilides was saying. "There is no scar. Not a blemish, not a mark upon her." He put his hand on the girl's shoulder, indicating that she should turn around. She jumped skittishly at his touch.

Mucianus was still staring at her. Suddenly, he drew his sword and with its point raised the robe at Alexandra's feet, offering it politely to her.

She took the linen, held it to her body.

"How much?" He had not taken his eyes from her.

"A virgin, my lord. No one has touched her. No one but you has even seen her. I've been saving her. You know I keep an eye out for my patrons."

"How much?"

"Look here. The doctor's certificate. A virgin. She is a virgin, my lord. How many are there to be found?"

"How much, Basilides?"

"See what a gentle creature she is. I guarantee she is in perfect health, free from fits, not thievish nor—once she learns the tenderness of your protection—prone to run away. She is not despondent and has never attempted suicide. A gentle creature, my lord. All day long, like a little bird, she sings softly to herself and never complains. Also, her teeth are sound." He took a deep breath. "Twenty thousand denarii."

Mucianus looked straight into her eyes. "What is your name?" he asked in heavily accented Aramaic.

"Diana," Basilides said. "I call her Diana."

"What is your name?" the Roman said again, ignoring the slave merchant.

"Alexandra. You may speak in Latin if you like. The common language of Judea is rather ugly, don't you think?"

"And educated," Basilides said quickly. "She is learned, noble master."

Mucianus did not take his eyes from her. "Beautiful lips like yours would be better suited to the tongue of poets," he said in Greek.

"As you wish." She answered him in kind.

He smiled. "This talent will cost me another thousand denarii, you know. Very well." He nodded to Basilides. "Deliver her to my apartment in the Praetorium." He held up his hand. "The cost is of no importance now. We shall settle later. I know you will deal honestly with me, flesh peddler." He smiled thinly at Basilides. "Won't you?"

The man bowed.

Mucianus made ready to leave. "I dine with Vespasian tonight. Bring the girl on the tenth hour. Let me know when you have some boys. I am told the Galileans are exceedingly strong. No redheads." And he was gone.

She stood on the steps of the great white palace that had been home to Tiberius Alexander, Gessius Florus, and all the other governors Rome had sent to Judea. The general Flavius Vespasian occupied it now; and she was going as a slave to the quarters of one of his commanding officers. Was this where it all led? Back to Caesarea? To be concubine to her people's enemy? Had she survived death and defilement for this?

As a child she had played on these steps with her brothers until the soldiers chased them both away....

"Come, come," Basilides said impatiently. "What are you staring at?" His eyes narrowed. "I trust you are not considering a dash for freedom. You would not get far."

"No," she said, "I will not run away," and followed him into the palace.

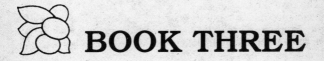 **BOOK THREE**

FLAVIUS VESPASIAN reached for the silver cup at his side and raised it to his lips. The cup was worn and plain except at the rim, which bore a simple motif that had long been out of fashion. The general smiled. "I would offer you some of my 'ambrosia,' Mucianus, but I know your taste runs to sweeter drink."

Licinius Mucianus did not hesitate to agree. "I had my fill of legionary's brew when I was a pup in the field, and I didn't like it then." He made a face, as though the mixture of cheap, vinegary wine and water had in fact touched his tongue. "I confess that your preference for our soldiers' *posca* makes me wonder if you have not spent too many years in battle under the sun. I suppose it is politic, however, seeing how the men worship you."

Vespasian frowned. "Worship? My men respect me, as I respect tham. I drink what they drink because this is what I like. Clears the head and the bladder. But see here, have more of this fancy wine I had brought in for you. Cost more than a denarius or two. Don't say we are not friends." Without waiting for the servants to come forward, he briskly filled his friend's goblet from an ornate gold pitcher. Then he raised the silver cup. "Caesar. Rome. Victory." That done, he drained his cup and set it down firmly on the edge of his chair.

Mucianus was familiar enough with his host to be unperturbed by the slight scowl on Vespasian's weather-beaten, bulldog countenance. The man was famous for his dour expression, which did not necessarily denote anger toward any particular party. Once, when Vespasian asked a well-known wit who always made jokes about people, "Why not make one about me?" the answer had been: "Gladly, when you have finished relieving yourself."

But the general seemed restless tonight; and as he, Mucianus, had another engagement he was eager to attend to, he shortly rose to take his leave. "I thank you for the excellent repast." In fact, he had never had a worse meal. Vespasian was inordinately fond of garlic, and the food had been heavily spiced with the bulb. The man's peasant tastes had long ago caused Nero's court to refer to him as the Old Farmer. Well, Mucianus thought, remembering the meat that had been served and the scarcely palatable *posca* that Vespasian had heartily consumed throughout the evening, farmers' guts must be like iron. He, on the other hand, had a monumental case of heartburn.

"It grows late," Mucianus continued as Vespasian looked at him in surprise. "If we are to have our wits about us at that meeting in the morning, perhaps we ought now to say goodnight."

"Ha! You don't fool me."

Mucianus looked startled.

"Sweet wine makes you sleepy." Grinning, Vespasian rose and patted his own flat belly. "I know how you gentlemen of Rome laugh at my fondness for plain stuff—but look. See, you are weary as a woman, and I—ten years your senior—can last the night and fight at dawn. That's what comes of your fancy food and sweet wine."

Mucianus smiled wanly. He swallowed a hiccough. "I would not boast of being fond of plain stuff if I were you. At least not in the presence of your oriental princess."

"Who? Berenice? Oh, she'd understand how it was meant. Besides, she's carrying on with Titus now. Has the boy bedazzled."

"Titus? I thought you and she—"

He brushed the past aside. "The liaison was—as you might say—politic. Must say I didn't mind. The woman's quite fascinating. The body may be soft, but her mind is sharp as steel. We both knew what it was about. Hospitality, you might say. Besides, I made it clear I am no Julius Caesar—and Rome has had enough of Cleopatras. We get along splendidly."

"And Titus?"

"Ah! That is a different matter. The Thunderbolt has struck." He smiled, obviously not minding the fact that his son had taken the woman from him. "Titus is a good boy. It is rare these days when a father can say that his son is his best friend. But that he is. My friend and my most trusted adviser.

By Mars, the way he fought at Gischala!" His eyes were bright with love, though he allowed himself only a pleased grunt.

"The princess Berenice is a superb specimen of womanhood," Mucianus remarked. "A bit Junoesque for my taste—"

"Yes, she's a fine-looking lady. The best of her race."

"She's not really Judean, you know. That is, the Jews don't consider her so. They call her—and her brother Agrippa—Herod's children. I believe they do not accept the line."

"I have a prisoner—a friend of Titus's in former days—who has mentioned that fact. Now, this Josephus fellow is himself a very pure-blooded, aristocratic Jew." He shrugged. "As if it matters. The man is in chains like any fisherman of the Galilee."

"Not exactly, from what I've seen."

"Ah, yes, that's right, you met him. No . . . not exactly. As I told you. He is Titus's friend. And a very interesting fellow. Clever. Exceedingly clever. His tactics at Jotapata were brilliant."

They were out in the hall now, Vespasian having decided to walk a bit with Mucianus. He was restless tonight. As they neared the officer's apartment, they caught sight of a portly man advancing toward them. He had a young woman with him. The pair caught Vespasian's eye even as he noted Mucianus signaling to the man, who bowed slightly in return and led the girl away. "Yours?" the general inquired, watching the girl's departing figure.

Mucianus laughed hesitantly. "Yes, I bought her today. Now, there is an example, I daresay, of real Judean nobility. I can tell you that girl is hardly common. She speaks Latin and Greek, as well as the horrendous dialect of this province. Most likely she is some priest's daughter."

Vespasian grunted. The girl had turned at the doorway to Mucianus's chamber. For a moment, two large, light-hued eyes beneath straight, winged brows met his in a solemn but piercingly direct gaze; then she was gone. He turned to Mucianus, who was hiccoughing behind his hand. "How much? How much did you pay? I'll buy her from you."

A hiccough splurted into a fit of coughing. As his commanding officer slapped him on the back, Mucianus managed to gasp, "You want the girl?"

"Yes. How much?"

The Roman wiped the tears from his eyes and blew his

nose. "Basilides asked forty thousand."

"Forty thousand? That's a lot for a piece of flesh—and not much flesh, at that."

"She's a virgin."

"Ah." His eyes softened, the knowledge awakening not lust but a faint glimmer of pity for the creature. He was determined now that Licinius Mucianus should not have her. "Very well. I will settle with the slave merchant."

"No, no," Mucianus said quickly. "She is yours. A gift." He put his hand to his breast, less a gesture of heartfelt friendship than a vain attempt to suppress the stabbing pains. Damn the man and his garlicky mutton! Mucianus smiled bravely. He wanted nothing so much now as to lie down—alone—with a cool, wet cloth on his brow. "Let me provide what Titus has taken away."

Vespasian laughed. The sound echoed through the hall like a dog's bark. "All right. All right, then. But you are too generous."

"Remember it when you are emperor."

Vespasian looked surprised. "What?"

"Nero's days are numbered. That is all I will say." That was all he could say—his legs felt weak.

"What about Galba?"

"The army will support no one but you. You are the man for Rome."

"Strange. . . ." He frowned. "The prisoner Josephus said the same. Naturally I rebuked him—it was no mistake on his part—and told him he would be sent to Caesar for punishment. 'Why send me to Nero?' the Jew replied. 'You are Caesar, and none other. Therefore keep me in chains if you will, but keep me with you, for only you may judge me.' Well . . . I dismissed his talk as politic—there is that word again—flattery, to gain my goodwill, I suppose. But Titus says the fellow has the power of prophecy. As you know, I have a loathing for astrologers and soothsayers—a man's an idiot to think what's in a chicken's ass or a goat's belly makes any difference to his life." He paused. "Are you all right? You look pale."

"I—the wine, I think. By your leave—" He disappeared inside the chamber. "I will send the girl to you," he called out before lapsing into a series of strange sounds that indicated some distress.

Vespasian waited a moment outside the door and then motioned to a palace slave. "You had better fetch a pot and some rags," he told the servant. "I believe Licinius Mucianus has just thrown up." His face brightened. "And bring the man some *posca*. With my compliments. That will fix him right soon enough." Whistling, he went off.

Alexandra followed the servant down the hall. Something had happened, but she was not sure what. There had been a few hurried words between Mucianus and Basilides, coin had changed hands, and the slave dealer had gone away. But now, instead of being left alone with the Roman who had bought her, she was being led to another part of the palace. She wondered if it had something to do with the man who had been speaking to Mucianus earlier. There was something about him. . . . He was not at all handsome and certainly not young, but he gave the impression of great strength and power—a certain solidity. What was the word the Romans used? *Gravitas*. That was it. The man possessed *gravitas*. No doubt he was another one of their commanders. One of their killers. That stern, scowling expression . . . Would a man like that have shown mercy at Tarichea? More to the point, would he be kind to one girl, brought to him now—if that indeed was her destination?

Since her meeting with Mucianus earlier that day, she had existed in a state of nervous excitement; she was curious, even eager to see what lay ahead. Resigned to the fact that all whom she loved were dead, that she was truly alone in the world, she was determined somehow to rise above the fate of a slave. But now, suddenly, the realities of her situation struck her. Suddenly, she was afraid.

The world is not the books you read, her uncle had said, *full of miracles and happy endings*. Men are cruel. They are cruel. . . .

You are nothing, the old woman had said. *You are a slave. You are nothing.* . . .

The Lord protect you from all evil. The Essene's blessing came back to her. *The Lord keep you from harm.* . . .

Alexandra took a deep breath. Head high, she entered the room that the servant had indicated.

There were not one but two men there. The first, facing her, was the man she had seen in the hall with Mucianus. The other had his back to her, but he seemed young; he was not dressed like a soldier. "There are twenty-four priestly classes," he was saying in a low, pleasant voice. "I know it sounds complicated, but these things are a way with us. We deem it of great importance to know who our fathers were and to be able to trace their steps in the years of ancient times. A Jerusalemite who cannot go back with certainty for at least four generations is of little social account."

Alexandra stared at the black, curly head. That voice . . . "Josef," she whispered, hardly daring to believe that it was really he. But who else could it be? "Josef," she said again, hesitant, but in a louder voice.

The Roman looked up.

The dark-haired man turned to her. He was frowning slightly, as if angered by the interruption. Then his expression changed as he realized he had been addressed by his Hebrew name. Puzzlement, wonder, curiosity, surprise—each took their turn in his eyes. Then the girl took a step forward, was out of the shadow that hid her features. Her lips were parted slightly, her eyes wide with wonder. He stared at her incredulously.

"Alexandra," he gasped.

She wanted to fly into his arms; but even now, as always, the sight of him made her shy. She stood there, trembling with joy. He was alive. He was here! He would save her. And then she saw his chains.

Gold chains. Attached to heavy, golden bracelets. More an ornament than a hindrance. And his dress was that of a Roman, plain but undeniably fine. She stared at him, hardly hearing what he was saying to the other man. She noted too that he was clean-shaven, as he had been when she first saw him, before he had sailed away to Rome.

"We . . . we were betrothed," Josef stammered, his composure shaken by the appearance of his all-but-forgotten fiancée.

"Betrothed?" the general echoed.

"Yes. Our families arranged for our wedding, which, as you can see, circumstances have prevented."

"Mucianus was right, then. The girl is no ordinary slave. I had her brought here because I thought you might be able to discover her identity." He laughed, pleased with himself. "I did not imagine how easy that would be. How is she called?"

"Her name is Alexandra. She is—was—the daughter of one Samuel ben Harsom, who was before his death a peaceful man and a friend to Rome."

"And what steps did her ancestors take in—how did you say it?—ancient times?"

"Alexandra is directly descended from the line of David the king. On the paternal side she is related to the philosopher Philo, and also to Tiberius Alexander, who now serves as Roman governor of Egypt."

Vespasian slapped his knee. "Ha! Damn me if I do not know a thoroughbred when I see one!"

"I am not a horse," Alexandra said.

The Roman turned to her, surprised. "Ah, yes," he remembered. "Mucianus said you speak our language." He turned back to Josef. "You say your families arranged the match. What are your feelings for the girl?"

Josef's mind raced for an answer. Vespasian had said that Alexandra was a slave. Where and when had she been captured? Never mind that now. Obviously the Roman could do with her as he wished—but would he feel the need to do away with his Jewish prisoner if he thought there was any love between Josef and the girl? On the other hand, if Josef said nothing, would his own stature be weakened, and his already perilous position eroded by contempt and abuse?

Josef spread his manacled hands as wide as the gold chain would allow and smiled sadly. "Is a prisoner permitted to have feelings?"

Vespasian reddened. "Unlike my colleagues," he said gruffly, "who seem to cherish the notion that Gauls, Germans, Britons, Nubians—and, of course, Jews—constitute a number of strange, subhuman species that by a mere quirk of the gods share the earth with civilized people, I have always held the view that the conquered races are yet human and that even slaves are made of flesh and blood. Perhaps that is why I am successful on the field. I do not underestimate the enemy." He pointed a finger at Josef. "Speak your mind, boy."

"To what purpose, great Vespasian? The generosity of your nature allows that I have feelings, but can I exercise those feelings? I am stripped of all action. Permit me, then, to cloak my heart, that I be not further unmanned before this company."

Vespasian was silent. Tapping his finger on the arm of his chair, he studied his Jewish prisoner and the girl, who had not taken her eyes from Josef throughout. He was struck by Alexandra's composure. If she guessed that her future was being decided in these moments, she betrayed no apprehension nor even any preference. She seemed only curious, like a physician watching the probing of a body. He had wanted to take her from Mucianus less from lust than from a desire to thwart that pederast, for whom, despite their long association, he had little affection. But now, even as he considered giving the girl up as a gesture of his humanity, he realized he wanted her. She was young, fresh; her face was unpainted, her hair loose and natural. She stood straight as an arrow, but despite her slimness there was a graceful flow of limb, a gentle curving from breast to waist to hip. In a country of burning summer and damp, bone-chilling winter, she was an incredible moment of spring. And the young man beside her, with his dark eyes looking straight ahead, that godlike profile and slender, smooth-muscled body—

The conqueror was looking in awe upon the conquered. Something about these two had taken the Roman aback. It was as if he could suddenly see those years of ancient times, those years that went beyond most mortal memory, far past the doings of his own Sabine and Etruscan ancestors. He felt as if he were looking at the remnants of some legendary glory, and felt eclipsed by their history. No wonder Cestius Gallus had been cowed before that damn Temple gate. And the girl was like the gate. Strange . . . he had not felt that way toward Berenice, who was, after all, princess of Judea. . . .

Josef cleared his throat. "The fact is . . . a Sadducee priest may not marry a widow or a woman who has been divorced or one . . . who is—has been—" He cleared his throat again. "Whatever else I may feel, my first duty is to our Law. . . ."

"The girl's a virgin." Vespasian stood up. "I would like to see a wedding as it is performed by members of your race. Foreign customs interest me. I will give you this girl, Josephus, as a mark of my amity toward the friend of my son Titus, and as a reward for your bravery at Jotapata. This should keep you occupied during your confinement here. I should not like you to grow stale from inactivity, inasmuch as I have 'stripped you of all action.' Well, not all, eh? Nor do I think it wise to let you sit around with time enough to conjure up such plans against me as you worked in the Galilee. Therefore, enjoy the contentment of a married man with my blessings." He turned to Alexandra with a wry bow. "Two is your lucky number, mistress, and a bad one for me."

"Two?" His meaning puzzled her.

"You have passed by two Romans in one night to reach the man you are obviously meant to marry. On the other hand, I have lost two beautiful women to two young men."

"Then," she said, smiling, "my lucky number must be three, for it is the third man I am to wed. Perhaps three will prove auspicious for you as well."

"Perhaps." He was beginning to regret his generosity. He turned back to Josef. "Instruct the servants as to your needs. We shall have the ceremony tomorrow. It will be a good entertainment for my guests. Meanwhile, you had better keep the girl with you." He grinned at the astonished young man. "I trust—tonight—you will not violate your...Law. Until tomorrow, then."

She was dreaming of the sea. It was that moment before night when everything turned pink and gold....Her brothers were wrestling on the sand, and the sky was red above the shore, and Josef was calling her. He was standing waist-deep in the water, calling to her....I must go back, she said. I must help prepare the evening meal....But he only laughed and called to her to come into the sea....All around him the sun was glittering. . . . The water was full of jewels. . . . and he was calling her. . . . calling her. . . .

"Alexandra . . . Alexandra . . ."

She opened her eyes.

Josef smiled. "What a good wife I shall have. Even in her sleep she talks of preparing a meal."

She sat up. "We are really to be married?"

He nodded. "I have just seen to the arrangements. There is a rabbi among the prisoners....Hardly the sort of ceremony either of us ever expected, but it will have to do."

She was silent.

"How were you taken? Were you kidnapped in Jerusalem? Your uncle—"

"Dead. Uncle Shammai is dead."

"I'm sorry. Strange....Even though I knew he was ill and suffering, I never thought he would actually—I mean, he seemed so—" He broke off suddenly and frowned. "Why did you not stay with my father?" His expression changed to one of alarm. "My father, is he—"

"He is well. At least he was when I left Jerusalem. I was captured at Tarichea," she went on quickly, and then proceeded to tell him briefly of the events that had befallen her, carefully omitting her reasons for leaving the Holy City.

Josef shook his head in amazement. "You were foolish to leave Jerusalem," he chided her.

"But this is where I wanted to be. With you."

He stared at her, recalling now the girl in the priest's garden who had surprised him with her frankness. "Alexandra . . . our lives dangle on the whim of others, forfeit at any moment. I am a prisoner of war, and you are a slave. Vespasian has given you to me because for the moment it amuses him to do so. He may very well take you back tomorrow—or have us both killed."

"I do not think so. I do not think he is that kind of man."

"Perhaps not." He sighed. "But who can say?" He threw his hands up. "Anything can happen. Anything at all. Don't be fooled by tonight. Our position—yours and mine—is quite precarious."

She nodded. He was right, of course, but as there was nothing either of them could do about it—

"May I have something to drink?"

"What? Yes, certainly. I am sorry, I did not think. . . . How long has it been since you have eaten?"

"I don't want anything, thank you. Only some water . . ."

"There is wine in the corner there." He watched her move to the table, pour a small libation into a goblet, and sip at the wine. Her dark hair shone in the light of the oil lamp. She was not beautiful in the ordinary sense, but there was something about her. . . .

She turned, and her eyes met his above the cup.

The Roman was a fool to give her up, Josef thought. But, in fact, had he?

"Did they—were you . . . harmed?" he asked softly.

"No. I was not beaten."

"That is not what I meant."

"Oh. No. . . . No man has used me."

"In any way?"

"In any way."

"I am glad," he said truthfully. He took a step toward her, his hand raised to touch her hair, then stopped. Were they being watched? Were they, tonight, players in a vicious comedy Vespasian had devised, even as tomorrow—if indeed there was a tomorrow for them—their marriage would be an entertainment for the inhabitants of the Praetorium? No, the general was not a nefarious Nero. Still . . . he let his hand drop. "Tomorrow," Josef said loudly in the event that other ears besides the girl's were listening, "tomorrow, in accordance with our Mosaic Law, I shall make you my wife. As you know, it is the custom of our people that bride and groom do not see each other the night before their wedding. However, as we are powerless to alter our circumstances here, I shall pass the night in this corner of the room, and you must sleep over there, on that pallet. Even though we are prisoners of Rome," he declared rather theatrically, "let us not forget that we are children of Israel and members of the priestly class, which must be an example to all others. Though we were among barbarians— which, fortunately, we are not—we shall still not be barbarians ourselves."

He waited. Silence. The girl was staring wide-eyed at him. He put his fingers to his lips and motioned for her to return to the couch. Silently she obeyed, watching as he went about the room drawing aside the hangings, searching for some hith- erto unnoticed window or opening. Satisfied at last that they were unobserved, he sat down in a chair at the opposite end of the room, first filling the wine goblet, which he took with him.

She wanted to talk to him, but he seemed lost in thought, unaware even of her presence.

He looked up and saw her watching him. "Go to sleep," he said gently. "No harm will come to you tonight."

She was sure of that. Josef was with her, was he not? And tomorrow, tomorrow she would become his bride. All the years of wanting him, waiting for him, dreaming of this moment, pretending as a child she was his wife...

It was meant to be, she told herself, and would have told him as well. What did it matter where they were or what circumstances? They were together. Finally.

Happily, she drifted off to sleep, forgetting that she had wanted to ask him about the gold chains.

Her euphoria continued the next day, through the preparations for her wedding and through the ceremony itself. She let the female slaves of the palace bathe and perfume her, hardly hearing their coarse jokes regarding her future husband's prow- ess—"considering his having," the women giggled, "like all Jews do, a piece cut off." But when the rowdy group attempted to see if she was "also mutilated," she put aside her good humor in order to slap on one curious girl and silence the rest with a fierce, cold look. They left her alone after that.

As she walked to the white canopy under which Josef waited, she saw no one but him. How handsome he looked! How fine and proud! She did not hear the murmurs of her Greek and Roman audience or see the trembling of the poor rabbi before whom she and Josef stood. Another time she would not have failed to note the red, sullen faces of the four Galilean prisoners recruited to hold the poles of the wedding canopy, of Josef's tight-lipped, self-conscious air. But it was more than the veil topped with its wreath of myrtle that clouded her view.

In his guttural peasant accent, the rabbi stammered out the ancient Hebrew words that would bind her to Josef ben Matthias. The bridegroom raised her veil. She sipped the wine from the wedding cup. It was done. She was his wife. Behind them both lay shattered cities and unburied dead; but Alexandra did not hear the voice of any ghost on this, her wedding day. So completely had she wrapped herself in the cocoon of fantasy that she could sit smiling among her "wedding guests"—her enemies and captors—and not heed what they were saying.

"I thought there would be more," one lady murmured, disappointed. "It was too simple, too plain. I thought there would be dancing at the least—some wild, wonderful, wicked dance for their desert god. How disappointing."

"I am sure your wild, wicked dance will take place," her companion assured her. "But in private, my dear. The Jews are known for their intemperate nature, particularly in matters of sexual indulgence. Among foreigners, of course, they put on an appearance of chastity and aloofness and make a great show of refraining from intercourse with those outside their race, but among themselves anything is allowed—even between sister and brother."

"Really? How intriguing."

"I see your interest is rekindled. Well, I am told that many of our Roman ladies have thus been drawn to the faith of Israel, and the first lessons they learn are to despise the gods, renounce the government, and think nothing of parents, children, and brethren."

"Oh, dear."

"As for that charming fellow there"—he gestured toward

Josef, who was in earnest discussion with Vespasian—"why, he is the very scoundrel that caused the empress Poppea to declare herself a convert to the Jewish god. Need I tell you the powers of persuasion the man must possess if he could sway that insatiable lady?"

"Poppea?"

"Poppea. Why do you think this Josephus is treated so well?"

"But I thought Vespasian despised the royal family."

"He does." Undaunted, the Roman continued with new logic. "Perhaps the Jew serves his own."

"Whatever do you mean?"

"Titus and this Josephus are as close as, shall we say, brothers? Despite Titus's infatuation with the oriental princess—who has entertained the father as well—the boy has been known to play both sides of the coin."

"Well, but who does not these days?"

"Vespasian, for one. The man is incurably old-fashioned. Do you see the silver cup in his hand? It was his grandfather's. Comes from the farmhouse at Rieti where the general was raised by his grandmother. He takes it with him everywhere, as if—can you believe it?—he were proud of that rough Sabine background of his."

"Yes, but do you think he knows about Titus and the Jew? Perhaps that is why he has made the Jew take a wife!"

"Hmnn. I think from the look in his eye that he favors the girl himself—although he has the dreariest reputation for fidelity, first to his late wife Domitilla, and now to his mistress Caenis. Yes, I do believe from those looks he casts upon our bride that she may well spend her wedding night outside her husband's bed."

"What a scandal...."

"Hardly. After all, one must do something amusing in the suburbs."

They were back in his room. The narrow pallet had been removed in their absence, replaced by a wider bed covered with clean, soft linen. There was a bowl of fruit, and wine. She saw now that the chamber was not large but was comfortably furnished. There was even a writing table. It was hardly a place one would expect to be provided for a captive—unless, of course, the prisoner was an honored one. (Would Agrippa have been thrown into a dark cell?) After all, Josef had been governor of the Galilee and commander of Judea's northern army. And yet . . .

The delicate clink of the golden chain drew her from her thoughts. He had removed it from the bracelets on his wrists, let it fall from his fingers in a shining heap on the writing table.

Something was not right in all of this. Tomorrow . . . she must give it thought.

He was checking the door and walls again.

"Do you think they will spy on us?"

"No . . . I guess not. But I want to be sure." He frowned slightly. "I have had my fill of being an actor today. Let us trust that our hosts"—he gave the last word a wry twist—"have found other entertainments for now. I am sorry," he said solemnly, "that you were subject to this farce."

"Farce? Was the wedding not real?"

"Oh, yes, real enough. According to the Law of Moses and Israel, we are husband and wife. I meant . . . the circumstances. . . ."

"I . . . I do not mind."

He looked at her. She had behaved splendidly, he thought. Not a quiver or a tear, not a stammer or a blush to lessen their stature throughout the interminable evening. She had moved with regal grace, sat with quiet dignity—a trifle flushed perhaps, but composed withal. He remembered now that petite yet queenly woman whose fiery hair had enflamed his boyish passions. He had begun by wanting to charm the woman and had in fact been overwhelmed himself, so much so that he had been grateful when his ship set sail at last for Rome. His infatuation with maturity had been satiated at Caesar's court, and he had long ceased to harbor fantasies of older, experienced females. But now the image of the beautiful, unattainable Devorah came back to him, and he seemed to see her spirit in her daughter's eyes.

"You behaved well," he said. "At least Vespasion and that crowd know now how a true princess of Judea conducts herself."

Her face shone. "I wanted you to be proud."

He smiled.

Blushing, she turned away, suddenly busy with the fruit.

As always he made her shy, turned her back into a thin, gawky twelve-year-old who whispered secrets to the sea.

"Will you have some?"

"What? Ah, the fruit. No.... Some wine perhaps."

She filled the goblet and brought it to him. "There are apricots . . . and almonds. . . ."

"No." He took the goblet from her hand, but instead of drinking from it, he set it down and pulled her to him.

His face was close to hers; the dark ringlets on his brow were hers to touch now, the thin nose, his lips, the cleft chin hers to trace with a finger, but she dared not....

"Are you tired?" he asked.

"No...."

"And are you well?"

"Yes."

"That is good," he murmured, seeming perhaps to smile.

Now, she thought, now he will kiss me; and she waited for this, for the heavy gold of a long-ago memory to return, for the honey feeling, rising, melting....

But his lips merely brushed hers, passing swiftly to her neck and shoulder. Like points of flame his mouth touched her, now here, now there, moving on her skin like small burning wings. She closed her eyes; she felt dizzy....

He pulled her robe apart, drawing it down over her shoulders while he kissed her neck and then her breasts. She trembled with new, delicious fear.... But it was not what she had thought it would be. . . . Where was the golden honey feeling . . . that deep, blinding force lifting her out of herself?

She twisted her body so that her face was close to his again, and wound her arms around his neck, pressing her lips to his. She could feel the shock go through him, and then his hands tightened on her and his mouth overpowered hers. His tongue moved between her lips, then deeper....

It was strange what she felt, not at all like the memory of that long-ago kiss, which was perhaps, after all, only an embellished dream, something she had conjured up herself. No, this was different from what she had remembered or imagined. . . . It was different . . . strange and wonderful . . . and she wanted it. It was not the other.... But she wanted it.

Tentatively, she began to explore his mouth with her tongue, at the same time moving her hand along the back of his neck, up into the thick, curly hair.

Josef drew away a little. He studied her a moment and then smiled that strange half-smile of his. "Alexandra," he said softly, "you are full of surprises."

He was skilled in the ways of love, with a sensuous nature and a demonic energy that, unchecked by normal activity, vented itself now in the girl's willing body. She pleased him. Although generally drawn to a more voluptuous type, and with a decided preference for the fair hair and blue eyes that were admired throughout the Mediterranean, Josef had to admit his bride had a beauty distinctly her own. A man might pass over her at first, but his eyes would return and would not leave again. It was clear that Vespasian had been drawn to her immediately; and whether the general's attraction would prove to be an embarrassment or worse was still to be seen. Meanwhile, he had set out for Jericho, leaving the newlyweds to enjoy their union in virtual isolation.

How many men, Josef wondered, gazing at the girl in his arms, would guess at the passion behind those cool, intelligent eyes? She was eager for experience—perhaps too eager—drawn by a consuming hunger to know what the world and she herself were made of. It was a hunger Josef knew only too well. In Jerusalem, he might have viewed this characteristic of his wife less tolerantly; certainly he would have treated her differently. But now, here, they were both orphans, cut adrift from ties that had once regulated their lives and conditioned their attitudes. She was his wife, but in bed Josef did not treat her as if she were.

Had Alexandra been worldly enough to know this, her particular nature would probably have made her glad that she had come to him in the manner she had. As it was, not knowing men were likely to be different with their mistresses than they were with their wives, she was happy. After the initial pain and small shock at the extent of true intimacy, she was able to embark wholeheartedly on an exploration of pleasure that went beyond anything she had imagined people could do or feel. For once her curiosity was not unfed; and in the darkness of her nights with Josef she knew a freedom that in all other things had lain outside her grasp.

And yet it seemed to her that there was always something missing, something she could not even name, something she searched for but never found in Josef's embrace.

TWO

The stone facade of Beit Harsom was almost white in the glare of Caesarea's sun. The house had been built of Jerusalem stone transported at great cost from the Holy City. But Samuel ben Harsom had wanted his Devorah to have something of her beloved Jerusalem.

The villa had been gutted in the fire that swept across the Jewish quarter the night of the massacre, its furnishings and treasures taken or destroyed, its windowpanes of Phoenician glass broken; crystal slivers of pale blue and green still lay on the ground nearly two years later.

Alexandra stood silently before the quiet house. Through the open rusted gate she could see the courtyard, the flowers there all grown to weed. The fountain was quiet, its pool filled with old, stagnant rainwater and spotted leaves. The great sundial was mottled with bird droppings.

A dirty child peered out from behind the gate; Alexandra stared at her.

A woman came out of the house and into the courtyard. "What do you want?" she asked in a harsh voice, pushing the child behind her as she spoke. Then she saw the soldier with the girl and stepped back. "What is it? I've done nothing wrong."

The man, a member of the palace guard, put up his hand to reassure her. He turned to Alexandra. "There is nothing here for you. Come away."

Silently she followed him. Suddenly she stopped. There was a side entrance to the house leading directly to the street. She ran there now. Attached to the wooden support of the stone archway was a small metal rectangle blackened by fire. She clawed at the *mezuzah* but could not free it. As the soldier rushed up to her, she turned breathlessly to him.

"Please . . . please will you get it for me?"

He looked at her and then at the metal box nailed to the side of the door. He took out his knife, then hesitated. "What will you give me?"

She was taken aback. "I . . . I have only the market money."

"I don't want your money."

She stared at him, uncomprehending. Then her eyes turned to ice, cutting through him like the blade of the dagger in his hand. "I have nothing to give you," she said.

Angrily he sheathed the knife. "Then you will get nothing." He caught her arm as she swept past him. "Don't be so proud. If I say I caught you trying to run away, they will brand that pretty skin of yours. A kiss, on the other hand, leaves no mark."

"I was not running away."

"Your word, slave. Anyway, what do you want in the Jews' quarter? There are none of your kind here unless they are slaves like yourself. Do you imagine anyone in Caesarea would harbor the likes of you or take your word against mine?" He paused. "The thing on the door . . . what is it? Jew magic? Filled with enough poison, I wager, to kill everyone in the palace. What if I tell them that?"

"Tell them?" she said coolly. "Tell whom? I am not a palace slave. I am the wife of the prisoner Josef ben Matthias, who is held in great regard and is under the personal protection of your commander, Flavius Vespasian." She wrenched her arm away. "Be careful you do not incur the wrath of your own master." She walked a few steps away, then turned, waiting for him to follow. "Shall we return now? I believe I will feel safer in the Praetorium."

They had no sooner departed than a woman dressed in black appeared. She stared after the soldier and the girl; then, making sure no one was watching, she took out a knife and pried the *mezuzah* from the archpost. Hiding the object in her skirt, she hurried away.

Josef was at the writing table when the door to the chamber opened. A woman stood there, tray in hand. He looked up and frowned. "What is it? My wife prepares our meals. Vespasian has consented to this and given us separate utensils so that we may adhere to our dietary laws. Who has sent you? What have you got there?"

"Only fruit and some freshly made goat cheese, sir. I recall you were fond of it once, sir, during happier times for you in Caesarea."

Alexandra came out of the curtained alcove that served as their bedroom. She stared at the woman a moment, then ran to her. "Hagar!" She threw her arms around the servant's neck and hugged her like a child.

"Enough! Enough! You will break my neck," the Greek woman protested in mock anger. Sternly she held the girl away from her, but there were tears in her eyes. "Little fool," she said. "Why did you go to Jerusalem? Why did you leave Jerusalem?"

"For him," Alexandra replied simply.

"Little fool."

She had taken work in the palace to be near the girl. Being with Hagar brought Alexandra a rush of memories that were all the more devastating after seeing Beit Harsom again. But she was glad the woman was there, and not only because her presence made her feel less alone. Despite the relative comfort of her position, Alexandra had not given up the idea of escape. Hagar would help them find a way to get back to Jerusalem; Alexandra was sure of that. Before returning to the kitchen, the woman had pressed an object into the girl's hands. It was the *mezuzah* from Beit Harsom.

"We must nail it outside our door," she told Josef excitedly. "That way the Romans will know we have not forgotten who we are or where our loyalty lies."

"Are you mad?" he exclaimed. "Put that thing away before someone sees it."

"But—"

"Alexandra, this is no place for acts of childish defiance. By all that is holy, woman, have you no understanding of our position? Do you imagine, because I am not in a cell with other prisoners and you are not in slaves' quarters, that I am less a prisoner or that you are not a slave?"

"But that is exactly why—"

"Get rid of it," he said, pointing to the *mezuzah*. "I mean it." Then, seeing the look in her eyes, he went to her and took her in his arms. "Alexandra . . . I know how much it means to you, that this small piece of metal containing the Lord's commandments is all that is left of your father's house. But surely you do not wish—your father would not, I know—that this precious souvenir become a warrant for our death. Yes, yes, it could well be that. Alexandra..." He brushed her hair with his lips. "Obey me, for both our sakes.... Hide the *mezuzah*. You see? I do not ask you to give it up. Do not show it to anyone. And be careful how you speak to Hagar. She is at heart a Greek. One can never be sure...." He lifted her up and carried her to their bed. "My little Zealot," he said, smiling as he put her down on the already rumpled linen. "Here is where you belong. This is the place for that wild spirit of yours."

THREE

"Well, there it stood," Vespasian said, "in the middle of the desert. A complex of buildings spread over a terrace that jutted out from one of the cliffs. You would not have believed your eyes. Courtyards, cattle pens, assembly halls, pottery works— even a flour mill and bakery!" He shook his head in amazement as his assembled guests murmured their wonder. "A community of men, women, and children in the middle of . . . nothing," he said finally, searching for a way to describe the desert wilderness. "Working under that burning sun, living in the harshest of conditions, and evidently happy as larks to be just where they were! Cerealis here thought they were lepers— didn't you? Yes, a colony of lepers."

The Roman shrugged. "Who would live in such a place if not forced by society?"

"But they were clean!" Vespasian exclaimed triumphantly. "Weren't they, Cerealis? Not a mark on any of them. Clean, and dressed all in white. Some of the cloth was pretty shabby, but it was all clean and plain white."

"Who are they?" the lady Livia asked. "What are they?"

"Holy folk," Vespasian said with certainty. "That is, I imagine the people in these parts consider them holy, like that fellow—what's-his-name—who was going around dipping any who'd let him in the water."

"Oh, they must have been Christians, then. You know how strange they are."

"They were Essenes," Josef said quietly. "You are right, great Vespasian, they are a holy brotherhood. They are some-times called the Pious Ones or the Community of the Poor, but they refer to themselves as the Sons of Light. They are a profoundly spiritual sect, given, as you have seen, to an austere communal life, pledging themselves to love of God, love of virtue, and love of man."

Vespasian frowned. "Then . . . they are harmless?

Josef hesitated. "No," he said finally. "The Essenes have long spoken of war—the War of the Sons of Light with the Sons of Darkness. It is prophesied in their scrolls."

"The Sons of Darkness—that is what they called us! And *Kittem* or *Kittum*—something like that."

"The *Kittim*. It means 'the Triumphant Empire.' It is their name for Rome, which"—again he hesitated—"they regard as an evil nation. The nation of the Ungodly."

Vespasian seemed relieved to hear this. "Good," he said. "The gods have not been offended. Rome's enemies have been destroyed. It had bothered me that they might have been innocent of this rebellion and that therefore their extermination—a necessary precaution in any event—might mean bad luck. I am glad to learn my first instinct was correct. You see, Cerealis? They were a Zealot pack after all."

"I could have told you that by the way they fought," Cerealis replied. "Holy folk don't jump at you with such terrible cries, not even to protect their women and children. Holy folk die quietly, with a bit of singing perhaps. Haven't you ever seen the Christians in the arena? I don't hold with their philosophy, but certainly they know how to die. The way holy folk—if they are holy folk—ought to die, if you ask me."

"There was a scriptorium," Josef said, leaning forward anxiously, "and a library—"

"You mean the building full of rolled parchment and hides?" Cerealis asked.

"I had it burned," Vespasian said. "The writings were strange. Some of the scrolls contained what seemed to be drawings of human parts. The men feared their magic and requested that the place be put to the torch, along with everything in it. I gave the order. It is always better to leave a happy garrison."

Josef sighed. "There was magic there, but a beneficent sort. There is nothing in the property of the Essenes that concerns itself with harming man, only with healing. They are wonderful doctors, famous for their miraculous cures. There are some of them as well who can foretell the future."

"Hmmn. I think, Josephus, from now on you shall accompany me wherever I go so that stupid mistakes like this one shall not occur again. In the future you must point out what treasures are to be spared. Especially when we go to Jerusalem."

"When do you expect to take the Holy City?" Josef asked. They were alone now, the others having taken their leave or been dismissed.

"I don't know. Word has come that a revolt against Nero has started up in Gaul. I shall wait here in Caesarea until the outcome is known. The delay is of little account, and my men can use the rest. I am told by my informers that Jerusalem is split by dissension and already at war against itself." He studied his Jewish prisoner's face; there was no change of expression. "It would seem your people have taken to doing my job for me. Perhaps I should leave the generalship of this campaign to your Hebrew God."

Josef was silent.

"Tell me more of these Essenes . . . these Sons of Light. . . . You seem to know them well. What do they do for water? They do not inhabit an oasis, and the lake nearby is unfit for anything. By the gods! What a strange body of water—if water it is. Changing color with the hours, throwing up black lumps of asphalt as big as bulls—"

"That is why the Greeks named it Lake Asphaltitis."

"Yes, well, I like your name for it better. The Dead Sea. It is so bitter I cannot see any living thing existing in it or any man able to drink from it. On the other hand, nothing can drown in it. I was told that the water's lightness would bring to the surface even the heaviest objects thrown in. Accordingly, I had some prisoners we took in Jericho cast in with their hands tied behind them."

Alexandra, who was also present, albeit forgotten by the two men, looked up at this, her startled eyes the same gray as the sea of which Vespasian spoke.

"By Mars!" The general slapped his knee. "Every one of the lot came to the surface as if blown upwards by a strong wind! No matter where we threw them in, they floated. Damnedest bunch of poor fish I ever saw. Some of them were screaming in pain as the water's salt went into their wounds." He caught sight of the young woman now. She was not looking at him but staring down at the floor, her fists clenched. His eye traveled up the length of her arm, rested on the small shoulder, took in the shining cap of hair.

"There is an aqueduct," Josef was saying, "that brings rain-water down from the highlands to supply the Essene settlement you chanced upon. It is cut through solid rock part of the way. I believe it was engineered with the help of the Nabateans—or at least through knowledge of that people's skill. As you may have noted, Qumran has quite a complicated system of cisterns, conduits, and tanks. Frequent ablutions, baths, and ceremonial purification are an important part of the brothers' regime."

"And sisters? There were women and children there—not so many females, hardly enough to go around—but a fair amount of children, again mostly male."

"The Essenes regard woman as a lascivious creature who would turn man away from the study of God and enslave him to lust and familial duties. Most do not marry. When they do, it is not for sexual pleasure but only for procreation, to continue the community. The brothers consider pleasure-seeking a vice and regard mastery of the passions as the highest virtue."

"Hmmn. I should imagine that lessens their appeal for many."

"On the contrary. Despite their strict tenets they draw many votarists, and because they own nothing individually but are pledged to care for all, their settlements are havens for orphans and children of the poor. Not all the young whom they train become brothers," he added. "I myself was their student."

"You!"

"I was sixteen." Josef smiled. "Ripe for revelation."

"How long were you with these Sons of Light?"

"Three years, taking into account the time I spent with Banus. A holy man who lived apart from the others," he explained. "One of their Righteous Teachers."

"And what sort of revelation did you come by through this experience," the Roman wanted to know.

"That I have little taste for the life of a desert ascetic," Josef replied.

"No, I do not expect you do," Vespasian commented with that wry scowl that passed for a grin. His eyes returned to Alexandra. "I daresay your confinement during my absence was not without its attendant consolations. Did the slave dealer lie?"

"Lie?"

"Was she a virgin?"

"Yes . . . yes, she was."

"And now?"

"Alexandra is, as you wished, my wife."

"And you, little one . . . are you happy?"

She looked up, startled by the question. Was he scowling or smiling?

"We are both grateful for your benevolence and your protection," Josef replied before she could say anything. "This inherent magnanimity will win the love of all Rome when you are Caesar."

"You go on with that, do you?"

"It is written in the stars now, but soon it will be recorded in the scrolls of history. You said yourself the tide is turning against Nero. 'Out of the East a man shall come to rule the world.' That man is you."

"Written in the stars, eh? I must tell you I have a loathing of fortune-tellers. And yet . . . I myself had a dream. . . . It was in Greece, just before I came here to Judea. . . . I dreamed my family would prosper from the moment when Nero lost a tooth. Ridiculous, eh? But on the following day, I was in the imperial quarters—and damn me if a dentist did not enter and show me one of Nero's teeth, which he had just extracted!"

"There is truth in dreams."

"Perhaps, perhaps. . . ." The man laughed self-consciously. "My father, you know, was always convinced a great fortune lay before me. There is an ancient oak tree—it is sacred to Mars—on the family estate outside Rome. Each time my mother was brought to bed with child this tree would put out a shoot. The first withered quickly, and likewise, the first child—a girl—died within the year. The second shoot was long and healthy, promising good luck. But the third shoot—mine—seemed, I am told, more like a tree than a branch. My father, Flavius Sabinus, observing other omens as well, went to my grandmother and said, 'Congratulations! You have a grandson who is going to become emperor!' And my grandmother said, 'Congratulations to you too—for going soft in the head before your old mother!'"

Josef laughed with him. "A formidable woman."

"Formidable? The best. The best of women. Raised me as the son of a Sabine should be raised." He sighed. "Women like that are rare these days. At least they are in Rome. I confess, this Judean campaign has revealed to me a type of female I thought no longer existed. Mothers and daughters braver than women have a right to be." He was studying the Jewish girl again. "And beautiful besides.... Hardly in keeping with the image one generally has, particularly abroad, of the people here. One does not expect to find heroes and heroines among Jews."

"It is said that the measure of one's courage may be found in the dimensions of one's enemy. Do you find it strange, great Vespasian, that of all the countries which Rome has placed under its 'protection,' only Judea—the frailest, the smallest, certainly the poorest, with no organized army, no great war machine—has dared to challenge the conqueror of the world? Perhaps we are not so mean as some would think."

"Oh, I have a fair enough opinion of you people," Vespasian replied. "I told you, I never underestimate the enemy. And I know you are not cowards. But you are fools. And worse, bad soldiers, reckless and undisciplined. You make too much of your victories. But your fire is quickly put out by the smallest setback. A first-class soldier never lets success go to his head. That is why failure never gets him down." He pointed a finger at Josef. "Your strategy at Jotapata was fine, fine. But you could not have beaten us, not with that rabble under your command. It seems to me there were times when they must have given you more trouble than my legions did—especially those suicidal maniacs at the end."

Josef laughed ruefully. "As you say, we are not organized. Inspired. But not . . . organized."

"Battles are not won by emotion," Vespasian said grimly. "They are won by efficiency and discipline. Well . . ." He yawned. "The whole business strikes me as being without reason. As far as I can see, Rome has treated you people well enough. Nobody's bothered your priests and precious Temple. You haven't been asked to sacrifice to the gods or to forfeit your own. Why, Judea is the only province in the entire empire where statues of Caesar have not been set up for worship! And now to start this thing, a war you cannot possibly win!" He shook his head disgustedly. "Personally, I have no great enmity toward you Jews. You seem decent enough to me, clean, respecting your parents, et cetera—I like that. But you can't seem to get it into your heads that to challenge the government is to invite disaster upon yourselves—along with anyone else who disturbs the order we have been at such pains to establish. And this disaster will be with the consent of the empire—and that is the world. The world is not with you. The world wants peace. Roman peace. The world wants order. Well . . . this thing is not our doing. You people will have to answer to yourselves for your own destruction."

"Men do not undertake war without reason, particularly one as desperate as this. You must imagine what the people of Judea have endured—"

"What? That little bastard Gessius Florus? You declare war on Caesar because of one rotten egg? Come, come. . . . If it was not one thing it would be another. Your history says as much. You Jews are never happy. And damned if I understand why. With the beautiful women you have . . ."

Josef spread his hands and smiled his crooked smile. "Perhaps it is our women who turn us troublesome."

Vespasian laughed. "There you have it! Keep you hopping, do they? Well, maybe we ought to import a few more ladies from Rome. Let them teach your females how to keep you quiet." He laughed again. "There you have it! We've finally found a way to end this damned war!"

"I am sure your Roman ladies would teach us fine manners," Alexandra said. "Why, in no time at all there would not be a woman in Judea who was not false to her husband."

There was silence in the room. Vespasian scowled. "You are bold, mistress."

"You have taken my home from me, my family, my country, my freedom. Boldness is all I have left."

Josef started to say something, but Vespasian waved him silent. He looked at the girl a long time. Then he said quietly, "I am not a monster, young woman. I am a soldier and a citizen of Rome. And your people have chosen to make war upon my government. This was not our doing. As for your family . . . I know something of your case. Your father was one Samuel of the House of Harsom. I have been informed that he was friendly to Caesar's representatives and that Rome bore him no ill will. In fact, your family was under the procurator's protection. That is why you have been given in marriage to Josephus and not made common use of. I speak plainly, girl." His eyes bored steadily into her, but with no hint of cruelty. "Your father was an honest and a reasonable man who tried to keep the peace. I respect that. And your family was not destroyed by Rome but by the citizens of Caesarea. An unfortunate occurrence. You have my sympathy." He stood up and clapped Josef on the shoulder. "We will talk more. . . . I like to learn as much as I can about those I must battle. Now, you Jews puzzle me. I confess it. You can be the most logical people, the most realistic, and yet...I confess, you puzzle me. But your women..." He laughed ruefully. "I think I am too generous; it can be a fault....Well, we shall see how generous you will be to me." He nodded in Alexandra's direction. "She has spirit. I like that. Well, good night." And he was gone.

He wants her, Josef thought. *Why is he waiting? Why hasn't he summoned her to his bed? Is he taking this marriage seriously?*

He looked at the sleeping girl illuminated by moonlight.

He wants you. . . . But in what way? . . . As mistress? Or daughter?

Vespasian was a farmer at heart, descended from that old Roman stock the poet Horace called "a manly breed of yeoman-soldiers, taught to turn the stubborn earth with Sabine mattocks and to carry cut logs at the bidding of a stern mother." That was Vespasian, all right—a man of simple tastes, adhering to an old and highly moral code, with a sense of honor and duty that kept him faithful to Caesar despite the fact that he despised Nero.

But would his sense of decency extend itself to prisoners and slaves? He had cast bound men into the Dead Sea to see if they would float, apparently without a thought to the possibility of their drowning. He had enjoyed the attentions of the princess Berenice without caring that Agrippa might be offended. Why would he hesitate to take Alexandra?

It was already whispered that the Jewish prisoner and his "bride" were house pets of the general and his son. To make matters even more intriguing, Vespasian had had a document of marriage *sine in manum conuentione* drawn up for Josef and Alexandra. A Roman bride given *in manum*, or "into the hand," of her husband left behind all family authority. But a marriage contracted "without entering the husband's authority" meant the woman remained under the authority of her father or legal guardian. In which case, Josef mused, the husband had no rights to her property.

That was it. Vespasian had discovered the fortune Alexandra was heir to and declared himself not her owner—if she was a slave she possessed nothing—but her guardian. There was nothing to indicate Samuel ben Harsom had been an enemy of Rome, for there was no record of his brief imprisonment by

Gessius Florus; had the man lived he would undoubtedly have joined those other wealthy Jews who fled to Agrippa or to Rome's protection. Therefore, Vespasian could present the proper documents to the courts in Rome and lay claim to all property and goods belonging to the girl—which, in Italy as well as in Greece, Egypt, and Africa, were considerable. Despite the war, Samuel's businesses outside Judea had not been confiscated, for in his lifetime the man had been honored with the Roman title of knight.

So it was money that had brought them this consideration.

No, there was something more....

It had something to do with the grandmother at Rieti. And possibly something to do with Alexandra's rather interesting personality, which had obviously had an effect on the Roman. Who would have thought that Flavius Vespasian, commander of the Roman legions in Judea, conqueror of Gaul and Britain, and quite possibly the next emperor of Rome, was a man subject to the powers of woman?

Or was he waiting for Josef to send Alexandra to him?

The legions rested from their labors. In addition to the Galilee, Emmaus and Samaria had been occupied, and all Perea crushed as far as Machaerus. Jerusalem was still to be taken, but meanwhile that city had its hands full with warring Zealot factions and class revolution. Even as Vespasian waited for the fortunes of Rome to be played out across the sea, escapees from Jerusalem found their way to Caesarea, eager to tell their tales of terror at the hands of Judea's "Army of the Poor."

Meanwhile, life in the seaside Hellenic center continued as it always had, except now there were no hated Jews sitting on the city council or living in finer homes than the rest of the populace—or in fact anywhere, unless they were slaves or beggars or prisoners of war being used for city labor. Filled with red-cloaked soldiers and officers and their families, Caesarea began to resemble Rome even more. The theater and the arena were filled daily; the shops did fine business, and the brothels ever better. Combat was waged in the arena from morning to evening, with the legionaries obsessively following and betting on their favorite charioteers.

"For us, Jerusalem is the most beautiful of cities," Josef remarked. He was following Vespasian through the crowded market as they made their way to the theater. "But I am sure there are many who consider Caesarea the finest place in Judea."

"It is more to our taste," Vespasian agreed. "Although I have only seen your Jerusalem from a distance." He looked around him. "If one did not know better, one might think oneself in Rome or Greece." He pointed to a figure of Artemis. "That statue, for example. I thought you Jews forbade the setting up of images."

"We do. But it has been said that the first Agrippa, who embellished Caesarea even more than Herod did, was a Jew in Jerusalem and a Greek everywhere else. To demonstrate his fondness for art he even had statues made of his three daughters—including one of Berenice, which used to stand here. He loved this city. In fact, he even took part in theatricals here, and it was during one of these that he was struck dead in his mask of gold—By the Lord, the rabbis said, for his blasphemous conduct. More likely he was poisoned by one of his enemies."

"He was not liked?"

"Neither in Jerusalem nor in Caesarea, despite his attempts to please both. When it was learned that he was dead, some soldiers here took the statues of his daughters up to the roof of one of Caesarea's best-known brothels and pretended to have sex with the figures—before a loudly appreciative audience, I am told." He took his seat. "I thank you for your kindness in allowing me to join you today. It has been a long time since I enjoyed the pleasures of theater as I was fortunate enough to do in Rome."

"I am also fond of the drama—although one is hard put to find the Greek classics played anywhere today. I do not care much for the modern writers—they are too much given to sensationalism and violence, or to comedy of the grossest nature, with no redeeming wit. That reminds me . . . a friend of yours has arrived here. An actor. One Aliterus."

He was a large man—a mountain of a man—but nimble as a dancer, with small hands and feet that seemed to be always in motion. The jowly face was dominated by eyes that appeared ready to leap from their sockets, the bare brow embellished with two question marks of hair brought forward from the sparse crop at the back of his skull. He had a number of chins and a mouth of pure elastic that stretched anywhere from grin to grimace with infinite nuances and exaggerations. He was the Roman actor Aliterus, born a Jew and a slave, risen to wealth and popular acclaim by virtue of his comic genius. Friend of Nero and Poppea, he was the one who had brought the young Jerusalemite Josef ben Matthias into the inner circle of the imperial court.

He was in top form as Josef entered the room and had already reduced Alexandra to gales of laughter. Even Hagar's lips were twitching. "I'll have you know a comedian's training is a strict tradition," the actor was expounding. "There is more skill to be learned there than any mime will ever know, even though those little rosebuds are so glorified. Why, an actor must learn correctness of expression"—fury, pain, and ecstasy sped across the man's countenance with lightning speed—"Apt delivery. Modulation of voice. Deportment. And the play of eye and hand," he added, illustrating each in turn. "You laugh, do you? Look, I will show you.... For example, the pace of walking must follow the nature of the role—slower for old men, soldiers, and married women ... and quicker for slaves, maidservants, and fishermen." Having executed the appropriate movements to perfection, he sat down with a flourish. "So you see, we actors take our parts seriously. In fact, after a particularly affecting scene I have often left the stage weeping myself."

"Unlike the audience," Josef said, "unless theirs were tears of laughter. For there is no greater source of merriment in all the world than you possess, you great rhinoceros!"

"Josef ben Matthias! Soul's delight!" The actor swallowed the man up in a gargantuan embrace. "So! Here we are again! Together in the sacred land of our Fathers! When are we going to see the Temple? How far to Jerusalem? That's a pretty piece of jewelry," he said, noting the golden chains. "A new fashion? Doesn't it get in the way?"

"Not if you know magic," Josef replied. "Watch!" A wave of the hand, and the chains fell from their bracelets.

"Good boy! You remember the tricks Alcibides taught you. He said you had the gift, that your fingers were as nimble as that evil brain of yours."

"Never mind Alcibides. What are you doing here?"

"You are not pleased to see me?"

"Pleased?" He grew serious. "You have come to a theater of war, friend, a place where a Jew's life is worth less than a piece of cheese. Why have you left the Imperial City? And why, in the name of all that is holy, have you come here?"

Aliterus shrugged elaborately, his eyes rolling upwards. "What shall I do in Rome? I am not good at lying—I haven't the wit. I don't know how to read the stars. And I am not skilled enough to hire out as an assassin for some young puppy who would like his father knocked off. Anyway...I have always had a preference for tragedy. There is not a manager in Rome, however, who will let me play a hero's part—the shortsighted, money-hungry buggers! And I had to spread my wings—artistically, that is. Well, the place for that is far from the critic's eye."

Josef raised an eyebrow, exchanging a quick glance with Alexandra, who was listening in utter fascination. "You consider Judea an out-of-town tryout for your talent? Aliterus, no more of this absurdity, I beg you. You see my own position—"

"Not so bad as you might imagine. Titus is on your side. And Vespasian knows you acted without choice, that to do less than you did would have been dishonorable. He would care less for you, believe me, if you had not fought as well and as long as you did. And when the time is proper—"

"But why are you here?"

Aliterus grew solemn, but even now his expression seemed a comic exaggeration of gravity and sorrow. "Caesar has lost his love for actors. Paris is dead, and I assure you I was next on the monster's list. I do not think Nero has many days left himself, but his enemies despise those who were in his favor as much as they hate the emperor. The situation is quite mad. I was surrounded, I tell you. It was a pure case of Scylla and Charybdis—and I am no sailor as Odysseus was, although it seems I have begun my wandering....So I said to myself, 'Aliterus'—even I call myself that, you see—" he said in a low aside to Alexandra, who was smiling again. "Illustrious Star." He spread his hands modestly. "It seems you are in danger of being plucked from the heavens by everyone around. It is time to make an exit—a simple one, no applause necessary."

Josef did not laugh. "But to come to Judea! Haven't you heard, man? There is a war—"

"You would not know that in Rome." The actor shrugged. "You are party to a provincial rebellion, in case you did not realize. I do not believe even the Senate is aware how many men Rome has sent to put down this 'little insurrection'—or how many legionaries have already been lost."

"How can that be? When I was in the Imperial City—"

"You were at court, dear Josephus. We are speaking now of what the general populace has been told and what they can bring themselves to believe." He shrugged again. "Judea is not the first topic of conversation in Rome these days."

"No . . . I don't suppose it would be," Josef said with some bitterness. For a moment, Jotapata had come back to him, those dry, dirty days filled with death and fighting. "But surely you knew," he pressed the actor. "And yet you came—"

"It was not my doing," Aliterus admitted finally. There was a strange look on his face. "Fate . . . or perhaps your Hebrew God has had a Hand in this. . . . We will talk of it later. Not now . . . not now." And that was all he would say.

FOUR

She stretched luxuriously, turned, and saw that she was alone in bed. Puzzled, she sat up. "Josef?" No answer. She sank down under the coverlet again and waited. Silence. He was gone. Where? Had Vespasian summoned him? Was he off with Nicanor, or Titus again? She pulled the sheet over her head. There was a strong, earthy smell in the darkness, the pungent odor of a man and a woman and the sea inside them. She threw the covering aside and sprang from the bed, shivering as her feet touched the tile floor. She wanted a bath. And something to eat. But later, clean and fed, when he had not yet returned, she grew restless and began to pace the room anxiously.

She had free access of a kind within the palace, but the place was not without danger for her. There was so much intrigue going on; everyone and everything was the cause and carrier of gossip. None of it was to her taste. Even the classic beauty of the building held little allure for her, not with the ocean at once so near and so far, beckoning and always beyond her grasp. What fools the Romans were, she thought, to build so many pools with all that water nearby. Shutting themselves away from the wind and sun, preferring the feel of cold tile and marble to warm, soft sand. Well, at least the Romans were clean. Certainly they spent enough time in their baths, although Aliterus had hinted that other things went on in those bathing pools. What? What could they do with no women there? Unless they brought in slave girls . . . or boys. Aliterus had spoken of boys. But what could men do with boys? Probably all they did was sit around and talk about who was sleeping with whom or which gladiator had the biggest muscles and which charioteer the best team. What fools these generals seemed to be. How could they have conquered the world unless everyone else was an even bigger fool?

Vespasian, however, was different. Alexandra was finding

it hard, despite her position, not to admire the man. He seemed so much more sensible than those around him. He had a great love for making jokes, even at his own expense, and his wit was not bad—although, she thought with a smile, he made the most dreadful puns. Sometimes it seemed that she was the only one who caught on to his deliberate misquotes. Once he had remarked, hearing her laugh while everyone else looked puzzled, "To think I had to come all the way to Judea to find someone who understands Aeschylus as well as I." She shook her head now, smiling at the memory. Vespasian was someone her own father—her mother—would have liked.

Her father and mother. Her family. The days at Beit Harsom . . . Jerusalem . . . Tarichea. . . . It all seemed so far away now, as if nothing existed but this sheltered palace life and her hours with Josef. The war was so distant. Was it still going on? Was it real? Was she still Alexandra bat Harsom? Or . . . something else? What was she? Who was she?

Her eyes rested on a wax tablet and stylus lying on the writing table. Vespasian had begun to allow Josef to go among the prisoners seeking out those who might be friends or possess valuable knowledge. In this way Josef had been able to obtain medical attention for some men who had become sick and to win respite from the cross for others whom he knew. It made Alexandra proud to think that despite his own imprisonment Josef still served his country. The gold fetters no longer disturbed her; she ascribed them to vicious humor on the part of their captors. Josef could easily break those chains; but if he did, where then could he go? The chains were a symbol of his captivity, less real than what they represented, perhaps, but painful all the same. As for Titus's affection, Josef had told her of their friendship in Rome before the Judean revolt. "He hates this war as much as I," Josef had said. "His only wish is for peace. A world at peace."

She sighed. Half the day was gone, and Josef still had not returned. Where could he be? Where was Hagar? Aliterus? She determined to seek them out, to find somebody to talk to, at any rate. Suddenly she had an idea. Grabbing up the wax tablet and stylus, she hurried down the hall searching for an entrance or stairway that would lead below the building to the cellar dungeons where the prisoners were kept.

A guard stopped her. "Where are you going?"

She held up her tablet. "I must bring this to Josef ben Matthias. He is questioning the prisoners."

"Who?"

"It's all right," another guard said. "It's the general's Jew she means. Let her go."

He hesitated, then let her pass, saying something in a low voice to the other. She could hear them both laughing as she made her way down the stone steps leading to the underground cells. Daylight disappeared, the air became cold and clammy; it smelled of pus and urine and vomit.

The cages were crowded, although most of the men taken in the Galilee had already been disposed of, shipped off to Corinth to work on Nero's canal or given to the allied kings in reward for their loyalty. Still, as Licinius Mucianus had been heard to remark, there seemed to be an unending supply of Judean "meat," and if things kept up, the slave market was bound to be glutted. "You would think that after Jotapata, Tarichea, Gischala, and all the rest, these people would be sensible and quit their mad war. Yet still the Jews persist. They seem determined to fight until there is not an able-bodied man left to lift a sword."

Slowly Alexandra passed among the ragged mass of her countrymen. Whatever she had come to do or see was completely wiped out of mind now. Earlier she had wondered if the war was real. She knew now that it was.

She felt a tugging at her skirt. She jumped.

"Water . . . miss, please . . . can you bring some water?"

"I . . . I'll try . . . yes . . . yes, of course."

She ran from the place, sped up the stairs and through the hall until, breathless and faint, she was leaning against the door to her room. Trembling, she pushed the door open, entered the simple but comfortable apartment. Somewhere during her flight she had dropped the writing tablet and stylus. She would have to go back. . . .

The room was empty, quiet. Sunlight poured in through the high-set window. There was a bowl of figs on the writing table.

She closed her eyes. "Forgive me," she whispered. "Forgive me . . . for having forgotten."

She went back, taking a pitcher of water and the figs, which she wrapped in a square of linen, thinking even as she did how stupid it was to bring so little to so many.

They pressed around her now, their iron fetters scraping and clanking, the sound mingling with their murmurs. She did not know who took the water or the fruit; both were gone in an instant. "I'm sorry I have no more," she apologized. "I did not realize—I will try to bring more. Tell me what you need."

"She speaks the tongue of Judea," one of the prisoners said. "You are a Roman?" he asked her.

"No, no, I am Judean. I am a Jew." She went up to the man. "Who are you? Where do you come from? Is there anything I can bring you?"

"You always did enjoy giving handouts," a voice said with a bitter laugh. "Bring? Bring us freedom. Bring us that if you can."

She spun around. "Who are you? Who spoke? Do I know you?"

A young man pushed forward. "Know me?" he repeated. "I doubt you would remember, daughter of Samuel ben Harsom. You never cared much for poor Galileans, though you ate my mother's soup quick enough and pretended to be friendly to my sisters."

She looked deeply into his eyes, desperate to remember. "Aaron!" she exclaimed. "You are Avram's son . . . from Bersabe!"

"So you do know me."

"Of course, of course! When were you taken? How long have you been here? Your father—"

"My father is dead. Too late he learned I was right."

"I'm sorry," she whispered. "Your mother? Mary?"

"I don't know. Fled with the others. Or killed. Or . . . taken and sold for slaves."

"I am a slave," she said, almost eagerly.

"You?" He stared at her, incredulous.

"I was taken at Tarichea and sold to Vespasian. All my family are dead," she added.

"Good," he said. "I mean, it is better that they do not know what you have become."

"Oh, no, it is not what you think. Truly the Lord has looked after me. I don't know why, but He has. Vespasian gave me away to Josef ben Matthias. So you see, I have not dishonored my family or our people. We were wed according to the Law, and although Josef is the Roman's prisoner—"

But his eyes had narrowed. "You are married to Josef ben Matthias? Commander of the Galilean forces? The one at Jotapata?"

"Yes! Yes, the very one! Josef is here, Aaron! Don't you

see? He will save us! All of us! I will tell him you are here—"

"Save us?" He uttered a short, ugly laugh. "That traitor? He would as soon help any here as kiss a corpse."

"What are you saying? No, no, you misunderstand. I speak of Josef—"

"Ben Matthias. I know of whom you speak. His own family has cast him out, declaring him dead. He has betrayed all of us. Even now he continues his treason."

"He is a prisoner!"

"Prisoners are down here," another man put in. He jerked his thumb upwards. "Not up there."

"You . . . Elijah. . . ." Aaron called the man over. "You know what happened at Jotapata. Tell her."

"Yes, I know what happened. . . ." The man came forward, stared at Alexandra a bit, and said, "After the town was taken, your general from Jerusalem hid with a bunch of his rich friends in a cozy cave while everyone else was being put to the sword or locked up in chains. But he decided to let the Romans know where he was after learning that they planned to make him king of Judea." He let the others have their laugh at this, then continued. "Well, maybe not that, but he knew he had nothing to fear from Rome. And when the legionaries found his hiding place they just helped him out friendly as can be—and killed everyone else there so no one could say he had plotted the whole thing. Only . . . one of the people the soldiers left for dead wasn't, although she died soon after. She crawled off a ways, and our raiding party found her. She told us what happened."

"It isn't true!" Alexandra cried. "Josef told me what happened. They made a pact to kill themselves before the Romans got to them, and they drew lots so that only one would be left at the end with the sin of suicide. The Lord willed Josef and one other remained, but the man, thinking to get a reward, turned him over to Vespasian."

"Bullshit," Elijah said, and turned away.

"It isn't true, Aaron! I know it isn't true!"

"Josef ben Matthias has been publicly declared a traitor," Aaron replied. "The council in Jerusalem—his own friends, his own father—has done this. Everyone knows he went willingly to the Romans."

"Then why is he in chains? Why is he not permitted to leave the palace or even his quarters without a guard? Why does he try in every way to persuade Vespasian of the rightness of our cause and the truth of our beliefs? If you only knew what these Romans think of us, what lies they tell each other! If Josef did not teach Vespasian otherwise, the man would surely believe that we are monsters. Oh, Aaron, you are wrong! All of you are wrong! Josef has not betrayed us! I know he has not! Look," she continued in a low voice, "I think I know what he is about. I have heard the questions he puts to Vespasian and Titus, the things he asks. . . . He is just waiting for the right moment, Aaron. I am sure of it. He is learning their plans, and soon, very soon, he will engineer an escape and return to Jerusalem. And he will find a way to set all of us free. Why else would he ask permission to go among the prisoners as he does? It's a signal. A sign to let you know he is here, that he is one of you."

"He has told you this?" Aaron was unsure now. She seemed so certain. He had always thought her spoiled and selfish, but he knew she was not one to lie. And Jotapata had held out for so long, longer than anyone had believed possible. Could the man responsible for such a triumph, limited though it was, throw that glory away? He sighed. He was so desperate he would believe anything now, and the looks on the faces of his companions mirrored his own feelings. It was better to believe in the crazy hope the girl held out than to dismiss utterly the possibility of freedom.

"He has not spoken of this to me," Alexandra admitted. "But I know him. I know it is what he is thinking and planning. Everything he does and says makes his intention clear."

"What's going on?" One of the guards pushed through the small crowd gathered around the girl. "Planning a revolt?" he asked mildly. "Or a little entertainment? Who the hell are you?"

"One of your spies," Aaron said loudly. "You think you can send someone to remind us of our sisters and wives, that we will grow soft and tell you everything you want to know— Get her out of here!"

"Come, miss." The guard took her by the arm. "You had better come away before these animals get ugly. Jews have no respect for women."

She allowed him to lead her away but managed to look back and saw Aaron nodding at her, his eyes signaling his newfound hope.

• • •

"You must talk to them! You must tell them they are wrong! I know it is dangerous, but you must let them know you have not abandoned our people!"

"Who? What? What are you talking about?"

She sighed in exasperation. "You haven't heard anything I've said. Why are you so preoccupied? Josef, please. . . . I spoke to some of the prisoners today. They think you are a traitor. They say you betrayed them at Jotapata. And everyone in Jerusalem believes it as well, even your father!"

His face paled. His eyes burned dark and dangerous. "Who told you this?"

"I told you . . . I went among the prisoners. I know one of them. He is—"

"You what?" He grabbed her arms. "Why did you go there? Are you mad? What did you hope to find? What were you looking for?"

"I don't know. I was lonely. I wanted to be with my own kind—"

"They are your kind? Rabble and riffraff?"

"They are Judeans!" She was shocked. "Soldiers fighting for our country's freedom!"

He said nothing, his mouth a tight, grim line. Suddenly he let her go and turned away.

She stood there, confused, rubbing her arm where he had gripped it. "They . . . they said—"

"I know what they said . . . or I can guess." He clenched his fists. "Did you know," he said bitterly, "when it was thought that I had died in Jotapata, I was loved as I had never been in life? I am told that for a whole month the wailing never stopped in Jerusalem. It seems, however, when it was discovered that I had not been scourged and crucified or tortured in any way, my head cut off—or, at the very least, that I had not fallen on my sword in honorable defeat—why, then I was reviled as a coward and a traitor! As if . . . as if my death . . . would have meant something more than a moment in time. My own family lit candles," he continued, "and my father said the prayer for the dead, casting me out of his life forever. So much," he concluded in a choked, angry voice, "so much for the love of . . . Jerusalem."

"Then you must tell them—"

"I will tell them nothing! I do not excuse myself, ever! Excuses are weakening."

She admired his pride; she understood it. "Well," she said

softly, touching his back, "perhaps there is no need for you to say anything. I spoke with the men. I told them what is in your heart. I am sure they believed me. Aaron knows I would not lie."

He turned back to her, his burning eyes boring deeply into hers. "What did you say? Tell me, Alexandra. What did you say to them?"

"I told them you were not a traitor, that you are only here to spy on the Romans. I said you had a plan—you have not spoken of it, but I know you do, Josef! I know it!"

He walked to the writing table and sat down. "What else?"

"I told them you would find a way to free them. Oh, Josef, it gave them such hope! If only you could have seen their faces!"

He was silent a moment. Then: "To whom did you say this?"

"I spoke with Aaron—he is the son of my father's old friend Avram. A few of the others heard us, but I am sure Aaron has told them all by now."

"You little fool. You stupid, meddling little fool. You are not to go near the prisoners again, do you understand? You are not to speak to any of them, especially this Aaron. If the guards should hear you or get wind of this..." He was pacing up and down now. "I have enough enemies in this place without your adding fuel to their schemes against me. If Vespasian thinks I am a spy... well, in the end it would be this Aaron's word against mine, and who is he? I can always count on Titus, and yet..."

She stared at him, too stunned to move. It was true... the things the prisoners had said . . . those terrible things. . . . But it couldn't be. It couldn't be. . . . "What . . . what happened in Jotapata?" she asked faintly.

"I told you what happened in Jotapata."

"You said the Lord saved you."

He uttered a short laugh. "Well, didn't He?"

She sat down, gripping the side of the writing table like a shipwrecked sailor hanging on to a raft in the midst of a whirling sea. "I said it was a trick... that you were waiting, learning Vespasian's plans. . . . I told them . . . you would find a way to escape from here . . . return to Jerusalem . . . lead us to victory." The words choked her. Tears began to fill her eyes, but she forced them back. "I thought... I thought—what does it matter now what I thought?" she asked angrily. "I only

despise myself more when I think how I believed you, how
I . . . adored you. . . . *Josephus*."

"You have been with me nearly a year," he said calmly.
"Surely you have realized long before this moment that I am
a prisoner in name more than fact."

"I did not believe it. I thought it was a trick. I thought you
only pretended this friendship with Titus and Vespasian."

"I have always admired Rome—even as your own father
did. Surely you knew that. It was he who first said Judea would
fare better in Roman hands than under self-rule."

"We are past the scholar's choice," she replied, "long past
discussion at a dinner table. Our blood stains this land. A
ribbon of it runs from the feet of one dead Jew to another,
from north to south, Dan to Beersheva. Your Romans defecate
on us. They make our holy places into lavatories and brothels.
They hang us up alive and turn us into pitiful gladiators for
their cruel amusements. We may have failings—and you have
spoken often of Judea's faults—but whatever our weaknesses,
we do not kill for sport. We do not crucify living flesh or make
an obscenity of men's deaths, though they be our enemies."

"You need not remind me of all this, Alexandra. I am still
a Jew."

She remembered what the guard had said. *"Their* Jew."

"I am my own man." If he was angry he did not show it.
"I work in my own way. If, like the others, you choose to
believe I am a traitor, then do so. Someday you will realize
that wars are not settled finally with blood. If I had fought to
the death or killed myself, what cause would that have served?
What would have been the gain?" He shrugged. "We die, and
history remains."

"I know only that my father is dead, and you remain! My
mother is dead, and you are here. My brothers are slain, and
you are alive, friend to their enemy. I have no family, no
home—I cannot even put a stone on my parents' graves. I have
nothing now . . . not even you."

"You have everything! It is all before you, can't you see?
I will get back your father's land and ships! I will give you
Beit Harsom!" He paused, excited now. "Nero is dead. The
news arrived this morning. Vespasian's command is termi-
nated, and he must wait to have it confirmed by the new
emperor or make his own bid for the throne. Soon Vespasian
will wear the wreath of Caesar—I know it! The legions will
support no other. And when that time comes . . . he will set me

free and give back your wealth—and mine—and more! But we don't have to stay here. We can go to Rome, Alexandra. Rome! There is a city for you! There is a world!"

"And if Vespasian does not become emperor? What if he is usurped? What if he is killed? Yes, and by a Jewish sword. . . . The war is not over. Jerusalem stands. Our forces could attack even now. We could still win."

"Win? Defeat the army of Rome? Or win a respite from retribution—which would come as soon as Italy resolves her internal affairs." He laughed. "Alexandra . . . use your head."

"Jerusalem—"

"Jerusalem will fall! Those inside its walls pray even now for the steady hand of Rome to rescue them from the insanity that prevails there. Haven't you seen the stream of deserters? Haven't you heard their tales of the terror within the Holy City? One faction warring against the next . . . Jew killing Jew . . . mock trials, executions, illegal confiscation of property— the Temple is in the hands of ignorant peasants who will next set up a village stonemason as High Priest! Thus do the followers of Menahem the Sicarius take their revenge for their leader's death. There are at least three different Zealot bandit-murderers pitting their mobs against each other, fighting for control of a city that in the eyes of Rome, the rabbis—and certainly the Lord—has already doomed itself." He took a breath. "Don't be a fool, Alexandra." He drew her to him. "You suit me. I know you are not stupid, as most women are. And you are . . . besides . . . pleasing to me. I should like to keep you with me." He ran his finger down her arm. "Daughter of the House of Harsom," he whispered, "am I not Josef ben Matthias who slept on your father's roof, who walked with your brothers, who returned from Rome only to serve our people?" He took her face in his hands. "Trust me, Alexandra. I swear to you that I still serve our God." He smiled now, that strange half-smile that might even now be mocking her; or perhaps it held sadness that he should be so misunderstood. "I know you loved me once—even as a child, you have said. But I was not there to receive that love. Now that you are my wife, let me know the sweetness inside you, for I have great need of it."

His arms closed around her, his mouth pressed against hers; and willingly she gave herself to him. All that mattered were those last words he had whispered; the rest was talk for Roman ears. There were spies everywhere; they would repeat everything to Vespasian. Hadn't she heard a sound at the door, the rustling of a Roman tunic, the scraping of a guard's sword? But she knew the truth now. She had been right; it was all a trick. Josef was planning a rebellion within Vespasian's own camp. He would organize the prisoners in secret; they would escape, and he would lead the forces in Jerusalem, unite the people of Judea, and drive the Roman legions away forever.

I work in my own way, he'd said.

How stupid she had been not to see that. How foolish she had been to doubt him.

She was correct in only one thing: Vespasian did not succeed Nero. The elderly Servius Galba assumed the throne, ruling less than seven months before he was assassinated in the Forum.

Upon learning several months after the fact that Galba was emperor (it took fifty-four days for imperial couriers to reach Caesarea from Rome), Vespasian dispatched Titus to Italy to pay homage and to learn what new directives were in store for him. Again the expedition to Jerusalem was put off, and military activity suspended.

Alexandra did not visit the prisoners again. She realized her presence among them might ruin Josef's plans and agreed with him that the Romans must not suspect he was anything but what he appeared to be. But each day she waited for a sign that the revolt she dreamed of was at hand. Each day she waited to hear that escape was forthcoming. Each day she tried to guess how the man she had married would implement the daring schemes she ascribed to him.

Time passed, and Josef did nothing. She grew impatient. The turn of political events in Rome was to their advantage here in Judea. The moment for action was now, while the legionaries were on holiday, their officers partaking of theater and oil massages and sportive combat among themselves. More than one occasion had passed when it would have been simple—or so she thought—for them to flee or get to the prisoners below. At last, unable to keep still any longer, she asked Josef if he had managed to speak to Aaron again.

"Aaron?" He was reading over something he had written; it was a history of Herod's reign.

"The prisoner I told you about. The son of my father's friend."

"Oh, that one. He is long gone," he replied carelessly.

"Gone? Did he escape? Was he set free?"

"No . . . taken to the arena, I believe. You remember when Vespasian made that big fuss about his Thracian gladiators going soft? He set up a special set of matches. . . ." He looked up, suddenly aware of her intense stare.

"You killed him," she said slowly.

"I? I had nothing to do with it. The fellow was a trouble-maker, as I recall. The guards got wind that he was planning to stir up a prisoners' revolt. Shipped him and his gang off to the arena, where I imagine the poor fools got their fill of fighting at last."

"You killed him," she said again. "You took what I said and used it against him. Aaron was right. You are a traitor."

He sighed. "I have not killed anyone. You forget, I am a prisoner myself."

"You are a traitor."

"Alexandra—"

"You had those men killed because you were afraid they would undermine your position with Vespasian. You murdered them as surely as if you'd run a sword through their hearts."

"If what you say is true, then it is not I but you who are responsible for their deaths. Yes, my dear wife, you. If you had not filled that poor peasant's mind with such ridiculous hopes, he might be alive today—although I doubt it." He shrugged. "It was the arena sooner or later for him in any case. It just happened to be . . . sooner."

She covered her eyes. She could not bear to look at him. Her hand was shaking.

"The important thing," Josef was saying, "is that nothing has changed. Galba is dead, and Otho warring with Vitellius, who claims the throne as nominee of the German legions. No matter which of them wins, I tell you Vespasian will be the emperor in the end. And we will be free."

She stumbled to bed. She felt cold, filled with the same sick feeling she had known once before in Caesarea and then again on the beach at Tarichea.

"Are you all right? You look ill."

She did not answer him. She lay there, leaden, her eyes burning with tears.

He went to her, stood over her, staring at her a moment. Then he took her in his arms. "Don't cry, Alexandra," he said stroking her hair. "You mustn't blame yourself for Aaron's

death. It was bound to occur, and I think he preferred it to
slavery. As for you . . . there is nothing to fear. Just do as I say,
and all will be well. I will look after you. I will keep you safe
with me. You are my wife, and you shall give me sons of the
line of David. Don't cry. . . . All will be well with us. Don't
think of today. Think of tomorrow . . . when you will be a fine
lady in Rome with slaves of your own. . . . It will come to pass.
You will see. . . . It will come to pass."

She loathed him now. The love and admiration she once felt
had turned to hatred, a cold, consuming passion that obsessed
her. She nurtured it, feeding it even as she fed upon it; it was
all that kept her alive now. She lived with the hope not of
freeing herself but of getting revenge, of seeing him punished
and Caesarea in flames.

And yet, that cool, objective brain of hers realized that Josef
was sincere in believing the course he had chosen was right,
not only for the sake of his own life and fortune, but for what
he called "the greater good." He meant it when he said he still
served the God of Israel, and he often spoke of his intention
to write a chronicle of this war with Rome so that history
should not be misled as to the truth of events.

What Josef was doing, Alexandra thought suddenly, was
forsaking the present for posterity, becoming apologist to the
world for his people and his religion. How often had she heard
him expound before Vespasian and an assembly of gentiles
upon the nobility of Jewish thought and customs. Once he had
narrated a long history of the tribes, always pointing out the
Israelites' constant struggle for freedom and human dignity,
cleverly refuting the distortions and lies that abounded.

"The Jews have long been in revolt not only against Rome
but against humanity," Cerealis remarked one night. "A race
that has made its own life apart, irreconcilable—that cannot
share with the rest of mankind in the pleasures of the table or
join in their libations and sacrifices—is separated from ourselves by a greater gulf than divides us from the distant Indies."

"He is right," Mucianus agreed. "They are obstinately loyal
to each other, for example, and always ready to show com-
passion to their own kind—but they feel only hatred and enmity
for the rest of the world. When have you ever known a Jew
to be honest with one not of his race? It is no wonder the good

people of Caesarea took their revenge finally. The Samaritans and Syrians," he added, "also hate the Jews for their unkind ways."

"Unkind?" Josef asked politely. "As you gentlemen have such knowledge of our customs, you must know our Law forbids us to withhold aid to any man. We must furnish fire, water, and food to all who ask, point out the road, not leave a corpse unburied, and show consideration even to declared enemies. Even in war—if, for example, we had invaded Rome rather than the other way around—we are forbidden to burn up the country or cut down the fruit trees or despoil those fallen in battle."

There was a silence. Mucianus shrugged.

The tribune Nicanor smiled. "Josephus has great powers of persuasion. The late Poppea was quite ready to forsake the gods for his Hebrew deity, so convincingly did he proclaim his Lord's virtues."

"Well," the Judean replied modestly, "it was not my doing but the truth of the case. The fact is, our beliefs are in harmony with the wisest of the Greeks' teachings. Pythagoras and Plato had the same notion of the nature of God—that He is unbegotten and immutable through all eternity, superior to all mortal conceptions, and though known to us by His power, yet unknown as to His essence."

Vespasian grunted. He was himself a Stoic. "Poppea, eh? I can just see her pointing out the road and leaving cherries on the tree."

"In any event," Cerealis went on, "from what I have heard here in Caesarea, all good philosophy aside, the Greeks have a real grievance against the Jews. When you learn what it is, we shall see where your sympathies lie.

"It seems," he said, settling himself more comfortably among the cushions, "that when Antiochus entered the Temple in Jerusalem, he found a man reclining on a couch, a table before him laden with every manner of food. The man fell at the king's knees begging to be set free, saying he was a Greek who had been kidnapped by the Jews and shut up in this place, where he was being fattened on feasts of the most lavish description. And do you know why?" Cerealis leaned forward. "Because every year the Jews kidnap a Greek, fatten him up, and then kill him on their holy day." He nodded solemnly. "They sacrifice him to their God—the one with the unknown essence—and eat his flesh and drink his blood." Cerealis popped an olive into his mouth and delicately spat the pit into his palm. "What say you to this, Josephus?"

A faint smile played across the young man's face. "I say it is strange that the story concerns only a Greek." He reached into the dish of olives, brought one to his lips. "After all," he murmured, "why should that race be the only object of our alleged conspiracy against the whole world?"

Vespasian laughed. "Good! Good!" He turned his attention to the girl in white linen, who was sitting, as he liked her to do, near his hand. "And what do you say, little one?"

Alexandra raised her eyes to his, then looked across to Cerealis. "I would think," she said coolly, "that anyone professing to know our customs would realize a Jew could not possibly make a meal of a Greek, nor for that matter, a Roman."

"And why not, little one?"

"Because," she replied, "we are forbidden to eat that which is unclean."

"You are an arrogant bitch, wife."

She smiled.

"You are lucky, Alexandra, that Vespasian finds you intriguing—otherwise you would not have further opportunity to insult him." He poured the wine with a quick, angry hand and quaffed the drink at once. Despite the shock that her remark had generated, Vespasian had not rebuked her. And when Mucianus said, "It is a pity you did not stay with me, my dear—I might have taught that tongue pleasanter uses," Vespasian had barked, "So you would be a teacher, Mucianus? Any man who stores his jewels in the toilet has something to learn himself."

Josef frowned. "And then, that remark you made about the Hasmoneans having no right to the throne except through the affection of the people. You know how Titus feels about Berenice. You as much as called the woman a usurper."

"She is. She is also a—"

"Never mind." He sighed. "The future depends on Vespasian believing I am sincere. A partisan wife does not help my cause. Fortunately it was the Roman who gave you to me, and he seems to find it amusing that you contradict me. But all jokes wear thin, remember that. And if I denounce you,

you will find yourself playing your tricks in the Roman's bed.
When he tires of you, you will be passed on, perhaps finally
to be humiliated in the arena. They do that, you know. In
Rome, I saw them take a German girl . . . They stripped her
. . . and let the gladiators have her for sport between the
fights." He shook his head sorrowfully. "I should be sad indeed
to see you end like that."

"You are a swine, Josef ben Matthias."

"Be careful, Alexandra. The rabbis are not against a proper
beating administered now and again to a wicked woman."

"I, wicked! It is you who are evil!" She lifted her chin.
"Beat me, then. It could not make me hate you more."

Quickly he was on her, his eyes fierce and dark, his hand
like a claw gripping her wrist. "Why are you such an idiot?
Don't you see what the future holds? Don't you know what
lies in store for the people of this land? Believe me, whatever
you have seen till now is nothing compared to what will be.
Once the Roman machine has begun to roll, it does not stop
until there is nothing left to crush. There is no victory for
Judea. No hope. Caesar will destroy even the little that remains.
The Chosen People will perish—and for what? For the dream
of continuing their own corrupt dynasties, inept governments,
holy palaces that drain the poor? Caesar need not vie with God,
don't you see? The issue is after all political—it always has
been. One can be a citizen of Rome *and* a Jew! And better to
serve Caesar than that pack of holy hypocrites in Jerusalem."

"You lie!"

"No, it is you who lie. To yourself. I know you, Alexandra.
I knew your father and your uncle, and I know what they
thought and what you were raised to think. I know you can
think—your mind speaks so coolly and clearly through those
eyes of yours. You know your country and your people for
what they are, and you despise them! The meanness, the nar-
row-minded patterns, the ridiculous taboos—and with all of
this, an arrogance totally out of keeping with their situation."

"What do you know? What do you know of the people?"

"I know them. I led them, and I know them. They worship
their own stupidity."

She would have struck him, but he caught her arm and
pushed her back on the bed. His hands were like iron bands
on her wrists, but she would not cry out in pain. She would
not cry for him.

"I was born a Sadducee," he said. "I have been a Pharisee. And I have lived with the Essenes, those holy freaks. When I was still a boy I went into the desert with Banus, who, they said, spoke to the Lord Himself. And still I seek more. All the learning in man's possession is not enough for me, and I don't care who is king and who is not, which god sits in the Temple and what men attend him, so long as I am free to live my life as I wish. Free to see and learn and taste and know—a little— what it is all about. And that is what you want. That first time, when I made you my wife, I knew what you were. You are not ruled by man or God, Alexandra, but by your own curiosity. Even as I am. We are the same. Above all we seek to live, to learn, and to love."

She hated him for these words and twisted desperately to be free, but his hands cut across her wrists like metal. And now, she realized, he wanted her; she could feel the heat coming off his body onto hers. And she also realized, horrified, that she wanted him to take her.

His mouth came down hard, brutal, on hers; and she lay still.

He lifted his head, mocking her with that crooked half-smile. "You see?" he whispered. "I know you. I know what you are and what you want." But he would not release her hands, and his mouth was everywhere.

All that night she existed in a fever. Again and again they came at each other with a vicious, murdering hunger. Like animals they fought each other, thrilled each other, toyed with each other for all that red-shadowed night. Her hair stuck to her back, her body ached, pleasure mixed with pain. And sometimes she seemed to see herself and to wonder, Who is this creature, from where did she come? She had a vision of herself with lion paws, crawling on the hot desert sand; then it was night, the moon full and white, the wind rearranging the dunes, tearing through the flimsy tents. . . .

Afterwards she felt unclean, as though she had betrayed something in her self.

Her life was without order or meaning now. Day turned to night, and the oil lamp by the bed burned darkness into dawn. Was it spring again or summer? She rarely went outside the palace. There was the pool, the dinners with the Romans, the bed . . .

In the end she had ceased to fight him, seeking only to obliterate her thoughts and feelings in the fires of sex, learning to hate herself as much as she hated him.

FIVE

Hagar studied the girl, her own expression emotionless as always, her black eyes a pool whose depth could not be measured. Alexandra was becoming more indolent every day; she seemed to float, lethargic and uncaring, through her waking hours, then sleep for long stretches at a time. She had taken to strange diets, eating at odd hours, sometimes not eating anything at all for a whole day. She dawdled and she picked, she stared through people and was rude to everyone. Hagar was concerned. More and more, Alexandra was taking on the personality of a slave. She was thinner than she had ever been, and yet her body had a new feline grace. Although she was thoroughly unpleasant, she had never been so alluring. Hagar watched the faces of the men who saw the dark-haired girl, with her finely chiseled features, her large, light eyes so totally devoid of warmth. They all wanted the little monster now, Hagar thought. Alexandra's disregard for those around her—for herself—had endowed her with a certain real power. Men sensed she cared for nothing, and they found this contempt exciting. Not so Hagar.

"Your hair looks as though you have not combed it for a week," the woman said.

Alexandra shrugged. "I haven't. What for? It only gets tangled again . . . in bed."

Hagar chose to ignore this. "Come here," she said. "Let me arrange it for you. When you were small you never would hold still for anyone. But sometimes, at night, you would let me comb your hair. . . . I think it brought you pleasure."

Alexandra looked sideways at her. As a child she had loved to sit while Hagar combed through her hair, for it was then that the woman would tell stories, strange wonderful tales . . ."All right," she said indifferently, and sat down.

Hagar found the ivory comb and began to run it through the girl's dark hair. The locks were a deep, burnished brown, almost black, but in sunlight the color of dark wine.

Alexandra closed her eyes. She let her shoulders fall, relaxed. "Tell me a story, Hagar."

"You are too old for stories."

"No, I'm not. Tell me a story. I need a story."

You need a shaking, the woman thought. Aloud she said, "Shall I braid it? Your father always liked to see your hair braided. He said you looked as he thought Rachel must have looked to Jacob."

The light eyes flew open. "Stop it."

"What have I said?"

"Just stop it, Hagar." She got up from the chair. "Don't give me any memories. They do not make me happy, and I am tired of hurting."

"Pain tells us we exist."

"Oh, I'm alive, all right. I just don't want to think or feel or remember. I don't even hate Josef anymore." She smiled wryly. "Perhaps I am becoming a Christian. I don't hate anyone."

"This is not good."

"Don't be silly. It's wonderful. For the first time in my life I'm free, really free. Who knows? I may even become empress of Rome—or close enough to it." And, laughing at the woman's expression, she swept out of the room. But once she was outside, her laughter stopped. The pillared hall stretched before her, quiet, empty, her steps on the marble mosaic floor the only sound to be heard.

Why didn't she run away? It would be so easy. . . .

"Vespasian likes you near," Josef had said. "He has made you his daughter, I think. Don't throw this away, if not for me, then for your own good—even for your precious prisoners. Who knows? The Roman might just give you the Temple as a gift." He had lowered his voice. "This is what I meant when I said there are other ways to fight. . . ."

Josef.

Josephus.

Was he really a traitor or . . . something else? "History," he said, "will look more kindly on us as a result of my writings. I will tell the truth about this war."

But what did it matter that generations to come would speak well of the people of Israel if there were none of them left? What good would a noble memory be to a dead nation?

There were those who still fought, who breathed the air of real freedom. Zealots, Sicarii. . . . Why did she not join them? Even if she were killed in the attempt, wouldn't death be better than living like this, with no purpose, no identity, a stranger to herself?

All her life she had moved under some unseen guiding hand. She had always felt the presence of the Lord and found Him, if not in the houses men built for Him, then in the sun and sky and sea . . . in the rain, the stillness of twilight, the hills outside Jerusalem. But now she felt the Lord had forgotten her.

Or had she lost sight of Him?

Why was she here? Escape would be simple. . . .

Did she still believe in Josef, still, despite all else, love him?

Did she hope to get back the land and ships that were her birthright? To restore Beit Harsom?

Or was she simply afraid? Afraid to be caught, to be hurt . . . humiliated. . . . Afraid to die. . . .

And was she curious? . . . Yes, even as Josef had said, was she possessed of some black demon curiosity, so that she wondered what it would be like to live in Rome . . . to lie in Vespasian's leather arms . . . to make love with an uncircumcised man?

Had God forgotten her indeed . . . or did she make Him turn away His eyes?

There was an inner courtyard in the palace, with a garden of classic Greek design. It was adorned with statues of gods and woodland deities, and had a small tiled pool in which brightly colored fish swam, shimmering incandescent in the water. Trees of various kinds screened the sun, the light falling dappled on the grass and pool.

She walked slowly up to a statue of Pan clasping a nymph in abandoned embrace. She reached out and ran her hand down the stone bodies, wondering bemusedly if a sword of lightning would burst from the sky and strike her down for this impious act—perhaps hoping one would.

There was a sound. She turned quickly but saw nothing. A breeze rustled through the trees; it was the leaves that cast those shadows on the ground.

"Mistress . . . mistress . . ."

She saw him now, a little man, his shoulders hunched forward.

He raised his hand. "Don't be afraid." He came closer. "I am a Jew," he said, smiling, touching his breast. "I am a Jew."

"What do you want? Who are you?"

"I am Tobias. Before the war I was a merchant here in Caesarea."

"I am from Caesarea. I do not recall—"

"The city is large. One cannot know everyone. My business was small, not like your father's. Ah, yes, I know who you are. You are the daughter of Samuel ben Harsom and"—he paused significantly—"the beautiful Devorah."

"You knew my parents?"

"Only your mother. We spoke a few words now and again. My . . . business—brought me sometimes to the Praetorium, and I saw her here."

"I think you are mistaken. My mother never visited this place. She had no reason to."

"I think perhaps she did," the man said smoothly, still smiling. "The noble Gessius Florus often looked to her for, ah, advice on Judean affairs. She was a clever woman," he added. "As wise as she was beautiful. And I see that you are from the same mold."

"I don't think I understand—"

"There is no need to pretend with me. I am Tobias. I am your friend. I, for one, am glad to see how favored you are. Word gets around. . . . Titus is fond of Josephus, but not so fond as Vespasian is of you." He nodded. "You have done well for yourself, better even than your mother. What is a procurator next to an emperor? You are astonished. . . . But surely you believe Vespasian will be king of Rome? I tell you, I am glad for you." He moved even nearer. "Look . . . we are both Jews, you and I." He lowered his voice conspiratorially. "You need friends, people you can trust, people who won't betray you. This is a world of intrigue and schemes and jealousy. The princess Berenice can tell you that. You need friends. As for me . . ." He smiled again. "What I shall be to you

. . . perhaps you will be to me. You will let Vespasian know what a loyal servant I am, how faithfully I have served Rome. I will be your friend . . . and you will be mine. Yes?"

"Toad. Worm." Shock had turned to fury. "I am no friend of yours, and you are none of mine!" Her chin was up; for the moment she had become the girl she once was. "Go away from here, and pray the Lord does not squash you like the insect you are!"

The smile faded. "You are indeed like your mother," he snarled. "Perhaps more so than either of us realized."

"Don't you ever mention her again!" She was livid. Fists clenched, she took a step forward, causing the startled little man to stumble backward. "If I hear you speak of her in any way—if I suspect you are even thinking of her—I will tell Vespasian you are a Zealot spy!"

"That is how you would repay friendship, daughter of Harsom? Very well, I will remember this. I should have known a Sadducee still thinks he is better than anyone else, no matter what dirt he wallows in. You are no better than I! And your mother—" He was about to add what he thought of Devorah, but the look in the girl's eyes decided him against it. Departing hurriedly from the garden, he turned suddenly and said, "At least I am not a slave!"

It was quiet once more, the green garden giving no evidence of the earthquake that had just occurred.

Alexandra turned and saw Hagar standing there, watching her. "Is it true?"

"Yes."

"My mother . . . slept with Gessius Florus? My mother . . . was that man's—" She could not go on.

"Whatever your mother did, she did for you! Yes, and for your brothers and your father! For him! Why do you think your family escaped for so long the misfortunes that befell so many others? Nothing is free, little owl. Nothing is without a price."

"You sound like Josef now," she said bitterly.

"No. I do not say that everything can be bought. I say everything must be paid for."

"As my mother . . . paid for us?"

"She did what she had to do. But it killed her. She was dead before those filthy animals ever touched her. Do you understand? She was brave . . . but she was not strong. You must be both. Do you understand?"

The girl nodded. She was sobbing now.

Hagar took her in her arms, rocking her like a baby. "Growing up is not easy," she said softly. "Is it, little owl?"

SIX

Near the end of spring in 69, Vespasian, restless with waiting for new directives from Rome, moved in the direction of Jerusalem but let the city alone. Instead he launched a campaign against those parts of Judea not yet conquered. The toparchies of Gophna and Acrabetta were occupied, the towns of Bethal and Ephraim garrisoned. Roman cavalry stamped out all resistance in the immediate environment of Jerusalem, slaughtering hundreds and taking prisoners by the score. Cerealis meanwhile ravaged Upper Idumea and burnt the ancient city of Hebron to the ground. Except for Jerusalem, which according to all reports was bleeding itself to death in vicious civil war, the only strongholds left in rebel hands were the Herodium, west of the Dead Sea; the fortress Machaerus, on its eastern shore; and the Masada, from which the Sicarii carried out raids along the sea's west coast.

Returning to Caesarea, Vespasian learned that the sybaritic Vitellius was now emperor, his legions having beaten Otho's forces in northern Italy. Otho had committed suicide.

The news did not please Vespasian. He was a loyal citizen of Rome, but it was difficult for him to accept Vitellius.

"He has turned the Imperial City into a camp, filling every house with armed men," said Titus angrily. He had just returned from Rome. "It seems he brought not only his own army back from Germany but a whole mob of hangers-on. They are laying waste to everything."

"The man's a disgrace," Mucianus muttered. "He has always let discipline go and joked about the excesses committed by his men. Of course they love him—he lets them do exactly as they please. I have heard he has such a taste for torture that he rewards his soldiers for inventing new means."

"The fact that he has been a fixture for so long at court," Cerealis added, "says something of his nature. Both Caligula and Nero admired him greatly. Why, I believe it was he who taught Claudius to play at dice."

Vespasian turned the silver cup in his hand. "The man's a first-rate prick," he agreed.

"The legions—our legions—are angry," Titus said. "Our men are saying the soldiers in Rome live in undeserved luxury, voting anyone they fancy to the throne, while it is they, here, they who have toiled so long and hard in their country's behalf, who should have the privilege of appointing an emperor. They say"—he paused significantly—"they have a candidate whose right to the throne is stronger than Vitellius's, just as they are far better soldiers than those who appointed him."

"I do not want a civil war," Vespasian replied.

"No contest will be necessary," Mucianus said quickly. "Do you think the Senate or the people would prefer that gluttonous lout to you?" He leaned forward earnestly. "Do you think they want another childless man? Wise men know the best guarantee of peace and stability is a line of excellent princes."

Vespasian looked at his son, who returned the gaze calmly, his eyes devoid of greed or ambition. Vespasian smiled, pleased. But he shook his head. "A crown is a heavy burden. I have never sought office for myself, as you know. I prefer the safety of private life to the dangers that go with exalted position. I do not mean outside assassins but the corruptive nature of power itself. I like to think of myself as a simple man. I would not like to find out I am not. Still . . ." He shook his head again. "Vitellius!"

"You have my three legions," Mucianus said in a low, tense voice. "You can count on the two in Egypt under Tiberius Alexander's command."

"Agrippa is with you," Titus put in. "You will have the backing of all the East and, I think, as much of Europe as is safely out of Vitellius's reach."

"Your brother Flavius Sabinus, who is prefect of the urban cohorts, can look after things in Rome," Cerealis added.

"And there is Domitian!" Titus exclaimed, smiling as he named his younger brother.

Vespasian did not answer right away. "I must talk to Tiberius Alexander," he said finally. "Meanwhile our business in Judea is not yet finished. We can delay the siege of Jerusalem—time only strengthens our position with regard to that, seeing the rebels in the city persist in weakening themselves with the calamitous divisions. But do not think we can let it go entirely. If—the gods protect me!—I do take the throne, then I want my reign to begin in orderly fashion, with an end to this damn war. So, gentlemen, while you dream of Rome, do not forget Judea. People have a way of getting stabbed when their backs are turned. The knife of the Sicarius is short, but its reach is long."

He knew they called him Iron Guts and the Farmer. It didn't bother him. Better those names than some of the ones hung on Nero and his kind—the little prick. Well, at least he had known how to die like a man. And now Vitellius. . . . It was too much. Rome deserved better.

But was he the man?

He was a soldier, not a king, and he had an instinctive distaste for office. For years he had postponed his candidacy for the purple stripe already earned by his brother Sabinus, until finally he was driven to become a senator by his mother, Vespasia Polla. She was a strong woman, he reflected, but not so strong as Tertulla, his paternal grandmother, who had brought him up on her estate at Cosa. How he wished he might speak with that good woman now, or with Caenis, his mistress of many years. He had a penchant for strong women, women he could talk to as well as enjoy physically. He liked honest women. Now, the princess Berenice was beautiful and intelligent but dangerous. Very dangerous. Titus must beware, particularly if the Flavians became Rome's royal family. The memory of the serpentine Cleopatra still haunted many in the Imperial City. Well, but Titus was no fool. Obviously he was caught up in Berenice's considerable allure, but he knew his first duty was to Rome. Another, lesser man might forget that, but not Titus. He, Vespasian, would stake his life on that.

Now, he could see Titus as emperor. . . . Yes, Rome could do far worse than Titus or Domitian. But he, Vespasian . . . !

And yet, what had the Jew Josephus said that first time he came before him? "You think you have taken a mere captive, but I come to you as a messenger of greater destinies. Had it not been the will of the Lord that I make known to you His decree, that you will be Caesar, I would have fallen on my sword back there, as any general would have done."

"So I am to be Caesar, am I?" Vespasian had laughed.

"Yes. And after you, your sons."

If ever anyone was intolerant of soothsayers, it was Vespasian; but the young man had fought too well and long at Jotapata to be a mere charlatan. Moreover, he had been Titus's friend before the war.

"Why do you make these prophecies?" Vespasian had asked the prisoner later. "Do you think I will treat you better for it? If you know as much as you claim, then you must know as well that I am not a man to be taken in by messages supposedly not of this earth."

"Very well," Josef had replied. "Since you do not care to hear what heaven foretells, I will tell you what men say. They say Nero is not fit to rule."

Vespasian had frowned. "You speak of Caesar."

"I speak of Nero. Caesar is Rome, and Rome cannot be Nero."

"Strange talk from a Jew."

"I believe in the Lord God of Israel, great Vespasian. Nothing and no one can or will ever induce me to say otherwise. But government and religion seem to me different things. As the saying goes, 'Let us render unto the Lord that which is His, and unto Caesar that which is Caesar's.' To me, Rome represents the highest achievement of man's civilization. I would fight to preserve that civilization as I would to protect the Lord's Temple."

So the fellow loved Rome. It was no sham; Titus had vouched for the Jew's affection. He had said how torn Josephus was when the war with Judea began, how sadly he had sailed for home.

"You fought hard enough at Jotapata," Vespasian had remarked, studying the man for signs of deceit. "If you did not believe as a Zealot, why, then, you fought like one, boy!"

"It was my duty. I could do no less—for myself or for my father's honor."

It was a good answer. Still Vespasian had pressed him. "But you knew you could not win. Why didn't you surrender? Why did you go on to the end?"

The fellow had smiled that crazy, lopsided smile of his. "So I could look you in the eye now. So you would know that I am no coward," he continued, serious again, "that I allowed myself to be taken only because . . . there are things I must do."

"Such as?"

The smile had returned, full now. "For one, tell you that you are to be Caesar. When the time comes and you are in doubt, remember my prophecy. It is the will of the Lord, and it will soon be the determination of the world."

The will of the people. . . . Certainly it seemed to be the will of Mucianus and Cerealis, of Agrippa and possibly Tiberius Alexander. The last was the key. Egypt was vital; if she withheld her corn, there could be famine in Rome.

Meanwhile, there was Judea. And Jerusalem. Well, if it was meant that he should return to Rome, Titus could finish things here. That would please him, no doubt, give him more time with his oriental beauty.

Vespasian grunted. It was almost a laugh, almost a sigh. Well, he thought wryly, Caesar—if he was in fact to be Caesar—was certainly not behaving like any of the past Caesars. Going to bed alone . . . He sighed deeply now. He could use some soft company tonight. That girl with the gray eyes, the one he'd given away like a damn fool—what had possessed him to do that?—where was she tonight? In the arms of the husband he'd given her, that's where. The more he saw her, the more he cursed himself for not taking her. She was a slave, wasn't she?

No. She was a brave, honest girl. How Josephus cringed at her honesty. He would not tame that one. Vespasian doubted any man could. How delicious, though, to try. . . .

He could summon her.

No. He would not behave like Nero. He had given her in marriage to the man her family had picked for her because he pitied her condition, the fact that one so young and lovely, a girl of noble birth, had through circumstance been sold as a slave.

No. He would not command. He wanted no cold, fearful woman beneath him, no stiff, dry body to sheathe his sword, no wounded animal eyes. He'd had his fill of conquered flesh in Germany and Britain. When he was a young colonel in Thrace . . . he'd raped a woman only once and even now regretted it.

He wanted the girl. But he would not command. She must come to him herself. Willingly.

The Praetorium was filled with people. Suddenly there were emissaries from all parts of the East. As legion commanders and foreign kings came to the palace in Caesarea, Berenice assumed the role of Vespasian's hostess, sweeping across rooms full of dazzled guests, as beautiful as any legendary queen. It was not difficult to see why the Flavians, like so many others, had fallen under her spell. It was also quite clear that the woman was as much in love with Titus as he seemed enraptured by her. Titus was in his late twenties at the time, and Berenice was nearly forty; but the two were equally bright-eyed, and so caught up in each other that they seemed oblivious to the rest of the world. To those who knew her, Herod's daughter had never been so beautiful; she was radiant as she leaned even closer to hear the young, fair Roman speak. One person, however, was unmoved by this show of tenderness and affection; Alexandra viewed the two with equal distaste.

As if sensing the cold eyes on her, Berenice looked up, saw the girl staring at her, and drew back, startled. Titus turned to see what had drawn his love's attention but only noticed Josef. Smiling, he beckoned to him. Bowing obediently, his gold-manacled hands clasped together, the Judean prince advanced. But Alexandra did not move alongside her husband. She was staring at someone else now.

Sitting by Vespasian was a dark man dressed in the robes of a prince of Arabia. He was perhaps forty years of age, well built, and graceful as he illustrated his conversation with many gestures. Such a man—a sheikh of the Quraysh tribe in the south—had been a guest at Beit Harsom. He had sought out Samuel as a dealer in spices and frankincense, an especially dear commodity. Caravans from his land brought these items to the markets of Judea, from there to be shipped to other parts of the world; and his tribe had grown prosperous through trade. But as men began to sail past Egypt to India, returning with shiploads of more cheaply bought spices, the Quraysh began to worry about the competition. If it had been a matter of another tribe, the intruders could have been dealt with; but India was far away, too far for the camel and the horse and the curved sword to reach. Accordingly, a tribesman named Pangar had come to the House of Harsom seeking a covenant of trade. Samuel had given his hand to it, drawing up a contract that ensured the Ishmaelites, as they were called, a market for their goods "for as long as there were sons of Quraysh and sons of Harsom." Later, Samuel told his family that he had agreed to the deal for two reasons, the first being the quality of the goods and the excellent conditions. But, he added, he also felt he ought to do something to make up for Abraham's poor treatment of Ishmael. "After all," Samuel had said, "Pan-

gar and I are brothers, for if Abraham had not listened to his
wife we would be under the same tent today." To which Devorah, echoing Sarah, had remarked with a shudder, "Not if
I had anything to say about it."

Alexandra smiled at the memory, remembering how they
had all laughed at her mother. Pangar had stayed in their "tent"
many times. She and her brothers had looked forward eagerly
to his visits, for he always brought wonderful gifts and even
better—to her mind—stories of his people. He called the Lord
"Allah" and had besides, like the Greeks and Romans, many
other gods to whom he prayed. He came from a place called
Mecca, which his people had proclaimed a holy city, like
Jerusalem, in memory of "the Black Stone which fell from
heaven in the days of Adam." From far and near across the
desert, the tribes of Arabia came every year to offer sacrifice
there. "Even as your people go to the great Temple in the
mountains, so my people must make their *hajj* to the Black
Stone of Ka'Bah," Pangar had told them. "It was Father Abram
who built the Ka'Bah. He had come to see his son Ishmael,
and he found the Stone and embedded it in its Holy Place.
When you make your *hajj* you must run around the Stone seven
times, then kiss it, and you will have luck for a full year."

It had been nearly five years since Pangar sat at the white
marble table in Beit Harsom. How well Alexandra recalled that
last visit, for the men had talked of Rome and the wisdom of
alliance with Caesar. The Indian market had cut deeply into
Arab trade. Pangar's people, Samuel had suggested, must look
to a commitment from Rome.

She studied the lean, dark face of the man beside Vespasian,
with its high-bridged nose and heavy-lidded eyes. Could this
be her father's friend?

"Alexandra, come here to me." Vespasian held out his hand.
She took a step forward. "Closer, closer. Here. Sit." He patted
a cushion beside him, and she took her place upon it. The
Roman put his arm around her; it was heavy, the color of
leather, with a mat of white curls running from elbow to wrist.
"Josephus." He waved him over. "Come and sit. Have some
wine. That cannot offend your faith. Drink up, drink up. 'No
songs can please nor yet live long which are written by those
who drink water.' You too, little one. Here, you shall drink
from my cup." He was slightly drunk. She tried to shift the
weight of his arm from her shoulder. The man was heavy.

The Ishmaelite raised polite eyes. There was no sign of

recognition there, but she was sure he was the Quraysh prince she had once known. She wondered if he realized who she was.

Vespasian hugged her to him.

Better that Pangar not know my name, she thought, *than that he see how low the House of Harsom has fallen*.

"A pretty one, eh, Pangar? A beauty. Keep your end of it, and there will be plenty for you in Jerusalem. Ah, I like the women of this country! I admit it! Only decent things around. Eh, Titus?" Not waiting for an answer from that quarter, he continued. "You're a lucky dog, Josephus. I swear I ought to make an end of you and take this girl under my protection. No, keep your mouth shut. Don't worry, I gave my hand on it. A Roman soldier does not break his oath, but you ought to return the favor, Josephus. Time someone around here was kind to me... kind to an old soldier. Will you be kind to me, little one?"

"Great Vespasian." Pangar placed his hand on his heart. "King of men. Bestow an honor.. Allow me to send you a daughter of my tribe. None can serve man's pleasure more sweetly than one of our black-eyed maidens—one, say, just entered into womanhood." He leaned forward and whispered something in Vespasian's ear that made the man smile. Alexandra took the opportunity to slip out from under the Roman's arm. Josef was smiling too, as though he were part of Pangar's conversation or at least knew what was being said. Alexandra started to rise. Josef caught her arm and forced her down again; he was still smiling, his eyes never having left the Roman and the Arab.

Vespasian started to laugh.

"This talk will go better without me. . . ."

"No, Alexandra. Stay, little one. I like you near me. I am sorry if you have been offended," he said gravely, seeing that her lip was trembling. "I am an old soldier. I see little of modesty. Too little. In the old days, Rome had real women, women of virtue and honesty. My grandmother was one. A simple woman. Honest . . . loving . . . a farmer's wife. But worth a hundred empresses of Rome." He raised the silver cup. "This was hers. I take it with me wherever I go."

"'A woman of valor, what is her worth?'" Josef recited. "'Far above rubies. . . . Strength and dignity are her clothing. . . . She laugheth at the time to come.'"

"'Strength and dignity'—I like that. Good. Very good, Jo-

sephus. For once you Jews have got it right." He looked at
Alexandra for a moment, then tipped her chin up with his
finger. "Give me a clear-eyed girl with no nonsense to her.
One who is too honest even to mask her . . . hate." He dropped
his hand. "Go away, girl. Go . . . before I act like Nero when
I am not yet Caesar."

Josef did not leave with her. He stayed long at the feast, and
she had fallen asleep when at last she seemed to hear his voice.
He was talking to someone. There was a strange scent in the
room, the odor of an unfamiliar spice. She peeked through the
alcove curtain and recognized the tribune Nicanor, reclining
on the couch. Josef was sitting with his back to her. There was
something burning in a small dish; every now and then the two
men took deep breaths of the smoke, passing the plate between
them.

"I had made up my mind," Josef was saying, "that I would
serve the Lord better than any man has ever done." He laughed
softly. "I was paid for my presumption. You see, I thought
the way to begin was first to learn what each sect considered
the proper way. . . . And do you know what I found out, Nicanor?" He laughed again. "I found out that it was all a lie.
Sadducee . . . Pharisee . . . Essene. . . . It was all a lie."

"Then you do not believe in the God of your people?"

"Believe? Oh, yes, Nicanor! I believe in the Almighty!
More than anything I believe in the existence of the Divine.
But what, you may ask—and pray do—is the nature of that
Divine Existence?"

"Well, there is Zeus . . . and Mars. . . . Why do you laugh?
Even your own writings say that man is made in the likeness
of God."

"No, no, Nicanor, you are not listening. You must listen."
He leaned forward earnestly. "Haven't you ever felt—in battle,
perhaps—that whatever meaning exists in this world we inhabit
is only . . . stuff . . . things we have made up ourselves,
arrangements we have devised—like those roads you are forever building—to keep from colliding with ourselves?"

Nicanor murmured something, but it was lost to Alexandra
as he bent to inhale the strange incense.

"The Temple stinks to God," Josef said suddenly. "Look
at this." He went over to a deep chest in the room and began
pulling various items from it. Alexandra gasped as she saw the

robes of a Temple priest spill from his hands. "Look at that," Josef was saying. "Scarlet thread . . . purple dye . . . silken tassels and gold pomegranates. . . . What have they to do with anything divine?"

"I thought they were prescribed . . ."

"By men!" Josef exclaimed, and, laughing, he threw the robe over Nicanor. "By idiots who cannot see beyond their own desires." He sat down again, his head flung backward, a dreamlike expression on his face. "When I went into the desert with that crazy old man, I saw the mockery we had made of our fathers' revelations. At night, in the desert, you can almost touch the stars. They are so near . . . and yet . . . so distant. You hear a sound. . . . Is it the pulse of the earth or the beating of your own terrified heart? Silence. Only . . . terrible silence.

"In the desert, there are no words, Nicanor. No language, music, or preposterous art to shadow the one Reality, the one Presence. There is no pretense, no sentimental concern for our frailties. There is only Knowledge, and pure, mathematical indifference to our schemes." He paused. "I can no more believe in a human god than you can take seriously those ridiculous figures cavorting on Mount Olympus."

"Well . . ." Nicanor laughed uneasily. He had wrapped himself in the priest's robes and sat now like a child rolled up in a blanket. "Many stories are absurd. Still . . ." He cleared his throat. "It does not hurt to offer a libation now and then." He giggled. "I used to wonder about old Zeus taking so many disguises. I mean, I can understand wanting to be a bull. But a swan? An idiot bird? Of course, that's not half so ridiculous as some of the things our late beloved Nero tried. Do you know, he once had this mad idea of tying everyone to stakes— naked as babes, of course—and then the little bugger darts out dressed all in animal skins, growling and snarling, with this bear's hide over his head and back, and runs about sniffing and nibbling away at one and all. Well, you know, it could have been quite wonderful if one did not know the man was mad. I mean," he said, wiping tears of laughter from his eyes, "what if he had actually bitten something off? He was capable of it. Quite capable." He sat up, pointing his finger at Josephus. "Now, there was someone with less reverence for the gods than even you. Nero despised all religions—he raped the Vestal Virgin, you know—except for one. Wait a moment, what was it? Ah, yes, I have it—the cult of Atargatis, a Syrian goddess,

I believe. Anyway, he soon changed his mind about her, which he demonstrated by urinating on her sacred statue one day and calling on everyone else to do the same. You ought to have seen the line happy to oblige." He fell back laughing.

Josef smiled. His eyes went far away. "Yes," he said. "We want to obey. To do and think what others tell us to do and think. Because then *there can be no blame*. Who among us is brave enough . . . strong enough . . . to belong only to himself? . . ."

"My dear Josephus," Nicanor said dreamily. "You are still in the desert."

"Perhaps. Perhaps I will always be. . . ."

"Now you are melancholy."

"Am I?"

"Tell me what happened after your little holiday with the holy man."

"I did not go back to the Essenes. I returned to my father's house, where for some months I sat like a stone in my room, unable to take part in any normal activity. I was haunted by the desert . . . by the Silence I had found there." He got up again, restless now. "The feeling passed. But I was changed, determined to go beyond the realm of things that men know or dare to transgress. I had become, as I am now, impatient of a world defined by others' fears."

"And so you came to Rome."

Josef stared at him. "To Rome? Yes," he said with his half-smile. "Yes, I suppose Rome is part of it." He leaned over, took a deep breath of the pungent smoke, then sat down again, smiling. "Yes. . . . I demand the right to live as I choose. Without boundaries or taboos. Without tribe."

Nicanor left soon after this, and Josef came to bed.

"You are awake. I had forgotten you were here." He smiled at her. "You were listening, I suppose."

She nodded.

"Did you understand?"

"I'm not sure. Some of it."

He began to remove his clothing. "It might go better with us if you had an understanding of me," he mused. "I do not expect you ever will, and I suppose it does not really matter. Still . . . we are here, the two of us. . . . We could be of comfort to one another." He leaned over, touched her lips with his finger. "No ... don't talk. It is better with us when there are no words."

But after the lovemaking he said, "Tell me what you want, Alexandra. Tell me what you really want."

She lay there, silent.

He laughed softly. "Don't you trust me with your heart's secrets? I suppose I can't blame you for that. You know, sometimes I think you are quite extraordinary. There is a restlessness in you that is not natural to women. I like it," he admitted. "We are well suited, for all the difference of our beliefs. No, don't pull away. Let us not debate that now."

Still she did not answer.

"There is a mystery to you," he mused. "I feel it when I am in you, that as much as I possess you, I never really have you. And the feeling lingers. . . . The gentiles have many words for lovemaking, but in Hebrew there is only one: 'to know.' And I do not know you, Alexandra. You are my wife but yet unknown to me."

"I thought I pleased you."

"That is not what I mean." He turned on his stomach, studied her face a moment, then said abruptly, "You are not happy with me. The fact that this marriage has kept your honor—saved your life, even—means nothing to you. I am no longer governor of the Galilee, general to your Zealot mob. I belong to Rome now. Like a dog. And you belong to the dog." He rolled over on his back again with a strange laugh. "If you only knew ... The day they put their fetters on me, they struck deadlier ones from my heart. When they led me chained like an animal to Vespasian, all I could think was, 'I am free ... I am free.'"

So now, at last, she knew. "You hate being one of us. You hate being a Jew."

"No!" What anguish there was in that denial. "No ... but I want it to be part of me, not all of me. Not ... all."

She was ashamed for him and yet, despite herself, sympathetic. She had felt the bondage of being a woman, fought against the limits set for her sex. It had never occurred to her that for men there were other prisons. But now, suddenly, she realized how many cages there were. For everyone.

"You asked what I seek," she said slowly. "You said once you knew what I wanted. You said ... we were the same. In some ways I suppose we are. I too want knowledge. I want to know—I must know—what it is all about."

He said a strange thing then. He said, "Don't look for answers, Alexandra. Seek knowledge, not answers."

"Daughter of my friend Samu-el. Blessings of Allah upon thee." Pangar, sheikh of the Quraysh tribe and commander of Vespasian's Arab auxiliaries, touched his heart in greeting.

"*Salaam*, great prince. Will you take water to cool your throat, bread to warm your stomach? My hand is open in peace."

He smiled as she recited the desert salutation he had himself taught her. "The daughter of Samu-el does not change no matter where her tent is raised."

"My house is yours. I am afraid it does not consist of much these days, only this small apartment. But you are welcome here as you were in Beit Harsom."

He bowed slightly. "May the God of Abram lead you always to water. May He be host to Samu-el for all eternity."

"You know my father is dead."

"May he walk with Allah. Yes. My own heart is wounded for all that has befallen my friends."

"Yet you align yourself with Rome."

He made an apologetic gesture. "Rome rules the world. Even at your own table as much was said. Did not your father tell me that rebellion against such great power was foolish? I must think of the welfare of my people."

"Yes, I guess you must."

He took a step forward and in a low voice said, "I am in your debt, daughter of Samu-el. When you saw me, you were silent. I honor our friendship as I do my name—but, you understand, it might be harmful in the eyes of Rome."

"I would imagine Vespasian knows you were once welcome in a Jewish home. There are enough informers and spies in this place to populate a city."

"He knows only that I bring him ten thousand horsemen."

"To kill the people of Judea."

He spread his hands again. "I must think of my own people."

She nodded. There was nothing to say. She felt tired. She tried to smile. "I am honored that you remembered me. I did not think you would."

"Who could forget such eyes? They are the eyes of Al-Uzza, goddess of the morning star. Besides, who was it always begging for a tale, asking about my people, wanting to learn our language? I am glad that you are safe and well. I have been told you are the wife of the one they call Josephus. It is a good alliance. The *jarr* is a clever man, and Vespasian is fond of him. Until this war is settled, the Roman cannot be open in his regard, but you will do well for yourself. One day I will sit at your table again, in the city of Caesar perhaps. I would like to see this place, although I confess I cannot stay long in these tents of stone. I am a man of sand after all."

Shifting with the wind, she thought.

"Daughter of Samu-el, like the Roman I cannot be open in my regard. But I am in the debt of the House of Harsom. Someday I will balance the weights."

"I may hold you to that, great prince."

"What is it?" He lowered his voice again. "If it is within my power you have only to ask. . . ."

"Help me leave this place."

He was astonished by her request. "Where will you go? You are safe here. Your bed is soft, your table full. The *jarr* is in no danger. But outside . . . this land wears the face of death. Soon they will starve in the city of your God. They will kill each other for a meal of grass as now they kill each other for gold. You must not leave Vespasian's protection."

"Protection! I am a slave! The golden bracelets Vespasian sends me might as well be iron bands, this necklace of jade a yoke around my neck, a slave collar! No, I am not mistreated. But can I live like this, like some pet cat existing by virtue of another's tolerance?" She shook her head, her eyes cloudy and troubled. "To sleep on cushions woven by my family's murderers . . . to eat meat salted by the labor of Jewish slaves . . . no. . . . No, Pangar. My place is not here. You said you were in my debt—in my father's debt. Help me, then. Help me to leave this place."

"You ask me to help you die."

"Only to escape . . ."

"You seek death, daughter of Samu-el."

"Death is many things. I am dead here."

"I will take you with me. My kingdom is not unpleasant, and my wives will be kind to you. You shall be my daughter. I will make you a princess of Arabia."

She shook her head. "Such honor is not for me."

He sighed. "Where would you go?"

"I don't know. I have heard that there are places outside Jerusalem where my people are still free, where they continue to fight the Roman."

"I know of only two. Vespasian has not turned his attention to them because he wishes first to settle the matter of Jerusalem. But when he decides to look to them—"

Eagerly she took hold of his arm. "Where? Where, Pangar?"

He hesitated, but her eyes compelled him to answer. "One is called Machaerus," he said slowly. "The other is near the Sea of Salt. But it is desolate. It stands alone in the midst of nothing but sand and rock—"

"How is it called?"

"Masada. It is called the Masada."

SEVEN

The victories at Jericho, Hebron, and elsewhere had filled the prisoners' cages to overflowing. Titus had a special fondness for the arena, and as Vespasian's fortunes seemed about to take an upward leap, a series of gladiatorial games was announced "for the amusement of the multitude, and dedicated to the god Mars."

"We are expected to attend," Josef said.

Alexandra regarded this bit of news with shock and then dismay. "Surely Vespasian cannot suppose we wish to watch our countrymen die."

"I asked to be present," Josef said. "If I am to write an accurate account of things, as I propose to do, then I must see it all. There is no other way."

"But it is cruel..."

"Life is cruel. War is cruel. History, however, is dispassionate. At least it ought to be. Don't you see, Alexandra? There is no better way to reveal monstrous actions than to record them as they are. Those of us who have seen certain things or are in a position to view them have an obligation to relate them." He paused. "I know what others will think when they see me by the Roman's side. You, at least, will know the truth."

"Shall I be your apologist, then," she asked, "as you would be for our people?"

He smiled. "No. I told you once—never make excuses. Certainly not for me."

She said nothing, watching as he went over his papyri.

Vespasian had given Josef the writing tools he requested and even allowed him to interview many of the prisoners and soldiers. In this way the young Judean passed much of his captivity. Sometimes Alexandra accompanied him or later transcribed his notes, adding her own impressions to his. Although

Josef did not like to acknowledge any woman's intellectual capabilities—or, in fact, any female ability other then sexual gratification and pregnancy—he was no fool when it came to taking advantage of gifts at hand. By a quirk of nature this girl had a fine, retentive mind, and he did not shirk from putting it to use.

For her part, Alexandra was glad of the task and welcomed the access to the prisoners, trying hard to ignore their suspicion and contempt, learning not to listen when they called her ugly names. Hagar had confessed finally that she had never seen the dead body of Benjamin ben Harsom; and Alexandra had come to hope that her brother might somehow, somewhere, be alive. So she followed Josef into the prisoners' cages, asking when she dared for any news of Beni. But if any of the men had indeed heard of him, they would not say.

And now how many of them would be taken to the arena for one final hour in the sun before eternal darkness?

"There is no need for me to attend the games," she said. "You will do well enough without me."

"No, you must come. Vespasian made a special point of mentioning your presence. No doubt you will sit beside him." His voice had suddenly become cold. "I think the Farmer is getting ready to reap his harvest, or at least to pluck one apple from the tree."

She reddened. "What will you do?"

"I? What will I do? No, my dear wife, the question is rather 'What will you do?'"

"What should I do?"

"Well . . . you could kill yourself, I suppose, to save your honor and mine. It is the classic solution. Though I can't imagine you committing suicide. Some action like Judith's would be more in keeping with your character, I think," he added, recalling the Maccabean heroine who, when called to the bed of one of Antiochus's generals, got the man drunk and cut off his head. "You like that, don't you?" He pointed his finger at her. "Well, don't try it."

"Are you worried for yourself?"

"For you, believe it or not." He looked away. He knew she thought his "prophecies" only a trick or show, a way to gain power for himself, but in fact he often had premonitions of things to come. He had seen the Romans taking Jotapata in a dream that graphically portrayed them walking through the misty, silent town in the first hours of dawn. Awakening, he had led Saul and the others to the cave, thus escaping the soldiers' first fury. And he had known that Vespasian would become Caesar as far back as his days in Rome, where he had looked at Titus and had a sudden sense of what was now coming to pass. Now, looking at Alexandra, he had another premonition. She had escaped violence twice in her young life, but he had a flash vision of her surrounded by great calamity from which there was no escape. He saw a fire...flames....

"Can you not tell him I am ill?"

"No. I think you had better come. There are many strangers roaming the palace now, men from Egypt, Arabia, the Syrian territories. It is better for you not to remain here alone."

"I don't want to see anyone gobbled up by lions! Aliterus says—"

"That is Rome. And Nero."

"Aliterus told me they make prisoners fight each other. He said if darkness fell before the audience was satisfied slaves would be set afire to light the arena. Human torches, Josef!"

"Sometimes they do these things," he said uneasily. "In Rome, there are even special theaters where the center is an entire lake on which whole fleets of ships fight. They call these places *naumachiae*. It is quite wonderful," he said, getting enthusiastic now. "They fight to the end..." His voice trailed off.

"Josef, who mans these vessels? Slaves? Prisoners of war?"

"That is the way things are," he said impatiently. "Anyway, Vespasian's taste runs more to chariot races and gladiatorial combat. He likes professional fighters. And before you start to feel sorry for them, let me tell you they enjoy the best of everything. Why, they are treated like gods, I tell you! The uglier they are, the more women they have."

"Do not confuse the Circus with the Theater," Aliterus said. "The one caters to the vilest of common tastes, the other is forum to the gods."

Alexandra was familiar with the writings of the Greek playwrights and, unlike her uncle, the Sadducee priest Shammai, did not consider the theater an unholy place. She could not believe that a man like Aeschylus would have directed his energy toward a base form.

"The classic dramas are rarely put forth now," Aliterus acknowledged, impressed with the girl's literate questions.

"They are not to the public taste. Today, everyone in Rome wants comedy—the broader, the better—and spectacles, of course. Everything must be lavish beyond description. If one does see a *Medea*—which is fairly modern, you understand—it is only to witness the sacrifice of real children."

"How can you be part of that?" Alexandra wondered.

"I am no tragedian," he replied, not understanding. "Although I tell you I could play Oedipus to make the gods weep."

In the end, despite her protestations, she went to the arena, driven by her curiosity, which was not to be denied, for all her noble talk. But then, her curiosity had been a family joke, her father avowing that her first word had not been *imma*, "mother," but *lamma*, "why." Her younger brother had been the same, although his passion for discovery was more physical than academic. Beni was forever crawling into or on top of things, she recalled. As he was small and agile, he generally managed to escape the various prisons he put himself in, but more than one clay vessel had to be cracked open to free his fingers or foot. Alexandra had been "the owl." Beni had been "the monkey."

Family memories had begun to stir again despite her determined attempts not to think of the past. The night before the games there had been a grand dinner in the palace. Among the guests was Tiberius Alexander, former procurator of Judea, present governor of Egypt, commander of two Roman legions, and cousin to Alexandra bat Harsom.

Next to Josef ben Matthias, who would be known to future generations as Flavius Josephus, and after the royal siblings Agrippa and Berenice, this nephew of Philo, this son of a man whose esteem among Jerusalemites was no less for his having contributed the gold plating on the Temple doors, was perhaps the most infamous Romanizer and renegade Jew of the time. As procurator of Judea, he had executed hundreds of Galilean rebels and was responsible for the capture and crucifixion of James and Simon, sons of Judah the Galilean. It was his men who had searched the hills for Menahem the Sicarius outlaw, who had raped and murdered Judah's daughter and killed her husband, leaving an orphan son named Eleazar ben Ya'ir. As governor of Egypt, Tiberius Alexander had ordered troops into the Delta quarter at the outbreak of the Judean revolt, ostensibly to quell the riots there, but in reality effecting the massacre of most of Alexandria's Jewish community. Rome had no reason to doubt his loyalty.

Yet even as Alexandra, seeing him in the Praetorium, was reminded of the House of Harsom, the Egyptian governor, noticing the girl, began to think of his own childhood.

"You find her interesting?" Vespasian inquired gruffly, seeing his guest's searching look, and nodding in Alexandra's direction.

"Those eyes . . . I thought for a moment . . . Who is she?"

"The daughter of a wealthy Jew who was killed here in Caesarea along with most of his family. The man was not Caesar's enemy and had a rather distinguished background. Alexandra was brought here as a slave, but out of respect for her deceased parent I have allowed her to become the wife of my prisoner Josephus, whom you already know."

"Those eyes..." Tiberius Alexander murmured again. "Who was her father? Is there a family name? It is not customary for Jews to have one, but sometimes, if they are persons of note, they will refer to themselves as being of a certain house or line."

"I can tell you that," said Josef, who was near enough to overhear their conversation. "My wife is the daughter of Samuel ben Harsom. I believe," he added significantly, "that in Alexandria there stands a villa in whose door or gate is carved the likeness of the new moon, the emblem of that family."

"And I know it well!" Tiberius Alexander exclaimed. "Why, we are kin! Now I understand. . . ." He turned to Vespasian excitedly. "I have seen such eyes as that girl possesses only once before. My grandmother had gray eyes. Why, the woman could look right through you! I remember, as a child, thinking she must be some strange magic creature because of the light that shone from her face. When she loved you, she was all sunlight. But when she was angry—" He shuddered. "I think she was the only woman I ever feared."

Vespasian laughed. "You had a grandmother too, eh?" He found the idea very funny. "Alexandra, come here."

She hesitated, then came forward, aware of many eyes on her and of whispering as well. She was dressed simply, as a Judean woman, and not in the gown and coiffure of a Roman lady, despite Josef's preference for that classic style. She did not like ornaments; necklaces and bracelets reminded her of slave symbols. Josef, however, had insisted that she wear the jewelry Vespasian had sent her. A silver chain dotted with rough-cut turquoise stones circled her neck. Earrings of delicate silver filigree peeped out from the veil of smooth, dark hair like stars suddenly appearing through the clouds in a midnight sky. A green silk cord was knotted around the waist of her white linen robe, the braided ropes reaching to her knees, ending in tassels caught with tiny silver bells. Her gown, cut straight across the neck, with full sleeves covering her arms, was of fine, soft fabric; and though hardly as revealing or provocative as those worn by the other women present, it still could not disguise the girl's supple, slender figure or fluid movements.

Berenice watched her, herself gorgeously attired in silk shot with threads of gold and embellished with multicolored embroidery, wearing a king's ransom in necklaces, rings, and bracelets. Reclining, her tall, full-breasted figure supine like that of a cat or rare tiger, she cast a quick look at Titus and nervously touched her hair. The "most desirable woman in the East" put on a small, mysterious smile—the one that masked frown lines—and thought with a sigh how well youth was served by nothing more than youth.

"Alexandra," Tiberius Alexander said with a smile. "We are even similarly named. We are cousins," he said, turning to Vespasian. "It gets a bit complicated, but we are indeed related."

"I think not," Alexandra said coldly.

"Why, yes," the man told her. "It is through the esteemed philosopher Philo, of Alexandria. His mother—"

"If you are familiar with Philo," Alexandra said, "then you may recall these words: 'Kinship shall be measured not by blood but by likeness of conduct.'"

"Ah." He sat back. "Then you do know who I am."

"You are Tiberius Alexander, governor of Egypt and former procurator of Judea."

"And a Jew once as well."

"Really?" she said politely.

"Cast out," he continued with a smile, "by my own family."

"On that we agree. I thought you might mistakenly believe it was you who did the casting out."

He did not react to this but looked around the room and said, "It seems that is not all we agree on, little cousin. Neither of us has any quarrel with Rome."

She flushed at this. "I am not here by choice." She looked squarely at Vespasian. "You have been kind to me. But I am not here of my own will."

"And where would you be?" Tiberius Alexander said suddenly. "Jerusalem? Do you know what they would do to you there, Alexandra bat Harsom? They would strip you naked, tie you to a horse, and send the animal through the streets of the Holy City, for you to be jeered and abused as a Sadducee princess, one whose father sat at the table of Rome, who exploited and betrayed the mass of common folk. John of Gischala and Simon bar Giora would fight over the right to execute you as they are fighting now over your house and belongings. Your patriotism is commendable," he said, "but misplaced."

"Would a man who has turned his back on his God and his people say otherwise?"

But he was not angry. "You see?" he said to Vespasian, smiling. "You see what the women in my family are like?"

The Roman nodded, smiling too. He was thinking how he would like to twist his hand in that dark hair, to still those lips with his own, to hold her young, smooth body to his and tell her to be at peace, that he would care for her, keep her from any harm. . . .

"Your father's reputation went beyond Judea," Tiberius Alexander was saying to the straight-backed girl. "There were none who knew him and did not respect him. I would say this legacy has proved more valuable to you than all the worldly possessions he acquired. Why can't you be governed by his wisdom? He never wanted war. And he saw no need for the isolation of Judea as something outside and apart from the power and protection of Rome."

"My father was a fool," she said bitterly. "He thought that all we had to do was be civilized and even the barbarian would see how absurd it was to think of us as monsters. He said if we were understanding of incomprehensible situations, tolerant of the prejudice against us—in short, if we led the just and virtuous life that Torah demands—why, then it would surely follow that the world would welcome us in its midst and let us live in peace." She took a deep breath. "You know how the Greeks and Syrians have treated us. You have seen how little Rome thinks of us. You cannot tell me there is any race on this earth that does not wish us dead."

"Perhaps," Tiberius Alexander said softly, "it is because you do not always follow Torah."

"Who else must submit to such judgment?" she retorted.

"Tell me what people does not transgress. And yet, what nation is there whose existence depends on its goodness? Are we to be allowed to live only so long as we practice virtue?"

"Look to Jerusalem," Tiberius Alexander said. "You have heard the reports. You speak of the barbarian. Who is that? Rome? The Greeks? The Syrians and Egyptians? Or is it your own Zealots?"

"We have a right to fight among ourselves. Yes, and to each and every mean, petty action men and women everywhere are heir to. That is our right. It is our right to be a people. Our own people."

The apostate frowned. "You do not know what you are saying."

"I am saying that it is not for you or anyone else to judge the people of Israel. I, for one, will leave that to the Almighty."

"Then watch, little cousin, how He will cast you down."

"Not forever." She shook her head stubbornly. "Not . . . forever."

The sun was as hard as diamonds. Reflecting off sea and sand, it glared down like a ferocious golden beast on the spectators in the arena. On the shaded side of the stands Vespasian and Titus, with their guests and entourage, sat sheltered under the canopy of the official podium. The princess Berenice sat beside Titus; and by Vespasian's hand, giving more fuel to the already rampant gossip, was the slave girl called Alexandra. Many stories were circulating about the young Jewess. One rumor had it that she was Vespasian's illegitimate daughter, whom he had fathered during his governorship of Africa with a mysterious woman who later came to Judea, and whom he now enjoyed incestuously. Another story said that the girl was Tiberius Alexander's illegitimate daughter. Still a third claimed that Alexandra was Berenice's half-sister, the illegitimate daughter of Agrippa I. All tales seemed to agree on two facts: the girl was a bastard and Vespasian's mistress.

"I don't know what he sees in her," one of the ladies present muttered. "She has the coldest eyes."

"Well, it seems the Flavians have a taste for orientals," her companion said.

"Yes, but *she's* a queen—and hot enough to melt the throne on which she sits, from what I've heard. Three husbands, was it? And her own brother?"

The two women being discussed stared straight ahead, looking neither at each other nor at those whispering about them.
They had seen each other many times in the palace but had
never spoken. Berenice had known the disquieting effects of
Alexandra's gaze; but she was not one to admit the power of
any female but herself. Like many women who struggled for
recognition in a world of men, she had no fondness for those
of her own sex.

Vespasian was in high humor. Tiberius Alexander had
pledged his support; his own legions in Caesarea had saluted
him as Caesar. In a day or so he would leave with the governor
of Egypt to receive the homage of the legions in Alexandria
and then continue on to Berytus for a council of war. The sun
felt good on his bones; it was the damp he minded most now.
The girl sitting on the steps at his feet warmed his blood even
more. He had been a fool not to take her. She was wasted on
anyone else. Despite his age he was as strong as any young
pup. Hadn't Berenice marveled at his strength, admiring the
square, muscular body whose younger version she now worshipped? He would call the girl to him. Tonight. Yes, tonight.
Perhaps he would take her with him to Egypt. . . .

Josef ben Matthias squinted into the sun as he looked around
him, mentally taking note of the place and all its occupants.
He was excited, less by the sport about to begin than by the
knowledge of what lay ahead. His future status was all but
guaranteed. Vespasian had as much as promised he would be
set free. And when that happened . . . he would melt the gold
chains, buy something pretty with the precious lump—perhaps
in the famed markets of Alexandria. Vespasian had said something about taking him with him. . . .

A cage of men was lifted from an underground chamber to
one end of the arena. The bars were unlocked, and the first
group of prisoners stepped out, blinking at the light, shielding
their eyes from the harsh sun. They looked around them, confused and distracted by the crowd, which began to whistle and
call to them. Some of them had been given heavy armor, but
these men stood uncertainly, as if not knowing how or in what
direction to point their swords. Guards pushed them to the
center of the ring, prodding them with lances. Some of the
men reacted angrily to this, which pleased the audience greatly;
they shouted excitedly for combat to commence. Suddenly,

one young man stepped forward. Advancing toward the podium, he dropped the great sword in his hand and cried, "*Sica! Sica!*"

The crowd began to murmur, delighted with this sudden drama.

"What is he saying?" Vespasian turned to his son.

"I am not sure," Titus replied. He stood up and motioned for the young man to come closer.

Alexandra had not been paying close attention to these events. When the Judean captives entered the ring, she had instinctively looked away, ashamed for them and ashamed of herself for being in this place. Vaguely she saw one of the group disassociate himself from the rest; and now, hearing his petition, she was moved by curiosity to study him as he came near.

"I believe he is asking for a dagger," Titus was saying. "He is no doubt one of the Sicarii we caught near Jerusalem and prefers to fight with his own weapon."

The young man was in front of them now. He was of average height but slightly built, so that he appeared smaller than he really was. His bare arms were thin but sinewy. His stance was firm and very proud. "*Sica*," he said again, grimly. "Give me the short knife."

Alexandra leaned forward. The boy's face was deeply tanned; a scar ran down one cheek. His eyes, however, were exceptionally clear and light, and his dark hair, struck by the sun, was the color of deep wine. There was no mistaking the resemblance. He might have been her twin.

She did not know if she cried out his name or whispered it. Vespasian turned to her in surprise. The young man in the arena looked back at her; startled, he mouthed her name.

"He is my brother," she told Vespasian in a hoarse voice. "My brother, Benjamin." And she fell on her knees to the Roman and embraced his legs.

Vespasian bent his head to her, and she whispered that she would do anything, anything he asked, if he would but release her brother. Vespasian tipped her face up, and she saw the pity in his eyes and hated him for it, hated him for seeing her cry, hated him for everything. But still she whispered, "Anything . . . anything you wish of me . . ."

The crowd had begun to whistle and call again, impatient for the spectacle to begin.

"I cannot free him," Vespasian said gently. "It is not done.

I cannot break the rule. But if he fights and lives, he shall have his freedom." He looked at Titus now, who nodded; for Benjamin was in fact his son's prisoner.

Vespasian rose, lifting his hands for silence. "The Jew has asked for the short knife. He shall have it." To the boy he said simply, "Win and you are free."

The gray eyes were still grim. "And my sister," he demanded in a firm, low voice, a voice with the same steady quality as his eyes.

Vespasian was startled by the request. He had long ceased to think of Alexandra as a captive. But he nodded finally and sat down again.

A dagger fell at the young fighter's feet. He picked it up and grinned. "God is king!" he shouted defiantly. "Freedom is all! Death is nothing!" And with a wild, joyous cry he ran back to his companions, who seemed to have taken heart now. Echoing his words, they raced to the center of the arena, perhaps hoping that they too might win their freedom.

The crowd was in an uproar; they sensed the heightened urgency of this combat. Here was a fine show! What madmen these Jews were, to think they might best the gladiators of Caesarea and Rome! Why, look at the size of those Nubians. There were Vespasian's prized Thracians—and just look at that big Gaul! You'd think the Jews would not be so happy to see such as these.

But they were. The sight of the Gauls and Thracians had lightened the hearts of the captive men, who had feared only that they would be forced to fight one another.

Josef came forward now and took Alexandra's hand. If she had bothered to look, she would have seen the agony in his eyes and wondered if perhaps he was thinking that he might well have been one of the men in the ring. Or was he remembering a child who had wrestled with him on a sunlit beach, a child grown into a man who would not have to make use of the skills he, Josef, had taught him that bright, long-ago day?

The men in the arena had begun to fight, and Alexandra had eyes only to seek out the figure of her brother. He was the center of attention. She could hear all around her the wagering for and against his life, mixed with speculation as to his identity and hers. How she wanted to close her eyes, to cover her ears, to hide her head; and yet she could not look away or shut out the sound of the excited, betting crowd. "Oh, Lord," she found herself praying, "don't let him die here! Don't let my brother die in this arena before these animals!"

It was a fight those present that day would long speak of, one that old legionaries would relate when they swapped campaign tales. "There was this fellow," they'd say, "a lad with hardly a beard, but braver than most men I've seen."

Beni was fighting well. Titus, watching him, declared the battle as good as anything he'd seen in Rome; while Vespasian, whose whole body seemed to echo the maneuvers on the field, would call out every so often, "Well done! Well done!" and slap his knee.

The boy was pitted against a *retiarius,* or netter—the largest man Alexandra had ever seen; indeed, the image of David and Goliath came to many minds that afternoon. The *retiarius* wore no heavy armor but carried a net and a three-pronged lance. With the net he would seek to cover his adversary, rendering him helpless so that he could spear him like a fish with the trident. Yet each time the giant cast out his net he covered only sand, for Beni was as quick as the netter was big. The boy moved like a dancer or a bull-jumper; and each time he evaded his foe the crowd went wild. Now he was here, now there, nimble as could be. Once he fell, and the crowd stilled as the net came down—but there! he had rolled away and was on his feet before the *retiarius* could cast out again! The crowd roared. Alexandra's head begun to buzz with the tumult. Beni had been called monkey, but now he was like a serpent, so smoothly did he move, so cleverly did he elude the netter. Again and yet again he escaped the deadly web and lance.

"If only he had a spear or long sword," Nicanor murmured, shaking his head. "If he comes close enough to use the dagger he is done for."

"But he would not be so fast with a heavy weapon," Vespasian said excitedly, his eyes never leaving the fight. "He is playing for time, I think—By the gods! Did you see that? A hundred denarii the lad pulls through!"

"Done!" shouted Titus.

Alexandra's eyes began to burn. The arena seemed filled with a strange ballet, and she began to see it all as through the mist that rises from the desert sand. Josef was gripping her hand so tightly that it had become quite numb.

Suddenly all rose to their feet with a great shout, and she with them. Beni was on the ground. For some reason he did not move as the net covered him, or even when the *retiarius* drew back his arm to cast the lance. But in the moment when the trident flew, he managed to turn aside so that only his shoulder was speared. He was still alive. The netter would have to come close now for the kill, and as the man bent to pull out the lance and strike once more, Beni thrust upward. The gladiator fell alongside the boy and rolled over, a dagger in his stomach.

Everything happened quickly after that. Vespasian seemed to signal to someone, rising simultaneously and pulling Alexandra up with him. Vespasian swept along in his great strides. Then she was in a rough chamber, a cool, damp place filled with the smell of many men. The sounds of the arena echoed dimly through the rock walls, and the light from the barred opening cast checkered shadows on the dirt floor. Beni was laid out on a table, and two men were pulling the broken trident from his flesh. He cried out once and then was still. She ran to him. The lance was out; his chest was covered with blood. The men were trying to staunch the wound.

"He's alive," one of the attendants said.

She looked at Vespasian and saw him exchange glances with the man. "They must burn the wound," she said. "Why haven't they begun?"

Vespasian shook his head. "It isn't in the shoulder, Alexandra. Your God has kept him alive for you, but not for long, I think."

As if in answer, Beni opened his eyes. They were the clear gray of morning, the color of day's first light.

"Will you leave us?" she asked the men.

They left the room, Vespasian as well.

She wiped Beni's brow. His eyes were so clear, so full of light.

"Alexandra . . ."

"Yes . . . yes, I'm here."

He managed a smile. "We won. . . . We won, Lexa. Wouldn't father be proud?"

"Father . . . Shimon . . . Joshua. . . . If only they could see what a hero you have become. I'd like to see Shimon push you now."

"Will the Roman keep his word?"

"You are free, Beni. You have won your freedom."

"And you?"

"Yes. . . . You have freed me, too."

"I thought you were dead. I was caught in the market. . . . They drove us to the dock like sheep . . . worse. . . . I dove off the breakwater. No one saw. I hid in the water... managed to climb aboard one of the ships . . . hid there. . . . Lucky it didn't put out to sea. Then . . . swam . . . and swam. Lived with Galileans . . . the Sicarii. They're not what we thought. . . . They're . . ." He pressed his lips together, swallowed. She gave him water, raising his head so that he could drink. "I'm tired. . . . I'm tired, Lexa. . . ." He lay back with a sigh.

"You must sleep now."

"Not yet . . . not yet. You're beautiful, Lexa. . . . You're beautiful. You look like . . . mother. . . . Don't worry, I'll take care of you. . . . Ma . . ." He swallowed. "Everything will be all right now. I'll take you . . . to Ma . . . Ma . . ." He began to cough, and the blood spilled out of his mouth. His eyes turned the color of slate. Then he was still.

His body was placed in a coffin of soft limestone, interred, with Vespasian's permission, in the hills of Beit Shearim beneath Mount Carmel. In the sarcophagus she placed the *mezuzah* from the house in Caesarea.

He was seventeen years old.

Thirty days of mourning were prescribed by Jewish Law. During that time, Alexandra was visited by a man who had fought beside Beni in the arena, and earlier in the Galilee. Vespasian had granted manumission to all who were victorious in the ring that day; thus several prisoners had won both life and freedom. More than two hundred, however, had died before the bloodlust of the cheering crowd was satiated.

Shem had stayed to see Beni buried and to talk with Alexandra. He felt he owed his life to the dead boy because of the courage Beni had put in his heart and the generosity he had inspired in the Roman. And so he sat with Alexandra and told her what he knew—how brave Beni had been at Gamala, how he had never lost hope during their captivity, how he had often spoken of escape and of rejoining the Judean forces.

"He would not fight with John or Simon," Shem said. "He seemed to think that each was bad although committed to our cause."

"What did he intend to do, then?" Alexandra asked. "That is, if he had been able to escape."

"He spoke of joining the Sicarii," Shem said.

"Then he did plan to go to Jerusalem."

"No, ma'am. He wanted to ride with ben Ya'ir. You see,

Jerusalem is a bit of a mess right now. Between the goings on there and what's happened to the rest of the country, there are only a few places left in Judea where a man is really free. The Sicarii—or what's left of them—have taken over a place way out near the shore of the Dead Sea. Every day more people come to them—there are many Essenes there, too, who fled from Qumran. Anyway, that's where your brother—may he rest in peace—wanted to go. To the Masada."

The Masada. That was what Beni had been trying to say. He had tried to tell her he would take her to the Masada. Pangar had also spoken of the Zealot fortress, but in the most discouraging terms. "Tell me about this place," she asked. "Tell me about this—Masada."

While Alexandra sat in mourning, still another person called on her. It was the princess Berenice.

She came softly into the room, with none of the imperial aloofness for which she was famous; yet more than ever she reminded Alexandra of a kind of great, legendary bird, the sound of whose wings beating together must surely be terrifying.

Berenice was a tall, big-boned woman, amber-complexioned, with heavy, hennaed hair flowing girlishly on her tawny shoulders, the color startling against her dark Idumean skin. Three times a bride, wife, the rumors went, to her unmarried brother, she was perhaps the most hated yet most adored woman in Judea, and she had beguiled every Roman procurator who had ever come into her presence—including Gessius Florus, who, it was said, had called off his troops in exchange for a night of her company. Her appeal was all the more amazing since eastern taste usually ran to young maidens, those barely into womanhood. To touch a girl before she menstruated was taboo, but one did not wait long thereafter. Berenice was nearly forty years old, living in a climate and time where women as a rule did not age well, and she was still considered the most dazzling, seductive creature in the East. Titus, who was himself a handsome, muscular product of Rome, and certainly no naive boy, albeit twenty years younger than his mistress, had been totally swept off his feet.

The princess's face was grave and gentle as she stood before the girl. Her golden, uptilted eyes were soft with sympathy, and in a low, courteous voice she expressed the sentiments appropriate to the occasion. Alexandra thanked her shortly; and a silence grew around the two women like the shadow of the hours. Berenice hesitated, started to leave, then turned back. "You don't like me, do you?" she asked suddenly. Before the startled girl could reply, she went on. "I know what you think of me. Strange . . . that I should give it any thought. I have never cared in the least for anyone's opinion. But I find myself wondering how you see me." She gave a short laugh. "Wondering . . . why I care at all."

Alexandra gave her a searching look but said nothing, her silence more damning than any words.

Berenice flushed with anger. "Go on," she said. "Tell me what a wicked woman I am. Say all the dirty things you whisper about me in the streets. I am my brother's wife, Vespasian's whore, Titus's mistress. . . . Why don't you say it?" She laughed drily. "You are silent. Why? Because . . . I am princess of Judea. No matter what else you may call me, I am still your queen." She raised her tawny arms, smiling with satisfaction. "The blood of the Hasmoneans runs through these veins . . . yes, in these arms that circle the neck of Rome." Her hands dropped to her side. "Thanks to my grandmother Miriamne," she continued factually, "who was murdered, as you no doubt know, by my grandfather Herod, called the Great. Ah, yes, I know what you say of him! A badly circumcised barbarian. An Idumean with a Nabatean mother, whose people were chasing goats across the desert while your fathers' fathers were annotating the Law. That may be. But we sit above you now. We, the sons and daughters of the goat chasers. Your precious descendants of David are the shepherds now. Your priests of Zadok are eunuchs to my family's whim. You despise us, but we are your royal house, the House of Herod. And I . . . am Herod's daughter." She paused. "A pity, that. I ought to have been his son."

Still Alexandra said nothing. The woman seemed to be in a kind of private torment that Alexandra's presence fed and yet, perversely, comforted.

Berenice was pacing back and forth now. "Your husband—Josephus—is a traitor."

"Yes."

"So. Even those who trace without question the infinite purity of their blood may look to Rome."

"So it seems."

"Your father looked to Rome."

"My father . . . was mistaken."

Berenice stopped her pacing. "I knew your mother," she said suddenly. "I was jealous of her. That hair . . . those eyes. . . . She was very beautiful. I can see her in you despite the difference of your coloring." She sighed. "How slender you are. . . . You look as though your bones were made of glass. You are so young. . . . When I was your age I had already known two husbands . . . old men with sour breath and sweaty claws. They were horrible . . . horrible. My youth was squandered on old men, sold by my father to insure the security of his kingdom, to fatten his treasury. I never knew what it was to feel . . . anything. And now . . . ." She lowered her head like a penitent. "He is so young," she whispered. "So beautiful. And he says he loves me. Could he love me? Could anyone . . . really love me?" She fell silent for some time, remaining motionless, her head bent forward, until Alexandra thought the woman had forgotten her. A stain appeared on Berenice's bodice, as though a tear had fallen there; but when the princess raised her head, her face was composed, her eyes calm. "We shall be staying in Caesarea until Titus returns from Berytus," she said. "You are welcome to abide under our protection. I suspect you would prefer to leave this place. I do not advise it. The world you hunger for—your Zealot Judea— is a hard, terrible place." She paused. "Don't be a fool. You are in an enviable position. Yes, I envy you myself. Your future is quite promising. Josephus has played a clever game, and I think he has won it. You are young, beautiful, and most important, you pose no threat to anyone. Rome will take to you. I believe you and Josephus may even become celebrities there, exotic additions to the local culture. And as long as Vespasian bears this fondness for you, well . . . ." She shrugged delicately. "You are in Caesar's favor. Surely you realize what that means. Well . . . ." Berenice turned to leave, but Alexandra's voice stopped her.

"Thank you for your advice. There is one thing, though. . . ."

Berenice lifted an eyebrow questioningly.

"About your Hasmonean heritage. Miriamne's blood does not entitle you to the throne of David any more than Herod's does. The Maccabee was not of the anointed line. The blood that runs through your veins—every drop of it—is the blood of usurpers. You are not the royal house of Judea. You rule nothing. Rome owns the world—you've said so yourself. And you are not an Israelite. The world may call you Jew, but you are not one of us, either by heritage or by inclination." The sharp gleam left the gray eyes; they became soft, dovelike. "You came here, I suppose, out of sympathy. It is discourteous of me to speak so. But I have a passion for truth. For facts, at any rate, that cannot be disputed."

But instead of being angry, Berenice merely smiled. "Look to yourself," she said softly. "Look to yourself, Alexandra bat Harsom. You will find it is a perilous thing to be a woman alone."

EIGHT

Josef was jubilant. "He did it before all of them! Titus, Cerealis, Mucianus—all of them! So there would never be any doubt! He had my chains struck, Alexandra! It is the equivalent of full pardon—Titus suggested it. Vespasian has set me free! He has gone on to Italy now—Titus will finish up here. I am to accompany Titus to Jerusalem, and afterwards—afterwards we sail for Rome!" He was rummaging through the chest, tossing articles of clothing every which way. "My notes— where are my notes? I have some things I want to record before I forget. I thought you were keeping everything in order—ah, here they are!" He gave her a quick look. "Are you all right? I am sorry I could not stay with you after your brother—Well, but Hagar looked after you, didn't she? She always does. You may take her to Rome if you like. I think we can count on her loyalty. But you must get someone else to do your hair, someone who knows the latest styles. I want you to start putting it up like the women at court. And your clothes must be changed; they are monstrously provincial. It doesn't hurt to bare a shoulder now and then. You have very nice shoulders. And we must get you some good necklaces and things—I know you dislike jewelry, but you don't want people to think we're poor, do you? People never respect you if they think you are poor."

"Josef—"

"Eh? By the gods, where is that stylus? Can't you see to things? Can't I depend on anyone but myself?"

"Josef, please . . ."

"What? What? What is it? Ha! You should have seen Titus's face when he found Berenice had not returned to Tiberias but was waiting for him. The man's in love, I tell you."

"Josef." She took a deep breath. "I'm leaving."

"Don't start that again. Well, here is some parchment, at any rate."

"No, I mean it. I want a divorce."

He put down the stylus. "You what?"

"You must divorce me," she said firmly. "You can write the decree yourself—you were trained as a priest. You can say anything you like. I don't care."

His face darkened. "A divorce," he said angrily. "You dare to ask—yes, I'll divorce you!" He grabbed the roll of parchment and hastily wrote something on it, then threw it across the room at her. "I ought to have done this long ago! I took you— I married you! A Sadducee priest marrying a common slave! I saved you—and you have done nothing but fight me all the way. I ought to let you go. Yes, you deserve what is waiting out there. Go on, go back to Jerusalem. Go. Go and die with all the rest, with madmen and murderers and idiots like yourself. Divorce! What do either of us need with a divorce! You will be a corpse soon enough!"

She turned white at this outburst but said nothing. Her eyes fixed him like beacon lights. As suddenly as it had begun, his anger subsided. He went to her.

"Alexandra . . . I know you are still upset about Benjamin." He sighed. "That was a sad, a very sad thing . . . and that is why I will not listen to you now. You are alone in the world. I am too. We are both of us quite alone. . . . But we must forget the past, forget Jerusalem, forget Caesarea too. We will begin our own house. I have not minded that you have not yet conceived, because I did not wish my son to be born of a slave and a prisoner. But now . . ." He drew her close to him. "We must give this matter great attention," he whispered, running his hand down her arm. "My nights have been lonely. . . . Surely you have missed me. I know what a sweet appetite you have. . . ."

"No. . . . No!" She pulled away from him. She was trembling.

"Alexandra . . ."

Slowly, she turned back to face him. "I honored you," she said. "Once, I thought you were the bravest, the finest man in all the world. When people said it was a sign of weakness that you had been Sadducee, Pharisee, even Essene, I thought only that your quest for knowledge was three times greater than any ordinary man's. When it was whispered that you lingered in Rome, that you were the empress's lover, I thought only of the danger you defied in that unstable atmosphere in order to free those in whose behalf you had been sent. When you counseled peace, I thought you wise. And when you accepted command of the Galilee, I thought you courageous and dedicated to our people. When I saw you with Vespasian, I rejoiced because you were alive. And when... when others said you were not taken but had gone willingly, I called them liars . . . liars. . . ." She looked away.

He was silent. Then he said, "Am I so odious to you now?"

"No more than I am to myself."

"Why do you seek to punish yourself? Why this guilt? Now I know what this is about! Alexandra, that you live while others have died is a miracle, not a curse. You ought to thank the Almighty. I swear, it would be enough to make a man a true believer, seeing how you have been spared."

"But don't you see? It must be for something, for some reason or purpose!"

"I told you once not to look for answers. Life and death are accidents. Besides, why insist on logic in a history swollen with absurdity? All right," he said suddenly, "I will give you your reason. Our class, if not our nation, will soon be extinct. The rich—the Sadducees—will all be murdered by Zealots, and the poor will undoubtedly be killed by the legions in the battle for Jerusalem. Our country has sentenced itself to annihilation. You seek a reason for your existence. It is this: You will live. You will bear sons and daughters who will not only preserve their Sadducee birthright but will enjoy a favored position in the world as well. Alexandra, you have been given a chance to lift yourself up from the anonymity of existence, to take your place in history beside Vespasian, Titus, Berenice, Agrippa, and Josephus. Yes! When Jerusalem is dust of the future, those names will still be spoken."

"What is the glory of man beside the glory of God?"

"It is the shadow of a shadow," he acknowledged. "But it is something! Wait..." He took her hands in his. "Believe me, the glory of Israel is gone forever. Jerusalem is even now a dream in the eyes of old men. Soon they will sit in mourning for their Temple. The Chosen People shall be homeless—beggars and slaves because of this folly begun with Rome. Despised by those whom they themselves rejected, without a nation of their own, they will disappear among the peoples of the world and be no more. Or, if any still exist, they will be the lowest of the low."

"And you and I? The sons and daughters of whom you speak? What will they be then?"

"Exceptions."

She stared at him. He was smiling at her. She shook her head, angry now. "The children of Israel are not yet gone from the earth, Josef. We have lost many battles, but the war is not done, and we are not all dead. It may be the Lord will be merciful. Perhaps He will send a leader"—she could not keep the bitterness from her voice—"one who will not betray us as others have."

"A messiah?" he mocked.

"A man."

"You dream."

"Perhaps."

"Where will you go?" he asked suddenly.

"Away . . . from here."

"Jerusalem will fall," he warned softly.

"Then," she said, "we will build it up again."

He smiled. "You talk like a Zealot."

"Perhaps, after all, I am one."

"No more than I." He paused. "Where will you go, Alexandra?" he asked again, curious now. "What do you want?"

She answered both questions: "To seek my self."

He stared at her, then shook his head. "You go too far," he said quietly. "You push yourself toward experiences you ought not know. The further you go, the less possible it will be for you to return to that existence which history and natural choice prescribe for a woman—and which, after all, may be all you are capable of handling."

"Perhaps. But I must find that out myself."

Again he stared at her, a look whose meaning she could not interpret. Then he smiled the curious half-smile she had grown to know so well. "A pity," he murmured. "If only we had come together in different circumstances. Another time, another place . . . I might have loved you."

"Yes," she said. "Another time . . . another place."

There was little she wished to take with her—nothing, in fact; and she left the packing to Hagar. The woman was determined to accompany her wherever she might go. "I let you out of my sight once, and look what trouble you found for yourself," Hagar said grimly.

"How is it you did not come with me to Jerusalem after my parents were killed?" Alexandra asked.

The woman sniffed. "How is it you never asked me? You just up and went. I returned from the market one day, and you were gone, along with the Christian wine merchant. I thought he had persuaded you finally to go with him to Pella."

"No," Alexandra replied, "although he tried hard enough."

"You see no merit in the ways of the Nazarene, then?"

"In his ways, yes. I am sure the man was honest. Nothing he seems to have taught is contrary to the essence of the Law but rather to be at the very heart of it. All that Lukas told me reminded me very much of Hillel. But Hillel never offered himself as anything but a teacher. And that is what bothers me about the followers of Jesus—their fanatical adoration of the man. That is why the rabbis call them *meshokim*—heretics. The Lord has always sent prophets, teachers, and leaders—but it is blasphemy to raise any man to be a god."

"And the messiah?"

"I don't believe in a messiah, Hagar."

"You do not think your God would send a Son?"

Alexandra grinned wickedly. "Why a son? Why not a Daughter?"

Hagar threw back her head and laughed. "Truly you are *my* daughter," she said. "Mine, and the Good Goddess's!"

There was another who would be leaving Caesarea. To everyone's surprise, Aliterus made known his intention of accompanying Alexandra. He wanted, he said, to see Jerusalem.

"Wait, then," Josef said when he heard of the actor's plans. "Come with Titus and myself."

Aliterus shook his head. "I do not wish to see the City of David as an invading foreigner," he said gently. He smiled, then sprang up and struck a pose as though afraid he had appeared too serious. "I have always researched my roles with great care," he announced.

"Research?" Josef asked. "Research for what?"

"For the part I was born to play. The role of a Jew."

It was impossible to ascertain whether the man was joking. Josef frowned. He did not like to think he might be the butt of the comedian's humor. "I have never understood why or how you ended up here in Judea," he said testily. "What you've told me is as strange as anything I've ever heard. Nor do I understand why you failed to accompany Vespasian back to Rome. The man assured you there was no danger, and I imagine the populace there would quickly welcome you back to your old glory. Yet you insist on remaining here, and now—now— you want to go to Jerusalem! Go, then," he said angrily. "Go with Alexandra. I see you are both obsessed with...with strange quests. Go to Jerusalem. I shall forget I ever knew you—as you both, it seems, have forgotten me."

The actor and the girl exchanged glances.

Josef sighed. "Do not stay long in the Holy City, my friend. And do not let it be known to anyone who and what you are, or they will surely hang you for a spy."

"I shall not die in Jerusalem," Aliterus said with great certainty. "I cannot tell you why, but I know it for a fact."

Josef shook his head. "You are mad . . . mad . . . both of you."

"Why didn't you go back to Rome with Vespasian?" Alexandra asked later. She had grown fond of the stout comedian but could see no future for him in Judea.

"Why won't you go there with Josephus?" he asked in return.

"I am Judean."

"Well, then . . ."

"But you are not—"

"My mother was a Jew. I think my father was too, from certain things I remember being said. But all I have to remind me of them is a certain distinct part of my anatomy. I want something more." And that was all he would say.

Josef obtained papers of safe conduct written in Titus's hand for all of them. "These should protect you from the soldiers on the road," he said, handing over the rolled parchments in their official cases. "I have nothing to give you that will likewise protect you from others you will meet," he added, looking at Alexandra. "I suppose you had better trust to the protection of the Lord. They say He looks after fools and children."

She smiled and, leaning down from the white mare on which she was mounted, kissed him lightly. There was another scroll in her possession. He had agreed to their divorce and in a calmer moment had drawn up the official document. "Don't be angry," she whispered. "Think what fun you'll have in Rome without a wife to answer to."

"I wouldn't have answered to you in any case," he replied; but he smiled.

She waved to him as they rode off, and he raised his hand in parting. She was on a beautiful horse that had been a gift from Pangar. The Ishmaelite had called Josef the *jarr*. It meant, Alexandra had learned, a man who leaves his own tribe to live with another, or one who, having left the protection of his own tent, wanders from place to place. The *Jarr*. The Stranger. It was, Alexandra reflected, a good name for Josef.

She had seen Vespasian once more after Beni's death. He had come to her that very night, finding her alone in the room where her brother's body, wrapped in white cloth, lay in its limestone coffin. There would be no death mask, no images carved on the sealed casket. Only the boy's name and the inscription Alexandra had requested: "Death is nothing. Freedom is everything. The Lord alone is king."

For some time the general stood beside the girl. He was glad to see she was not weeping. She was in fact quite still, and silent; and more beautiful, he thought, than any creature he had ever seen.

He cleared his throat. "I leave for Egypt in the morning. Josephus will be accompanying me. I should like to have you come as well. I think you will be happier away from here.... You must have many sad memories of Caesarea. Come with us, Alexandra. It would be best."

"I cannot," she said simply. "My brother must be buried. I must say the prayers for him and sit in mourning. There is no one else to do it, you see."

He frowned. He did not wish to appear insensitive, still . . . "Surely there must be some way."

"No."

"Well, then, you can join us later. In Berytus, perhaps."

She did not answer.

"Well, then. It is settled." But he did not leave.

"Now that you are to be emperor of Rome, will you call off this war?" she asked suddenly.

"I cannot," he replied even as she had earlier.

"Why? What more is there to destroy? You've said yourself our civil war has weakened Judea so much that resistance against your troops could only be minimal. 'Why march against Jerusalem,' I've heard you say, 'when the Jews there are already killing each other off?' You cannot believe Judea is any threat to Rome. There is no chance we would invade your Imperial City."

"You pose a greater threat to Rome than military occupation. What would the Britains think if Judea goes unpunished? What will the Thracians do? We would be forced with revolt on every side. I cannot turn my back on such consequences. That is why I could not let your brother go free," he blurted. "I wanted to, for your sake. But I could not. I cannot disturb the order that has been established by those before me. There are rules one must follow. Certain acts reap certain consequences. There must be an order to things," he repeated. "Whatever I may feel, my first duty is to that order. To Rome."

"Then you know what mine is."

He smiled sadly. "Will you fight against me, my lovely Alexandra? What a pity. If ever two people could be happy with one another . . . Forgive me, I ought not to speak so. I am, after all, your country's enemy, and old enough to be your father."

"I have never looked upon you as a father. I mean . . . I do not find you . . . unattractive."

"What? This old puss?" Still, he was pleased. "Alexandra," he began again. He sighed. "Forget your mad countrymen, your sad Judea. I will give you the world. . . ."

"I cannot. And if I could—or did—you would not want me."

He smiled sadly. "I have been told I am old-fashioned . . . that honor, virtue, duty to gods and family, are mere antiquated notions, concepts that may have been necessary once but are hardly worthwhile in this modern, sophisticated civilization we have wrought upon the world. Seneca has said it is wrong to think our age peculiar for vice, luxury, desertion of moral standards . . . that these are faults of mankind, not of any age, and that no time in history has been free from guilt. Well, perhaps. But perhaps it is time we all returned to my 'old-fashioned' ideals. Rome has brought order of one kind to the world. Perhaps, now, we must look for another kind of order."

He bowed. "I shall look forward to seeing you in Berytus," he said, knowing as he spoke that he would probably never see her again.

NINE

The house stood on the outskirts of Caesarea, behind the breakwater. An old woman was sitting in the doorway, gumming a crust of bread. The place seemed otherwise deserted.

"Is this the house of Basilides?"

The old woman squinted. The girl was standing in the sun, the light making a halo of fire around her hair. "Eh? Who?"

"Basilides. A dealer of slaves. He was from Rome. . . ."

The hag nodded. "My master was from Rome. Gone back there, too."

"He has gone back to Rome?" Alexandra asked, dismayed.

"That's what I said. I may have no teeth, but I can still talk plain enough. Yes, he went back to Rome. Gave me my freedom before he left, although what I am to do with it I do not know." She shrugged. "What's freedom anyway but harder work? What do you want?"

"There was a girl here—"

"Lots of girls."

"This one was . . . well, she was small and thin. . . . Her name was Lilah."

The old woman blinked. She shrugged.

"You must remember her," Alexandra urged. She was beginning to feel apprehensive. Had Basilides taken Lilah with him? Why had she waited so long? "Your master was . . . fond of her."

"Fond of lots of them. Fond of me too once. That was a long time ago. . . ." She laughed noiselessly.

"This girl was a Christian," Alexandra said desperately. "She—"

"Wait . . . wait. Yes." The woman nodded. "I know the one you mean."

"Has she gone with Basilides?"

"That one?" She shook her head. "Not her. Why? What do

you want? I am in charge here, so you had better tell me." She stood up. "What do you want?"

"I want to buy her. Look, I have money—"

"Can't."

"If it isn't enough I'll get more. I have some rings—"

"Dead. She's dead. The girl's dead."

"No . . . no. . . ."

"See for yourself. She's buried over there. We put her in the ground last spring. Over there . . . where that white stone is. I put it there myself, to keep the spirit from rising. I don't like ghosts wandering around my house." She spat over her shoulder and jabbed the air, her thumbs clenched in her fists. "Look, there's flowers growing where she's buried."

There was indeed a small patch of wildflowers pushing out of the sandy soil marked by a large white rock.

"She begged not to be burned. She was always asking that. Said only the bodies of criminals could be burned."

"That is the Law of Israel. . . ."

"Eh? You mean the girl was a Jew?"

"I don't know. I thought . . ." She shook her head. "I don't know."

"Niko dug the hole and put her in."

Alexandra looked up at the big man who had come to stand beside the old woman. He said nothing.

"I put the stone there," the woman said again, hopefully, thinking this might merit a few denarii tossed in her lap. But the lady did not answer or even look at her. Shrugging, she went back to her doorway.

"Oh, Lilah," Alexandra whispered. "I'm sorry . . . I'm so sorry. . . . If only I'd come sooner. I could have found a way—I should have found a way. I've been so selfish . . . pitying myself, beating my breast about this war and this nation . . . when it would have been so simple just to help one person. Oh, Lilah . . . Lilah . . ."

"Don't cry."

She looked up, startled. She had forgotten the man was there.

"Don't cry," he said again. "She is not sad. Lilah is not sad. She is in heaven. No one can hurt her now. She is with the Master."

Alexandra stared at him.

"She is with the Master," he said again. "She is in heaven."

Alexandra sighed. She wiped her eyes with the back of her

hand. "Well, you are right about one thing. No one can hurt her now." She turned to go, then suddenly stopped. Stooping down beside the girl's grave, she found a sharp stone; she hesitated a moment, then scratched the outline of a fish on the white rock. When she stood up, Niko was smiling at her. She took out the bag of coins she had brought to buy Lilah's freedom and pushed it into his hands.

"They are in Pella," she said.

His eyes told her he understood. He bowed his head in thanks.

As she walked past him, she heard him speak once more.

"Will you . . . walk that way?"

She turned back again and shook her head. "No," she said softly. "I must go . . . another way."

BOOK FOUR

THE ROAD was crowded with soldiers and refugees going in opposite directions, the one group returning to Caesarea, where they would rest for the duration of the winter, the other pushing toward Jerusalem.

The legionaries were tired, as foot soldiers always are, but they marched with orderly precision under the watchful eyes of the mounted centurions. Every legion still in the East was converging on Caesarea now in order to assemble and regroup under Titus's command. In the spring they would move out again—one giant, united force—against the very place to which they now turned their backs and the very people whom they now passed. The irony of the situation was not lost on the soldiers.

"See you in Jerusalem!" a young private shouted to a family huddled by the side of the road, splattered with mud kicked up by the centurion's horse. "See you in the Temple come spring!" He laughed. "Look at that, will you?" He jerked his head toward another group waiting silently for the soldiers to pass. "Did you ever see such a sorry lot? Nothing but cripples, old folks, dirty brats, and the ugliest women a man could lay eyes on."

The grizzled trooper marching beside him shook his head. "Don't be fooled by what you see here, boy. There's plenty of able bodies left in Judea, more than enough to cut out our hearts. They're holed up in Jerusalem, waiting for us, or hiding, the gods know where, with the Sicarii, damn their hides. As for women, there's plenty of good ones in Jerusalem, from what I hear. Real high-class ladies, as far as being Jews goes. But you just take a peek under some of them cloaks and hoods we're going by right now, and I warrant you'll find a nice enough piece sooner than later. They dirty 'em up on purpose. Make 'em look bad so's we won't take notice." He grinned at the boy's expression. "Agh, it's an old trick. I seen it done in Gaul and Thrace, most everywhere, I warrant." He shrugged. "Me, I take no mind of an ugly face. Pussy is pussy, as my old sergeant used to say. Who's looking for a wife?"

The young soldier looked at him with fresh respect; then, turning his head, he began to study with new interest the civilians by the side of the road.

A man with a bundle in his hands and another at his feet grimly watched the parade of Rome's finest. When he was certain the last legionary had gone by, he spat into the dust and said, "All right, let's get going."

A girl peeked out from behind his back.

"I said it's all right. They're gone. Come on, pick up that pack. It will be dark before you know it, and we have a ways to go."

The girl came around in front of him. She picked up the bundle on the ground, then hesitated, looking up at him with an anxious expression.

"Well? What are you waiting for? I said we could go on now. What is it? You want me to go first?" He sighed. "Don't worry...I won't leave you. The Almighty knows you are no prize, but you are a creature of the Lord same as everyone else, and I will not abandon you. I said I would take you to Jerusalem, and I will."

She dropped the bundle, grabbed his hands, and kissed them.

"Stop that. Stop—now look what you've made me do. I've dropped my own pack. Come, we must be on our way. It's not just soldiers we've got to worry about. There's always robbers wherever you go—war doesn't stop them. And there's wild beasts too. Hungry dogs and the like. It's best not to get too far behind the others." He sighed. "And I wouldn't mind hearing a voice other than my own. Feels like I'm talking to myself half the time." He picked up his bundle and started off, trudging down the broad seaside highway that branched off at Lydda for Jerusalem, the girl walking silenty behind.

"Come here," he said after awhile. "It's bad enough wondering if I'm just talking to myself, without seeing another face as well. Makes me feel like a fool, and I know I must look like one. Come on, walk beside me." He gave her a sideways glance. "That pack heavy?"

She shook her head in vigorous denial.

"Good. There's nothing I can do about it anyways. Got my

own load, as you can plainly see. You got one eye that's blue and the other brown, but I guess you can see all right. The Almighty knows what two-color eyes mean, but I guess it can't hurt anyone. I don't guess you're much different from anyone else except you can't talk and got those funny eyes. I mean, looks like you've suffered same as all of us. Maybe more," he added thoughtfully. "You were a sorry sight when I found you." He paused. "If that pack gets too heavy, let me know. I guess I can carry both if it comes to that. All right, all right, walk faster, will you? By the time we get to the Holy City those Roman pigs may just decide to turn around and join us there, the Lord forbid. No, let them come. Time we gave them a taste of their own. You'll see, once we're in Jerusalem, everything will be all right. That's the Lord's city. You don't think the Almighty would let any harm come to His very own city, do you? Or to His people there? No...Jerusalem's the place to be. I'm going to join up with Simon bar Giora once we get there. I would have done it sooner, but Leah..." His voice faltered. "I promised her I wouldn't go off, you see. I promised...." His voice trailed away again. "She ought to have come with me," he said suddenly, angrily. "I begged her. But she loved our little cottage.... She wanted the child to be born there. She...well, I couldn't ask her to ride in her condition, could I?" He sighed. "So we stayed. And now, no house, no Leah, no..." He swallowed. "Take your time. Why do you walk so fast? Jerusalem is two days away. There is no reason to hurry. We will be there soon enough. Besides, what is there to fear? A man with nothing...a girl who cannot speak.... What would anyone want with either of us?"

Aliterus was singing a very bawdy song. Hagar's lips were set in a disapproving line, but her eyes shone with amusement. Alexandra was listening carefully to the lyrics, her expression so studious that Aliterus finally broke off singing and exclaimed, "By all the gods, girl, you are the first I have ever known to wear a scholar's face to that piece!"

"Some of the words are unfamiliar," she confessed. "Or else their meaning is different from what I think it to be."

He laughed. "There are two meanings, one of which is proper in polite company, the other proper to the song. But there are some, ah, vulgar idioms that I doubt you would know. For example—"

"Never mind," Hagar said. "She knows enough words now in half a dozen tongues—and most of them more proper for soldiers than ladies."

"And you?" Alexandra retorted.

"I do not make use of the stupid names men give to the things they do with women. Such words are belittling and reveal the speaker's fear of the Great Mother. A good curse, now—that is a thing of value. But men do not know how to curse."

Alexandra laughed. Giving the white horse a friendly kick, she urged him into a brief gallop, pulling up after a bit to let Hagar and Aliterus join her. She was staring dreamily at the sea when they rode up.

Aliterus studied her with interest. Despite her marriage to Josephus, and whatever she might have experienced as a slave, there was something virginal about the girl, something fresh and unused. It was this quality, no doubt, that had attracted Vespasian—that, and the girl's frank manner. She was certainly not Josephus's type, Aliterus thought, recalling the licentious young man he had known in Rome. And yet, in all that time in the Praetorium, the comedian had not once known the captive Judean to be false to his bride, despite many opportunities. A goodly number of ladies in Caesarea had found the Jewish prisoner exceedingly attractive, and his gold chains hardly repulsive. The lady Livia had even confessed to a rather intriguing fantasy she had regarding those chains. Well, the chains were off now. Josephus was a free man, and no longer lord to this slim girl with the great, gray eyes, this . . . singular young female who had thrown aside not only a handsome husband whose prestige was rising but also the affection of the man who would soon rule the world.

For what?

But who am I to ask? Aliterus thought. *Even now, as she stares so intently across the sea, is she wondering why a fat clown rides after her, singing his dirty songs as we go off into what must be, at the very least, an uncertain future? Or is it that fools love fools for company?*

"Dost wait for King Neptune to rise from the waves, sweet maiden?" He pulled alongside her, a large, clumsy rider on a horse that seemed too small for him. "Or were you thinking of Josephus?"

She turned to him, surprised. "No."

He wagged his finger at her. "I wager he is thinking of you,

Alexandra. And I will wager that you are the first woman ever to leave him. That alone would make our Josephus regret he let you go."

She smiled. "I don't think so."

"I am surprised he did not give you something by which to remember him."

"I don't want anything for remembrance' sake."

"I did not mean a trinket." He glanced significantly at her figure. "I meant...well, you were together nearly two years...."

She looked startled. Without answering, she turned the horse away from him and pointed to the road ahead. "We leave the sea at Joppa and move inland to Lydda, where this road will join the main one that runs parallel to it now—and which I have avoided because it is the one the legions take. As you can see, this old highway is not much used, being narrow and so near the water."

"Alexandra, I'm sorry. I ought not to have—"

"That's all right." She turned around, checking to see if Hagar was behind them. "There are a number of ways one may travel to Jerusalem," she said, as they continued their journey. "The best highway leads straight from the Galilee to the Holy City, but it cuts through Samaria, and therefore we must avoid it. I remember traveling with my father from the Temple to Bersabe in the north. We took a road that led from Jerusalem past Bethany to Jericho, where we had to ford the Jordan River. There the road led to Gilead, and from there, one could go southwards—or else continue into the Galilee. It was quite roundabout, and dangerous too, but it was better, you see, to face whatever robbers there might be—and that we did, as I remember—than the Samaritans."

"I am told there is great hatred between the peoples of Judea and Samaria," Aliterus said, "but are not both Jews?"

"As if that ever stopped a fight," Hagar said, coming up to them now.

"The Samaritans reject all the books of the Bible except the first five," Alexandra explained. "Also, they do not recognize Jerusalem as the center for our faith. They have their own temple on Mount Gerizim. They are a mongrel breed," she said, dismissing them with a typically Sadducee shrug. "There has been much intermarriage with desert tribesmen, Babylonian colonists, and worshipers of profane gods. It was in Samaria that Ahab reigned with his wife Jezebel, in their ivory palace.

The king favored the old gods of Canaan, and his wife openly worshipped Baal. Samaritans serve as soldiers for Rome now—there are many of them in Caesarea. I do not think," she concluded, "that even the gentiles would call them Jews. But certainly that is what the Samaritans call the people of Judea."

"You do not call yourselves Jews?"

"Certainly not. One is a Jerusalemite or a Galilean or simply a Judean. Those of our faith who live in other countries call themselves Israelites. It is the others—the gentiles—who call us Jew."

"I must remember that when I am in Jerusalem."

"No matter now." She sighed. "There is nothing a slave loves more than to call another 'slave.' I think it is the same with us now."

They made their camp by the sea that night, dining on cheese and bread and dried fruit that they had brought with them from Caesarea. Hagar made a fire on the beach and took out three eggs from the pack on her donkey, cooking these with herbs from a little bag she wore tied around her waist. Aliterus brought out a skin of wine, and Alexandra contributed almonds, which she was partial to. After the meal they leaned back against their bundles of belongings and gazed, content, at the sea or the fire or the star-bright sky. Hagar got up after a bit and went to stand by the water's edge, murmuring something in a strange tongue neither of her traveling companions could comprehend. The woman lifted her arms high above her head, as if to embrace the moon. Then she crouched down on her haunches, staring into the waves that licked the sand at her feet but never seemed to touch them. She was silent now, and far away from the things at hand.

Neither Aliterus nor Alexandra seemed to find Hagar's behavior strange; in a way it was comforting, as if what she did was somehow protective. Long ago, Alexandra recalled, she had stood beside this woman from Crete, calling to the sea and the moon with the silent voice of her heart, forgetting the wisdom of the rabbis: "Be careful what you ask of God, lest your prayer be granted."

She had asked for Josef. *Give him to me,* she had whispered to the moon that long-ago night. *Make him mine.* And now, as then, his face rose before her, the classic head with its crown of black curls, the dark eyes that could be piercing as a shaft or dreamlike as the midnight sea. She saw the straight nose with its arrogant arch of nostril, the same nose that to a lesser, more delicate degree had been her mother's—was, in fact, her own. A Sadducee nose. Then she saw his mouth, and even now her body tingled as she recalled his kiss and the sweet fire she had known in his arms.

The bastard, she thought somewhat helplessly, unconsciously mimicking Vespasian's tone. Why couldn't the man be plain? Why hadn't his crimes turned him as ugly as the evil he perpetrated?

He had come late to their chamber that last night they were together, having dined with Titus. She was standing by the window when he entered, her pale profile clearly outlined against the dark sky.

"Are you praying?" he asked.

"No," she said without turning. "But I think it is the new moon."

He walked over to the window and stood beside her there, looking out. "So it is," he said. "You begin your journey with the new month. That should bode well." He paused. "Titus will personally lead the legions against Jerusalem," he said in a low voice, not looking at her. "I am to accompany him. In the spring, when the army is fully assembled and the rains have ceased, we will move out. Do not tarry in the Holy City, Alexandra. Celebrate the Passover elsewhere. Do you understand?"

She did not answer or even turn to look at him.

After another pause he continued. "It has been decided that the Temple must not be left standing. It is too precious a symbol and might be a rallying point in the future. The very distant future," he amended wryly.

She turned to him now. "They would really destroy the Temple?"

"A lesson to the world. There is, after all, nothing dearer to our people." He shook his head, as if suddenly frightened. "I will talk again with Titus," he said in a troubled voice. "Perhaps there is something I can say...."

She sighed. "Why are you here, Josef? Why do you stay? It would be easy for you to leave."

"You know my reasons." He was calm again.

"They call you friend and brother. How can you bear it?" she wondered softly. "My father's ashes are scattered on the sand where you once walked with him. My brother's blood stains the arena. Josef... why are you here?"

He had seemed to study the sky as though measuring his

words against the slice of moon. "I thought you knew," he had said absently.

But I don't know, she thought, staring into the fire Hagar had built. *I will never know.*

"Do you hate him?"

Aliterus's voice startled her. Had her thoughts been so transparent? "Hate?" she echoed. "Of whom do you speak?"

"Josephus, of course."

She did not answer for awhile. Then, slowly, she said, "I don't know. Part of me does." She was silent again. Suddenly, angrily, she said, "Yes. Yes..."

Aliterus nodded. "Actors can be difficult to live with, but not so hard, I think, as those who should be actors and are not. Why do you look so shocked? The man has the body, the voice, the ability to hold an audience—and the desire to do so. Josephus would have made an excellent actor."

"An actor!" The suggestion was tantamount to lumping him with thieves, pimps, and whores. Then she realized that Aliterus was himself a follower of Thespis; but before she could say anything to show the comedian she did not think poorly of him, he sighed.

"Strange..." he murmured to no one in particular. "We make them laugh, we make them cry, we pull them out of their miserable lives for the space of a golden hour—and for this we are despised, distrusted, catalogued with scoundrels of the worst kind. Yet it is a noble profession, I tell you. Merchants traffic in mortal stuff, none of which lasts forever. But an actor offers a treasure that can never be destroyed, something that cannot be held in the hand and yet is more real than any object purchased at the marketplace."

"And what might that be?" Hagar asked, returning to the fire.

"A moment, madam. A memory. A dream."

She made a sound that was not very encouraging.

"Tell me about Jerusalem," Aliterus asked Alexandra, coming out of his reverie.

"Jerusalem.... What do you wish to know?"

"Whatever you will tell me. Sometimes I think...I have already seen this place."

"Where?" Hagar asked sarcastically. "In your actor's dreams?"

But he chose to ignore this. "Tell me about Jerusalem," he said again.

Alexandra leaned back against her rolled-up blanket and

stared at the sky. "I was born near the sea," she began, "and I love the smell of it, the air full of fish and foam and the song of the birds that walk the shore at day's end. I love the sun that hangs over the water before night, ready to drop like a red ball, like a child's toy, but fiery. . . . But the air of Jerusalem is also sweet. And the sun hangs over the city like a new coin . . . until it melts into the hills and houses, spreading its gold like honey. . . .

"I was nine when my father first took me there alone. My brothers had all been there before me—even Beni, who was younger than I—and it was a sore thing in my heart that they had done something which I had not. By that I mean the chance to accompany my father on one of his business trips. You see, we all went together to Jerusalem for the three pilgrimages that are required each year—one at the time of the Passover, one for the festival of Shavuot, and one for Succot. The journey to the Holy City and the Temple is called *aliyah*, which means 'to go up or ascend.' As we approach Jerusalem, you shall see why.

"Well, my father had a shipment of pepper—which, as you know, is a dear commodity—and he wished to attend personally to its disposal. I pressed him to take me along, and as he loved me and was always kind to me, he consented at last.

"He always took this coastal route, avoiding Samaria and the central highways which, as I have explained, are wider and easier to traverse but vulnerable to the legions, and in those days to robber bands.

"How well I remember that journey! The almond was all abloom, the white flowers falling on our shoulders like some beautiful, soft rain. The road was full of children and lambs, and the very air seemed filled with the songs of the pilgrims traveling to the Temple. You see, even when it is not a holy time, there are always people going to Jerusalem. Sometimes they go for the redemption of a firstborn son, or to register a marriage, or to offer sacrifice to ensure the blessing of the Lord on some journey or business venture. There are always Nazarites too, as they are called—penitents who shave their heads and make certain vows and come to pray in the Temple. But mostly, everyone is happy. No one in all the villages we shall pass would turn away a pilgrim to Jerusalem or fail to offer water, food, and lodging for the night. That is their *mitzveh*, you see. Their good deed.

"It was late in the afternoon, I remember, when we came to the Arch of Accounts outside the city, where my father began his business transactions. We'd had our first glimpse of Jerusalem—as will you—from Mount Scopus. It is an unforgettable sight. The city seems to hang in the air like a jewel suspended in the midst of the stony hills. Well, you shall see for yourself, and then you will understand why it is called the City of High Places, and why we do not simply go there but 'ascend unto' it.

"It was, as I said, late in the afternoon. The sky was streaked with the colors of the bleeding sun—all red and gold, and yet softly pink. I mean, it was a tender fire, if there is such a thing. And then, even as we watched, the gold in the sky seemed to come down like a veil or cloak upon the rooms and towers of the city. Everything turned to gold. The smallest pebble became a fiery nugget, the rocky hills fields of precious ore. The very walls of the city in the distance before us looked as if they were made not of stone but of shining metal. The palace spires seemed to be plated in golden armor. It was all gold. A city of gold.

"'Ten measures of beauty hath the Lord bestowed upon the world,' my father recited. 'And nine of these are in Jerusalem.' Behold perfection," he said.

"I looked at him with awe, as if he had become a sorcerer, as if he had somehow commanded this miraculous sight. His eyes had closed. Softly, he murmured prayers, thanking the Lord for our safe journey, praising the Almighty for His greatness.

"Like a thief, with my heart pounding, I bent down and 'stole' a pebble while he prayed. I kept it tight in my fist as we made our way into the city and to the house of my uncle Shammai, who was a priest of the Temple. I could not wait to be alone, and when at last I was, I opened my hand to look at my treasure—and saw, of course, that it was only a common stone. For some reason I was not disappointed. Instead of throwing the thing away, I put it with my belongings.

"I waited all the following day. The visit to the Temple, the marketplace, conversations with my cousins—all of it passed like an interminable dream. But finally, at last, the sun began to flame in the sky, and the walls of my uncle's courtyard warmed to a rosy hue, and I drew out my pebble and watched, content, as it turned to gold.

"Jerusalem is like that stone. From afar it may seem to hang in the sky like a piece of heaven itself, but from within it may appear not nearly so beautiful as Caesarea or Rome. And yet, even as you think how disappointing it is, how ordinary, something will make you fall under its spell. For some, it is the sight of the Temple. For me, it has always been the play of light and color, the changes that occur with the rise and fall of the sun, and that moment when everything turns to gold. It may be something else for you. I do not really know what you seek in Jerusalem, Aliterus. But, as Plautus says, 'The poet seeks what is nowhere in all the world . . . And yet—somewhere—he finds it.'"

He was quiet for some time. Then he said, "You did not cry when your pebble proved not to be true gold. Why? You were only a child."

"Because I realized that magic is something no one can touch, that it is not the thing changed but that which changes it. But surely you know that. If you can do what you say an actor does, then you are yourself a kind of sorcerer."

"Magic. Sorcery. Nice words for a Jew—and the daughter of priests, as well," Hagar said.

"I learned them from you," Alexandra retorted in the banter that passed for affection between these two. "And I would be careful with those incantations to the sea," she added. "'Thou shalt not suffer a witch to live,' remember?"

Hagar sniffed. "We are not in Jerusalem yet. As for you," she told the actor, "you would be wise not to mention your profession in the City of David. I have been in this land long enough to know that the people of Judea may be as harsh to those who deviate from their ways as they claim others are to them. Besides, you speak with an accent that is not of this region. So take my advice and keep your mouth shut as much as possible."

"I'm afraid she's right," Alexandra agreed. "No one would believe you are a Judean, and if they did they might still kill you for a Roman spy."

"Roman?" Aliterus raised his eyebrows. "But I am from Alexandria. A poor survivor of the Delta massacre."

Alexandra smiled, but she shook her head. "I am at odds with Josef on many things, but on this we are agreed. I do not understand your being here, Aliterus, or why you have waited until now to make your *aliyah*. It may well be the last journey you ever take—and not by fault of Rome."

"If I am meant to die in Jerusalem, then be it so," the actor responded calmly and without theatricality. "I have placed my life on the wings of the wind—or, if you like, in the hands of your God. We shall see what fate provides." And again he would say no more.

The following day they began to see others on the road and to glimpse the first of a string of devastated towns and villages. This area had once been fertile plain, with scores of thriving hamlets and a large, healthy population. But where in happier days the oak and cedar would have sheltered them from the sun, where olive trees had once raised their branches like the arms of graceful dancers on the hills, where there had been rich earth and grass and flowers and all manner of living, growing things, now there was only the muddy, trampled ground, the charred remnants of what had been dwellings, the bones of dead animals, the bodies of birds shot down not for food but for sport, and stumps of trees that had been cut down to build siege towers and platforms for the Roman war machines. As they moved inland and nearer to Jerusalem, the scenes of recent destruction grew even worse.

The shock of seeing the despoiled land made Alexandra silent. Aliterus, who had been in high spirits, saw the look in her eyes and stopped his chattering. But Alexandra had no words for him. How could she make him understand what had been done?

A tree was sacred. The vilest insult one Judean could spit at another was to call him a "cutter of trees" or "the son of a cutter." When a child was born, the parents made a planting: a cedar for a male, an acacia for a girl. When the child was grown and ready for marriage, the tree's branches would hold the wedding canopy and its wood make the couple's house. In this way, the Law instructed, the earth would not be depleted. "For the world was not a barren place when we came into it," Alexandra could hear her father saying. "As our fathers planted for us, so must we plant for our children." So, too, the Law decreed that after seven years' use a field must lie fallow, unturned and unharvested—not, Alexandra would have told Aliterus, because the people of Israel were lazy, as their enemies claimed, but so the earth might rest and renew itself.

Was it the long years of desert wandering that had given the Israelite his deep love for the land? she wondered. How many kings of old had risen with the sun, like farmers, to see if the vines had budded, the pomegranate flowered? How many scholars had paused in their prayers to gaze with joy upon the green fields, while lovers since the days of Solomon had sent their whispers out on the morning wind? "Arise, my love," they had called, "and come away. . . . The time of singing is come. . . . The voice of the turtledove is heard in our land. . . ."

No song but lamentation now. No voice but wailing for the dead. No dancing at the harvest, only the marching of troops along the road and the cries of the hungry and the hurt.

How long would the face of Judea be scarred? Alexandra wondered. How long before the land would be green again?

Lord, what have they done to the earth? she cried out silently. *What have they done to Thy fair daughter?*

To the people on the road and even to the soldiers there was something uncommon in the presence of the girl riding the white mare. "She was beautiful," they would say later, "but with strange eyes. Eyes that were not there, or so full of light or tears that you could not see them." And as the days and the years and the centuries passed, a legend would take wing: the legend of the *Shekhinah,* the One with No Eyes.

The *Shekhinah* is the Bride of God, the dispelled and displaced Jews would tell their children. She is His wife and His daughter; and when the people of Israel incur the Lord's wrath, it is she who speaks in their behalf. Wherever Jews wander, the *Shekhinah* wanders with them, blinded by tears of sorrow for the plight of her people. And every night, at midnight, she talks to the Lord, reminding the Almighty of His covenant, begging Him to be merciful and to return His chosen children to their home.

With time, the figure of the blind, beautiful woman would merge with other concepts. The *Shekhinah* would become synonymous with the Shabbat Queen, embodied in the Jewish wife or mother as she lit the Sabbath candles. She would be Torah to the scholar, embraced as a bridegroom embraces his bride. She would be the Spirit of Love and Beauty; and it would be said that when a man and a woman made love and were in love, the *Shekhinah* was present, and each was beautiful.

But while the small province of Judea was waging its war with Rome, while Jerusalem and the Temple still stood, while the children of Israel still clung to the land promised them by their Lord, there was only a young woman riding a white horse, her gray eyes filled with sorrow and pain.

There was nowhere she could turn for comfort. If she took her eyes from the devastated countryside, she saw the people on the road; and if the burnt, barren earth brought tears, this stream of pitiful humanity brought even more.

Like the young legionary before her, Alexandra saw few men unless they were old or crippled. She saw no attractive women; young girls were heavily veiled, and as the soldier had said, their faces purposely dirtied to make them even less appealing. Most of the pretty girls of the villages had been taken for legion brothels, appropriated by officers, or sold into slavery. Two boatloads of young men and women had already been shipped off to Rome's houses of prostitution. Thus, Alexandra's beauty, her unmarred appearance, and—thank to Titus's documents—her immunity from the soldiers set her quite apart from her fellow travelers.

Hagar took in the horde of old folk and children, the one-legged boys, the women with haunted eyes, the ones who wandered dreamily or feverishly with untold tales of terror locked behind their too-bright eyes or in the babbling of their tongues; but she said nothing. As always, it was impossible to tell what she thought of what she saw. Her main concern seemed to be that no harm should befall their little group, and she counted the bundles on the animals regularly, making sure nothing had been stolen. She was wary of everyone she met.

Aliterus won the affection of all with his ceaseless clowning. He told his story of the Delta massacre to many an appreciative audience and was convinced that the tears and horror he conjured up were due to his latent talent for tragedy. When someone asked how he happened to have a paper that made soldiers go away once they looked at it, he merely winked and proceeded to draw a half-denarius from the questioner's ear.

The night was dotted with the fires of the roadside camps. It was a time of sharing: food, fire, and tales. Hagar had made a broth from dried lentils; none who approached was turned away.

"Your pot seems boundless," Aliterus remarked as she ladled out the soup to a family from Bethel.

"No one who asks may be refused. It is the Law. This I learned in the House of Harsom. The homeless and the hungry must be cared for, but they must not be made to feel beholden. It is the Law." She turned to Alexandra. "At least the soldiers have not despoiled the wells. Even so, we ought to take water with us from now on. I do not know this countryside. We must be prepared for anything."

"There are many rivers and wells between here and Jerusalem," Alexandra replied. "There is no need to worry until we reach the wilderness. But as you say, it is best to be prepared. I will fill the skins."

"In the morning. You must stay close to the fire tonight."

"Are you worried? We have papers insuring our safety."

The woman let out a laugh. "And when it is too dark to read? Or if a man cannot? Besides, those things are meant to protect us from the soldiers." She looked around significantly. "I see no legionaries. Only men."

"Most of whom do not even have all their limbs."

"There is only one limb you need worry about—and unless that has been lost as well, you had better stay by the fire. In the morning we will fill the skins." She jerked her head toward Aliterus. "Perhaps the fat one will help. That is, if he can do more than recite silly words that are too long for understanding or sing his blasphemous songs."

"I, a water carrier? You are talking to a star, madam. I do not carry props." He shrugged. "However, members of touring companies must all do their share. Ask what you will." He bowed. "I am your servant."

Hagar grunted. She cast a glance at Alexandra, who was lying down now, her head resting on her arm. "Do not take off your shoes," she reminded the girl. "They are the first things to be stolen."

"I have them on."

Hagar grunted again. "You did not eat much," she said.

"I'm not hungry."

"You look pale."

"How can you tell? It is night."

"I can tell."

"I am near the time of my blood," Alexandra said with some uneasiness. She shifted her body away from the woman. "That's all."

Hagar gave her a keen look but said nothing.

Alexandra bit her lip. The fact was she was long past her time of menstruation, and there was no sign of any discharge. Furthermore, her breasts felt sore. In an effort to distract herself, she turned her attention to Aliterus, who was trying to settle his large frame on a couch of blankets and bundles. "Are you beginning to have second thoughts about this journey?" she asked, amused, as he tried to make himself comfortable.

"Are there no inns where one might pass the night? Surely there must be many places where a weary pilgrim can stay."

"There is a large garrison in Joppa," Alexandra replied. "From what was said on the road, it seems best to avoid the city. In any case, the inns are never clean, and the food is always suspect. One can never be sure the owner has kept strictly to the laws of *kashrut*."

"You mean the mixing of meat and milk?"

"There is more to it than that." But she did not elaborate. She felt queasy at the thought. "When we journeyed to Jerusalem, we always stayed with friends along the way. But now . . ." She shook her head sadly. "I would not know where to look or whom to ask. Everything that I remember seems gone . . . destroyed."

"Then Judea was not always like this?"

"Oh, no! Apollonia was a lovely little town. And Antipatris—why, Herod build that city in honor of his own father." She sighed. "You would not know now how beautiful it once was."

"Then Jerusalem may also be changed," he said thoughtfully.

"I do not know what you will find in Jerusalem," she confessed. "The war has altered everything. But let us not speak of that. Tell me of Rome. Josef said it was the most wonderful place he'd ever seen."

"Yes, it is beautiful enough . . . and cruel, too. A city of a thousand pleasures, that above all."

"Only for pleasure?"

The question startled him. "Well, that is all anybody seems to want nowadays."

"But you want more. You would not have left otherwise."

He laughed. "You have a way, Alexandra, of cutting through the mask. I can understand Josephus's discomfort."

"A strong woman needs a strong man," Hagar said.

"And you, madam?"

"I have no need for any man."

"Tell me about Rome," Alexandra asked again. She settled herself in for a good story. "Tell me why you left there."

He did not answer.

"It is time to talk, Aliterus," she urged softly. "I have a curious nature, and I have let you go long enough. We will part soon, and we may never see each other again, so now you must reveal your mystery to me. Neither Hagar nor I am the sort to spread tales, and there is only us and the night to hear you speak. Come, tell me your tale."

He sighed. "All right. As you say, the time has come to talk."

"My old master, may his bones rest in peace, was the actor Appeles. He bought me when I was no bigger than a candle-stick, and just as thin. I was his pet for fourteen years, but I managed to slip away now and then to the girls of the house. Appeles wanted me to be a tragic dancer, but he was soon forced to admit that the circumference of my talent, as it were, lent itself to something else. And I have always had, it seems, an ability to make people laugh.

"Well, I'd managed to save up my freedom price from the coins tossed my way, and I could have left the world of my master, but an actor's life suited me. In Rome, a star actor can live as well as a charioteer—or even a Caesar.

"Well, I soon made my way to the top. The world is always looking for a laugh, and anyone who can give it to them is worth his weight in gold—you may imagine, then, how rich I became. But my talents have never been recognized in full. I have played the clown, but in my heart I am Aliterus the tragedian. Oh, what an Orestes I might have been! Or Aga-memnon! The world has missed its chance, I tell you, for I could move an audience to such tears as would fill a hundred waterskins, as would turn whole theaters into lakes!

"But I ought not to complain. From a poor circumcised mouse of a slave I became a millionaire, my name known to every citizen of Rome. I had a villa with twenty bed-rooms . . . slaves, servants, friends, lovers, the choicest roles, a guaranteed claque, and the favor of the emperor. It was the last that proved my undoing.

"After the execution of the actor Paris, I began to have my fears. Paris was the emperor's close companion—his lover, in fact—and his teacher in the art of dancing. Caesar, however, suddenly took the notion that he should excel in this art before all others and therefore decided there should be no rival to his talent. And so . . . goodbye, dear Paris.

"Who then was theater's brightest star? A rhetorical question that modesty forbids me to answer. And there was Nero, sud-

denly proclaiming that comedy was the only form that truly
won the hearts of the populace. Would I follow Paris?

"But the days passed, and Nero treated me more fondly than
ever, his hand on my shoulder as we discoursed upon the
popular satires and gossip of the day. 'You must teach me your
art," said he. "I have never seen such a knack for timing as
you possess. You know exactly when to speak and when to be
silent, and there are more laughs in your pauses than in your
speeches.' Well, this was all true. But I disclaimed any credit,
saying it was all in the writing—and besides, it was he, Nero,
who was master of phrasing, as could be heard in his magnificent singing performances. The gods forgive me for such a
lie.

"Now he became coy and flirtatious. His hand left my shoulder and took a southerly route. 'You are such a large man,'
he said, sighing like a maiden. 'How weak and helpless you
make me feel.'

"I protested his affections. I have had my favorite boys, but
this was dangerous ground. I had as soon lie with an adder.
'I am unworthy of Caesar's love,' said I. 'A fat, ugly clown
people laugh at, not a slender mime of such great beauty that
I might dare to offer even a smile to Caesar.'

"'You are beautiful,' the little snake replied, stroking my
arm and fluttering his eyelids. 'A man among men. A Zeus
upon whose back Europa would be happy to lie. I shall prove
this to you.'

"Trembling, I waited to see if he had it in mind to imper-
sonate Europa or if I was expected to get down on all fours
and bellow like a bull. But he only said, 'Who would you say
is the most beautiful, most virtuous, most lovely and desirable
woman in all Rome?'

"I hedged a bit, not knowing what he wanted me to say,
just wanting to keep my head still fixed to my shoulders, but
I finally named a lady renowned for her beauty and virtue—
the wife of a senator who, I may add, was as famous for his
forays into the pleasure pits of the Imperial City as his wife
was for her goodness.

"Nero applauded my choice. 'Well done,' he said. 'The
lady's character and charm are legend, and to my knowledge
she has never played her husband false. Surely if this woman
took a lover he would be a man of extraordinary power and
beauty. And then, imagine, if her lover left her—why it would
have to be for one even more beautiful than she.' Once more

he began to caress me. 'Would not the final pair be magnificent, the embodiment of all that is wonderful?' It is the mathematics of a madman. But I murmured yes to all he said, never dreaming what drama his evil genius had conceived.

"One night soon after, a woman was escorted to my estate by several of the emperor's private guard. Her face was veiled, but I knew at once she was the lady whom I had earlier named. I do not know by what means Caesar compelled her to this nocturnal visit, but she quickly let me know she had come to do my bidding. I tell you, I was stunned! What was I to do? The woman was weeping—I had no wish to cause her any sorrow. She was a very respected lady, most beauteous and proud—so very proud, as befits the wife of a senator and the daughter of one of Rome's oldest and most honored families.

"I begged her not to cry. But she only said, 'How can I not weep? I am thrice cursed. First, that I am forced to stain the honor of house and husband by this deed. Secondly, that I do so by consorting with an actor. Thirdly, that this actor is a Jew.'

"I had resolved not to touch her. We had been cast in a comedy of the blackest nature, yet I had no intention of doing other than playing at my part. I would have told her this, and she could have taken some comfort in knowing that no matter what others would think, she had not in fact been unfaithful to her husband—a man, as I say, totally undeserving of such consideration. But her words cut through me worse than any knife, and in anger I would have taken her—but for the thought that such action would indeed make me as vile a creature as she already considered me to be.

"I did not say a word, therefore, but left her and went alone to bed. I determined to tell Caesar that I had spurned the female in order to be true to him, who was my heart's only passion. How monstrous it is when we must plan our words to accommodate tyrants. . . .

"In the morning, though, I found her dead. She had opened her wrists while I slept.

"The rest is all a jumble of events. I fled, hiding for some weeks with another actor. . . . Somehow he obtained passage for me on a ship destined for Greece. Nero had accused me of murder. . . .

"But the ship came here to Judea. It was your father's vessel, Alexandra, its ownership assumed by Flavius Vespasian. I did not learn this until I arrived in Caesarea.

"It is a curious story, I know. I don't understand it myself. It is all like a dream to me now. Rome . . . Nero . . . the theater and the world I knew . . .

"But one thing haunts me even more than the strange circumstances that brought me here—and that is the loathing with which that woman regarded me, and the realization that while I have never been a Jew to myself, it seems I have always been one to others.

"Perhaps it was all meant to be. Perhaps now . . . in Jerusalem . . . I shall discover what it is that I am already accused of being."

Alexandra pointed to the road ahead; it seemed to unravel like a slender ribbon up into the hills, disappearing finally among the towering trees. "Now we begin our ascent," she said. "We have left the sea behind us, and now we shall also leave the plains of Judea, climbing higher and higher to Jerusalem."

They were soon enveloped in a leafy darkness. The air seemed to change; it became cool and sharp as they wound their way higher and higher, following the narrow road into the midst of the whispering trees. Suddenly there was a parting of the green shadows, and the earth rose and fell all around them. Stony, terraced hills rose up like Gaea's breasts; there were groves of olive trees on each of them. And in the distance ahead, towers gem-topped by the sun, encircling walls crowned with gold, perched among the clouds like an impregnable fortress and at the same time like an enormous, unattainable jewel, was the City of High Places, Jerusalem.

The ancient psalmist had written, "As the mountains are round about Jerusalem, so the Lord is round about His children." And so it seemed now to Aliterus. From the heights of Mount Scopus, Aliterus could see the stream of people flowing through the city's gates—not only refugees from the burned-out towns and villages but also pilgrims from all over the land, and even from other countries, who had come despite the war to pray in the Temple. There seemed no reason for them not to; the city's wall and location and the very aura surrounding it gave it every appearance of being invincible. Set so high among the clouds and so deep in the hearts of the people, it did indeed seem close to God. Surely the Lord would not allow this wondrous place, this thing of special beauty, to be destroyed.

Despite Josef's warning and his own knowledge of Titus's

intentions, Aliterus gazed longingly upon Jerusalem; and he
could not help feeling, like any poor soul approaching its gates,
that there was no safer place in the world.

He could not tear his eyes away. It was as if he suddenly
became aware of a hunger he had not even guessed he felt. He
could see in great detail the city's tower-topped wall and, even
higher, the Temple itself, its gilded spires stretching toward
the sky. Behind the Temple the houses of the city huddled
together like the tiles of a mosaic; behind them were the palaces
of the princes and priests, with their white roofs and colonnades. Higher still, behind all these, was the dark line of Jerusalem's protective wall climbing to the top of Mount Gareb,
mounting ever upward in a series of great steps crowded with
towers.

Alexandra stood beside Aliterus, not unmoved by the awesome sight of the mountain city; but for her Jerusalem was
already lost, already ashes.

She had dreamed of it the night before, dreamed too of
Berenice . . . and it seemed to her that Berenice was Jerusalem
and the city was Berenice. For Jerusalem was like a
woman . . . like a queen whom all men desire.

*How long have we flocked to her, died for her . . . sent our
sons to sacrifice at her altar?* Alexandra wondered. And for
what? Did the Lord dwell more in Jerusalem than in the hills
outside her gates? Could the Almighty be found in the Temple
and not in the villages of the Galilee or the cities of the plain
or the desert—or even far across the great sea? What was
Jerusalem, after all, but a fragment of a small corner of a
fraction of God's Kingdom?

Or was it, rather, the center?

"The sages believe Jerusalem is the heart of the whole
world," she told Aliterus. "The city sits upon the heights of
mountains, and it is on Mount Moriah that the Temple stands.
In the Temple, in the Holy of Holies, there is a stone from the
time of the first prophets. Some say it is from the time of
Creation. It is called *Even Ha-Shetiyah,* 'the Foundation
Stone,' for it is thought to be the base and the very center of
the whole world. Of course," she added in that factual, academic way she had, "*shetiyah* also means 'drinking,' and some
say the stone is so called because beneath it is hidden the source
of all the springs and fountains from which man drinks."

"*Shetiyah,*" he repeated, enjoying the feel of the word in
his mouth.

"Some say that when King David dug the foundation for

the Temple he found a stone with the name of the Lord on it resting on the mouth of the abyss and put this stone into the Holy of Holies. But others say the stone was always where it is now, that the world was founded on it. For Isaiah writes. 'Thus saith the Lord, *Behold I lay in Zion for a foundation a stone.*'"

But Aliterus did not seem to be listening; he was looking again toward Jerusalem with the eyes of the psalmist who sang, 'O city of God . . . All my thoughts are in thee!"

"The rabbis believe Caesarea is the nemesis of Jerusalem," Alexandra said suddenly. "They say that as long as one of these two cities stands, the other is doomed to fall."

"Which one?" Hagar asked practically.

Alexandra laughed. "Well, I suppose Titus would give one answer—and Johanan ben Zakkai another."

"Who is Johanan ben Zakkai?" Aliterus asked. "One of your Zealot generals?"

"Far from it. He is a rabbi, and opposed to war of any kind—even," she added with a trace of bitterness, "one that would make Judea free."

"Well," Aliterus checked the pack on his horse. He was impatient now to enter the city. "Shall we be going?"

"I must leave you here," Alexandra said.

He stared at her a moment, uncomprehending. Then he said, "Before we left the palace . . . I heard you talking with the Arab prince . . . You said something about the desert. I have been wondering all this time when we would come to it and why we have not."

"There is no desert for you to cross. I'm sorry if I misled you. I never meant to go to Jerusalem. I am going to a place called the Masada."

"You have family there?"

"No, I am alone. I have no kin anywhere in Judea."

"But you had relatives in Jerusalem. I remember Josephus saying—"

"My uncle is dead. My cousins were killed in the first fighting. There may be someone left, but I do not care to find out. My uncle's house and all our property have doubtless been taken by the council, and if I went to claim them they would just marry me off to one of their kind." She paused. "There was a time when I would have fought like anything for my inheritance, but now I am glad to be unencumbered by it. It is something that belongs to the past. Besides, I would grow lonely in that great house."

"I do not think you would be alone for long," he joked. "Some young, strong Zealot would come along—" The sudden fierce look in her eyes stopped him.

"I'll never be any man's slave again. Not by war, and not by love."

"Well," he said, taken aback by her stern tone. He changed his tack. "In Jerusalem, you could pray in the Temple."

"If I had a mind for prayer I could do it anywhere—yes, even standing here. Anyway, the wilderness is probably better suited to praying to Abraham's God than any Temple."

"Is that what this is about?" Hagar asked, an eyebrow raised incredulously. "We go into the desert to pray?"

Alexandra had to smile. "No, Hagar. We are not going where we are going in order to pray."

"What, then?"

"To fight, Hagar. To fight the *Kittim*."

And so the two women took their leave of Aliterus and continued their journey until they reached the edge of the great wilderness that is the Judean desert. They stood before it, looking out on the harsh, desolate land; and Alexandra felt something heavy lifted from her, and was happy in the sudden stillness of this place.

TWO

They slept at the edge of the desert. They had ridden far away from Jerusalem, until the cultivated land sank to rolling hills and waterless vales. Wells became few in number; but here and there they had found cisterns of rainwater with which to fill the skins. For hours they had traveled up and down steep ridges, each barer than the one before, until they came to a rocky slope descending to a wide, bare plain. Here they had made camp.

For a moment there had been an antelope poised against the moon, its large eyes staring into theirs; then it was gone, and there remained only the howling of jackals and the harsh laugh of a hyena to pierce the darkness. Hagar made a ring of stones and twigs planted in various designs, which she said would guard them from snakes and other dangers. They made a fire to keep themselves warm and to keep away the animals. Nights were cold here on the brink of the wilderness; vestiges of the desert's diamond wind cut through their cloaks and scraped their bones. The moon was full; it cast a cool light over the scene, heightening the lines of the landscape, making everything seem unreal.

Hagar rocked back and forth on her heels as she crouched beside the fire. Her eyes were full of old dreams, and Alexandra felt sure she would spin a tale or two as she used to do in Beit Harsom. What wonderful stories she had told then! Myths of woodland sprites and wild centaurs, of brave young kings who found their way out of labyrinths, of adventurers saved by beautiful princesses. Hagar had also spoken of the bull-jumpers of her native Crete and of the priestesses of the snake and of her Good Goddess. "Your Lawgiver thought to have cast her out," she told Alexandra. "But the Good Goddess will never fade from the hearts of the people. She is the Mother, and she will live for all time."

But tonight Hagar was not thinking of her goddess or of kings and minotaurs. She was thinking of her youth and of the manner in which she had been brought to Judea.

."He was a Phoenician," she said, "and captain of his ship. A big, dark man with eyes like fire and arms as thick as trees. Ah! I tell you, he was beautiful! His body was covered with tattoos—that is the way with his people—on his right arm was a blue snake that he could make dance like a thing alive. I was young. . . . My breasts were high, and heavy with the sap running in them. . . . And he found me on the beach, standing in the water with my skirts pulled up . . . and those eyes of his pierced my belly like a knife until my thighs ran wet from love. I was a woman from that day, from that hour he took me, when the sun sank into the sea and we lay together on the sand, me and my tattooed man. He said I was beautiful. And I was. Yes. . . . I was beautiful. And night came and we counted the stars, and he told me the name of each, and which to follow to the land of the yellow-skins, and which to the country of Caesar, and which one would lead him back again to his own kind. And he told me stories of all the places he had seen and the treasures he had won and lost. And he promised me necklaces of gold and earrings of silver if I would go with him. He said I would be queen of his ship . . . that I would sail with him to the edge of the world.

"So I went with him onto his ship, and he loved me there. But when we put in at the port of Alexandria, the dog sold me to an old Babylonian who tried to cover his stink with sweet perfume. I ran away from the wretch and hid in a ship. It was your father's vessel. And so it was I came to Judea.

"It is the Law of your people that all who seek refuge must be granted it. Escaped slaves may not be returned unless they are criminals—which your father in his wisdom saw that I was not. So it was I became a part of your household and worshiped your God. Your mother had no milk for you, and since I had just been delivered of a dead child—son of a miserable sailor who gave me too much wine one full-moon night—I gave you suck. Your brother Beni also drank at the breast of another— a miserable Syrian creature who would have stolen the lids off the pots had I not kept these sharp eyes on her."

"Did you never see the Phoenician again?"

She laughed happily. "The miserable dog. No—or I would have stuck his privy parts together on the point of my knife like shish-kebab!" But her eyes gleamed fondly. "The dog. Ah! There was a man!"

"But he sold you!"

She shrugged. "That is the way with men." She smiled a strange smile. "Listen to me, little owl. Once, only once while you draw breath in this world, if the Good Goddess smiles upon you, you will meet the one who is the you outside yourself. The man to whom you must give your life. The man for whom you would die. You know it from the first. Even if he speaks not a word to you, nor you to him, or if the words between you are harsh . . . still, you will know each other. Be it in the first cool hours of morning or in the white heat of noon or in the darkness of night, you will find each other. And you will follow. Though he beat you, though he sell you, though he kill you. There is no other way. So it must be." She sighed. "This is the weakness of woman. This is why, though she is closer to the gods than man can ever be, she has such a low position on this earth. She is born to serve one man. And if it be not her husband, then it will be her son."

They awoke next morning to find the fire out, the horses gone, and everything not in the bundles they had used for pillows stolen while they slept.

Alexandra believed they had been robbed by children; there were gangs of them all around, hungry little orphan-outlaws whose own youth had been stolen. If grown men had come upon them, she felt sure they would have been killed or attacked. But then, there was no telling in these times, she said.

Hagar cursed man and child of every known race, calling down upon the unknown thieves an assortment of ingenious afflictions whose scope and detail would have filled any listener with awe.

Alexandra tried to calm her. "It is no more than a day's journey to the Masada. Pangar said we must follow Lake Asphaltitis—the Dead Sea, they call it now. We should reach the oasis of Ein Gedi first, and we can rest there. No, do not bother with all that," she told Hagar, who was taking inventory of what remained. "It will be hot enough without loading ourselves down like donkeys."

But Hagar continued to rummage through the remaining bundles, taking certain items that she tied up in a cloth and attached to the cord around her waist. Finally she hurried after Alexandra, who had already started.

The morning dew had lifted. Ahead of them stretched the silent sand and tawny cliffs. Hagar looked up at the sky. The sun was beginning to burn through the clouds. She hoped they did not have far to go.

The ancient Israelites had called the Judean desert Jeshimon. It meant "devastation." The land, Hagar thought, had been well named.

It was a veritable wasteland, a place untouched by any kindness of nature. The terrain before them seemed contorted, ridges running in all directions, hills torn apart by the dried riverbeds called wadis. There was nothing but stones and sand and the sun beating down hard. Often the ground sounded hollow underfoot; the limestone surfaces were blistered and peeling, the rocks bare and jagged, glowing with dull heat. There were places where steam rose from the earth, where boiling springs bubbled up, giving off the stench of sulphur.

"It is said to come from the gates of Gehenna," Alexandra told Hagar. "The place of the dead."

The woman's eyes widened. For some time she had been clutching hard at a small, curiously shaped stone she had picked up. Now, as she followed Alexandra across the silent, harsh landscape, she began to see the girl with new respect. It was no easy journey. It took time and skill to cross the deep ravines that cut the hill paths; even then it was difficult, and the sun was relentless. Yet Alexandra was calm; she led the way with a strange surety, without fear or apprehension. It was as if she somehow knew this place, had always known it; as if this thirsty, broken land of crags and shelves, with its deep wadis and towering cliffs, was something she had already seen— perhaps in some recurring dream; as if the sand and stones she trod upon now were the stuff of her bones, the grit of her blood. She smiled at Hagar, as if to say that the woman's talismans and amulets, her innumerable gods, even her Good Goddess, were of no account here. They had entered the domain of Yahwah.

"In the desert there is no pretense," Josef had said. What there was was this Presence, this Reality. An unrelenting Eye staring down, merciless as the sun . . .

Strangely exhilarated, Alexandra started to laugh but stopped as sudden pain cut across her back and into her stomach.

"What is it?" Hagar asked immediately.

"Nothing." She drew in her breath. "I must have been walking too fast."

"Too fast! You wander as in a dream."

"Do you fear that we are lost?"

Hagar studied the girl thoughtfully. "No," she said at last. "No, you are not lost. You go as you must go. I only hope," she added drily, "the journey does not take forty years, as it did for your Lawgiver. I do not find this place very pleasant."

"We should be nearing Ein Gedi. There will be water there."

But the oasis did not appear. Far to their left they could make out the mountains of Moab and sometimes catch glimpses of a deep blue sea, but there was no sign of Ein Gedi. The sun was directly above their heads now, the air heavy, motionless. They had been walking for hours. Then, suddenly, the sea burst upon them in all its turquoise length; and they tumbled, exhausted, down a mountainous stretch of craggy limestone, flint, and marl to the broad beach of *Yam Hamelach*, the desolation, the howling waste of Jeshimon made bearable by the presence of this salt sea.

But the water gave no succor.

They could not drink it or even refresh themselves by bathing in it; for it was a strange, warm liquid, oily to the touch and foul-smelling. A hedge of driftwood, bleached and glittering with salt, girdled the lake like the bones of dead animals or men. The shore was devoid of life—there were not even any birds—but for the presence of great swarms of insects that sent the women running inland.

"What do you suppose they have for dinner when we are not around?" Hagar muttered, slapping at her arm. She sighed wearily. "This is a miserable trick. I am an old woman. What am I doing here in this miserable place?"

"Be quiet," Alexandra replied irritably. Scratched by thorns, bitten by mosquitoes, she was quite as sore as her companion. Moreover, the hand she'd dipped into the Sea of Salt was throbbing with pain, and it was all she could do to keep from gagging at the pervasive odor of sulphur. But Hagar was right, she thought. What a cruel trick of God or nature this body of water was, placed here, so temptingly, in the Dead Sea Valley.

"It is madness to travel during these hours," Hagar said

now, squinting up at the sky. "We must wait until the sun is lower."

Alexandra looked around, then pointed toward the cliffs. "We will find a cave or at least rest in the shadows."

Hagar grunted her approval, but they had gone only a short distance when she let out a gasp. Looking up, Alexandra saw a man standing before her. She was so startled to see him that she did not think to be afraid, despite his formidable appearance. From a face that was burnt deep brown, two eyes like black holes stared at her. A thick black beard covered the entire lower part of his face, and above it his cheekbones jutted out like the bones of a skull. One hand rested on the bow slung over his shoulder; the other touched the hilt of a dagger stuck through his belt. He wore the breastplate of a Roman soldier, but he spoke in Aramaic with the guttural drawl of the Galilee.

"What are you doing here?" he demanded. "This is no place for women to be wandering about. Are you lost? Are you come from Ein Gedi?"

"We seek the place called the Masada," Alexandra said forthrightly, evenly meeting his eyes.

He blinked. "Masada?"

Her heart jumped anxiously. "You . . . you do know of it, don't you?"

He did not reply. His face was blank.

She tried again. "A man named Shem—from Gischala—he spoke of joining the Sicarii there. He knew my brother. They— he—That is—" She stopped. Suddenly she did not know what to say. Had it all been for nothing? Were they lost? Was the story of the Masada only that—a story?

"Who is you brother?"

"He was killed in the Roman arena. He fought in the Galilee. He . . . he bought my freedom with his life. Please . . . there is no other place for me to go. . . ."

"There is Jerusalem." His eyes were guarded. "Why do you not go to the Holy City?"

"My brother wanted me to come to the Masada. Those were his last words."

The hand came away from the knife. "How are you called?" he asked in a softer voice.

"Alexandra."

He stiffened. "A Sadducee name."

"Yes."

"You are the daughter of—?"

"What does it matter?" she said wearily. "They are all dead."

He was quiet a moment, trying to digest the strange assortment of facts come his way. Then he jerked his chin toward Hagar. "And you?"

"I too have no one in this world," Hagar said quickly. "I met this one on the road and decided to come with her. Maybe I will find myself a husband on this Masada, eh? There will be plenty to cook for, I warrant." She looked him over disdainfully. "You are not much more than a burnt bag of bones."

A grin split the black beard. "Well, now, mother, perhaps there is a future for you with us. And you too, miss. But I promise you no soft beds." He looked critically at the slender girl. "I still think it would be better for you to go to the Holy City. It is a hard life here. I can see you've had your share of troubles, but what you have endured thus far may be as nothing compared to what lies ahead."

Alexandra raised her hand to shield her eyes from the sun. It was very hot, and she wished that he would let them get on. She did not feel well. "What is death?" she asked. "Freedom is all. The Lord our God will provide for us."

His eyes lit up. He took her arm. "Come, then," he said.

Yigael—for that was his name—declared it was too hot to proceed further. "We must wait to make the climb, yet not so late as to see the sky turn black. The path we must take is not an easy one," he added in a tone that suggested the ascent would be more difficult than they had bargained for. "We are not far, as you can see." He pointed to a cliff some quarter-hour's walk ahead. "That one, jutting towards the sea. There is the Masada."

Alexandra and Hagar followed the Zealot scout across the dry, stone-filled wadis to a cave a few meters up the foot of one of the great cliffs. It had obviously been used before. Letters in Hebrew script had been scratched in the walls; the ashes of a fire long cold were still on the ground. Some clay vessels and a pile of lentils were heaped in a corner.

Yigael went to one of the urns and removed its cloth covering. He tipped the jar to his lips and drank deeply of the liquid stored within. Then he passed the vessel to Alexandra. The water was cool, surprisingly sweet. Hagar next quenched her thirst; and then, as one, all three sank wearily to the ground.

The wall of the cave was damp; a shiver ran up Alexandra's back. She tried to conceal it and also her pain, which had returned even more acutely. She felt Hagar's eyes on her. "I am tired," she murmured self-consciously. "It is the heat. . . ."

Yigael was sitting on his haunches, his arms resting loosely on his knees; he was directly across from the two women but with a clear view of the entrance. He nodded in agreement. "It is not fit for humans here. I left Magdala three years ago, but I am still not used to this accursed place. I do not know how the Essenes can stand it as they do. They work outside even with the sun straight above. Me, I'd rather settle in Ein Gedi. It's green there," he added wistfully, "like Magdala used to be."

"Essenes?" Hagar was puzzled. "Desert people? Are they Jews?"

Yigael was shocked by her ignorance. "The Holy Ones are closer to the Lord than you and I will ever be. Where did you say you came from?"

"Caesarea," Alexandra said.

He spat on the ground. "Roman gutter! I didn't think there were any of us left alive there." His eyes narrowed. "I thought all the Jews of Caesarea had been murdered."

"Or sold."

He looked away from her direct gaze, his face reddening beneath the tan.

"You ask a lot of questions," Hagar said. "How do we know what you are? How do we know you have not led us here for some mischief?"

He was about to answer her indignantly but stopped. Her eyes had narrowed. She pointed to the entrance of the cave, where a dark figure stood silhouetted against the white sky.

Yigael jumped up, his hand on his knife. He peered intently at the newcomer a moment, then let his hand drop. "*Shalom*," he said, sitting down again.

"*Shalom*." The man came forward, blinking at the sudden darkness of the cave.

Yigael waved his hand in the direction of the two women. "They seek the Masada. They are runaway slaves, I think."

The man turned to them. "You are welcome." He had a gentle voice.

"This is Jonatan," Yigael said. "He is one of the Holy Ones, as were his father and mother before him. There was a great settlement of Essenes right around here. The *Kittim* destroyed it last spring. They keep a garrison there now. You did well to avoid it."

The one called Jonatan said nothing to this but went to the clay vessels and briefly inspected them. He did not drink from any, however; instead he drew a skin from his belt and raised it to his lips. He seemed to take a drop, a mere mouthful. Alexandra saw now that he was young, not much older than herself, and that his face was as gentle as his voice. He was a shade of dusty brown all over—hair, eyes, skin, even his once-white tunic. He had very fine, straight hair.

"The one they call Banus," she asked suddenly. "Is he still alive?"

"No." He could not hide his surprise.

"I knew someone who once lived among Essenes," she explained. "He spoke often of the 'holy hermit.'"

Jonatan was even more startled by this.

"Did you know Banus?" she asked.

"No."

"I wish I could have."

Jonatan swallowed. "He would not have spoken to a woman," he said, and turned away.

Little was said now. The two men conferred briefly in low voices and then fell silent. Alexandra was too weary and full of pain to care what they said. Her stomach was full of knives, and the odors of the place were making her dizzy. She leaned forward, away from the wall, with a noticeable shiver. Her back was wet.

Hagar moved closer. "What is it?"

Alexandra shook her head. "Nothing . . . nothing."

The woman studied her briefly, then let out her breath. "I should have known. . . . Why did you not tell me?"

"What? That I am tired?" She tried to lean away. She could smell Hagar's scalp, the oil the woman rubbed into her hair. She smelled . . . blood.

"We should never have left Caesarea."

"Be quiet. If you say one word I will kill you, I swear it. If they think I am . . . they might not take us with them."

"Better to be left behind than for you to be lying dead on that accursed mountain."

Alexandra swallowed. "I am not going to die. I told you, it's just the heat. I'm tired." She tried to laugh. "What do you think, I am an old mule like you?"

Yigael came over to them. "Now." He pointed to the entrance of the cave. The light outside had softened. "We must reach the top of the Masada before night falls."

The women got to their feet and followed him outside, where Jonatan was waiting, scanning the horizon.

"We had better take the Snake," the young Essene said. "We are nearer to it."

"There is another path," Yigael said as they made their way across the sand and stones once more. "It is easier to climb, but earlier Jonatan saw some riders to the west. They may be *Kittim*—Roman soldiers. It is best if we go straight ahead."

They went quickly now, the two women following Jonatan, and Yigael keeping watch behind.

The sky was a soft, rosy gold, no longer the blazing white it had been earlier, but for all its tender warmth, the sun cut through her eyes. Her head throbbed, and each pebble underfoot was a small lance tearing into the muscles of her legs. Alexandra had thought the distance short; but they seemed to go on forever, on and on across the dry, rocky land. And then, suddenly, when she had begun to think this march would never cease, there it was before them. A great, flat-topped rock. A mountain rising up from the sand.

The Masada.

Yigael stood beside her, looking up at the formidable piece of landscape with fond awe. He grinned. "Well, little one," he said, pointing to the narrow path that encircled the mountain, winding up and around it like a snake, "we shall see now if that soft flesh hides the heart of a Zealot."

Alexandra accepted the challenge and started forward eagerly, pushing ahead of the startled Jonatan to begin the ascent. It was not long, however, before she was forced to allow the Essene to take the lead. She had begun too fast, as any experienced climber could have told her; moreover, she had no knowledge of the way ahead. There were many hazardous spots, places where it was necessary to rely upon the skill and aid of the two men, where a show of independence would have been not only foolish but dangerous.

The air was growing cooler now; she gulped it down, but it was hard, rough-edged stuff that hurt her throat and chest. Beads of perspiration stood out on her forehead like cold rain, and the pain in her stomach and back deepened each time she took a step forward, each time she thrust herself upward, her

fingers digging into found crevices, her arms embracing walls
of stone a dizzying height above the ground.

But she did not stop. She went on. Nothing could make her
turn back now. It was a matter of her very life to reach the
top. No, she could not turn back, and she would not stop. The
sun burned behind her eyes; her body was in torture, the pain
in her loins becoming so intense that finally it turned sweet
and she felt drunk, intoxicated with an excruciating ecstasy,
filled with a sudden, strange, mad exhilaration. It was as if
she moved somewhere outside her body, inside yet outside the
pain and heat and weariness. And in the sweetness of this pain,
she wondered with a sudden flash of clarity what she was
looking for and what she hoped to find.

I seek my self, she had said.

Her self. In the desert? On a mountaintop? With Zealots,
Sicarii, Essenes? . . . She would have laughed aloud had she the
breath for it.

The light was fading quickly now. It would be night in a
matter of moments. The mountains of Moab had turned from
lavender to slate, but the sun inside her head was bursting into
a thousand suns, like flowers, like petals of gold ripping open
her flesh. She could feel Hagar at her back, breathing hard,
but sure and steady behind her. "I am here," the woman seemed
to murmur. "I am here. . . ."

The light was slipping away. A sudden, consuming wave
of pain made her stumble and cry out. She was falling . . . and
then there was a hand reaching down for her, pulling her up
and over the top as the light disappeared. All the suns exploded,
and it was dark . . . dark. . . . Blessed darkness.

THREE

A thick cloud of black smoke hung over the city; the air was pungent, sharp with the scent of incense and the unmistakable stench of burning flesh. Aliterus stiffened in alarm and looked about, trying to determine the direction of the fire, but he could see nothing unusual in Jerusalem's busy streets. Despite the ominous sky and strangely spiced air, the haggling in the marketplace went on without a lull. Tradesmen shouted their wares; mothers called after lost children; water carriers bearing skins upon their backs sang of their services; a scribe sat in a doorway quietly penning a letter for a man who could not write. The coppersmiths hammered, the fullers fulled.

Aliterus caught the sleeve of a passerby and nervously asked, "Has something caught fire?"

The man looked startled. Then, looking up at the sky, he smiled. "Ah! It must be the smoke from the Temple altar that you speak of. Yes...the priests are making sacrifice. It's always dark like this," he explained, "when the wind blows from the east. They say you can smell the blessed scent clear to Jericho. Are you not from Judea?"

Aliterus caught his breath. The man's expression was pleasant enough; there seemed to be no animosity or suspicion in his voice. "No," the actor said. "But I have come a long distance to see the Temple. To make my *aliyah*," he added, remembering Alexandra's words.

The Jerusalemite smiled again, spreading his hands wide in greeting. "Blessed are they who seek the Lord. Welcome to His City, Jerusalem, City of Peace." With a nod he moved off and was quickly lost in the crowd.

Aliterus stood there a moment; then he sighed. City of Peace indeed. Hardly a man on the streets was not armed. Stern-faced gangs, their thumbs tucked into heavy leather sword belts, were everywhere. Their very beards were menacing.

345

Aliterus scratched his own new-grown whiskers (a smooth-shaven face was the sign of Rome). What would he not give for the sight of a centurion's crested helmet or a red-cloaked trooper one could count on to keep order. But there were no more legionaries in Jerusalem, no mounted Gaulish or Numidian auxiliaries to curse the crowd for not giving their horses room, no Roman soldiers clearing the way for condemned men being taken to Golgotha, the Place of the Skull, with the beam of the cross upon their backs.

The city teemed with travelers, pilgrims whom no war with Rome or terror tales of fratricide could sway from their holy task; Aliterus need not have worried that his position was unique. Jews from Babylon, in trailing black robes; men from Phoenicia, in tunics and striped trousers; children of Israel from Anatolia, in goat's-hair cloaks, and from Persia, in precious silk shot through with gold and silver threads—all crowded the narrow streets alongside refugees from every part of Judea, the proud Jerusalemites, and the omnipresent Zealot soldiers.

Intermixed with the great throng of people was a large number of animals—donkeys, their hooves tapping up and down the cobbled steps, cattle and sheep being driven to sacrifice. Aliterus did not have long to stand and contemplate the situation; the tide of men and beasts quickly pushed him aside. Instinctively his hand went to his breast and then to his belt. Satisfied that his papers and money were safe, he continued to walk along until he grew tired. Then, his eyes smarting from the heavy, dark air, he found a spot, sat down, and leaned heavily against a stone wall smoothed by the backs of untold numbers of beggars who had rested in its shadow.

Aliterus closed his eyes. So this was Jerusalem. A noisy, stinking city jammed to the walls with people, half a mile high in the sky. The stage managers in Rome, thought the actor wryly, could take a lesson from the God of Israel. From afar the place seemed to hang from the clouds like a piece of heaven itself. Close up, however, Jerusalem was not particularly beautiful, especially to anyone who knew Rome. The houses, for example, were unimpressive; they clung to one another, often overlapping. The rooftop balustrades required by law to prevent a fall were a nice moral touch, but certainly no architectural achievement. There were a few gardens—here and there a fig tree might be seen rising from a courtyard—and no statuary of any kind. Carved reliefs seemed limited to impressions of grapes and pomegranates, for it was forbidden among the Jews to depict anything that might be construed as an idol.

The streets of the city were exceedingly narrow; the marketplace was lined with traders' stalls, each with its own crowd, and it was hardly possible to move without receiving an elbow in one's side or sandal on one's foot. There were in fact two markets in Jerusalem: one in the Upper Town, where the great and priestly families lived and where the wealthy shopped, and the Lower Town market for the more numerous poorer population. Few litters dared to challenge the traffic of either. Aliterus, accustomed to the opulence and variety of the Imperial City's shops, would probably have found little to astonish, interest, or amuse him even in Jerusalem's more elegant quarters. Herod's Palace—that magnificent structure, with its white colonnades and green lawns, its coppices of trees traversed by long walks, fountains, and bronze statues, its luxuriously furnished rooms and courts trimmed with alabaster—had been burnt to the ground by the Sicarii at the outbreak of the war. Likewise, most of the Hasmonean palaces and Sadducee villas had been destroyed or turned into garrisons by the Zealot factions. The Hellenistic legacy that Judea's aristocracy had embraced and that had endowed Jerusalem with the kind of grace and beauty Aliterus found appealing was looked on with abhorrence by the Zealots, and it had therefore been destroyed as far as possible. Left standing, however, was the one piece of Herodian magnificence that even those stern hearts dared not deface, though they had defiled it: the Temple.

But for the moment Aliterus had forgotten the Temple. Forgotten, too, was the fact that his presence in this unappealing place was due to no whim of the gods—Fate could be held accountable only to a certain point—but to his own determination. Sadly he sat in the shadow of the great wall that surrounded the City of David, not the least diverted by the sights and sounds around him, wondering why in Hades he had ever wanted to come here. The stench alone was enough to kill a man. Although it was forbidden in Jerusalem to have open-air ovens or to fertilize trees and flowers with manure, there was still—besides the "blessed scent" emanating from the altar of sacrifices—a noxious odor. Though the open places were swept daily, as required by law, garbage filled the alleys, its smell mingling with that of hot cooking oil, along with a general profusion of herbs, spices, onion, and garlic.

Aliterus emitted a large, melancholy sigh. Years slipped away, and for a moment he was back in the marketplace of

Rome, remembering the taste of a stolen sausage that an always hungry slave boy had burned his tongue on. The contrast of what he had been to what he had made himself, and of that to what he had now set himself amidst, suddenly struck him; the past was interwoven with the smell of frying bread.

Moreover, he was hungry. Again he sighed. The local eating houses were so proud of their fare: fresh or salt fish, fried locusts, hot vegetables, soup, pastry, fruitcake, wine, Egyptian beer. But what was all that to a man who had seen a slave enter a dining room bearing a peacock roasted in its feathers, the tail outspread so that the creature looked as if it had but alighted for a moment on a silver dish? What were jellied wine and smoked fish to a man who had at one sitting nibbled on cold wild boar with pickled vegetables; downed oysters, shell-fish, shrimp, and two varieties of turbot; dined on wildfowl, the liver of a white goose fattened on ripe figs, shoulder of hare, broiled blackbirds and wood pigeons; and topped it all off with a final course of red apples and black mulberries "gathered before the sun is high"?

Another great sigh. What would he not give for an apple now? They were a delicacy in Judea, imported from Crete, and since the war in short supply. Of course, there was plenty of everything in Caesarea. Titus and Josephus would be feasting right now on some lovely supper. What a topsy-turvy turn of events. He, Aliterus, in Jerusalem, and Josef ben Matthias—the actor's own handsome Josephus—in Rome, so to speak!

I have come here, Aliterus thought, *like one aspiring to an audition, an actor in search of a role. Meanwhile, the play-wright has vanished. God of Josephus and of my own mother as well, You had better provide me with a stage direction now, or cue me, if You please. The fact is, I have lost my place in this script or wandered foolishly into the wrong theater.*

"That's Micah's place."

The actor's eyes flew open. One hand to his chest, the other at his belt, he quickly looked up to see who had spoken.

It was a one-eyed beggar. "Where you're sitting now," he said. "That's where Micah sits—or used to, at any rate. No need to worry about him, though. He's dead. Arrow through the heart, courtesy of Simon's men. A neat trick had it been done on purpose. But it wasn't. Just an accident during the fighting. Sit down, sit down. No need to be afraid. John's in the Temple, and isn't a son of a Sadducee anywhere in the city would start trouble now that Sophas ben Raguel's been arrested. The council has promised a trial—but you wait, he'll turn up dead before that ever comes to pass. Tripped over his own *talith* and strangled accidentally, they'll say." The beggar laughed drily. "As if any in Jerusalem would believe that old story." He looked Aliterus over, squinting through his one good eye. "Well, where are you from?"

"Outside Judea. I have come to see the Temple."

"Then what are you doing sitting here? Leave the space to them as has no legs to walk but can still stretch out a hand for alms. . . . Where outside Judea?"

"Alexandria. I am from Alexandria."

"No, you're not," the beggar said calmly. "Not that it matters to me. Well, you're not going to pass up the honor of giving a shekel to a poor beggar in Jerusalem, are you? My blessing is better than my curse."

"I think I am already cursed," Aliterus muttered, rising to leave.

"What, had a hard time of it, have you? Look at me, with only one eye and not a bite to eat since yesterday. Half my regular customers were killed by the legionaries, and the rest have been done in by John or Simon's men. Not to speak of the friends I've lost in this war. Poor Micah. He never knew what hit him. That's what comes of being too lame to move out of trouble's way. Well, come on." He poked Aliterus with his cane. "Give me a shekel now, a couple of denarii, whatever you like—I'm not choosy. In return I'll give you something better than a blessing or a curse."

"And what might that be?"

"Advice." The outstretched hand closed around the coin Aliterus dropped into it. "Good. I thank you, sir. The Almighty will reward your kindness as He rewards all acts of charity."

"You said you had some advice for me."

"And so I have." One bright eye peered up at Aliterus. "Simon holds most of the city—all of the Upper Town and most of the Lower. But the Temple is in John's hands—except for the inner courts, which the militant priests protect. Our glorious defenders like nothing better than to fight among themselves. It is not uncommon for one of their arrows to pierce the heart of a poor innocent like Micah. Yes, even in the Temple courts. So take care as you pray. Many like you who have come from the ends of the earth to offer sacrifice to the Eternal have been struck down before their very offerings." The beggar nodded sadly. "What was once the house of God has become the burial place of His children."

Startled, Aliterus stood dumbly.

"Another thing," the old man said. "At the Temple gates, foreigners are searched."

"I bear no weapons."

"A letter written in Roman characters, even a bill of sale, is enough to hang you nowadays."

Aliterus stared at the beggar.

"They will search you at the outer gate and again at the entrance to the inner courts." He held up the denarius Aliterus had given him. "In the Court of Gentiles you must change this for the coin of Israel. Caesar's image is forbidden within the Temple grounds. Though it lay in the darkness of your pocket, it would not be hidden from the Eye of the Almighty."

"But where—"

"Oh, don't worry, you'll hear the voices of the money-changers quick enough, though they're not as loud as they used to be. The rates are fixed by law, but in the old days an ignorant man might lose in the exchange. At least the council has put a stop to that." He fished through his rags and brought out two coins, which he displayed in his open palm. One was a crudely rounded silver disc engraved with a chalice and the inscription "Jerusalem the Holy." The other coin was bronze with a vine-leaf design. As Aliterus bent nearer to examine it, the beggar's hand quickly closed around it. Indignant, Aliterus straightened and turned to go. This time he felt a bony hand tugging at his cloak.

"Wait," the beggar commanded. "I'm not finished with you. Unless, that is, you are determined to get yourself into trouble."

Aliterus turned back slowly. "Truly it is said that rich men of Tyre are not so haughty as the beggars of Jerusalem."

"The arrogance of the streets. Tongues that taste little food grow tart. Besides, as you said, I am a Jerusalemite. But let's get down to business. After you have done with the money-changers, you must buy something for sacrifice. A couple of pigeons will do. Anything grand will mark you a rich man, and that is a dangerous thing to be these days. A few pennies should do it."

"Well, thank you," Aliterus said with a bow that made the beggar grin. "I shall be off now. And since you seem to know everything, you may as well tell me which way leads to the great Temple."

"Why, follow the animals," the beggar replied, waving his staff at the passing parade. "Braying or praying, they're all going to the same place. And more than one," he added grimly, "I guarantee won't be coming back."

Aliterus hesitated.

"Scared you, have I?"

"No," the actor said slowly. "I have come too far not to see this through. Follow the animals, you say?"

"Oh, you won't get lost. There is a saying: 'All paths lead to Jerusalem. And in Jerusalem, all streets lead to the Temple.'"

"I thought all roads led to Rome."

"Not in Judea, they don't. Besides," the beggar added, "all you have to do is look up to find your way."

"Up?"

The beggar jabbed at the sky with one long finger and then leaned back against the wall, closing his one good eye as if to say, "That's all you get from me for a denarius."

Aliterus raised his eyes obediently; and then he saw it. Gleaming, shining like a star, like a sculpture carved from snow, set atop the hill called Mount Moriah, its gold-spiked roof like the rising sun, with no hint, no murmur, of murder or blood or carnage of any kind to mar the peace and purity of its facade, there sat the Temple Herod had erected upon the foundations of the one built by Solomon and razed by Nebuchadnezzar.

It was a glorious sight. The most sophisticated eye could hardly fail to appreciate its beauty, the grandeur of its structure and setting; and Aliterus was duly awed. He was standing as he had on the hill outside Jerusalem, gazing upward, his heart in his eyes, when a silence enveloped the city, as dramatic in its suddenness as the sight of the Temple had been. The seven silver trumpets of the Levite priests had rung out from the gate of the Men's Court, signaling one of the day's three ritual pauses. In the hush that followed, Aliterus became aware of a soft buzz of prayer in many languages. Then the moment passed; the discordant sounds of common life resumed, and all activity that had for a spellbound moment ceased began again.

Aliterus slipped into the crowd pressing toward the Temple, his flesh still tingling from the sound of the silver trumpets. Moving forward, he looked up at the sky, which was no longer and foreboding but clear and marvelously golden. He sinned. "Well done," he whispered with a wink, as if to some fellow actor. "Your timing is excellent."

On the heights of Mount Moriah lay the threshing floor of Ornan the Jebusite. It was here that the angel of the Lord revealed himself to David the King, who had provoked the wrath of God.

The Book of Chronicles relates, "And David lifted up his eyes and saw the angel of the Lord standing between earth and heaven with a drawn sword in his hand stretched out over Jerusalem."

Then David fell upon his face and said, "It is I, Lord, who have sinned and done wickedly, not the people. Let thy hand be not against Jerusalem but against me. . . ."

Then the angel commanded David to rear an altar unto the Lord on the threshing floor of Ornan the Jebusite. And David built there an altar and offered burnt offerings and called upon the Lord. And the Lord answered him by fire upon the altar.

It was over the threshing floor of Ornan that King Solomon, son of David, erected the great Temple of the Lord, renowned throughout the ancient world until its destruction by the Babylonians. Centuries later, determined to establish himself as a Jewish king, Herod took it upon himself not only to rebuild the sacred structure but to surpass in splendor that which had gone before. The same mind that set itself to the construction of Caesarea and to the remarkable conception of the Masada spared nothing in the design and building of the Second Temple. Ten thousand laborers worked on the elaborate colonnade surrounding the summit of Mount Moriah and the least holy parts of the building proper. As none but priests were permitted to enter the inner chambers of the Temple, one thousand Levites were trained in masonry and carpentry.

The Temple was the center of Judaism. There were synagogues scattered all over the Mediterranean world in places where the children of Israel congregated—at Alexandria in Egypt, at Antioch in Syria, at the trading cities of Asia Minor, in every town and village within Judea—but the Temple was the House of God among His people, and the only place where the High Priest performed his offices. Every Israelite, no matter where he lived, paid a half-shekel yearly for maintenance of the Temple, for the incense and the sacrificial animals and the vestments; rich men gave more. As poor as they were, already taxed by Rome, the inhabitants of Judea paid willingly, knowing that there could be no Temple outside the Promised Land; and the inhabitants of Jerusalem paid with pride, for it was the Temple that made their city holy.

Aliterus was hot and tired and hungry, but as he climbed Temple Hill he felt a resurgence of the excitement he had experienced outside Jerusalem. The summit was ringed with portico pillars, each cut from a single block of whitest marble, and so large it would take three men with outstretched arms to encircle one of them. Their tops, spreading into the stone foliage of Corinthian capitals, supported intricately carved ceilings paneled with fragrant cedar. The whole area, called Solomon's Porch, encompassed a circuit of some three quarters of a mile, open to the sky, and paved with stones of every kind and color.

As he strolled down the long, majestic aisles, pausing between the rows of fluted columns to drink in the view below, Aliterus felt a sense of peace unlike anything he had ever known before. His fatigue had disappeared, his belly had stopped its growling; it was as if he had left his body somewhere at the bottom of the hill. The view to the east stretched all the way to the mountains of Moab on the far side of the Dead Sea. Below him were Jerusalem's wall, the rocky valley of the Kidron, and on the far side of the river, the road to Bethany, a silver sliver winding through dark green groves of olive trees.

He could have stayed there indefinitely, spirit refreshed by the quiet beauty of the landscape, at ease in the familiar Greco-Roman setting, but his desire to see the Temple proper drove him on. Passing three rows of pillars, he entered the Temple's outer area, commonly called the Court of Gentiles.

His serenity was instantly shattered. The place was a madhouse: jostling mobs . . . the cries of the moneychangers . . . the smell of dung from the sheep and oxen lowing across the court . . . the fluttering wings of the soon-to-be-sacrificed doves and pigeons against the bars of their wooden cages . . . the entreaties of the beggars propped against the wall, bony arms outstretched, crying, "A shekel! A shekel! Twice blessed is he who remembers the poor!"

It was unbelievable. A ruckus such as this in the vicinity of Jupiter's temple was punishable by death—and yet, how pious the Jews professed to be! Was this how they worshiped their God? In the midst of this mad bazaar?

Momentarily forgetting the one-eyed beggar's instructions, Aliterus began to make his way across the broad grounds toward a stone balustrade that concealed a second court. As he approached, he saw that it was carved at regular intervals with inscriptions in both Latin and Greek. But before he could come close enough to read them, a hand closed upon his arm and a voice said, "No foreigner may enter the sacred precincts, upon penalty of death."

Aliterus turned slowly and smiled at the Zealot guard. "I did not think," he said jovially, "that any foreigner might enter Jerusalem, let alone set foot upon Temple ground. Caesar himself would not dare attempt it."

The Zealot smiled. "Truly he would not. Not so long as John of Gischala is here."

"John? I thought I heard the name Simon—"

The Zealot frowned. "John is the only one who can lead us to victory. Simon bar Giora cares only for himself. If he did not, would he make war upon his own people? He cares nothing for freedom, only for plunder." He put his hand on his sword belt. "I do not like to say this, but Jews like Simon give us all a bad name—him and his criminal followers."

Aliterus nodded sadly. "I have heard stories—"

"They're all true. I tell you, the Lord will not smile upon us until Judea is purged—of Rome and of men like Simon bar Giora."

Aliterus raised his hands in supplication. "I shall offer sacrifice to that. May the Eternal hear my prayer."

The Zealot clapped him on the back. "You do that. And while you're at it, you might ask the Almighty to send a plague upon the priests up there." He jerked his thumb toward the sacred precincts. "They're as bad as Simon."

The inscription, which was the same in both languages, repeated the Zealot's warning: No foreigner might enter within the balustrade and embarkment around the Sanctuary. "Whoever is caught will have himself to blame for his death, which will follow."

Entrance was not only forbidden to gentiles; those who had been defiled through contact with a corpse were likewise prohibited, an ordinance rendered ironic by the war. Also banned were women in the time of their menstrual period. Everyone—Judeans and pagans alike—had the privilege of entering the

Temple Mount and the Court of Gentiles, which was broad enough to accommodate an assembly of thousands and had been used for this purpose by kings and procurators; but those afflicted with leprosy, venereal disease, or any other contagious affliction were totally barred from the area and in fact from the city.

Aliterus had changed his money for the coin of Jerusalem and purchased a dove, which he carried with him in a small wooden cage (the cage was to be returned after sacrifice, whereupon Aliterus's penny deposit would be given back to him). Climbing the fourteen steps up to the courts beyond the balustrade, he passed through high double doors completely covered with gold and silver. He was now in the outermost portion of the Temple proper, the Women's Court. There were men here as well, but a woman might proceed no further. The rites of the Temple were not for the eyes of the daughters of Eve. Excluded from ritual, they made up their own prayers, calling to the Lord in their own way as they held their children close or laid their cheeks against the wall that isolated them, whispering their thoughts to the stone. Aliterus had been searched in the outer portico and again by a Levite guard at the gates to the Women's Court, but no quantity of armed, hostile men— or even the words of the beggar at the city wall—could have brought the war home to him as vividly as did the sight of these women in the Temple. Hardly a one was not in mourning. Widows, mothers bereft of sons, young girls whom death had robbed of their betrothed, victims of the legionaries and the strife among their own leaders—did any man in the worst battle suffer more than they? Who would not be moved to pity by their wailing, by the tears they shed in this place?

Aliterus studied the women, searching his memory for an image of his own lost mother. He had been three or four years of age when he was sold, and yet now it seemed to him that he could recall a smiling face, a warm breast, the smell of milk. . . .

Most likely she was dead. Perhaps not. What had become of her? All these years he had never given her a thought, not since the first dark nights after he had been taken from her. His name had not been Aliterus then, it had been something else; he could not remember what. He had hated her, he recalled suddenly, watching impassively as a group of women tried to keep one of their number from striking her head upon the ground in a hysterical fit of grief.

I hated you, he thought, *because you let them take me, and I embraced my new master because he wanted me. He became my father, and his ways became my ways, and I never thought of you again until today. I was too young to know how you must have suffered.*

The heart had gone out of him. Once more he stood uncertainly, not only an alien in this land of Judea but a stranger unto himself—this large man with melancholy eyes and woeful face. And then he heard a sound—men singing somewhere in the distance. He raised his eyes, searching for the singers, and just as the silver trumpets of the Levites had led him to the Temple before, so now their voices raised in song beckoned to the great gate leading from the Court of Women to the Court of the Israelites.

As in a trance, Aliterus crossed the Women's Court, mounted the semicircular flight of fifteen shallow steps at the western end, and passed through an enormous double-doored gate of Corinthian brass decorated with gold and silver plating. Mesmerized by the music, unaware that he had left his caged dove behind, he allowed himself to be searched once more by the guards in the gate room. They waved him on, and he continued to follow the sound, which came from still another court beyond the flagstone wall farthest west. There was a platform at the entrance; here the Levites sang their daily hymns.

Aliterus advanced toward the sound and the singers, but he was stopped at the entrance to the *Azarah,* or Court of Priests. Unless he was a priest or a Levite, he could not enter this court were he Agrippa himself or even the legendary David. But as the *Azarah* was on a higher elevation, Aliterus was able to watch the ceremonies that now took place.

There were sacrifices daily: a lamb before sunrise, one before sunset, and various offerings in between by private citizens for reasons detailed in the Torah. While Aliterus stood watching, a wealthy Persian gave custody of a pair of lambs into the hands of a Levite, who led them up to a primitive altar, a mass of rough stones fifty or sixty feet square, its four corners jutting out like horns. Behind it, at the far side of the courtyard and on a terrace, was the Sanctuary itself. A flight of steps ascended to its enormous doors of gold, above which hung golden vines and clusters of gold grapes, each bunch big as a man. The walls of the building were of white marble; from the pinnacles rose sharp gold spikes that prevented birds from perching on the roof and soiling it, and that looked from a distance like rays of the setting sun. Before the entrance hung a veil of Babylonian tapestry wondrously embroidered, with the whole vista of the heavens worked in the design.

It was gorgeous. Even the Roman Tacitus had commented on its magnificence. But it was the altar that Aliterus kept coming back to. Against all this fine, polished beauty, its rudeness was a shock. "We come from the desert," Alexandra had said. The desert. The wilderness. Long before there had been a Rome or even a Greece. Somewhere back . . . time past thought . . . a single man had made an altar of stones, built a fire, made a sacrifice to an Unseen Deity. . . . And the man had become a tribe, and the tribe a nation. . . .

It was that primeval gathering of rock, not the marble and the gold, that was the key.

"'And if thou wilt make Me an altar, thou shalt not build it of hewn stone. For if thou lift up thy tool upon it, thou hast polluted it.'"

Aliterus turned to the man who had spoken. It was the same man who had stopped him from entering the Priests' Court. His eyes were not unkind; there was something familiar about him. Aliterus turned back to the sacrifice now underway, wondering who the man was and how he had been able to divine the actor's thoughts.

The lambs of the Persian merchant had been slain; a priest standing over each had lifted the animal's jaws and with a single stroke drawn his knife across its throat. The killing, as prescribed by ritual, was done in that one stroke; the victims had not uttered a single cry, as was also prescribed.

Some of the blood from each animal was caught in a basin of gold and handed up along a line of priests until the last priest, standing at the sacrificial rock, took the basin and dashed the blood against the stone. The blood ran down the altar toward the drains at the lower end, disappearing into the channel that would carry it off to the Kidron.

While the sacrificed lambs were being hung from a rack and flayed, Aliterus turned again to the man beside him. "Is that the High Priest?" he asked, gesturing toward the one who had emptied the gold basin of its contents.

"The High Priest participates only on the Sabbath, at the new moon, and on feast days. His robes are much finer than any you see now."

"Of course, of course," Aliterus said hurriedly.

The wool had been carefully peeled from the lambs, their bellies cut, and the viscera, fat, kidneys, and "caul above the liver" extracted and placed upon a fire altar. While the offering steamed and burned, Aliterus watched the priests rub salt into the flesh of the lambs, remove the right forelegs, and cut the cheeks from the animals' heads. These were set aside.

"That is the priestly tithe," the man beside Aliterus explained. "It is the priests' due from the people, from those who offer sacrifice."

"You say these things as though you think I do not already know them," Aliterus snapped.

The man smiled apologetically. "You said you were a stranger in Judea. I thought perhaps you might be a stranger to our ways as well. Living in *Gola,* even the most pious may not have the complete knowledge of the rites. Forgive me if I have insulted you."

Aliterus stared at him. Now he remembered! It was the man in the marketplace who had welcomed him to the "City of Peace."

"It is you who must forgive me," he said at last. "The tales I have been told—the fighting within the city—have made me suspicious of all and everyone."

"Suspicious?"

"That I might be suspect."

Laughing softly, the Jerusalemite accompanied him back to the Court of the Israelites. "I see. Be at ease, then. You have nothing to fear from me." He stopped, seeing that Aliterus had halted and was looking back. "You wish to see more?"

"The singing. I would like to hear more of that. I have never heard such music. . . ."

"Yes, the Levites are wonderful musicians. In the old days—on feast days and Shabbat—there would be song throughout the night . . . the sound of the lyre and the voices of men raised to heaven as sweet as any bird." He sighed. "Those days are gone."

"Perhaps—when peace comes—they will return."

"From your mouth to the Ears of the Almighty." He studied Aliterus, whose expressive features could not mask his inner turmoil. "What is it? The sacrifice? No need to be ashamed. Many do not like the sight of blood, no matter how consecrated—"

"No, no—I have seen worse, I can assure you."

"The ritual, perhaps . . ."

"I am no stranger to that. Why, I saw an *Iphigenia* once—" He stopped, cleared his throat. "No," he continued finally, "it was not the rites."

"The splendor of the Sanctuary, then. You are over-whelmed—"

"Overwhelmed?" Aliterus faced the man squarely. "I am shaken, sir, to the very depths of my being—and by what, I cannot say. I have not seen your God, or even the inner chambers of what you say is His house. From what you have told me, I shall never be allowed to set foot within the Sanctuary. What I have just viewed is, I admit, an extraordinary temple covered with a lot of gold and silver—which, I must tell you, I have seen elsewhere in both greater and lesser degrees—within which a bunch of bearded fellows in fine linen did in a couple of dumb animals and dashed some blood against a pile of stones." He caught his breath, frowning. "Frankly, I expected more."

"Then why," the Jerusalemite asked calmly, "are you, as you say, shaken to the depths of your being?"

"If I only knew," Aliterus murmured. "The music," he said suddenly. "It was the sound . . ."

"Surely you have heard singing before."

"Not like that. And you may take my word for it, I have heard the most acclaimed artists of the world performing at the very height of their careers. But never have I experienced, have I felt—It was as if my very soul had been lifted upon the back of a winged steed and set flying towards the sun! Memories, feelings I did not even know were mine, are even now rushing through my head and heart. . . . I must hear them sing again! I shall wait here until they commence once more."

"That may not be wise," the Jerusalemite cautioned. "The Levites will not make another appearance until the evening sacrifice. Things have been quiet the last day or so, but from the anxious way the guards are pacing back and forth, I would say we would do well not to linger. Either Simon has decided to attack John's forces again, or John is ready to go after the priests. In either case, you and I would only be in the way, don't you think?"

"Assuredly," Aliterus agreed, remembering the beggar's warning.

"Where are you staying?" the Jerusalemite asked as they began their descent from the heights of Mount Moriah.

"I have not taken lodging yet."

"Then you shall come with me and stay at my house."

"You are kind."

"No more than you. If I were a stranger in your country, would you not take me in, as is the Law of our people?"

"Yes. Of course."

"Well, then." The man smiled. "In truth, I am being selfish. You interest me. I warn you, you shall pay for your lodging with long hours of talk. There is much I would ask you."

"And I, you."

"Then it is a marriage made in heaven. Tell me, how are you called?"

"The only name I know is the one my master gave me. Aliterus."

"You were a slave?"

"Long ago. In Rome. My mother, I am told, was of the faith of Israel. My body bears the mark of Abraham's covenant." He looked at the Jerusalemite, who was silent, head bowed. "I suppose now you will denounce me to your council on suspicion of being a spy."

The man looked up, surprised. "Denounce you? Do I look as if I would do that? Be at ease," he said, as he had earlier. "I am no Zealot captain, only a poor teacher. I am called Johanan ben Zakkai." He looked about as if catching a whiff of something ominous in the air. "Come. We had best be on our way. Something tells me trouble is about to break out— as though we have not had our share. Let us be on our way," he said again.

The rabbi's apprehension proved correct. They had no sooner reached the bottom of the hill than the fighting began. Arrows rained down from Solomon's Porch; in the streets of the city below, groups of men ran at each other with drawn swords or heavy clubs. "Follow me." ben Zakkai said; and Aliterus, wondering at the man's calm in the midst of this sudden chaos, stayed close behind as they made their way through the narrow streets and alleys. The market was littered with the fallen bodies of men, women, and children who had been caught in the sudden outbreak; flames sprang up as the Zealots put the torch to the shops and houses of their enemies. This was no battle such as Aliterus had seen staged in the Roman Circus or as an embellishment to some classic drama; and yet he had the sense of being an observer, of being audience to something that despite its apparent danger could not harm him in any way. Had he become so jaded, he wondered, that he had not even the sense to fear for his own life? Or did he rather believe that Something or Someone was protecting him and would see him to safety?

The stout arm of Johanan ben Zakkai suddenly shot out, barring the way. They were in the narrowest of alleys, nothing more than a small opening between two rows of houses through which they could only pass in single file. The rabbi had stopped; he took a step backward, forcing Aliterus back as well. Peering over the man's shoulder, Aliterus managed to catch a glimpse of the battle ahead.

"We can go no further," ben Zakkai whispered.

"Do we turn back, then?" Aliterus asked, also in a whisper.

Before the rabbi could reply, a man burst into the alley, sword drawn, his face a ferocious mask. Suddenly the anger in his eyes gave way to amazement and then concern. "Uncle?" he asked. "Is it you, Johanan ben Zakkai?"

"The son of my brother Barriah," the rabbi murmured, letting his breath out. He turned to Aliterus. "We are saved, I think."

"I am most honored to meet you, general," Aliterus said quickly.

"He isn't a general, and don't be so honored." The rabbi's eyes took in his nephew's bloodstained sword. "There is little honor in this work," he said softly and with sadness.

Ben Barriah took an angry step forward. "Not in your eyes," he said tersely. "But surely in the Lord's sight."

"You speak for the Lord, nephew? That is a large step up from the council."

The Zealot did not bother to answer. "Stay close behind. I will try to get you safely to your house. What are you doing here anyway? I sent word advising you to remain close to home."

"I have been to the Temple."

"The Temple! You might as well put your head in the mouth of a lion."

"You see," ben Zakkai said, turning to Aliterus, "how greatly we enjoy the blessings of freedom now that we are rid of Rome."

"We are not rid of Rome," ben Barriah replied. "The legions will attack when the rains stop. Lucky for us they are afraid to get wet. We need this time to put our own affairs in order."

Aliterus stepped over the trampled body of an old woman. "How energetically you clean house," he murmured.

Fortunately the man did not hear this. He had turned back and was staring in the direction of the Temple. "The fools!" he cried. "They've set fire to the storehouses! All the grain—" Forgetting everything else, ben Barriah rushed toward the scene of the blaze.

"It's all right," ben Zakkai said. "I think we are out of it now. Only a little further—"

But Aliterus did not answer. He had stopped and was bending over the body of another cut down in the brief but brutal fighting. The beggar lay sprawled face upwards, his one good eye open in death, shining like a blue jewel or small mirror of the sky above. One hand was also open; inches away from the upturned palm lay several scattered coins. Aliterus picked one up. It was the small bronze piece the beggar had not let him see earlier. It had been struck in the third year of the Jewish revolt. There was a vine-leaf design on one side of the coin and a chalice on the other. The Hebrew inscription read: "For the Freedom of Zion."

FOUR

The darkness was lifting; she was beginning to see faces, hear voices; only nothing was clear. Was she back in Caesarea? Jerusalem?

There had been the sudden consuming wave of pain and then . . . nothing. . . . Once her body had given up the unformed mass in its womb and was her own again, empty but at peace, she felt no further discomfort from that quarter. It was the pain behind her eyes that would not go away. For days she lay wracked with chills, flushed with fever. This was the time of the long darkness, an interminable night filled with dreams and memories. . . .

The house was burning. . . . Tongues of flame enveloped the white marble table. . . . She could feel it rocking like a boat beneath her, and suddenly she was swimming in a phosphorescent sea, past her father and mother . . . Beni . . . Lilah . . . their bodies floating silently down. . . . Then the rush of the sea became the roaring of a crowd, and she was in the arena, stripped, naked under the stinging sun. . . . She was a slave. She was being sold. . . . She tried to cover herself and looked toward the podium as if someone there might save her. . . . Josef was sitting there all alone, smiling and nodding to her. She tried to call to him, but no sound came out, and he did not move. . . . He saw her but did not move; he only sat there smiling and nodding. . . .

Darkness again . . . the night turning green. . . . She was in a field; there was the smell of grass, the feel of roughhewn stone under her palm and something hard at her back. . . . There was a man. Was he kissing her? . . . Or was it only soft spring air she felt on her lips; caressing her. . . . No, no, it was someone; she could feel him on her, but she could not see his face. . . . It was beautiful, more beautiful than anything. . . . She

363

could not see his face—she had to see his face. She had to see him. . . .

She began twisting from side to side, and suddenly, eyes wide and staring, she was sitting up in a strange bed. She blinked, confused. The room was some kind of palace chamber. There was a man standing beside the bed . . . a tall man with dark eyes and golden hair. Alexandra looked at him, puzzled. He leaned forward, put his hands on her shoulders, and gently pushed her down. She felt a soft, cool wind across her throat as she lay back. With a little sigh, she closed her eyes and slept.

Tenderly, with infinite care, the young Essene called Jonatan Ha-Taleh inscribed the words of the prophet Ezra on the skin he had prepared. It was a painstaking job, but Jonatan was happy as he worked. It was a blessed task, this copying and transmitting of the Divine Knowledge—and an important one. A slip of the pen, a dot of ink mistaken for a vowel, or worse, a word omitted, and an entire text could be corrupted. No wonder the young scribe always said a brief prayer before sitting down at his writing table.

As always, the words he penned filled him with joy, and not only for the vision they transmitted; in their very formation he felt his own soul take wing. Sometimes it seemed to him that each letter had its own face and character; they were like people, like old friends. They stood together like a little army sometimes, and sometimes they ran together like happy children. Sometimes the letters seemed like lovers to him, embracing, reaching out for one another. . . .

What had made him think of that? What did he know of lovers? How could he dare to sully his holy task with such impure images? How had such a thought come into his mind? Look, see where his wicked hand had left a blot upon the scroll. . . .

Controlling his anguish, he lightly touched his finger to the speck of ink that loomed so monstrously before his eyes and drew it up into his own flesh. He gave a sigh of relief. The scroll was only slightly marred. But the happiness he had felt earlier was gone. He got up from the chair and went to pour water from a small pitcher into a copper basin. He could wash the ink from his hand, but could he remove the stain from his soul? Troubled, the young man bent his head, but he had hardly begun to pray when a voice at his back caused him to open his eyes with a start. Turning hastily, he met with a pale but smiling face and two large, luminous eyes.

"Hello," the girl said again. "Have I startled you?"

"Yes."

Alexandra smiled. "Sorry," she said cheerfully. "I've been out exploring, and I saw the writing table through the door. I was curious. I've been looking for you anyway," she added.

"For me?"

"Well, I don't know anyone here but you and Yigael, and there's been no welcoming committee—"

"I did not know you were up and about. I do not think the others realized it either. You were very ill."

"So it seems. I cannot believe how long Hagar says I've been abed. It was the sun, she says, not the other. That took care of itself."

He cleared his throat. "I am happy you are well. I gave the old woman a certain potion, but she would allow only her own remedy to touch your lips. She has served you well."

"Yes . . . once more. . . ."

He cleared his throat again. "I must ask you—if you are— if you have been—" He stopped, reddening.

For a moment she stared at him, puzzled. Then she understood. "It's all right," she said with a weary sigh. "I have been to the *mikve*. I am 'clean.'"

His face still red, he nodded energetically, as if to say thank you. "The ritual bath is prescribed after such time as . . . I mean . . ."

"I know what is prescribed," she said a bit testily. "I would have bathed even if it were not."

"Forgive me," he said in his gentle voice. "I did not wish to make you angry. You must understand. . . . I am bound by certain rules. It is not just the Law. I have taken vows."

"I know. You must tell me all about that."

He was startled by this.

"But come and walk with me. You can explain everything— all the sights, I mean."

He was even more startled now, but before he could reply she had reached for the scroll on the table. "What's this? May I look? Oh, but it's beautiful! What a wonderful hand you have! I have not seen such fine script since—" She stopped. "Well, for a very long time." She began to read aloud in her pure, perfect Hebrew.

It was the Essene's turn to be amazed. "You read wonderfully well," he blurted.

"Yes, I know," she replied matter-of-factly, going through the other rolls on the table.

"Your father was a priest?"

"He chose not to be. But my grandfather served the Temple, and my uncle, and others before them, *ad infinitum*. I come from a rather illustrious Zadokite clan. What's wrong? Are you bothered that I am a Sadducee?" She looked up.

"You spoke in the tongue of the *Kittim*."

"I have spent the last two years among the *Kittim*, as you call them."

"I am sorry. It must have been very difficult."

"It's done with. That's all that matters. I'm free now. And I want to do whatever I can to liberate Judea. That's why I've come here. To fight."

He could only stare at her. He had little experience with women, but he could not believe that any female would say the things this one did.

"Was it you who stood by my bed when I had the fever?" she asked.

"I? No, it is forbidden. A man may not go near a woman at such time as—I wanted to," he said suddenly. "But . . . it is forbidden to me."

The look in her eyes made him lower his own. He did not realize she was not condemning him but merely wondering about the identity of the man she had seen. Perhaps it had been a dream after all. No . . . she had felt those hands on her shoulders, strong, gentle hands. If it was not Jonatan, who, then, had it been?

Later, returning to the quarters assigned to her and Hagar, Alexandra caught a glimpse of a tall man with a distinctive catlike stride. He was narrow-hipped but wide-shouldered; his hair and beard, streaked by the relentless sun, were all shades of gold, from light to dark, in startling contrast to his skin, which had been burned deep bronze. She watched him, fascinated by his leonine walk and appearance, wondering why they seemed somehow familiar to her, when she saw him go up to a tall young woman with long, flaxen braids and converse with her in an affectionate, easy manner. For some reason that irked her. It was really a scandal, she thought, tossing her own smooth, dark hair back from her shoulders, how many Amorite women the Galileans had taken to wife. She watched the handsome couple a moment more and was about to turn away when she saw several of the Sicarii approach the man and address him familiarly but with a certain respect.

Suddenly she knew that the blond man was none other than Eleazar ben Ya'ir, a lone, already legendary fighter in his own right, whose search-and-rescue missions and daring raids against Caesar's legions had made him a hero to Judea and a wanted man in the Roman camp. Vespasian was not the only one to put a price on the Galilean's head; ben Ya'ir had been declared an outlaw by the council in Jerusalem, and there was talk that Simon bar Giora had vowed to kill him. But there none of Simon's men, Hagar had told Alexandra, would join in an attack against the man from Masada—not so much from fear as from admiration. "There is only one man in all Judea," Yigael had told Hagar, "who can lead us against the *Kittim,* who alone can unite us in victory, and that is Eleazar ben Ya'ir. I myself," he had added, "would follow him to the edge of the earth and beyond. And none that I know would do differently."

Benjamin ben Harsom had felt the same way, Alexandra thought, recalling now the words of the prisoner Shem, who had come to her after her brother's death. And Beni had never even met ben Ya'ir! What kind of power did this golden-haired giant have over people? she wondered. If he was truly the man to lead the forces of Judea, why was he here, apart and cut off from the majority of his countrymen? Why had he refused to align himself with the governing council, and was that the reason he had been declared a criminal? Why did Simon bar Giora—the Zealot leader with the largest following—why did Simon hate him so?

"I don't like him," she announced later to Hagar. "He is arrogant and too sure of himself. That lordly way he struts around, as if he thought himself some kind of king!"

Hagar, who was busy patting balls of dough into round loaves, glanced sideways at the girl but did not answer.

"Oh, he's handsome enough," Alexandra went on. "I suppose . . . if one cared for that type. And judging from the way the women here look at him, I would say enough do. But then," she added with a dramatic sigh, "the *am ha'eretz* have never been known for their exquisite taste."

"Spoken like a true princess of Judea."

Alexandra blushed.

"Ben Ya'ir has been kind enough to you," Hagar said now. "There is no need to turn up your nose at him."

"Kind? To me?"

"Many a night while you tossed and turned with the sun-fever, he stayed at your side, keeping watch."

"Eleazar ben Ya'ir?" She could not hide her surprise.

Hagar nodded. "And put water to your lips and on the cloth I held to your brow."

Alexandra stared at the woman, open-mouthed.

"You would have fallen to your death—and most likely taken me along—had he not caught you and carried you here."

Alexandra was silent. Then her chin came up. "Even so—"

"Even so . . ." Hagar set the ball of dough aside. "What do you want?" she asked, folding her arms across her breast. "Another bald bird to fly after you like the Roman eagle? Maybe you miss the one that was your husband. . . . He was fine enough. And friendly too." She spat. "If Eleazar ben Ya'ir is treated like a king around here, it may well be that he is worthy of such attention." She laughed suddenly. "I tell you this, little owl, if these breasts were ripe apples I, for one, would not wait to offer him a bite!"

"Dirty old hag."

"True enough," Hagar replied, laughing still. "But at least I know a cucumber from a pickle!"

With a show of disgust, Alexandra brushed past her, the woman's laughter trailing after her into the bright sunlight. She did not know what angered her most: Hagar's attitude or the man who had inspired it.

So Eleazar ben Ya'ir had tended her in her illness. Why, then, was he so indifferent now? Here she was, up and about, and not so much as a simple hello had he sent her way. After all, it would be only common courtesy to welcome her to the community. How dare he behave as though Alexandra bat Harsom did not exist! Unless . . . That big blond creature was probably his wife. . . . No, wait, Hagar had said he was not married . . . something about this pleasing the Essenes but making the Sicarii unhappy, as they wished for a continuation of the line of Judah of Gamala, called the Galilean. (Had she not heard that name before?) Was the man an Essene, then? No, he would not have spoken so familiarly to the blond girl if he were—not if the scribe Jonatan was any indication of how the Essenes behaved toward women. Nor would he have watched over Alexandra as he had after her miscarriage. An Essene would have stayed away; in fact, most men would. . . .

Pondering these things, Alexandra found that she had crossed the summit of the Masada and was at its northern end. She had surmised that the site was shaped rather like one of her father's ships, very narrow in the north, like a prow, somewhat less narrow in the south, and broad in the center. If it was to be a kind of Ark it was not a bad one; for the area was large enough to accommodate comfortably palaces, villas, storage houses, public baths built in the Roman manner, a swimming pool—and an even greater number of people than the several hundred now residing on the rock fortress's heights.

Most of the structures seemed to be concentrated in the northern half of the summit. The southern half was lower and was bare for the most part, except for a profusion of gardens. Perhaps Herod, seeing that the soil of Masada was as rich as any valley's, had reserved this section for agriculture. In any case, it was here that the Zealots cultivated and tended their vegetable patches.

Surrounding the mountaintop was a casemate, a double wall some twelve cubits high, divided by partitions into a series of rooms, and topped at various intervals with towers, twenty-seven in all. It stopped at the northern tip, reaching only to the southern section of the beautiful palace that stood there. This wall appeared to seal off any approach to the buildings; however, Alexandra finally discovered a narrow passageway, next to which was a bench. There was no one about. An air of quiet, like the weeds that surround uninhabited, long-deserted buildings, hung over the place.

The palace was empty, stripped of whatever treasures it had once held, and of all furnishings except for a single crude pallet in one of the rooms. There were only four chambers, but they were magnificent, the walls and ceilings adorned with paintings, the floors decorated with fine mosaics. Emerging from one of the several corridors that connected the rooms, Alexandra suddenly found herself on a large, semicircular porch with a breathtaking view of the area. Ein Gedi was a green patch to the north. Beyond and eastwards, across the Dead Sea, rose the lavender mountains of Moab. To the west she could see as far as the hills of Judea. And now, looking down, she saw with astonishment and delight that the palace contained three separate terraces and that she was at the apex of a three-tiered dwelling perched impossibly upon the highest, narrowest, most northerly section of the mountain.

Wondering at the effort and expense of this construction, at the skill and ingenuity of Herod's engineers, Alexandra sought a means of descending to the other levels she had discovered: the middle terrace, extending out some sixty feet below; and about forty-five feet below that, the bottom and most northerly terrace. There seemed to be no way of reaching them, however. At last, returning to the passageway through which she had first entered the palace, she found a broad set of steps that brought her to the rear of the middle terrace. The staircase was cut into the mountain rock, hidden from the outside by the foundation walls.

The lower terrace proved even more delightful. Here, artists had given the plastered walls the appearance of marble paneling; more frescoes in the Herodian or Roman style further embellished the walls; and the Corinthian capitals that topped the terrace pillars were covered with gold. Most astounding of all, perhaps, there was—on the slope of this steep rock more than one thousand feet above the Dead Sea—a private bathhouse in the finest Roman tradition. It was a place worthy of Caesar.

Dreamily, Alexandra leaned against one of the fluted columns and stared at the strange, still world she had become part of. The great golden cliffs rising from depths far below stared back with their dark cave-eyes; everything was silent in the pure, dry air.

She closed her eyes; for once, she had no questions. She had the feeling that if she fell now she would simply tumble over the terrace wall and out into the quiet, empty space. Somehow it did not seem to matter.

She felt rather than heard his presence.

Turning, she saw a tall figure descend the steps that joined the three terraces. A man with golden hair emerged from the shadowed stairs.

Eleazar ben Ya'ir.

He seemed as startled to see her as she was to see him, but he nodded a curt greeting as he came forward. "*Shalom.*"

"*Shalom.*"

She waited, but he said nothing more. He walked to the edge of the terrace and, leaning his arms on the protective wall, stared out at the still scene. The silence of the land seemed to envelop him, to set him beyond idle conversation. But she wanted to talk to him; and so, finally, clearing her throat a little, she said, "I have not had an opportunity to speak to you since my arrival here."

No reply.

She cleared her throat again, wondering at her own nervousness. There was something about his presence, something disturbing; it went beyond her surprise at meeting him here. "I . . . I wish to thank you for all you have done." The words tumbled out in a rush.

He looked at her briefly. Then his eyes went past her once more, locked into the horizon, and became one with it. "I did nothing. All are welcome here."

She was taken aback by the terse reply. "Hagar said . . . that is, I am told you were kind to me when I was ill. I wish to thank you for your courtesy."

He seemed to smile slightly. "Courtesy," he repeated, almost to himself, as though the word held some private humor.

Alexandra felt her face grow warm. The man was impossible. Why did he make her feel like such a fool? She was about to say something sharp but decided against it; turning, she took a step toward the stairs. His voice stopped her.

"No, don't go." He turned to face her. "Sorry. My thoughts are elsewhere. I didn't expect to see anyone here," he confessed. "The others avoid this place. They think it is cursed."

"Cursed? But why? It is so beautiful."

"They are frightened by a sound that echoes through the halls at night. They say it is the voice of Herod." He shrugged. "I say it is only the wind. In any event, no one will stay here, even though this is the coolest spot on the Masada and there are good quarters above."

"There is a pallet in one of the rooms."

"It is mine. I come here when I want to be alone."

"If you prefer solitude now—"

He did not answer; he was looking out across the horizon again, as if he had not heard her.

She hesitated, annoyed by his indifference. But, remembering what Hagar said, she decided to try again. "How did all this—this Masada—come to be?"

"Herod. The Masada was to be his refuge. Only now it is ours." He turned to her once more. He had deep-set, very dark blue eyes. She had seen eyes like that before. . . . "There is a man among us whose father's father was one of the king's masons. He told us what we would find here." Warming to her obvious interest, he continued. "The Romans had stationed a small garrison by the western ascent. They'd done some plundering, but not enough to make any difference to us."

"Romans? Did you kill them?"

He stiffened. "Do you think they made us a gift of the Masada?"

"No, I mean, how did you do it? I should imagine the soldiers would have little difficulty picking off anyone trying to climb up."

He leaned back against the pillars, studying her. "We came up behind them. In the night."

"Behind them?"

"I told you, the garrison was by the western ascent. We used the Snake Path, the same one you took. The *Kittim* hadn't even bothered to post a lookout. Either they didn't know the path existed, or else they thought no one dared use it. It was pretty well overgrown."

She shuddered, recalling her climb. The way had been difficult enough with light to see. But at night!

"The path is guarded now," he was saying. "Although we have cleared it so that it is visible, I assure you Vespasian will find it difficult—if not impossible—to put this knowledge to use."

She looked up, not sure of his tone. His eyes were the color of the sea far from shore. They had taken on a curious gleam. The sun, she thought, must have moved.

He stared back at her for what seemed a long time. Then, abruptly, he said, "You spoke in your fever."

"Yes?" She was still puzzled.

"Two names. Vespasian. Josephus. I know the second as well as the first—and may they both be damned!" His eyes never left her. "The old woman has told me all. Frankly, I am not satisfied."

Once more she felt her face burn. "Satisfied? With what?"

"With you. The House of Harsom was friendly to Rome. This war was not to your family's liking."

"My family was murdered."

"Not by the Romans, but by the gentiles among whom you chose to live. After which I am to believe you were taken as a slave."

"That is true."

"I think not. I think Vespasian merely took under his protection the sole surviving child of a friend and ally. That, furthermore, he did not use her as a slave but made himself her guardian and even gave her a husband." He suddenly uttered a short, ugly laugh. "What a party that must have been! Berenice . . . Agrippa . . . Vespasian, Titus, the traitor Josef . . . and you!"

She swallowed. "Go on."

"Why did you leave Caesarea? Why would you give up your soft bed, your fine linen, your rich food—Caesar's protection!—to live on a desolate mountain with people your class has always despised? What is our freedom to you? What have you to fight for? Would you come here if you were not sent?"

His meaning was clear now. "You think I am a spy. . . ."

"I must consider it," he replied grimly. "There is something in your favor. . . . One of the men has told me of your brother, how he fought in the Galilee and how he died. For his sake I will believe you are here as one of us. For his sake I will say nothing of what I know. The others would look even less kindly upon your alliance with Josef ben Matthias, particularly those who have come to us from Jotapata."

"Say anything you like," she replied coldly. "It would be an exquisite irony to have survived the *Kittim*, as you call them, only to be killed by Jews!" Head high, she brushed past, leaving him to the solitude he desired and, she thought, deserved.

He was not the only one to view her with suspicion. There was a noticeable lack of Sadducees in the mountain fortress, though many there were the unwitting descendants of the priestly and even the princely Davidic line; but these, their own heritage obscured by Herod and the Hasmoneans before him, had little love for Judea's ruling class. For a brief period the population on Masada had included a daughter of one of Jerusalem's great houses, a poor, mad creature whose family, escaping the vengeance of the Zealots, had fallen prey to the legionaries at Qumran. The soldiers had kept the girl for some time—how long would never be known—leaving her at last to wander into the desert and die. The Sicarii scouts found her and brought her back to the Masada, but she did not live long after that, and never, Miriam told Alexandra, spoke a word of sense.

The tall, fair young woman with long braids and sea-blue eyes was one of the few to come in genuine friendship, seemingly unperturbed by Alexandra's background and aloof man-

ner. To Miriam, all that mattered was that the new arrival was
an orphan and, even more pitiable, had been a slave. Jonatan,
the Essene Alexandra had met in the cliff cave, proved to be
another, if hesitant, ally. At times the soft-spoken scribe appeared to be engaged in some kind of personal struggle as he
strove to converse with the gray-eyed girl; but Alexandra put
this down to natural shyness and conditioned restraint. At least,
she thought, he did not look away or turn his back to her as
did the other Essenes. But for a very few, such as Miriam and
Jonatan and of course Hagar, Alexandra would have been as
isolated on the Masada as she had been in the palace in Caesarea. As the days passed and it became more and more clear
to her that "fighting the *Kittim*" had for her no true basis in
reality, she began to wonder why she had come to this place
and what sort of future there was for her here.

"We are safe," she told Hagar, "but, oh, it is so boring!
Nothing to read or do, hardly anyone to talk to. . . . Miriam is
so sweet and solicitous I could choke her—and Jonatan never
tells me the things I want to know. Your great god, Eleazar
ben Ya'ir—what an arrogant, insufferable man!—does not
even deign to grunt a greeting when I pass, and his men get
all red in the face whenever I talk to any of them, or else they
growl at me as if I'd committed a crime. None of their wives
have any wit, you know. All they talk about are the children,
as if nothing else existed, not even the war! We might just as
well be in some stupid little village like Bersabe." She stopped.
Bersabe. What made her think of that? She sighed. "We're so
cut off from everything . . . everyone. I thought it would be
different. I thought . . . oh, Hagar! What shall I do today? What
shall I do tomorrow?"

"You might try learning to bake bread," the woman replied
calmly. "Or take your turn tending the crops. It is work that
must be done."

"Bake bread? Plant vegetables? Have I come all this way
to be a cook and a farmer? Is that how I shall fight Rome?"

Hagar shrugged. "Soldiers must eat."

"But I want to be a soldier! Why not? There was Devorah
in the days of old—and Judith! What about that island you
used to tell me about, with all the women warriors?"

Hagar nodded. "King Theseus took one to bride."

"Yes! Yes!"

"But that," Hagar reminded her, "was not Judea. And you,"
she added flatly, "are no Amazon. It would be better," she

concluded, "if you learned to bake bread. Perhaps the others would distrust you less if they saw you were willing to share their life here."

"What the others think of me is of no importance," Alexandra replied imperiously. "All I want is the chance to strike back at Rome. I don't care a fig for anything else. But from now on I will help prepare the food and work in the gardens—only because there is little else to do around here!"

Hagar smiled but said nothing.

Alexandra was in fact helping to plant one of several pomegranate bushes Yigael had excitedly brought to the rebel community (the roots wrapped in cloth dampened in Ein Gedi's life-giving spring) when she was summoned to the western palace. It was the largest building on Masada, standing on the edge of the rock close to the ascent the Romans had used when they controlled the fortress. The Sicarii used it as an administration building, and it served as the dwelling quarters for Masada's "first families." There were a number of more modest villas close by. Perched on hillocks, with a magnificent view of the Dead Sea, these small palaces were no less ornately decorated than the larger palatial residences; they had been intended for members of Herod's family. Alexandra and Hagar had been assigned an apartment in one of them. Still, the girl thought as she made her way down a long corridor, she would prefer to stay in the three-tiered palace at the rock's northern tip. She had no idea why she was being called to Sicarii headquarters, but it seemed an opportune time to request the change. Surely there was no reason she should be denied—unless, she thought with sudden anger, Eleazar ben Ya'ir simply wanted to be obstinate.

He was waiting in what had originally been intended as a throne room, standing behind a large table over which were spread a great many charts and rolled parchments; some, her quick eye noted, had been appropriated from the Roman camp. Next to him stood a burly red-haired Zealot whose broad chest was covered by a leather vest thickly studded with nailheads. Many of the Sicarii had adopted this kind of armor or wore breastplates taken from the legionaries they killed. Ben Ya'ir, however, seldom wore more than a short tunic of homespun girded with a wide leather belt. Over this he sometimes added another tunic of leather, as when he disappeared on a sortie or raid against the Romans. At such times he carried a simple, rather old-fashioned bow, a quiver of arrows slung from his shoulder, and the short knife stuck through his belt. All the men on Masada carried the *sica*, Essenes as well as Daggermen. In fact, Alexandra thought as she glanced at Jonatan, who had preceded her into the room, it was difficult at this point to tell one group from the other. The Sicarii had even fallen into using the Essene calendar, which was based on the sun rather than the moon and divided the year into three hundred and sixty-four days.

Ben Ya'ir barely looked up. He took a leather parchment case, the kind entrusted to couriers, and rolled it across the table. "We took this from the *Kittim*. As you have spent some time among the Romans, perhaps you can interpret it. Jonatan tells me that though you are a woman you are able to read and write in many languages."

Though you are a woman. He could not have endeared himself more. "Yes, I read Latin. Also Greek, Aramaic, and the holy tongue of our fathers. Only one thing I cannot do," she said pointedly, "and that is read what Galileans write; and that must be either because they leave out so many letters or because they have invented a new language known only to themselves."

He grinned. "Why, I thought you knew—Galileans don't know how to write at all."

"That must be why I am so rarely asked to decipher their words." She reached for the case, realized her hands were stained with soil and, dismayed, quickly wiped them on her skirt. He seemed to take no notice of this, although there was a suspicious twinkle in his eyes. Sternly, Alexandra opened the parchment case and unrolled the document, scanning it quickly. She was eager to translate the message despite her dislike for ben Ya'ir. The Sicarii would see that she could be of use to them. It wasn't as good as wielding a sword, but it was better than planting beans. She went over the document a second time, wanting to be sure she had it right.

"This may be of some importance," she said at last. "It concerns the deployment of forces in the advance against Jerusalem. More particularly it deals with the garrison at Qumran and"—she looked down at the parchment again—"the stationing of another garrison at Ein Gedi." She looked up to find him staring impassively at her. She looked at Jonatan; he was also silent. "You could cut them off," she suggested. "You would have to. I mean, I have seen how you make use of Ein Gedi for supplies. Horses, for example, when you need them."

The redhead muttered something, but ben Ya'ir ignored him.

"Read it to me," Eleazar said, never taking his eyes from her. "Word by word."

She did as he wished, wondering how he could remain so stoic.

"Is that all?" he asked when she had finished.

"Yes."

"You are quite sure?"

"Yes...." His intense stare made her scan the document again, searching for something hidden in the lines, some word she might have missed or misread. "Ah," she said, looking up with a smile, "the milk message!"

"What?"

"A message written in milk. At the bottom, after the signature. It is a rather common practice among the Romans. If you dust it with charcoal you will be able to read it. I suspect it is only a note of endearment. It's rather common among the officers."

Ben Ya'ir was staring at Jonatan, whose amazement mirrored his own. The redhead had uttered a short exclamation.

"I did not know," the Essene said, startled. "I never would have guessed."

"That the soldiers sometimes love each other?" Alexandra asked, amused by the reaction of the men. But something in the way they were looking at one another made her own smile fade. "It was a trick," she said slowly, "wasn't it? A test.... You knew all along what was written here—all, that is, but the note written in milk, which none of you could see! But the rest of it—you were testing me!"

"It is not the first of these things that has come into our possession," Eleazar ben Ya'ir admitted. "I would be a poor soldier if I had not made it my business long ago to learn the enemy's tongue. Although," he added with a sheepish smile, "I confess I knew nothing of words written in milk. A good thing none of us have eaten meat today." He took the parchment from her hand and ran his eyes over it, touching the invisible message with his finger, nodding as he felt the slightly raised letters. "You read very well," he told her, passing the document to his aide, who bent over it in furious study though he could read not a word. "But I suppose with families of the upper class there is every opportunity for daughters to be indulged in their education. Tell me," he said with a friendly grin, "can you also cook?"

She was too enraged to answer.

Jonatan touched her arm. "Don't be angry, Alexandra. This was my idea. I knew you were not a traitor. I wanted to prove it."

She ignored him. Her eyes were fixed on Eleazar ben Ya'ir. "And if I had read the report falsely?"

His voice became as cold as hers. "You would not have remained with us."

"You would kill me, I suppose." *Shall you kill me, then?* . . . Words spoken long ago. . . . Why did they now come back to her? That scowling, red-haired Zealot—hadn't she seen him before?

"You would have been escorted to within sight of the *Kittim* at Qumran and left there to join your own. The legionaries get very lonely. I am sure they would appreciate your company. As for this"—he took the parchment back, nodding for the redhead to leave—"it is weeks old. Jonatan forged the date. We have already seen to it that there will be no Romans in Ein Gedi." Again unrolling the document in question, he turned his back to her and began to study it.

Trembling with anger, she picked up the parchment case and said, "Here, you forgot this."

He turned around. His eyes widened. He ducked.

The case went sailing past his head.

They glared at each other a moment. Then, regally, completely unmindful of the smudge on her nose, which she had inadvertently rubbed with a dirty finger while studying the Roman document, she swept out of the western palace.

She burst in upon Hagar, white with fury. "Why did we come here?" she cried. "Tell me, why did we come? I am a fool," she went on before the startled woman could reply. "I am the greatest of fools. . . . Why did I come here? What did I hope to find? Tell me. You know everything. Tell me, why am I here? No, don't say it. Josef was right. I should have remained with him. Only I hate him. I hate them all. He was right, though. They are not worth the effort, I tell you. They deserve everything that has happened to them—and whatever more comes, they deserve that as well." She had been pacing frantically back and forth; now she sank wearily to the ground. "Oh, Hagar, what is to become of us? It is all so useless. I don't belong here, and I never shall. And I'm not a man, so I can't take up a sword and go out to do battle. I don't even ride very well. Berenice was right—and Josef. I ought to have stayed with Vespasian if I really wanted to do some good. I could have asked for favors, I could have—Oh, but that is odious! I can't live like that! I'm not like Josef! I won't be like him!" She closed her eyes. "I don't belong here," she said again. "I am an outsider here just as I was in Caesarea. I will always be one."

Hagar had said nothing to all this; now, the girl's tirade seemingly done, she merely chuckled in what Alexandra considered an infuriatingly knowing manner.

"That's right," the young woman grumbled. "Go on, enjoy yourself. Only just remember, you are stuck here too, and if these idiots decide to roast me, your head will be upon the spit as well!" She turned on her side, resting her head on her arm and staring into the embers of the small cooking fire. Suddenly she seemed to see a day long ago in a spring that would never come again . . . the hills full of flowers . . . the Galilee dotted with lush fields and thriving towns. . . . In the distance ahead lay the blue Kinneret, its waters calm. . . . At night, couples danced around the fire, embraced beneath the tamarisks. . . . The well . . . a tall young man with golden hair and eyes the color of a dark sea . . .

"I know a potion." Hagar's voice slid across the room, soft as a snake. "It will make a man die for a woman's love."

She sat up. "Are you mad? What do I want with such things?"

The old woman shrugged. "A man in love looks to his woman's safety. He keeps her from harm. If you are afraid . . ."

"Don't be an idiot. I am afraid of nothing."

"I think so," Hagar replied quietly. "Of others, no. But of yourself, yes, you are afraid. You have courage, little owl, to fly out into the desert, to withstand loneliness and abuse, even to face the enemy with a sword. But you are afraid to become a woman. I have seen this in you. You fear your own nature."

"If you mean, do I want to become like you—or Berenice, or my mother—no, I do not want that. I hate the lies and trickery, the poses and pretense. I hate your potions!"

She shook her head. "You choose the smallest part of it."

"Then tell me, Hagar. Tell what it is to be a woman."

"I cannot. You must find it for yourself. You must open yourself to it and not be afraid."

"You mean love, don't you? Well, I have been in love." She sighed. "I used to dream of Josef ben Matthias.... You don't know what dreams I had of him. I loved him long before I married him—and hated him long before I left him."

She spat. "Dreams! The love of a girl is in dreams. The love of a woman is real. It is flesh and blood. It does not deny a man his odors, his sweat, his fears and wounds and weaknesses. Do not speak to me of love, Daughter of Harsom, when you mean your childish fancies."

"I loved Josef once."

"Never! You loved your dreams."

FIVE

Day had barely dawned, but laundry was flapping in the breeze, and the smell of baking bread came wafting on the morning wind from the window of Johanan ben Zakkai's house. It was more than a house. It was a Beit Midrash: a place of study. Filled nigh to bursting with the rabbi's colleagues and students, the rooms and courtyard of the plain but immaculately kept abode were the scene of constant debate, discussion, discourse, and even song. As Aliterus, only just risen, strolled outside to take in some of the sweetness of the sun, Joshua ben Hananiah was already giving instruction to a child no more than four years of age. Carefully the rabbi dipped a finger into a small pot of honey and drew something on a flat dish. Then he took the child's hand and, pointing the boy's finger, guided it over the letter he had made. "That is an *aleph,* Sami," Rabban Joshua said. "*Aleph.*"

The boy hesitated, but the temptation was too great; without answering, he popped his sticky finger into his mouth.

Rabban Joshua smiled. Gently he took Sami's hand again and this time dipped the boy's finger into the honeypot. Now he guided the hand onto the dish. "*Aleph,*" he repeated. "Let us make the letter together. *Aleph.*"

The child looked down at the dish and then at his finger, "*Aleph,*" he said with a grin, and once more popped his finger into his mouth.

Rabban Joshua nodded. He looked up at Aliterus, who had been watching, and said with a smile. "The first taste of learning must always be sweet."

The kitchen bustled with activity; there was always something baking or frying or bubbling away there. Johanan ben Zakkai often joked that his wife's stove was like the eternal flame of the Temple altar. Well, what was the poor woman to do, with the house constantly filled with people come from far and near to drink of the wisdom of the famed Johanan ben Zakkai? So while they were at it, they had a little soup. Scholars needed looking after. They immersed themselves so in Torah that they never knew when their breath was bad. The best thing to do was take a plate of something and shove it under their noses.

This philosophy had come to be well illustrated in the person of the rabbi; for if Johanan ben Zakkai's head was in heaven, his feet were firmly rooted to the ground. He was a large man, about the same size and weight as Aliterus. Now that the actor's beard was fuller, there was more than a passing resemblance between the two men—enough so that another visitor to the kitchen was forced to take a startled second look at him before saying with a laugh, "I was about to take issue with you for disobeying my instructions. But I see you are not Rabban Johanan, whom I have just left lying abed with strict orders to remain there. Are you brother to the rabbi? A cousin perhaps?"

"Would that I were," Aliterus replied, for his fondness as well as his admiration for ben Zakkai had steadily increased in the days since he had first come to know him. "I am only a journeyman here, however, a poor wayfarer seeking knowledge."

"Well, you have come to the right place for that," the man said, accepting a cup of hot milk curdled with spiced wine that one of the women in the kitchen now brought forward. "But you would be doing a kindness to Rabban Johanan if you allowed him to rest today."

"He is unwell?"

"He is in perfect health. It is his only luck. A lesser man would have fallen apart long ago, especially since the death of his son." The man fell silent, as though reluctant to draw the attention of the women in the room to that subject.

"Then what is the matter?"

"According to him, nothing. His good wife informs me, however, that he nearly fainted upon rising this morning. I am sure it is only a question of too much debate and not enough sleep. But I have advised him to rest today."

"You minister to the sick?" Aliterus asked.

"I am a physician, yes. If you ever have need of my services, just ask anyone here to direct you to the home of Solomon ben Ya'ish."

"Oh, no need for that," Aliterus replied with a broad wink. "I have learned how to make a poultice or two in my time."

Solomon ben Ya'ish looked at him curiously but said nothing.

The practice of medicine was not highly regarded in Rome and was usually given over to slaves, but Mesopotamia had a medical code some two thousand years old that went far beyond Aliterus's poultices. It was the law of the Sanhedrin that every town in Judea, and indeed every community of Israelites, have a resident physician-surgeon or access to one. Jewish doctors knew the Egyptian techniques for operating on the human brain and for performing tracheotomies. They were the first to operate on the human eye for cataracts; they used needles for suturing, had catheters, surgical scissors, and forceps of varying sizes, and had invented a ratchet for dilation. The doctors of Judea knew how to seal off arteries, performed hysterectomies, understood the necessity of amputation in the event of gangrene, and made use of a variety of anesthetics they had developed. Doctoring was considered a distinguished profession, for the ability to save a life or relieve suffering was a *mitzveh*, a blessing or good deed. It would not be long before Aliterus realized that Solomon ben Ya'ish was no mere clever slave or learned servant, but a man of some distinction and a certain quiet dignity. Accompanying him outside, he did not fail to observe the respect with which ben Ya'ish was greeted.

Stopping by the bench where Joshua ben Hananiah still sat with his young student, the doctor inquired about the rabbi's leg, which evidently had been troubling him. With a shrug and a smile Rabban Joshua passed it off. "I am sure you have more to concern you." He tapped his knee. "In any event I have one sure way of knowing when it will rain. So this, too, is for the good. But tell me, Solomon ben Ya'ish, how is it with the fighting in the city? What is happening with our people? How many wounded did you attend yesterday? How many more will there be today?"

The physician let out a deep sigh and shook his head. "What can I tell you that you do not already know? It is madness, Rabban Joshua, utter madness. All the buildings round the Temple have been burnt to the ground. The storehouses, all the grain—enough to support us through years of siege—it has all gone up in flames. It will be our undoing—if any of us are still alive when the Romans come."

"But the Temple is untouched?"

Ben Ya'ish gave a bitter laugh. "With scores of dead in the courts, the Sanctuary peopled by 'priests' carrying daggers, the

Holy Gates manned by armed Zealots—do I dare say the Temple is untouched? Let us say, the Temple stands, Rabban Joshua. Untouched?" Sadly, he shook his head.

Joshua ben Hananiah sighed deeply. Then he smiled. "Never mind. All will be well. The Eternal One will not abandon His people, and the Temple will remain forever. For on three things has it not been said the Age stands? On Torah, on the Temple service, and on acts of piety. These three things constitute the very foundation and base of the world, Sami," he said, turning to the child beside him and stroking the boy's hair. "So long as the Temple service is maintained the world is a blessing to its inhabitants. Yes, and the rains come down in season and all things grow and prosper as is their wont. There is no service more beloved of the Holy One, blessed be He, than the Temple service."

"That now remains to be seen," Solomon ben Ya'ish said drily. "In case you hadn't heard, the powers that be have decided the High Priest must be chosen 'democratically,' by lot. With nearly everyone of noble blood imprisoned or murdered, there has been little opposition to this, and the golden bells and pomegranate, as of last night, adorn the person of one hitherto anonymous fellow named Phanias, who, I am told, before his induction into the priestly order, served as a village stonemason. John's gang seems to find this high sport. I doubt the Lord is equally amused." He shook his head. "The High Priest of all Israel a bumbling idiot tripping over his robes, without sense enough to know he is being made sport of! Could the men of Caesar have played a crueler joke? Can this too, Joshua ben Hananiah, be for the good?"

Joshua ben Hananiah said nothing but continued to stroke the hair of the child beside him.

Aliterus cleared his throat. "If the Temple service is one of the things upon which the Lord's favor is contingent, what will happen now that it has been profaned? What would happen," he continued hesitantly, "if . . . if there ceased to be a Temple?"

At that moment a cheerful voice said, "The words of the Torah are far more precious to God than burnt offerings and sacrifice. No matter who officiates at the altar—even if there were no Temple service at all—the world would still be sustained. How? By Torah, my friends. By acts of loving-kindness and by prayer. He who prays offers up his own fat and blood."

"I thought I told you to stay in bed," Solomon ben Ya'ish said, trying to appear stern.

Johanan ben Zakkai spread his hands and smiled. "What? Miss this sunshine? And are we not to discuss the matter of Sophas ben Raguel today? For what cause has the council seen fit to imprison him? Come, let us walk together to the *Beit Din*."

"There will be no meeting of the Court of Judgment. Ben Raguel and his brother Levias as well have been found dead in their cells. The Sanhedrin has become as great a travesty as the Temple."

"The Sanhedrin did not accuse ben Raguel, imprison him, or pass judgment upon him," ben Zakkai reminded him.

"No, but we are powerless to prevent such things from occurring. The people do not know which way to turn or whom to believe. John is maddened by what happened at Gischala and Gamala, and every Galilean with him believes his own family perished because Jerusalem refused to send help. They have a grudge against the city as deep as anything they feel toward Rome. Every Jerusalemite of note will be murdered before they are through. Simon is just as bad; the only difference is that he doesn't care what part of Judea you are from. If you are rich, if you or your family have owned slaves, then you are his enemy." The physician sighed. "The tragedy is that both in their way love Judea, and each—I am forced to say it—has a real grievance. If only they could put their hatred aside! If only someone could make them understand they cannot hope to revolutionize society until we first achieve political independence. Together, our people united, we could fight a real war against Rome! But now . . . we are like a body full of broken bones, consumed by the poison of our wounds." He sighed again. "With ben Raguel dead, no one will dare to speak out now."

"I can hear you plain enough, Solomon."

The man shrugged. "I am tolerated, Rabban Johanan, because I am needed to patch up their stupid cracked heads and because I belong to no side. If I tried to rouse the people against John or Simon or both, I would be cut down in a minute."

"The blessed Hillel used to say, 'Where there are no men, thou, strive to be a man.'"

Ben Ya'ish smiled wryly. "He also said, 'If I am not for myself, who then will be?'" He shook his head. "It isn't that I'm afraid, old friend. But I am no leader, no general of men. I am a doctor. I do what I can the way I know best. Like you."

Johanan ben Zakkai said nothing. He watched the tired

physician depart, staring after him thoughtfully. "'If I am not for myself, who then shall be?'" he recited, echoing the words of the man he himself had called *rabban*, "master." Then he raised his hand and, with a pointed finger punctuating each word, added, "'And being for myself, what am I?'" He turned to Aliterus. "Solomon ben Ya'ish left out the most important part."

Aliterus had entered a world unlike any other. Not because it was a community within a community, seemingly immune from the hatred and despair and chaos that now characterized the rest of Jerusalem. Not because the inhabitants were morally perfect beings—which, despite their striving for goodness, they were not. Not because nowhere else was there so serious a concern with law; certainly Rome was not without legalism and casuistry, which was after all the basic stuff of a well-ordered existence. It was, Aliterus thought, watching these sages in their discussions—Johanan ben Zakkai, the acknowledged leader; Joshua ben Hananiah; the sternly righteous Simeon ben Nathaniel; the brilliant Eleazar ben Arak; the saintly Jose, called "the Priest"; and ben Zakkai's favorite, Eliezer ben Hyrcanus, whom he likened to "a plastered cistern which loses not a drop"—it was like being in the presence of some disembodied yet not dehumanized activity: intellect reacting to intellect. These men worked their brains the way athletes worked their bodies, exercising the muscle of their own understanding the way others strengthened their limbs, reaching out even as a runner strove for quicker time, a jumper for greater distance. And what eager reaching out there was in the give-and-take of their dialogues! Everything, no matter how trivial the subject, was argued in an attitude of deepest conviction that the discussion was an attempt to fulfill God's own commandment.

"'The words of the wise are as goads, and as nails well fastened are those that sit together in groups.'" Ben Zakkai said one day, quoting Ecclesiastes. "Even as a goad directs the beast along the furrows, so the words of the Torah direct man along the paths of life," he explained to Aliterus.

"But a goad may be withdrawn," Aliterus pointed out. "May the words of the Torah be withdrawn?"

The rabbi was delighted. His eyes lit up; his entire body seemed filled with joy. "The timid cannot learn," he had told

Aliterus at the beginning of their relationship. "Do not be afraid to ask questions. Neither can the short-tempered teach. He who pushes you away or calls you fool is not worthy to be heard." So now he said, leaning forward eagerly, "Well thought, my friend. But the verse states, 'and as nails well fastened.' Even as that which is well fastened cannot be removed, so are the words of the Torah not removable."

It was the beginning of Aliterus's acceptance into the circle of scholastic debate. Sometimes he had to wonder if what transpired was an earnest religious exercise or no more than intellectual athletics for its own sake. But, as one of the rabbis said, if a man could not come up with a hundred arguments for declaring a snake clean—though Scripture categorically declares it unclean—he would lack the necessary skill to open a capital trial with reasons for acquittal. "Which is an absolute requirement," Eleazar ben Arak said. "Capital cases must begin with reasons for acquittal and may not begin with reasons for conviction."

However, caught as they were in the midst of what could no longer be called anything but civil war, it did not seem that any of them would again have the chance to argue for anyone's acquittal. The Council Chamber of the Sanhedrin, the supreme court and legislative body of all Israel, was in the hands of the Zealots now. Those members of the *Beit Din* who were Sadducees no longer served or in fact existed. The high priests who sat in the Chamber of Hewn Stone in the inner courts of the Temple were now appointed by John or sanctioned by his word. Men like Solomon ben Ya'ish, who were generally respected, and those of ben Zakkai's circle were allowed to keep their positions but were in fact overruled by the young "scribes" who now declared themselves to speak for the will of the people. Scholarship in the law, wisdom, appreciation of justice and mercy—all the elements that had for so long been the criteria for acceptance into the Court of Judgment—had been superseded by this one ability: to "speak for the will of the people." No longer could the judges of Judea agree that "a Sanhedrin which passes the death sentence more than once every seven years is too hotheaded."

Often the sentence of death came after the fact. John was an impatient man. As for Simon, his followers held their own "kangaroo courts," while others—mere criminals masquerading as patriots—perpetrated all manner of crimes without worry of apprehension. Jerusalem was dominated by fear, less of Rome, perhaps, than of the terrorists who claimed to be her savior.

"When the Messiah comes," Eleazar ben Arak said, "these evils shall be set right. Now it is as the prophet Isaiah wrote—'The people's leaders are misleaders, and they that are led are confused.'"

His words were borne out by a young man who came to the house of ben Zakkai one day, accompanied by a girl. He was a sturdy fellow, with the plain, open countenance of one who works the land, looking up at heaven now and again to see when it might rain, but without expecting any divine message to make itself known to him. He understood the basics of the Law—certainly the Commandments, which for him seemed quite enough—but was an unusual sort to come to the house of the sages, hat in hand, obviously troubled, and anxious to pose a question to the rabbis. The query, when it finally made itself known, proved to be practical rather than academic. Still, it took a bit of time for him, stumbling and fumbling in the doorway, to make his intention clear.

"The fact is," he said at last in his guttural northern accent, "I wasn't sure if you were the man to see or not, Rabbi ben Zakkai. But back home in the Galilee, we sort of got used to going to our teachers for advice, seeing as there are no priests in the fields, and even if there were they wouldn't pay much mind to one like me. Oh, they tell you how much tithe you are to give and what kind of sacrifice you must make for this and that—that is, if you could afford to make sacrifice, not that I don't wish I had the money sometimes to get the Lord to listen to me. . . . But I mean, it was always our rabbi we went to when we had some trouble, and we hoped he could set it right—not with the Lord, maybe; I guess only the priests in the Temple can do that—but I mean, you know, when your neighbor says your fence is on his land, or maybe one of the village boys has been stealing eggs. . . ."

He cleared his throat, looking around the room uncomfortably, obviously wondering what reception he, a member of the *am ha'eretz*, could expect from a Jerusalemite who, if not a priest, was certainly not without a formidable reputation. But this Johanan ben Zakkai didn't seem so bad; there was an encouraging look in the rabbi's eyes. And so, after another pause, the young man said bluntly, "I came to Jerusalem to fight alongside Simon. My wife and the child in her belly are both dead. My house was burned to the ground. Everyone I knew, everyone I had . . . they're all gone. The village where I was born . . . it's nothing but ashes now. Ashes and piles of stones, and the earth not fit to seed for who knows how long. . . . So I came here. Because they won't stop until they have Jerusalem, too. I know that. And they mustn't have it. They must not do what they did to my village. Not to Jerusalem. Not to the Temple. Me, I can build another house, wait a bit and make the earth good again, or plant a crop anyhow. Even . . . even take another wife. . . ." His voice trailed off, and he looked away a moment. "But the Temple," he said suddenly, "that's another matter. The Temple is the Lord's House, and Jerusalem is His City."

"Do you not think the Lord can protect His own?" Johanan ben Zakkai asked softly.

"Well, I suppose He can. Still, I'd like Him to know I'm on His side. That's the thing of it, rabbi. I came here to fight for the Lord. For Judea. Against Rome. I didn't know Simon was waging war against John of Gischala or that the priests in the Temple were against Simon. I can't make heads nor tails out of it all. And how can I draw my sword against men of the Galilee? Simon says John wants nothing more than to belittle and enslave us the way the old nobility did. What gives him the right to say that? I never knew anyone in the north who cared a fig to be master of anyone else. Seems all we've ever fought for—even before Judah the Galilean—was that no one of us should bow to anyone but the Lord of all men."

"What does John say to this?"

"Says it's a pack of lies. Says Simon is angry because the Galileans aren't under his thumb like the others. One of the fellows I know—he's from a village near mine, he's one of John's men—he says we shouldn't think twice about sticking a knife in any of Simon's gang, that they're all escaped criminals and slaves who, now that they have their own freedom, care nothing for Judea's freedom and just want an excuse to go around robbing folks and doing all the things was done to them. But I don't know. . . . Some of the men I've met . . . the way they've suffered, some of them with marks burned in their flesh and the Lord knows what burned behind their eyes . . . well, I can't see turning my sword on any of them. Not when the only men I care to fight are men of Rome." He shook his head as if the whole matter was too much for him. "And the priests in the Temple! They're the worst! Shooting

arrows down at us and calling us names not fit to be said in
the streets, let alone in the House of God! Why, most of them
are not true priests anyway. My friend says they're all Levites
who just want to get back at the HaKohans for lording it over
them for so long and making them do all the Temple dirty
work. He says they've been killing off just as many Sadducees
as the others. Now, that's another thing. Dragging off the high
and mighty the way they have—even if it is because they want
peace with Rome."

"Who says that?"

"Everyone. John. Simon. The soldier-priests. They say it
was the Sadducees sold us out right from the beginning and
that they'll do it again now if we let them. Still . . . I don't feel
right killing them. I mean, they're Jews too, aren't they? Besides, it's not what I came here to do."

Johanan ben Zakkai nodded. "What do you want of me?"
he asked. "If you wish me to advise you about which party to
align yourself with, I can only say none. And I must tell you
that although I am not a wealthy man or a Zadokite, I am for
peace with Rome."

The Galilean stared at him. "After all they've done to us?"

"What they have done, my son? Or rather, what the Lord
has worked?"

The man's face turned red; then he blurted, "It is certain
I have transgressed in my lifetime, for there are rules and laws
that I know you rabbis say we of the *am ha'eretz* can in our
ignorance never fulfill. But I can tell you there is nothing I
have ever done—no, nor any of my friends and family—that
would warrant such vengeance as has been wreaked upon us.
My wife . . . the babe in her . . ." He choked on the words,
had to stop. "No," he said finally, angrily. "I cannot believe
that they or I did anything so terrible as to cause . . . to cause
. . . what happened in my village."

"The sins of the people of Israel are many. Perhaps the Lord
has seen fit to punish all of us for the iniquity of our generation.
Surely nothing Rome has done to us is as bad as what we now
are doing to ourselves. The very Temple, which is our link
with heaven, has been polluted. By whom? Not by Rome, my
son."

"It was Rome destroyed my home and killed my wife and
child!"

"The fallen are our sacrifice, and more precious to the Lord,
blessed be His name, than anything offered upon the altar of

His Temple. Their altar is a greater one, and their blood shall pave the way for the Age to Come. When the Messiah redeems Israel, it will be in the name of all the innocent slain."

"The Messiah, eh? I doubt I'll live to see him, rabbi, the way things are. I just hope I stay alive long enough to give some back to Rome. Anyway, I've come here to ask you to look after this girl with me. Near as I can make out she's from Bersabe, or round about there. I found her hiding in a well, all wet and shivering. She can't speak, nary a word, but she understands what you say to her well enough. I can't keep her with me, not the way things are. Some of the men have started pawing her—they have the notion comrades ought to share what they've got, if you know what I mean. Well, she's not much, but I guess she's been through enough." He swallowed. "I don't expect anyone would want to marry her, but seems to me she ought to be in a decent place with other women around, where people will be kind to her. That's what the Lord wants, isn't it? I mean, the homeless have to be taken care of, don't they?"

Johanan ben Zakkai nodded. "She is welcome to stay in this house."

The man gave a sigh of relief. "Good. That's settled, then. Here, you," he said to the girl, who had been pressed against the wall silently watching throughout. "I want you to stay here, understand? There's nothing for you with me, only more trouble, like as not. You stay here with these people, understand? Don't worry, you'll be all right. No one's going to hurt you." He looked back at ben Zakkai. "She...she's not feeble-minded, so you needn't think that because she can't speak any..." His voice trailed off. "Well, I'll be back when I can to see how she is, if that's all right."

"Of course. Of course."

"Well, then..." He pushed the girl forward and without another word disappeared out the door.

They called her Hadassah—"little turtle"—and she proved to be a good and willing worker in the house. Some were put off by the fact that she had one blue eye and one brown, but Rabban Johanan declared himself above such superstition and forbade any mention of "evil spirits" in the girl's presence. He seemed to feel that her silence was a sign, perhaps an indication that their prayers for Jerusalem fell on deaf ears. He had become convinced that the city was lost, even though it had not yet been approached by Titus. And, though he dared not say it, he felt in his heart that the Temple too was doomed. But he spoke cheerfully of the future, perhaps trying to persuade himself as he strove to convince others that the Eternal One had not deserted His people and the city He loved. It was all a prelude to the coming of the Messiah, the Anointed One, who would rid Jerusalem of the evil within, rout the Romans, and from the throne of David, to which he was the rightful heir, establish his kingdom with judgment and justice. The land of Israel would be "a shining light unto all the nations," and men throughout the world, seeing how blessed it was to live in peace, would banish all evil and dwell in righteousness.

Meanwhile, the factions in Jerusalem continued their destruction, and Titus, in Caesarea, gathered his troops around him, preparing for a final confrontation with the people who had dared to disturb the *Pax Romana*.

SIX

She was turned away, her long dark hair spilling over her bare shoulders, flowing down her naked back like a smooth, dark river. She came around slowly, and he saw her breasts, the pink nipples like small flowers. . . . His eyes caressed her throat, and she let her head fall back as if his mouth had touched her. Her body seemed to arch as she brought her head forward once more, her lips slightly parted. . . . He saw her eyes now, like pieces of glass or mirrors, and in them two tiny figures of a man. The figures grew, became larger than the girl, merged. . . . It was himself, naked, moving toward her, reaching for her. . . .

"No! . . . No!" Jonatan sprang up and out of the dream. He stared into the darkness, shivering a little as the cold night settled on his shoulders, wide-eyed with fear. But there was nothing before him. It was the beating of his own heart that thundered in his ears. With a sigh he brought his legs up to his chest, slowly crossed his arms on his knees, and wearily bent forward. His head shot up. Horrified, he pushed the blanket away. It was wet. He had spilled his seed. Trembling now with shame as much as with cold, he bolted from bed and grabbed a cloak to cover himself as he stumbled out of the small chamber.

If he had wished to hide himself in the night, he could not; for heaven seemed lit by a thousand stars, and the moon shone round and full. He looked up at the sky, blinking like a man staring into the sun; then, ashamed, he turned his eyes downward. The wind slashed through his thin cloak like a whip, but he did not move. He wanted his flesh to be scourged. He was barefoot; stones cut deep into the soles of his feet; and he was glad too for this pain.

He stumbled across the moonlit plateau like a blind man, making his way finally to the lookout tower by the eastern ascent. "I'll take the watch," he told the surprised guard. Gratefully the shivering man relinquished his post, hastily taking off before the Essene could change his mind.

It would be a long, cold night. Again Jonatan looked up at the star-strewn sky. Heaven seemed so near, closer still from the lookout tower. "So near to Thee," he whispered. "And still, so far away."

"Good morning, Jonatan. Wasn't it cold last night? I woke up stiff as could be. But it is lovely now, out here in the sun!" She sighed contentedly.

When she smiled her whole face lit up, he thought. Her eyes were like stars; they were the sun shining. . . .

"Did you shiver in your bed, too?"

"I . . . I do not mind the cold."

"Or heat, judging from the way you work all day." She laughed. "I sometimes wonder if you are really flesh and blood. Don't you feel anything?"

He swallowed. "We are trained to raise ourselves above . . . above the elements."

"Ah, yes." She nodded thoughtfully as she fell into step beside him. "The mind controls the body. It is part of your Knowledge."

"It is part of our training," he corrected her gently. "True Knowledge is attained by very few."

"Teach me," she said suddenly. "Teach me, so that I may attain it."

It was not the first time she had put forth this request, but he was still shocked by it. "I have not attained True Knowledge myself."

"Then teach me what you know."

"What I know? But I know nothing."

"I doubt that. Besides, the first step to Knowledge is to admit one knows nothing. Well, isn't that what your Righteous Teacher would say?"

"How did you guess?"

"Because they all say that, all the philosophers. The Greeks certainly. Well, will you make me an Essene?"

The idea made him smile.

"You might begin," she said eagerly, mistaking his smile for acceptance, "by teaching me how to withstand heat and cold."

He shook his head. "I cannot."

"Why?"

"You are a woman—" Her look stopped him from continuing.

"If we are to be friends," she said coldly, "do not ever begin anything you wish to say to me with those words."

"Alexandra, please—" He caught up with her, was about to touch her arm, thought better of it, and said, "I'm sorry. I did not mean—What I meant was—" He took a deep breath. "It is not that I think you are incapable of understanding." He looked around before continuing in a low voice, "It is forbidden to pass on the . . . the things you wish to know. To any woman. I would be expelled from the Brotherhood."

"Your mother was an Essene."

"No. She was a member of our community, but she was not . . . trained. None of the women are. They are only to bear children."

She made a disgusted face. Then a new thought struck her. "Did you love her?"

"My mother? I did not know her very well. As soon as I was old enough to leave her breast, I was taken to live with the other children under the guidance of our teachers."

"What was that like? Were there girls as well as boys? Did you all sleep in the same room? Did you learn Torah?"

"Male children lived apart from . . . from the females. But we were all schooled, as is the Law of Israel. I began my study of Torah at the age of three. In many ways my education was no different from that of your own brothers."

"I doubt that. My brothers—and I—learned Greek as well as Hebrew. We were permitted to read anything we had a mind to, even that which the rabbis considered blasphemous."

"I also learned Greek, and the language of the *Kittim*, as well as how to decipher the word-pictures of the pharaohs. Also," he added modestly, "I have received instruction in certain tongues not spoken in our part of the world. Some, in fact, that have ceased to be spoken at all."

Her eyes widened. "Really? How so?"

"Wisdom does not limit itself to one people. There are many wonders to be learned, many cures that can be worked and that are known even in the far-off Indies."

"Now you have really made me curious! Oh, Jonatan, you must tell me all that you know! You must!"

He stared at her. Had Eleazar been right? Was she a spy

after all? Had the Sons of Darkness sent forth this creature to ensnare them, to steal their secrets and their souls? Lilith came in the night, she . . .

"Why do you care?" he asked finally. "What will you do with such knowledge?"

"Do with it?" The question surprised her. "I don't know what I would do with it. But at least I'd have it. At least it would be mine."

"For what purpose?"

"Must knowledge have a purpose?"

Jonatan did not answer. He was transfixed by the sun on her hair, by the purity of her profile silhouetted against the sky. Her eyelashes rested on her cheek like dark feathers. Her lips . . .

He swallowed, shifting his weight, aware of the throbbing, hardening muscle sending fire along his loins.

"I want to know," she said slowly, thoughtfully, "I suppose because I am capable of knowing. Or at least I think I am. You test your novices. I want to test myself. I want to be the best I can be, Jonatan—the most I can be. All my life other people have set limits for me—limits for a woman, limits for an Israelite, for a member of the priestly class. Well, I will set my own limits—if I must have any at all. Being free . . . means more than not being a slave."

He did not reply to this but looked at her with new respect, albeit mixed with fear. But whether that fear was of what she was or of his own longing for her he could not, would not dare to, say. Still, he did not avoid her, and she in turn never ceased to ask him for instruction in the ways of the Essenes.

One day she said mischievously, "If you will not tell me your secrets, I'll just have to come up with a few of my own. Then we can make a trade."

"Trade?"

"Well, you have something I want. Now, if I possessed something you wanted, we could make an exchange." She had to laugh at his expression. "You see, I am the daughter of a businessman."

He smiled weakly. "You do not have to give me anything." He felt suddenly ashamed. "Knowledge ought to be property of all who seek it. And friends should give things to one another without price."

She looked up, almost shyly, he thought. "We are friends?"

"Yes. . . . Yes, we are friends."

"You will not think of me as a woman?"

"I will . . . try."

She smiled. "It was good of you," she said softly, "to try to persuade Eleazar ben Ya'ir of my honesty."

"I am glad you are not angry with me for that. I am against trickery—it is not our Way. The Brotherhood holds that the accuser must come forth openly against the accused. But I wanted Eleazar to see how wrong he was to doubt you, and I think now he knows this. Eleazar is a very fair man."

"He is a terrible man."

"No, not Eleazar."

"The Sicarii are nothing but bandits and murderers. How can you align yourself with them?"

"When the *Kittim* destroyed Qumran, Eleazar and his men searched all the hills to find those of us still alive. They brought us here, to the Masada. But," he added, "I have been with Eleazar for many years. It was the wish of Nathaniel, our Righteous Teacher, that I be always at his side."

"Why?"

"In the days to come you will know the answer to that. In the End of Days, all will be clear." He felt uncomfortable. He had already said too much. No wonder the teachers warned against women! How easy it was to let their soft voices lead one on, to look into their bright eyes and forget the True Light. Still, he felt compelled to say, "The Sicarii, as you call them, are not as they once were. Those who believed as Menahem did died with him in the Temple—or went off to follow Simon bar Giora."

"Tell me about Simon," she asked eagerly. "They say he has gathered an army of thousands, nearly all of them freed slaves. I know he was here on the Masada for some time. What is he like? Can he beat Titus?"

"Simon is like the others," Jonatan said after a pause. "He will not vanquish Rome. Only the Sons of Light will defeat the Sons of Darkness."

"Who, then, are the Sons of Light?"

His natural humility prevented him from replying. Instead he glanced around the mountain community.

"You!" she exclaimed. "Oh, Jonatan, how I wish I could believe that! Once I thought—my brother was so certain—But you are so few and they are so many!"

"One man may have the might of many if the Lord is with him."

"The Lord! Oh, Jonatan . . ." She turned away.

Once again he was frightened. What creature was this to doubt the Almighty? But when she turned back to him, there was such anguish in her eyes that he could never believe she was Satan's minion, never doubt for a moment that she was human—only a young woman, after all, who had suffered no less than any of them.

"So the righteous shall vanquish the wicked. For surely the Lord rewards and punishes according to merit." She gave a short, bitter laugh. "Let me tell you something. My parents were killed on the Sabbath day. I defiled the Sabbath. I disobeyed the Law and my father's command—two evils thereby running off for a swim. That act saved my life. Later, I broke the Law again—and my word—by dressing as a boy. Did the Lord punish me for this? I found myself on a beach full of corpses—but I lived!"

"You were taken as a slave."

"And again I transgressed. I broke the laws of *kashrut*. I ate whatever food was given to me—and it was more than that I didn't care. I was curious. I wanted to know the taste of their food. And so I ate it. Do you know how the Lord chastised me? He delivered me straight to the arms of the man to whom I had been betrothed. I shall not even begin to tell you how Josef ben Matthias has been punished for his sins. That alone would be enough to test the faith of your Righteous Teacher!"

Instead of being angry, he smiled that gentle smile she had come to know so well and said, "Nathaniel would only ask you to look past the first level of these experiences."

"What does that mean?"

"There is no pain in death, Alexandra. Sorrow—the real agony—belongs to those who still must live. Even worse, to those who must see and remember."

She bent her head that he might not see her suddenly trembling lips, but when she raised her eyes to his again she was defiant, even angry. "I had a friend—a slave, a Christian girl. She said her Christ was her strength, but she clung to me to keep away the cold, and in the end her Christ did not save her nor set her free. But I could have . . . I could have. . . ."

"What happened to her?"

"She died."

"Then she is free."

Alexandra could only stare at him.

"We must trust in the Lord," Jonatan said, his voice gentle

as always, but strong in conviction. "We must lean on Him and live by the words He has set forth for us to follow. This is what the Almighty wants of us—not the slaughtering of bullocks over sacred fire, not even, I think, the everlasting hymns of praise to His name. The Lord has chosen us to receive the Knowledge of the ways by which man must live. When we live by His commandments we are strong, we are the Lions of Judah—and nothing can enslave us or defeat us."

She bent her head again. "How like my father you sound," she whispered. "'Live by Torah. Trust the Lord and live by His words.' But that did not save him, Jonatan. Nor my mother, nor my brothers, nor those I have called friend." Suddenly she bent down and picking up a handful of soil, said in a firm, angry voice, "This is what I trust. What I can see and hear and touch with my own hands. I trust Simon bar Giora and John of Gischala to lead us against Titus, to drive him all the way back to Rome! I see no angels, no messiahs come to show us the way—only men willing to fight for their freedom. And that is good enough for me!"

But he only said in his gentle voice, "Simon and John will fail. Jerusalem will fall. It was long ago ordained."

"And will you then fly to Israel's rescue like angels from this mountaintop?" she asked wryly.

"The great battle at the End of Days will not take place in Jerusalem."

They walked in silence now. She bit her lip. "I suppose now . . . after what I've said . . . you no longer wish to be my friend."

"Of course I am your friend." He turned earnestly to her, started to say something, stopped. Finally he said, "I would like to be more . . . more than your friend."

"More than a friend?"

He drew in his breath. Her eyes were clear as mirrors. What did he see in them? What did he really want? "Your brother," he blurted. "Let me be your brother."

The idea delighted her. Thereafter she seemed to change when they were together, to grow even younger when she was with him. It was as if the fantasy of having a brother once more had transformed her, turned her back into a happy girl living by the sea. Impulsively she would squeeze his hand or, coming up behind him as he worked, hug him in appreciation of the exquisite letters that flowed from his pen. She did not know how her affection pained him. When he drew back stiffly, she only thought him shy, never dreaming how he wrestled with his desire for her in the long, cold nights.

One day, restless and in a fine mood, she said, "If you're really to be my brother, let's see how well you do in a race. I'm not as fast as I once was—I know it comes of getting older and growing breasts—but I wager I can beat you to the storehouses. Well, are you game?"

He could only stare at her in utter astonishment. After all this time, he still did not know what to make of her. One moment she was a woman, the next a child. And running! It was unseemly! She would kick up her skirts, and he would see her legs!

Was that what she wanted?

Lilith had many tricks, many ways by which to ensnare man. It was not unknown for evil to come in the guise of childlike innocence or to create trust by awakening pity. There was the illness she had suffered upon coming to the Masada, the bloody mass her body had spewed forth.... Was that the product of some demon seed? Was her own soul engaged in battle with Belial? Or had she come to tempt him, to...

She was smiling, waiting. Her eyes were so clear.... No, he could not believe she was evil. He was drawn to her through his own weakness, his own unworthiness. She was not evil. She could not be evil.

But, he thought with a sigh, she was certainly strange.

"All right, then!" She had, to his horror, hitched up her skirt. "Ready. Set. Go!" With a laugh as mercurial as her movements, she sped toward the storehouses, not waiting to see if he followed—which indeed he did not. Somewhere in flight she sensed herself alone and, looking back over her shoulder, promptly thudded into something large and extremely sturdy. The collision knocked her to the ground. She immediately sat up, pushed the hair out of her eyes, and looked up quizzically, only to find Eleazar ben Ya'ir standing before her, seemingly absorbed in a study of one long, bare leg stretched out in the dust. Hastily she pushed her skirt down, and just as hastily he reached down and lifted her to her feet.

"I—I'm sorry," she stammered. "I didn't see you."

He frowned. "Are you all right? What happened? Why were you running like that?"

"I—I—" Embarrassment gave way to anger. Who was he to demand explanations from her? Brushing the dirt from her dress and deliberately ignoring his question, she said, "I would ask something of you."

"Yes? What is it?"

"I would like to move into the north palace."

"You do not care for your quarters?"

"Oh, no, it isn't that! They're fine, really. But the hanging villa is so beautiful! And you said yourself no one cares to live there. Well, I do. I'm not afraid of any ghosts and—"

"No."

"But why? What harm would there be? What can it matter to you where I sleep?"

"It doesn't." He paused. "If I let you stay in the north palace—alone, as you would be—it might prove too great a temptation to some of my men."

"You are concerned for my safety?" This was a surprise.

"Not so much as I fear for my men."

She regarded him a moment, then said drily, "I suppose I ought to take that as a compliment. I never expected to hear the grandson of Judah the Galilean—who, it is said, fears no man on earth—admit to the power of a woman."

"I admit only the power of circumstance."

"And passion?"

It was his turn to redden.

She smiled. "But perhaps you have no knowledge of that. Perhaps you are like the Essenes, with no feeling or desire for women. If so, you ought to be glad to put me out of sight. Unless . . ." Her lip curled wickedly. "You did say you often went to the palace to be alone. Perhaps," she said innocently, "I would intrude upon your . . . solitude."

The dark blue eyes stayed calm. "You will remain in the place you have been assigned. Where," he added, "I can keep an eye on you."

"Oh, you are a fool!" she exploded. "Do you still believe I am a spy? Do you dare to imagine I would set myself up like a harlot to entice those unintelligible baboons you call your men—in order, I suppose, to learn whatever secret plans you have to lead your ragged little army against Titus? Can't you get it through your thick head that I came here to fight Rome? And because I believed—I was told—that this was the one place in all Judea where an Israelite was free! I did not know the people of Masada were subject to the arbitrary decisions and suspicions of a petty, stupid dictator, or I would have gone to Jerusalem and taken my chances with the council! I might just do that. They say Simon and John hate all Sadducees, but their animosity could not be worse than what I have encountered here!"

His hand shot out, halting her departure. "It could," he said. "It is." He did not tell of the reports that had come back to him of Simon's "Freedom Fighters" looting and raping at will, of John's men strutting through the Holy City, perfumed like whores, killing at random. Those who had been slaves in the great houses of Israel would not hesitate now to take their revenge on the "haughty daughters" of their old masters. "You will stay with us," Eleazar said. "And in the place you have been assigned."

"You—you are—"

"A petty, stupid dictator. Yes, I know. You've already told me."

"I could say worse."

"I'm sure you could." He grinned. "But I thought ladies of your class had finer manners than that." The smile disappeared as quickly as it had come. "You say you want to get back at Rome. All right. But if you would fight for Judea, then first learn to love Judea."

"But I do!"

He shook his head. "You are angry because Caesarea was taken from you and because your class cuts no corners with Rome any longer." He held up his hand before she could protest. "I do not say you have not suffered. But what are your few years of misery"—he nodded in the direction of a group of Galileans carrying rations from the storehouses—"compared to the generations they have known?" His eyes drove steadily into hers. "We may not possess the learning and the fine ways of the Zadokites, but we, the *am ha'eretz*—this ragged army of unintelligible baboons—we are Judea."

He turned away now, but her voice stopped him.

"You may be Judea," she said, "but so am I!"

He could not conceal his surprise. They stared at each other a moment. Then she said softly, "Perhaps, Eleazar ben Ya'ir, you ought to heed your own advice." And with that she turned and left him, missing the smile that returned fleetingly to his face.

"You mustn't be angry with Eleazar," Miriam said. "Despite

his words, I know he has only your best interest at heart. He thinks only of others, never for himself."

"The man's perverse," Alexandra replied. "If I asked for shelter from the rain, he would tell me the sun is shining. And if I sought refuge from the sun, do you know what he would say?" She took a wide-legged stance, crossed her arms in front of her chest, and said in as deep a voice as she could muster, "'Fool. Do you fear the heat of the moon? Or can't you Sadducees tell the difference between night and day without a slave to guide you?'"

Despite herself, Miriam had to laugh. Then she said, "I know Eleazar has been hard on you—I don't know why, really; he is so gentle with all the others. But he has so many things to worry about. I know how he has changed these last years, become quiet and somber. He hardly ever laughs the way he used to, and sometimes I see him staring off into the distance as if—as if—" She broke off and fell silent, suddenly as somber as the man she spoke of.

"Perhaps he wishes to leave this place," Hagar suggested.

"Oh, no! Eleazar loves the Masada! I know. I can tell."

"More than Jerusalem?" Alexandra asked.

"Why should he love Jerusalem?" A voice came from the doorway. It was the red-haired Zealot, Joav.

Alexandra turned to look at the man, but she did not say anything.

"Why should any of us love Jerusalem," he went on. "All it has ever meant is trouble."

"Is that why you stay away?" Alexandra asked. "Because you fear trouble? From whom? The council? Or Titus, who will soon be there?"

"You think I am afraid?" He took a menacing step forward.

"I think the Roman legions do not present nearly so enticing a picture as helpless travelers on the road. I think you stay here because it is safe, and I think you—and your beloved leader— hate not me but yourselves, because you know it is the cowardly thing to do!"

He glared at her a moment, then turned and left.

Hagar looked at Alexandra, raised an eyebrow, but said nothing. It was Miriam who broke the silence at last. "You are wrong," she blurted. "You are wrong."

"Am I? Then why aren't we joined with the forces in Jerusalem? Simon and John are going to need every bit of help they can get. From what I've heard, no one here has the slightest intention of leaving the Masada. And if Jerusalem falls, how long do you suppose it will be before they come after us?"

"The Masada is impregnable."

"Then we'd have to spend the rest of our lives here. Do you want to spend the rest of your life here?"

"I would not mind," Miriam said softly. "I could stay anywhere if . . . Eleazar was also there."

Alexandra studied the flaxen-haired girl. "You love him, don't you?"

"All my life," Miriam confessed.

"The beast. Why hasn't he married you?"

"We are cousins."

"The Law says nothing against this."

"We grew up together. Eleazar has looked after me since I was a small child. He thinks of me as a sister."

Hagar nodded. "That is the way of men. I have heard it said that for this reason the God of Israel made Adam fall into a deep sleep while Eve was born. For had the man watched her creation, the woman would not have awakened love in him."

"Eleazar does not stay on the Masada because he is afraid," Miriam said. "He is not a coward!"

Alexandra shrugged. She had already surmised that, but she wanted Miriam to talk. "Then why?"

Miriam sighed. "I can only tell you what I know. I don't understand all of it—I am only a woman—"

"Don't say that," Alexandra snapped. "Don't ever say that."

Miriam stared at her, then went on. "Well . . . the first thing you must know is that Eleazar cannot go to Jerusalem. The council would have him killed."

"Why?"

"They have ascribed many crimes to him that in truth he did not commit. My uncle Menahem— But that was long ago, and Eleazar had nothing to do with it!" Miriam sighed. "Still, whenever someone is robbed or murdered, it is always the Sicarii who are blamed."

"What about Simon and John?"

"I do not know John of Gischala. Simon was with us for a time. He has a very beautiful wife, and he is a very jealous man. I can tell you for certain that it was she who was bold, always going out of her way to ask Eleazar this or that. He tried to avoid her, and I know he never—" She stopped, looked at Alexandra, looked away. "You see, I know Eleazar," she said softly. "I would know if he . . . cared for someone. And with Simon's wife, never! But it was more than that that made Simon jealous. You have seen how it is here. The people love Eleazar. He has this power in him. He makes you feel special, that you can do anything. And you believe it. And you believe in him. Do you understand?"

"*Charisma*," Hagar said. "The power of the gods."

"Don't be blasphemous," Alexandra said. But she was more intrigued than ever. "Go on," she told Miriam.

"I do not know this word *charis*—"

"It is Greek. Go on."

"Well, Simon spoke of an army. A great battle against the *Kittim* such as the Holy Ones have prophesied. He spoke of uniting all the people of Judea into one army, and since this was Eleazar's own desire, he believed in Simon and gave his allegiance to him. But Nathaniel—"

"Nathaniel. Jonatan's Nathaniel?"

"Yes. The Righteous Teacher of the Brotherhood. Nathaniel said that Eleazar must be leader of this army in order to ensure the blessing of the Lord. But Simon wanted to be general."

"What did Eleazar want?"

"He was willing to follow Simon. Until . . . Ein Gedi."

Before Alexandra could ask what happened at Ein Gedi, Miriam said, "I really must go. I promised Batsheva I would help her with the new baby. We're going to give him a bath. Would you like to come and see?"

"No, not really."

"I almost forgot," Miriam said, turning at the entrance to the small chamber. "I came to ask you something. Would you, could you—" She stopped, evidently not knowing how to phrase the question.

"Yes?" Alexandra prompted, wondering what request could so unnerve the tall, calm girl.

"Could you teach me to write? And to read as well?"

"Certainly! But have you had no schooling? It is the Law that all must be taught—even in the Galilee. Was it because you are a female—"

"Oh, no! Our village had its school and teacher. But you see, we were forced to move out into the hill caves in order that the soldiers might not find us. One day we would be in the hills, and the next back in the village, and so on and so on, until finally, after Eleazar's parents were killed, we moved to the hills with my uncle for good. My father was also killed then. My mother had died giving birth to me," she added.

"And you have never learned to read or write?"

"Eleazar used to teach me, when he had the time for it. I know how he admires your ability, and I thought—"

"Admires my ability to read and write?"

"In so many different tongues, yes. He has a great love for learning."

"And he admires my abilities. . . ."

"Oh, yes! He told Joav you think like a man."

Hagar snorted derisively at this. But Alexandra smiled and said, "I will teach you, Miriam. And anyone else who wishes to learn."

"Well, the Essenes instruct the children, but they will have nothing to do with females after a certain age. I think there might be others—Batsheva, for instance—who would like to learn." Miriam laughed self-consciously. "I know it is frivolous—there are so many other things to do—but—"

"Learning is never frivolous. We are the People of the Book, remember? How can we follow the Word if we cannot read it? How can we pass it on to our children if we cannot write it or speak it with clarity and comprehension?"

"But that is for men to do."

"No, Miriam, I think the Lord meant it for everyone."

After the girl left, Hagar said, raising an eyebrow once more, "I hope Batsheva says nothing of this to her husband."

"You don't think he will be proud of her?"

"I think he will beat her. Maybe rightly so. Her duty is to pass milk to the babe, not the Word of your Lord."

"Hagar, I shall never understand you."

"It is simple. You cannot be both sky and earth, little owl."

She always knew when it would rain; she could smell it hanging in the air like some green perfume. In Caesarea, when she was a child, and later in Jerusalem, the showers came suddenly, ribbons of gold with the sun shining through. There would be two, three, sometimes four a day. Then it would rain all night, and the morning would be washed clean. The ground was greener in winter than in summer, when everything was burnt brown. There were always rainbows in the sky, and the puddles ran with mud rich and dark as gravy.

As winter wore on, the rain grew harsher, and the days were gray with a dampness that gnawed at the bones even though the braziers were kept lit. But nowhere were storms fiercer than in the desert wilderness. The winter wind howled across the desolate land like the wrath of the prophets, and the rain fell out of the sky as if some giant hand had slashed through heaven, ripping the clouds apart with great flashes of fire and thunder. The rain seemed to fall on the dry, dead land with a vengeance, as if it had some sense of what miracles it must work to make anything grow here; and it could kill as easily as it bestowed life. Flash floods, sudden terrific waterfalls cascading down the sides of the towering cliffs, turned the dry ravines into deathtraps. In seconds, wadis became rivers; the force of one of these gushes of water—coming, it seemed, from nowhere—was more than enough to sweep man and horse under. Their bodies would be found days later, miles away from where they had been caught by the torrent. Little wonder that Titus chose to wait the winter out. Even away from the desert, there would be trouble. Horses were easily crippled in the mud; progress would be slow and miserable, the legionaries sluggish and as prone to fight among themselves as with any outside force. Besides which, it was nearly impossible to make plans or adhere to calculations when the weather was so unpredictable—as was everything in Judea, the disgruntled Roman might have added.

But Alexandra, for one, always knew when it would rain; and now she waited for it gladly, needing it as much as the gardens she'd helped plant, knowing even before the sky, darkening, began to drum, that a storm was about to break.

Suddenly, the first flash and shot of approaching rain sent the women scurrying to shelter like foxes to their holes. They grabbed up the startled children as they ran, causing more than one babe who had laughed delightedly at the show of lightning to stiffen with alarm and begin howling in terror. Their cries were soon lost in the wind, which rapidly achieved gale force. It sounded as though a hundred birds had suddenly taken flight, but it was the flapping of cloaks and veils and her own wind-whipped skirt that Alexandra heard, not the beating of giant wings. Her heart beat fast too; she was excited by the sudden activity and the anticipation of the approaching storm. On a sudden impulse she started to make a dash for the terrace of the north palace but she had gone only a few steps when the first heavy drops fell on her face. The rain quickened, the drops became fine and hard; in a matter of moments she was thoroughly drenched. She started to laugh. Raising her arms above her head she began to twirl around like a dancer, mouth open, drinking in the rain. Suddenly she became aware of a tall figure rushing up to her, his hands cupped to his mouth. She could not make out what he was saying.

"What?"

"Get inside! Take cover!"

She shook her head and laughed.

Ben Ya'ir started to say something, but the thunder obliterated his words. He cast a worried look upward as another bolt of lightning flashed through the nearly black sky. "Are you mad?" he shouted through the wind. "Take cover!"

"No!" she shouted back. And laughing, she began to spin around again.

He took her arm now with such force that she lost her balance and would have fallen had he not caught her to him. Still she laughed.

"Fool," he said, staring at her with a look she did not comprehend.

There was another crack of thunder. She laughed, and the look in his eyes turned to one of unmistakable anger. With an oath, he lifted her up, throwing her over his shoulder like the sacks of grain he had been transporting from the storehouses when the storm broke, and carried her out of the rain. Once inside the shelter he had chosen, he dumped her on the floor and turned away.

She saw with surprise that they were in the north palace. He had built a small stove in a corner of the room; it covered a section of the fine mosaic. She stared at the fire but made no move toward it. Instead, she ran her finger along the colored tiles, watching with curious, detached interest how the drops of water falling from her hand intensified the colors of the stones.

"Here." He threw a blanket in her direction, then turned away again, angrily pulling off his leather tunic.

She hesitated, realized she was shivering, then also turned away and took off her cloak and outer robe. She hesitated again. Then, defiant, she pulled off her shift and wrapped herself in the blanket he had given her. The fabric was heavy and rough—not, she thought suddenly, like the fine woolens she had known in Josef's bed. Holding it around her with one hand, she spread her clothes out to dry, then moved closer to the fire. The sudden warmth made her yawn. Dreamily, she began to braid her hair.

"Why do you fight me?"

She looked up, startled. He was sitting on a narrow pallet, drying a fine bow he held across his knees. The light from the fire fell half across his face; his eyes were like the coals she had been staring into, and his hair was darkly gold. His hair was like points of flame, and she wanted to touch it to see if it would burn....

"Why do you fight me?" he said again.

"I don't."

He grinned. "You do." He grew solemn again. His eyes were dark, like coals. "Is it so difficult to take orders from a Zealot, a worthless Sicarius?" He paused. "Or do you still despise the Galilean who kissed you once, long ago, in the village of Bersabe?"

She looked down. "I did not think you remembered," she whispered. She dared not look at him now. But she could sense him moving closer.

"For a long time I have carried your eyes with me. Only ..." He sighed. "There has been so much to think about, so much to do. I have had little time for any woman. And yet, sometimes, I would see you . . . those nights I could not sleep. . . . I would close my eyes and see yours. And I would sleep." He spoke softly, wonderingly, as if he could not himself believe what he had said.

Still she dared not look at him. His voice, so soft, almost a whisper, yet something she could feel on her skin ...

She felt him touch her hair. He had moved to the floor beside her, and now, with a lazy finger, like a schoolboy, he began to poke apart the braids, pulling her dark hair loose. The fire was hot on her face; she wanted to tear off the blanket. But she was naked....

"I remembered," he said. "And you ... did you never once think of that fellow who gave you such a hard time?" His voice was easy now; there was a smile in it.

"Perhaps."

His hand dropped. "Or have your thoughts been for the man who was your husband? Did you love him?"

"Love a traitor?" She could look at him now. "I have no husband."

"Then marry me."

She could only stare at him in disbelief.

"Josef ben Matthias is dead. He has been cast out from us, and he is dead. There are but a few who know of your marriage. The rest know only that you were a prisoner of Rome and that you escaped. I want you to be my wife, Alexandra bat Harsom. I want you."

She could not speak. Every muscle of her body, every nerve, was throbbing. She could feel his desire as strongly as if he had put his hands on her. It was like a power emanating from his body, like fingers on her skin; and somewhere inside she died a little, melting into bits and pieces of gold and honey.

But when he reached for her, she resisted, for his arms were strong and hard, and for a moment she was afraid. Then, like one coming out of a dream, she saw his eyes . . . dark, with a kind of pain in them . . . and she knew who he was and what he would be to her . . . and that once, long ago, he had touched her, and nothing had ever been quite the same.

For how long had she carried the memory of him with her, not even knowing it was he whom she sought?

"Why do you fight me?" he murmured yet again. And then his lips found her and drew her down, down into the sea. . . .

SEVEN

"There are three ways by which a woman may be acquired in marriage," Johanan ben Zakkai said. He was writing out the *ketubah* for Hadassah and Sheptai. The latter, having deposited the girl with the rabbi, had decided he wished to make her his wife. "By the giving of silver to her father; by *shtar*, or writ; or by *bi'ah*, *usus*, which is to say, actual possession. After that, a feast is held in which the *Kiddushim*, or consecrations, take place. Sheptai, you must say then to Hadassah, 'You are consecrated to me according to the Law of Moses and Israel,' and Hadassah will be your wife."

Sheptai nodded.

"You are obliged to support her from that moment on. If she is taken captive, you must do your best to ransom her. If she becomes ill, you must provide her with medical care. If she dies, then you must see to it that she is buried properly and with dignity. If she transgresses the laws or appears unveiled or with loose hair, you may divorce her, and she will forfeit the *ketubah*. On the other hand, if you put her away from you out of anger or simply because you are displeased, then you must answer to the terms of this contract, in which you pledge all your porperties as security for Hadassah against death or divorce."

Hadassah began to gesticulate wildly at this.

"I know, I know," Rabban Johanan said gently. "You care nothing for such things and would as soon do without. But you must know, my child, it is forbidden for a man to live with his wife without a *ketubah* even if she wishes to surrender her privilege in this respect. It is for your own good, my child, believe me."

Sheptai shrugged. "It doesn't matter," he said. "I have nothing to give in any case. The house you've got written up there

411

is burned to the ground, rabbi. It's not like . . . like before, when I had something to my name."

"From the dust of the earth we were created," Johanan ben Zakkai said. "From the ashes and waste that cover this land, grass shall yet grow, the trees will give fruit, and houses of men like you will rise once more."

"You never lose faith," Aliterus marveled later. "But I haven't your conviction. The fact is, I don't believe in any of the gods. I've seen too much, you see."

Johanan ben Zakkai studied him a moment, then said, "That first day, in the Temple courtyard, you were struck by something—you admitted it then. And even before that, I think, you felt something . . . something that made you embark on a long and dangerous journey."

"My coming here was, I assure you, beyond my own choice," the actor replied with a flourish of hand, an old gesture he had not employed for some time now. "I was escaping the wrath of Caesar—with no intention, I might add, of ending up in Judea."

"But here you are. And here you have chosen to stay. Why?"

Aliterus was silent for a long moment. Then he whispered, "It's true. Something leads me on, I dare not say what. I am not ready to say it. But watching you and those around you, I find myself thinking how much better the world can be than it is now. How much better we—all of us—can be. It seems such a simple road to follow. But then, listening to those who come before you—all the problems that beset even the most ordinary, uncomplicated of lives—and hearing the answers you give, the way you and the others see so many sides to each issue . . . why, then it becomes complex. And I am lost. Perhaps if I believed . . . perhaps that would be enough. . . ."

"It is not faith that redeems us, Aliterus—the Lord requires much more. It is the fulfillment of His Commandments. Faith, after all, is God's gift to us. To believe in something outside yourself, something greater and more wonderful than anything man can touch, is to possess a wonderful treasure. It is food when you are hungry, fire when you are cold, strength when you are weak. Faith is God's gift," he repeated.

"Your God demands acknowledgment," Aliterus said. "The first thing your children learn to say is the *Shema*: 'Hear, O

Israel, the Lord our God, the Lord is One.' He takes joy in t.
Temple service."

"He takes greater joy when we live according to the rules
of behavior He has set forth for us to follow. Do not kill. Do
not steal. Honor those who have brought you forth. Deal justly
with others. Do not bow down before idols and images fashioned by men, for they are the work of a lesser hand, and
imperfect and profane. This is what the Lord wants."

"But there are so many laws," Aliterus said. "There must
be hundreds. How can a man possibly hope to know them all?
How can he help but transgress, if unknowingly?"

"A story is told of our blessed teacher Hillel," Joshua ben
Hananiah said. He had entered the room while Aliterus was
speaking. "A Roman officer came up to him one day as he was
on his way to the Chamber of Hewn Stone and said, 'Rabbi,
if you can tell me whilst you are standing on one foot all there
is to your faith and what your God demands of you, then I will
renounce my gods and follow yours.' Whereupon Hillel did
as the Roman asked. He balanced himself on one foot and said,
'Do not do unto others what you do not wish them to do to
you. That is the Law. All the rest is commentary.'"

It was an unusually harsh winter, as if nature and God had
conspired with Rome to ravage the troubled and suffering land.
Although the weather delayed Titus's advance, even that
brought no relief to Judea. The warring factions in Jerusalem
seemed not to care about the real battle they would have to face
in the spring. While the legionaries rested and regrouped in
Caesarea, while Titus, fortified by the advice of the renegade
Jew Josephus and of his chief of staff, Tiberius Alexander, met
daily with his officers to plan strategy, Simon and John continued to confuse and demoralize the anxious city.

The damp, cold weather was not the sort to lift anyone's
spirits, but as Simon bar Giora stood looking out the window,
watching the rain pelt the street, he hardly seemed aware of
the wind whipping across his face or whistling through the
room. Though not a particularly large man, he was well-muscled, his thick arms and torso giving the appearance of great
strength and stature. Deep creases ran like wadis down the
sides of his face; his dark eyes seemed nearly hidden behind
prominent cheekbones, giving him a faintly oriental look. He

was not a handsome man; he was, in fact, ugly. But there was something compelling in his features, something oddly attractive.

"Why don't you close that window," Solomon ben Ya'ish suggested. "The wind will put out the fire."

Simon bar Giora drew the lattices shut and turned to the physician. "How is she?"

"Your wife is fine. Some womanly trouble, but nothing that cannot be healed. I must tell you, though, that once I remove the diseased organ she will not be able to bear children."

Simon bar Giora stared into the iron brazier. "Look at that," he said. "Fire wherever you want it. The rich carry it around with them. They can sit anywhere they like and have warm feet." He looked up at Solomon ben Ya'ish. "She could not bear children before this, so I guess that doesn't matter, does it? Each time she thought she was with child...each time it came to nothing. . . . And she would cry and cry. . . ."

"Yes, well, this is the reason why."

"I don't like the idea of her being cut. If she can't have babies, all right. But why must she be cut?"

"The disease could spread. She would likely die."

Simon slapped his fist into his palm. He was silent a moment. Then he nodded his consent. "They did it to her," he said suddenly, darkly. "Rome and Jerusalem. Her father could not pay the tax," he explained. "He was a poor farmer with many children to feed. So he sold her to get out of debt."

"Sold her to Rome?"

"No. It was the Roman tax made him do it. But he sold her to one of the high-and-mighty families here. They were supposed to use her for household duties, but the son took her for his mistress. She had not even seen a dozen summers when he took her. In this house. In this very house." He gave a short, bitter laugh. "I swore I'd make her mistress of this place, and I have! My only regret is I didn't personally strangle that bastard Zadokite! Seems the procurator took care of that for me. Crucified him along with the others after the market riot." He laughed again, then grew sober. "He did it to her. He made her this way."

"No one did it to her, Simon. It is a common ailment among women. Perhaps, if I had seen her sooner...Never mind. But it has nothing to do, I assure you, with her having been a slave."

"A slave? She was a whore! He passed her around, he——"

Simon broke off. "They'll pay," he said grimly. "They'll all pay for it, Rome and Jerusalem both. They think we're nothing. They think we're animals, good only to tend the fields and grow the food they get fat on. To pull their litters. To work their mines. To pleasure them in bed. Well, no more of that! Rome will learn we mean to be free! And every man, woman, and child in this city that ever owned a human being will learn what it is to bow to those they once called slave!"

The physician sighed.

"You find fault in this?"

"Hillel says, 'Do not judge a man until you have stood in his place.' I have never been a slave. I can only guess at the hurts and grievances you carry in your heart. But I know that you—and John—are destroying Judea."

"Judea! It is Jerusalem I would wash clean!"

"Jerusalem is Judea! What else is there? A few scattered villages by the mercy of heaven yet untouched? One or two mountain fortresses in the desert that Rome could hardly care about? Here is the government. Here is the Temple. If Jerusalem falls, there is nothing left."

"Jerusalem will not fall."

"It is already in the worst state of disorder and panic. At our best we are hardly a match for Rome. What are we now? Every day there are more bodies. . . . You fool, can't you see what you are doing? Save your strength. Save Jerusalem's strength. Get together with John, work out your differences. Or put them aside until we see what Rome has in mind."

Simon bar Giora turned away. "And I say to you, save your strength, physician. If anything happens to my wife—"

"Don't worry," Solomon ben Ya'ish said disgustedly. "I know what I'm doing. Which is more than I can say for you," he added.

Simon bar Giora stared at him a moment, then turned back to the window and the rain.

In a chamber of the north palace, a young woman stood and watched the driving rain. All was quiet but for the wind and the drumming of water on the terrace outside. A sudden river streamed down a nearby cliff, leaping towards the Dead Sea in a series of spectacular waterfalls. All the wadis west of the Masada had overflowed their banks; the ground below was nothing but mud and water. The desert fortress was like an island, more than ever isolated, cut off from the rest of the world.

There was little activity atop the mountain. The aqueducts so ingeniously constructed by Herod's engineers had done their work; the cisterns were full. Through the long, dry summer there would be water to drink, to fill the ritual baths and the swimming pools, to keep the gardens green. In the long, dry summer, the people would bless the winter rains. But now the days were gray and grim. It was not unusual for the south wind to reach gale force, and the low-lying areas of the summit had become one huge pool of water. Except for the Essenes, no one bothered to do much more than to try to keep warm and dry. The famed—or infamous—Sicarii raids had been curtailed, even as Roman action had ceased due to the weather. People slept, huddling together against the dampness and chill; they sharpened their knives and polished their bows, told each other stories of the past, dreamed of the future, and prayed.

The Essenes, with their superb organization and discipline, had fallen quite naturally into leadership of the community. There was, after all, no one else to tell the people when the holy days fell or what to do on those occasions. Also, the Brotherhood did not revolve around the Temple, which it considered a profane instrument of false priests, and it abhorred the business of animal sacrifice, not only because of the act itself, the taking of life, but as a means of expiation for sin. It became easier, therefore, removed as they were from altar and priests, for the people on the Masada to adhere to the philosophy and practices of the Essenes, while not forgetting the teachings of their own rabbis in the towns and villages from which they'd come. Prayer became more structured; there were congregations daily in the synagogue that Herod, out of respect for his Jewish wife, perhaps, had constructed on the western side of the summit. Religion took on a plain, sober quality; with no priests to intervene, the people on the Masada dared speak to God themselves. The *am ha' eretz* had merged with the Holy Ones; added to the simplicity of their lives was a new piousness that the most earnest student of the Law might envy.

But old ways did not die. Men were men, and those who had once been known as the Daggermen were hardly content to remain forever in the wilderness singing songs to the Lord and hoeing weeds. Restless, they waited for spring, even as Titus, in Caesarea, measured the days. Nor did the men on the Masada adopt the celibacy of the Essenes. These were family men. Life meant home and hearth, and that meant a good woman and children to call your own. There were marriages on the Masada, sometimes amounting to no more than a declaration by the man. But that was enough. The *ketubah*, or marriage contract protecting the woman's rights, was hardly considered necessary by the Essenes, who in any case did not believe in personal property; and unless a woman knew better, brides went without. Although Alexandra cared little for the material objects the contract promised, she felt the principle of agreement was important, that it was a mark of respect and consideration. Laughingly, Eleazar had told her to draw up whatever she wished.

"All I have is yours," he had said. "The desert, the sea . . . this palace, if you like, as no one else seems to want it. Take it all and be my wife," he had murmured. "You always were."

"I am your betrothed," she corrected him.

"You are my wife. But have it your way. I never realized you Sadducees were such sticklers for protocol."

"My wedding to Josef was a farce, an amusement for the Romans. This time it must be as it would have been if—if my family were here."

He had looked at her with understanding. "It will be as you wish."

She turned from the window now, watching him still asleep on the blanket they'd spread on the floor. They were together constantly, meeting in the palace all else feared. Their union was intensely physical, yet somehow it transcended that, was more than simply touching. The force of his desire, his hunger for her, was unlike anything she'd ever known. It lifted her out of herself, made her—*both sky and earth*, she thought suddenly.

She stared at him, asleep by the fire, his hair lit like gold by the flames, and wondered at this man she hardly knew yet knew so well, and at the feelings he had awakened in her.

He seemed to feel her eyes on him. He opened his, looked back at her, and with that stare drew her to him.

She knelt beside him. Still without a word he reached up, twisting his hand in her hair, drawing her down to him, her mouth on his. She had a sudden image of the waterfall outside; a wave of heat had begun to course through her body like the river tumbling down the cliff. She was falling . . . falling. . . .

He released her and drew back a little, staring at her. Then he smiled. "Must I win you every time? Always it's as if there had been no time before. You hesitate, as if you were afraid...."

"Do I?" She laid her head against his chest. "I didn't know. It's just that you are so strong...."

He stroked her hair; his hand had moved down her back, caressing her. "I don't want to hurt you."

She closed her eyes. His hand was so warm. She rubbed her cheek against the golden hair that covered his chest. She could hear his heart beating. "It isn't that. You make me feel so helpless, so... out of control." She raised her head, looked up at him. "I swore I'd be no man's slave. And yet... it seems I can deny you nothing."

He drew her on top of him. "And how do you think I feel?" he whispered.

She put her arms around his neck and bent to kiss him, but a sound made her straighten. "Listen!"

"What?"

"Don't you hear it? The strangest sound..."

"It's the wind. Only the wind."

"No, listen! It's as if someone were calling. Or moaning..."

"It's the wind, I tell you—"

But she had already gotten up, was poised at the door, listening. "Sshh. There it is again." She turned back, eyes wide. "It's Herod," she announced in a dramatic voice. "The ghost of Herod..."

"I didn't know you believed in such things," he said sharply.

She laughed. "But it is! Everyone knows how evil he was. They say he loved only one person, the princess Miriamne. My uncle said he made her his queen because she was Hasmonean and her blood ensured the succession of the line. But my mother said he loved her very much. She was very beautiful and kind to all the people. The king could not believe that she was faithful to him, although everyone knew she was as virtuous as she was lovely. But his passion made him insane with jealousy, and he ordered her killed. Afterwards he went mad and dreamed of her constantly, calling her name over and over through all the lonely nights left to him."

Eleazar was silent.

Alexandra hugged herself excitedly. "Do you think perhaps they were here together, in this very room? They were! Yes, I'm sure of it! I think he had this palace built for her. It's too small to be anything but a private villa. And it is so beautiful. Oh, yes, Eleazar! This must be Miriamne's palace! And that sound . . . it isn't the wind at all." She shivered with delight. "It's Herod calling to her. 'Miriamne . . . Miriamne . . .'" Her voice echoed through the empty rooms.

He did not smile. His face was pale and tense. "Why do you talk such foolishness? Ghosts. The dead are dead. They cannot walk. They cannot speak."

"I was only playing." The troubled look in his eyes surprised her.

"Alexandra . . ." He reached out for her.

Wondering, she came back to him. Once more she felt the desperate need that seemed as much part of him as his strength and magic. For there was a power he possessed, a king of golden energy that was impossible to resist. Within the circle of that power, engulfed by that force, she had no will of her own, no memory, no consciousness of anything but the moment and the feel of him on her, about her, in her.

Josef had been subtle in love, clever and titillating; but Eleazar was the dream that came on the wind of the summer nights and the storm that broke upon the desert. He was all things, nameless and perfect; and even as she loved him she was afraid of him and wondered at his beauty.

Several moments passed in silence, then Eleazar spoke. "My uncle was an angry man," he said. "He hated the Romans who had taken everything from us—our home and our land— after the death of my grandfather Judah, called the Galilean. He hated the king and the princes and priests who helped Rome, who, in fact, despised us as much as the legionaries. I think he even hated the Galileans who were permitted to return to their villages after my grandfather's revolt. And whatever he hated was, he said, that which the Lord also hated.

"My uncle had fits. I mean, he would fall into a kind of swoon and thrash around on the ground like a wounded animal. Afterwards, he would speak words he said he had received from God. He said the Lord was angry with us for bowing to Caesar and for allowing the Temple to be in the hands of the ungodly. He said that whenever he had the falling sickness it was the Lord's own anger that had entered his body, that even as he would have bitten off his tongue had we not placed a stick between his teeth, so would the voice of the Lord be gone forever from Israel if we did not free Judea.

"Nobody needed much urging. If it wasn't the boot of the

legionary, then it was the whip of some prince of Israel across our backs. Even while we were in the hills of the Galilee, not yet banded together in true war, escaped slaves from the Houses of Boethus or Ananus found us and joined us. And we all of us dreamed of a new beginning. I admit it, we wanted to destroy more than the arm of Rome."

"Was that why you aligned yourself with Simon bar Giora?"

"Yes. I believed in Simon. 'No man shall make himself master of another,' he said. Well, that was what I thought. Back in the hills, it was what we all believed." He sighed. "If only it were as simple as that. But it always comes to more. . . ."

"Did it come to more with your uncle?"

"My uncle. I loved him, Alexandra. And I would have killed him if Joav had not held me back." He fell silent, his eyes dark and troubled.

She put her arms around him. She did not know what to say to him.

"The Temple," he said suddenly. "No one can tell me God was there. Not in my lifetime. And the priests! Butchers! Skilled at carving up oxen and rendering the fat. They said they served God, but what about the people? Butchers and cooks, that's all they were." He passed a hand before his eyes. "Butchers . . . every one of us . . .

"Eleazar . . ."

"There were bodies everywhere. In the courtyards, even in the Sanctuary. They had not even bothered to drag them away. Old men lying there . . . cut down in the holiest place of Israel."

"But you had nothing to do with that."

"Then why do I feel guilty? No, I ought to have known. I ought to have seen it coming. The way my uncle spoke, the things he said, the way he acted . . . I ought to have known."

"Could you have stopped him?"

He stared at her. "No," he said finally. "Probably not. But I could have tried."

He was pacing back and forth, his movements fluid but contained, emanating that certain power she found fascinating. Even now, in this agony, he was something splendid to behold.

"Even before that, back in the hills, I ought to have seen it. Most of us had banded together because of a cause we felt was just. But there were those who had a brutish nature, men who came to us and were no more than outright thieves or worse. There are men who like to kill. They take a joy in blood. It is like a fever with them, and you hear them laughing in the battle. Beware of a man whose eyes show three white corners, my father used to say. There is a love of death in that man's heart. He will lower his head like a bull before a charge, and though he speaks softly to you his hand is always ready at his sword."

"Is Simon like that?"

"Simon is an angry man—like my uncle—but he does not lust after blood for its own sake. At least I did not think so until—" He stopped.

"Until Ein Gedi?" she prompted.

Again he stared at her. Finally he nodded.

"What happened there?"

"We had word the soldiers wanted to take over the place and set up a garrison. An advance party had already entered Ein Gedi. More legionaries were on the way. I took one group of men to stop them on the road. Simon went into the village. I guess he felt the people there were friendlier to the soldiers than they had a right to be. I think what really bothered him was the fact that his wife had once wintered there with the young prince who owned her. She often spoke of it, saying how well treated she had been even though she was a slave. Well, Simon's men destroyed the place. I mean, they leveled it. Men, women, children. They tortured the soldiers for information, finally killed them all. They came back here loaded with loot, drunk, dragging women with them. . . .

"I thought there would have to be a fight. I was ready for it. He and I. There and then. After Jerusalem I'd vowed never to raise my sword against a Judean. But I couldn't let the Masada become a camp for murderers. And I knew Simon could not hold his men in check, that furthermore he had no wish to do so. It would just be one gory massacre after another. Judeans, Romans—it would not matter which. His hatred spilled over all the boundaries—it was greater than whatever love he bore Judea and freedom.

"He chose not to fight. He just laughed and said I hadn't the heart for war. He's right, I don't. I can't see how anyone could. It isn't fine or pretty. I don't even know if battles accomplish what they're meant to do, except maybe for a short while. There are times a man has to fight. Without freedom you might as well be dead. But it isn't as simple as I once thought. . . ." His voice trailed away. He was staring out the window, as if he could see something in the night beyond the darkness.

"Simon rode off to Jerusalem . . . without a care, without a thought for those he left behind in Ein Gedi, as if they had never existed, were never men and women, old and young, never more than bodies that had come before his wrath like . . . pieces of dirt kicked aside."

The wind echoed through the palace; he listened to the sound it made, then said, "The dead are dead. There are no ghosts calling to us. It is only the wind. Only the wind."

EIGHT

The almond was in bloom; in the north, anemones had begun to cover the hills, while in Jerusalem the afternoons settled once more on the rooftops and towers with a shower of gold, the sky clear and gentle. In the wilderness, flowers of every color dotted sudden green expanses; the Judean desert had come alive with a new and rare beauty. The Masada itself was testimony to spring, its fruitful soil fulfilling the promise of the rain. The whole of Judea seemed reborn, spirits uplifted, hope for the future renewed. Once again the roads leading to Jerusalem were filled with people. The Passover was near, and it was time for the children of Israel to make their pilgrimage to the Temple. Not far behind, sometimes passing the parties of Jews headed eastward to the Holy City, came the men of Rome. Titus had begun his march.

He had his own legion, the Fifteenth—the one he had brought from Alexandria at the beginning of the war—plus the Fifth, which Vespasian had stationed at Emmaus, and the Tenth, from Jericho, which had wreaked destruction upon the community of Qumran. Each legion had been replenished, partly from the detachments from Egypt and from the forts on the Euphrates, so that they were at their full complement of over five thousand men each. Also marching to Jerusalem was the Twelfth Legion, the famed Thunderbolt, which had retreated four years before under Cestius Gallus, and now, reconstituted, was eager for revenge. With the cavalry units, the mercenaries, and the auxiliaries furnished by Agrippa, Pangar, and the other monarchs of the region, Titus had a force amounting to more than sixty-five thousand men—more than Vespasian had had when he descended on Jotapata.

As pilgrims thronged through the city's gates, they brought with them the news of Titus's advance, of the great numbers of soldiers on the road, and of the whole formidable apparatus of the Roman army, which was drawing closer and closer to Jerusalem. Before the war, the hills outside the mountain city were always covered with tents during the Passover; but now no one dared remain beyond the safety of the walls, and Jerusalem was swollen with Jews come to observe the *Pesach*. Every house and hostel was full; and though a siege was imminent, for the present the main concern of all was not Rome but the Lord God of Israel.

The unleavened bread must be baked and eaten, the sacrifices performed, the telling and teaching of the age-old ritual maintained. More than ever the house of Johanan ben Zakkai and those of his neighbors were scenes of constant activity as the women swept and scrubbed every corner. Traditionally, the entire city was cleaned before the Passover, the pocked roads resurfaced, the sepulchers white-washed—the beggars were even handed new clothes—but little of this took place now. Simon and John were still feuding; with the storehouses burned, the governing council's main concern was gathering together enough food to feed the masses swarming into the city. For the moment, there was no lack of meat—all male Jews within fifteen miles of Jerusalem were required to come to the Temple on the first day of the *Pesach* bringing with them an unmarred lamb not less than eight days old. Generally, two hundred thousand lambs were sacrificed on this one day, commemorating the departure from Egypt, when each male family head had slain a lamb and sprinkled the blood on the doorposts and lintels of his home so that the Angel of Death might recognize it and pass over.

There was plenty to drink, and the stores of nuts and figs were still ample; but the special flour for the unleavened bread was in short supply. It was therefore with gratitude and surprise that Johanan ben Zakkai accepted the two precious sacks his nephew brought to him.

"Be sparing in your use," ben Barriah advised grimly. "There won't be any more."

"This is enough for the eight days we are commanded to keep," Johanan ben Zakkai observed. "More than enough."

"It isn't the Passover I mean. Caesar's men are on the march. Only the Lord knows when we'll be able to open the gates of Jerusalem again."

"Then the great battle draws near."

The Zealot chief nodded. "There's time still. The Romans like to build their camps first, give everyone a look at their great strength and power. You will be able, I think, to eat your *Pesach* meal before any real fighting begins. Unless, that is, I can talk John into joining in a little surprise welcome. I'm going now with my men to see if we can't work some mischief on the road." He turned to leave, stopped, turned back. "There's bound to be a siege, uncle. Keep something aside for that time."

"Whatever I have will be shared."

"You're very generous," his nephew said suddenly, bitterly. "Would that you cared to spread a little courage and hope around as well."

"But I have only hope. I will never believe that the Lord has abandoned His people."

"I'm talking about Jerusalem. I'm talking about Rome. I'm talking about this war, the real reasons for which everyone seems to have lost sight of. I could never understand how you, of all people, could be content to see Jerusalem, to see the land of Judea, ruled by men who do not believe in the One God and who spit on those that do."

"I do not see such men," the rabbi replied calmly. "They do not exist for me. They never have. And they have never ruled Judea. Only the Eternal One can do that."

"Tell that to those who have suffered under Caesar. Tell that to the sons and daughters of the men the legionaries have crucified." He laughed harshly. "Oh, uncle, you live in a world that does not exist. You live in a world of words. But how I wish you had the right words for our people! You could erase so much doubt and confusion if you would only speak in our behalf."

Ben Zakkai was silent a moment. Then he said, "Once, I went walking with my teacher, Hillel. We passed by a stream, and floating on the water was a human skull. I do not know how it came to be there, but my teacher stared as if it were a sign for which he had been waiting. The flow of the stream brought the skull to the bank whereon we stood, to our very feet, and Hillel raised it out of the water with his own hands and said, 'For drowning others, so you have been drowned. And those that drowned you, they also shall be drowned.' I know the bitterness you must feel, son of my late brother. You have lost a father. I have lost my son. But there is no end to violence but more violence. We cannot be that which the Lord commands us to be if we raise our swords."

"The Lord commands us to defend our faith and our families and our very lives. You are wrong, uncle. I have not become what I am out of bitterness over the death of my father at the hands of the procurator. I was a Zealot long before that. I would be less than a man if I did not demand freedom—the most simple basic liberty—for myself and my countrymen. I don't care what the Greeks and the Thracians and all the other countries have accepted. Judea belongs to Judeans and none other. Jerusalem will not be another of Caesar's toys."

"Jerusalem can never be that. No man can be king of Jerusalem. No walls can encompass the City of God. Whatever happens, Jerusalem will live as it has always lived, in the hearts of those who love her."

Ben Barriah sighed. "You talk of shadows. I speak of substance. Dreams and memory may live beyond the flesh, but we still must make the best of our lives." He turned to go.

"Will you join us for the Passover feast?"

The man turned back. "Yes. Thank you."

"*Shalom*, then. Go in peace."

Ben Barriah had a sudden image of the scene he would soon lay eyes on, the troops of legionaries marching toward his city hopefully, unaware of the band of Zealots who would be waiting for them in the hills. He smiled tiredly. "*Shalom*," he said.

"We do not reckon the months and years as governed by the moon," Jonatan was saying. "Many generations past it came to our Teachers that it was more orderly to count by the sun. They divided each year into fifty-two weeks, which in turn are divided into four seasons, each consisting of three months thirty days in length. An additional day must be added to every season as a link between them. According to these calculations, holy days such as the Pesach fall on exactly the same day of the week in every other year. Now you know why we celebrate the feast days at different times than the rest of Judea."

"Shabbat as well," Alexandra noted. "I remember it was said that the Brotherhood rested while the rest of us worked, and toiled when we observed the Sabbath. I must admit your reasoning is logical—and of course you need not rely on the runners from Jerusalem officially proclaiming the new moon.

Was that why the Teachers made their own calendar? To break with Jerusalem?"

"The breach came before that. The Brotherhood has never recognized the house Herod built as the Lord's Temple. Nathaniel says that only when the priests are perfectly versed in all that is revealed in the Law, when their works are truth, righteousness, and loving-kindness, when they preserve the faith with steadfastness and humility and atone for sin not with the fat of sacrifice but by the practice of justice—then shall the House of the Lord be truly established."

"Then shall it be an Assembly of the most Holy for Aaron." Eleazar had come up behind them; he was buckling on his sword belt. He slipped his arm around Alexandra's waist and, unmindful of the Essene, brushed his lips against her hair. "What are you teaching her now, Jonatan? I must tell you that for all your good intentions, I do not think you will make her a member of the Community."

Jonatan smiled. "But she is a member of this community. We all are now. I was explaining how we measure the year," he said.

"A practical thing, that," Eleazar said. "Especially useful now."

"Useful?" Alexandra asked. "How so?"

"The *Kittim* know we will defend ourselves but never attack on *Shabbat*," Eleazar explained. "However, as you now know, some Judeans observe one day of rest, and some of us"—he winked—"another."

"So you will truly surprise the soldiers."

He nodded. "Truly. I hope."

"Do you think you can stop them from reaching Jerusalem?"

"They are already there for the most part, setting up their camps and war machines. No, I cannot stop them altogether, Alexandra." He grinned. "But the *chev'ra* and I—our gang—may be able to kick a little dust in their mouths."

"Will you go into Jerusalem?"

The smile disappeared. "I have vowed never to set foot in the city again."

"But if the council pardoned you—"

"For what?" He shook his head. "No, I cannot. I will never turn my back on our people, but I must do things my own way, the way it feels right." He hugged her to him. "When I come back, we will have a proper marriage. I've waited long enough for you. Besides, now that Nathaniel is back, he might start wanting to check your bloodline. Four generations if the daughter of a priest, five if not, eh, Jonatan?"

"I am a descendant of the House of David," she said, astonished. That sort of investigation was only necessary when one married into a priestly family. "My great-grandfather was High Priest, and my uncle—"

He caught her to him. "Don't worry," he said with a grin, "I'll take you in spite of your faults," and kissed her right there in front of Jonatan.

If this display of affection disturbed the young Essene, he did not show it. In fact it moved him, filled him with a kind of sweet-sad pleasure. He had come upon them in the palace of Herod, thinking to find only Eleazar and seeing instead the man and the girl locked in embrace. Fascinated, frightened, enthralled, he had watched, seeing his own dreams come to life. And with that image finally real, his horror became unreal. When at last their love was spent, he had turned aside and wept for the beauty of it, for the miracle of man and woman, and for himself that he would never know their ecstasy, never be able to bring to the experience of flesh the joy and innocence that made it holy. For it was he who was corrupt; the teaching that had conditioned him would forever make his love less than what he had seen in that palace chamber. Three things there were too wonderful to comprehend—*"Yea, four which I know not," a sage had written. "The way of an eagle in the air, the way of a serpent upon a rock, the way of a ship in the midst of the sea—and the way of a man with a woman."* Jonatan watched the girl stare after the departing figure of the tall, golden-haired man. She would never be his wife. But he was now and would always be her brother.

"Eleazar will fare well," he said gently.

"Yes," she answered absently. "I know he will." But something else had caught her eye. The fine weather had brought more people to the Masada, and among the newcomers was a man who seemed somehow familiar. Each time she saw him, Alexandra searched her memory for some clue to his identity, but still she could not place him. It was clear the man knew who she was; he had given a curious little nod of greeting that seemed to signal recognition; yet he had not spoken to her or approached her after that initial salute. She watched him join the group about to follow Eleazar down the mountain and wondered again who he was.

Jonatan was also preparing to leave.

Alexandra pressed his hand; she knew her kisses made him shy. "Be careful, Jonatan."

He smiled his sweet, gentle smile. "'He that is everlasting is the support of my right hand.'"

She sighed. "And Eleazar's too, I pray. Oh, how I wish I were going with you! How I'd like to stick it to the *Kittim!* That for Caesarea! That for Tarichea! That for all the rest!" She sighed again. "Never mind. With all the husbands away, I can hold a proper school. Miriam says there are more women who wish to learn to read and write." She paused. "You don't think she hates me, do you? I mean, because Eleazar and I—"

"I know she does not. I think, in a way, she is glad. Miriam is free now." *And so am I*, he thought.

She stood with the other women, watching the men ride off on the horses brought from Ein Gedi, smiling to see Eleazar on the white mare Pangar had given her. One day, soon after the rains, the animal had shown up at the foot of the mountain. Alexandra liked to think of the mare as Eleazar's mount now.

"Tread firm and sure," she whispered to the steed. "Be swift in battle and bring him home again." And even as she thought these things, she noticed the stranger riding behind Eleazar and again searched her memory.

"Tobias!" she exclaimed.

Hagar turned round in surprise. "Who? What?"

"That little weasel in the garden of the governor's palace. I didn't recognize him because he was clean-shaven then. Now he has a beard. What is he doing here? Oh, Hagar, it could be a trap! The raid—If Tobias is here, it can mean no good! I must get word to Eleazar! He must know who this man is!"

"Whoa! Hold on, if you please. You cannot catch them now. Besides, a small band of crazy mountain men is not going to get Flavius Titus worked up into sending any spies around— as you yourself have pointed out. Not when the Roman has got his eyes fixed straight for Jerusalem. This Tobias may just be looking for a place for himself, a place where he's not known." She frowned. "But you are right about one thing. His presence is sure to mean trouble."

• • •

Alexandra awaited Eleazar's return with mounting anxiety. Not only did she fear for his safety, but now she was desperate to reveal to him Tobias's identity.

Days passed. It was nearly a week before the band of Zealots was spotted making its way across the desert to the Masada. Hagar came to tell Alexandra the news.

"I saw the white horse," she said.

The girl nodded. She was too excited to speak, too excited even to run out to greet him. In his absence she had realized for the first time how deep were her feelings for him. The time without him had seemed like an eternity. How was it possible to go a day without his touch, without the sound of his voice, without knowing that if he was out of sight he was still somewhere near? *I love him*, she thought. *I truly love him*. She had never said the words to him. And now he must know. She must tell him.

She waited for him, trembling with her own happiness, anticipating his smile, the look in his eyes when she told him, those dark blue eyes with their own special light. He would be dirty and dusty, but he would take her in his arms...

But when he appeared in the doorway of the room he seemed possessed by a strange humor. There was a wild look in his eyes, and he was breathing heavily. "Leave us, old woman."

Hagar hesitated, unsure.

"Go!"

The woman's eyes narrowed. She looked at Alexandra, then at ben Ya'ir. Silently she stole from the room.

Alexandra felt a strange fluttering inside her, a kind of sick and anxious fear. "Was there trouble?" she asked. "Did everything not go well?"

His eyes seemed to clear. "What? The raid...yes, it went as we had planned."

Then why this mood? She waited, but he remained silent, watching her as if he were debating what course of action to take. The fluttering in her stomach quickened. She felt enveloped in a strange heat and with it a kind of chill.

"I am glad you are not hurt." Now, now she must tell him all that was in her heart; but she was suddenly unsure and afraid. "I...I am glad to see you," she stammered breathlessly.

"Your sentiments are received with thanks." It was the old

tone of voice, the one he had used with her when they first met. "Would that they came from the heart. But then..." He took a step toward her. "Where there is so much beauty one ought not want more. It would be greedy to ask for honesty, loyalty—certainly not fidelity." He was but an arm's length away. "Any of those little virtues has a nasty habit of getting in the way, wouldn't you say?"

"What... what are you talking about? Getting in the way of what?"

"Oh..." He waved his hand casually. "Power, I imagine. The kind of things women go after. Wealth, of course. Comfort. Security. All the things a beautiful female would find hard to do without. And you are beautiful, Alexandra. You are very beautiful...."

She did not reply.

"You're like a piece of silver," he said, taking hold of her wrists. "So fine and delicate... but with the fire of life burning inside you...." He drew her to him now. "Your heart beats fast... like a little bird flapping its wings, wanting so desperately to fly away...." He put his hand on her breast; and she felt the fire of which he spoke, for his hand was a flame on her. "You always pull back," he murmured. "You are terrified of me, aren't you?" His hand dropped. "Terrified." Angrily he pulled her to him again. "Why do you tremble? Because I am a Jew? A Galilean? Because I am no Roman general or one who would kiss Caesar's sandal? You little whore... aren't I good enough for you?"

She was so astonished she could not answer.

He laughed harshly. "Good enough for here, I suppose. Go after the top man.... I suppose that's what your mother taught you. I should have known.... You Sadducee women are all alike. There isn't one of you who knows the meaning of simple honesty and decency." He laughed bitterly. "It was all a game to you. 'A proper marriage!' Betrothal, *ketubah*, the ceremony of consecration!" He laughed again; it was not a pleasant sound.

Like one possessed, he took her face in his hands, staring deeply into her eyes. "Nothing there," he murmured. "They're like glass. All I see is myself. Why don't you say something? Why are you silent?" His hands dropped, and he turned away. Suddenly, in a fury, he swept aside all that had lain on a table in the room. Alexandra felt numb, too weary even to be afraid when he started toward her again. He stopped. "All the way back here I planned what I would do with you," he said slowly, deliberately. "But you need not fear. I will not harm you. I will not touch you. I will not touch you," he said with disgust, "ever again."

He was gone. The weariness that had engulfed her now opened like a chasm. She sank to the floor. She felt weak and dizzy. And she began to cry. She had not wept so since the day her family was killed; but now, all the indignities and loneliness she had suffered since that time rose up in her like a monstrous wave, and she could not fight such a tide. But even as she wept, her tears changed; even as she cried, it was less and less with pity for herself and more and more with anger.

Tobias had done his work well; Alexandra soon felt the full effects of his slander. Women turned their faces away; men regarded her with a mixture of hatred and desire—the desire to avail themselves of that which the Romans had known. It was a look that said they would have liked to use her violently. Only Miriam and Jonatan remained constant, and surprisingly, the Essenes did not turn from her. After all, what she was accused of being was no more than the common frailty of woman. One did not chastise a lesser being for that which it was her nature to be—or at least that was Alexandra's scornful interpretation of the Holy Ones' continued acceptance of her presence on the Masada. She soon learned that their silence while everyone else was clamoring for her dismissal from the community bespoke a deeper sympathy.

The day the first green buds had appeared, a day wholly without rain, the one called Nathaniel had come out of the wilderness and made his way to the top of the mountain. Where he had been, how he had survived, what he had subsisted on during the cruel winter, he did not say. His robe was worn thin, bleached white as bone, white as the hair on his head and the long beard that seemed one with his garment. He carried a staff but walked erect. It was impossible to tell his age, except that he looked older than time and younger than anyone else. And now he stood in the doorway of Alexandra's room, where she had begun to isolate herself, and beckoned for her to come to him. She obeyed, once more drawn into the timeless well that was his eyes as she had been long ago in another, younger spring. His look was calm, not intense, yet she knew it had gone deep inside her. After awhile he said softly, "Much evil has been done to you."

Her eyes filled, but she kept back the tears.

"A woman of beauty is like a piece of gold, poisoning men's minds so that they think without wisdom and act without goodness. Which is to be blamed? The beauty of the woman or the weakness of the man? What must be considered is the intention." He nodded slightly. "I have watched you, and though you do not walk with modesty, I see that your pride and arrogance are a cloak upon your wounds and not the lure of a godless woman. Yet . . ." He seemed to study her more closely. "You are not wholly innocent of men."

"I have been wed, Gracious Teacher, to a man of our race in the prescribed ceremony of our faith. We were both prisoners of Rome. But he . . . he was prisoner in name only. I thought I loved him once, but I know now that I never did. And when I saw that he . . . he . . . I had to leave him. There was no honor left, no—" She swallowed. "I could not remain his wife."

"You were given to Josef, the son of the Jerusalemite Matthias. Jonatan has told me of this."

She bowed her head. "Yes." She looked up. "But I have a divorce from him. I thought the document was lost, but Hagar has it." The words came in a rush now. She had not realized how much she wanted to talk about it. "We were kept in the palace in Caesarea. Whatever else, Vespasian was kind to me. I will not deny it. He was kind to Josef and to me and protected us from the intrigues of those around us. He never commanded me to . . . he never forced me to any evil." Her chin came up. "And I never . . . never," she said firmly. "I have never brought upon myself the shame and dishonor of which I am accused."

"You are accused of many things. Of being a friend to Rome in more ways than being its new emperor's mistress. Of being Vespasian's spy."

"I know the antiquity of my line makes me suspect of this treason. But don't you see? Whatever sons I may someday bear will be of the house from which all prophecies begin, the line of David. Do you think I would stain this hope?"

He smiled. "I wanted to hear you speak. I do not believe what has been said of you, but I am glad now that you have expressed yourself to me. There is to be a council. You will be called upon to give testimony in your own behalf. If you cannot satisfy Eleazar and his captains as to your honesty, you will be expelled from the community—or worse, depending upon their mood." He sighed. "There is nothing like a woman to bring out the beasts that sleep within man."

"I will not answer them. They may do as they like."

"My child . . ."

"It is easy enough to refute their lies by calling to account the one who has accused me. But I am weary of it all. . . . I am tired of man's infamy, his mean ways, his stupidity. . . . I have done no hurt to anyone here, yet they have been anxious to hate from the first. Why? Because I am a Sadducee? It is as stupid as the hatred the gentiles bear us because we are Jews." She shrugged. "Eleazar and his captains may do as they wish. They are as little in my esteem as the mob that murdered my family."

He shook his head. "You must confront your accuser. If you do not, who knows what larger acts of malignancy he may then commit? What other innocent soul shall then suffer for your pardon? Besides, you must not allow Eleazar to judge falsely. You must lift this evil from his heart."

"Evil is he who thinks evil. The treachery is his."

"A man in love is never wise." He smiled, and she felt a cleansing warmth flow through her cold, numb body. "Defend yourself," Nathaniel said. "The Lord loves those who speak truth."

It was not long thereafter that she was summoned to the western palace and led before a group of men who sat sternly awaiting her. Eleazar sat behind the table that had held the letter she was asked to decipher when she first came to the Masada. Joav sat at his right hand. Jonatan was in the room, as was Nathaniel, who could have sat beside Eleazar but chose instead to remain off in a corner. Alexandra recognized Yigael, who had found her in the desert, and several others whose wives had become friendly with her but who now, under orders from their husbands, shunned her. Tobias, however, was conspicuously absent.

"He is nowhere to be found," one of the men reported. "I have looked everywhere. If he has left the Masada, it will be difficult to seek him now, for the sun has gone down."

Eleazar frowned. "Strange . . . he knew he was to be here."

Jonatan stood up. "It is the law of the Brotherhood that a trial may not proceed unless accuser and accused are both present. It is clear to me this Tobias has run away. In any event, since you cannot find him to come forth with his claim, you must dismiss his charge and absolve Alexandra from any guilt. That is the law of the Brotherhood."

"Who said we were all Essenes here?" Joav growled. "I say we get on with it. I have heard enough to think we had better determine if this piece of baggage is fit to dwell among us— or fit indeed to live. I say we come to a decision now."

There was a murmuring at this, but Alexandra hardly heard it. She was staring straight at Eleazar, whose eyes were likewise fixed on her. Neither spoke nor made a move of any kind. They just stared at each other. Coldly. Like strangers.

"At least let her speak," Jonatan pleaded. "Give her the chance to answer you."

"What do you expect her to say?" someone said. "That she didn't sleep with half the men of Rome or conspire with that bastard from Jerusalem to betray the people of Judea? You think she'll tell us that her father never kissed Caesar's arse, and that her mother did not do even worse?"

Whether it was Alexandra's white face or the roar of laughter that greeted this, Eleazar seemed to snap out of the reverie that had held him silent. "Enough," he said tersely. The short command silenced the room. "With the exception of Nathaniel I doubt any of us would make the Sanhedrin, but at least we can conduct ourselves like decent men and not like pigs."

Several in the room grew red at this and nodded abashedly, but Joav would not let it go. "If you want to talk of decency—" the redhead began.

"Shut up, Joav." He turned to her. "Jonatan is right. Let her speak." He paused. "If she wishes to."

Alexandra took a step forward, her features a mixture of anger and contempt. Her gaze traveled around the room, fixing each man there with a short stare, in that glance taking full measure of these men who had assembled to judge her, making it quite clear that with few exceptions she found them far below the task. She was young, female, slender as a reed, but at this moment she possessed the power of a Berenice, every inch of her the Davidic princess that in truth she was. Devorah stood there at that moment, proud and unafraid. Samuel was there too, the quick, fine mind appraising the situation, sifting the possibilities of success and failure, instantaneously computing circumstance and response. And beyond this was someone else, a creature unique and full-grown, a young woman: Alexandra bat Harsom.

She had never in her life backed off from a fight.

"I have lived among you for some time now," she said. "And with me is a woman who was a servant in my father's house, a convert to our faith. This woman has cooked for you, cared for your children, and in every way made herself part of this community. So too, I have tried to give whatever aid I could, asking only that I might dwell among you, my own people, not subject to the insults of gentiles, not slave to anyone. Yet I have been treated more fairly by the *Kittim*, as you call them, than by you whom I sought. And the woman Hagar, who has done as much for any of you as a mother might—now you call her witch and keep your children from her. And all because a man has come here saying evil things of me. Where is this man now? Why does he not say to me what he has said to you? Or can he be afraid that I might throw his words back into his face? That I might accuse him of that of which he accuses me?"

She took a deep breath. "I knew Tobias in Caesarea. Many like him came to Vespasian. Jews, yes. Their tongues were like the beating of vultures' wings, and they told anything they were asked and said everything the Romans wanted to hear until Vespasian said, 'Why must I ride upon Jerusalem? The longer these Jews are left alone, the surer it is they will destroy themselves.'"

There was a murmur at this, but Joav spoke up angrily. "The opinion of the *Kittim* is of no importance here. As for spies and informers, we are interested in only one, and that is yourself. Were you sent by Vespasian?"

"How could I be?" she asked in disgust. What a pack of morons! "Yigael," she asked, searching out the man, "when you found the old woman and myself, did it look as if we had been escorted by soldiers, that we knew where we were or in fact where the Masada was?" Without waiting for an answer, she turned back to the others and said, "In all the time I have been here, have I attempted to gain any knowledge that would be of some military consequence? You know only too well that I have kept to myself and to the company of women or of the

Holy Ones, who," she added pointedly, "do not slip out from the shadows to attack a solitary female as no honest man would."

Some of the men shifted uneasily at this. Several had indeed made themselves bold; while Alexandra had always managed to elude their clumsy aggressions and, because of the circumstances, had pardoned their impudence, it was time to let this jackal herd know that nothing had been forgotten. Added to the pleasure of seeing them squirm was the sight of Eleazar turning pale at this announcement. Sternly he looked around.

"You are attempting to divert us from the true issue," one Abodiah said hastily.

She looked directly at him, and he knew that she remembered quite clearly the night he'd crept into her chamber, only to be doused with the contents of the water pitcher. "Very well," she said. "If I were a spy, if I had in fact gathered information the Romans need—though what that might be I cannot imagine, seeing this is not, after all, Jerusalem, and you, despite the love you bear yourselves, are hardly of much consequence to the Roman campaign—but if I had discovered some precious bit of news, tell me, how do you propose I had delivered it? To where? To whom? Have I ever attempted to leave the Masada? Have I obstructed any of your raids or given false information? Or have I rather told you all that I could to help you?"

"This is true," Eleazar admitted in a low voice. "I am satisfied she is not a spy. But"—he leaned forward, seeming to struggle with the words—"there are other charges."

"She is the traitor's woman!" someone called out angrily. Most of the men here were from the Galilee. Josef ben Matthias had been their governor and their general. As once they had loved him, so now they despised him.

"I am divorced from the one who calls himself Josephus." She hesitated. "The marriage was . . . arranged . . . by Vespasian, in the manner of a master with his slaves." She found it hard to speak now, but she knew she must go on. "I was taken at Tarichea and put aside to be sold into the household of the palace." She remembered Mucianus pulling off her robe, staring at her nakedness. She felt stripped now. Hot irons on her flesh could not burn more than the eyes of these men. She forced herself to go on. "Vespasian thought it would be . . . amusing . . . to see a Jew take a wife. But afterwards he . . . respected the marriage. I was never made to do anything dishonorable. And though I came to despise my . . . my husband's way . . . I was never false to him. My brother Benjamin won my freedom fighting in the arena . . . though he forfeited his own life. Still, I could not leave because Josef . . . my husband . . . was Vespasian's prisoner. But he too obtained his freedom . . . and I left him. He was glad to see me go, I think. He always said a partisan wife was not much help to him. He consented to a divorce. I have the document."

"Why did you not reveal this when you first came to the Masada?" Nathaniel asked.

"Tell everyone that I had been the wife of Josef ben Matthias?" She shook her head. "I was too ashamed. The calumny was his. But a woman suffers more . . . inside her . . . when the man to whom she has been consecrated . . . is of such little worth." She stole a look at Eleazar; he was staring down at his fists clenched on the table. The room was quiet.

"Well, but why has Tobias spoken ill of you?" Joav demanded, still angry.

"Why have you believed him?" she retorted. "Because I am of the class you call Sadducee? Or because I am a woman? Are all my actions, deeds, vows, rendered meaningless just as soon as a man—any man—says what he likes of me?" Again she took a deep breath. "As the Lord above is just, you have no cause to stone me, as I believe you had in mind. And you need not ask me to leave the Masada. I have already decided that I do not wish to live among you."

She had not failed to move them, and with Tobias gone (he was never seen again), there was nothing to do but dismiss the charges brought against her. Some of her accusers came to her to apologize. "The minute I learned you were a slave," one of the men said, "I could not find it in my heart to blame you for anything." He looked down as though suddenly recalling something he wished to forget. "Who can say what anyone would do if he were a slave?" Only when he walked away did she see the brand mark on his neck.

But Eleazar said nothing. In fact, she gave him no chance, turning abruptly away as he—she thought—came forward. "I want nothing more to do with him," she told Jonatan. "With any of them. It was a mistake to come here, I see that now. The sooner I am gone from this accursed mountain, the happier

I shall be. I tell you this, though; if anyone says one bad thing about my mother and father—you must tell me if they do, Jonatan—I will come back from wherever I may be and slit the throat of the man that said it!"

He smiled now. "I think you will come back without such cause."

"Never!"

"Never is a week of days," Hagar said, shrugging. To Alexandra's great surprise she had refused to leave the Masada. "I am too old to climb down only to climb up again," she had said, making it clear she thought Alexandra's self-imposed exile a temporary and foolish piece of business. As for Eleazar, she told Alexandra, "If he did not love you so deeply he would not have been so wounded."

But Alexandra was nursing her own wounds. She felt that every man she had ever cared for had betrayed her: her father by his peaceful counsel; Josef by his treason; Eleazar by his mistrust; even her brother Benjamin by dying and leaving her to face this Masada alone. She was hardly rational, but she was after all not yet twenty and had already experienced an inordinate variety of events that might well have tested the sanity and emotions of one older, stronger, and wiser. Which is not to say she had in any way lost her mind or sense of what was right. Perhaps her resilience was due to her youth. Perhaps it was because she was fashioned from strong fiber—a survivor, her father had called her. Perhaps it was simply that she was extraordinary, a human being whose natural curiosity, intelligence, and feel for life carried her ever onward, ever forward. It was this "fire of life" of which Eleazar had spoken—which had been part of the attraction Vespasian had felt, and which Josef had at once recognized—that gave her the special beauty that went beyond her youth and her already lovely features. Whatever weariness she felt, whatever sadness weighed upon her heart, she rode away from the Masada with her chin up, her back straight as steel, unmindful of the eyes that followed her departure.

"Where will you go?" she had been asked once more.

This time she replied, "To Alexandria, I think. I have family there." She did not mention the name of Tiberius Alexander.

"Do not go straight off," Jonatan had said. "The mind needs to rest. Stay awhile in Ein Gedi. I will come and visit you shortly, and we will talk."

She had agreed, too tired despite her show of strength to cope with more than the immediate future. She would rest in the oasis, swim in its cool, life-giving spring, dream perhaps beneath the feathery palms of what might have been.

Despite the memory of Simon's massacre, the residents of Ein Gedi offered a friendly welcome. Eleazar had come with his men in an attempt to repair some of the damage. There was still evidence of burned houses, but there were new buildings as well. Jonatan left her in the care of an elderly couple, then rode back to the mountain fortress, promising to return in a few days' time.

But only one day had passed before the old lady whose house it was said, "Someone has come for you."

Alexandra smiled. She was sure Hagar had followed after all. The woman made her life a misery, but she had to admit she missed the old witch.

No woman waited in the garden, however; and the man leaning against a tree was not Jonatan. There was no mistaking that tall figure, those broad shoulders, that golden head. He straightened as she came forward, his body tensed like a hunter's. For a moment, she was afraid he would spring at her, but then she saw him relax, standing suspended, it seemed, against the violet twilight.

"What do you want?" she asked.

"You."

"As always, there is little courtesy in your speech."

"And none," he rebuked her softly, "in yours."

Her mouth fell open. "You dare to accuse me——" She was so angry she could not go on."

"Alexandra . . ." He came forward quickly, his movements swift and easy, filled with the particular catlike grace that always fascinated her. Once again she felt the power he had over her—whatever hardness there was in her surely must break into little pieces now that she was near him again—but she resisted it, remembering how he had wronged her.

Night was falling on them, soft and dark and full of stars.

"Don't turn away," he said. "You have every right to. . . . But I ask you . . . I ask you to . . ."

She raised her eyes to his. Did he want pardon?

He swallowed. "Come back with me."

"No."

"Why do you make it so difficult?" he said in sudden

exasperation. "No—don't go." He sighed. "You are a hard woman."

"I have learned to be."

"Is there no softness in you? No forgiveness? Do you hate me so much, then?"

If he only knew. She moved away. "I am not chattel, Eleazar ben Ya'ir. I am not an object, not a thing that you may have when you want and toss away and then take back again. Once, you said you wanted me. And you took me. You did not ask how I might feel, if I loved you, wanted you . . ."

"There are things that need no words. You know as well as I that you belong to me. You have been mine for a long, long time. . . ."

"I do not belong to you! I will not!"

He drew her firmly to him. "Why must you always fight me?"

She wrenched herself free. "Why do you want me, then?" she retorted hotly. "Why don't you go to Miriam? Why don't you marry her? She is humble and devoted—she worships you! That's what you want, isn't it? Someone to adore you, to follow dumbly behind, silent, obedient. I am well aware that in our world women are accorded the legal status of children and idiots—but I am not a child. And I am not an idiot. I will not be treated as such."

"I would not ask a child to be my wife," he said quietly, "much less one who could not reason." He fell silent. Then he said, "All right. There is something I ought to say, something I want to tell you." He hesitated again and finally began, "I saw a young girl once . . . standing by a well, a baby lamb in her arms, and her eyes full of sunlight. A child and woman—and a cheeky little thing, to boot!" He laughed ruefully, then went on dreamily. "Behind you the hills of the Galilee were all green, covered with flowers. The sun was on your hair and in your eyes. It was late in the afternoon . . . everything still and perfect . . . lazy. . . . Do you wonder that I can see that day so plainly, as if it were now and you and I what we were then? I've carried it with me a long, long time. There were nights when it was more comfort than prayer. When all I could see were dying men, all I could hear were their screams . . . when I was afraid to sleep because of the things I might see in my sleep . . . I would conjure up your image and that moment . . . that memory of peace . . . and beauty. . . .

"You have been mother, sister, daughter, wife to me these bitter, bloody years. I didn't want to find you human. I didn't want to know that you had suffered like the rest of us; grown older, lost your innocence. I wanted to keep you by old Avram's well . . . with the lamb in your arms . . . where you were safe . . . and belonged only to me.

"And then I saw you again. You became more than a memory . . . and more beautiful. It was like a knife in my guts to know that someone else . . . I watched you in your fever, hating the man or men who were responsible, hating you for . . . for what? Being alive? Being real? And so I fell in love with you a second time, but even then half in love with the image I'd carried with me all those years. I moved the pieces of the picture around, that's all, to fit my need for you. I am telling you this, Alexandra, because I want you to know why I have acted toward you the way I have. Perhaps you think it womanish of me to speak so long and so plainly of the things inside me. But what is between us must be understood. It must be set right. I believed Tobias because you were not real to me. I did not want you to be real."

"And now?" she whispered.

"I love you," he said simply. "As you are . . . what you are . . . more than I dreamed you could be. I want you to be my wife."

But she felt the need to be cruel to him still. "That is the second time you have asked. And how long now may I count on your affection? Until the next man comes along to speak ill of me?"

His voice darkened. "By the Almighty, woman, I have opened my heart to you! What is it you want? Must I go down on my knees to you? Must I humble myself like a slave?"

Still she would not relent. Walking away from him, she said, "I do not want you humble, Eleazar ben Ya'ir. I do not want you at all."

He caught her arm and spun her around. It was dark—night—but they saw each other plainly. His grip relaxed. He nodded. "It is enough, Alexandra," he said quietly. "The thing is done. We have hurt each other enough for one lifetime." He smiled. "Toss your head all you like. The thing is done, I tell you. You will be my wife." And with that he caught her to him, and all the pain and bitterness left her, washed away forever in his embrace.

"*Anni vey dodi vey dodi li*," he said. "Say it. Say it to me."

She whispered the words against his lips, his hair, pressed them against his throat and chest. "*Anni vey dodi vey dodi li*. 'I am my beloved's, and my beloved is mine.'"

NINE

Titus drummed his fingers on the arm of the campaign chair—looking very much like his father at that moment, Josef thought. The young Roman frowned. "I ought to have expected that surprise attack," he said. "It was too quiet. I ought to. have realized it was too quiet."

"It was the Sabbath," Josef offered.

"Yes, well, that doesn't seem to stop your countrymen from the activities of war, does it? Six hundred of the best Roman cavalry routed by a bunch of bearded fanatics! I thought you said the citizens of Jerusalem were anxious for peace, that they have submitted to these insurgents only out of fear. I was cut off," he went on before Josef could answer. "Cut off from my own men! My only luck was that the gods were with me. How I got safely back to camp I shall never know."

"It was your own courage got you back," Josef said.

Titus sighed. "The worst of it is they will think they have won a grand victory—when it was all due to my own carelessness. It just prolongs the wait until they surrender, which is their only hope. I have no desire to drag this war out—or indulge in a grand, bloody finale. My father needs me in Rome. The sooner I can get this thing cleaned up and Judea set right again, the sooner I will be on my way. My dear Josephus, will they talk to you, do you think? You are one of them. Surely they will respect your advice. Tell them they need only make sincere allegiance to Caesar and abstain from any further troublemaking. In return, they may expect to go on with their lives and religious practice. The rebels will have to be delivered over, of course, and reparations made for the men and equipment we have lost . . ."

"And the Temple?"

Titus looked surprised. "The Temple? But you know that has been decided. Rome cannot leave Judea without a symbol

of its displeasure. That would be too much to expect, and a
bad example to the rest of the world. Better to level one building, wouldn't you say, than to execute thousands of men?
Especially when the labor of those thousands can mean revenue
to Rome. I know that's what my father would say. And you,
Josephus, how many times have you spoken against the hy-
pocrisy you feel your Temple represents?"

Josef swallowed. "It is true I have no love for the priests.
But the Temple . . . the Temple represents something greater. . . ."

"Exactly. That is why it must be destroyed. For the good
of Judea. For the good of your people, Josephus. There must
be no further thought of rebellion. It would only mean total
destruction."

Josef nodded. He knew Titus was right. But why did he
have this sudden queasy feeling in his stomach? This . . . fear . . .

"Talk to them, Josephus. Make them listen to you." He
clapped his hand on the young man's shoulder. "You can persuade anyone of anything when you have a mind to. See if you
can convince your Jerusalemites to abandon further resistance
before they regret their own folly."

Josef had already to the greatest degree worked it out to his
own satisfaction. If the Temple was in truth the House of God,
surely the Lord would not allow it to be destroyed. But even
as he thought this, Josef remembered the Silence he had known
in the desert with Banus. Did that Silence have a Hand? Would
that Hand—could it—stretch forth as it had for Abraham and
Moses? Or was there . . . nothing?

*In which case the great Temple is no more than a pile of
stones sanctified by a people's need for something holy*, Josef
thought. And as stones could be raised, so also might they be
leveled, and by nothing more divine than a sturdy Roman
battering ram.

As he walked back to his own tent, he passed groups of
legionaries clustered around small fires, playing their favorite
game of knucklebones or talking in low tones. He tried not to
take note of the looks they gave him, that mixture of suspicion
and thinly veiled contempt that would perhaps follow him
throughout his life despite his closeness to the royal family.
It did not really bother him. In one way or another he had
always been an outsider; Rome was the closest he had ever
come to finding a real niche for himself. He smiled, recalling

the days spent with Aliterus and that rascal crowd of artists and actors who were the only true family he felt he'd ever known. Titus was right. The sooner this stupid war was over and they were all on their way back to Rome, the better it would be. For Rome, with the strong, sturdy Flavians at the helm. For Judea. And for Josef.

John of Gischala stood before Simon bar Giora, his keen blue eyes taking in the width and length of the room, making sure they were alone before settling once more on his adversary. "The physician tells me your wife has had some trouble," he said.

"She is better now."

The grizzled Galilean held out a small bag. "Here. Some barley. She will need to keep up her strength."

"The House of Simon bar Giora does not eat unless all the people eat."

"The sick are above such consideration. The Law says so."

Simon raised an eyebrow. "I didn't know you were such a rabbi."

John grinned. "One becomes many things when the need arises." He set the bag of barley down, giving Simon time to adjust to the gift and to his presence. John was a man well over fifty; time and experience had combined to give him a certain understanding of the workings of men's minds. This, together with his natural energy and cunning, had made him a leader even before the war. He was a robust figure; in better days, the strong body had carried a "rich man's pouch," but now his thick leather belt was tightly buckled over hard muscle. Coarse white curls covered his head; his short beard was thick, a mixture of black and white hair. The leathery face had been deeply furrowed by years of labor in the sun, but the bright blue eyes, those "Galilean jewels," were as sharp and clear as any youngster's. He straightened up slowly now, hooked his thumbs in his sword belt, and said, "All right, boy, let's get down to it."

The muscles of Simon's face tightened, but he said nothing.

John waved a hand toward the door. "There are God knows how many Romans, Arabs, and assorted bastards out there wanting to cut our throats, and more people than Jerusalem has ever seen at one time packed tight inside the city, with hardly enough food to go around. Now here stand you and I, in the middle of all this, your men taking potshots at mine, and my boys forced to fight back instead of aiming their arrows at the legionaries as they should."

"Now, wait a minute. Your men haven't exactly been sitting around waiting to be attacked—"

"All right, all right. Let's not get into that now. I'm not here to argue with you, Simon. There's been enough of that. And I'm not saying I'm forgetting what's between us. But the way I see it, that's all got to wait—unless you want to settle things right now."

"You know what I want. Government in Jerusalem elected by all men of Judea. One man, one vote. No more councils of rich men and HaKohans telling the rest of us what to do. Land divided equally. Each man working for himself, not for the benefit of some fat priest or princely family. Slavery abolished. No man has the right to make himself master of another."

John sighed. "Simon, Simon . . . I agree there are inequalities. Who should know better than I? Look at me. I am no priest. My father was no Levite. I am a poor Israelite like yourself. I have worked hard all my life. Whatever I have has come by my own two hands. And let me tell you, no one—not you or anyone else—will take away my land, land I have watered with my own sweat and blood. My wife and children—blessed be their memories—went without so that I could buy that land. No man of Caesar shall take it from me, and no son of a slave either! I agree the rule of the kings and priests must be at an end. But that doesn't mean anyone can get what he wants without working for it! Or that you may take from honest men what they have labored long for."

"What you really mean is that there will be no kings and priests to rule Judea but one, John of Gischala!"

"The people can choose whomever they damn well want! But let them say their choice honestly and not be speaking with a knife held at their throats by one of your mob!" He stopped. "There it is again. And I told you I did not come for this."

Simon shrugged. "What else is there?"

"Rome. Outside. Waiting for us. And every day less food in the city, fewer men willing to hold out against Caesar. People are beginning to desert. They listen to that little pimp, Josef ben Matthias, standing outside the wall telling them they have nothing to fear from Titus, that we—you and I—are their enemy. And they are beginning to believe it is so. Simon . . . you're like a man at an inn complaining the food is not kosher while the house is burning down! Ben Barriah has already put us to shame with his stories against the camps. Even the Sicarii have managed to do some damage in the rear. While you and I sit here fighting, our men sniping at one another. We have already lost too many men this way—and too much time. I say we put aside our differences. It may well be that Rome will decide them for us. If at the end of this we are both still alive, then we will meet again. If not..." He shrugged. "Let it be the will of the Lord."

Simon studied him. "All right," he said finally. "But my men answer only to me."

John nodded.

"What about the priests?"

"I've taken care of them. My boys control the Temple now. Did you know they had a store of lumber hidden away in the Sanctuary? Said it was sacred timber. Well, I don't think the Lord will mind us taking it to build defense towers in His behalf, do you?"

Simon smiled. "For the first time, John, I think we are in complete agreement."

Protected by ravines on three sides, Jerusalem was pregnable only from the north, and there it was protected by a wall, begun by the first Agrippa to enclose the suburban area that had sprung up there. Although the wall had been left unfinished until the start of the war and then completed in a hurry, it was a formidable barrier. A second wall stood between the north suburbs and the city proper, and a third wall cut through the city itself, from Herod's palace on the west across the Valley of the Cheesemakers to Temple Hill on the east. As Tiberius Alexander pointed out, a single rampart would suffice.

Titus had stationed most of his forces on Mount Scopus—called Lookout Hill because it was the first point from which Jerusalem could be seen—and had placed the Fifth Legion six hundred yards to the rear for protection while the rampart was being constructed. The Tenth Legion was ordered to encamp about three quarters of a mile from Jerusalem, at the Mount of Olives, beyond the ravine that edged the city on the east. It was the Tenth that first felt the force of John of Gischala and Simon bar Giora's alliance.

After months of waiting, the Judeans were eager to attack, and they swarmed out of the city with blood-curdling yells, into the ravine and up the mount, where they caught the Tenth busy pitching camp. It would have been an embarrassing defeat for Rome had not Titus rushed additional troops to the scene and, after long, hard fighting, managed to drive the partisans back. The Roman was furious, and as this would prove to be only the first of many such sorties, Titus's temper did not mellow with time. His father awaited him in Rome; there was Berenice, whose alluring company he sorely missed; and these damned Jews were determined to drag out this stupid war, which they could not possibly win in any event! There was no doubting their courage—reckless courage, he called it—or the cunning of their stratagems and ambushes; but in the end they were outnumbered and outdisciplined. It would be a sad day indeed when the legionaries of Rome could not easily defeat such a pack of wild dogs.

Four days were spent in leveling the ground right up to the walls. Every fence and hedge that had once enclosed a garden or orchard was thrown down, every tree felled, every hole filled, every hill demolished. What did it matter if passing centuries would see the stripped land become as desolate as the wilderness surrounding the Masada? For now, the Romans could rest safely. Their view was unobstructed. There would be no more surprise attacks.

And now it was time to take the offensive.

First, Agrippa's wall was attacked in force: there were machines for firing arrows and javelins, machines for propelling hundred-pound stones, and there were the battering rams. The legionaries constructed three wooden siege towers from the timber they had collected and moved them up on ramps flush against the wall, overlooking the city. From here they could send arrows, spears, and stones down at the Jews while other soldiers hammered at the wall with the battering ram. John and Simon fought back; manning the wall, they flung firebrands against the engines and showered arrows on the men working the batterers. Small groups would spring forward and fall on the crews, then retreat. But the battering ram—affectionately named Victor by the troops—succeeded at last, and the Romans advanced through the gaps left by the collapsed wall. The Jerusalem forces withdrew to the middle wall separating the northern suburb from the city proper. It was late in May, and the siege was fifteen days old.

Five days after breaching Agrippa's wall, Titus breached the middle wall, and his men moved into a part of the city that had been one of the famed Seven Marketplaces of Jerusalem. Here, where wool and clothiers' shops had crowded together, legionaries and Jews fought in the narrow alleys, the inhabitants of the city defending themselves so well that the Romans were forced to retreat. Before attacking the middle wall, Titus had ordered all prisoners crucified in plain sight. If he hoped this demonstration might lessen the determination of the enemy, he soon learned it had as little effect on their will as Josef's admonitions for peaceful surrender. Fighting was fierce; the breach in the wall was filled with bodies. It took Titus four more days to break through a second time, but this time he stayed through. His work, however, had only begun.

The scholars in the house of Johanan ben Zakkai looked up in consternation as the quiet of their study was disrupted by Zealot soldiers. Only the rabbi kept calm, gesturing for his students to remain seated, meanwhile waiting for the intruders to make known the reason for their presence. These were not ben Barriah's men; from their accents, they were not even Jerusalemites; clearly they had no knowledge of the house they had broken into—or perhaps they knew and did not care.

"Orders from the council," the leader announced. "With food so scarce, all remaining supplies will be given only to fighting men. There are to be no more rations for the general populace. You must find ways to feed yourself unless you bear arms in defense of Judea. All deserters will be executed on the spot. Anyone caught trying to leave the city or hoarding food, anyone able-bodied and refusing to aid the defense forces, will forfeit his life. Do you understand?"

Johanan ben Zakkai nodded.

"I must search this house now to see if you are hiding any wheat or barley or corn."

"There is nothing. The rations have long been gone."

The Zealot looked at the group of men critically. "I've been in houses where there is nothing to eat," he said. "I know the look and the smell. None of you would be sitting here so calmly if your bellies were as empty as mine."

"But we are not wholly without sustenance. Torah is our food and drink. The word of the Lord is our bread."

At this moment another Zealot pushed the rabbi's wife into the room. "There's soup in the kitchen!" he exclaimed. "A big pot of it boiling away! And something baking too!"

The leader fixed ben Zakkai with a cruel smile. "The word of the Lord, eh?"

Frowning, the rabbi looked to his wife.

"It is only grass and herbs," she explained. "The children forage for them at night, beyond the wall."

"Grass and herbs!" the Zealot said. "Roman garbage, you mean! The children sneak past the guards into the camps. Garbage! They bring back Roman garbage!"

The woman sighed. "I do not know what it is. I do not care. It is food."

Her husband shook his head, astonished. "How could you?" he murmured sadly. "It is unclean ... unclean. Better to die than commit such transgression. How could you? How could you?"

"It is only grass," she said tearfully. "Herbs. Nothing more."

"This doesn't look like grass to me," the leader said now, catching in his hands the small loaf his companion threw to him.

"For the girl!" the rabbi's wife cried, pointing to Hadassah. "She is with child! It is the Law!"

The rabbi took a step forward. "I do not know how this bread came to be here, but what my wife says is true. It is the Law of Israel that pregnant women take priority over all others—"

"Not anymore, they don't." He bit hungrily into the loaf, then tossed it to his men, who quickly devoured it. "Fighting men come first. Look, I know who you are. It is only out of respect that I don't slit your throat here and now for this. I won't even report it to the council. But do you think this girl is the only one with a big belly? What good are all the babies born to us if their lives are taken away by the soldiers? Or worse, if they grow up slaves? Right now the legionaries are busy making earthwork ramps against the wall. Soon they will try to move up their war machines. What will happen to all the pregnant women then, with no one to defend them, and the Romans in our city?"

"But we will die anyway with nothing to eat," one of the scholars said. "We are no good to you. Let us leave the city. Surely the Romans will see that we are not soldiers. Titus has promised pardon for those who would leave in peace."

"Pardon, eh? Well you're not the only one believes that garbage. Go take a look from the wall at the way he pardons such as you."

"He is right," Aliterus said quietly. "I went to the wall this morning," he told ben Zakkai. "I wanted to hear this Josef speak. There must be hundreds nailed upon crosses, some in grotesque poses. I suppose the legionaries find the conventional methods boring by now."

"Deserters ought to die," the Zealot said stoutly. "If we catch any, you can believe they will meet their end. So don't anyone here try it."

"I have no plans to leave Jerusalem," Johanan ben Zakkai said. "Now or ever."

"See that you don't," the man replied. He turned to go, then stopped, remembering something. "Here," he said, drawing a scroll out from under his tunic. "I was told to give this *megillah* to you." He nodded to his companions, and without saying anything further, they all left.

The scholars crowded around ben Zakkai. His fingers trembling from weakness, he unrolled the document.

"What is it?" Aliterus asked. "More new rules?"

"'. . . Consecration of the House of the Lord in the days Of Zerubbabel. . . . The seventh day of Kislev, in commemoration of the great victory over Cestius. . . . In commemoration of the Hanukkah . . . of Purim, or the Triumph of Esther . . .'" The rabbi looked up from the scroll. "It is a calendar of festivals we are to observe as citizens of the independent State of Judea. A schedule," he explained, "of new feast days!"

"We must get him out of here," Aliterus said.

Solomon ben Ya'ish nodded. "The question is, how? Months ago I advised him to leave, but he would not. Why he stays I do not know. The Court of Judgment no longer meets—that is, the real one doesn't. The Temple is a travesty of what it once was. The new priests are so in fear of the council they don't know what they're doing—and even if they did know, it wouldn't mean much, seeing that most of them are untrained."

"Everything he loves has been corrupted," Aliterus mused.

"Except Torah."

"And what will become of the Holy Book with no Johanan

ben Zakkai to carry on its study? If he dies of starvation or is killed, so much knowledge will be lost forever. There is more to this faith of Israel than that which is written down. There is an entire spoken history, an oral tradition, if you will. . . . What am I saying? What do I know of anything? Only this. Johanan ben Zakkai must not perish. I know Titus, Solomon. I know what the Roman army is capable of accomplishing. And I know what will happen once the third wall gives way. Fight or surrender, it is all the same. Jerusalem is done. Finished."

The physician looked at the actor curiously. "Why do you stay?"

"How can I leave?" He paused. "It is true, once I got past John and Simon's guards—and if I could get straightway to Titus or Josef ben Matthias—well, as I told you, I have nothing to fear from them. In fact, I have a note in Titus's own hand assuring my safety." He laughed ruefully. "Now if only I had one from Simon or John . . ." He thought a moment, then said, "Perhaps there is a way, after all."

"For you to leave Jerusalem?"

"No," Aliterus replied. "Not I. Another."

The Zealot captain ben Barriah tried not to show his concern. It was unlike Johanan ben Zakkai to summon him unless it was a matter of grave importance. But then, the rabbi's nephew thought, who could say what was important to Johanan ben Zakkai? While others racked their brains trying to figure out a way to feed their families, Rabban Johanan worried over the meaning of a single word in an obscure phrase of scripture.

"Does he think I can pardon those the council has declared traitors to the cause? He must know I can do nothing in their behalf," he told Solomon ben Ya'ish. "Nor can I get him out of Jerusalem. I would be executed—and my wife as well—if I even tried."

"Your uncle doesn't need your help or the council's permission for where he's going," the physician said sadly.

Ben Barriah looked at him in sudden alarm. "You mean—"

"What did you expect would happen with nothing to eat for days but the thinnest soup and a crumb of stale bread? And even that he gives away to others. How long can a man live on prayer alone?"

"I . . . I did not know. They told me . . . they told me he

was provided for. He is an important man—"

"Evidently not as important as those willing to draw their swords against Rome."

The stunned Zealot passed his hand before his eyes. "I . . . I will see what I can do." Suddenly his hand dropped. He straightened. "Why should he be any different from the rest?" he said angrily. "It might never have come to this if he had lent his will to our cause in the beginning. We could have been strong, there would have been less confusion if he had led the way. He is always quoting Hillel. 'Do not withdraw from the community.' But what has he done? He's turned his back on us. Well, let him live in his world of words. Let his Torah sustain him."

"Your uncle is dying," Solomon ben Ya'ish said. "Do you want to see him or not?"

"Yes . . . yes, of course."

The room was dark. The figure of a man lay still upon the bed. Ben Barriah blinked in the dusky light, straining to make out the features of his uncle. The robust figure was shrunken now, the bearded face thin and somehow different. But everyone looked different now. Fear and famine had changed the very complexion of Jerusalem.

His voice when he spoke was hardly more than a whisper. "Nephew . . . is it you?"

"Yes . . ."

"Forgive me for asking you to come here. I know . . . how important your duties are . . . and I do not wish . . . your reputation to be tarnished . . . by consorting . . . in these quarters. I know what you . . . and your people . . . think of me."

Ben Barriah bowed his head.

"It is difficult to speak. But I must . . . I want . . . to tell you . . . you were right. And now you must hold firm . . . against the ungodly."

The Zealot nodded tearfully. "Yes . . . yes . . ."

"Too late . . . I realize my error. May the Eternal One, blessed be His Holy Name, judge me with mercy. May it be His will and command."

Solomon ben Ya'ish coughed.

"I must not . . . go on so. You have your work to do . . . and I . . . have mine. Mine, it seems, is to prepare for a journey which we all must take sooner or later."

"Uncle . . ."

"Sshh. I know what is coming. That is why I have sent for you. It is the Law that the dead may not stay even one night in the Holy City. Yet even now the bodies of those who have fallen or who have starved to death pollute our beloved Jerusalem. . . ."

"We have no choice—"

"I know . . . I know. May the Lord understand and forgive. But I beg you . . . do not allow my corpse to add to this corruption. As I have striven within my lifetime to keep the laws of our faith, help me now in death not to transgress."

"What is it you want?"

"Let my mortal remains be carried to the Mount of Olives, where your own father lies buried . . . there to await the coming of the Messiah and the New Age. 'For behold, a day of the Lord cometh . . . and His feet shall stand in that day upon the Mount of Olives. . . .'"

Ben Barriah looked at Solomon ben Ya'ish. "Even if I could get him through, there is a legion posted there. They would kill whoever was foolhardy enough to cross over, and likely throw the body to the dogs."

"Rabban Johanan's companions will carry their teacher to the Mount," the physician said. "They do not care for their own lives—they have already said as much—and perhaps their piety will inspire kindness."

Ben Barriah laughed harshly. "Kindness? Jerusalem is ringed with crosses. Above the moaning of children crying for food you can hear the gasps of crucified men and the screams of those being tortured. How like my uncle to worry about a final resting place while we are fighting for our existence." He sighed. "Never mind. I will do what I can. You are sure there is no hope?"

Ben Ya'ish shook his head. "It is a wonder he has survived this long." But after the Zealot had gone, he turned to his patient with a grin. "Not bad. You almost had me fooled. You do talk a lot, you know, for a dying man."

Aliterus sighed happily. "With my last breath I would not cut short such a scene. By the gods—excuse me—it was good to work again! What an improvisation! I wanted to get in that bit you told me about no worms eating the bodies of those buried on the Mount of Olives, but I hadn't the chance. Pity. It would have been a tasty touch. Never mind. I was brilliant enough, don't you think? What pathos! I've always known I had the feel for tragedy."

"You'd better get up before Rabban Johanan comes in and finds us in his bedchamber. I've managed to gather the things I need for that potion I told you about. It will make the rabbi sleep for several hours, and better still, slow down his heart so that he will appear to be dead. He is pale enough, I think. There is no need for the face paint you have suggested."

"Have you told the others?"

"Only Eliezer ben Hyrcanus. It is better if the rest believe he is really dead. Eliezer says Rabban Johanan has often talked of visiting Jabneh, where his mother was born. It is a pleasant seaside town, and—miraculously—untouched by the war. If Titus will let them settle there..."

"Pray God he will. I have written a letter that must be delivered to Josephus. But most important is the safe conduct in Titus's own hand. That should get them through."

"You could have used it yourself. If you managed to sneak past our own guards and revealed yourself to the legionaries—"

"I haven't the strength of limb or heart for such daring," the actor replied with a careless shrug. "I am too faint at this point to do more than rest in the care of the God of Israel."

"You are truly faint?"

"No more than anyone else, I suppose." Aliterus gave a sudden guffaw. "I have always refrained from eating before a performance," he said, "but this is ridiculous!"

One day later, word was given out that Johanan ben Zakkai had passed away. A great mourning went up in the city, and John and Simon, seeing how respected the rabbi had been, had no choice but to let the small group carrying his casket advance to the breach in the wall. One of the guards, however, not from Jerusalem, demanded that the body be uncovered. "Would you stare at the dead?" someone asked in horror. "Just making sure he really is dead," the guard replied, and would have run his sword through ben Zakkai's body had not ben Barriah come up then. Brusquely he pushed the man's arm aside. "Let him pass unscarred," he said hoarsely, averting his eyes from the pale, still face in the coffin. "But—" the guard started to protest. "Let him pass!" ben Barriah thundered. And so the body was carried through.

From a tower of the besieged wall, Aliterus watched the small group of scholars with their precious burden advance toward the waiting Romans. He saw Eliezer ben Hyrcanus go forward and speak to one of the soldiers. Something passed hands. The soldier gestured for the legionaries to take hold of the casket. Another soldier was sent running for Josephus. The Romanized Judean soon appeared and took the note, which he quickly read. As the legionaries led the small group of scholars away, Josef looked searchingly toward the wall that separated him from those he had once called his countrymen. With the tribune Nicanor at his side, he rode toward the wall and then back and forth beneath it, looking upwards as though searching for something or someone.

"There he goes again," a voice behind Aliterus said. The actor turned round as the boy pushed forward to the edge of the wall. He was no more than thirteen or fourteen years of age, a dark lad who most likely would have been thin even without the present famine. His big, dark eyes were bright with bitter anger as he watched Josef and Nicanor circling before the wall. " 'Put an end to your resistance, you wretched people,' " the boy mocked. " 'Do not compel Titus, who is in reality the Messiah come to save you—do not compel your kind savior to destroy you and your city!' " The boy looked at Aliterus. "Why doesn't someone kill him?"

Before Aliterus could answer, one of the armed men on the tower said, "Too far away. Watch, boy. See how carefully he has judged the distance. He stays just beyond the reach of our arrows—that's how much he loves and trusts his 'beloved fellow Judeans.' "

"He never was stupid," Aliterus murmured.

"What?"

"Out of range, is he?" the boy said, his eyes still on the figures below. Without another word he looked around, found a large stone, and fitting it to his sling, sent the missile flying. The stone hit its target squarely; Josef was knocked from his horse. Seeing this, others began to throw rocks and stones. Nicanor, rushing to Josef's aid, was struck in the shoulder by a Zealot arrow. A group of legionaries now ran forward, and under this cover Nicanor and Josef were carried back to the Roman camp. Nothing remained on the ground below but scattered stones and rocks and arrows. Aliterus looked around him. The boy was gone.

It was the middle of June, and four earthwork ramps had been completed. Two had been set against the Antonia, two against the wall of the Upper City. Until the start of the war the tower called the Antonia, high on the terrace above the northwest corner of the Temple enclosure, had been headquarters for the Roman garrison in Jerusalem. While the Fifth Legion had been busy building its platforms here, John's men had been tunneling underground, supporting the tunnels with the "sacred timber" John had appropriated from the Temple. The Judeans waited now until the legionaries brought their engines up on the platforms and then set fire to their own wooden props underground. As the props burnt away, the entire tunnel collapsed, the Roman platforms falling into the cavity with a thunderous crash. A dense cloud of smoke and dust arose; then, suddenly, a brilliant flame broke through, and as the Romans watched their work swallowed up in fire, the Judeans began to cheer.

It was Simon's turn now. The Romans still had two ramps constructed against the wall and had already brought up their batterers on this side. But Simon's followers streamed onto the ramps, fought their way to the engines, and set them on fire. As the flames shot up, legionaries came running from their camps to the rescue, but more Jews advanced from the wall to stop them. The fire spread from the engines to the platforms, and the Romans began to withdraw. With Simon before them, Jerusalem's defenders charged straight into the Roman camp, their number swelled now by reinforcements from the city. They fought long and hard, but, overwhelmed at last by the sheer number of their foe, they were driven back into the city. For John and Simon, however, their arms around each other's shoulders, the battle had been a victory. All the labor of the legions had, in a single day, been rendered useless.

Titus held a council of war.

"I say we bring the whole army into action," one of his officers suggested grimly. "A full-scale assault."

"We must rebuild the platforms," another said.

Titus did not reply. He looked to Tiberius Alexander, his chief of staff and most trusted adviser.

"Blockade the city," Tiberius Alexander said now. "Prevent the Jews from making sallies—and most important, from bringing in any food. Leave them alone in their Holy City, and they will starve to death there—or kill each other off as before."

"I don't like letting our men remain idle," Titus said. "This setback will prove demoralizing without some action to counter it."

"Then rebuild the platforms. But meanwhile throw a ring around the city."

"Impossible." Josef spoke up now. "You can't encircle Jerusalem with an unbroken line of soldiers. The size of the area and the difficult terrain make that highly impractical. The presence of the legionaries would tempt, not discourage, more sallies—and there is always the danger of the Sicarii making holes in the line. Even if you block the known paths, there are many secret ways out—I myself know only a few. There is always the possibility that provisions could be smuggled in."

"No," Titus said firmly. "No one must leave the city—and nothing must be smuggled into it. Tiberius Alexander is right. We must build our own wall around Jerusalem."

"But—"

"Not a wall of men, Josephus. An airtight siege wall of your own Judean earth. I must force these Jews to abandon all hope of survival and to surrender their city. In any event, if they do not, their hunger will make them weak soldiers. Yes, that's it. We will squeeze the life from Jerusalem. . . ." He jumped up. "There is no time to lose. The wall must be started today. Now."

"But it will take months."

"No, it won't. We shall have a contest, divide up the work among the units. Whoever finishes his section first shall receive my reward. When that is done, we will resume construction of the platforms."

One of the officers sighed. "It is a formidable task. A wall around Jerusalem . . ." He shook his head.

"Of course it is formidable," Titus said cheerfully. "Hadn't you heard? Little tasks are beneath the dignity of Rome."

The legionaries, as Titus had known they would, reacted with enthusiasm to the "contest." In three days the wall was finished; a great, ugly, earthen rampart almost five miles in circumference, coiling around Jerusalem far enough away to be out of range but near enough to constrict the freedom of the besieged inhabitants. There were thirteen garrisons at intervals along Titus's wall. The guards drew lots for periods of sleep, and all day and all night long they patrolled the space between the forts.

But hunger conquered fear. The troops had an ample supply of food that was brought from Syria and the neighboring provinces; and the soldiers would often stand by the wall, eating and drinking excessively in plain sight of the famished Judeans. Inside the city, children's bellies were swollen with emptiness; people fell in the alleys or crumpled at home. The streets were filled with corpses; it was impossible to bury them all. There were fights—killings—over a grain of corn. Gold was worthless; sacks of it were traded for a small bag of barley or wheat. Houses were broken into and searched for food, suspected hoarders beaten to make them divulge the whereabouts of their cache of crumbs. Desperate, many attempted to flee, pretending to join a sally against the soldiers and then running to the Roman lines, or making their way out by means of the numerous hidden passageways that led from the ancient city.

In the Syrian camp one deserter was discovered picking gold coins out of his own excrement, the conveying of one's wealth by swallowing it being an ancient practice. Immediately the rumor went round that Jews were arriving stuffed with gold, and it became a sport, if not a passion, for the Arab and Syrian units to get hold of refugees before the legionaries spotted them, whereupon they cut them open and ransacked their bellies. History notes that Titus, upon learning of this, delivered an admonition he felt appropriate to the occasion.

TEN

The city was wreathed in silence; it enfolded Jerusalem like a shroud. The dead lay quiet in the streets and houses, unburied, rotting under the silent summer sun. Quietly people moved about, searching for food, rifling the bodies of the fallen. The wind made no sound; there were no trees through which the mountain breezes might rustle; the countryside was quiet, bare, stripped of its wood and groves. Not a single tree or bush within a ten-mile radius had been left standing in the Roman search for timber. There were no birds, for there was nowhere they might perch or build their nests. There were no animals; dogs and rats were hunted and eaten as the law of life took precedence over the laws of *kashrut*. July crawled away, the days long and hot and silent, silent. . . .

But the silence on this August morning was special and strange. It awoke Aliterus, set him to wondering. Hunger had not dimmed his brain; after the first torturous days of doing without, he found he had no need for the quantities of food he had once thought it necessary to consume. He was hungry— his body groaned with emptiness; but his mind had become an even nimbler dancer than before. The outlines of shadows were painfully sharp. Colors, shapes, ideas, had become flashing images that had never before burned so brightly. He almost seemed to know what people would say before they came to say it—indeed, he felt as if he knew what was inside their heads without their saying a single word. Deprived of mortal sustenance, his senses were feeding on something else. They had been honed by his hunger. He understood now why holy men fasted.

He was beyond fatigue. He felt, on the one hand, as if he were going to die, and on the other hand, he knew he had never been stronger. Was it some power received from the God

461

of Israel that kept him going? Or was it all an illusion? Was
he, in fact, a raving, dying man?

He wandered around the empty courtyard of the house of
Johanan ben Zakkai, seeming to see the scholars and sages
assembled there. They were all gone now but himself and the
girl Hadassah. Not all the household had escaped to Jabneh.
Many were dead. Solomon ben Ya'ish was still in the city.
Sometimes Aliterus saw him, a ghost of a man wandering from
house to house, administering to the sick and dying as best he
could. Where did he get his strength? What kept him going?

How do any of us continue to go on, Aliterus wondered.
And why? Anyone with sense would know enough to die.

There was so little left. Nothing, in fact. John had broken
open the Temple storehouses and distributed to the crowd every
bit of sacred corn and the oil the priests kept for the burnt
offerings. There was nothing left now. For the people. For the
altar.

That was it. That was the cause of this silence.

Every day, at dawn, the silver trumpets rang out from Temple Hill, heralding the morning sacrifice. Every evening the
silver trumpets sounded again. Today, this morning, there had
been no such sound. It was the seventeenth day of the Hebrew
month of Tammuz; and for the first time in generations, the
God of Israel had received no sacrifice in the Temple of Jerusalem. Like His people in the city, the Lord went without.

"What would become of the world if there were no Temple
service?" Joshua ben Hananiah had once asked even as Aliterus
had. "What will become of us if the Temple, where the sins
of Israel are atoned for, is laid waste?"

"The world will always be sustained by Torah," Johanan
ben Zakkai had answered. "As for atonement, there is something better than the slaying of a lamb, and that is acts of
loving-kindness. 'For I desire mercy,' sayeth the Lord, 'and
not sacrifice.' By Torah, by acts of loving-kindness, and by
prayer, both the world and our people will forever be sustained."

"It is most significant," Josef reported excitedly. "Either there
are no priests to perform the sacrifice or no lambs to be offered
upon the altar. They have got to feel the shame of it. And they
must believe finally that the Lord has deserted them. How
could they even hope to have His favor now? Would God save

a city where He did not receive His due offerings? Now is the time to make a move."

"The platforms are finished," Nicanor said. "The men are tired; their strength has been sapped by toil. And they are frustrated by these constant hit-and-run skirmishes that have no decisive effect or end. Morale is not high. They need a good fight."

Titus looked to Tiberius Alexander.

"I don't know," the general said. "My impulse is to wait."

"They will try to burn the platforms," Nicanor said. "And there is no more timber—you may be sure of that. If the platforms go before we have the chance to take the offensive—"

"Yes, yes I know. . . ."

"Josephus feels the Jerusalemites will be despondent—godless, if you will—now that the Temple sacrifice cannot be performed," Titus said. He was impatient for a definite answer.

"Perhaps. But—"

"But what, man?" the young Roman snapped. "By the gods, they are your race! Don't you know your own kind?"

Tiberius Alexander's face grew red, but his eyes betrayed no emotion. "I understand," he said slowly, "how tedious this siege has become. The soldiers are anxious for a showdown. Rome beckons. But it has been my experience that calamity only whets the Jew's appetite for battle. You may discover that this race has an inner courage that surfaces when you least expect it, to rise above faction, famine, war, and disasters beyond number." He shrugged. "If it were up to me, I would give them what they want. Not out of natural sympathy, as you might suppose, but because it is the surest way to defeat them. Small in number, untrained, unfed, without the resources and equipment of any self-respecting army, they somehow manage to stand strong against a common foe. But left to themselves . . . my dear Titus, give these Jews their precious Judea— I mean, simply turn your back on them—and in a few years they will destroy themselves completely. That is because they have only one real enemy, and that is themselves."

The tower known as Antonia was razed. John's forces had put up a gallant defense, joined by Simon's men in close combat. But gradually the rebels were forced back into the Temple. They held their ground there, and Titus's men finally withdrew, unable to penetrate the holy complex.

Titus ordered the Antonia torn down and a broad roadway constructed by which his army could mount to the top of the hill. The Judeans placed on the Temple roof their own crude engines for throwing stones and darts, and they set fire to the part of the northern portico that had adjoined the Antonia, thus cutting away that which, left standing, might have provided a platform for the Romans.

Some legionaries impulsively climbed to the broad, flat roof of the western portico. There had been a bunch of Jews busy in this area earlier in the day, but they had gone away, looking tired and easy to beat. The soldiers did not realize until too late that the Jews had been packing dry kindling wood, pitch, and asphalt between the rafters and the ceiling of the portico. When the roof was crowded with Romans, the first of many flaming arrows came flying through the air, setting it on fire. The soldiers died screaming; some jumped to their deaths while their companions below watched helplessly. The portico's triple row of graceful columns, its gold-leaf ornamentation and cedarwood ceiling, lay in a tangled black wreck. The Court of Gentiles was no more. But the Temple proper had been untouched.

Hadassah cried out, the sound coming from deep within, from the dark red center of her being. She bit her lip, closing her eyes to the pain, trying to keep silent. She did not want to disturb Sheptai. The physician had pulled the arrow from his leg, cleaned and wrapped it, administered a potion to make him sleep.

"He is faint from the loss of blood," Solomon ben Ya'ish had told her. "I do not think there is infection. He must rest and—I know how absurd it is to say this—but he must have some nourishment. I have nothing to give you—I am sorry. Perhaps there are some herbs. . . . You might brew some water . . . make a broth. . . ." He had turned away. What could he say? There were no herbs. There was nothing. The ground had long been plucked bare of any blade of grass. Weeds, roots, twigs stripped of their outer bark for the succulent green flesh inside—what hadn't the hungry people of Jerusalem put into their mouths?

"Pity your time has not come," he had murmured. "You could feed them both from your breast—the babe and your husband. I'd milk you myself, God help me, to feed the children. What am I saying? You will have no milk. You will be dry like the others. And the baby will be—" He had stopped himself. There was little chance Hadassah's child would be born alive. He had already seen too many stillbirths this summer. But why add to her suffering? So he had patted her on the shoulder and said, "I am going to the Temple. Many have congregated there who are sick and fearful. I must do what I can to help them. If you should see Aliterus, make him understand where I have gone." Her body had seemed to jerk under his hand. The movement made him study her more closely.

"Do you know where the midwife lives? What, she is dead? Gone? Then listen to me now. If it begins, come to me in the Temple, in the Court of Women. It is early, but when the body has been abused . . ." He had broken off. "Sheptai will recover. He simply needs to regain his strength."

She had nodded, gritting her teeth against the stabbing pain in her back. The physician was needed by others. She must not keep him. She could look after Sheptai and herself. But Sheptai seemed to grow worse through the night. His lips were dry no matter how much water she gave him to drink, and he groaned and mumbled words, his head swaying from side to side. His forehead was hot, his breathing labored. After a time she could do nothing for him because the pains in her back became stronger and came more often, shuddering waves that swept through her whole body.

She had never seen a birth, but she had heard the women talking. People always talked more freely around her, as if they thought that because she never spoke she could not understand what was said. So now, when the time came, she squatted on the floor over the blanket she had spread there— there was no straw; that had long ago been eaten—bracing herself against a stool on one side and the table on the other. And as the man on the bed moaned in his fever she groaned in her labor, grunting and pushing until the baby was out, a small, still lump whose arms did not move, whose legs did not kick. She bit off the cord that bound her to the tiny corpse, cleaned herself, and tenderly washed the body of her dead child. She threw the blanket into the fire and turned back finally to Sheptai. His fever was gone, but he seemed to sleep only a dream away from death, so still did he lie there, so faintly did he breathe.

• • •

The men kicked open the door. "I told you I smelled cooking!" one exclaimed. "Look! There's broth on the fire! And bones on that plate! While the rest of us starve!"

Startled, the girl had turned around as they entered, but she was not in the least afraid, even as they advanced with murder in their eyes. She nodded eagerly and, running, fetched another plate, which she brought to them.

The men converged on her and then, suddenly, as one, withdrew. "It—it's a baby," one gasped. "Or what's left of one. A . . . a baby . . ."

Hadassah nodded energetically. She held the plate out, beckoning them to eat. But the men had backed off, making for the door. Horrified, they could not take their eyes from her. "Lord help us," one whispered, tears streaming down his face. "That it has come to this!"

Hadassah cocked her head to one side, her gaze a curious stare because they would not share her meal.

"She's mad," someone said; and then they were gone.

"Hadassah . . . Hadass . . ." Sheptai called weakly from the bed in the corner. She put down the plate and ran to him. "Is . . . someone here?" he murmured. "I thought . . . I heard men."

She shook her head and put her finger to his lips. Then, in a calm, housewifely manner, she began to feed him the broth she had prepared.

Aliterus stumbled through the sunbaked streets of the city, looking, like everyone else, for something to eat. People staggered alongside or behind him; sometimes one would stop and hammer at a door like a drunken man, begging for food. But no doors opened until small gangs, desperate, broke into the houses or shops, more often than not to be met by a roomful of corpses. Open-mouthed with hunger, Aliterus watched men and women put their teeth to anything, even filth picked up from the street. Faint and sick at heart, the actor wandered about, pushing past men fighting over a scrap to swallow, until he found himself on the outskirts of the city. He sat down on a large rock and was resting his head in his hands, feeling like a man who had just walked through Hades, when he caught sight of a boy emerging, it seemed, from the earth itself. He looked up. The boy was carrying a dead rat by the tail. He saw Aliterus, stopped, and drew forth a knife.

"Well, if it isn't young David," Aliterus remarked. He gestured toward the knife. "You're very versatile. What happened to the sling?"

"In my pocket," the boy said, recognizing Aliterus from the wall. "How did you know my name?"

Aliterus managed a laugh. "My mental powers have become as fine as your aim. Where did you get that—thing?"

"The sewer. You can always find something in the sewers." He brought the knife up. "If you're thinking of trying to take this from me—"

"My dear boy, I wouldn't dream of it. The feast is yours. I advise you to hurry, though. There are others whose appetite is not so delicate as mine. They'll tear you apart just for the tail."

"Let them try. I know how to take care of myself."

"Yes, I guess you do," Aliterus said, and fainted.

When he awoke he saw that the boy had built a small fire. Before he could say anything, the lad was at his side with something that looked like a piece of roasted meat on a stick. Without thinking, Aliterus grabbed the stick and stuffed the morsel in his mouth and gulped it down. His tongue was burned, and the roof of his mouth felt sore—even his teeth hurt—but he said hoarsely, "More. More."

The boy grinned. "Guess your stomach isn't as delicate as you thought. Here, have some water."

"More food . . . please. . . ."

"Drink fast. Isn't so bad after all, is it?"

"What?"

"The chicken."

"Chicken?" Aliterus groaned. "Oh, no . . ."

"Not as good as dog—I call that lamb—but with plenty of salt and pepper you can eat anything."

"Where would you get pepper? Only kings eat pepper."

"Then I have stolen from kings."

"Street brat."

The boy nodded, unperturbed. "It takes one, they say, to know one."

Aliterus laughed hoarsely. He held out his hand, and the boy gave him another piece of "chicken."

"You're not a Jerusalemite, are you?" the boy asked.

"I have not lived here all my life, if that's what you mean."

"You're not from the Galilee either. I can tell by the way you talk."

"You have an accent yourself. Where do you come from?"

"Alexandria, in the place they call the Delta. That's where all the Jews live. Or at least they did until they were murdered by the soldiers. I learned about the streets—and the sewers—in Alexandria."

"Yes, I remember hearing of the massacre.... Poppea thought it dreadful...."

"Who?"

"Someone I used to know . . . a long time ago. . . ." He leaned back against the rock and closed his eyes. Food—though it was best not to think what it was—had put warmth in his veins and a new fire in his brain. He felt dizzy. He uttered a short laugh. "A sewer banquet! Why," he went on dreamily, "I have been guest of honor at dinners where the fare comprised a hundred courses, each more opulent than the one before . . . where slaves of the most refined and gentle nature— not ragamuffins like you, but boys who could recite Homer better than their masters—would come and pedicure our toenails, bending their heads that we might wipe our hands in their lovely, perfumed hair....

"I have dined on peahen eggs and orioles . . . bears roasted whole . . . pastry tall as buildings. . . . I've drunk wine guaranteed to be one hundred years old—the genuine Falernian article, marked and all. Just think . . . wine lasts longer than men. Well, I've had more of it spilled under my table than most have in their cellars. I have been feted by millionaires, senators, knights, and Caesar himself, the little prick. I have eaten like a king in my time . . . loved like a satyr . . . seen my name scribbled with praises on the walls of a hundred piss-pot alleys! 'Bravo, Aliterus! The King of Clowns!'" He fell silent. "Imagine," he said finally, "what a state the world is in . . . when a man who can make people laugh . . . is as prized as Corinthian bronze...."

The boy snorted derisively. "From what I've heard, every beggar on the road was driven from a palace, and every slave is the son of a king. My father was a potter. I do not know what you were before the war, but I think my father did more honest work than you."

Aliterus looked up at the sky. "No doubt," he said. "No doubt."

• • •

Titus ordered the gates of the Temple set on fire. He had already put the torch to the remaining colonnade, and for more than a week the rams and batterers had pounded against the wall, but to no avail. The legionaries' ladders were pushed away; the rebels managed to kill every man who climbed up, and in the end they even captured the Roman standards.

As the soldiers piled burning faggots against the gates leading to the Temple courts, the silver and gold covering the woodwork melted and ran. In moments, a ring of fire had surrounded the Holy Place. For a day and a night the flames took possession, while Judeans within and those outside the wall of fire could do nothing but watch in utter helplessness.

"I'm tired," the man from Gischala said. He was with Simon in the High Priest's chamber. "Blood and killing, left, right, before you, behind you—all around nothing but death and the dying. . . . Gischala, Gamala, Jerusalem . . . you, the priests, the Romans . . . keeping the food from babes in order to feed fighting men. . . . I'm tired . . . and I'm sick of it all."

"You've lost your faith," Simon said.

"Never had much to begin with. Not in the Lord, anyways. Can't see what He's done for any of us. And I don't expect He'll give me word now how to beat Titus. No, He's never come and chatted with me like He did with old Noah or the others. Has God talked to you, Simon?"

"Yes."

"Bull."

Simon looked at him briefly. "You're drunk."

"Not yet." John held up the silver urn, turning it in his hands so that the light played off the shining metal. "Sacred wine," he said. "The priests' own special store. Not half so good as what we have in the Galilee—that'll put you under soon enough. This stuff takes forever. Come, Simon, drink with me. It isn't food, but it will warm your belly. Put a fire in your eyes bright as the one burning outside."

"Why not?"

"Good! Good! And here's a golden cup. . . . How do you like that, eh? Silver and gold. Nothing but the best."

Simon stared at the goblet. "I am uneasy with such fine things. I never wanted wealth for myself. . . ."

"I know, I know."

"It was always . . . for the people. . . ."

"The people." John let out a laugh. "Every time some fellow like you starts talking about the people, I get the notion you think you're championing one big, helpless, kindly, put-upon creature. One face, one set of eyes, one pair of hands all reaching for the same thing. The noble, downtrodden people. Lord, boy, the people is you and me, and we're different as can be! 'The people'—" He stopped. "Forget it. Pay no mind. You know, they say when Adam planted the vine, Satan was there to help. The Evil One slaughtered a lamb, a lion, a pig, and a monkey, and made the blood of each flow under the grapes. That is why before a man takes a drink he is gentle as a lamb. One cup, and he is strong as a lion. A few more, and he becomes a pig. And finally he makes a monkey of himself."

Simon smiled.

"You're not angry. Good!"

"As you yourself have said, there are others to fight besides ourselves."

John shook his head. "It's over." He looked around the room. "This place is finished."

"It can't be. It is the Lord's House."

"It is my house! A soldier's tent, that's what it is. Legionaries camped in the courts outside—and the Sanctuary our garrison. Our battleground."

"The Lord has not left his people. We fight for what is right."

"This place has turned you into a priest, Simon. Or better still, a rabbi. You ought to take your place in the Chamber of Hewn Rock with ben Zakkai and the others."

"Johanan ben Zakkai is dead."

"As we all will be soon."

"Not I."

"You are so sure?"

"I fight for what is right. Let your wine make you a lion. My strength comes from the Lord. 'Do not let my people be slaves,' He has said to me. And I have heard. And so I act." He nodded at the door. "They'll put out the fire in the morning, then clear a path.... We must not give them the chance to come forward. We must attack as soon as the fire is out."

"Agreed. There is a chance we can fight our way out. Down in the city it might go better for us."

"That means giving up the Temple."

John shrugged. "It is already lost—unless the God of Israel

cares to whisk what's left up into the clouds. Besides, I don't want to die here. I'm an old man; I don't mind dying. But not here. I've had enough of this place." He paused. "I've faced Titus before. He respects bravery. You and I would not fare so badly. Of course he's got Josef around, and Josef hates my guts—as well he should." He laughed. "I did my best to kill the Jerusalemite when he was governor of the Galilee. I never did like him. But Titus plays fair with officers. The Romans are funny that way. They think nothing of slaughtering civilians, but enemy generals get decent treatment. Strange, the military mind . . ."

Simon raised the priestly goblet to his lips. "If we get out of here . . . I'd like to take my family and those close to me back to the wilderness. If we could live in peace there, not as slaves . . ."

"Back to the Masada?"

Simon put the goblet down. "No. Anyway, I'd have to kill Eleazar ben Ya'ir first."

"So?"

Simon shook his head. "No man can kill him," he said slowly, "I was ready to once. But my hand would not go to my sword . . ."

"Maybe you're afraid he'll kill you. I've seen the grandson of Judah the Galilean in action. He rides out of the hills like the wrath of God." He sighed. "I wish we had him with us now. Wouldn't it be grand to see him swoop down on Titus at the head of a column of angels, riding like the wind with his crazy Sons of Light!"

Simon stared at him. "Do you think he is the Messiah?"

"Why, no," John replied, surprised. "Just a damn good fighter. The Messiah!"

"My hand would not go to my sword . . . and I hated him. . . . The Lord knows I hated him, for all we spoke of being brothers. Son of Light, the Holy Ones call him. He brushes it aside, uneasy in their love, unwilling to take command. What does he doubt?" He looked at John. "Eleazar ben Ya'ir will not come to Jerusalem. Not because of the council's decree or because he fears me. Even when we were making our plans together, he intended to stay outside the city. He said his presence was a . . . pollution. He said the city must be destroyed in any case. He said there must be a New Jerusalem, cleansed of all the old sins. That's what I wanted to do . . . build a new Jerusalem. But he couldn't see that."

"Well, maybe he'll let you come back to the Masada after all. They say he never turns aside those who come to him. Who knows? I may soon be asking myself. It's not a bad idea. If we could get out of here in one piece and make it to the Masada . . . why, a bit of rest and food—I hear they have everything there—and my boys and I would be fit soon enough to give this thing another try! All we have to do is wait a bit, make them think we're all through, and then—"

Simon grinned. "I thought you were tired. I thought you were sick of it all."

John sighed. "I am tired, and I am sick of it. But what choice is there? By what right do these men of Rome come into our land? They say they are here to teach us a lesson. Well, by the Almighty, let them learn one too!"

At dawn the next morning, the rebels, with what seemed new strength and confidence, plunged through the East Gate against the Romans camped in the Outer Temple. The Romans closed rank, sheltering themselves behind a wall of locked shields, but the raiding party had got the best of them. Anticipating the collapse of the line, Titus, who had been watching from the site of the Antonia, rushed to the rescue. After three hours of hard fighting, the Romans finally overpowered the partisans, forcing them to withdraw once more into the Inner Temple. At this point, one of the legionaries snatched up a blazing piece of wood and, climbing on another soldier's back, hurled the brand through a window in the northern part of the Sanctuary, where it landed somewhere in the chain of small storage rooms that surrounded the Holy Place. In a short time, the little rooms and the treasures they held were ablaze. Priests, Levites, Zealots—all rushed to put out the fire, with no thought for their own lives. Insane with fury, John and Simon slashed with their swords at any Roman within reach, spurring their followers on to renewed battle. But the fire had excited the legionaries; they sensed the day was theirs, and they charged ahead, falling on the Jews who had taken refuge in the place they thought protected by heaven itself, slaughtering people even in the midst of prayer. The steps of the terrace on which the marble Sanctuary stood became clogged with bodies, and round the altar the heap of corpses grew higher and higher.

The Holy Place itself had not yet caught fire, and the Holy of Holies was still untouched, but the flame and smoke and heat from the burning chambers surrounding them was intense. Realizing there was little time left, Titus led his staff inside the building and, with the aid of the one called Josephus, had his men remove certain treasures for his own safekeeping, to be delivered to Caesar as proof of victory. Looting on a less official scale was meanwhile going on right and left as soldiers surged into the burning chambers to grab the money and treasures that were legend. As Titus and his aides withdrew, someone pushed a torch into the hinges of the great gold entrance doors. From within a flame shot up, and the Room of God became an inferno.

Below in the city the people looked up and saw their Temple burning. All of Temple Hill seemed enveloped in flames from top to bottom; it appeared to be boiling up from its very roots. Through the roar of the flames they could hear the war cry of the Roman legions, the shouts of the Temple's defenders encircled with fire and sword, the groans of the fallen, the shrieks of those cut off above. And the cries from the hill, from the top of Mount Moriah, were answered from the crowded streets below as Judeans began to moan and wail, seeing their Sanctuary in flames.

After a violent struggle the partisans had managed to burst through into the Outer Temple and from there down into the city. Many priests had in the end behaved with more courage than their detractors would have cared to believe. Some of the younger ones tore the gold spikes from the Sanctuary roof and threw them at the Romans. Then, seeing they were about to die by the sword, holding hands and crying out the name of the Lord, they leaped together into the fire.

One colonnade of the Outer Temple remained untouched. Thousands had taken refuge here, mostly women and children and those who were ill or injured. Despite the carnage and destruction all around, Solomon ben Ya'ish moved calmly among his patients, speaking softly to them, comforting this one or telling that one how to care for his wound. Aliterus had said that Titus was a fair man—an "honorable boy," the actor had put it. Surely the Roman would spare the mass of sick and hungry people huddled here. But the legionaries were beyond instructions now, or possibly they had been given none. Perhaps the fury of the soldiers at the humiliations they had suffered—including Cestius's retreat years earlier, the boiling oil thrown at them in Jotapata, the slaughtering of their night guards by Sicarii, the rocks thrown at them by mere children,

ew brats"—together with their ingrained hatred for this
rac with their Faceless God, had swept away whatever natural
humanity these men might have possessed. The colonnade was
fired from below. No one escaped.

Fighting spread to the city as the Romans pursued John and
Simon. Having seen the advantages of fire, the legionaries set
many buildings ablaze, butchering anyone who ran out. In the
days that followed, Jerusalem would be totally destroyed as
her conquerors indulged in an orgy of blood and fire. The
Romans would bring their standards into the smoldering Temple area and sacrifice to them there, hailing Titus as *imperator*.
Their banners would also be set upon the towers of the wall
surrounding Jerusalem. Over one million children of Israel
would perish in the course of this long siege and battle. Eleven
thousand prisoners would die of starvation. Of the nearly one
hundred thousand left alive, the handsomest and tallest would
be kept for the triumphal procession in Rome. Others would
be sent to the mines or the galleys, and great numbers would
perish in the arena. So many slaves would be taken that the
world market would suffer a ten-year glut; and the soldiers
would leave Judea with so much loot that the price of gold
would be cut in half.

But for now the fires raged and the fighting went on. In the
houses, in the streets, in the ashes of the city, Judeans fought
and died, refusing still to yield, refusing to surrender.

They followed the boy through the sewer. "They won't search
here for a few days yet," David said, his voice echoing through
the darkness. "But the guards at the earthen wall may not be
standing so fast now. They will be looking toward the fire
instead of keeping their eyes to the ground. If we can get past
them—"

"If we first get out of here alive," Aliterus muttered. He
held his hand to his nose, trying not to gag.

"It will be worse tomorrow and the days that follow. Then
the stink will be of the dying as well as everything else."

Aliterus gazed after the boy, wondering how he knew so
much. But he said he'd lived through the Delta massacre,
perhaps in like fashion, by hiding in the sewers of Alexandria.

"Come on, come on," someone behind said. "I can't take much more of this."

A woman wept.

"You'll have to," the boy replied. "This tunnel is the longest one out of the city, but it will take us far from the soldiers. Once we're out, there are only the guards to worry about."

The small group shuffled behind him. A child whimpered in fear. Often there was the sound of wretching as people became nauseated by the stench and the slime, despite their empty stomachs. The sounds of war had retreated; the refugees moved in silence, in darkness, clutching at one another behind the stalwart boy whose step never faltered. At last, blinking at the light, like moles they emerged from the underground labyrinth. They were outside Jerusalem. The Temple was still burning, a crown of flame atop the smoking city, bright as blood against the fire-darkened sky. Some of the women began to weep again as men offered up prayers and lamentation.

"Quiet!" the boy hissed. He pointed, and they saw the guard in the distance, patrolling the ground between the earth wall's stations. The band of Judeans scattered among the rocks, waiting until the soldier had passed. Then, silently, a few at a time, they made their way past the patrol point into a ravine where they could hide until night. The boy stayed behind for some time. When he appeared at last, his knife was stained with blood. He wiped it without a word and stuck it into his belt.

"I will take you away from this," Aliterus murmured, moved to pity. "There need be no more war for you. We will go to Jabneh. You will be safe there. You will live with Johanan ben Zakkai and learn the Law and live in peace."

"Never!" the boy responded fiercely. "I am no coward to hide from Rome beneath the cloak of those who are too weak to be of any consequence. Everyone knows what women scholars are."

"You are only a boy—"

"No, it is you who are the child," David replied more calmly. "Go to your rabbis if you like. I will find John and Simon."

"They may be dead."

"Then there are others! In Jerusalem, I heard talk of the fortress Machaerus. They say the people there have sworn never to surrender. And there is another place, in the desert. They call it the Masada. The Sicarii are there, and they would rather die than submit to Caesar. I will go to them."

Aliterus shook his head. "It is over. Why can't you understand—"

"It is you who do not understand," David said. "It is not over. It will never be over—until Jerusalem is ours once again!"

ELEVEN

The tenth day of the Hebrew month of Ab—the very day and month that, centuries before, had seen the Temple burnt by the Babylonians—dawned hot and still in the desert wilderness. It was the end of August, a time of heavy, stifling heat and the dry wind the nomads called *hamsin*. But on this day, the wind held still and the sky seemed to darken early. A feeling of restlessness pervaded the Masada; uneasy, the people there went about their tasks as though awaiting some soon-to-come calamity. Even the children were fretful; they seemed bothered by something more than the heat.

Alexandra's scalp tingled. Since her return to the Masada and her marriage to Eleazar some months before, she had felt a sense of peace she had not known since childhood. On this morning, however, she had awakened with a strange, sick chill that would not let go. She was not ill; no, it was more like the feeling she'd had the day of the massacre in Caesarea and again in Tarichea. But there was no word from the scouts that Titus was advancing. How could there be? The legions were encamped around Jerusalem, waiting while the city bled itself in famine.

Jerusalem.

She raised her eyes to the sky and saw now the dark clouds forming to the North, the smoke spiraling up from the Holy City. Impulsively she ran to the northern palace to stand breathlessly on the terrace there, her body straining forward. A red haze lit the sky. There was little doubt in her mind now as to what it all meant.

She ran to find Eleazar. He had been in the western palace with Joav, but now he seemed to be alone there. He was pacing back and forth. She started to go to him when a voice stopped her.

"There is nothing you could have done, Son of Light. From

the God of Knowledge comes all that is and all that shall be. Before ever these things existed their design was established, and when, as is ordained, they come into being, it is in accord with this glorious design. It is part of the Mystery to come." Nathaniel stood in a corner of the room, his white-robed figure illuminated in the darkness of the shadows as by a beam of sunlight fallen through the window.

Eleazar shook his head. "I ought to be there. I am no different. Their sins are my sins. I ought to be with Simon now."

"In every age, a handful, a remnant—a few who hold fast to their faith—must remain. For their sake the Covenant endures. For their sake it is eternal."

"I am unclean! My hands are covered with blood!"

"Judgement is with the Lord, Eleazar. Trust in Him, as I do. The most mighty wisdom is that which trusts in the Almighty and leans on His great loving-kindness. Rejoice, my son! This day has been appointed from ancient times! Jerusalem has been the abode of Belial. It has been a stronghold of the ungodly, an abomination in the land, and a great blasphemy among the children of Israel. Let it be gone from us now. It is the will of the Lord."

Alexandra stole from the palace. Outside, the sky was red as blood, and people stood about staring up at it and talking together in low tones. They all seemed to know. Jerusalem was burning. The City of David, perhaps the Temple too, was in flames.

In the seaside town of Jabneh, Johanan ben Zakkai stood facing the east, gazing upwards at the strangely colored sky. Jabneh was quiet and pleasant, a far cry from the violent atmosphere of Jerusalem these last years. For some reason Jabneh had been untouched by the war and even by the careless destruction wrought by the procurators before that, as if its gentleness provoked a like response. It was a good place for scholars to congregate, a place where, disturbed by nothing more startling than the splendid sunsets over the sea, they might pursue their quiet studies and search for truth. More and more it seemed to Johanan ben Zakkai that the spoken tradition which was the wealth of the Pharisee rabbis and which had been so contemptuously dismissed by the Sadducee priests must be put in written order. The sayings of the sages—particularly the wisdom of Hillel—must be collected into a *Mishna*, or body of oral lore; together with *Halakoth*, the traditional statements of law; a *Midrash*, or exposition of the Five Books of Moses; and all the proverbs, parables, and narratives that were *Haggadoth*— or exposition of a non-halakic character. It would take years— it would take generations—but it must be begun; for this *Talmud*, this study, would guard the faith of Israel as no Temple or army of soldiers ever could.

Johanan ben Zakkai looked toward the east, where the House of the Lord and the Holy City were crumbling away, devoured in fire, consumed in blood. The great walls surrounding Jerusalem had not held back the foe. *But we will build a wall around Torah that no one can destroy*, he thought. His heart beat fast at the thought of the happy work ahead; still, as he gazed at the fiery horizon, he mourned for what was now forever lost.

Eliezer ben Hyrcanus had come out of the house, puzzled by the red-and-black sky. Seeing ben Zakkai standing so quietly, he hesitated, stopping before he reached the rabbi's side. But ben Zakkai seemed to have sensed his presence and said without turning, "Put ashes upon your head, my son. Rend your garments and remove your shoes. Today is a time of mourning."

"But of course it is," Eliezer ben Hyrcanus replied, wondering. "It is Tisha ba'Ab, the day of the destruction of Solomon's Temple by the Babylonians. Have you forgotten, master? We began the fast last night."

"I have not forgotten. Do as I say, my son. And tell the others that as we lament for that which was destoryed in our fathers' time, so now we must mourn that which is destroyed in our own time." He turned now, and the young man saw that while the rabbi was speaking softly, the tears had begun to course from his eyes. "The days of the Second Temple are no more," Johanan ben Zakkai said. "Jerusalem is taken from us again. Go. Tell the others, that they may weep for what is lost." He turned back to the fiery sky. "Weep, Zion," he whispered. "Weep . . ."

"Are they saints," Alexandra asked, "or madmen?"

Eleazar looked at the dancing men. The Essenes were in a frenzy of joy, in a very delirium of ecstasy. The prophecies had been revealed. The final battle of the Sons of Light and the Sons of Darkness would soon commence; the Messiahs of

Aaron and David—priest and king—would appear; and from the ashes of the Holy City, the New Jerusalem, like the phoenix of legend, would arise, reborn in virtuous splendor. The End of Days had begun.

Were they madmen? Or saints?

Eleazar shook his head. "I wish I knew."

They stood watching the jubilant dancers, she with curiosity, he with a look she had come to know but could not yet define. A group had gathered in the synagogue to mourn the destruction of Jerusalem and to offer prayers for the fallen. Whenever the Holy Brotherhood outside paused in their singing, the lamentations of those in the synagogue trailed out into the night.

"What will happen now that the war is over?" Alexandra asked. "I mean, to us?"

"We go on," he said simply. He turned to her, and even in the darkness she could see the torment in his eyes. "I knew Jerusalem must perish. I knew it long ago, not because of the prophecies—I knew it for myself." He sighed. "We must wait now. Wait, and hope they will forget about us."

"And then?"

"We begin again. It is not over, Alexandra. No matter what has befallen Jerusalem or the Temple. So long as some of us—so long as one of us—remains free, then someday all of us will be free."

She looked at him. The anguish was gone. His eyes were calm and sure; and she believed him and believed in him.

Jonatan came to stand at their side.

"You are not dancing?" There was no rancor in Eleazar's voice.

The Essene shook his head. "These events have made me think of Qumran. I confess I could sooner weep for the loss of the library of sacred books than for the Temple that Herod built."

"Well, I, for one, shed no tears for Jerusalem," Joav said, joining them now.

"No, I suppose not," Alexandra murmured.

But the giant redhead paid no attention to her. He was staring at the night sky that still glowed from the fires in the distance. "They laughed at us," he said slowly. "The Jerusalemites always laughed at us. They ate the wheat we grew, the fish we caught—and laughed at us for being farmers and fishermen while they were Hasmoneans and "*nashi*," great princes!

They said we did not keep the Law, yet when we came to the city with our hard-earned shekels for a Passover lamb, they nudged each other and winked and asked for twice what we had. And when we could not meet their price, they said we did not love the Lord and were bad Jews." He looked straight at Alexandra. "We had a little synagogue in Magdala. Not a grand place, but every stone of it was laid with loving hands. The *Kittim* burned it to the ground. Let others weep for Jerusalem. I weep for the synagogue of Magdala."

There was a pause; then Alexandra said, "My mother was a Jerusalemite. She loved the city, and I know it pained her not to live there. But she loved my father, and he would only live by the sea. She often spoke of Jerusalem, of its white glass and jellied wine, of its streets of shops and how as a girl she would wander through the Seven Markets with her cousins, stopping here and there to try on a necklace or taste a candied fig. They say the marketplace of Caesarea, where I grew up, has the finest assortment of goods and services in all Judea— or at least it once did. But my mother never enjoyed shopping there, and I think I know why. It is why I weep for Jerusalem, why what I am saying is not really as frivolous as it may seem. Jerusalem was ours. Whatever else it may have been or seemed to you to be, it was ours. It was us. It was Israel. No place can be better than the people who live there, and I think Jerusalemites are neither better nor worse than people everywhere. It may have been the Lord's own City, but it was only people, after all, who lived there."

"Then why mourn?" Jonatan asked.

"Because," she said again, "it was ours. The only place in all the world where not even Caesar dared bring his standards, where even now, I know, Titus the Conqueror must tremble to touch the Veil of the Sanctuary, just like Pompey before him. My mother was born to a freedom I never knew, growing up as I did among those who, at best, tolerated our presence. Your 'freedom' in the Galilee was only a shadow of what she had—and now, with Jerusalem lost, you may not even know that again. You may think you hate Jerusalem, Joav, but I cannot believe you do not feel—as we all must—that something has been taken from us that can never be replaced."

The three men were silent. Then Eleazar said softly, "I would weep if I had any tears left. Not for the city, but for the people there. You all know from those we've managed to bring back the way they've been suffering. It will be worse now.

Worse than Jotapata or Tarichea or Jericho or Qumran. . . . It is best not to think how the men of the legions will celebrate their long-awaited victory, but I guess we all know only too well what they'll do. We had better make ready to leave at dawn. There will be those who manage to make their way out. We must find them and help them, bring them here if they want. No questions asked. If they are alive, it is enough. Do not ask how they managed to escape or what they did to live. It doesn't matter." He looked at the followers who had now grouped themselves around him. "If you want to avenge the dead, stick your steel into the *Kittim*. There are no more Sadducees, understand? No more priests, no more Jerusalemites, no more followers of Simon or members of the council. There is only the living. And the dead. Our business now is to take care of the living. And for ourselves, to survive."

Later, when Eleazar and Alexandra were alone, he made love to her with a passion that exceeded even what they had known together before. Each thrust of his body was an affirmation of more than their love; it was an attempt to will her to believe in the future. "It is not over," he had said. Had he meant the war? Or their own lives?

But she needed no command to have courage. When they'd ridden back to the Masada from Ein Gedi, alone in the desert, they had taken vows that were more sacred to her than their marriage celebration later atop the mountain. Whatever the future brought they would face together; and so long as they were together she did not fear the future.

He held her close throughout the night. "I should not say it," he whispered. "It is selfish of me—but I thank God you are here and not in Jerusalem."

In the morning the sky was still red, and gray smoke mingled with the white clouds above, as it would for days to come. The quiet of the wilderness seemed an illusion, but miraculously no legionaries sprang at the small group of survivors who had somehow managed to escape.

Aliterus put out his hand to help the limping Sheptai across the rocky ravine. David was far ahead with the Sicarius scout, while Hadassah was next to scramble across the wadi, silent and nimble as a cat. Behind her others came. Aliterus waited until they had all gone past; still, he hesitated. Jabneh was to the west, near the sea. He looked at the line of refugees shuffling deeper into the desert, where he could just make out the thin figure of the boy who had twice saved his life. With a small sigh, Aliterus started after the others. Suddenly he paused and, turning, looked back one last time at the burning city.

"Jerusalem lives in the heart," Johanan ben Zakkai had once said. "No man can be king of Jerusalem, and no walls can encompass it."

If that was true, Aliterus thought, then no man could destroy it.

He smiled.

It was something to think about.

BOOK FIVE

THE DAY promised to be splendid. The sun was out, and so, it seemed, was most of Rome's populace. Josef felt particularly fine this morning, and his good humor was in no way diminished by the respect and seeming affection with which so many greeted him during the course of his walk. Why, he had but paused to scan the latest gladiatorial posters when Trebatius Priscus rushed up, exclaiming, "Flavius Josephus, praise to Fortune I have found you! You must put in a word for me with Caesar—he is sure to listen if you..." There followed the dreary tale of the man's equally dreary suit, which Josef listened to in all apparent earnestness. Finally, promising to speak of the matter to Vespasian, he moved off under a barrage of thank-you's, fully aware that Priscus would later refer to their meeting as a conversation with "the emperor's Jew." Josef smiled to himself as he stopped to examine an exhibit of paintings executed in decidedly Pompeian style. As he ducked into a merchant's shop for a look at the man's "pearls from farthest Arabia," he decided that Trebatius Priscus could call him Jupiter's monkey for all that it mattered. Proceeding to the establishment of Cornelius Julianus, where a new shipment of Megaric marble had arrived, Josef noted with characteristic wryness what a thick skin he'd grown since those days of being "Matthias of Jerusalem's second son."

The Megaric marble proved to be the day's first disappointment. But feeling now the need to acquire something—anything—Josef placed an order for a figure of Hermes that Titus had admired, executed in Pentelic marble with a bronze head. Recalling a particular landscape gardener whom Titus had likewise praised, Josef asked Cornelius Julianus's opinion of the man.

"My dear friend Flavius Titus," Josef remarked with studied

casualness, "assures me he has the knack for making the coolest and greenest of retreats."

The art dealer allowed himself a respectful grimace. "With all love to Titus, the one you speak of has a passion for ivy that is beyond reason, if not bordering on true madness. There are pieces that lend themselves to greenery—Diana, in the Greek style, adorned with natural flowers, would be charming. But to see a noble Hercules or Mars smothered by monstrous vines, choking, as it were, on green coils..." He shook his head and sighed. "But it is the fashion. It is the fashion."

Josef laughed appreciatively. "What is fashion," he asked, "when we speak of art? One is for the moment, the other for all time."

The Roman expressed his gratitude with a slight bow. "It is a great pleasure, Flavius Josephus, to deal with a man of your sensitivity. No doubt your new estate will be an exquisite reflection of your exquisite taste. How goes the construction?"

"Oh, nothing left to do now but the baths and another promenade, I think. A paved colonnade gives a certain dignity...That reminds me, I must see to the stuccoing today...."

"You must be anxious to move in."

"Well, one needs a place to entertain...where one can work without distraction. I like the city too much, I fear. There is always something to do when I ought to be at my writing table. As you know, Caesar has allowed me the use of the house he occupied before becoming emperor. It is comfortable, albeit a trifle Spartan. I hesitate to change that which the great Vespasian has honored with his presence, but in time, in time..."

"Knowing the love our Caesar bears you, I doubt he would mind whatever innovations you care to make. If I can be of service, I am at your disposal."

"Well, we shall see...."

"I would of course be willing to forgo a certain amount of profit for the honor of working on such a project."

Josef smiled. "We shall see," he said again, and bade the man farewell.

As he continued his walk, he was once more aware of the many eyes upon him. Few people in Rome did not know of Flavius Josephus these days. Now that the Judean war was over, he had been honored with Roman citizenship and the right to call himself Flavius. To the holdings Josef had claimed in Judea, Vespasian had added more land and a state pension.

Josef was rich now, he enjoyed the affection of the ruling family, and he moved in the very best circles. He was of course still a "Jew," but his background did not seem to matter at this point. It was, after all, a period in Rome when all honor went to the rich—a society where, as Horace put it, Queen Money ruled.

The extremes of Roman fortune were apparent as Josef made his way from the Aventine to the part of the city known as the Quirinal. Shops full of silver and ivory gave way to mules and porters, muddy pigs and barking dogs, and the ragged proletariat that was the rank and file of the World Conqueror.

Reaching the place he sought, he was greeted by a stout, perspiring man. "I am sorry to bring you here," Basilides said, mopping his face. "It must be at least four miles up and down hill. My apologies."

"No matter. You said a new group was in."

"Yes...only last night. Truly it would be better to wait until they are bathed."

"Never mind that. You are sure I am the first to see them?"

"May the gods strike me if you are not." He led Josef into a room that held a group of women and girls chained to one another. They were gray with fatigue and fear and despair. They looked, Josef thought, like a spilled sack of potatoes, like colorless lumps on the floor.

Josef walked up and down the line of women, his eyes searching yet guarded. If he felt any emotion, he did not betray it. In Jerusalem, when the killing and the plundering had finally ceased, the captives were herded into the ruins of the Temple, and Titus permitted him to enter the prison yard. He'd walked like this, up and down before rows and rows of men and women and children. So many had been killed....It was hard to believe so many were left. He'd found his own brother among the prisoners, and about fifty friends of his youth. Titus had pardoned them at his request. Later he had managed to free nearly two hundred more. Three he'd rescued right from the cross; of these only one survived, and he made straightway for the desert, vowing vengeance on Rome and Josef. A crooked smile crossed the Jerusalemite's face as he recalled the gratitude of this man he'd saved from death. But then, his own brother had spit on him.

"This is the latest shipment," Basilides was saying. "They are a bit seaworn, as you can see, but I assure you—with a little rest and care they will blossom like flowers after the rain. I cannot attest to their characters at this time. The point must be marked upon a bill of sale. I cannot be held responsible should one prove thievish or sickly. Dear sir, I beg you, wait. I do not like selling what I cannot vouch for. I have a reputation to maintain. Come back with me to my estate. You know by now what fine stock I carry. What is your mood? A gentle nature? Or do you prefer the wild bird to the tame, someone who'll scratch your back to ribbons, eh? I know how young Domitian likes his tigers."

But Josef was not listening. There was a girl with her back to him, a slender thing with long, dark hair. He reached out, his hand seeming to tremble as he touched her shoulder to turn her around. She shrank away, her dark eyes filled with terror. His hand dropped.

Basilides did not miss the look in Josef's eyes. "Is there someone in particular..." He stopped. Better not to remind the emperor's Jew of the past. He cleared his throat. "Why not return with me to my house? I have some stunning new beauties. Now that the German revolt has been quelled, we're starting to get some quality stuff, not this penny-a-pound Judean trash. Blond all over, if you get my meaning." He watched Josef go up and down the line of females once more. "There would have been more, but one of the ships sank. Yes, hadn't you heard? Somehow the prisoners took control, killed the crew, and then, seeing it was all to no avail—no port would receive them—they set fire to the vessel and jumped into the sea. Boys and girls alike. The captain of the sister ship said there was nothing he could do. What a waste. The ship, I mean. The market is flooded enough with flesh these days. Since the war, it's a buyer's market. The only ones willing to pay a fair price are the Jews themselves. Why, I must have unloaded thousands of Judeans on the Jews of Rome, who have straightway set them free. I've just concluded a deal with some representatives of the Jews in Alexandria, and I have little doubt the slaves I'm shipping to Egypt will be freemen when they arrive. Foolishness, if you ask me. The Judeans have always meant nothing but trouble. Set these rebels free, and they will start another war. I say this because I know you agree, Flavius Josephus."

Josef smiled his strange half-smile, slightly sad, slightly mocking. "You forget, Basilides, that it was I who arranged the meeting between yourself and the Synagogue Committee to Purchase Prisoners. Some might say I did so to expedite a new revolt."

It was Basilides' turn to smile. "Or for the percentage you took."

"Percentage? Why, I thought that was a gift, a token of gratitude for bringing to your attention the fact that every community of Israelites has a charity committee, and that furthermore, in times like these, there isn't a single Jewish matron who would not melt down all her rings and necklaces for the purchase of these slaves." He shrugged ever so slightly. "Isn't it amazing what, in the right circles, penny-a-pound trash will bring?"

"Indeed. Pity the other ship sank. Imagine . . . hundreds throwing themselves overboard. . . ."

"The *Kiddush ha-Shem*," Josef said softly.

"Death before dishonor, I suppose? Well, the only sure thing in life is death, they say. Speaking of which—and of surprises as well—I sold a young female to Dolabella some weeks ago. He, being past his prime, decides to buy a husband for her and breed himself a houseful of little slaves. Does he come to me? No. Somewhere he avails himself of a lad who, he tells one and all, is a perfect match. The old fool. Turns out the boy is the girl's brother—they were separated in Jerusalem—and both up and kill themselves. Serves Dolabella right, I say." He followed Josef outside. "I regret you did not find what you were seeking."

Josef shrugged. "It was a thought, a whim. Of no importance really. Just . . . a thought."

The slave merchant nodded. "There will be other shipments. Meanwhile, please convey my warmest greetings to Caesar, and do not fail to let him know I am at his service."

"Vespasian is a solitary man. Still . . . that girl inside . . . it seems to me that once he was fond of a similar creature."

"Take her. A gift. With my compliments."

Josef smiled. "I would not want you to suffer any loss—"

"What loss? Let me think of it as a small investment."

"You have my gratitude."

"Say friendship, rather." He accompanied Josef into the street. "I will have the girl cleaned up and sent to you." He hesitated. "If there is someone in particular you would care to have me look for . . . you can count on my discretion. . . ."

"A gray-eyed girl, Basilides. Slender, with smooth dark hair and the gray eyes of Athene." As though he feared he had said too much, he hurried off.

Basilides stared after him. A girl with the eyes of Athene! Would that the gods would favor him so again! And yet . . .

He shuddered. One brush with destiny was enough.

Josef was melancholy when he returned to the villa. He seemed oblivious to the numerous servants and slaves anxious to attend him, or even to the beautiful hetaera Claudia, who now came forward with a pitcher of iced wine. Recognizing Josef's mood, Claudia wisely said nothing. Instead she set the wine within reach, sat herself at his feet, and removing his sandals, began to knead his insteps with her supple fingers. He leaned back in the chair and closed his eyes.

After awhile, she said in her soft voice, "I have asked Trebatius to send over one of his library slaves to help glue pages. He will bring some bits of parchment for title pieces."

Josef nodded.

"Servilia tells me the whispers grow against Berenice. The people love Titus, but they fear the oriental princess. They begin to speak again of Cleopatra and the trouble she wrought. It would be best, the people say, for young Caesar to send the Jewess back to her own land. I know he loves her, but he must show Rome he loves Rome more."

Josef opened his eyes and looked at her.

She smiled at him.

He smiled too. "Let down your hair."

Without a word, she began to remove the combs that held the golden curls and coils in place, until her hair fell upon her shoulders in sensual disarray. She was kneeling before him, her hands on his knees. Her fingers began to make warm roads up his thighs. She smiled.

Thoughtfully, Josef studied the beautiful courtesan. She was one of the loveliest women in Rome, spoke a number of languages, sang and played the lyre in pleasing fashion, and was ever obedient to his will. But for some reason, as he looked at Claudia, the soft smile on her lips a promise of the pleasure to follow, he thought of the girl Alexandra, who had been his wife. Vespasian had given him all the land and property that had been Samuel ben Harsom's, even the villa in Caesarea. Caesar had asked about Alexandra; when Josef replied that she had "run away," he did not seem surprised, seemed even to smile slightly at this information.

Josef's lips tightened. It had been a mistake to let her go. She was, after all, a descendant of King David—or had been. The line was pure, unbroken; together with his own Hasmonean blood . . . there was none more fit to bear his sons. He had always gotten what he wanted; it was annoying to be denied this. He sighed. He would have frowned, but his irritation was melting in the heat of Claudia's caresses. He closed his eyes again, but a sense of loss remained, and a feeling as close to sorrow as he might ever know. It suddenly occurred to him that in all their time together—nearly two years—he could not recall ever seeing Alexandra smile. And suddenly he wished he could have seen her happy. Considering the fate she had no doubt met in Jerusalem, it would be better to remember her that way.

The young woman could not contain her laughter as her husband, with a grimace, handed back their infant son. Eleazar started to laugh too, while Hagar rushed up with a cloth to wipe the front of his tunic. Hagar took the baby away, and Alexandra, still grinning, helped him mop himself up.

"Well, that's the first time anyone has done that to me," the commander of Masada said. "Cheeky, like his mother."

Alexandra laughed again. "I'm sure if he knew who you were he'd have been more respectful."

He caught her to him. "Never mind that. As I have been dampened by my own son, why don't you help me dry off?"

"But I am."

"Not like that, woman. Here, I'll just take off this tunic, and you—"

"Eleazar, we can't! It is the Law. We may not lie together so soon after the birth of the child. Only after the prescribed number of weeks has passed. And then I must go to the ritual bath, and only then may we—"

"Since when have you become so pious?" he grumbled.

"Oh, no. Hagar says the Law is for the good of the woman. She says that is why Israelite women do not sicken and die while they are still young, as so many others do."

His hands tightened on her waist. "I would not want to harm you," he said. "Still . . ." He sighed, glancing down at her newly voluptuous figure. Her breasts pushed tightly against the front of her robe as though they would burst through the cloth at any moment. He sighed again and put his finger to one clearly outlined nipple. "Look," he whispered, "You are wet too."

She laughed. "That's not for you." She put her arms around his neck and kissed him. "That is for your son."

"I think I'm beginning to resent that boy. How many weeks did you say? Are you sure you have the right count?"

"Umnn." She leaned back against him, his arms tightly encircling her. "Do you realize, Eleazar, little Beni is not only descended from King David but through you from the line of Aaron as well? The messianic prophecies say— What is it?" He had dropped his arms and moved away from her. "What's wrong?"

"Don't talk about that."

"Talk about what? What's wrong?"

"I want no talk of messiahs, do you understand? Or descendants of David or Aaron or anyone else."

She stared at him, astonished.

"Look, I'm sorry," he said quickly, going to her once more. "But there is enough confusion here without talk of messiahs or priestly lines. It's bad enough with the Holy Brotherhood forever going on about their great battle at the End of Days, without getting everyone excited about some blessed presence. I don't want you to bring up Beni's lineage again, not to me or anyone else."

"Are you—do the Essenes think you are the Messiah?"

"What?" He whirled around to stare at her.

"The day the Temple fell...I saw you with Nathaniel. I heard what he said. He called you the Son of Light. Are you their leader? Are you their Messiah?"

"What do you think?"

"I don't know," she said slowly. "You don't act like an Essene. You don't act like any man I've ever known. I did not realize you were of the priestly class until we were to be married. Nathaniel said you broke the law of the Ha-Kohan by marrying a divorced woman."

He grinned now. "Not at all." He shrugged. "How could you be divorced when the man who was supposed to have been your husband was dead?"

"Josef? Dead?"

He nodded solemnly. "Twice."

"Twice dead?"

"Absolutely. When it was thought that Josef ben Matthias had died at Jotapata, were not candles lit? Did not his family sit in mourning? Then, when it was discovered that he had not been killed but had gone over to the *Kittim*, didn't his father cast him out as dead, and didn't his family light candles and mourn a second time. You see? Twice dead."

She had to smile. "Even so—"

"Only I have the right to say whether you lay with a man before our marriage."

"Eleazar. . . ." She went to him and put her arms around his waist and leaned her head against his chest. "I love you."

He stroked her hair. "You ought to know better than anyone if I am an Essene or not," he said softly. "In any case, breaking the law of the Ha-Kohan, if that is what I have done, ought to finally convince Nathaniel that I am a tainted mortal at best, and no angel warrior." He sighed. "Sometimes I wish for his sake—for all of us—that an Anointed Messenger would appear. The Lord knows I am not he—only a man put in a position of which I would gladly be free. But as long as everyone around here seems to think I know what must be done, then I must do what I can to keep things going. There must be no talk of messiahs or miracles. Our business now is to survive. To heal wounds and put ourselves in order. To teach the children, so that when the time comes that we can leave the Masada, we will not be ignorant or forgetful of freedom's cause. And we must unite as one people. It was our own divisiveness that destroyed Jerusalem and lost the war."

But even as he spoke the Masada was divided; for in the year since Jerusalem had been razed, the population of the mountain fortress had swelled to nearly a thousand men, women, and children from every class of life and every part of Judea. Essenes and Zealots had been joined by refugees from Jerusalem, who included not only Jerusalemites but also many who had come for the Passover and been trapped inside the Holy City. There were some, like the boy David, who were from Alexandria, as well as Jews who had come running from Antioch or elsewhere in the wake of Judea's destruction, when the rest of the world felt licensed to heap its scorn and pent-up anger on the Israelites in its communities. And there was even a man from Rome: the actor Aliterus. No longer was the population of the Masada united, even loosely, in thought and behavior.

The Essenes were content to carry on with their austere

lives in like surroundings. As more people came to the Masada, they vacated the buildings and moved to the harsh chambers of the casemate wall; but in time they had to share even these dwellings with ordinary families. They never complained. They worked the gardens, prayed, and sang, awaiting the great battle at the End of Days. *"My eyes have gazed on what is eternal,"* they sang, *"on wisdom concealed from men, on knowledge and wise design. . . . My light springs from the source of His knowledge. . . . And the light of my heart, the mystery to come."*

But others were not so serene.

It was, after all, no Eden on that mountaintop, for suffering does not ensure nobility, nor hardship make all men saints. To some, hearing of the Masada, it may have seemed that the people there dreamed only of freedom and of an end to Roman oppression. But they also dreamed of fine houses, good food, robes of silk, bracelets of gold. The ordeal of war had made them—with the exception of the Essenes—fanatics for the trappings of life, the creature comforts, the luxuries—and even more, the blessed, homely things. A flower in a clay vessel. Warm bread. A baby's first step. The embrace of man and woman. This was the common stuff of life; yet how precious it had become, how dear. When the men returned from patrol their wives held them close, as if for all time; when they left again, the women glued their eyes to the retreating figures, sometimes remembering another man or even another life. A marriage, the birth of a child, heralded song and dance.

But there was divorce as well; sometimes the Masada became too much for one of the partners, and the man or woman left, hoping the Roman danger was past, that a better life might be found somewhere in Judea or in the outside world.

And there was death. Wounds that never healed, a scout who never returned; the victim of a knife fight over a woman; the old; the sick. They were quickly buried in a cave below the surface of the plateau.

No one mourned long. The business at hand was life. Survival. "The best revenge," Eleazar would say, "is to outlive our enemies." There were those who did not agree, who would have rushed pell-mell at any Roman garrison only for the satisfaction of confrontation, with no thought of what it might mean to the rest. Eleazar held them back. "We must wait," he said. "We must grow strong." Even so, the Sicarii went on raids; it would have been asking too much to deny the men this. Eleazar made certain they were carefully planned attacks, engineered to wreak as much damage as possible without loss. Thus, Roman guards were often discovered with their throats slashed, or a cage of slaves might be found suddenly, mysteriously empty, or a shipment of meat to the garrison in Jerusalem would be delivered spoiled. No single Roman dared venture out alone into the desert wilderness, not even to pursue runaway captives, for the legionaries who had done so or had been foolish enough to ride off to Ein Gedi's delightful spring had all apparently vanished from the earth. Such disappearances were duly noted in dispatches sent to Rome by the officers in Judea, who reported the existence of "small pockets of resistance."

But guerrilla raids were not enough for the boy David. He wanted war, and he began to pay close attention to what the Essenes said and to dream with them of a great battle. He did not, however, share the Brotherhood's respect for Eleazar ben Ya'ir. As he watched the man go about the daily business of community administration—mediating quarrels, assigning housing, checking the storehouses—and even more, as he watched the legendary Sicarius warrior playing with his infant son or standing easily with his arm around the woman with light eyes, David's initial admiration turned to disappointment and then contempt. It would have made little difference had he known how ben Ya'ir shared his distaste for administrative politics, and little difference that in the months to come it would become obvious that anyone interested in keeping the Masada at peace had to be a skillful politician.

There were the Essenes, for instance. True, they went about their own business; but there was the matter of their calendar, which caused fresh confusion and rankled those members of the priestly class who still clung to the authority of the Temple. It did not please these Sadducees, furthermore, that their rank counted for nothing in the new community.

Among this group was one Aqavia, of the family of High Priests, who had survived the bloodbath in Jerusalem by hiding in one of the Temple's many underground passages. He had nearly starved to death there but was finally led forth by his servant, Iddo, who nursed him back to health and brought him to the Masada. This servant took upon himself the airs of his master, and when it came time for him to present himself at the storehouses, he balked at his allotment.

"But this is for Kahana Raba Aqavia," Iddo protested.

Joav, whose job it was that day to dole out provisions, barely looked up. He'd heard it all before.

Iddo continued his attempt to impress the sturdy Zealot with his master's credentials, but to no avail. "You don't understand," he said finally. "My master was a priest of the highest order. He is a very important man."

"Of course he is," Joav agreed cheerfully.

Iddo let out a sigh of relief. At last, he'd gotten through.

"Who isn't?" the Zealot went on. He leaned forward a little. "On the Masada," he said carefully, "everyone is important."

That evening, while Eleazar sat at dinner, Kahana Raba Aqavia stormed into the room and began to berate him for the humiliation he had suffered that day. "Have I survived the terrors of war by the grace of the Almighty only to be ridiculed by mere Israelites?" the priest demanded. "Has no one here any respect for a priest of the Temple?"

Eleazar suppressed a smile. The story of Iddo at the storehouse had quickly made the rounds of the camp, to the great amusement of all. By midday everyone was saying, "Hadn't you heard? On the Masada everyone is important."

"Joav meant no disrespect," Eleazar said now. "But you must understand that no one gets special treatment. Rations are given according to need, not title."

"You put me in the same class with *am ha'eretz*? My fathers' names are in the Book! We are counted in the return from exile! We—"

"*Nashi*," Eleazar said, trying to soften his words by calling the man prince, "try to understand. The old ways are gone. It is the Year One for us. If there were to be a ruling class on the Masada, it would be those of us who came here first, by choice, not driven before the army of the *Kittim* like orphans in a storm. But there are no princes here. No priests as in the days of the Temple. There are no fatted oxen on the Masada— and if we had one it would not be offered up on an altar, and the best parts given to you and your kind, but divided among all the people with the choicest parts drawn by lot. That is the way it is here, and this is the will of the people. No priorities. No exceptions. You are one of us, or you are not. But come, let us not quarrel. We ought rather to be giving thanks that you are alive and with us. Come, sit down and take supper. My wife is making a dish I know you will like. It is called an omelet—something she learned from the Romans. Come, join us."

But the priest remained standing. "The will of the people, you say? Very well. We shall see what is the will of the people." And with that he left.

Joav stared after him in anger. "How can vermin like that remain alive when so many good men have died?"

"It is hard for him," Eleazar said thoughtfully. "All he has left is his pride. Take that away and he would not last long."

"Then let him die!" Joav exclaimed.

"No." He glanced up at Alexandra as she brought supper to the table. It was his favorite meal: eggs with pieces of cheese cooked in the middle, a salad of chopped vegetables flavored with a bit of oil, bread baked only that morning, and milk fresh from one of the Masada's goats. But as he looked at the slender young woman serving him, he suddenly thought of the life she had been born to and what she had known in the past. He caught her hand, no longer pale and smooth but deeply tanned and weathered by work. "It must be hard for you here. Do you miss the fine life you once led?"

She looked at him with surprise. She had never been happier in her life. She put her arms around his neck, smiling as she felt his lips against her palm. "Better a dish of herbs where there is love," she said, quoting the proverb, "than a fatted oxen in a house full of hatred."

But in the end the priests received their tithe; for Aqavia persuaded the people that to deny them this was to incur the wrath of the Lord—and it was, after all, only the Lord's grace that permitted the Masada to exist. The Essenes concurred in the tithing, which was prescribed in Torah. Eleazar bowed to the will of the community, but he was clearly disgusted with the turn of events—which next saw a Levite named Hillel going about gathering the "Temple shekel" for a "building fund for the restoration of the Temple in Jerusalem." The Essenes refused to take part in this, and their separateness was respected. When it was seen, however, that the Pious Ones were exempt from the Temple tax, many persons came forward declaring themselves to be of the sect, and a quarrel arose as to who was an Essene and who was not.

The situation was aggravated by the case of a young man whose betrothal to the daughter of a newly arrived family Aqavia had stopped because of differences in class. The young man began to protest angrily one day, and since it seemed the time to air grievances, several put forth the view that housing for some was better than for others, and so on and so forth. Words flew back and forth between Sicarius and Sadducee, Galilean and Jerusalemite, Judean and Babylonian—another moment and fists would be flying too. Suddenly there was a tall figure in their midst; and a voice thundered above the insults and accusations, "Enough!"

They turned to stare at him, the Sicarii quieted by the appearance of their commander, the young people and the women awed by the sight of the golden-haired man; even the priests were taken with the princely figure. It was a good thing Eleazar was so handsome, Alexandra thought amusedly. Beauty certainly had its effect.

Ben Ya'ir looked around angrily, as though daring anyone to say another word. The plateau was silent.

"Now, look," he said in a low voice, "I know this isn't the best of all possible worlds. Some of you are used to better. And let's face it, some of you have been used to worse. But if things are bad now, you better believe they won't get any finer. There will be more coming to join us, I have no doubt of that. The only places left in Judea that do not answer to Rome are Machaerus and the Masada. And we may still have to face Rome. But it isn't the *Kittim* I fear so much as what is happening among us. I see the beginnings of corruption. A lowering of morale. Hatred between groups, and just plain, ugly behavior all around. Is this how it will end? Tell me, *chev'ra*, is this what we fight for?"

The group stood silent, ashamed.

Eleazar turned to Aqavia. "Temple priest, you know so well the laws of milk and meat, of tithing and sacrifice. . . . But the laws of community life, of respect for the institutions and instruments of the community, have you forgotten these?" He turned to all now. "It seems to have been decided that I should be your leader—and you know I have never asked for this. If you wish now to have another lead you, then choose one among you. I offer no resistance. But if I am to be in command, then there will be one law on the Masada, and it will be this—no longer will a man call himself Pharisee, and another Essene. No longer will one be a Galilean, another a Jerusalemite, and one an Egyptian, or Benjamite. There will be no division among us in this way. No marriage shall be prohibited for reasons of class, and no one asked to be another's servant. After all," he said suddenly, with a smile, "you will remember that one man—only one—was brought forth at the time of creation so that no one thereafter could say, 'My father was greater than yours.'"

There was appreciative laughter at this.

Eleazar nodded. "Let us remember that we are all equal in the eyes of the Lord and are judged by the Almighty not by our names but by the deeds we have done." A sudden light came into his eyes. Watching him, knowing him as she did, Alexandra felt the power he projected as much as anyone there. At a time like this, he seemed to be something other than himself, something more than an ordinary man. She knew he was aware of this power, that he was afraid of it, shied away from it, as though he feared the use he might make of it. She sighed. Perhaps, if he had led the forces in Jerusalem . . .

Would it have made a difference?

Men had been willing to die for Simon; they still spoke of him with love, knowing that he and John had been captured finally by the legionaries.

Would it have made a difference if Eleazar had been in Jerusalem?

But he had stayed away even as she had, perhaps excluded not so much by events as by an unspoken conviction that *neither was meant to be there*. She had been spared at Caesarea and again at Tarichea, had survived the trek across the desert to this mountain in the wilderness, to receive on the Masada a reward of happiness she hardly thought she deserved. And Eleazar, too, was unscathed by battle, as though he had been kept alive for some purpose—perhaps for the New Beginning he promised. Or—she did not want to think of it—for the Great Battle at the End of Days.

"The world outside calls us Jews," he was saying. "All right. Let us call ourselves that now. Let us say it with pride and love. Let us make the word not an insult or mark of shame but a badge of glory, a triumphant testimony to our faith in the One Living God. This I ask you now. This must be the law of the Masada. Priests shall receive their tithe, as it is written in Torah, but in no other way shall a man hold himself apart from his brothers. We will be Jews here. All of us. If not, we won't have to worry about Rome—we'll end up destroying ourselves." And then he did something remarkable. "*Anni Yehudit*," he said suddenly. "I am a Jew."

The priest Aqavia gasped. Eleazar had spoken in Hebrew, the holy tongue of the Bible. Moreover, he had dared use the sacred language to pronounce the profane name given to the children of Israel by their enemies.

Everyone was staring at Eleazar, astonished and mesmerized.

"*Anni Yehudit*," the tall, golden-haired man said again. "Say it! Say it with me!"

And as one they said it, not in Aramaic or Greek or in the tongue of Syria or Egypt or Rome, but in the one language common to them. "I am a Jew," they said; and the sound of their pride and faith rang out in the barren world above the sand of centuries and the desolation of Jerusalem, rising higher than the tears and kicks and blows they'd suffered, higher even than the incense of the Temple had ever risen, or the smoke of that burned building, to rest at the feet of God with all the words of all the sages, none of which was more beautiful.

"*Anni Yehudit*."

For the first time, they were really one.

But it was not enough for the boy David. One day he disappeared from the Masada, and it was thought that he had gone to Machaerus to see if the rebels there were more inclined to wage real war. He returned in a week's time. He had not gone to Machaerus. He had been in Jerusalem.

"The city is leveled," he reported. "There is nothing left but the western wall that once enclosed the Temple. They would have destroyed that too, but an Ishmaelite king called Pangar, whose business it was to raze it, failed to do so. The legionaries said Titus was very angry, but the Ishmaelite argued that he left the wall only to show what greatness was conquered by Rome."

"The legionaries told you this?" Eleazar raised an eyebrow. "That was friendly of them."

David grinned. "What had they to fear from a poor, 'lame' boy?" He grew suddenly serious. "There is only the Tenth Legion, with a few troops of horse and companies of foot. They do nothing but play at dice and search for treasure which they say is still hidden in the ground. They have many cages of women and boys and have turned Temple Hill into a place for their pleasure."

Eleazar nodded.

"But there is only the Tenth! They grow fat and lazy. They—"

"I know who and what is in Jerusalem," Eleazar said softly.

"We could take them! We could take back Jerusalem!"

"For how long? No, it is too soon, David. We are too few."

The boy stared at him a moment. "You are afraid!" he blurted. "You sit here on your mountain holding a baby on your lap while the *Kittim* laugh at us and spit on our holy places and do everything they can to show how little they think of us! Well, maybe they are right to look down on us!" Choking back his tears, he ran from the room.

It was Alexandra who finally found him on the terrace of the north palace. Eleazar had refused to live here after their marriage; it was the one thing he had denied her. He thought it might seem that he was putting on kingly airs, and so they had remained in the Zealot headquarters. As always, the view here filled her with great peace, but the young boy staring fixedly ahead obviously did not share her pleasure.

"David . . ."

His shoulder twitched as if to say, "Leave me alone!"

"Won't you talk to me?"

He turned around and glared at her. Why had she come? It was all her fault Eleazar ben Ya'ir had become so weak. Everyone knew what a great *bacchur* he had been until he was so foolish as to get married. The Essenes were right. Women sapped men's strength, made them soft and weak. "I don't talk to women," he announced.

"Well, you will talk to this one." Her chin came up. "You may think an extra bit of flesh between your legs makes you better than I—but it is the stuff inside his head whereby I take my measure of a man." She smiled at his shocked expression.

"You—you wouldn't understand," he mumbled, his face red.

"Why not?"

"Because you are a woman!"

She sighed. "And even the Jew must have his Jew. . . ."

He stared at her. She was certainly strange.

"David . . . I do understand. More than you could know. You are young and angry, and you want to hit back. But it isn't the fighting you want. It's the dying. I know . . . because for a very long time it was what I wanted. I came to the Masada seeking death. And instead I found life."

"Life!" he cried. "Waiting here like cowards for them to come and find us! We could take Jerusalem now! We could take back the Holy City!"

"And hold it for how long? Eleazar is right. We must wait. We must gather up as many of our people as we can and wait."

"Wait! For what? The messiah?"

She was taken aback by this. "Why, no. For them to forget about us. For the *Kittim* to forget about Judea."

He had never considered the possibility. He was silent for some moments. "And then?" His eyes were the eyes of a child after all, a boy waiting for the happy ending to the bedtime story.

She smiled. "We begin again. Even now Jews all over the world are stripping themselves of their possessions in order to buy back as many slaves as possible. Eleazar has had a report that the community in Alexandria is pledging support for a renewed confrontation. Just think, David! If Jews everywhere band together to fight Caesar—not just Judeans—why, think how strong we will be! And perhaps others will follow, countries that are tired of bowing to the Golden Eagle and want to be free!"

For a moment his face lit up; then he sighed and shook his head. "It will take too long. I'll grow old and slow. And what happens if I marry someone like you? Then I'll have to worry about you, and it will be harder to go out and fight. No, no, it must be now! Now, while I can still see what they did to us in the Delta and in Jerusalem! Don't you see? It has to be now!"

She wanted to reach out and touch him, but she said simply, "I understand."

"You don't! You can't! Hating them is the only thing I have! It's what kept me alive in the sewers and later in the ship to Judea, where those filthy sailors used me, they——" He broke off, choking on his rage and tears. "I used to help John. . . . I would find out things for him. . . . He never knew what I had to do to make the soldiers friendly." He clenched his fists. "But it didn't matter as long as I could kill them afterwards. And it doesn't matter now. I don't think about it. I just think about hating them and killing them. And then I'm all right."

"But you're not all right! Once, Eleazar told me he thought every time you kill someone you kill a little piece of yourself. And the more you kill, the more dead you become, until finally you're just a ghost surrounded by the ghosts of all you have slain. You think your bitterness makes you a great *bacchur*— a warrior—but all it has done is make you old before your time and empty of all you should feel."

"I told you you could not understand."

"But I do! I was a slave, David. I was stripped and sold. All the time I lived in the Praetorium—and before that, when my family was killed in Caesarea, and when I was taken at Tarichea—I thought it was hate that kept me strong, kept me alive. But it wasn't. It was love. The love I had seen and known in my family." She paused, suddenly seeing all who had been dear to her. . . . Her father and brothers . . . her mother, who had fought the only way she could . . . the Christian girl Lilah, who could bear anything in this world for the world to come . . . even her uncle, who had tried so hard to make her future secure. . . .

How many people had given her a little piece of themselves, making her braver and better than she would have been without them?

"Love doesn't make you weak," she said. "It makes you strong."

"I wanted to take him to Jabneh," Aliterus said, "to Johanan ben Zakkai."

"He would not go?" Alexandra asked.

"He wants to be a *bacchur*, not a scholar. He asked how I could admire Rabban Johanan after he had deserted Jerusalem—those were David's words. 'How could he ask anything of Titus? And why should those old men live while so many others died? Why didn't ben Zakkai stay to give courage and hope, to lead the people—if not with the sword then with the Book?'" Aliterus sighed. "What could I say?"

"I don't know," Alexandra said. "I think I agree with David."

Aliterus shook his head. "One thing I learned in Jerusalem is that the ways of the Lord cannot be written with a single word. I believe the rabbi performs God's will, just as Eleazar does by being here—and even, I think, as does our dear Josephus, with his 'histories of truth.' Each serves in his own way. One in Jabneh. One in Rome. One on the Masada. Three roads, each by itself only a part, yet all part of the same thing."

For two years following the destruction of Jerusalem they harried the Romans, using the Masada as a base for their guerrilla

operations. It was not the all-out battle that David wanted, but
it was enough to make Rome take notice, and enough for
Vespasian to order a thorough "cleanup" of the remaining rebel
strongholds. A new legate was sent to Judea, Lucilius Bassus,
whose first act was to secure the submission of the fortress at
Herodium. Then, concentrating all available troops, hitherto
widely dispersed—including the Tenth Legion—he marched
against the fortress Machaerus, east of the Dead Sea. In 72
C.E. Machaerus fell, victim to massacre. Every man who had
not perished in the battle was killed, every woman and child
enslaved. Only the Masada was left; but Bassus died before
he could march against it, and a new military governor was
appointed. His name: Flavius Silva.

Except for the desert fortress, the rest of the country had
been reduced to impotence. Caesar instructed his procurators
to sell all Jewish territory, treating Judea as his own property.
He imposed a tax on Jews everywhere, ordering them to pay
each year to the Capitol the identical sum they had previously
paid to the Temple at Jerusalem. The specter of poverty stalked
the streets and fields of Judea even more than before; and with
the horror of Machaerus now on every tongue, no one dared
whisper of revolt. Yet on the Masada, Israel lived. The isolated
fortress had become more than a refuge; it was home now, a
little world—the last sovereign community in Judea, and the
only place in all the world where a Jew was truly free.

Of course, the Zealots still had themselves to live with, and
being a stiff-necked people, they did not always find that easy,
despite the gentle presence of the Essenes and Eleazar ben
Ya'ir's skillful mediations. Yet if the people on the Masada
fought among themselves, they had become a family. A
chev'ra. For finally they had no one but each other. There was
talk of Alexandra giving support, of Berenice working a miracle through Titus's love, even of the Jews in Rome rising
against the Empire. But no one really believed any of this
would come to pass. The Jews of Alexandria would send money
to buy back Jewish slaves, but the passing of gold from hand
to hand was the only action they would take. Berenice would
gamble only for herself. And the Jews in Rome, albeit subject
to discrimination and often degradation by the populace, still
boasted of their "citizenship" in the Empire. No, there was no
one else.

And so they came to the Masada, like pilgrims to a Holy
City. Men with eyes shining, whole families that had trekked

across the sand and wilderness—they came as if they were giving themselves to a new City of David, as if they were following a dream.

For their part, those on the Masada looked upon the idealistic newcomers as though they were mad. Here were palaces and pools, but also dirt and fear and the harsh winter and the pitiless sun. One did not starve, but neither did one feast. The Masada was no magic kingdom, but a hard, desperate place where the only miracle each day was that it still existed.

And those who came with shining eyes, who spoke the name Masada as if it were some holy word—how quickly the light died in them and a flame rose instead when they saw the quarters they were assigned and the work they must do. "But I am so-and-so," one would say. Or, "I gave up such-and-such to join you here. You expect me to live in this? Why can't I have a room in that palace over there? No, I will not move until you find a better place for me than this casemate chamber!"

The old-timers were astonished at such behavior; their joy at seeing their number increase quickly turned to anger. And it finally came to pass that when some poor soul made his way to the fortress, he was greeted with testy words and a wary welcome that made him wonder if he had indeed joined compatriots.

But this too changed.

One day the dust rose in the distance, and they could see, like locusts flying out of a cloud, the first of a long train of men advancing toward them, and hear the beating of drums. Rome had not been blinded by the desert sun, nor had Caesar chosen to look away from their small world. Jerusalem was devastated, the Temple destroyed, the countryside laid bare, and the population of Judea decimated, scattered, enslaved; and still Caesar was not satisfied.

Even more than before, the people of Masada were like a handful of stones against the might of Rome. They were not quite a thousand in number, but alone in all the world they had not bowed to Caesar.

Was the vanity of Rome so great that even this small number must be subdued? Or had these people with their One God somehow become important?

First one, then another, and finally the entire population of the Masada gathered at the wall to watch the *Kittim*, like ants, make their dark trail across the sand. There were hundreds of them, thousands—centurions on horseback, foot soldiers trudging behind, standard carriers and auxiliary archers, and after them scores of slaves and animals carrying supplies, wagons full of food and water, even women. Silently, the Jews watched them approach, the great noise of the marching mingling with the pounding of their hearts until the air around them seemed to thunder with a thousand drums. Silently, they watched them come.

It had begun.

TWO

"The war," Flavius Silva declared, "is over." The Roman paused, searching the heights of the Masada for some sign of attention, or recognition at least, of his presence. He knew they were there—these last survivors of the fallen free Judea that the Jews had dared to proclaim—though nothing moved on the casemate wall. They were there all right, out of sight for the moment perhaps, but listening, he felt sure, to his every word.

"I have not come here to tell you what you already know," the general continued, annoyed that he had to speak against the wind, which had shifted curiously within the hour. "I daresay there are those among you who have seen what Jerusalem is and what little remains of your cities and towns. There is no point in staying where you are," he continued tersely. "No one will come to your aid. Your Temple has been destroyed, and I think even your God has forsaken you. But Caesar has not. Come down from your mountain. Return to your land and begin now to rebuild what you have yourselves, in your folly, destroyed. Turn over to our command those among you who are criminals of war, and the rest of you will be returned to your former homes, with no more given on your part than a pledge of allegiance to Caesar and Rome." He paused, aware of the hollow sound of his voice. "You cannot exist separate and apart from the world. And you cannot continue your resistance. You cannot, nor will Caesar allow it. Come down," he said finally. "Make your peace with us—or suffer the consequences."

He waited. There was only the sound of the wind sweeping across the desolate sands, and the faint echo of his last words.

He waited a moment more, then turned his back and walked away.

The real artist Rome produced was the engineer, for the genius of this empire lay not in painting or literature but in the practical fulfillment of her enormous needs: Tremendous, indomitable buildings worthy of the world's capital. Amphitheaters where eighty thousand people could watch a spectacle. Baths that could accommodate three thousand at a time. Bridges and aqueducts. Soaring arches. Massive piers. And the mighty Roman road, monument of a dogged army marching through uncharted forests, over mountains, across deserts, to the very edges of the known world. There was perhaps no other people as capable as this one in addressing "insurmountable" obstacles—"impregnable" fortresses such as this piece of rock called the Masada. And there was perhaps no one commander more suited to lead the assault on the one remaining stronghold of Jewish rebellion than General Flavius Silva.

He was no relative to the royal house, despite the similarity of name, but he was a man after Vespasian's own heart. A good soldier and, moreover, what Vespasian and other Romans would consider a good man: loyal to Rome, to his family, and to the gods. But more than this, which was perhaps what Vespasian had seen in him, Silva was a consummate technician.

Silva realized he was faced with no easy task—he would have to fight the desert as well as the Jews—but he was remarkably confident, especially considering the arduous journey he had taken just to reach this desolate spot. If those around him could have peered into his heart, they would have seen a bubbling well of excitement that, given the man's generally emotionless exterior, would have surprised even those officers who knew him best. The fact was, this thin-lipped Roman, hardly given to passionate excesses of hate or love, was aroused by working out strategy, by problem solving—more so than by any woman or foe, though he was not indifferent to either of these. During the long campaigns away from home, his tent saw its share of "body warmers." As for his attitude toward Rome's enemies, he was not a bloodthirsty man although he'd done his share of killing, reasoning that a foe left alive was someone who would undoubtedly have to be met again. But he took no joy in the fighting or the charge. He did not like to sweat. Nor, it might be added, had he much fondness for the field, with its accompanying discomforts—such as the flies now buzzing freely around his face. But he kept his composure, despite the heat and the presence of these infernal insects, as he perused his charts. Not so the others in his tent. He could hear Crassio, that stalwart veteran of the Tenth, cursing under his breath, while Antoninus Marcus, the young tribune he had chosen to be his aide, was trying in as dignified a manner as possible to keep a fly from landing on his nose. The boy was bobbing and weaving like a cautious fighter. Silva suppressed a smile.

"Better get used to it, Marc," he said. "It won't get any better."

"Yes, sir, commander," the young man replied with a slight sigh. He shifted his weight as if he thought he could somehow shrink away from the weight of the heavy brass chestplate.

"This is a real hellhole," Crassio remarked, "if you'll pardon my saying so, sir. Seems to me, with your record, Rome might have come up with a better reward than this stinking province, not to mention the job before us. Again, pardon my saying so."

"Not at all, captain. I consider the challenge an honor and a mark of Caesar's esteem." He did not add that Vespasian had privately confided his doubts as to Lucilius Bassus's ability to take the Masada, and his opinion that by dying the military governor had taken the easy way out. "I will tell you that the emperor considers the maintenance of the *Pax Romana* in Judea to be of primary importance to the welfare and security of the Empire. You, Crassio, have been here long enough to know that trouble always comes from Judea. As for me, all I know is that the Sicarii were the first to start this war, and they will be the first to start another if we give them half a chance."

Crassio nodded. "I'm with you on that, commander. It's just—well, I've been here close to seven years now, and I've had my fill of Judea. Seems to me, though, this place is about the worst of it. The men of the Tenth are not ones to complain, but isn't one of them won't be glad to leave this putrefying desert. The rumor's gone round that this here's the spot where lepers are born."

"Heat rash, Crassio. It is to be expected in these parts. The Greek surgeons will attend to any so afflicted. Just see that no one panics."

"There is a Jew among the slaves whom I believe to be one

of their doctors," Antoninus Marcus said now. "Perhaps he would be better acquainted with such ailments."

"Have him brought to the surgeon's camp. We must not waste talent."

"I know the one you mean," Crassio said. "With your permission I'll fetch him now."

"Fine. You may also inform my officers that I will expect them here within the hour for a briefing. You may omit to so inform the Nabatean chief and the leader of our Arab archers. When I say officers, I mean Romans. Oh, and Crassio—" He looked up at the legionary with as friendly a smile as he could muster. "It is well to remember that while we can do nothing about that which fate sends us, we can do everything about the way we take what is sent. Only a fool finds fault with a place. A balanced temper, Crassio, is the only answer."

"Yes, sir."

"Very well, then. Find your doctor and report back." He turned to the waiting tribune. "Now then, Marc, come have a look at these charts. This is your first time on the field, and you must learn as much as you can." He paused. "I knew your father well, Antoninus Marcus. There wasn't a better soldier. I wish I had the centurion Jocundus with me. But as I have his son, I shall do my best to teach you what he would have taught you, and hope that you will prove an honor to his memory."

"I will do my best, sir."

"That is all I ask. Now, have a look at these. As you can see, what I have in mind is the construction of a siege wall surrounding the Masada—"

"A siege wall? You mean like the one Titus employed at Jerusalem?"

"Good boy. You've not let that slip by you, have you? No, not quite like that. That is, not for the same purpose. A siege will not weaken these rebels. Unlike Jerusalem, they have quite enough water and food—more, I daresay, than we have down here. Before the war we had a garrison on the summit, so I am acquainted with the Masada's system of cisterns. Moreover, I have been told that the soil atop the mountain is remarkably good. No doubt the enemy has put it to use growing food for his table. No, to subjugate these people through siege would take a very long time indeed—more time than I think wise to spend in this hellhole, as Crassio so aptly called it."

"Then why a siege wall?"

"Perhaps I should say 'circumvallation.' Yes, that is more precise. Why the wall? To prevent escape, of course. And to inspire fear. When this is over, I expect every single Sicarius to be accounted for. Not one of their number must be left alive, particularly their leader. Now, here you see the placement of our camps. The two largest are here—one in the east, and one where we now stand, in the west, outside my proposed wall. I want the Tenth divided between these two camps. There are to be four smaller camps for the auxiliaries—this one to bar passage through the wadi, that one to guard the exit from this other wadi, and so forth. There must be one camp to guard the Snake Path, and another here in the southwest. I believe it is possible—if highly unlikely—to descend from or climb up to the fortress from the southern edge, so we want to watch that. The promontory there upon which one of our camps will be situated provides an excellent lookout post for the entire southern sector. But it is here, where we now stand, that I consider the most vital spot. The western approach. Remember that, Marc. In time, after the wall is built, I will explain further. In any case, from this spot we might possibly prevent the enemy from going down to their cisterns—which, as you can see, are cut into the western slope. That can do no harm. So, there you have it."

The young tribune shook his head in awe. "Excellent, sir. Most excellent. The camps provide quarters for the troops, dominate possible escape routes, and are in the best position to defend themselves against surprise raids."

Flavius Silva smiled. "Take note of something else, Antoninus Marcus. We are in Judea now. But if we were in Africa or Gaul or the far-off Indies, the plan of each camp would remain exactly the same as the one you inhabited while in training. There is no excuse for any soldier—not the youngest novice—to plead confusion or uncertainty regarding his place, his immediate superior, and his duty."

"Yes, sir."

"Now, I want the slaves put to work immediately on the wall. I have taken into account the amount of labor lost in our journey here, and calculated further losses due to exertion, heat, discipline, *etcetera*. I estimate no serious shortage. A certain number of men must be set aside to bring food and water from Ein Gedi or beyond. We will no doubt lose a percentage of the work force through these journeys. I want to be kept fully informed of the number at all times. I can always send for more slaves, but I don't want delays, so I must know if we are falling below my calculations. Is anything wrong?"

"No, sir. It's just . . . well, I know the toll our journey across the desert has taken. It is very hard for them . . . pushed and chained under this fierce sun . . . some of them barefoot, and the ground like fire underfoot. I mean, when you see how they suffer, it is hard . . . I mean, to think of them as . . . simply numbers. . . ."

"Yes, well, I'd trade them if I could for some nice clean machines—if there were any—to do their work. I'm not keen on slaves myself, particularly when they are former fighting men. Highly undependable. One must constantly revise. Don't worry, Marc, they're tougher than you think. I know how it is the first time out. But don't be fooled. You'll stop to help one who for all the world seems to be dying and suddenly discover the man's got strength enough to grab your throat. And not let go."

"Yes, sir."

"Now, why don't you indulge in a bath and some rest? I know that brass *lorica* is the latest issue, but I suggest you wear a leather tunic here. It won't chafe as much. Just be sure you stay out of the reach of a Sicarius arrow."

"Yes, sir. Thank you, sir."

"You might investigate the goods some of our camp followers are offering. I understand they've one or two rather decent females. Just be sure the surgeons check the women over each time. Understand?"

"Yes, sir." They were at the opening of the tent. The young man paused. He looked up at the mountain before them. "General Silva . . . may I ask you something?"

"Yes?"

"You said yourself the war is over, that Judea has been vanquished. I myself was witness to the triumphal march in Rome. I saw Titus crowned with laurel. Commemorative coins have been struck. The treasures of Jerusalem's Temple are even now in the palace of Jupiter, and the renegade leaders have been executed."

"That is so."

"Forgive me, I know I must sound stupid . . . but why, then, are we here?" His gaze traveled up to the Masada's summit as if drawn by something irresistible. "And why, sir, are they there?"

Flavius Silva's eyes also traveled up the side of the rock fortress until they reached the top. "Antoninus Marcus," he said calmly, "I have gotten where I have gotten because I have never interested myself in why. Only in how. For me, it has always been enough to know a thing can be accomplished—or rather, to see if it *can* be accomplished and in what way. Reasons are unimportant. But I will tell you this. They"—he gestured with his head at the western summit of the Masada, where a group of children had gathered to watch the legionaries below—"are up there because, unlike you, they do not believe the war is over. They have refused to come down, to make allegiance to Caesar, or even to admit they are subjects of the Roman Empire. They have a motto, I am told. 'Death is nothing. Freedom is everything. There is no king but God.' Their God, of course. A nameless, faceless being who has picked the Jews, if you can believe it, to be His chosen people."

"Chosen for what, I wonder," the young tribune muttered as he watched a group of slaves stagger past, their arms filled with rocks and stone.

"Don't waste time with philosophy, Marc. Don't indulge in investigations that seek to find out things which nobody can know—or things which nobody needs to know. On the field, facts are all that matter. And the fact is, those rebels must be destroyed. They have been using their Masada as a base for forays against our new settlements and army units. More importantly, it is Caesar's belief that their very existence may spark the embers of rebellion all over again. We must never forget that the defenders of that mountain are among the most daring, zealous, and desperate people to resist our forces of law and order."

They were walking through the camp, where the forces of law and order were busy setting up tents over low foundation walls of rubblestone. Each of these mess units could accommodate eight to nine soldiers and had its own sleeping and eating arrangements. There were hundreds of these *contubernia* surrounding the Masada, for more than ten thousand troops had come to deliver Rome from the ominous threat of the thousand or so men, women, and children occupying the rebels' nest atop the mountain. Added to this force were more than five thousand Jewish prisoners who would be used to bring food and water and to work on construction. Shacks of the many camp followers and tradesmen who were invariably to be found trailing the army were at the rear of the camps, along with the soldiers' brothels.

Antoninus Marcus cast a backward glance at the Masada. He could feel, he thought, hundreds of eyes on his back. He remembered the group he had seen at the casemate wall. Not one of those "daring, zealous, and desperate people" had looked to be over ten years of age. "They are only children," he murmured.

Flavius Silva had heard him. "Children," the general said flatly, "grow up."

"Afraid, are you?" Aliterus said. "Why, that's nothing down there. I'll give you something to be frightened of." His rubber face stretched into a scowl to end all scowls. His eyebrows lowered ominously as he began to growl, "Who are these Zealot brats that dare disturb Captain Manducus, head of the Praetorian Guard? What? Are these the little rascals who would unseat Caesar? Where's my sword? Let's have a go at them!" As he fumbled with the stick that was his sword, it somehow got caught between his legs, and with a "Whoops!" and a "Whoa!" the actor executed a few nimble stumbling steps before taking a large and very gleefully received pratfall. "Why, you little devils! Laugh at Captain Manducus, will you?" he cried, brandishing his stick at the crowd of laughing children. "I'll get you now, see if I won't." Lurching to his feet like a wounded rhinoceros, Aliterus charged after his youthful audience, who ran every which way, squealing in joyful terror, their real fears forgotten.

Joav managed to catch little Avigael before she banged into his knees in her escape from the "Roman captain." Gently the burly Zealot picked up the four-year-old daughter of Shem and Rebekkah, gave her a kiss, and set her down again. Then he turned back to Eleazar, resuming the conversation as though no interruption had taken place.

"Look at them down there. What are they doing, building some kind of wall? They must be crazy to think they can starve us out the way they did Jerusalem. It will be fun, though, to see how well they last down there."

"They'll manage. They always do."

"Still we might send them something. A few sacks of garbage, for instance, raining down on their heads, might serve to let them know our tables are not bare. Or better still, a shower of arrows. What are we waiting for?" he said impatiently. "Why don't we let them have it? Our archers would welcome the practice."

"In the first place, they are out of reach," Eleazar replied. "Besides, as you said, their siege wall cannot harm us. Let them use up their strength in its construction."

"It isn't *their* strength that's being used up," Alexandra pointed out, coming up to them. "The sweat of the slaves—Judean slaves—builds their wall. Anyway, I don't think they want a long siege. They would be harder put than ourselves by any extended stay in the desert."

The men were silent. Joav had long since come to respect the intelligence of this gray-eyed woman. Besides, she had lived among the *Kittim;* she knew their minds.

"The new procurator, this Flavius Silva—I heard Vespasian speak of him—Silva served him in Africa. He is—let me recall Vespasian's words—a man of great thoroughness. He does not begin another task until he has finished the first. Therefore, I do not believe he will attack until this wall is completed. I have already ruled out the possibility of the wall being a diversion."

Eleazar nodded his agreement. "Too arduous a task for a mere distraction. Besides, they are working on all fronts, which would likewise keep us on guard all round. You said 'attack.' You think they plan an assault?"

"Yes. And I think the wall is to prevent escape."

"Attack!" Joav exclaimed. "They would be as foolish to do that as to think a siege will weaken us in position. Even now, our people are placing the rolling rocks in position. Just let the *Kittim* try to climb up the Masada! We will send our stones as well as our arrows down on them. They will be crushed or sent falling to their death."

"There are many of them. At least ten to our one."

"It doesn't matter," Eleazar said. "Joav's right. The advantage lies with us because of our position."

"Well, if you agree they do not want a siege and you don't believe they are planning an assault, what do you think they are doing down there?" she asked tartly. "You think the Tenth Legion is sitting around waiting for the messiah?"

Eleazar grinned. "You see, Joav, what a hard thing a woman is? That is because the Lord made her from bone and not soft earth, as He did Adam. No, wife, I do not think the *Kittim* are waiting for a miracle to deliver us to them. And I don't think we ought to be sitting around waiting for one to deliver us from them. I think you are probably right. I think this Flavius Silva is planning to attack. I just can't figure out how he thinks to reach us."

"Perhaps he means to lure us down," Jonatan suggested, joining the little group now. "They promised freedom to the people of Machaerus if they would surrender."

"And you know what came of that," Eleazar said. All levity had disappeared. "Who would be so foolish as to believe any Roman now?" He studied Jonatan. "What does the Brotherhood say?"

"The battle must be here, on the Masada, not below. The wall does not matter. We were agreed even before the building of it that there would be no attempt to escape. We have no wish to avoid the confrontation for which we have girded ourselves so long. But we do not think it wise for anyone to abandon the Masada. The women and children would slow down your exodus. There is no water for miles. You would be easy targets for the *Kittim.*"

Eleazar nodded. "The council of captains is, as you know, of the same opinion."

"Nathaniel says the men are to be commended for not desiring to leave the females and young ones and attempt to lose themselves in the wilderness."

"No, we stay together." He put his arms around Alexandra's waist. "Well, then, *chev'ra.* It seems there is little we can do but wait to learn what the *Kittim* have in mind for us."

It was not long before they knew.

Its sheer rock face made the Masada almost totally inaccessible. Only two tracks led all the way up. The Snake Path, in the east, was of no value to an army. The western path was more negotiable, but at its narrowest point a sturdy tower stood in the way of further progress, and from there it would be easy for the Zealots to pick off soldiers filing upward. Behind the tower, however, was a spur of rock, very broad and very prominent, that jutted out a considerable distance and because of its unusual paleness was called the White Cliff. The spur was several hundred feet below the top of the plateau, but there was room on it to build a ramp, which was precisely what Flavius Silva intended to do.

The fashioning of his circumvallation was itself no mean task. Six feet thick, built on parts of slopes that were by themselves quite treacherous, further fortified by a dozen lookout towers, it had taken months and the lives of many slaves to construct. No less impressive were the eight camps established at various points round the base of the fortress. Each camp had its own command post, dais and ramp for the reviewing officer, altars for sacrifice, marketplace, treasury, and even an *auguratorium* from which the priests could determine good and bad omens by watching the stars or the flight of birds. General Silva made it a point to sacrifice to Caesar every morning, and though he dared not look up for fear of being blinded by the rising sun, he knew he was always watched by the people on the Masada. He wondered if they were impressed.

"I remember," Aliterus said, "that once we were discussing omens and auspices—whether a man could really rely upon the liver of a goat or a sparrow's heart to tell him what he must do on what day and at which hour—when Josephus, with that crazy, crooked smile of his, told the story of Mosollamus, a Judean archer with Alexander the Great's cavalry. Well, during one of the Macedonian's campaigns this Mosollamus noticed that a number of men were going to and fro on the route, up and back, holding up the entire force while they checked with a seer at the front who was diligently peering at something in the distance. Mosollamus rode up to the seer and asked why they had halted. The seer pointed to a bird in a tree alongside the road and explained that so long as the bird remained in that spot the troops must halt. If he flew forward, they could advance. But if he flew backward, then they must retreat. The Jew then, without a word, drew forth his bow and shot the bird. Needless to say, the seer began to berate him for this, but Mosollamus said calmly, 'What are you so angry about? If that bird could not even take care of itself, how do you expect it would guide us on our march? And if it had been gifted with divination, it certainly would not have come here, for fear of my killing it.'"

Alexandra smiled. "I know the story. It is mentioned by one Hecataeus of Abdera, who wrote a book about our people. Josef read it when he stayed at Beit Harsom before sailing to Rome."

"I wonder if he is down there now in one of those camps."

She shook her head. "He has feared the desert ever since the time he spent with Banus. No, Josef is not in Judea. He has washed his hands of the past. That is what I don't understand, Aliterus," she said suddenly. "The war is supposed to be over. Oh, I know we cause the occupying army trouble, but not enough to bring these thousands of troops out to besiege us. Look how many men there are down there! And the equipment with them—timber, rope, armored plating! Why, it must cost a fortune! And you know how stingy Vespasian is. I don't understand it," she said again. "This huge show of force, the building of that wall—why, this is preparation for a major battle! And they must know we have less than a thousand men on the Masada. Why? Why are we so important?"

"Before I came to Judea," Aliterus said by way of reply, "I had no idea of the extent of this little provincial rebellion, as the Senate liked to call it. Rome's troubles with Judea were never spoken of as amounting to a war. It was more a kind of 'police action,' or so we were led to believe—something one of the legions could take care of quickly. Meanwhile, more and more men were sent to Judea. The general populace had no idea how many Roman soldiers were being lost. You may accept Caesar's march of triumph as open admission of your countrymen's valor. A sort of grudging admiration, if you will. Of course," he mused, "the new Caesar could hardly have been involved in anything less than a grand war. The gods do not take part in minor enterprises."

"Vespasian a god. . . . Old Garlic Breath. . . . How he must laugh at it. . . ." She became sober.

"What are you thinking?"

"I am thinking that if Rome has declared the war over, then it will want no evidence to the contrary. Every man at Machaerus was slain. There were no prisoners. I think—" She looked up and saw Eleazar standing in the doorway. She ran to him, threw her arms around him. "Eleazar! They mean to kill us all! They will kill you!"

He held her tight. She was trembling. "It's all right," he murmured. "It's all right. Of course they mean to kill us," he joked gently, "but we won't let them."

"Eleazar . . ."

"Look at me. Look into my eyes. I promise you, Alexandra, I give you my word, the *Kittim* will not touch you. Not you or the baby."

"Eleazar . . ."

"Do you believe me?"

"I—"

"Do you believe me?"

She sighed. "I believe you. But you don't understand. It isn't that I'm afraid. I mean, I am, but—it's not for myself—it's for all of us."

He smiled then and drew her to him again. "Thank you," he said softly.

She closed her eyes, feeling his heart beating against her cheek. It was like the beating of her own heart. "They must not destroy us," she said. "Not just us—as people—but what we have here. What we have become. We are all that is left. They have taken Jerusalem . . . the Temple. . . . They must not take the Masada."

His voice was sure. "They won't."

Aliterus cleared his throat. "As the sages always say of Israel, 'You can cut the flowers but not the vine.'"

Eleazar looked at the actor and nodded. "The Lord will be our rock and our fortress. So long as we believe in Him—and in ourselves—why, we are a match for anyone!"

There was a psalm he had always liked. The words came to him now as he made the rounds of the casemate wall and sentry towers.

When I behold Thy heavens, the work of Thy fingers,
The moon and the stars which Thou hast established;
What is man, that Thou art mindful of him?
And the son of man, that Thou thinkest of him?
Yet Thou hast made him but little lower than the angels,
And hast crowned him with glory and honor.

Eleazar sighed. What was man indeed that the Almighty should take note of him? Had the Eternal One listened in Jerusalem or Jotapata or Machaerus? Did He hear the moans of his sons dying under the Roman whip as they toiled for the *Kittim?* He shuddered slightly. *Only a fool believes there is no God,* he reminded himself. He climbed the tower overlooking the western ascent. The fires of the Roman camps dotted the night below, red twins of the white stars above. *And*

we are in between, Eleazar thought, *waiting to learn what the
ungodly intend as well as what the Lord wants.* He paused on
the steps of the tower, stretching his hands on the supports like
a man trying to hold up the world. He closed his eyes. *Show
me the way,* he prayed. *Guide me....*

He opened his eyes, let out his breath. Slowly he climbed
to the lookout. Jonatan was there, his lips moving ever so
slightly. Eleazar had to smile.

"Are you praying?" he asked.

Jonatan turned to him. "'*And I said, mighty men have encamped against me with their instruments of war. And the
glittering of their lance was like fire which devours the
wood....And like the roaring of many waters was the tumult
of their voices. . . . But though my heart melted . . . my soul
was strengthened through thy covenant.*'" He smiled too, a
smile as gentle as the nights in Galilee so very far away and
so very long ago.

How was it, Eleazar wondered, that this young Essene,
desert born and bred, reminded him now of the Galilee? It was
like Nathaniel's eyes; one looked into them and saw things one
had thought were hidden away forever or locked deep in the
heart.

"We are being tried," Jonatan said. "This is the testing."

Eleazar seemed not to hear. "We need a plan," he said.
"Sitting here, waiting for them . . . it's all wrong. We need more
than the strength of our resolve. Or our faith in the Lord."

"You are wrong," Jonatan said simply. "That is all we
need."

Eleazar looked at him now, his jaw set in a grim line. "The
Kittim should not have been allowed to take the White Cliff.
We did not try hard enough to stop them. But what can you
do when half your fighting force is convinced the spur is not
important, that no Roman will ever make it to the top of the
Masada?"

"Even if everyone believed as you do, I do not think we
could have kept the *Kittim* back. The way they lock their shields
above their heads, our arrows just glance off. And no matter
how many we hit, there are always more to take their places."

"Joav thinks their being on the spur is of no consequence,"
Eleazar said.

"Nathaniel says everything is of consequence."

"Jonatan . . . I have studied the writings of the Teachers. The

Great Battle at the End of Days is written to take place in some plain—the Valley of Jezreel, for instance. Armageddon. We cannot fight on the Masada in the manner prescribed by your manual. We are not an army but the remnants of several armies, and the best we have ever been able to do is a kind of hit-and-run attack, which in these circumstances we are incapable of performing. If the *Kittim* manage to scale our mountain, we have very little to hope for. We number less than a thousand—half of whom are women, children, and men too old or ill to fight. If each man here had the strength of ten, we would still be outnumbered—and hindered by the helpless ones we must protect. Oh, we'd give them a fight!" He caught his breath. "We'd give them a fight," he said again, "but what would be left? Who would be left? And for how long?" He shook his head. "They must be prevented from breaching our wall. We must keep them below, far below. They have destroyed the aqueducts that fill the cisterns, but we can exist many years with the water we have, and we could devise other means of catching rainwater. Joav is right. The desert is our ally, and the sun our best weapon. When the wind comes, they will choke on the white dust. In the winter, they will be swept away by the rains—see how they have foolishly pitched their tents on the sides of the hills! And when summer comes again they will burn again and beg their commander to be gone from this place. And all the while they will see that we are strong and unafraid, that we laugh at the wall they have built—who would be foolish enough to leave the Masada?—that we pity them all they must suffer, the heat, the flies, the lizards, the diseases that disfigure their bodies. . . . And all the while our archers will be waiting in the towers, waiting for an opening in that scale of shields. We will wear them out, Jonatan!" He threw back his head and laughed. "All this time I have been telling everyone our best revenge is to outlive our enemies. I never realized how right I was!" He looked up at the sky, where the stars still twinkled palely in the graying morning. "We must begin our attack today," he declared. "We have been silent too long, huddling together like lost, frightened sheep, waiting to be shown which gate leads to life and which to death. Now we must find our tongues. As the day breaks behind us we shall begin our friendly little talks with the *Kittim* below. With their eyes blinded by the sun, they may even think that it is the voices of their own gods they hear." He grinned, then suddenly grew serious. "It is a small way to fight. I pray it is the right way."

"The Lord will not desert us."

"Nor shall we desert him." He looked down at the Roman camps, where the fires were beginning to smolder in the dawn. "We must keep them down there," Eleazar said. "They must not find a way up the Masada."

"The lesion is here, inside the thigh," Flavius Silva said. "There is another, smaller one, as you can see, above the navel." He was careful to keep his voice calm. It would not do to let this Jew sense his concern. He cleared his throat while the man inspected the sores. "Well, what do you think?"

"There are similar marks on your back. Do you feel a burning sensation? Does it itch?"

He nodded. It was all he could do to keep from clawing at himself. But not one of his own men had seen him scratch his body, and neither would this Jew.

"What do your own physicians say?"

"I have not mentioned this ailment to anyone. You will say nothing of it." He paused. "I could have your tongue removed, of course, but that would only raise the suspicion that you possess information I wish no one to know. And that is exactly what I want to avoid. Therefore, you will be silent—or see ten of your companions executed. Is that understood?"

"Yes."

"Well?"

"It is not the leprosy."

Silva let out his breath. "You are sure?"

"Dead flesh gives no sensation. Besides, there would be a certain look in the eyes, a peculiar brightness. . . . No, general, you are not a leper."

"Then what, Jew?"

"I have a name," the man said calmly, washing his hands in the basin of water provided for this purpose. "It is Solomon ben Ya'ish. Forgive me for suggesting such familiarity, but after these last few years I think I need to be reassured of who I am. Especially now that I have resumed my profession."

"From what I understand you never relinquished it, Solomon ben Ya'ish. The slaves call you the Healer."

"Would that I were. I do what I can. It is rarely enough."

"It had better be enough now. Well, what is your cure?"

"A bath, general."

Silva stared at him, then jerked his head toward the oval campaign tub in the corner of the tent. "Fresh water brought daily from the springs of Ein Gedi."

The physician shook his head. "No, general. You must bathe in the waters of the lake."

"That stinking, sulphurous sea?"

"There are elements there that heal the flesh. Herod came often to these shores to soak his ailing body, and it is said that only after bathing in Yam Hamelach—the Sea of Salt—did Sarah, the aged wife of our prophet Abraham, conceive Isaac. Each morning you must immerse your body in its salty water, being careful not to let even one drop touch your eyes. Then return to your tent and bathe in clear water. The lesions will cease to spread, and they should disappear in a week's time. Meanwhile, if you grant me access to your own physicians' store of herbs and ointments, I may perhaps be able to make a paste that will ease your discomfort."

"Take what you need. If you do not find it, make note of it, and it shall be fetched."

"As you will."

Flavius Silva studied the man, trying to determine if what he had said was the truth. "If this is a trick . . . if there is some flesh-eating beast in that Dead Sea . . ."

Solomon ben Ya'ish smiled. "No creature dwells in it. Nothing can live there."

"Yet the water heals?"

"Great are the workings of the Lord. Many are His miracles, General. This world is His creation, and therefore there is some good in all its elements. How could it be otherwise?"

The Roman was taken aback. "Good in everything?" He smiled wryly. "In that case, you will have to admit that there is good in us who are your enemy."

"I admit only that I believe there is a purpose for everything. I myself am hardly wise enough to recognize what that purpose is. I just try to deal with things as they come."

"Well, you had better think how you will deal with things if you are lying to me now."

"General Silva, I could have easily told you what you most feared to hear—that you have become leprous. I wonder now why I did not. Surely such news would have upset your sleep a bit, and that might be some consolation for the lives I've seen lost under the whips of your overseers. But I have not lied, and if the remedy I have prescribed fails, why, then do what you will. I have survived the burning of the Temple—how, I shall never know—two years of slavery, and now the desert. As far as I am concerned I have already lived too long. Kill me, and be done with it."

"No, you shall live. The legionaries trust your skills more than those of the Greek butchers I brought with me. I think I trust you too. You speak like a man, not like a slave."

Solomon ben Ya'ish sighed. "Slaves are men, General. And if you think your soldiers would look any better to you stripped to a loincloth, sweating in the sun, moving rocks and sand with their tongues swollen dry in their mouths and their hands raw and bleeding, their wrists and ankles ringed with sores from the iron cuff and the chain—if you think your people wouldn't then look like animals, as you've made my people look, then I'd say you were not a very realistic man."

She was sitting so quietly that he did not see her at first; but he was no sooner aware of her presence than the Nabatean was in front of him, sword drawn. Marc took a step back, but it was out of surprise, not fear. "Put that away," he said evenly. "Your life is forfeit if you but raise your hand against a Roman officer."

"Officer? Officer? Ah! Officer! You come from Big General? Girl for Big General. I let no one else take her. Bring from city of Jews for Big General."

"I am the tribune Antoninus Marcus. General Silva has asked me to bring the female to his tent."

"Good! Good! I come too. Soldiers hungry men. They jump at piece of meat. I come."

"That won't be necessary." He stole a look at the girl. She was still sitting there, her hands resting on her lap. The palms were up, and he would have thought she was studying them, looking for some injury perhaps; but she was staring straight ahead.

"I come," the Nabatean said firmly. "I bring letter back to city that girl is with Big General. If not—" He paused and passed his hand in front of his throat.

"All right, come along then." He gestured at the girl. "You, there," he began in his newly acquired Aramaic.

"She speak soldiers' tongue," the Nabatean said. He grinned. "Little General in Jerusalem teach her. Now she learn from Big General."

Little General. That would be Larcius Lepidus. This was just the sort of gift he would send. For some reason the young tribune found himself annoyed. His irritation grew as he escorted the girl to Silva's tent. What a stupid-looking trio he had become part of, he thought as he led the way through the soldiers' camps, the girl behind him, and the Nabatean drawing up the rear. Marc felt his face grow hot as the legionaries whistled and called out explicit invitations and vulgar endearments. He was the only one not laughing by the time they reached the general's tent. He spoke quickly to the Praetorian guard, anxious to be finished with this business, impatiently drumming his fingers on his belt as their arrival was announced. With a sigh of relief, he saw the tent flap drawn back and motioned for the girl to enter. Their eyes met briefly as she passed him. He turned away, gestured for the Nabatean to follow—he would give him his saving letter—and strode off, still vaguely disturbed.

He had expected to see fear in her eyes, or shame, or sorrow. He would have understood anger, but there had been no expression of feeling at all. It was as if she had looked past him or through him, as if he, the Nabatean, the soldiers—even Flavius Silva, military governor of Judea—did not exist.

She was a slave. A whore.

Why, then, was it he who felt ashamed?

Day and night the hammering went on, a constant, dull droning in the ears, as the slaves, like worker ants, toiled on the wooden scaffolding to support Silva's earthen ramp. It was late August, the Hebrew month Elul, and at eight in the morning the sky was already white with heat.

Alexandra hurried to the water cisterns. There was perhaps another hour or two in which to finish heavy chores. By ten o'clock the heat would be so intense that one hardly cared to move; and generally one did not. She was behind schedule now. It was best to get to the cisterns as the sun rose so that the light was in the Romans' eyes, blinding them when they looked up. It was still early, but she would have to move carefully. Impatiently she swatted at the flies that were always there on the plateau. The only consolation was that the flies were on the ground below as well, along with scorpions, lizards, and other disgusting creatures. At night the legionaries heard the cries of the jackal and other animals of the wilderness, terrors that they on the Masada did not have to fear.

Nor did the soldiers have the comfort of the Masada's pools and abundant water. At the beginning, groups of them would sometimes hike to the shore of the Dead Sea, thinking, no doubt, to refresh themselves with a swim. They would return to camp more uncomfortable than when they had left, and as they could not indulge in the luxury of a freshwater bath, the salt on their skin would disturb them for hours. Alexandra smiled at the thought. In time the Roman general had seen the wisdom of allowing small, privileged groups to depart in rotation for Ein Gedi, where they might refresh themselves in the oasis's clear springs and waterfall.

Alexandra sighed, wistfully recalling the days she had spent there with Eleazar, how they had climbed the cliffs to the spring's source and bathed in its cold, clear water, swimming in its fern-dappled pools, frolicking under the waterfall, filling their mouths with the sweet water, and then . . . lying together in the rushes that pillowed the caves behind the pools. . . .

She closed her eyes, suddenly very aware of her body under the white linen robe, the way the cloth brushed against her thighs as she walked, the sudden slight breeze lifting her veil to touch her neck. . . . How curious, she thought in that detached, academic manner of hers, that the desert heat, so terribly incapacitating for most things, was for one particular, intimate activity so strangely exhilarating. Even now, a scant few hours since he had left her, she missed Eleazar's body on hers. . . .

He was always up before dawn now. First to arise and last to bed. Every night he made the rounds of the Masada, climbing every tower, talking to the night guards and to the people in the casemate chambers, hearing their complaints, their fears, their prayers. Every morning he arose even before the stars had faded from the sky, and made the same tour. And every day he watched the Roman road creep up the side of their mountain, pounding his fist into his palm in helpless anger and frustration.

There seemed no way to stop the building of that ramp. The

soldiers were careful to stand away to the sides, letting the slaves toil in the middle, so that the rolling stones Joav and the others sent down harmed only the prisoners and caused little injury to the *Kittim*. Seeing that they were killing their own brothers, the defenders of the Masada had finally abandoned this tactic, relying instead on the skill of their archers. But the Romans countered with a barrage from their Syrian and Arab archers, who always gave full cover to the men on the ramp. The Zealots had to content themselves with clever sniping whenever the opportunity presented itself. The boy David, who had traded in his knife for the bow Eleazar gave him, proved despite his youth to be a most accurate shot.

But we are like those flies buzzing around the Kittim's face. Alexandra reflected. *We annoy but we do no real damage*. Still, she could think of no way to stop the building of the ramp. Night after night she listened to Eleazar speaking softly beside her in their bed, trying out this scheme and that in the air above their heads. "Even if we were to make war on our own people—send the stones down on the slaves—the *Kittim* would only bring more to work on the ramp. Besides, I haven't the heart for it, and neither, I am glad to say, do the others. It is bad enough to see how they fall under the whip or from thirst and heat. Shem recognized his cousin yesterday, working on the ramp. He called to him, and sure enough, his cousin looked up and shouted out his name. That earned him several lashes. Shem went to pieces. Later, we talked and talked. What could I tell him? Can we mount a rescue of his cousin? And if for him, why not the rest? The best we can do is leave them alone."

"But they are working toward our destruction," she had reminded him softly.

"I will not have their blood on my hands."

She descended the steps of the cistern now, taking one of the torches on the wall to guide her way. At water level she put the torch in the wall niche and filled her jar. The place was cool and dark and damp. She paused a moment, listening to the echo of her own breathing in the rock chamber. She waited in the near-darkness as if she thought some answer, some saving idea, might come to her here. But there was only the sound of her breathing—a slight, rushing sound like the one she used to hear when she put a seashell to her ear. She used to think, when she was a child, that what she heard inside the shells was the voice of the Lord, and that if she was very good or very clever, she would be able to understand what He said. But no matter how hard she tried, she never had been able to make out any words.

The bright sky outside the cistern made her blink. The camps below the Masada were shimmering in the heat, and the workers on the ramp seemed to sway back and forth like melting images. What would she not give now to swim in the sea as she had when she was a child . . . or to return to Ein Gedi with Eleazar . . . to lie with him again on the rushes behind the waterfall, in the cave where David had hidden from King Saul? . . . They could hide there now from the *Kittim*. . . .

Dreams. There was no way back to the sea, and no way now to Ein Gedi. There was no way off the Masada.

Her heart came up in her throat.

It was the first time she had ever stopped to consider that there was no escaping this mountain. This was it. For the rest of their lives. There was no place to go, no way to run. Their only chance for a future lay in vanquishing the more than ten thousand men that made up the Tenth Legion of Imperial Rome and its auxiliaries.

"Have you the water?" Hagar asked. "Good. Took you long enough. There, there, little love," she crooned to the child in her lap. "Here is your mother now, with food and a lovely bath for you as well."

Absently, Alexandra took Beni from the woman and gave him her breast. She did not particularly feel like feeding him at the moment, and she hoped he would finish quickly. She looked down at the child sucking greedily away. "Monster," she murmured. "Here, try this one." She switched him to the other breast. He didn't miss a drop. She had to laugh.

Hagar was pouring the fresh water into a basin. She inspected it carefully for signs of scum or dead, floating insects. Satisfied the water was clean, she straightened and stood waiting, her arms folded across her chest.

"I think he's finished," Alexandra said.

"You mean, you'd like him to be finished. What kind of mother are you?"

"A good mother. A bad cow. Anyway, isn't he getting too big for this?"

"Women of Judea nurse the children until they are three years of age. It is their pride to do so."

Alexandra sighed.

"You are like your own mother," Hagar observed.

"I hope so."

The woman's eyes seemed to soften. "Come, give me the child."

"Not yet." Perching Beni on her knees, she began to pat him softly on the back. After awhile he let out a healthy hiccough, and the two women laughed.

Alexandra readjusted her robe while Hagar lowered the child into the bath. He immediately began to make gurgling sounds, kicking his feet as Hagar swirled the water around his chubby body.

Alexandra smiled. "I really love him," she said. "I love you, little Beni, did you know that? I never knew I could love anyone the way I love you, baby boy. Sometimes, at night, holding him in my arms, Hagar, just the two of us, and everything dark and still . . . I think nothing can be quite so perfect . . . nothing, not even what I have with Eleazar. It's as if everything is suddenly in place. And I feel as if I'm one with everything there is . . . the sea and the sky and the desert and all the animals and birds. . . . I feel as if I know everything there is to know. . . . And then there's that awful smell telling me Beni has to be cleaned up again, and I think, Oh, Lord, there's got to be more than this! Tell me I won't have to spend the rest of my life smelling sour milk and urine and sitting for hours while this little parasite sucks away my life!" She sighed. "I suppose it's just me, of course. I can't imagine Miriam ever feeling that way."

Hagar chuckled. "She would be the odd one if she didn't. Every woman feels as you do."

"Truly?"

Hagar nodded. "But enjoy him while you can, little owl."

Alexandra stiffened. "What do you mean?"

"They grow up sooner than you can imagine, and you are left with the memory of their innocence and beauty, which for a short time belonged only to you." She looked up at Alexandra. "What did you think I meant?" she said carefully.

"It sounded as if . . . someone was going away."

Hagar said nothing for some time, removing the child from the bath and wrapping him in clean linen. "We must leave this place," she said at last in a soft voice.

"You know that is impossible. There is no way—"

"There is always a way."

"Not this time, Hagar. Believe me. I have searched every corner of my mind. There is no way. Besides, Eleazar would never leave—"

"Then go without him."

Alexandra stared at her a moment. "You are nothing but a Greek after all," she said angrily. "Do you think I would leave him? Or the others? You old witch, even if you found a way out for us, do you think I would go without the rest?"

"They would go without you," Hagar replied calmly.

"Some of them, yes! But not all! And it doesn't matter. I do what I think is right."

"And what is right, little owl? Death? You owe the others nothing. You owe your child everything. You owe him life."

The gray eyes had become beacons of cold light, but the dark eyes of the Cretan woman did not waver or flinch. Finally Alexandra said, "I know you say this because you love me and you love the child. But do not speak of it again. I know what I owe my son. I also know what I owe my people and my God."

"The Good Goddess—"

"I do not serve the Good Goddess, Hagar. I am of the line of David, and the daughter of many generations of priests. I serve the God of my fathers, the God of Abraham and Isaac. The One God, Creator and Redeemer of us all."

Hagar had stepped back as if struck. Now she raised her head, perhaps seeing for the first time this slender girl she had raised as a daughter. "Long ago I learned the words of your faith," she said slowly, "but they have never dwelled in my heart. If you, whom I know so well, you, who are like a piece of my own flesh, can say this to me, then I must seek new thoughts. We shall speak no more of the time ahead. Let me stay with you as your servant, daughter of Harsom. That is all I ask."

Alexandra went to her then and put her arms around her. "Of course you shall stay. What would Beni and I do without you? But hadn't you heard, Hagar?" she asked with a smile. "There are no servants on the Masada."

Hagar grunted, pleased. "Tell that to the women," she retorted.

• • •

General Silva waded into the waters of the Dead Sea. It was soothingly warm; by ten o'clock it would be hot. White slabs of salt protruded from the lake like pieces of ice, their alabaster surfaces catching the sun like mirrors. Slowly the Roman moved through the still, blue-green water, his feet padding across the strange, soft, salt bottom of the lake. When he was chest-deep, he slowly brought his legs up, his arms spread wide so as not to tip over, and as though sitting in an imaginary chair, began to rock gently back and forth.

The water was like oil on his flesh; there was the smell of sulphur and of salt, the feel of the sun overhead. He wanted to close his eyes, but he dared not. That was the danger of the lake, the hidden death. It was a lie that one could not drown in this Dead Sea. When Vespasian had thrown prisoners into the deep center of the lake and seen them float to the surface, he did not understand how the warm, oily water could lull a man, make him fall asleep, so that he fell forward and indeed floated, but face downwards. Even now, scarcely minutes after his immersion, Silva could feel the energy draining out of his body, the salt bergs glittering harshly before his eyes. Carefully he set his feet on bottom again and waded back to shore. His aides came forward with vessels of clear water, which they poured over him. Back at camp he would take another bath in water brought from Ein Gedi.

Solomon ben Ya'ish had not lied. The lesions had disappeared from his flesh; still the general went daily to the lake, fearful of any recurrence of the rash.

It seemed to him as they rode back to camp that Antoninus Marcus had become too quiet. He was a serious young fellow to begin with; it was this quality that had drawn Silva to him, apart from the fact that he was the son of the centurion Jocundus. But this silence was something more, the beginnings of an introspection that could lead to no good. One's first time away from home was always hard, and being assigned to Judea was no added bonus. It must be difficult, Silva thought amusedly, for a handsome young Roman, feted and adored by mothers, aunts, and paramours, saluted and cheered by the populace, to find himself in the one place on earth where a Roman was most despised. Was it a shock to young Marc's ears to hear some of the epithets hurled down by the inhabitants of the Masada—along with the bags of refuse, filth, and other unspeakable matter? Had tough veterans like Crassio gotten to him already with their little tricks designed to humiliate and harden new officers? Was the boy homesick? Was he eager to finish the obligatory six months as a tribune before returning to Rome, perhaps eventually to run for the Senate as just about every other young fellow was doing these days? The Senate? No, Silva thought, not the son of Jocundus. He would be a military man, like his father before him.

He made a point of pouring wine for the young tribune when they were back in his tent. "Join me in a libation, Marc." He raised the goblet high. "Caesar. Rome. The gods."

Antoninus Marcus murmured something and passed the goblet before his lips.

"Is something wrong, Marc?"

"No, sir."

"You have become distant. I appreciate a lack of familiarity, but at the same time I find myself wondering lately whether you are paying any attention to my words."

"Have I committed some error, sir?"

"No, no. None that I can see, at any rate. Look, boy, your father was my friend. I have no son of my own. I would like to feel that I—well, if there is anything bothering you—"

"No, sir, nothing. Just the heat, I suppose. It's so strange here. . . . How can they live up there on that mountain with nothing around for miles and miles? . . . No trees . . . no birds except those black vultures that return periodically to peck at the dead." He cleared his throat. "By the way, sir, have you given thought to Solomon ben Ya'ish's suggestion regarding the slaves?"

"What was that?"

"He suggests that by allowing the workers to rest four times each hour—and perhaps giving them a drink of water at that time—you could increase their effectiveness. The guards could further make use of the delay to check their condition and call for replacements as they are needed instead of waiting until men drop."

"Four times each hour. He really does want to slow us down."

"It is the heat, general. It is taking its toll. It is inhuman—"

"Inhuman? You talk to me of being inhuman? Have you forgotten how your father died? Have you forgotten he was murdered by some of the very men, no doubt, for whom you now feel such pity? By the gods, Marc, I cannot believe this. You, if anyone, ought to be wielding the whip out there on that ramp!"

"I have been taught . . . not to hate. . . ."

"Hate? I don't hate those poor creatures out there. I'm talking facts. Justice, Marc. Justice." He surveyed the young man briefly, then turned away, busying himself with his charts. "That will be all, tribune."

"Sir—"

"Yes? What now? More suggestions from the Jew doctor?"

"It's about the girl."

"What girl?"

"The one Larcius Lepidus sent to you. I have her in a tent behind the tradesmen since you do not seem to wish her lodged here. But the men have been asking—that is, what must I do with her?"

"Do? Why, anything you like. Lepidus ought to know I have no time for such nonsense now."

"Shall I send her back to him?"

"No, no, that would be a waste of more time. No, she is here; she might as well serve some purpose. Let her pleasure the officers. A gift from their general. You may take charge of it." He looked up briefly. "I daresay a tumble might cheer you up as well. Do you good, Marc. Make a man of you."

Night in the desert was a black cat with soft fur and the breath of a breeze purring across Antoninus Marcus's eyes as he waded into the darkness beyond the campfires of the men. He had set her tent far back, behind the tradesmen and camp followers, almost hidden from view by a rocky precipice. The Nabatean still guarded her; he grinned as the tribune approached.

She was sitting as he had first seen her, the palms of her hands facing upwards in her lap. He knew she had heard him enter the tent, but she did not move or speak. He walked around the tent, at a loss as to what to do or say, until he found himself standing before her. She did not look up but continued to stare at her palms.

Why was he here? He felt like a fool. Why hadn't he turned her over to Crassio or one of the others and been rid of her? He was about to storm out of the tent when she looked up at him. His anger melted. There was a campstool in the tent. He pulled it over and sat down abruptly.

"I don't know what to do with you," he confessed. "I mean, I know what I have been ordered to do, but . . . I can't. I've

seen the way they are with the women in the camp. You are
so young.... What is your name? Can you understand my
words?"

"My name is Michal. Yes, tribune, I understand."

"That's right. I remember now. The Nabatean said—" He
stopped, staring at her. She had risen from the pallet and was
removing her robe. She moved stiffly, mechanically, like an
old, tired woman. "I didn't mean—" he whispered, and stopped
again. She was standing before him, naked in the shadows,
motionless, waiting. Her body was young and smooth; in the
faint, dusky light of the oil lamp, she was like a piece of amber.
He felt his own body stiffen with desire.

"I know what you mean," she said.

He rose from the chair, angry again, and brusquely reached
for her. She was a prisoner, a slave. Why shouldn't he do with
her as he liked? The general himself had suggested it. But as
his hand touched her shoulder, he felt his anger once more slip
away. Her skin was so smooth under his fingers. His hand
slipped down her arm, all the while drawing her closer to him.
He bent his head, touched her lips with his; but her mouth was
cold. He stepped back to look at her. This time the emptiness
in her eyes did not make him angry but filled him with sadness.
Gently, he took her face in his hands and began to kiss her
again, softly, sadly, with infinite care, as if she were very
precious to him. He could feel something go through her body.
Was it shock? Fear? She seemed to tremble, and though she
made no move to resist, he could feel her struggling against
him. And all the while he was kissing her, gently drawing her
back to him. Suddenly he felt her lips part—she seemed to
sigh—and a sweet warmth rushed into him; he felt flooded by
the sweetness and the warmth, and he knew that she was his.

Night was their blanket. He lay beside her in the aftermath of
desire, his body still warm from hers, but not uncomfortable.
These were the short, cool hours of the desert. Even before
the sun rose, the air would begin to grow heavy again, but now
there was sweet respite. For the moment he could forget where
he was, who he was. His eyes began to close; he was floating
away....

"I did not know ... it could be like that."

She had spoken softly; he could not be sure if she had

spoken to him or to herself. He turned his head to see her. She was staring up at the place where the sky was. He put his hand on her thigh; she seemed to shiver.

"Michal . . ."

She turned her face to his. "I wish . . . you had not come here to me."

"Why?"

"Because now it will be even worse with the others."

"Others?" The dream was gone now, wafted away with the last night breeze. He was in a tent on the perimeter of the Tenth Legion's camp in the Judean wilderness, lying beside a female who was the property of the Roman Empire.

"It would have been better not to know, not to feel. . . ." She began to cry softly, trying to control her sobs, as though she begrudged even this flowing of tears.

He drew her into his arms, pressing her wet face against his shoulder. He stroked her hair. "There will be no others. You are mine now. You belong to me. There will be no one else."

She raised her head. "I belong to you?"

"And I'm not so bad, now, am I?" He hoped she would smile.

But she only sighed. "Now I belong to you." She laid her head against his shoulder again. "But for how long? And then to whom shall you give me?"

"I will give you to no one." But she was crying again. And he lay there, holding her in his arms, watching the light fill the tent, feeling more confused than ever.

"It may interest you to know," Flavius Silva said, "that Vespasian has decided to establish an academy in Rome for the instruction of physicians. Henceforth, no one shall be allowed to call himself a doctor until he has gone through the academy and been found fit by it. Evidently, that foot wound Caesar received in Jotapata has convinced him the Empire needs to take a more serious view of its healers. I am in full concurrence. I mention this now to you, Solomon ben Ya'ish, because I want you to know that I am pleased with your work. I have been thinking of sending you to Rome when this is all over, with the recommendation that you be given a teaching position in Caesar's academy. Frankly, I would prefer to keep you with me in Caesarea. But, to be truthful, I must tell you that as a Judean in Judea, life will not be as pleasant for you as it could be in Rome. The choice, however, is yours."

"Thank you, general."

"Well, do you know what you want?"

"I think I will go to Rome, if it be your pleasure to send me. There is nothing here. My family are all dead or . . . lost to the winds of war. There is nothing to stay for. I would be glad to serve you in Caesarea, but perhaps in Rome I can bring honor to your name by my work and hence advance the general's position."

Flavius Silva smiled wryly. These Jews were not stupid. How smoothly this one made it seem that what was to his advantage was to the Roman's advantage as well.

"So be it, then. Let us hope we finish our task here quickly. Then off to Rome with you, and back to Caesarea for me—or perhaps a new assignment in some more hospitable part of the world."

"You do not find Judea to your liking?"

Silva stared at him. Was the man making fun of him? "It is hardly a pleasant place."

"Pleasant? No, I suppose not. Of course, had you seen it before the war . . ."

"I cannot imagine this province appearing attractive," the Roman murmured. "Nor has there ever been one procurator who had anything good to say about it."

"No, I suppose not," the doctor said again, politely.

"Even the fame of your Jerusalem seems exaggerated. I find it hard to believe in the splendors of which you Jews once boasted."

"Yes," Solomon ben Ya'ish agreed. "It is hard . . . now. But once it was beautiful. Every day was different . . . every hour the sky changed. One minute it was full of roses, and then it was all gold. Birds perched on the courtyard walls and sang." He had finished bandaging the arm of the soldier sitting on the bench before him. He waved the legionary away and smiled. "'If I forget thee, O Jerusalem . . .'"

"What?"

"'. . . let my tongue cleave to the roof of my mouth and my right hand lose its cunning. . . .'" He motioned for the next man to come forward. "That is one thing you cannot take from us, general. Our memories. And we are a people with a long memory."

"I have no desire to take anything from you," Silva replied. "You forget who started this war. As for me, I think I can say I take a dispassionate view of the situation. As far as I can determine, you Jews have gotten only what you deserved. And those people up there have no one but themselves to blame for the inevitable end."

"Inevitable?"

"Of course. When a Roman sets his mind to something— and believe me, I have set my mind to this! At first, it was just another assignment. But once I saw what I must face—" He slapped his fist into his palm. "Oh, I will take that mountain! I tell you frankly, the people up there hardly matter to me anymore. It is that mountain. . . ." He straightened, surprised at himself for this sudden display of emotion. It was unlike him to speak so, especially to a foreigner. He cleared his throat. "Well, I shall take it," he concluded lamely.

"What do you intend to do with those you take prisoner?" Solomon ben Ya'ish asked.

"There will be no prisoners." He turned away, annoyed by the look in the other's eyes. "Perhaps you have forgotten who dwells atop that mountain. Those are the people who lost your precious Jerusalem for you. After what you have suffered, do you wish them to go unpunished? Your own kind denounce them. The Jew Josephus declares the Sicarii to be the most evil of men—fiends, who would destroy the world, to say nothing of Rome—and assuredly they have destroyed your world. Josephus was most adamant in persuading Caesar of the need for their extermination. Now, then, I am reasonably sure of your honesty, Solomon ben Ya'ish. Can you tell me you did not suffer as much under the rule of those who declared themselves Jerusalem's liberators as you do now, victim of their rebellion?"

The Jerusalemite did not answer.

Satisfied, Silva left the tent.

The doctor continued to administer to the soldier on the bench, but in his mind he was seeing something other than the flesh and bone before him. He had spoken of the beauties of Jerusalem, but now he saw the mock trials held by the Zealots . . . good men dragged off the streets or from their beds to be thrown into prison and executed for the sin of class or name . . . daughters of priests paraded naked through the market . . . houses ransacked and burned . . . Judeans fighting in the Temple courtyard, brother against brother . . . the famine . . .

children with swollen bellies dying in the streets while John's men searched the houses for hidden grain and tortured suspected hoarders...

In the end they had rallied against the common, greater foe. But what evil they had meanwhile done to themselves....

"We have our memories," he'd said. "Good ones and bad ones," he ought to have added if he was as honest as the general thought.

I do not have the pride of the vanquished, he thought. I cannot convince myself of our righteousness, even knowing our cause was just. When I think of Simon—with all his good intentions—I think of the innocent felled by his private war, and all the heroics he inspired against Rome pale beside that memory. It is the same with John and all the others. In the siege of Jerusalem I heard brave men cry out as they rode against the legions, "Remember Jotapata!" But all I could remember was Josef ben Matthias going over to Vespasian.

I am a cynic, Solomon ben Ya'ish thought, calling for the next patient to come forward. Perhaps it was a disease one caught from opening others' flesh and seeing that underneath the ridiculously thin armor of skin, men were all the same. Blood and bone, the same vessels leading hither and yon, the same pockets of muscle in greater or lesser degree. *We are all the same,* he thought. *Judean and Roman, gentile and Jew. The Lord made us all.*

What did it matter, then, where he went or to whom he gave his skill? He had been plucked from death a dozen times, but whether in accordance with God's will or by sheer chance he was no longer certain. (What had made him leave that corner of the courtyard moments before it was set afire?) Nor had he any wish to see the rabbi ben Zakkai. Let those who still believed, believe. As for himself, he would go to Rome, immerse himself in science, and forget the past.

When, as a boy, he had announced his intention of becoming a physician, his father had blessed him and sent him forth to study, with the reminder that his endeavors would always be "to the glory of the Most High." For the Lord, his father said, was the One Creator and the True Healer. Whatever young Solomon would learn, either from others or through his own perceptions, was through His grace and must therefore be to His everlasting glory.

Well, he had become a doctor of men. And he would be one now, not for the God of Israel, but for man. He had watched the Roman general poring over his charts, scratching his diagrams in the sand, making battle plans with bits of rock and stone to represent war machines and men. Silva was not a deliberately brutal man. He did not hate the people on the Masada. But he had been given something to do, and he would do it. The fact that the task before him was one that other, perhaps lesser men had determined nigh impossible had only stimulated Silva's energetic mind. He did not ask why; he did not care how many suffered in the process, how many slaves died in the desert, how many legionaries dropped daily from the heat, how much money it cost to transport and build his vast machinery. He was a man with a single purpose. Solomon ben Ya'ish would also become a man with a single purpose. A man of science.

Was it not the only sensible thing?

THREE

When the scaffolding was complete, the slaves began the arduous task of covering it with earth and stone. Day and night they trudged back and forth, a never-ending line; for Silva was determined not to endure another summer in the desert. He hoped, in fact, to finish his ramp before winter set in; and to this end his officers drove the slaves relentlessly. Thousands of them died at the foot of the Masada; and as quickly as they dropped they were replaced from the seemingly inexhaustible store of flesh and blood at Rome's disposal.

Watching the white road grow, the men and women atop the Masada saw the suffering of their countrymen, their brethren below, who seemed now more like pitiful subhuman creatures than like the men they had once been. Their hearts were filled with anger even more than with fear for themselves, for they did not yet believe their God had deserted them. There would be a miracle. They would not be taken. Had not the Righteous Teacher of the Essenes, Nathaniel, prophesied their victory over the *Kittim?* Had not Eleazar ben Ya'ir promised they would not become slaves? No, they on the Masada would be saved. But what of the men below? Where was their help? How long would it be in coming? And why, some wondered, trembling at their own questioning, did not the Lord, seeing how they suffered, reach forth His hand to save them?

They tried to do it themselves. They threw flaming torches down on the scaffolding, but the charred timber was replaced with new, and one hundred slaves were executed in plain sight. Then several men managed to descend the southern slope one night (one fell to his death), creep into the soldiers' camp, and slit the throats of nearly a dozen sleeping legionaries before they themselves were taken. In the morning they were crucified where the remaining inhabitants of the mountain could see their punishment clearly, while for every soldier slain, twenty more slaves were killed. And now, despite the songs of the Essenes, the grim reality of the situation took hold of the people of the Masada. They could not hope to overcome ten thousand men. They could not stop the building of the ramp. And the prisoners whose labor worked toward their destruction were more than slaves; they were hostages.

It was the time for the New Year, of harvests and festivals of thanksgiving. But while the Romans took advantage of the comparatively comfortable weather, the Judeans debated and argued among themselves as to what course they should take. Some now were for surrender, or at least for talking with the Roman commander. Others bitterly denounced such "traitors," reminding them of what had befallen the men of Machaerus who had believed surrender would save their wives and children.

"But that was Lucilius Bassus," one man pointed out. "This Roman may be different."

"They are all the same," Joav growled, to a murmur of consent.

"Simon and John sent word to Titus that they would cease the struggle if he would allow them and their followers to escape to the wilderness. They pledged not to raise arms against Rome in return for the right to live away, alone, as men of Israel. Titus replied that losers did not dictate terms," Sheptai said, "and that they had better be prepared to fight for their lives."

"But that was Titus," the first man said. "This man is not Titus."

"And from whom do you think he gets his orders, then?" Pampras the mason shot back. "From the prophet Elijah?"

"It is my feeling," Eleazar said slowly, "that Titus won't help. They mean to kill us, as they did at Machaerus. Our women and children may survive as slaves, but I don't think we can count that a blessing. I did not believe the Roman when he first sent his greetings, and I do not think now, no matter what he says, that he will discuss terms. It is far too late for that. All this time . . . all those men. . . . Look down there. That is a siege tower. And that one there I warrant is a stone thrower. Oh, no, *chev'ra!* Surrender would spoil this Roman's fun! He is not about to let that happen! But if any of you wish to give yourselves up"—he shrugged—"then that must be a matter for you to decide. I have never asked anyone to stay with me whose heart was not in it."

"No, Eleazar," Joav said. "If only one family goes down—if but one man—then we are all weakened. The *Kittim* must not think any of us has lost his faith. That would give them courage."

"He is right," Sheptai said. "In Jerusalem, John and Simon killed those they caught trying to go over to Titus. They even executed the deserters' families so that others would not follow."

"I am not Simon! Or John!" He drew in his breath, trying to control his anger. "All right. You know how I feel. I will abide by the decision of the majority."

The vote was taken. The number who would have defected was surprisingly small. The council of captains thereupon declared the matter closed. "Anyone caught trying to leave Masada will find himself accommodated quickly," Joav warned, gesturing toward the casemate wall with his thumb. "Top to bottom. Fast."

There were scattered murmurs of "dictator" and "Is it Jerusalem once more?"; but as winter set in, the spirits of the besieged lifted, and they began to feel again that the Lord was working with them. They did not mind the storms and gales when they saw how the army below was hit by them. As Eleazar had noted, the legionaries' tents were situated on the slopes of the hills, where they could not always escape the force of flash floods. Work on the ramp went slowly now, halted by the rains and by the necessity of recovering the animals and equipment that were swept away as wadis became rivers. The soldiers' tempers were not improved by the laughter of the Zealots as they watched the *Kittim* running about, slipping and sinking in endless mud. They traded curses in the wind, the Judeans looking down and the Romans looking up; while the Nabatean and Arab archers sat, indifferent, in their tents, many meters of cloth wrapped around their heads and faces to protect them from the wind-whipped sand that stung the flesh like stones.

"This is the first time I have ever prayed for a long winter," Joav said. "By the time spring comes—even if they do finish their white ramp—they will be so tired and weak they will hardly be able to fight. One more summer, and they will crawl up the ramp like dogs just waiting to be kicked!"

"Do you intend to kick the siege tower as well?" Alexandra

asked drily. "Be careful. You might break your toe."

"Bah! That heap of sand will never hold anything. The tower will slide back on them, you'll see."

"And if they get it up?"

Asshur, who had survived the siege of Jerusalem, shuddered. "May the Lord protect us. In Jerusalem, I remember, they had machines that threw darts and stones. You've never seen such stones. Each must have weighed a talent, yet they were borne through the air maybe two furlongs, if not farther. They knocked down rows of us. The only thing was, we could tell when one was coming. The stones were white, you see, besides which there was always a great noise when they shot one out. Our tower guards would call, 'Baby on the way!' and we would throw ourselves flat on the ground. It worked until the Romans smartened up and started blacking the stones. It was harder to see them then."

"The thing that worries me is the battering ram," Yigael, the scout who had first found Alexandra, admitted. "You ever see one of those monsters in action? There isn't a wall can stand up to one for long."

"You are smiling," Alexandra said to Eleazar. "What is it that amuses you?"

"Nothing, really. Something Yigael said about the ram. It reminded me of someone I once knew."

"Who?"

"Someone who was once a friend. The captain of the Temple guards. I told you about him. . . ."

"Ah, yes, I remember. He was also called Eleazar."

"Eleazar ben Ananias."

"The son of the High Priest. Whatever happened to him, do you suppose?"

"I don't suppose. I know. He was killed at Machaerus." He pulled one of her braids. "You're right. There really isn't anything amusing in all of this."

Two days without rain. Three. It was the end of December, the Hebrew month Kislev. The *Kittim* ought to have been swimming in water; instead they were working on the ramp. The weather was unseasonably dry. Was the Lord forsaking them?

"The Eternal One sees all," the priest Aqavia announced. "He knows when His people stray from righteousness."

"What are you talking about?" Eleazar wanted to know.

"Your Nathaniel says the Almighty protects the Masada because those on it are the last of the just, whatever that means. Well, I will not cast aspersions upon the Brotherhood, despite the blasphemy of their calendar and their low regard for the Temple—may its glory endure forever in men's hearts—but I do know this community is not without its own *Kittim*, its own ungodly."

"*Kittim?* Here?"

"The one who calls himself Aliterus is a Roman."

"Aliterus is one of us. He was a slave in Rome."

"He was an actor! A puppet prancing shamelessly for the amusement of gentiles, mouthing words that praise their gods!"

"I told you once," Eleazar said calmly, "this is a new world. What men were before they came to the Masada no longer matters. All that counts is what they are now."

"So? Then it may interest you to know what he is now. And what he is doing."

"What is he doing?"

"I don't know!" the priest exploded. "But I know he is up to something evil. It could not be otherwise. The children gather around him. They whisper and giggle until I pass by, and then they become ominously silent. Who knows what he is telling them or teaching them to be? He is up to no good. It cannot be otherwise," he said again.

Eleazar cleared his throat. "I will look into it," he promised, and then pretended to be busy with other matters until the priest took his leave.

Once he had gone, Eleazar frowned. He knew of Aliterus's past. It was not the actor's old profession that worried him, nor did he imagine for a moment that Aliterus might be singing the praises of Mars and Jupiter. What bothered him was something Alexandra had said in response to his wondering if Aliterus had left a wife in Rome. "Not a wife," she had replied with a laugh, "but possibly a husband or two." Eleazar felt sure nothing "unnatural" was happening in the community—and yet, with children one might never know. The priest was not the only one to notice a conspiracy. Eleazar had also seen the tightly huddled, excited little groups, had been aware of their silence when they saw him approach. He frowned again, determined now to find out what was going on.

It was Aliterus himself who soon cleared up the mystery.

"As you know," he said one day, "the Feast of Lights draws near. One of the last things the council in Jerusalem did was to declare the Hanukkah a feast day—and while I have no desire to perpetuate the memory of the council, I think it would be good for us all to think now of the Maccabee and perhaps be inspired by their courage."

Eleazar looked at him in surprise, then nodded. "I think so too. But you obviously have something in mind. What is it?"

Aliterus smiled. "A grand surprise," he said, opening wide his arms. "That is, it was to be a surprise. But I am not deaf. I hear the grumblings of our Temple delegate. He is not one to keep his opinions to himself."

"What do you mean?" Eleazar asked, purposely keeping his face blank.

"I know what he means," said Yigael, who had been listening to this exchange. He turned to the actor. "What are you up to with our children? They follow you like cubs to honey. What's going on?"

"The children are preparing a, a—let me try to think of a word that will not offend you—a spectacle!"

"A what?"

His voice dropped. "A play," he said meekly.

"Play?" Yigael was puzzled. "What are they playing at?"

"Being Judah the Maccabee and his followers," the actor said quickly. "They have been rehearsing—I mean playing—for weeks, and on the first night of the feast they will show you something wonderful indeed! Oh, say you do not mind!"

"Why should I mind?" Yigael asked, still not sure what was going on.

Eleazar was less confused. "I think what Aliterus is trying to tell us is that the children—" He hesitated, himself unsure how to put it. "The children wish to celebrate the Feast of Lights by telling us the story in their own way."

"Yes, yes," Aliterus agreed. "We have been going off together to learn the words. They want their fathers and mothers, you see, to be proud of them—and surprised too, of course."

"So that's it!" Yigael understood at last. "Well, I see nothing wrong with that. Do you, Eleazar? Want us to be proud of them, do they?" The face behind the thick black beard had turned red with pleasure.

Eleazar grinned. "I think my son is too young to be involved in this. It's up to you and the others."

"I can't see the harm," Yigael said again. "I would have put my foot down before, but the wife said she didn't mind having an extra moment to herself while the boy was so busy with his friends. And now that I know why... Besides"—his voice softened—"the children have known so much of hardship, so little of play. The days to come will be even more trying. If this can take their minds off... what is down there..." He said no more.

Eleazar nodded. But later, when they were alone, he said to Aliterus, "I warn you, actor. If there is one blasphemous word or action—"

"None! None," Aliterus reassured him. "Every word spoken is from Torah or the Book of the Maccabee."

"It is only words then?"

"There was always singing in the Temple," Aliterus reminded him.

"What else?"

"The sister of Moses led the women in dance when the children of Israel had been delivered from Pharaoh."

"I'm warning you, Aliterus. One step out of line, and I won't have to throw you over the wall. Aqavia will do it for me."

Aliterus smiled.

The Lord is God, and hath given us light.
Order the festival procession with boughs,
even unto the horns of the altar.

There was a hushed silence atop the mountain. Nearly a hundred children stood in the center of a ring of light, completely encircled by scores of small oil lamps that had been carefully placed on the ground. Beyond these footlights sat parents and friends, amazed and entranced by what they saw. Aliterus stood off to the side but in plain view of his small thespians, mouthing the words they spoke, nodding encouragement, now and again waving frantically for some young soldier of the Lord to get back in line. He was more than pleased with the evening's proceedings; he was proud, more proud perhaps than he had ever been of his own greatly applauded accomplishments. There was, he thought, something to be said for art. Despite the rabbis' fears and the priests' denunciations and the abhorrence of ascetics like the Essenes, there was something to be said for an endeavor that, if only for a brief space of time, opened men's hearts, made them laugh or cry, made them think, made them feel.

Made them human.

It was as Rabban Johanan had once said: Judgment had to be based on intention.

More children were filing into the ring now, carrying oil lamps. They had found some old, unused iron spikes in the storerooms and attached small torches to them. Eight of the older boys came forward with these and drove them into the ground. Then the boy David came forth with a ninth spike, whose torch was lit. His voice had deepened considerably since the time Aliterus had first seen him on the wall in Jerusalem. There was the beginning of a dark shadow on his upper lip. His eyes had always been older than his years; tonight, they were the eyes of a young man. A proud young warrior. *I must stop thinking of him as "the boy David,"* Aliterus realized with rueful affection.

"We kindle these lights to commemorate the miracles that the Lord achieved for our fathers in the days of the Maccabee." He brought his torch over to the first spike and lit it. "Blessed art Thou, Lord our God, King of the universe, who hast sanctified us with Thy commandments and hast commanded us to kindle the holy light." He returned to his place and drove the spike into the ground.

"Blessed art Thou, Lord our God," the eight boys said now in unison, "King of the universe, who didst perform miracles for our fathers in the days of the Maccabee, at this season."

Then all the children said, "Blessed art Thou, Lord our God, King of the universe, who hast granted us life and sustained us and brought us to this season."

There was singing now, adults joining the children in the verses of the Hallel, the psalms praising the glory of God.

Aliterus looked around at his audience, their features strangely clear in the moonlit night, golden in the haze of the torches and the oil lamps. There was the priest Aqavia, his suspicious eyes closed contentedly as he swayed and nodded and sang. There was Joav, the red-haired giant, bellowing out hymns with the same great force that sent the rolling rocks down on the hated *Kittim*. Next to him stood fair Miriam, looking longingly at the children who would never be hers.

Over there sat the mute Hadassah, suckling her newborn daughter. Sheptai sat next to her, frowning slightly, his eyes far away.

There were Shem and Yigael and Zidon and Asshur and Nimrod and Heth . . . their wives and daughters. . . .

And there, sitting cross-legged on the ground, leaning against the broad-shouldered man with the mane of gold, was Alexandra. Her son, Benjamin, lay in her lap, asleep and all but forgotten. But no, she had moved her hand down to reassure herself of the child's presence. At the same time, Eleazar put out his arm, drawing her even closer to him. Aliterus could not take his eyes away from them; it was as if he hoped by staring at them so to keep their image with him forever.

A low voice in his ear made him jump.

"You have done well," Hagar said.

He turned to the Cretan woman and bowed slightly. "Your praise, madam, is to be cherished."

She was not looking at him, he realized, but staring at the children. "I see a girl-child in the ring of lights," she said. "And over there, another."

"There are many in the group. They would not be dissuaded. They said their mothers had thrown oil upon the soldiers at Jotapata and stuck knives into the legionaries in the streets of Jerusalem. I told them a mixed assembly was the surest excuse for Aqavia's wrath, but they shouted hotly at me—things about women named Devorah and Judith and Hannah, with her seven sons." He shrugged. "What could I do? Even the lads were cowed. By everything holy, I've never seen a more willful bunch of females!"

Hagar smiled slightly. "All the children here are spoiled." Briefly she scanned the audience of beaming parents. "They want them to have everything . . . while they can." Her gaze returned to the children. "Do you ever think of your old gods?"

"Jupiter and Apollo? Hermes and all the rest? Why, they were only masks an actor sometimes wore."

"I remember, in the place where I was born . . . the chants and the dancing and the fires of the temples. I remember darkness . . . and the taste of wine . . . and the heat of the fires and the chants and the dancing. I remember the sun burning the backs of the bull-jumpers, the way their oiled bodies arched as they ran and leaped, while our own hearts pounded hotly to see them." She looked up at the moon, full and white. "No children," she said flatly. "No songs a child would sing. The Good Goddess gave her daughters comfort but never the strength to be like these daughters of Israel. What is the meaning of this God whose name is never spoken, whose face is never seen, that He can be Lord to man and woman, parent and child?"

"Listen. . . ."

"*The Lord is for me*," the children were singing. "*I will not fear. The Lord is my strength and song.*"

"It is said," Aliterus told Hagar, "that when the Eternal One made known His desire to give Torah to the world, all the people of the earth gathered together, each nation asking to be the guardian of the Holy Words.

"'Give Torah to us,' spake the kings of the west, 'and all our gold and silver we pledge to Thee.'

"'Give Torah to us,' spake the kings of the east, 'and incense and spices, which are our great wealth, shall we pledge to Thee.'

"'Nay,' said the leaders of the northern nations. 'Look to us, Almighty, and our great armies and fierce warriors will forever protect Thy blessed gift.'

"And those of the south said, 'Choose us, Lord, and the fruits of the earth shall we place at Thy altar, along with precious gems and objects of wondrous design.'

"And so each and every nation and tribe put forth its request and pledge. But Israel was silent, for of all the peoples gathered she was the smallest and the poorest. Then, finally, the Almighty spoke and said, 'Tribe of Abraham, have you naught to pledge? Know ye, I must have guarantee that my Torah will not be abandoned but cherished for all time.'

"Then Israel said, 'We have no gold to give, Lord, nor gems nor great domain. But if Thou wilt give Thy Torah to us, we will give Thee our most precious possession, which is our children. And they shall be Thy surety and our bondsmen for all time.'

"And so it was that the Lord gave His commandments to the tribe of Abraham, choosing the Israelites to be His people in return for their promise to teach Torah to their children, thereby assuring its perpetuity and safekeeping. So it is as the sages say," Aliterus finished softly. "'The world rests upon the breath of children.'"

The lights on the Masada illuminated the sky above the mountain so that to those below the plateau appeared to wear a halo or crown of light. Michal stood in the opening of the tent, gazing up at the rock fortress.

"Michal. Michal . . . what are you doing there?" Antoninus Marcus sat up and rubbed his eyes. "I must have fallen asleep. Is the hour late?"

"No, it is early. The night is before us."

He smiled and held out his arms to her; but she was not looking at him. "Michal . . ."

"The Feast of Lights," she said softly. "They have kindled the first flame. . . ."

"What are you talking about?"

"Sshh. You can hear them singing." She listened a moment, then closed her eyes, humming softly.

"Come back to me."

She opened her eyes then and returned to his embrace.

"Tell me about your Feast of LIghts," he said. "Is it a happy occasion?"

"Most happy. We celebrate the miracle of the Temple."

"What miracle is this?"

"It was after the war against Antiochus the Syrian. He tried to make my people give up our God and worship false idols. Many were killed for refusing to bow down, until finally the family of the Maccabee drew all the people together to fight against the Syrians. And Antiochus was defeated."

"Is that the miracle?"

"When the people came to the Temple, they saw that the soldiers of Antiochus had defiled it. Unspeakable filth covered the floor. The walls were covered with crude words. The sacred utensils had been broken, and unclean animals allowed to roam inside. In the very center, on the altar, was a statue of one of their dead gods."

"And the miracle was that all this disappeared, right?"

She laughed. "It was no miracle! The people worked very hard for many, many days cleaning the Temple and repairing what had been broken. But at last all was ready for the rededication of the House of the Lord and the lighting of the eternal flame." She paused.

"Don't stop now. Go on!"

Michal smiled. "Well! The priests searched but could find only one undefiled cruse of oil with the seal of the High Priest. It had only enough oil to burn one day—and it would take a full week until more could be brought. And then the miracle happened. The oil in the lamp burned eight full days, and the Temple was not in darkness."

"A fine miracle indeed," he agreed. "But how do you know

someone was not adding oil when the rest were not looking?"

"Because there was no other oil! Oh, you are teasing! Even so . . ."

"Even so . . . ?" His lips had found her shoulder.

"One believes . . . or one does not believe."

He pulled her down on the bed. "Do you believe?"

Her eyes were open, staring straight into his. "Yes."

He sat up. "After all that you have lived through?"

"Yes."

He ran his hand through his hair. "How much stronger is your faith," he wondered, "than mine."

"You believe in the One God?"

He stared at her a moment. "I don't know . . . what I believe in."

But she was listening to the singing again, her eyes far away. "Come," she said, and led him from the bed to the opening of the tent. "Look how the light glows atop the mountain! And the stars, see how bright they are. Look over there, at that one star! It is so much larger than the rest. It is like a jewel up in the sky."

He nodded. "Like the star over Bethlehem," he said absently.

"You know of Bethlehem?" she asked, delighted. "My father was from Bethlehem."

"Was his name also Jesus?"

"Jesus?" She shook her head. "I know no one by that name."

"It would no doubt be different in Aramaic," he said, more to himself.

"You know a man from Bethlehem called Jesus? A Jew?"

He nodded. "He was born in Bethlehem but lived most of his life in your Galilee. No, I never met him. But I know about him. My mother, you see . . . never mind." He laughed a little, uneasy. "Come back to bed."

"Not yet . . ."

He was already under the blanket. "Do you wish you were up there with them?" he asked suddenly.

"Yes."

He was hurt. "I thought I made you happy."

She turned to stare at him. Her mouth opened, then closed. "Happy?" she echoed at last, flatly.

"You said you had never known such feelings as when we are together."

She moved slowly to the bed and sat down. "I . . . am

a . . . person," she said finally, struggling to find the words that would make him understand. "The time with you is good . . . but these are moments, and moments do not make a day . . . or a life. One day you will return to your country—"

"I will take you with me."

"To Rome? To be a slave?" There was no joy in her voice.

"Not a slave. My family does not keep slaves."

"A Roman without slaves? You are poor, then, or your family is strange."

"We are not poor. But, yes, I suppose we are . . . different. Once, when I was a child, I saw four hundred slaves executed. One of them had slain their master. The authorities knew who the murderer was but decided that all the slaves of that household were to be punished as an example to other slaves. They killed them all, whole families of them, old and young, men and women. Because only one had committed a crime." He paused. "My mother wept. Later, she told me that though they had suffered death here, they would live in heaven, to sit beside the Christ. . . ." He stopped, startled by the words that had escaped his lips. He gave a short laugh. "Well, now you know," he said. "The family secret. My mother . . . is of the same persuasion as those who call themselves Christians."

She was trying to read his eyes. "That is a bad thing to be?"

"In the eyes of Rome it is! My mother could one day find herself in the arena along with captives from your Judea, and from Britain and just about everywhere else we've planted the Eagle. No matter the illustrious heritage of her line—a good, strong, Roman military line, I might add."

"But why?"

"She is an enemy of the state. Vespasian does not actively pursue the Christians as Nero did, but the edict remains."

"And you?"

"What about . . . me?"

"Are you an enemy of the state?"

"I am a tribune of the Tenth Legion of Rome, aide to General Flavius Silva, military governor of the Roman province of Judea. There is no reason for anyone to doubt my loyalty to Caesar."

"But if the things you believe—"

"I told you," he said, reaching for her again. "I don't know what I believe."

• • •

"What does it mean?" Silva asked. He gestured toward the Masada, where the sound of singing was clear in the night. "They've never done that before. That glow in the sky... some ritual before attack? Some sort of barbaric magic to frighten the troops?"

"Barbaric?" Solomon ben Ya'ish looked wonderingly at the Roman. Each morning Silva stood on the dais of his tribunal, surrounded by standard-bearers. One of the bearers wore the skin of a leopard like a helmet, its jaws open above his head, the body of the animal hanging down his back. Another man had on the skin of a wolf. From time to time a goat would be brought and killed, its entrails examined to determine good or bad fortune. The body would then be offered in sacrifice to a gilded statue of Victory flanked by small portraits of Vespasian and Titus. Barbaric? Aloud Solomon ben Ya'ish said, "They celebrate the Feast of Lights. It is a happy occasion."

"Really? I did not know you people had glad festivals. I thought it was all moaning and praying to the wind. Happy, you say?"

"A commemoration of an earlier time, when foreign oppressors were driven from our land. Perhaps more important to some, the feast recalls the Hanukkah, or Rededication of the Temple."

"And I suppose up there they are thinking that someday they will have another Temple, eh?"

"I do not know what they are thinking... up there."

"I can tell you now there will be no more Temples for the Jews," Silva said matter-of-factly. He looked up. "Well... there, that ought to douse their lights. It's begun to rain."

Alexandra stood in the doorway of the palace, where she was sheltered from the sudden storm. Behind her she could hear snatches of conversation still going on despite the lateness of the hour. The children's pageant had gladdened everyone's heart; afterwards people had gathered in friendly groups, sharing wine and fig cakes and memories of other, happy times. But inevitably, as they reminisced, someone brought up the war, and then they all began to speak of it, each with his own tale of horror. Soon it seemed to Alexandra that the talk had become a grotesque contest as to which among them had seen the most violence.

Disgusted, she had taken her leave, gratefully breathing in the cold night air, the sweet smell of the rain. How strange, she mused, that those whom one might most expect to be mad were not, while those who had seemingly suffered least in these terrible times were so often the ones who made the most noise. *But who can measure pain?* she thought. *Who can draw up a ledger of human loss and give a true accounting? Does the death of a child weigh more heavily on the scales than the death of a husband? Is the loss of maidenhood commensurate with that of an arm or leg or eye?*

"Why did you leave?"

She leaned back into his arms. "I couldn't let them spoil this night. Why must the old men always cry? I'm sick of hearing about Jerusalem and the Temple. I don't want to know how Ezra's brother died, or that Nimrod's mother was trampled to death, or that—oh, why won't they forget! Or at least let the rest of us forget. Just once. Just one night."

His arms tightened around her. His lips brushed her hair. "No," he said softly. "We fight, Alexandra. . . . We die for freedom, and when freedom is ours we forget what we fought for and why. The Maccabee drove out the foreign king and his gods—and then our people raised up their own tyrants and polluted the Holy Place. The princes and priests of Jerusalem grew fat on the offerings of the *am ha'eretz* and forgot how their grandfathers ate grass and lived in caves while the battle for freedom was going on. Even now, while we stand here— all that is left of a free Judea—even now . . . some sigh for the 'good times' before the war, forgetting all that happened to make us fight, forgetting even what happened at Machaerus. No . . . let the old ones remind us. So that with every breath we take we say, 'Never again!' "

She lowered her head, chastened, but not for long. "I only asked for a night," she reminded him. "Just one night."

He nipped her ear. "A reasonable request."

His tone had lightened; and for a moment she had a vision of the young Galilean she had met so long ago, with his impudent grin and brash manners. The daredevil eyes brooded more often than not in these days, a dark and troubled sea; and there were streaks of white in the tawny gold head. She suddenly realized how much he, more than any of them, must want a moment away from war and death.

"Shall we attend to it?" he was murmuring in her ear.

She turned in his embrace and put her arms around his neck. "With all my heart."

FOUR

Winter ended, and work on the ramp was renewed. The slaves were driven mercilessly now, and the tempers of the soldiers seemed to grow meaner each day. Zealot snipers like David rarely missed. *But what were a hundred men killed compared to the thousands left?* Eleazar thought.

"You worry too much," Joav said. "As high as they dare to build their road, they will still fall short of reaching our wall. Many Romans will die in the meters between the end of the ramp and the top of the Masada," he promised.

But Eleazar took little comfort in this. Day and night he searched his mind for ways to sabotage the Roman effort; but he could find none, and neither could his captains.

Eight months had passed since the day they first heard the drums of the Tenth Legion and saw the sun gleaming on the brass chestplates of the *Kittim*. Eight months watching them build their wall and their machines and the ramp to reach them. Eight months of trading insults and threats, of sniping, of small and daring but hopeless confrontations. Eight months of watching their brothers below turn from proud men, farmers and fighters, into wretched beasts of labor.

They had laughed at the *Kittim*, knowing how time would take its toll on the desert's intruders; but time was taking its toll on them as well. Another, subtler war was being waged while the preparations for armed battle took place. As the mound of white earth crept nearer, their tension grew as well. There were moments when it seemed they all must be thinking the same thoughts, when a strange silence pervaded the plateau and the only sound was of those below working toward their destruction.

Only the Essenes went about their business as though nothing unusual were occurring, and the face of their spiritual leader, Nathaniel, seemed to grow more radiant each day.

"Guide me," Eleazar pleaded with him. "You are so sure. But hope dims in the people's eyes. What can I tell them? What must I say?"

"Say always what is in your heart, Eleazar. You have never lied to anyone. The Lord knows this, and I know it as well. Say, then, what you know to be the truth. Say what is in your heart."

"In my heart?" He laughed harshly. "Fear is in my heart. There are brave men on the Masada, but"—he made a gesture in the direction of the Roman camp—"facts speak for themselves."

"What facts are these, Eleazar?"

"We have no mighty war engines. We are outnumbered many times over. There are women here and children. . . . I fear that finally we will be overwhelmed."

The white-haired Essene nodded. "Look at me, Eleazar. Tell me, can you see me clearly?"

"Why, yes," he replied, startled by the question.

"There is sufficient light in this room?"

"Why, yes," he said again. "It is quite bright."

"Yet what is light in this room may certainly be dark as compared to the brilliant sunlight outside. Is that not so?"

"Yes . . ."

"So it is with your 'facts.' There is but one truth, Eleazar, and that is the Lord's truth." He closed his eyes and recited softly, *"My footpath is over stout rock which nothing shall shake. . . . For the rock upon which I walk is the truth of God . . . and His might is the support of my right hand."* He opened his eyes. "The Sons of Light must battle with the company of Darkness to make manifest the might of God. Tell the people, Eleazar, that the Lord will deliver their souls when their distress is unleashed, just as He will direct thy steps to the way. Tell them, Eleazar, the victory will be ours."

But Eleazar's heart was not lightened. He left Nathaniel with a heavy step, walking away woodenly, without direction, until suddenly he felt a light touch on his arm and, turning, saw Alexandra.

"I've been looking everywhere for you," she said breathlessly.

He had to smile. "Have you been running again? You know it is unseemly—"

"Oh, don't start that! Besides, I hate the word *unseemly*."

He grinned. Nothing would change her, not even the threat of ten thousand legionaries. On a sudden impulse he swept her off her feet and started to walk away with her in his arms.

"Eleazar! Put me down! Now who is being unseemly?"

"Did I ever tell you? I hate that word. Well, where shall we go? Tiberias? Ashkelon? Back to Ein Gedi?"

"Oh, to the sea, of course! There is a cove of rocks on the beach of Caesarea . . ." Her voice trailed away.

He set her down, and for a moment they just stood there looking at each other, the game ended. "I'm sorry," he said finally. "I thought we were safe here, all of us. I thought all we had to do was wait. . . ."

She touched his arm again. "We are safe. I'm glad we did not run. Or surrender. No matter what happens."

He was about to answer when he felt another tug. This time it was the woman Batsheva. One child clung to her robe, while the latest issue was tucked under one arm. "It is good to see you smile, *Adoni*," she said, shy of him but encouraged by Alexandra's presence. "There is nothing to worry about, is there? The Lord will not forsake us, will He?"

"What do you think?" he responded softly.

"I think it is good that you are smiling."

He grinned now, put his finger on the button nose of the infant in her arms. "Who is this little one?"

"That's Sara," Alexandra said.

"Sara, eh? What a beauty this one will be! Tell me," he joked, "should I make a match for my son now, or is she already spoken for?"

Batsheva smiled, pleased but still shy. "There is time, plenty of time for such things." Her face became serious. "Will there be . . . time?"

"I don't know," he replied.

"I will not give them my children," she said suddenly. "I will not give my Boaz and my Sara to them. You must promise me that. You must give me your word that no matter what happens the *Kittim* will not get our children."

"What if I cannot keep my word?"

"You will. Everyone knows you do not lie. If you say the children are safe, then I will believe it."

He stared at her. Finally he said, "Rome will not have the children of Masada. I pledge this to you."

"Now," she said, "I will also smile."

"We can fight too," Alexandra said when Batsheva had gone off. "We can throw hot oil on them and fight with knives if need be. Don't shut us away when the time comes! Please, Eleazar! At least let me be with you when it happens."

He tried to make light of it. "I suppose you'd like me to give you lessons with the sword."

"Yes, I would," she replied gravely.

"Alexandra. . . ." He sighed. "Give thanks to the Lord that you have never had to take a life."

"There are some lives I wouldn't mind taking."

"I too, woman. But it doesn't make me glad." He took her hand and led her onto the terrace of the north palace.

The place was never deserted now; there were always children playing here, running up and down the hidden staircases, hoping to astonish the legionaries below by being on one terrace and then suddenly on another. Three little girls sat cross-legged in a corner now, their heads together, whispering and giggling. They jumped up when they saw Eleazar descend the stairs and quickly ran away, their faces crimson. Alexandra smiled; but Eleazar did not seem to take notice, so deep was he in thought.

At last, with great difficulty, he said, "If I could, I would send you to safety . . . you and Beni. But if I find a way for you, can I not also find a way for Batsheva and her children, and all the others?" He sighed and ran his hand through his hair, a man in a deep, private struggle. "But if you wish it," he said finally, "I swear I will get you out of here."

Even as he spoke, she saw the pain in his eyes, and so she smiled, saying softly, "Do you think my love is less than yours, that I care more for my own life than for you, or that life itself without you is worth anything to me?" Her chin came up. "Or do you doubt my courage?" she challenged lightly. "Perhaps you think your Sadducee princess trembles so before the army of Caesar that she cannot take her place at her husband's side like any good woman from the Galilee?"

He grinned now, the darkness gone from his eyes, so that they were as blue as the sea she so longed to behold. Gripping her arms tightly he said, "I doubt neither your courage nor your love. But we both know what it will be like if the soldiers reach us. We won't be able to fight off all of them. Even if every woman and child here could by some miracle wield a sword, we are still outnumbered, greatly so. Unless all of

...aniel's angels descend from heaven or the prophets' army ...ry bones rises up from the grave to help us, we haven't much of a chance. And when it happens . . . if they take you . . ." He stopped, took a deep breath. "I have been thinking. . . . You have friends in high places. Josef ben Matthias must be doing well for himself. You said Vespasian was kind to you. I could arrange a meeting with Silva . . . say we took you as hostage. They need not know you are my wife, or that Benjamin is . . . my son. . . ." He was stumbling over the words, a man fighting against reality, a man pretending to himself that what he planned was possible.

She turned away so that he would not see the tears in her eyes. "It is a long way between here and those who once knew me," she managed to say lightly, with a careless shrug. "I doubt Vespasian would remember me—or that Josef would care to. Why"—she turned back with a smile—"I don't think they would even recognize me now. I am as brown as a Numidean, and my hands as rough as any country girl's. I think not even a foot soldier of the Syrian cohorts would want me."

He laughed now and hugged her to him. "You are more beautiful than ever!" He took her face in his hands. "You are like the rose that blooms in the desert, more rare and lovely than any flower in all the world. You have bloomed here," he said, his lips coming close to hers. "You have become a woman."

Jonatan sat cross-legged like a tailor, sewing skins together with linen thread. Messages and contracts might be written upon parchment or papyrus, but the words of the Holy Books could only be inscribed on leather. When a scroll of scripture became too worn to be used, it was not destroyed but rather buried in the *geniza,* or pit, under the floor of the synagogue. To destroy a religious scroll was forbidden—not only to the Essenes but to all Israelites—for the word of the Lord was a living thing; it was life itself. One of the ways in which the Romans and other enemies persecuted Jews was by tearing or burning books of the Bible before their eyes. When the legions were first sighted approaching Qumran, Jonatan had taken many scrolls and hidden them in caves high up in the cliffs, where they would be safe from the *Kittim.* It was that act which had saved his life.

"Mordecai the tanner says he will have more skins for you

by evening." Alexandra stood in the entrance to the tiny case-mate chamber, with Beni in tow.

He looked up. "Please..." he said lamely, gesturing nervously at the toddler, who had begun an instant examination of the room and all its contents. "If you don't mind..."

"Oops! Sorry! I forgot." She swept the child up. "Come here, Beni. We don't want you knocking over any inkwells like last time. Naughty monkey." She grinned at Jonatan. "It's just that he's so curious. Well, I'll let Miriam take him to the pool. She said she wanted to. Wait here, I'll be back. I want to talk to you."

He breathed a sigh of relief as she spirited the child away. She was not gone long, however; returning, she began to read the hides he had left out to dry. She was, he had long ago learned, a compulsive reader.

"Everyone is so busy," she said. "You are at it day and night. The tanner too—and not just because of your requests. Amnon the potter . . . the baker . . . everyone is working as if there will be no tomorrow."

He barely looked up. "You ought not to have let Miriam take the child to the bathing pool," he said in his gentle voice. "It is unclean. The children relieve themselves in the water. He will get the eye sickness."

"I know." She sighed. "But he must have friends. I want him to play with the others. You will just have to make that ointment again."

"I need the black mud of the sulphur springs. There is no way to get it now."

"Well, I'm sure Hagar will come up with something. She always does. Besides, nothing may happen. I told Miriam to keep his face out of the water." She peered over his shoulder. "You sew a finer line than I. What neat stitches. They are almost as beautiful as your script."

"All work is holy."

"No, it isn't."

He smiled and shook his head.

"I know you love your work," she said, suddenly curious, "but have you never wished to be something other than a scribe . . . or an Essene?"

"Once," he said, not looking up. "There was a time I doubted my worthiness, when I did not know if I was fit to serve the Brotherhood."

"But you were born to the Community!"

"Yes...I never had the choice. Why are you surprised? You told me once you used to wish you had not been born female. And your Josef, for all his words in Israel's defense— did you not say that he secretly wishes he were not one of us?"

"Yes..." She thought a moment. "Eleazar never wanted to be a soldier, even after what happened to his mother and father. He thinks of himself as a farmer. Can you believe it?"

He smiled. "Yes."

"But not in the Galilee. That is what is so strange. He loves the Masada, Jonatan. Truly loves it. And the wilderness around us. He says that if the Romans let us be we could build a new Jerusalem right here...that we could make even Jeshimon green if we were left in peace."

"The Nabateans tend gardens in the desert. At Qumran we unlocked many mysteries of their water supply. And you see for yourself how the Masada is provided. It is not so strange as you think, Alexandra."

"But trees and fields and cities where now there is only this desolation—"

"If the Lord were to smile upon us, if we were returned to His favor, would not anything be possible? What we speak of is only a small miracle for the Creator of the World."

She was silent, remembering how Eleazar had looked out over the empty sand and silent sea. "All my life I have been made to fight," he had said. "I was a *bacchur* even before I was thirteen, while that which I wanted—to make things grow—has always been beyond my reach. I used to think, 'When this is over, when they are gone from our land...' But I think now I will never know the kind of life my father knew." He had turned abruptly to her and smiled. "What does it matter? We are free. We are alive. In these times that should be enough for anyone."

Absently she reached for one of the scrolls on the writing table. "Do you believe in dreams, Jonatan? I mean, do you think the thoughts we have while we sleep may be more than our own thoughts?"

"The first divination is of dreams."

"Listen, then. For three nights I have dreamed of Jerusalem. The first night I saw it as it was when I was a child. The second night I saw a desert, but I heard a voice saying clearly, 'Here is his Holy City, but where now is thy beloved king?' I took this to mean the desert was Jerusalem destroyed—and the king referred to was David. For *David* means 'beloved.'"

He said nothing, but every muscle in his body had tensed. He felt a chill on the back of his neck. But he did not move.

"And then, last night, I dreamed again of Jerusalem. I saw the road we took, winding our way up into the hills, going higher and higher.... I could hear the trees rustling, the pine and the cypress.... I saw the sun fall dappled on the olive groves. . . . And I saw the towns outside the city . . . the women at the wells who gave us water... the men pausing in the fields to press a coin in our hands for the blessed, *mitzveh* journey to the Temple . . . children gamboling alongside like lambs. . . .

"But I clung to my father, for he was alive and beside me in this dream. And I spoke anxiously to him, saying the city had been destroyed, and everything around it...yet here were people smiling and happy, and the earth was green, as it was before the Romans came.

"My father only smiled and pointed in the distance.... And there I saw Jerusalem, more beautiful than before, and a stream of people going up to the city, old and young, and all happy and singing songs. And I saw that the walls of the city were no more, but that it was ringed with wondrous buildings of white stone, tall as mountains. The parched and treeless earth that I had once seen now seemed a dream within my dream, for everywhere it was green . . . and I felt the sun on my face. . . .

"My father took me to that high spot where as a child I had first discovered Jerusalem's gold, and as he had then, he closed his eyes to the beauty before us, rocking back and forth on his heels, murmuring prayers. I looked around.... I could smell the fragrance of the earth.... Everything seemed bathed in soft colors, as after a rain.... But the sun was shining, and people, thousands of them, were coming into the city, their arms around one another, their voices raised in song.

"'But this was destroyed,' I said.

"My father opened his eyes and smiled. 'From ashes comes forth life. From the four winds, breath for the slain, that they shall live again.'

"'Is it the Messiah?' I asked. 'Has the Messiah come?'

"And my father laughed with great joy. 'Yes,' he said. 'The Messiah has come.'

"'Who is he?' I asked. 'What is his name?'

"'Israel,' he replied. 'He is Israel.'"

She had finished speaking and now sat quiet, still lost in

the dream she had recounted. Finally, she raised her eyes to his. "You know of these things," she said, her voice barely more than a whisper. "What does it mean?"

He did not reply but took the scroll that she had been holding absently in her lap. Straightening the thin, pale leather, he began to read.

> Thus said the Lord God: When I have cleansed you of all your iniquities, I will people your settlements, and the ruined places shall be rebuilt; and the desolate land, after lying waste in the sight of every passerby, shall again be tilled. And men shall say, "That land, once desolate, has become like the garden of Eden; and the cities, once ruined, desolate, and ravaged, are now populated and fortified." And the nations that are left around you shall know that I the Lord have rebuilt the ravaged places and replanted the desolate land. I the Lord have spoken and will act.

"Ezekiel," Jonatan said. "For three days now I have been driven by a force outside myself to prepare a new scroll of the prophet."

She stared at the manuscript. "What does it mean?" she asked again.

"I think it means . . . we are not to lose hope."

"We, on the Masada?"

"We are part of something greater than ourselves, Alexandra."

She stood up. "I must tell Eleazar. I meant to tell him of my dream this morning, but somehow I forgot. And now there is your scroll. I must tell him."

"Yes."

She hesitated at the entrance to the room. "You said before that once you were not sure of your calling. What made you change your mind?"

He smiled his sweet, gentle smile. "I prayed . . . and the way was shown to me."

FIVE

"The bank has been raised and is solid for some two hundred cubits," Flavius Silva said. "Even so, it is not sufficient for the use of the engines, as I had once thought. A platform will have to be built at the top of the ramp. It must be at least fifty cubits high and equal to that in breadth."

His engineers nodded, quickly beginning a discussion among themselves as to the elements that would go into the platform's construction. Silva listened to them awhile, then finally said impatiently, "It would take months to get and bring more timber, while the area abounds in rocks. The slaves will lay stones for the platform." He turned his back on them with a disgusted look, catching Crassio's grin as he did. *This place is getting to me,* he thought. It was not like him to bark at his men, particularly his corps of engineers. But he was so close to getting what he wanted—and so infuriatingly far from it. At least twenty yards of the original footpath lay between the top of the white ramp and the casemate wall. The ramp had to be level with the wall, the siege tower above it so that his archers could shoot down. He needed a higher, level base.

It was spring in the rest of the world, while it was nothing but flies and sun and white dust. Another month, and the heat would be unbearable again. His men could take another summer in the desert—the Roman soldier could take anything if he had to—but it would be a cruelty. Besides, he could not allow the situation to remain as it was much longer. There had been letters from Rome. Life in the Imperial Palace seemed to have made Vespasian lose all memory of the Judean desert, to forget its hardships and his own statements regarding the tenacity of the Sicarii, as well as his eagerness to see them exterminated. Now all he seemed to care about was how much money was being sent to outfit this "little expedition."

It was interesting, Flavius Silva thought drily, that the farther one was removed from Judea, the easier it seemed—even to veterans of the long war like Vespasian and Titus—to round up and do away with "a bunch of Jews."

Someday, the Roman thought wistfully, *I will be equally forgetful . . . until such time as I am in the baths with a glass of wine in my hand, or watching some charioteer . . . and an attendant slave's sad face or the dust blown round the ring reminds me of these hellish months.*

Unless, he thought, always the realist, *I end up here forever—or am rewarded with duty in some equally unattractive outpost for failing to put an end to these rebels.*

He looked up at the Masada. Only when one approached it as those who would attack it had to come, through the waterless wilderness of Judea—that bit of Hades risen to earth, that hell with the sun shining into it—only then, Silva thought, could one feel its complete remoteness, its savage height, its power to turn would-be besiegers to despair.

It was the Gorgon's head . . . magnified to a mountain.

But I'll take you, he thought. *Not because Caesar fears you or to advance my own position, but because I want you. Because I know it can be done. And if it can be done, it should be done. And I will be the one to do it.*

But meanwhile, he needed to get away.

"We spotted the white horse again," Crassio said.

His heart took a sudden leap. "Where?"

"To the north. The men chased her, but they finally lost her."

"Again?"

"She just disappears, sir. And we have to be careful with our own animals. It's too easy for them to stumble and break their legs crossing the wadis. We've already lost more than a few that way."

"I want that white horse. We must have the spring races to honor Mars, and I intend to be riding that mare."

"She's wild, sir."

He shook his head. "One doesn't see horses like that in Judea unless they belong to some nomad king come for trade or war. The mare belonged to someone once. By the gods,

I've never seen such a beautiful animal!"

"Well, general, the last we caught sight of her she was heading toward Ein Gedi. I could take some men and—"

"No! I'll do it myself. I could use a ride today. Stir up a little dust of my own. Soldiers like you and I aren't used to all this sitting around, are we, Crassio?"

The legionary grinned. "Shall I come with you?"

"No, you stay here and keep things steady. The workers keep moving when you're around."

"Well, I guess they know I have a long whip and a quick wrist," he drawled, pleased.

"A long whip, eh? That isn't what the men of the Tenth used to call it."

Crassio grinned again. "Wouldn't know what to call it anymore. Doesn't seem to have much use outside of peeing in the sand."

"Aren't the camp followers supplying your needs?"

"Nothing but putrefying bags of bones. Love here's gone dry as the desert, and the itch gets you bad, if you know what I mean. It's the waiting does it, mostly. If you can't fight you might as well screw, and if there's no one to screw, then let's at least take those mother-dogs up there."

"Soon, Crassio," Silva promised. "I know how difficult it's been for everybody. Only a bit longer, and we'll be out of here. But not before we take a look at what's atop that putrefying mountain, eh? I trust you may find some females there more to your liking. Seems to me I've heard you and your companions discussing the merits of the Sicarii women."

"Well, sir, by now anything looks good. Except that dead meat at the rear of the camp."

"I didn't realize. I'll have word sent to Lepidus in Jerusalem to ship out a wagon or two. That's one supply order he ought to be able to fulfill without his customary delay."

"Thank you, general. It will keep spirits high."

"Not at all." He was anxious to be on his way.

"There is something, sir. . . ."

"What?"

"Well . . ." He cleared his throat. "Way back in the northwest sector there's this tent. It's at the bottom of a wadi—you can hardly see it. One of the Nabateans stands guard there. There's a girl inside."

"A girl?"

"The same as was brought to you way back. But perhaps you have forgotten her? The young tribune has been seeing to her needs. He won't let anyone else near her. We all thought it was your orders. But..." He cleared his throat again. "It's been a long time, sir. As I said, perhaps you have forgotten her."

The thin lips became an even narrower line, but the Roman's eyes remained without expression. "Yes, you're right.... I'd forgotten. Tell Antoninus Marcus he will accompany me to Ein Gedi. You may take charge of the female yourself."

"What would the general have me do with her?"

He spoke without emotion. "Anything you like."

Crassio's report had disturbed him much more than he let on. As he recalled, his orders to Marc had been rather vague, not much different from what he'd just told Crassio. Perhaps the boy had kept the girl, thinking his commander might change his mind, might want her back. *In which case,* Silva thought irritably, *he might at least have reminded me of her existence.* No, it was obvious Marc was using her himself. Fair enough. But why not share her with the others? Hadn't he told him to do that? Hiding her away... it was not like Marc to be selfish. If anything, the young tribune was generous to a fault.

He thinks he is in love with her.

Silva sighed. A Roman officer in love with a Jew-whore. There was nothing strange in gentlemen finding themselves captivated by hetaerae; more than one emperor had been enamored of these cultured courtesans. But this girl was only a common slave, unlearned, without charm, and—as he now recalled—cold as a clam.

Good Jocundus, for your sake I am trying to be father to your son, remembering how you fought beside me in Thrace and Africa, remembering how you kept the letters from your Julia, saying sadly how you had married the legion more than the woman you loved. And now, what of your son? The qualities are there, Jocundus. They are there. Despite his youth, he commands respect from the men. They are fond of him, as they were of you. And that is a gift for a soldier. It is good when you are fighting beside those who love you. They don't love me, but I don't think they hate me either. Vespasian once said the trouble was I didn't inspire men. Frankly, I've never felt the need. I can do without daring and sweaty heroics. It isn't bravado that wins wars, but the facts at hand and the time to figure things out. Oh, I know they all think me mad with my ramp and platform—certainly the Zealots on the Masada think so. But they don't know what I know. They think their God is going to save them, but I wager they don't know how. Now, I do know how my machines work and how my men work and what they have to work against. And in the end, Jocundus, mathematics will win. Mathematics and might. We have the means and the strength. They have only the will. I am not interested in breaking anyone's will, because it doesn't matter. Not so long as we have the means and the might to stay on top. Or in this case, I should say, to get to the top.

He allowed himself a smile at this small joke, his spirits lifted again. He would talk to Antoninus Marcus. But for now he was after the white horse.

It was after the rains had stopped that the mare began to come around. She was first sighted pawing the ground of a high plateau at the very edge of a deep wadi, a spot more suited to a goat than to a horse, Silva thought. As quickly as she appeared she was gone, only to return the next day at another inaccessible place. She seemed always to be looking toward the Masada, trying to come closer to the mountain fortress, but always running away when the legionaries tried to catch her. Despite his talk of a nomad king, Silva knew the horse must belong to someone on the Masada, but he did not care to keep that thought. It annoyed him to think of a Zealot outlaw owning such a beautiful animal, particularly one he was determined to have for himself. But the horse was as elusive as the top of the mountain. No one had been able to catch her.

He had begun to dream of the horse, seeing her in the night rearing up on her hind legs as though she thought she could leap from her narrow precipice to the casemate wall of the Masada; and he had awakened thrilled and full of longing to possess her. He had offered a reward to whoever would bring the mare to him. But it didn't matter now; he would get her himself. He was sure of it.

With uncharacteristic fervor, he urged his own stallion on, cheered by the sight of Ein Gedi's date trees and the green expanse of the oasis ahead. His back was to the Masada, his thoughts all on the white horse. For the moment nothing else mattered.

• • •

"There she is," Plinius said. "Next to the tall one with fair hair." He was with Crassio in the small camp that had been built facing the southern tip of the Masada. The camp was perched on a high plateau at the edge of a deep wadi. Looking across the steep chasm, the legionaries had a tantalizing eagle's view of the fortress's defenders. Crassio could see now the large palace of Herod, the storehouses, the lanes leading from one part of the rampart to another, to the reservoirs and numerous outbuildings. What was more intriguing was the number of women who always seemed to be gathered near or going to the southern wall. The reason for this was the location of a *mikve*, or ritual immersion bath, adjacent to the south water gate. It was not the only *mikve* on the Masada, for the Essenes had their own pool, as was required by their laws of cleanliness. This one, however, had been set aside for the women to use after their menses and on other occasions, such as childbirth. The legionaries did not know why so many females at one time or another made their way to the south gate; they only knew it was a good spot to watch for them.

"There she is," Plinius said again. "I tell you, she sounds as if she just stepped out of Caesar's court. Varens and I were, ah, calling to the ladies the other day—you know, letting them know how friendly we could be in other circumstances—and that one answers back plain as the nose on your face. I near fell off the cliff when I realized she understood all that we said—which wasn't, I admit, the same as I'd say to your sister or mine."

Crassio shrugged. "They're just Jews." He wet his lips. "Wouldn't mind wrestling with one, though. It's been a long, long time."

"There's women at the rear—"

"Vermin, you mean. Dead, putrefying holes. I'd sooner stick it in that white horse the general's mad for than give it to one of those sluts." He squinted across the wall. "Hey!" he called. "Hey, little sparrow! Won't be long now, little darling. Soon you'll have a whole one—won't that be nice?"

"What do you mean, a whole one?" Plinius asked.

"They've all got a piece missing. Haven't you seen? Animals, Plinius. Animals. No real man would let anyone cut a piece off. Come on, darling!" he called again. "Come fly to your big eagle. I've something lovely for you!"

The female had looked up at the first sound of his voice.

Sighting the soldiers on the precipice, she cocked her head and said clearly, in their own tongue, "So you have something for me, do you?"

"Why, yes, little darling. Just what you need. And your friend as well."

"And I have something for you," she replied. "A knife to slit you from anus to mouth, since it is clearly impossible to determine which part of you is which."

Plinius could not still his laughter.

Crassio grinned. "You need educating," he said, which he then proceeded to provide by means of several fanciful suggestions and soldier definitions, ending his lecture with a casual visual display.

The female remained imperturbable. When she had determined that he was finished with his demonstration, she calmly gave her own unflattering appraisal of his anatomy, culminating with succinct instructions as to what he might do with his exposed member and where.

Plinius found it all better than the theater he'd been to in Rome, but Crassio was no longer amused. "Come later to the western gate of your wall," he called across the chasm. "There, on the white ramp, I will instruct you further. Bring your friends. I promise you will see something interesting."

"If it is more of what you've just shown, I would not call it interesting. Besides, we are forbidden to look at pig meat."

His smile was no longer pleasant. "The ramp," he said again. "You will not be bored."

"You oughtn't to talk to them," Miriam said, still flustered. "What did he say? What was he doing?"

"Never mind."

"What strange gestures!"

"Yes . . . men can be strange. I wonder why they always— oh, never mind." Alexandra shrugged, uncomfortable. Despite her bravado, she felt sickened by the confrontation with the Roman. "He said we must come to the ramp, he would show us something there. He said to bring everyone."

"What do you think it could be?"

"I don't know. Probably something disgusting. But we'd better tell the others."

"What did you say to him?" Miriam was curious.

Alexandra smiled slowly, recalling the Latin epithets that had come so easily to mind. It was wonderful, she thought, to be blessed with a good memory. Particularly when one had grown up in a garrison town. She turned her large, clear eyes on Miriam. "Oh," she said innocently, "I just told him that the Lord would punish him and all the *Kittim* for their evil ways."

It was, as Flavius Silva had thought earlier, spring everywhere but in the colorless sea of sand. Not a bird could be seen flying in that bright sky; but at this moment the air was heavy not with heat so much as with tension.

A crowd had gathered at the western gate of the casemate wall directly above the ramp; men had climbed to the top of the ramparts and the towers. Legionaries were clustered together below, some of them sitting on the sides of the ramp. Slaves lay sprawled on the ground or huddled on the sides of the ramp, not knowing why they had been given this moment's rest, but grateful for it.

It was Crassio who broke the silence. He stood in the center of the white ramp and spread his arms wide. "I see you have all come to see my surprise." He spoke in a normal tone, knowing the unusual acoustics of the area would carry his voice to the top of the mountain. "Well, I won't disappoint you." His voice deepened. "Look now, you lepers' sons, at what is to come. Mark it well in your brains, you stinking vermin. Because what you see now you will see a hundred times again when we get to 'you." He turned back to his own men and nodded, and Plinius brought forth the girl.

She was clearly frightened, too much so even to struggle as Plinius pushed her onto the ramp.

"Don't be shy," Crassio said. "Plinius, I do believe the lady needs an escort."

Grinning, Plinius took the girl by the arm and dragged her up the ramp.

"That's better." He looked up at the casemate wall, reassuring himself of his audience. Confused, the girl took a few steps forward, as if she thought she was being allowed to join the besieged.

"No, no," Crassio admonished, and pulled her back to him. That action seemed to shake her out of her trance, and with a sudden cry she swung at him. Instantly his arm shot out, the back of his hand knocking her to the ground. She did not move.

As this happened, the men on the ramparts raised their bows, only to be immediately confronted by a row of archers on the ramp, who had sprung to cover the Roman.

"For every arrow that descends five of your lepers will be killed," Crassio warned.

There was a pause. Then the men on the wall lowered their weapons.

"Now, then," Crassio said cheerfully. "As I was saying—"

When they saw him mount the unconscious girl, most of the onlookers left the wall, not wanting to witness her shame or give further delight to the Roman by their presence. Some stayed, however, mesmerized as the mouse is by the serpent, while some were still trying to find a target for their arrows. Their anger and frustration grew as they saw the legionary replaced by first one and then another of the *Kittim* until more than twenty Praetorian guards had lain with the girl on the ramp.

"We should have killed him when he first stepped out alone," Yigael said.

"Not just him. All of them," Shem added.

"You heard what he said," Eleazar reminded them. "Five slaves for every one of them."

"Cheap enough," Joav said now.

"No life is cheap."

Joav turned to him. "It isn't the girl, Eleazar. We are all unmanned by this. The *Kittim* know that."

"And what do the slaves know?"

"They are more dead than alive. It would be a blessing to put them out of their misery. The girl too."

Before Eleazar could answer, Yigael said, "Look! They are gone."

She lay where they had left her, a small bundle of flesh and ragged cloth. Suddenly, however, the body in the middle of the ramp moved; slowly the girl pushed herself up on her arms. She looked around, dazed, a line of dried blood at the corner of her mouth. She tried to get to her feet, only to stumble and fall. She finally managed to raise herself up again and began to crawl up the ramp toward the gate of the fortress.

Yigael could stand it no more. Before anyone could stop

him, he started down the footpath that had been part of the original ascent. He had not gone far, however, when a Syrian arrow caught him in the shoulder. There was an instant barrage of arrows from the other Zealots as Eleazar and Joav dragged him back to safety. During all this, the girl had continued to crawl up the ramp, oblivious to everything around her. She was nearing the top, only a few yards away from the Sicarii footpath.

Crassio had watched her progress with a faint smile. Now, casually, he signaled the archer farthest up the ramp. The arrow struck dead center; she fell forward, the shaft protruding from her back.

It was at this moment that the young tribune came riding through the camp, his horse gleaming with sweat. Returning from Ein Gedi, Flavius Silva had casually informed him that the girl Michal had been given over to the camp. Antoninus Marcus rode to the ramp site, drawing up at its base, his chest heaving with exertion and anguish. As two men emerged from the rocky Zealot path at the top of the ramp, the archers took careful aim again.

"Stop!" Antoninus Marcus cried, his left hand upraised.

Obedient, the soldiers held still.

The men on the footpath halted a moment, then continued to descend to the ramp. One lifted the body of the girl in his arms and retreated back to the fortress with her while the other, bow drawn, covered his back. Only after they had disappeared inside the casemate wall did the tribune turn away.

A few days after the girl Michal was slain, one of the slaves working on the ramp made a break for freedom. It was not a sudden thing. By means of biblical phrases that the legionaries did not comprehend, the Judean prisoners and the inhabitants of the Masada had been communicating with each other for some time. Now, however, the verses from Isaiah that Shem called to his cousin below were meant to convey more than just hope: *"Therefore with joy shall ye draw water out of the wells of salvation. . . . And in that day shall ye say, 'Give thanks unto the Lord'"* followed by *"Cry aloud and shout, thou inhabitant of Zion. . . . For great is the Holy One of Israel in the midst of thee"* was the signal for the workers on the ramp to cause a disturbance during the water break.

Accordingly they set to fighting among themselves, and in the confusion that followed Shem's cousin made a dash for the footpath. Rocks laboriously carried to the top of the ramp for Silva's platform were suddenly rolling bottomward; men were falling every which way; whips were cracking on bare backs and swords were laid flat against shoulders as shouts and cries from every quarter filled the air. It was only a matter of moments before order prevailed, but as the dust settled, Crassio, who had been in the midst of the fray, caught sight of the prisoner making his way up the footpath. Cursing, he whistled for the Syrian archers, but as he gestured at them, two startling things occurred. The first was that as he raised his hand, the Syrians were felled by arrows; and then, before anyone could make another move, a sound came through the air that froze all but the man still scrambling toward the casemate wall.

The sound drew men, women, and children to the wall; it stunned those on the ramp and in the camp below. It seemed to emanate from the mountain itself, to swoop down like an eagle from the sky, to skim along the still waters of the Dead Sea, to bounce off the mountains of Moab and the silent golden cliffs, reverberating throughout the vicinity like a mighty trumpet blast.

Eee-yah-wahhh!

For a moment, no one moved.

Silva had rushed from his tent. "What is it?" he asked a legionary.

The soldier had visibly blanched. "The cry of the Sicarii." He pointed to the Masada.

The Roman general looked up, fully expecting to see an army of men, but there was only a long figure standing on the footpath halfway between the top of the plateau and the ramp.

The sun was to the Zealot's advantage. Silva had to shade his eyes with his hand as he strained to see the man coming down the mountain. What he saw was a tall, broad-shouldered figure whose golden head seemed aflame in a halo of sun. The man wore a white tunic and leather *lorica;* his feet were shod in sandals. He stood in the middle of the narrow path with easy authority, but there was no mistaking the tension in the well-built body or the determination in the slightly lowered head. This was a man poised for battle.

Crassio, halted momentarily by the Sicarius cry, was now advancing grimly up the ramp. No one else moved. There seemed to be an unspoken knowledge, acceptance, and agreement among all present as to what must happen next. Instinctively, Silva had raised his left fist; he had only to open it and the soldiers would charge up the ramp. But now, slowly, he lowered his arm, his eyes still on the man on the footpath.

The legionary at his side had turned; his sword was out. Silva was aware of other eyes waiting for his command.

"Sir?" the legionary asked.

He shook his head. "No," he said slowly. "Let them fight." The soldiers' eyes brightened.

"To the end," Silva added grimly. He glanced at Antoninus Marcus, who had now come beside him. "I will wager fifty denarii against your ten," he said casually to the young tribune, "that Crassio will split the head of yon Sicarius. That ought to be a bet to your liking, Marc. You see, I give you leave now to cheer for the other side."

The tribune did not answer.

Crassio had reached the end of the ramp and climbed atop the still incomplete platform of stone. He stood there with his legs spread wide, hands on his hips. "Well, come on down," he called, brandishing his sword. "I see you are jealous of the treatment one of your bitches received from me. Come down, then, and learn a legionary's love."

The tall Sicarius waited until the laughter had subsided. "Why don't you come here," he invited in a dangerously soft voice.

"Bah!" Crassio waved his sword at the footpath. "That's no place to fight! Come down to the platform, leper!"

"Ah! You want to fight," the man said again in that soft voice. "Why didn't you say so?" And with a leap and yet another chilling cry he was on the platform, crouched and tense, a lion ready to spring. The sun caught the point of the *sica* in his hand and sent forth rays from the Roman's sword and helmet as the two adversaries circled one another, so that the combatants seemed to be encompassed in a sphere of light.

They were fairly evenly matched in size, although Crassio was perhaps the heavier of the two. Whatever grim pleasure the Roman may have felt at this encounter was no match, however, for Eleazar ben Ya'ir's controlled rage. Those who knew him best, hearing the soft, deadly tone in which he had answered the legionary, had shuddered slightly, recognizing what that voice meant.

Alexandra had rushed to the casemate wall with the others. Finding no place where she might see what was happening, she ran to the synagogue adjacent to the western ascent. From there she had a clear view of the action below. She uttered a small cry when she saw him locked in combat and, without thinking, stretched forth her hand as if she might draw him back. She could not do so, but neither could she turn away. Once, she had been forced to watch her brother fight in the arena. No one was forcing her now; still she watched and, in that curious way she had, found herself removed from personal reality. Eleazar became a stranger, the same stranger who had stormed into her room when he suspected her of disloyalty, the same beautiful stranger who took her away with him in the dimensionless world of their passion. In moments of love she had always been a little afraid of him, for he invaded her self as much as he entered her body, and she had to trust that he would not hurt her in any of the many ways one human being can hurt another. She wondered if all women felt this way, or if it was only that he possessed some extraordinary power.

Now, abstractedly, she watched him plunge his dagger into the Roman and then, as the man fell, pick him up and with another great cry throw him over the side of the ramp. It was a strange cry, she thought. It sounded almost as if he were calling the sacred, unspeakable name of the Lord: Yahwah.

A sudden silence had enveloped the area. He was like a statue of gold, a magnificent animal surveying a miniature world below. She could almost feel the energy that had radiated from him only a moment before draining out of his body now, as if he were lying beside her after the spent force of his love.

She had wondered why he feared his own strength and the power he knew he had over people. Now, in this moment, she understood. If something existed, it could exist for evil as well as for good, for death as well as for life.

He was only a man, no angel warrior, as he himself had said. Unless, she thought, warrior angels—and demons—existed in all men. And then, with a start, she realized that the man she had been watching with such fascination was her own husband and that he might very well have been killed before her eyes.

He looked tired as he came up the footpath, oblivious to the cheers and hugs of the people whose valor he had vindicated by his prowess. He did not see David's adoring eyes, for he was looking at her as she ran toward him. The bloodied knife was still in his hand. He dropped it, not seeing David pick it up and tenderly wipe it clean. He was looking at her, and there was no joy in his eyes.

Another dream to waken him in the night, she thought. *Another ghost to haunt him.*

He reached out, drawing her through the crowd. "Are you all right?" he asked anxiously.

She opened her mouth, then closed it without speaking. Nodding, she laid her head against his chest. She was trembling suddenly.

"I knew it was ben Ya'ir," Flavius Silva declared, triumphantly sweeping Solomon ben Ya'ish's chess piece off the board. "The man who killed Crassio today . . . that man and only he is Eleazar ben Ya'ir."

"It surprises me that you have never called for a meeting with the commander of the Masada," ben Ya'ish observed.

"What for?" the Roman responded—a trifle angrily, the doctor thought. "He has his job to do, and I have mine. Besides it was made abundantly clear very early in the game that they have no intention of abandoning their position. If there had been a change of mind, then ben Ya'ir would have called for a meeting, I assure you."

"You never thought to lure them down?"

"After Machaerus? Lucilius Bassus took care of that for me. Of course, I hoped when they saw the wall and the ramp they might be so motivated by fear—"

"—they would descend like lambs." Ben Ya'ish grinned. "Ah, no, General. You never thought that. You have been prepared for battle from the first."

"I have set my mind on a . . . a decisive finish . . . to this Judean episode," Silva admitted carefully. "For the good of the Empire, of course. You know," he added a bit grimly, "there are those who think my preoccupation with 'my machines,' as they call it, borders on the amusing. I should be pleased to show certain parties in Rome just how effective machines and proper thinking can be. There will come a day, doctor, when we shall have no need for heroic gestures, for soul-stirring cries such as the one let loose today, or for tall, handsome champions. Someday, a hand—a very ordinary, even insignificant hand, an anonymous hand—will set in motion, in some yet unknown manner, some monstrous engine . . . and an opposing army will vanish in the dust."

"You are a man of vision," the Judean noted.

"There are many who would call me mad. That is why I said nothing of the way in which I intended to take the Masada until there was no one around to counter my means." He looked up from the board. "Let them surrender? Not in a thousand years. They will all die—to please Rome. But not until I scale that mountain."

"The white horse has been spotted again, sir," said Antoninus Marcus, entering Silva's tent.

He jumped up. "Where?"

"I don't really know," Marcus admitted. "A soldier in the southern sector saw her just about the same time one of the Arab bowmen in the eastern camp claims he sighted her."

He sank down again. "Demon mare. . . . She haunts my sleep. . . ."

"Is there anything, sir—"

"No. No, you can go, Marc. Yes, go. Go out into that soft, evil night and . . . never mind. Good night, tribune."

"Good night, sir."

When he had gone the general turned to the silent man sitting before the chessboard. "What is happening, Jew? What is happening to me? What is there in this dry, dead, forsaken land of yours that twists my thoughts? I am a calm man, I am a practical man. I do not waste my time in musings or philosophies or vague sentimentality. Yet here I am, driven with longing for a horse—a horse!—and an ugly piece of rock!" He drew himself up, a rather undistinguished-looking man with thinning hair and a narrow mouth. "There is no value," he stated flatly, "in discussing things which are of no vital concern to a thinking man. I am anxious, that is all. The platform is nearly complete, the engines and siege tower ready—I shall be getting out of here soon, Jew. Tell me," he said with a sudden change of tone, "why do you suppose he has been hiding himself all these months?"

"Who?"

"Their leader. Eleazar ben Ya'ir . . ."

"They say he is a modest man."

"No one who commands the masses is modest."

"I would not say there are masses on the Masada, General.

A thousand . . . maybe two . . . no more than that, and probably less. Perhaps you are confused . . ."

"No. I am not confused. Lucilius Bassus may have been confused, but I am not. I know all about Eleazar ben Ya'ir. Perhaps that is why he has not made himself more obvious," he mused. "He knows we know about him . . . and still thinks he can escape. . . ."

"But you have said no one can escape."

"And no one will. When this is over I must be certain that the leader of the Sicarii is dead. That, as far as Caesar is concerned, is the whole point of this operation. All these instigators—but particularly the one called Eleazar ben Ya'ir—must be wiped out." He smiled thinly. "And now I know who he is. . . ."

Marc found himself walking toward the place where her tent had been. He passed soldiers throwing dice in the light of their fires; he could hear the laughter that sometimes emanated from their tents, along with cursing and bits of tall tales and time-embellished exploits, random sentences that floated out into the night. Farther on, he passed the traders' camp and the tents of the craftsmen and peddlers and pimps. He passed slaves, chained together, sleeping in the open, or sitting with dead eyes, rubbing their sore limbs. He saw a juggler and a naked Numidean dancing for coins, and a gathering of Arab bowmen around a fire, the sweet, strange smell of their incense wafting upwards. And finally he was alone in the dark, empty, skylit world that seemed no more real to him than the one in which he slept, took his meals, and went about the business of war.

The wadi pitched steeply down, a dried riverbed with a few sparse clumps of green. No clue to the tumultuous flow of water that had careened along its bank but a short time ago. No hint of the life that had stirred and stretched and dreamed in a small tent here. She was gone; and he was empty, dry like the wadi, every word and thought crumbling in his head like the small stones underfoot, which were not really rocks but only broken, seared earth.

He thought of his father and wondered how that man whom he had not known well but had loved nevertheless, if only for the love others bore him—he wondered how his father had come to grips with a soldier's life, a soldier's reality. Had he ever been part of anything like that which had taken Michal's life? No. No. . . . But surely he had seen such things. Surely he had known. How could he have lived with it?

To serve one's country was a noble thing. But was simple-minded brutality any service to Rome? Was this why his mother had wept over her husband's profession, perhaps more than over the long separations? Was it why she had wept when her son entered the military? He'd never wanted to hurt her, but he had chosen his father's path over hers, believing it was the right thing to do, even thinking that by doing so he might better protect her.

From what must I be protected? he could almost hear her asking. *From these Judeans who want nothing more than to be left to themselves and their God?*

No, mother. Not from these Judeans and their god, but from your god. Your Man of Peace. Your Savior. In the name of your Christ you may one day find yourself thrown to wild beasts as in the time of Nero, or my sister, Lavinia, thrown to beasts like the ones that devoured Michal.

He was suddenly afraid. Not for his family, but for himself. He felt so cold, so empty. He had tried so hard to put away his mother's teachings, and now he realized, frightened, how well he'd succeeded. The precipice upon which he stood was more than a rock jutting over a dried riverbed; it was the line between himself and the soldiers on the ramp. Between himself and Crassio, or even Flavius Silva. He knew he did not fear death in battle. What filled him with this sudden cold terror was the vision of himself going on, living, working, pleasuring himself, but always empty inside, loveless, without regard for those around him. Paying lip service to Caesar and the gods in matter-of-fact ceremonies like the rituals Silva presided over each morning. What was religion to this Roman and others like him but a decidedly legal, businesslike exchange of favors? *Dead men*, Marc thought, *saluting dead banners*.

He stood alone in the desert, a solitary figure suspended, it seemed, amidst the towering cliffs and stark ravines, a man on the edge of an abyss more terrifying than the sharply sloping wadi he peered into. He felt dizzy and, lifting his head, saw how brightly lit the sky was, how perversely rich and beautiful its patterns of clouds and stars and moon were, contrasted with the barren landscape below. There was that one star again, so much brighter than the rest. He remembered how he had stood with Michal looking up at it.

I am the light of the world. . . . He that followeth me shall not walk in darkness.

Who had spoken? Startled, Marc looked around. There was no one. It was only his own thoughts, echoes of words he had heard as a child and put away when he became a man. It was memory speaking, his mother's voice. Yet he felt strangely comforted.

Why had she and men and women like her been declared enemies of Rome? What was there in the teachings of these Christians that forced them to meet secretly, like the criminals the state declared them to be, so that he had been ashamed and had turned away from his mother and put out of his mind all that she had told him? Now, against his will, those teachings were flooding back to him, as the wadi would be filled in winter; he began to recall scattered phrases, to hear the hymns sung softly in those dark catacombs where he had followed behind, clinging to his mother's skirt. He remembered the man his mother and sister had been so excited to see, how pleased his mother was when the man had lifted young Marc onto his lap. What was his name? Paul. . . .

Other images came back to him. He tried to push them away, as if he feared he might fall into some deadly trap, yet at the same time he welcomed them and the sudden warmth they brought. As Michal had struggled silently against his love, so now he struggled against something he both feared and wanted.

I am the way, the truth, and the light. . . .

She had given in at last and in that surrender freed her prisoner heart; so too he suddenly broke through the bars that had held him in a cold, dark night and felt his heart opened and filled with light. It was as if the stars had fallen into his hands; his fingers tingled with new life. His breath came easily, and he wanted to laugh, to hug the mountains, no longer forbidding.

Michal was gone, but he was no longer alone, and he knew he would never be alone again.

In the somewhat worn splendor of the general's campaign tent, Flavius Silva, that good citizen and enterprising soldier of Rome, tossed fitfully in his sleep. As on so many other nights the image of a white horse disturbed his rest, prancing, tantalizing, before him yet always out of reach. He saw himself running after the beautiful, elusive animal, an ordinary man, not very athletic, albeit hardy, as a military man was wont to be. . . .

He was chasing the white mare again. Running, running . . .

SIX

"I've been to hell and back," he said. "I was there when they burned the Temple and all of Jerusalem. Three solid days of fighting from the Hill down to the streets of the city and the Citadel. Three days without food or sleep . . . just running . . . and killing . . . and running again. I must have passed out finally. Woke up to find a legionary standing over me. He pushed me into a crowd, and we were all herded back into the Temple. When I think on it, it comes to me that I might have escaped then. But to tell the truth I was too weary, and for the others it was the same.

"They told us only those who offered armed resistance had been killed. The ones who'd been taken unresisting would live. But the first thing they did was weed out the old and the sick and get rid of them . . . no need for me to tell you how. Then they took away all the females and shut the rest of us up in the Court of Women, where we were separated into groups. Those under sixteen or so were put in one corner, older men in another, and many of us into yet another. I learned later that the youngsters were sold. Another group was put in irons and sent to Egypt.

"Many died in those days. If a guard did not like you, he saw to it you got no food. And there were many guards who did not like us. Some of our people willingly chose starvation rather than eat that which was unclean. In any case, there was not even enough corn to fill so many mouths, although for the guards there was always plenty. A great number of bullocks had been herded round the altars. The Roman sacrificed them to his gods and divided the meat among his soldiers for a victory feast. For three days they celebrated. We could smell the roasting meat . . . and we heard the cries of the women. . . .

"Meanwhile, those who had hidden themselves in the sewers were discovered and taken, the ground was torn up, and all who were trapped were killed. When they marched us out of the city, we had to step over the bodies in the streets. The stench was so foul I had to hold my breath and would have closed my eyes but for fear of stumbling over the dead.

"My group was taken to Caesarea. There we learned that Simon had finally been captured. John, starving to death with his brothers in the sewers, had given himself up and asked for mercy. They would let him live—in a cage, they said, for the rest of his life. Simon was set aside, for what purpose I shall soon tell you.

"In Caesarea, we were told it was the birthday of Titus's brother, Domitian, and that we had the privilege of helping him celebrate. At first we thought it was a joke. Would the guards give us cake and wine? But this was not the case. No, they feasted while we fought, and the number who perished in combat with wild beasts or in fighting each other or by being burnt alive was more than I dare count. But my group did not take part in this Roman entertainment or in later shows when Titus also celebrated his father's birthday.

"After some months, we were shipped off to Rome. I will not tell you what it was like in the dark hold of the boat, chained and crowded together, with no air and little food, or how many of us perished in that voyage. . . . It is something I have tried hard to forget. . . .

"But in Rome the sun shone for us. We were given food and made to bathe, and fresh clothes were brought to us. And this man came among us—this painted monkey, this cockroach. His name was Fronto—Fronto the Cockroach. He was the same one who had gone among the prisoners back in the Temple courtyard, saying who should go here and who there. And now he was here again, putting his hands on us, studying our faces and bodies as no decent man does. Now, I have never thought myself handsome, but I saw that all of us who had made the journey from Judea together were of a good height and perhaps stronger than most. Some were indeed comely. I began to fear that we were to be given to the pleasure of painted monkeys like this Fronto, but for the moment this was not the case.

Instead we were ourselves painted and perfumed and given grand garments to wear. Dark stuff was put around our eyes, like the stuff whores and dancers wear, and our wounds and scars were covered with flesh-colored cream. Strange, you say? Wait.... I could tell you tales of torture and cruelty beyond belief, but for each of these you no doubt have a story of your own. But for what I am about to tell you now, I warrant you have no reply.

"It was for a parade! A show! The streets were decked with garlands, the air was sweet with incense. There were throngs and throngs of Romans on every side, waving banners, cheering....

"Nothing you might imagine can equal what I saw that day. There were platforms that moved on wheels, and some of us rode on these and some marched. They called the platforms stages, and some were as high as mountains and hung with curtains of gold and true scarlet dye. Different scenes of war were shown on these stages—they had us pose like dolls, with clay weapons. Here would be a green countryside afire, there whole formations put to the sword! They made some of us stand as though ready to flee, and on each stage was the commander of a captured town posed as if he were being taken. There were even ships, on wheels, with masses of slaves pulling them forward! And treasures! Gold and silver, chests filled with jewels, hangings and embroideries carried by dozens of men. And finally they brought forth the Temple's treasures . . . the silver trumpets of the Levites . . . the seven-pronged lampstand of gold . . . And the Book of the Law. . . ."

The silence of the group gathered around the fire deepened. There had been sighs and murmurs while the escaped slave spoke, but now no one made a sound, no one moved.

"Vespasian rode behind," he continued after a pause. "And Titus behind him. The entire procession came to a halt in front of a great white temple, and the crowd, which had been cheering and throwing flowers into the air, now became quiet. Vespasian and Titus mounted the steps of the white temple, and Simon was dragged before them. They had let him march with us while John was carried forth in his cage, but now they dragged Simon away, a noose around him, knocking him about in the worst way. Then they took him away . . . and killed him . . . and brought the news of his death back to Vespasian. And the crowd cheered again as they were shown his body."

No one spoke. The quiet rose, thickened.

"Agh!" He spat into the fire as though to rid himself of some vile taste. "What sort of people are these that find delight in others' misery? To make a show! An entertainment!"

No one answered.

He sighed. "Afterwards, we were sorted into groups again. I fought in the circus for a time. I tried to escape—me and a Numidean, together. They killed him, and I caught this brand on my neck. Then I was back in a ship as a galley slave. I would still be there if Silva hadn't needed strong arms. The rest you know." He looked up. "When I saw Shem and the rest of you, I knew that what had kept me alive was not a dream. It had not been a lie."

"What dream?" Shem asked. "What lie?"

He did not answer his cousin but turned instead to Eleazar. "In the arena, in the galley, in the prisons, and in the mines . . . wherever the children of Israel are slaves . . . word passes from one to another that there are still free men in Judea, banded together upon a mountain called the Masada, led by one named Eleazar. We would whisper it as we passed each other in our chains. One word. *Masada*. It was water to parched lips."

"How can this be?" Eleazar asked, amazed. "How do men so far away know of us?"

"On the ship and later in Rome, before they killed him, Simon bar Giora spoke of you. He told us not to lose hope. He said you would not give up our cause and that Rome would never take you. Even as they dragged him away to his death, he called to us, 'Remember! Masada!'"

Eleazar turned away, blinking back the tears that had come suddenly to his eyes.

"That is why," the man who had escaped said now, "you must kill our brothers below. We have spoken of it among ourselves and are agreed. We knew that if I managed to escape, many on the ramp would be killed in punishment, and we also agreed to this. For you must listen to what I have to say. . . .

"It is because of us that Rome is here. The word that Judean slaves whisper among themselves has made Caesar afraid. It is more than a matter of Judea. The Numidean told me of a man called Spartacus, who also fought against Rome. This Spartacus, was killed long ago. But you are alive, and the Masada has not been taken. It is our fault—we who are in chains—that Rome has decided the Masada must fall. That is why they destroyed Machaerus and killed all the men. The leader there was also called Eleazar, and the Roman general thought he was you.

"You must not keep your arrows from those that toil on the ramp," he urged again. "Otherwise you are lost."

Eleazar shook his head; he was dazed by all he had heard. "No . . . no. . . ."

"You must! I told you, we have spoken of it and we are agreed!"

"No. . . ."

Joav put his hand out. "Eleazar . . ."

"No!"

"The platform is almost complete," the escaped man went on. "Soon they will try to move up their siege tower. Slaves will be pulling the ropes. Shoot them down! Stop them any way you can. It is your only hope, and even now it may be too late. But you must try. It doesn't matter how many you kill or how many they crucify in retaliation. All that matters is that they do not take you. The Masada must not fall!"

Eleazar did not answer.

"Listen to me! It is more than for Judea! I know it sounds strange, but in Rome that Numidean became my brother! Yes! And all the others in their chains! Rome is everything the Lord hates, and we are the only ones who oppose her! They have burned Jerusalems from one end of the world to the other, and the Masada is the only spark left! Whatever it takes, whatever the cost, the Masada must survive!"

There was a great murmur of agreement at this, but as the moments went by and still Eleazar did not speak, the others too grew quiet and waited.

"When I was a young man," he said at last, "I thought it was all about ridding our land of the foreign oppressor. And it didn't much matter to me how we did that. But as time went on, I began to think that there was another, greater war than the one we were fighting for independence. We call ourselves Hebrews. That means 'warriors for the Lord.' We are pledged to hate that which the Lord hates and to love that which He loves. But how many have we killed, some in justice and some not? How many have we tortured for information? How many of our own have we murdered? Whatever it takes, you say. Whatever the cost. Have we, then, become no different from those we fight? And if we are no different . . . if we are no different, *chev'ra*, then what is it all for?"

"What you say is true," Yigael admitted. "But it is not to the point. You have spent much time with the Essenes, and you speak like one now, not like a man who must think how to protect himself and his family."

"I am no Essene, Yigael. I am a man like you, with a wife and a son. Not in their name, not even in the Lord's name, can I do what you ask me to do."

"But the slaves are willing," Joav said. "They have agreed to it."

"And do you think the *Kittim* would not bring more slaves? Shall we kill them too? Will they also be willing, do you think, to die for us?" He stood up. "Those of you who came with me from Jerusalem after the death of my uncle took the same oath as I. We vowed nevermore to shed the blood of our brothers, even though our own lives be forfeit. I hold every one of you to that pledge."

Later, Jonatan said, "You did well, Eleazar. The Lord's grace is with the steadfast."

He sighed. "Is it?"

"His grace and His strength. Don't torment yourself, my brother. We have both seen men at their worst, and we have seen them at their best. We cannot always be what the Lord intended us to be, but we can try. We can try."

The following day a curious thing happened. As the slaves struggled up the ramp with the stones for the siege platform, there came the sound of singing. It was a simple harvest song, like those sung in the fields to make the work go faster and seem easier. Startled, the soldiers on the ramp looked up; sure enough, the singing was coming from the casemate wall. It was not long before first one and then another and then all the workers on the ramp took up the song, and despite their weariness and pain, the old, familiar tune brought a moment's cheer. As they sang, their step seemed to quicken and their work developed a distinct rhythm. For the first time in all the months they had been here, the long whips in the legionaries' hands stayed looped, while the pile of stones atop the ramp finally began to take on the shape Flavius Silva desired.

The general had come to watch the work. Despite the sudden, efficient proceedings, he was not in a good mood. Word had been brought that the white mare was dead. The soldiers, spotting her on the outskirts of the camp, had finally encircled her and thrown a noose over her head. As one of the men reported, "Any normal animal would have stopped pulling, sir, as the cord grew tighter. But this one just went ahead and pulled against us until she broke her own neck. Never seen anything like it," he added.

Flavius Silva, hearing now the singing of the slaves and the besieged, raised his tired eyes to the Masada and muttered, "Fools! Don't they realize they are only working toward their own destruction?"

Solomon ben Ya'ish, standing beside him in the dust of this prophets' land, had also been looking up at the mountain fortress. His eyes rested now on a young boy who was singing with the others from one of the watchtowers. "They know they are going to die," he said softly. "Now . . . they will give others the courage to live."

SEVEN

The fifteenth day of the month called Nisan dawned in rather ordinary fashion. Eleazar had risen as usual before the last star had faded into the gray of morning and was gone before she could rouse herself from bed or even before the child awakened, hungry as usual.

The Passover was but a week or two away. The bakers had better begin to make the unleavened bread, Alexandra thought, stretching lazily, or they would never be ready for it. The apartment must be swept clean. And she must somehow get that stain removed from her good robe—she ought to have known Beni would throw up that mess Batsheva gave him. The thought of it made her want to throw up herself. She turned on her stomach, aware of the new fullness of her breasts and the aching in her armpits. *Here we go again,* she thought. She had not yet missed her menses, but she did not need this confirmation. She knew. After the first one, a women knew. Still, it was best to wait before saying anything. She was in no mood to deal with Hagar's fussing.

A sudden twinge of cold went through her like the blast of the trumpets awakening the legionaries below. She pushed the feeling aside, and with it any thought of foreign intruders. It was better to think of last night. They had stayed up late, talking and doing other things . . .

The platform on the ramp was finished. There had been a kind of celebration in the Roman camp—or perhaps it was a feast day to honor their god Mars, Alexandra mused. There had been the usual sacrifice and conspicuous prayers, as though Flavius Silva hoped to impress upon the Judeans that Great Powers were on his side. Then there had been horse races, with the hitherto idle cavalry doing their best to inspire fear and awe. But, as Eleazar had noted, horses and riding prowess wouldn't do anyone much good on the Masada, and that remark had served to lessen the tension of the watchers in the towers.

It was the sacrifice of the bullock that had disturbed the priest Aqavia—not that he thought the ritual would benefit the soldiers, but that he regretted he could not perform the same service for his own God. "I ought to have insisted on some sort of sacrifice," he had complained. "We could have made an altar of stone . . ."

"Butcher," Joav had growled. "Aren't you happy unless you hear some poor animal howling in pain?"

"Howling? Pain? You ignorant Galilean clod, do you dare suppose that what is done in the name of the Most Holy carries with it any suffering?" The priest was incensed. "There is no pain in the ritual death. The victim must not cry out even once. Otherwise it is for naught."

"How can this be?" Eleazar had asked, intrigued.

"First, the knife must be exceedingly sharp. Then, one stroke—only one, here, across the throat—and it is done. Light is gone."

"Can it really be so?" he had wondered later, in bed with her.

She had nodded. "I remember my uncle saying how important it was that the sacrifice be done correctly, that there be no pain. That is why there was always a rotation of the priests, so that one alone did not daily perform this duty. It would have been too much, my uncle said."

"One stroke . . ." he had mused.

"Yes . . . here. . . ." She had thrown back her head and put her finger on the vein in her throat.

Leaning forward, he had pressed his lips to the spot she had touched.

She had started to laugh. "That tickles. . . ."

"Sshh. The victim is not supposed to make a sound."

She put her arms around his neck. "Shall you kill me, then?" she had asked, smiling.

"No. We throw little fish back into the sea."

She had sighed happily. "Do you remember?"

"I should have taken you with me that day. I was half tempted."

"I wish you had. There would have been more time for us together."

"What are you talking about? We have all the time in the world."

"Do we?"

He had pulled her hair. "The rest of our lives, Gray Eyes."

Another blast from the Roman trumpets. Sounds of men moving about, calling and cursing as day began in earnest.

Eleazar had returned. "The boy's asleep?"

"Yes—oh, don't wake him, please. Just kiss him softly. Where are you going? You haven't eaten—"

"Later. We have work to do."

"You'll get all dirty again."

"You can scrub my back later." He smiled. "In Ein Gedi."

"I'll settle for the pool in the north palace. Is there anything left of it?"

"From the outside nothing looks amiss. But old Herod wouldn't find much to please him inside."

She sighed. "First the synagogue, and now this wall of yours. What ruin we've wreaked."

"It could not be helped, Alexandra. We have to make do with the building materials at hand, and even that isn't very much. The palace was not essential to the community, and we had to build a larger place of worship. As for the wall, you will soon see how necessary that is. I must go. We've got to finish our preparations before they bring up the ram." He kissed her, squeezed her arm. "You're putting on a little weight," he observed with a wink; and then he was gone.

She sat there a moment, smiling, and then got up. The noise of activity in the camps of the *Kittim* had grown louder; she pushed the sounds aside, listening instead for a sign that the child was wakening. He headed briskly for the western gate, a tall, broad-shouldered man with thick golden hair and beard. His eyes were bright, as they had been in the old days in the hills. The months of waiting and worrying were gone; he was a man of action again. His energy and confidence were infectious; they filled the hearts and hands of the men already at the western gate, who smiled when they saw him striding toward them. To a man of reason, a man like Flavius Silva, this Zealot cheer would have seemed perverse. They had come, after all, as the Essenes declared, to the End of Days. But as Crassio had once noted, it was the waiting that was more deadly than the fighting. And with the fighting, there was the chance of deliverance. The Great Miracle. The victory of the Sons of

Light over the Forces of Darkness. In any case, whatever was to happen would happen now.

Joav fell into step beside him. He was yawning.

"Didn't you get any sleep?"

The redhead made a face. "David had me throwing the dice 'til dawn, like the *Kittim* below. You cannot believe how that game grabs hold of you. Good thing I had nothing to wager. I would have lost all—and still gone on playing." He shook his head, amazed at his own newfound capacity for gambling.

"Dice, eh? Strange thing for a man of the Lord, Joav."

Joav shrugged. He knew Eleazar was teasing. "Couldn't sleep. Could you?"

Eleazar grinned. "I told you long ago, you should have married Miriam."

Joav did not answer. He had spotted David. "There's the whelp now. No red eyes for him. The young are blessed, I tell you. Nothing bothers them."

Eleazar smiled as the boy approached. "I hear you bettered my man last night."

"Oh, I always win," David said casually.

"Is that important to you, winning?"

"Of course."

"What would you do if you didn't?"

"But I always do."

"But suppose you couldn't." He stopped a moment, then continued, "Suppose you had to win—it was life or death—and you saw that you couldn't. Winning was impossible. What would you do?"

David looked up, surprised at the intensity in the dark blue eyes. He thought a moment, then said, "Cheat."

Eleazar stared at him; then he laughed. "Come on," he said. "We have work to do."

A fierce wind had risen from the south, as if the elements of nature had conspired to take part in the confrontation at hand. Sand and dust flew, the standards of the legions rippled in the wind; but for the moment, men on both sides were still, poised before battle. The sun was inching toward the west. Still Silva waited. And Eleazar ben Ya'ir, knowing the shifting light moved to the Roman's advantage, could do nothing; the enemy was out of range.

The main assault tower had been moved to the base of the ramp. Silva's corps of engineers had made their last inspection of winches, ropes, and tackle, and were satisfied that despite the steepness of the ramp and the tower's tremendous weight, the great war engine would arrive intact at its destination, right on schedule. If Silva's calculations were correct, the tower would be halfway up some two hours after it began to move, at which point the bowmen riding in its armored top would be within range of the Masada's ramparts, with the sun at their backs. As the tower rose the sun would descend. At precisely the time when the Masada's defenders might offer the most serious threat, the light would be directly in their eyes.

The great battering ram would be hauled up after the tower, and also catapults manned by one of the cohorts. Ammunition in the form of stones had already been stacked near the platform. More than ten thousand slaves were assembled along the ramp, some lying in the dust or resting against the larger stones. Legionaries with coiled whips stood at intervals near them to make sure that when the signal was given, they would haul at the tackles of the siege tower without letup or disturbance. In all, there were nearly twenty thousand human beings on or near the ramp waiting for Flavius Silva's command. The hills to the west were dotted with groups of camp followers come to observe the assault, and guards had been doubled all around the circumvallation lest there be any attempts to escape during the coming turmoil.

Still the general waited, with his staff, his standard-bearers, his Praetorian Guard, and a mass of tense, poised troops. He glanced at the sun, then at the Masada. There was, he noted wryly, no singing today.

Eleazar ben Ya'ir stood in the tower adjacent to the western gate and watched the massive cart and siege tower of the *Kittim* inch forward. The great rocks that the Zealots had rolled down from the heights of the Masada bounced off the massive structure like dust-stones but killed many of the slaves pulling the ropes to transport the engine. He had ordered that no more of the rolling missiles be employed.

There were times when the cart stopped of its own, sinking into the surface of the ramp or lodging against a half-buried stone. Then the legionaries would lay on with their whips until the tower was on its way again. They heaved the bodies of the dead, or of those still alive but unable to work anymore, off the steep sides of the ramp and whistled for replacements. Inside the lines of those pulling the tower were two more lines of slaves whose efforts set in motion the car supporting the great ram. If the tower fell backward, they would be crushed. Behind the ram came the catapults on sledges hauled upward directly by the strength of a hundred men straining along the five ropes attached to each sledge.

"What about our wall?" Joav said.

"Pampras says we must wait until we know the exact center of impact."

"You think it will work?"

Eleazar grinned. "It will be worth it just to see the look on their faces. Do you remember, in Jerusalem, when we saw the Greek's second wall?"

"But we finally broke through that one."

"If they get through, it will have to be a few at a time— which gives us a chance to even the odds."

"Can't we stop the siege tower? Our marksmen are good, Eleazar."

"With the sun in our eyes? Against an enemy we can hardly see? Look, Joav, how the *Kittim* are concealed behind the iron plates of their tower. And on the ramp they are hidden in their own dust."

"It is the wind...."

"You remember what Shem said about the throwing machines? Make sure no one is in the open."

But even as he spoke the great stones came out of the blinding sun, and with them the cries of men and women as the fifty-pound missiles began to rain down on the plateau. The battle had begun.

Flavius Silva was pleased; the operation was going exactly as he had envisioned. Even the wind was on his side. Now and then the dust subsided, and in those brief moments of clear sight, Silva saw many a soldier fall from a well-placed Zealot arrow. But no matter that the ramp was littered with legionaries' bodies; nothing was going to prevent the union of his tower with the fortress now. Content, he watched the stones loft upward from his catapults, arc, and descend behind the Masada's wall.

The tower was moving to within javelin distance of the west gate, but the Zealots would have little time to use its approach to their benefit. Soon the car supporting the battering ram would be drawn in through an opening in the tower's rear, the man swinging the ram perfectly protected. Once the ram's center was known, the man would adjust the slings accordingly. After that, a child could establish momentum with a simple rhythmic push.

For some time they had been forced to retire from the wall, not daring to lift their heads above the works while bowmen hidden in the tower sent forth arrows, and the other engines catapulted darts and stones. But as the great ram made its first battery against the wall, Eleazar shouted, "Now!" and everyone ran to the barricade they had prepared against this moment. Great wooden beams torn from the north palace had been laid together lengthwise in two parallel rows, separated by the width of a wall. Men, women, and children now set to work filling the space between the rows with earth. As the height increased, the men laid more beams across the long balks, like lattices, to secure them. Although they were still being pelted by quick-loaders and stone-throwers and arrows from the bowmen riding in the top of the siege tower, the people rallied, frantically tearing up the gardens they had so carefully cultivated, dumping more and yet more of the fertile earth between the timbers.

The casemate wall had not been built to withstand the ram, but it had been built solidly enough. The sun was red in the sky when a breach was finally made and a small section collapsed. But the jubilation of the Romans was cut short as they saw, behind the wall they had overthrown, yet another. They were stunned only a moment; as the ram had shattered the outer wall, so now it would destroy this one. But while the second, crude barrier appeared to be of normal construction, it soon became apparent that it was not. It was a soft, pliant wall capable of taking the shocks that broke down the stone. The yielding earth between the rows of timber absorbed the ram's butts, and the concussion shook it together, making it even more solid. The longer and harder the ram struck, the more compact this wall would become.

The monotonous pounding of the ram, which had shattered the desert stillness most of the afternoon, suddenly ceased. The catapults were still. The advancing legionaries had halted. On

the Masada, the people looked at one another, and then, as the
soldiers had done when the casemate wall was breached, they
began to laugh and cheer. Men threw their arms around their
comrades in labor. Earth-stained hands clasped one another.
Some of the people wept with joy. Eleazar picked Pampras the
mason up in his arms and hugged the wall's mastermind as he
would a bride. "Masada is ours!" the people were shouting.
"The Lord is with us! We are saved!"

Silva had left his command post and ridden to the base of
the ramp, where he received news of the setback. Immediately
he started up the ramp accompanied by five Praetorians. Halfway to the top he had to abandon his horse. As he trudged,
panting, up the path, the extraordinary marksmanship of the
Sicarii became apparent: there were, he noted, far more dead
than wounded. As he reached the assault tower, the soldier to
his right was shot down, the sudden inactivity of the catapults
having brought David to the rampart's towers.

With his remaining guard, Silva climbed to the top of the
armored tower, brusquely pushing aside one of the bowmen
so that he could peer through the window slit. The ram had
passed the crumbled masonry of the casemate wall and appeared to be jammed against a wooden barrier. "It won't give
way," one of the engineers was saying. "Each shock only
serves to pack it more firmly."

Silva frowned. There was no time to recalculate the position
and angle of the tower; every second of delay meant another
dead soldier. Briefly he considered storming the barricade. But
there was hardly enough room for even two assault ladders,
and the advantage would be the Jews'.

"The wall is made of wood," he noted. "It will burn nicely."

As the first volley of flaming torches streaked across the sky,
new silence descended on the plateau. Anguished, the people
on the Masada watched the fire spread along the wooden wall,
rapidly consuming what they had toiled so hard and frantically
to build.

"It's no use," Joav groaned. "The wind is with them."

Eleazar stared grimly at the burning wall. When he and
Pampras had decided on the barricade, they had not dismissed
the possibility of fire effecting what the ram could not; but
they had counted on the stacked earth helping to quench the

flames. The wind was blowing so strongly, however, that the fire would not be smothered, and there was no way those inside the wall could put it out. With the wall burned away, legionaries would stream into the fortress. . . .

But the desert wind was a fickle wind. Within the same hour it might blow first from the south and then from the north, shifting course as suddenly as it arose.

"I told you," Aqavia was saying. "There was no sacrifice! The Lord loves sacrifice. Even before the synagogue was built, an altar of stone should have been constructed."

Eleazar grabbed him. "Pray!" he commanded. "Here is your Temple and your altar," he said, pointing to the burning wall. "Pray to the Lord, priest! Speak for us!"

The Sadducee took a step back, opened his mouth, then closed it. Hundreds of pairs of eyes had suddenly fixed on him. Galileans who hated him, Essenes who distrusted him, Jerusalemites who before the Masada had never heard of him, and the children who made fun of him. Now all this grimy, forlorn mass of Israelites was waiting for him to speak, to say the words that would save them. He wet his lips.

"What—what must I say?"

"You know the way to salvation better than any of us, or so you have said. Our prayers have gone for naught. Speak for us!"

Aqavia looked intently at ben Ya'ir, trying to determine if the man was mocking him; but he was in deadly earnest. There was no scorn in any of the eyes fixed on the priest, only hope.

Despite his airs, he had been a minor figure in the Temple hierarchy, willingly unobtrusive in the turbulent days of civil war. But he was a Ha-Kohan, with the blood of Aaron, the Lord's first priest, in his veins. He had boasted of this heritage. Now he must be worthy of it.

"O Lord," he began, drawing himself up, "we pray Thee . . . let Thine anger and wrath turn away from Thy people! Lord! Thou hast chosen us from all the nations to be Thy firstborn! Thou hast named Israel Thy son . . . and hast chastised us as a man chastises his son, that we may be healed of foolishness and blindness and iniquity. We do not reject Thy trials and sourges! In the midst of our misery, still we abide by the covenant! For Thou alone art a living God, and there is none beside Thee. . . .

"O Lord! . . . Thou who workest miracles from everlasting

to everlasting . . . let Thine anger and wrath turn away from us!
Look upon our distress and deliver us, that we may serve Thee
and give thanks to Thy holy name and recount Thy mighty
deeds to everlasting generations. . . ."

"Look!" Joav cried, pointing to the burning wall. The flames
had suddenly bent away, in the direction of the siege tower.

"The wind has shifted!" Yigael exulted. He put his hand
out, testing the air as it hit his flesh. "It blows from the north!"

People ran now to the brink of the rampart, laughing and
crying with joy as they watched the soldiers hastily abandon
the iron tower, and the lines of legionaries begin to retreat
down the ramp.

"A miracle!" they cried happily. "A miracle!"

But suddenly, as quickly as it had veered to come from the
north, the wind swung to the south again and, blowing even
more strongly, carried and flung the flames back against the
wall, turning it into one solid blazing mass. The last hope was
quelled.

"I tried," Aqavia said brokenly. "He did not hear me. He
did not hear. . . ."

"He heard." Eleazar gripped the old man's arm. "The Lord
heard. And He spoke. For you, His priest . . . He spoke."

Aqavia raised his eyes at this and looked searchingly at
Eleazar. Then, slowly, he nodded and proudly walked away.

"What now?" Joav asked quietly.

Eleazar did not answer. His gaze was fixed on the frail,
white-robed figure of Nathaniel, who was leaning on Jonatan's
shoulder, one hand raised as if to embrace the raging fire. His
expression was one of complete ecstasy.

At that moment Eleazar could not be certain if he wanted
to strangle the Righteous Teacher or kneel before him begging
for an answer.

Nathaniel saw him. "The time is come, Eleazar, of which
the prophets wrote! Now is the End of Days!"

Eleazar did not move.

Suddenly, the white-robed figure seemed to slip from Jonatan's shoulder and fell to the ground. Immediately, Eleazar
was at his side, had lifted him up in his strong arms and carried
him like a child to the casemate chamber where the leader of
the Essenes had chosen to dwell in stark simplicity.

"Eleazar . . ." Joav was beside him again. "Wait. What must
we do? What shall I tell the others?"

Nathaniel opened his eyes. "Tell them . . . not to weep. Tell them . . . our triumph is near . . . that this night shall be our victory. . . . Tell them . . . it is so. . . ."

Joav looked at Eleazar.

Eleazar said nothing. Then, slowly he nodded.

"I am to say . . . 'Victory is ours'?"

He did not speak. The wall would burn for some hours. The legionaries would not cross over until morning. There was time before the end. Hope was still better than despair. And for a moment the wind had turned. Miracles were not numbered. In a world governed by the Almighty anything was possible. *I must believe,* he told himself. *I must believe. . . .*

He looked up. "No," he said, correcting the other gently. "Victory will be ours."

Joav grinned and ran to spread the word.

Eleazar looked back at Nathaniel, who was now resting on his narrow pallet. "Have you made a liar of me after all?" he asked softly, with a slight, sad smile.

The Essene's eyes opened. "Be at peace, Eleazar," he said, knowing what anguish lay behind the smile. "The Lord is with you. I know . . . you will find . . . the way."

She stood on the terrace of the palace a mad king had built for the princess he loved—a slender figure, deeply tanned by the fierce sun of this wilderness, with strange, light eyes beneath winged brows, and the fine bone structure of her own royal heritage. The wind had pushed her veil back, and now it whipped her dark hair around so that the long strands sometimes stung her eyes and mouth. She seemed oblivious to this discomfort and also to the sight of the men patrolling the circumvallation in the distance. She turned slightly so that her eyes fell upon the pewter stretch of sea and the dark mountains behind the water.

It is that time, she thought, *when the sun becomes a round, red ball . . . when the gulls return . . . and the sky comes down all pink and gold. . . . The last sand tower so lovingly bedecked with shell and stone is drawn finally back into the sea, its jewels scattered on the wet sand . . . hidden beneath . . . only to be returned tomorrow and gathered by another child. . . .*

What is this moment, she wondered, *that it is so perfect?*

The sea ebbs . . . flows . . . and time is only a whisper . . . the murmuring of the sea. . . .

I can see it all now . . .

Odysseus at the helm with the sky coming down on his eyes . . .

Myself as a child . . . playing by the water's edge in this hour I love best . . .

My brothers skipping stones across the sea, laughing as we race across the sand . . .

My father . . . standing on a hill outside Jerusalem, praying to a God who has not saved any of us.

The sky is red . . .

But it is not the sun burning a path to night.

The Roman fire eats at our wall. In the morning they will be upon us.

The Masada has fallen.

EIGHT

"This is not a victory toast," Flavius Silva said as he handed a cup of wine to Solomon ben Ya'ish. "You have conducted yourself most honorably during the months we have been together. But I am not insensitive to the feelings you must be having at this moment—or, indeed, before this. Besides, the thing is not wholly done. But I am confident tomorrow will be the last of it."

"You are certain of that fact?" Solomon ben Ya'ish asked carefully.

"I was certain I could take the mountain, and I have no doubts whatsoever about the Tenth Legion and auxiliary cohorts dealing effectively with the rebel forces on the Masada. There will be, I admit, a certain lack of precision in the killing...a certain wanton destructiveness—which it is only reasonable to expect, considering the months of waiting and the provocation my men have endured. I want you to know I take no satisfaction in the murder and rape of your people, any more than I would in the torture of some dumb animal. When the wolf preys, you hunt him down and kill him for the good of all. There is no need for prolonged cruelty."

"Why tell me this?"

"Because I want you to know I will not be able to stop my men tomorrow. It is something I must allow. It is...their due."

"The brutalization of one human being by another is not excusable, General. It is no one's due. All life is holy—and every human life has the sanctity of intrinsic and infinite worth."

The Roman smiled wryly. "Ah, doctor, will you disappoint

me? I have stood in wonder these months over the fact that you have never once succumbed to the temptation of preaching at me—which seems a rather common habit among proponents of the One God. In Rome, the number of dissenters from the old religion grows daily. Before the war, there were many converts to the ways of Israel. Oh, yes! Now, however, seeing how low you people have fallen, there is, I am glad to say, a general aversion to anything Judaic. Instead we have an increasing number of these Christians, whose beliefs, I fear, are not all that dissimilar to your own—whose leader in fact is a Jew."

"Really?"

"Am I to believe you are truly innocent of this? Never mind. It is not to the point. What matters is that I have succeeded in doing what I set out to do."

"Not quite. You said yourself, the thing is not over. There is still tomorrow."

"Tomorrow will bring no miracles. Your God will not deliver Eleazar ben Ya'ir and his stubborn followers out of my hands. The facts speak for themselves. You may put your faith in your God, Solomon ben Ya'ish—and you see where that had led you—but I put my faith in facts."

"They will all die?"

"If they put up the kind of battle I expect, assuredly. It is legend that even the wives and babes of the Sicarii fight with anything at hand."

"But one might survive. Or two, or three . . ."

The Roman shrugged. "I imagine the troops will try to preserve a few females. How long a woman might survive the combined lust of so many men is a mathematical problem I have never personally investigated."

"But you must take slaves—if only as witness to the effectiveness of your campaign."

"No. No slaves. The market is glutted already, and I see no need to populate my province with troublemakers. Not even as witness to my genius." He laughed self-consciously. "I am sorry, my good doctor. As I said before, I can appreciate what feelings you must have now. But you must permit me this heady taste of triumph. It is so much sweeter than any wine." He was, in fact, a trifle drunk. "Poor, plodding Flavius Silva. So what if he gets the highest marks from the teachers? So what if he has never lost a single campaign with which he has been entrusted? So, give him finally to be military governor of this putrefying wasteland, and let him go about capturing an impossible stronghold. Well...I did it!" He sat down abruptly. "Things are going to be different when I return to Rome. No more fair-haired boys getting all the glory. I've always gotten along with Vespasian. Well, now I'm going to ask for my due. My wife's uncle has a villa in Pompeii. I've never been one for the sybaritic life, but I'm beginning to think there is nothing wrong with a little luxury in one's old age. If one can keep one's head in harsh surroundings, certainly one can do the same in a pleasurable atmosphere." He looked up. "You shall visit me in Pompeii. Once you are in Rome..."

Solomon ben Ya'ish cleared his throat. "I have wanted to discuss that with you...."

"Well? What is it?"

"I am very grateful for your generous offer to send me to Vespasian's academy. But I have thought it over, and I would prefer to remain in Judea."

"Good! You shall accompany me to Caesarea."

"No, general," he said quietly. "With your permission...I will live among my own people."

Silva sighed. "Then...you are only a fool, after all. All right. Whatever you want." He turned away abruptly. "It is late. I am tired. You may go."

"Something else..."

"What?"

"If there are any survivors—yes, I know it is impossible! But if there is one alive, only one—"

Silva laughed drily. "Or two—or three—"

"Give them to me."

"You know my orders."

"General Silva, you are a realistic man, a man of fact, not fancy. One or two pour souls, in all probability more dead than alive, are not going to start another war. I have no family. I need...family."

The Roman was silent a moment; then he nodded. "All right. But no grown men."

"No men."

"And no more than ten."

"I did not expect you to be so generous."

"It is the men out there, sleeping in their tents, from whom you must not expect generosity. It is all up to them."

"Perhaps not," Solomon ben Ya'ish said softly, too softly for the Roman to hear, as he disappeared out into the night.

They were waiting for Eleazar when he emerged from the casemate chamber, nearly a thousand souls, old and young, men and women and children. For a moment he seemed confused, as if he did not know who they were or why they were looking at him. Then his eyes cleared, took on that curious shot of light, and he smiled reassuringly.

Nathaniel was dead. Eleazar would not tell the people of the passing of the Teacher of Righteousness; they might consider it further proof of the Lord's abandonment and a sign of their own end. He did not want them plunged into gloom.

Nathaniel had spoken calmly of his own dying, saying he could feel his soul slipping away, that his passage from earth was imminent. Almost conversationally, he mentioned that he was looking forward to the journey.

"Don't speak so," Eleazar had protested. "You will be here to see our victory and the return of our people to the New Jerusalem."

"No," the Essene had whispered, his voice becoming fainter with each passing breath. "I am ready to cast off this worn clothing. How I long to be free. . . ." Suddenly his eyes opened, and in a young, strong voice, with a rather mischievous twinkle, he said, "The trouble with you, Eleazar, is that you see death as an end. It isn't. It is the beginning."

So he stood now facing the people to whom he had promised victory, whom he had led in rebellion and isolated survival and fragile freedom, whom he had not allowed—if not by force, then by the power of his own personality—to surrender. At this moment, he was thankful that of all the eyes upon him not one pair was reproachful or accusing.

"We come up with nothing," Asshur said, breaking the silence at last. "Even if we could escape into the desert—which seems even less likely than before—we could not go far before they caught up to us."

"What did the Holy One say?" Esau, Shem's cousin, wanted to know.

Eleazar did not answer him. Instead, he said, "Go now to your dwellings, and speak to your wives and children as soldiers do before they leave for battle. Wash yourselves

. . . . Break bread together. Then let us all meet in our customary gathering place, in the center of the Masada, where all northern tracks meet. I will tell you then what I propose."

"But the *Kittim*—" Yigal began.

"The fires are bright in their camps. They will not come till morning. Those of us without family will keep the watches to be sure they do not mean to surprise us in the darkness. For myself, I am sure they will not. The night is ours. Go now."

They went off into the darkness, wondering at his words.

Eleazar turned to Joav, who had remained at his side. "Why do you wait, old friend? Miriam is alone. Go to her."

"I . . . I thought I would take the watch in the west tower," he stammered.

"There are enough men for that. Go to Miriam."

Joav sucked in his breath. Then he nodded.

Eleazar grinned. "And wash that dirt off your arms and face."

"It is good dirt," Joav growled. "Good Judean soil. But not as good as we had in the Galilee, eh, Eleazar?"

"No . . . not like the Galilee."

Joav raised his mighty arms and studied them in the darkness. Then he let them fall to his sides. "It is good," he said finally, "to die for the land you love."

"He thinks it will be a fight to the last," a voice said as the sturdy Zealot walked away.

Eleazar did not have to make out the figure of the priest Aqavia; he knew so well the precise accent of the Sadducee aristocrat. "Don't you?"

The priest's face emerged in the darkness. "There are ways . . . and there are ways . . . to make a stand."

"What way would you choose, priest?"

"The same as you, Eleazar ben Ya'ir," he said softly. "The *Kiddush ha-Shem*."

Eleazar did not reply.

"You have never reproached me for being alive," the priest went on, "but I know you must have wondered how I managed to survive what so many did not."

"It is not for me to pass judgment."

"Still . . . you must have your thoughts. . . ."

He shrugged. "You are not the only one from Jerusalem. There's more than one sewer rat among us."

"But they are not priests. To tell the truth, before I came

here, in all those years in the Temple, I don't think I ever really thought of myself as a priest of the Lord. It was simply a profession...inherited. I never felt touched by anything...divine. And I was never called upon to perform anything less mundane than compiling the lists of the tithe collectors or assisting in the daily, routine sacrifice offerings. Once every so often, it was my turn to dash the bowl of blood against the altar." He paused.

"After the war broke out, when the council was doing its best to exterminate the old guard, I could have risen to a more prominent position, but I chose to remain in the background. Time proved me correct. There was, you may recall, a rather quick turnover of Zadokites under John and Simon. Toward the end, there was a whole new group of very young priests. They came to me for guidance, and I turned my back on them. When the Temple was set afire, I saw them pluck the spires from the golden roof and hurl them like lances at the legionaries. When these were gone, they gathered themselves together on the sacred roof, clasped one another's hands, and jumped, singing, into the flames. And I? What did I do? There are secret passages in the Temple, some known to many, some to only a few. I had spent a long, long time in the Holy House, and I knew it well.

"With a few others—including the Temple treasurer—I managed to stay hidden for some time. We were finally forced through lack of food to surrender, and obtained from Titus a sworn guarantee of safety in return for handing over the sacred treasures we had hidden. Lampstands, basins, cups of solid gold...the vestments of the chief priests, with all their precious stones . . . purple and scarlet dye for repairing the great curtain . . . and the curtain itself, which hung in front of the Sanctuary's golden doors. What a work of art! Even now I marvel at it. The whole vista of the heavens was worked in its design. The mixture of its materials typified all creation. Scarlet thread symbolized fire, blue the air, purple the sea, and plain linen the earth. What a marvel! How the Romans exclaimed at its size and beauty. There was more...but why remind ourselves of the glory taken from us? Or rather, given away...

"I received the pardon granted to deserters and was left to fend for myself. My family's villa had been taken over by the partisans. My servant, Iddo, did indeed hide and care for me.

But it was not Rome from whom I hid.

"The war never made much sense to me. But then, I was one of those with nothing to win and much to lose. I understand now that there are needs other than those we sought to serve through the Temple. The young priests who leaped into the fire spoke of those needs, but I would not listen. And now, it is too late."

"No," Eleazar said. "You know what we must do. I will need your help."

"Then I was correct. It is the *Kiddush ha-Shem*."

"Yes."

"So be it." He let out his breath. "The red-haired one was right," he said with a smile. "It is good to fight the good fight."

She was waiting. The child too, munching away on a piece of bread. Benjamin looked up at his father and grinned, the boy's smile a perfect miniature reflection of the man's. He had Eleazar's eyes but his mother's dark hair, and he was already tall for his age. Eleazar started to go to him, then stopped.

"What is this?" he said, taking the sword from her hand.

"I want to be with you at the end. I'm not going to be shut up with the women while you're out there! I won't! You can't make me! I want to be with you—"

He pulled her close, quieting her with his kisses. Finally, he took her face in his hands and said, "You will."

It was the gentleness of his voice that startled her. "What is it?"

He put his finger on her lips. "Not now. We have so little time. Let me play with my son a bit. Then . . . we will talk."

They were gathered and waiting. Calling soft greetings to this one or that one, bestowing an affectionate backslap here and there, Eleazar strode into their midst and found himself on the rise that was nearly in the middle of the plateau and had come to serve as a natural forum. He looked over the crowd, seeking out the faces of those he knew best, those men who had come with him to the Masada; and when he spoke it seemed as though he was addressing them.

"*Cheverim*," he began. "Comrades. Long ago, we made a vow, you and I. . . . We vowed that we would serve no earthly

king. Death, we said, is nothing. Freedom is everything. We
will live as free men, we said, or not at all. And we swore,
all of us—you, Joav . . . Shem . . . Yigael . . . and the rest
of you—that we would die before we would allow ourselves
to become slaves." He paused. "The time has come, *chev'ra*,
when we must make good our word."

The men he had spoken to were silent; but one in the crowd
who was not of the Sicarii, albeit a hardy veteran of the war,
raised his fist and shouted, "We are with you, Eleazar. We
will fight to the last man!"

"No," Eleazar replied. "We shall not lift our swords against
these Romans. But neither shall they lift theirs against us."

There was a great murmuring at this. "What does he mean?"
people asked one another. "What is to happen?"

"Pampras, old friend," Eleazar said suddenly. "When we
spoke of the wooden barrier, you said, 'It must be like Israel.
For we are a people who become stronger with each blow.'
You see now our wall going up in flames. Still, it must be as
you said. The harder we are hit, the stronger we must become."
His eyes went round the crowd. "Some of us here were among
the first to revolt, but all of us are the last to fight against
Rome. Daybreak will end our resistance. We have no hope of
escape, and none of survival. But we can still better the *Kittim!*"
He looked straight at David. "We can cheat them of their
triumph. We can make the victory ours. While we are still free
we can choose an honorable death, in the name of the One
God, who alone is the true and just Lord of mankind. There
is but one course left to us, my friends, that is our right and
our privilege. The *Kiddush ha-Shem.*"

In the silence that followed, the wind seemed to mingle
with the crackling flames of the crumbling wall. One of the
great beams fell backward with a great thud. A child began
to cry.

"Everyone . . . is to die?" someone asked. "Women . . .
and children?"

"We are all soldiers now," Eleazar replied. "The smallest
child, the babe still in the womb, is a *bacchur* now, a warrior
for the Lord."

"No," Mordecai the Tanner said suddenly. "No! Not my
wife . . . my children . . . no! No, I can't! It is madness . . .
to kill one's own flesh and blood . . . no! No!"

"Would you rather the soldiers did it for you?" Aqavia

asked. "Or do you still think you can preserve your family when so many others have been destroyed? Where now is the City of our people? Where now the Holy Sanctuary? Old men with streaming eyes sit in the ashes of the Temple. And those in the enemy's hands, what of them? Who would not hasten to die rather than share their fate?"

"He's right," Esau said now. "I've seen men broken on the rack, tortured to death at the stake, half eaten by savage beasts and then kept alive to be their food a second time—just to provide amusement and sport! I've seen babies held aloft on the points of spears, and women—" He broke off and shook his head. "You're blind if you can't see what's coming. I'm alone—and I swore I'd die before I ever went back to them. But if I had a woman and child, I'd do the kindest thing I could for them . . . while it was still possible."

Eleazar had been staring at Alexandra during this. She was standing very still, and her expression was one of complete calm. Like one coming out of a dream, he raised his head and looked out among the people again. "I know . . . that what I ask of you . . . is hard. But the Lord's way is never easy."

"Is it the Lord's will that we must die?" David asked.

Eleazar looked at the boy. "We were born to die," he said softly. "But outrage, slavery—no law of nature says we must be subject to this." He looked around once more and suddenly seemed to grow even more erect and commanding. The golden head was flung back a bit, as if he were looking up at the stars. He began to speak again, his voice deep and resolute.

"The Lord has made His will known to us. The fire that was being carried into the enemy lines did not turn back of its own accord. But if the Almighty has taken away all hope of survival, He has still given us the time and the means for victory. Yes, victory! We have been very proud of our courage. But who is brave enough to see his beloved violently carried off? Who would hear the voice of his child crying for help while his hands are bound? Come! While these hands are free and can still hold a sword, let them do a noble service! Let us die as free men together with our families! That is what our Law ordains! That is what our wives and children demand of us, the necessity God has laid on us, the opposite of what the Romans want!"

They had begun to cheer even before he finished.

"Set everything afire!" Joav shouted. "Let there be nothing

for the *Kittim* to loot! They will get nothing! Nothing!"

This was greeted with even more enthusiasm.

"All right!" Eleazar agreed. "But spare one store of supplies as witness that we did not perish through want but because we chose death before slavery."

He was engulfed in a mass of people while others rushed about shouting, weeping. The wooden wall was only a smoldering heap now, but the plateau was suddenly alight with dozens of fires that had been started in every corner of the place.

In the midst of this sudden, frenzied commotion, Alexandra remained where she had been during Eleazar's speech. He would never know what strength she had mustered in that moment when their eyes met, how much it had taken for her to remain calm and unquestioning, while he spoke to the crowd—and earlier, when he had spoken only to her. Because even now, knowing he was right, knowing it was the thing for them to do—not only to spare themselves the horrors each and every one of them would taste, but also for a greater purpose— even now, every muscle, every nerve, every part of her being, rebelled against his proposition. Behind the great gray eyes a voice was screaming, "I don't want to die!"—and that voice, though she made no sound, was hers.

I don't want to die, she was still thinking. *Not now. Not ever. But, oh! Not now!* Life was too good, too sweet—even without the sea, without Beit Harsom, without books or any of the things she had once thought mattered. All that had come to matter in the last few years was staying alive; and strangely, existence stripped to this essential core had become infinitely more satisfying than it had been when embellished with so many worldly things. There was Eleazar, and little Benjamin— oh, Beni was becoming so interesting now! She didn't want to miss a moment of his growth! Instinctively, she put her hand on her stomach. *I'll never know,* she thought, *if you are the daughter I so want. Now, I'll never know. . . .*

She felt someone touch her arm. It was Aliterus. "Come," he said, and began to lead her away.

She followed, dazed. The lean-tos which had been built to house those newest to the Masada were already aflame, and men with torches were running toward the storehouses and the small palaces. People were openly embracing. A small group of children danced around excitedly, not realizing what the pretty flames portended. For the moment, though, Beni was safe with Hagar.

Aliterus was leading her away from the others to the relatively isolated *columbarium,* a circular structure of stone with niches like dovecotes in its walls. What use it had served in Herod's day was anyone's guess, although Pampras had said the niches were not to harbor pigeons but to house the cremated remains of Herod's pagan mercenaries. The children were fond of playing here and had come here to plan their Hanukkah celebration. Aliterus had placed several oil lamps in the shallow niches. Alexandra saw now that he had a knife. She took a step back.

"No, no," he said, seeing her sudden apprehension. "You have nothing to fear from me. Only stay a moment. I need your courage."

"I am not feeling very brave, Aliterus."

"I have never been brave," he admitted. "Except before an audience."

She knew now what he wanted. "Do not ask me to watch you die."

"You must. As you love me, stay. Someone must see my greatest role." He held the dagger aloft with both hands but hesitated. "A last speech. What must it be? Euripides? Virgil? What must Rome's 'dirty Jew' say? One good line, after all, is a lasting monument."

"You are cruel," she whispered. "Can I take pleasure in this? Do it quickly."

"No," he said softly. "This is my moment, Alexandra. That for which I was born. We must not cheat destiny of a good performance. Ah! I have it! There is but one fitting line. How strange that I have waited 'til now to say it. 'Hear, O Israel, the Lord our God, the Lord is One!" With a swift, sudden movement, he plunged the dagger into his breast and fell to the ground.

She was beside him instantly.

He tried to reach up, to touch her face. "Tears..." he whispered. "I told you...I could play tragedy." His eyes closed, and he was gone.

She rose then and left him, walking like one blind. The very plateau seemed unfamiliar, like the place the *Kittim* called Hades, full of smoke and flames and the lamenting of men as they held their wives to them for the last time, and of women who kissed their beloved murderers, and of children who did not understand but, seeing parents weeping, readily joined in. She was stumbling over things—bodies?—not caring where she walked, until a hand cut her short and Hagar's black eyes snapped her back to reality. The woman was holding Beni, and he clung to her, his eyes wide with terror. Immediately Alexandra took the child into her arms.

"Aliterus is dead."

"The fool," Hagar said softly. "They are all fools. Come, we must leave this place."

She shook her head. "My place is here." She had a sudden vision of the dead actor. "Perhaps . . . this is that for which I was born."

"Madness!" Hagar spat. "You were born to live! To love! To raise your child! Would you kill him? Would you kill your own blood? You Jews are crazy!" She put her hand on the young woman's shoulder. "Little owl. My gray-eyed daughter . . . come away from this place. We will find a way. But we must leave now!"

But Alexandra only shook her head again; for she knew there was no other place for her. "Take the child," she said. "Hide deep in the water cave. Take others if you will . . . children. . . ." She rubbed her eyes; they were so full of smoke. "In the morning, when the Romans come to claim their victory, show yourself—but only when you are sure to see Silva. Tell him what has occurred here. Tell it well, Hagar, as well as the tales you told me when I was a child in my parents' house . . . that the world may know what the Jews of Masada thought of Caesar and his Empire."

Hagar opened her mouth to speak and then closed it. Finally, in a voice suddenly broken and old, she said, "I will stay with you. You will have need of me on this journey."

But Alexandra would not allow her to remain, for she knew it must be as she had said. And she wanted her son to live. He would be without a father, without a country. But he would be alive.

And as long as there is one of us still in this world it is not over, she thought. *Someday . . . someday. . . .*

At last Hagar bent to her will. Alexandra embraced the child, trying not to let him know it would be the last time she would ever hold him; but he clung to her and looked wonderingly when she put him in Hagar's arms again. "It is late, little boy," she said softly. "Go now with Hagar, to bed. Soon I will be with you. I will always be with you. . . . That's right, little love, lay your head on Hagar's shoulder." She stroked his hair. "Close your eyes, baby boy. Close your eyes. . . ."

Hagar suddenly stretched forth one arm, and for a moment the two women clung to each other.

"Look . . ." Alexandra whispered, pulling away. "He is asleep. Take him to Jabneh, Hagar. Let him learn all that ben Zakkai would teach. But you must teach him too . . . who he is, and the blood from which he comes. Do not let him forget that he saw his first days here, on the Masada. That he was born free. And that he is the son of Eleazar ben Ya'ir."

Hagar nodded, tears streaming all the while down her worn and withered face. Alexandra kissed her again, and then, once more, the sleeping child, and bade Hagar be off. She could not bear to watch the woman's retreating figure, and she turned away, only to find the boy David watching.

She looked at him a moment, then said, "I know you have the courage to follow Eleazar's command. But are you brave enough to do what I ask?"

"What is that?"

"Go with them. Be my son's . . . Joav."

Their eyes locked in perfect accord. He nodded and went off after Hagar.

Alexandra made her way back then to the *columbarium* and, bending over Aliterus's body, pulled the knife from his chest. "It is not done," she whispered; and it seemed to her he smiled approvingly. Then she found a dead child whose hair and size were not dissimilar to her son's, wrapped the body in a blanket, and carried it back to the north palace. There, she waited.

The tribune Antoninus Marcus reported to the general's tent as ordered.

"What's going on, Marc?"

"There seem to be fires all atop the Masada, sir. The southern camp reports the whole place is ablaze."

"Despair," he said cheerfully.

"Your pardon?"

"They must be mad with despair. Dammit, boy. Why are you always so polite?"

"I don't understand, sir."

Silva sighed. What could he say? The young man's manner was correct. Impeccable, in fact. How could he tell him that he'd hoped for something more?

"I have no son," he said at last. "Your father and I were very close. I had hoped . . . particularly now, in this glorious moment of triumph . . . to be able to share . . ." He broke off, embarrassed. "I have sensed for some time a certain distance between us that despite the disparity of age and station, I had hoped my . . . interest . . . might serve to diminish. Are you angry," he continued bluntly, "because of the girl?"

He shook his head. "I am to blame as much as anyone. I kept Michal for my own pleasure when I could have sent her to safety. The sin is mine."

"Sin? What sort of talk is this? What sin? The only sin for which a Roman is liable is an act of malignancy against another Roman or the gods. What happened to the girl was not pretty, but you have made it a far more important issue than it is. Your thinking is wrong, Marc. It is all wrong. I sensed it long ago when you began to wax sentimental over the enemy out there. I tell you frankly, there have been moments when I've wondered if you haven't secretly wished our little rebels' nest might remain intact upon the mighty Masada. No, don't answer. I won't believe a denial, and I will not goad a man to treason. Let us not pursue this further. But I speak for your own good. For the love I bore your father."

"You are right. I was hoping . . . for a miracle."

The general stared at him. "A miracle," he said finally. "Sins, miracles . . . have you gone mad?" He strode to the opening of the tent and, holding the flap aside, said, "Look! There is your miracle! A road straightway up the side of that damned mountain, and my siege tower sitting atop it pretty as you please! Who would have thought such a thing was possible? The impregnable Masada! But I have taken her! I have gone where no man dared to go, and tomorrow I will exterminate what no one else so far has been able to rid this world of. Now! There is your miracle!"

The young man had followed the general to the entrance of the tent; he stood there now gazing up at the Masada. There was an angry red glow around the top of the mountain, and now and again Marc could see the tips of shooting flames and hear the cries of the people on the plateau. But as the flames grew higher, a sudden silence enveloped the mountain. *Perhaps hey are praying*, Marc thought. His face clouded as he realized that morning, and what it would bring, were not far away.

"Or do you doubt their defeat?" Silva asked sarcastically.

Marc continued to stare searchingly at the Masada. Suddenly, his face cleared, as if he could see something in or beyond the smoky red haze. "There was a man once," he said slowly, "who also was defeated. At least, it would seem that he was. He ended his life nailed to a cross. What more horrible death could there be? What is more low and despicable to us than crucifixion? Yet that man—if indeed he was a man—has made our symbol of contempt the symbol of his glory and the glory of all men." He looked at Flavius Silva. "They're going to beat you," he said softly. "The people on the Masada are going to beat you. I don't know how. I only know they will. In any case, I will not accompany you in the morning. I can no longer order one man to kill another."

"Do you realize what you are saying, tribune?"

He nodded. "I am prepared to take the consequences."

"Marc . . . listen to me. . . . It is this damned desert. Listen . . . you have the qualities. You can have a fine career—"

"No! Not as a murderer!" He shook his head. "And I can't— I cannot make Caesar my god any longer." He paused. "There is something I must tell you, something I ought to have said a long time ago. I am one of those who call themselves Christians. I believe in the teachings of Jesus. I believe in the Christ."

Silva was too stunned to reply. For a moment he considered the boy had gone mad, for here he was, calmly condemning himself as an enemy of the state. And smiling! But no, there was no look of madness in Antoninus Marcus's eyes. Would that he, Flavius Silva, military governor of Judea, general of the province's occupying force, honored husband, respected citizen, loyal devotee of Rome's gods, and conqueror of Rome's foes—would that he might look out upon the world with eyes so full of . . . peace.

But he was, after all, what he was; and the shock he'd experienced upon hearing Marc's words, the confusion he had felt at this sudden, unexpected revelation, quickly passed, to be replaced by a kind of grim determination. The general's back straightened; his features took on an even colder, more remote expression than the troops under his command were used to seeing. Still . . .

There was something in the air. It was like a fly or gnat he could only sense hovering about, like the faint buzzing of some irritating pest forever out of reach.

There had been something in the eyes of Solomon ben Ya'ish not unlike what Silva saw now in the face of Antoninus Marcus.

The slight movement of the general's hand might have been an involuntary gesture or the flicking away of some small annoyance. "I will not have my triumph sullied by martyrdom," he declared succinctly. "I have little doubt," he went on, "this . . . philosophy of yours . . . will lead you to a less than glorious end—in the arena, perhaps, as it has so many unfortunates before you. But not on my account, tribune. Not on my account. In any event, you may as well know I have long held the knowledge of your mother's . . . peculiarities. I suppose she must be blamed for this." He allowed himself a sigh. "I see that I was wrong to think you possessed the qualities that would have made for a career in Caesar's service. No doubt my affection for your father has clouded my judgement." He cleared his throat. "You shall return to Rome with my recommendation that you be excused from further duty. We shall say 'reasons of health.' Yes . . . the climate . . . these harsh surroundings . . ."

"Thank you, sir."

Silva nodded. He stared at the young man a moment more and then said, with an anger he could no longer control, "But on this I shall insist! In a few hours, when the sun rises, you will accompany me to the Masada. I want you by my side when I cross the Zealots' ravaged wall. Once and for all, for your own good, you will see for yourself that the God of the Jews and of your Christ has not delivered the people of Masada from the hand of Rome!"

It was quiet now. The dark, still heart of night.

She waited for him in the room where they used to meet before they were married. She had made a small fire and now knelt before it, gazing into the flames, no longer hearing the sounds outside the palace—perhaps because there had ceased to be any. She stared at the flames of the small fire and then at the fine mosaic floor. The rude Zealot stove had dislodged a chip of colored stone, and she could see the lines Herod's artisan had drawn on the rough floor to guide his hand.

Someone was coming into the chamber.

Eleazar. . . .

His face in the light of the fire, in the half-darkness, was like a stranger's. *Who is this man?* she thought. *What does he see with those eyes that look so far away?* . . .

Softly, she called his name.

His eyes found her; his face seemed to relax, to take on warmth. Without a word he went to her, raised her to her feet, and took her in his arms.

She closed her eyes, feeling his lips on her face, her hair, her neck, his hands warm on her body . . . feeling as always—and smiling even now at her own blasphemy—that if Yahwah was his Lord, surely Eleazar ben Ya'ir was hers.

At last he released her. "Benjamin?"

She hesitated, then pointed to a small bundle on the floor. Beside it lay a bloodstained knife.

"I . . . I wanted to spare you that," she stammered, holding on to his arm that he might not move closer to the small corpse.

He stared at her and then at the dead child for what seemed an eternity. Then he turned back to her. "Where is he?" he asked quietly.

"Safe."

"Alexandra . . ." He shook his head; he had no words to say. "I . . . cannot . . . I . . ."

"So long as one of us is free," she reminded him softly, "then someday . . . perhaps . . . all of us will be free. . . ."

He passed his hand before his eyes, a man so obviously wracked by so many emotions that she could not be sure what he would do. At last he said, "The law of Masada . . . all are equal here. Shall I grant you what I have denied the others?"

"Denied? . . . Did any ask of you that which I ask now?"

"No," he replied. "Not one."

"If any had—if Batsheva, for instance, had come forward and begged you to spare her child—would you have refused her?"

The gray eyes as always demanded total honesty.

He thought a moment, then said simply, "No."

She let out her breath. "Then let it be as you have said, Eleazar. Treat me as you would all the rest."

Again he looked long at her, and then he seemed to smile. "Oh, my son," he said softly, ". . . wherever you are . . . beware of clever women. And thank God for them." Then he put out his arms and drew her to him again, and for a long moment neither spoke.

"They are all dead," he said finally, "Jonatan . . . Joav . . . all. We made a pile of food so the *Kittim* would understand we did not die of want. The Holy Books have been buried. Everything else has been set afire." He sank to his knees, exhausted. "We drew lots. Ten captains to help me . . . take care of the rest. To see that it was done . . . as we had agreed. Then we were to draw again . . . for the last man . . . to strike the last blow. But they would not draw for this. 'We might fail in our resolve,' they said. 'But you will not.'" He passed his hand across his eyes once more. "And so I killed them . . . and set the western palace blazing." His hand dropped to his side. He stared at her. "And now I come to you, Alexandra, whom I love more than— I am here to kill you, Alexandra . . . and then to die beside you."

She did not answer but knelt beside him and put her head on his shoulder.

"And then it will be done." He was staring into the fire again. "No more priests . . . no more petty tyrants . . . no more Sicarii. All burned away. Done with. That the people of Israel may rise again, reborn and clean and true to their God." He sighed. "And I will never have to kill again. This last time, and never again. Ah, Alexandra . . . I am so covered with blood! . . . What will the Lord say when he sees these red hands?"

"You are His soldier, Eleazar. The Lord's own *bacchur*. You will take your place beside the others He has loved."

He smiled. "My Sadducee princess. You know you don't believe in a Throne of Judgment."

"Whatever will be . . . I will be with you."

He turned slightly, drawing her up on her knees. "Will you be there?" he asked, gripping her arms tightly.

"For all eternity."

"I love you."

"And I, you."

He drew her into his arms again, but this time it was she who broke the embrace. "It will be morning soon," she said softly. "You must do it now. Come, my love. I am not afraid."

"I am," he whispered. "For in that moment after, that moment before I die . . . I will be alone here. One man amidst the bodies of those he loved best and the ghosts of those he most

despised. Do not doubt that I will join you, Alexandra. Do not
doubt that we will be together."

"Always. For all time." And she believed it. For love, after
all, was the final measure; and in its light all things were
possible.

The fire was out. A light had begun to fill the room. Somewhere a bird was singing. . . .

His voice was like the whisper of the wind. "A
moment . . . only a moment. And we shall be free."

AUTHOR'S NOTE

Most of the characters in *The Tenth Measure* actually existed. As many readers will know, there was an Josef ben Matthias, later to be known as Flavius Josephus, and there was an Eleazar ben Ya'ir who led the Jewish rebels at the desert fortress called Masada.

Josephus revealed as much of himself as anyone is ever likely to know in his *Autobiography, History of the War Against the Jews,* and other writings. The traditional story of his escape from Jotapata, related in his own words, involves the casting of lots among the survivors hidden in the cave, each man to kill the other until only one was left to commit suicide—not unlike the final scene at Masada. Josephus says that as "luck" would have it, only he and one other were left, and he persuaded the other fellow to join him in surrender.

Thanks to Josephus, we know of Menahem and the Sicarii; Eleazar ben Ananias, captain of the Temple guards; John of Gischala; Simon bar Giora; ben Bariah, nephew of Johanan ben Zakkai; Gessius Florus; Tiberius Alexander, and others. While Josephus paints a uniformly black portrait of the Sicarii, Zealots, and Jewish insurgents, he also records acts of valor attributed to these men—his enemies—and tells how Simon inspired enormous bravery and unswerving loyalty.

The actor Aliterus appears in Josephus' autobiography. He was in fact a Jew, a favorite at court and with the Roman populace, and in fact introduced Josephus to Poppea. Aliterus' arrival in Jerusalem and subsequent events involving him are my own invention.

Vespasian, Titus, Agrippa, Berenice, Herod, and Miriamne were actual people, and the love affair between Titus and Berenice is history.

The Essenes have generally been considered the sect responsible for the Dead Sea Scrolls. Yigael Yadin's excavations give evidence of an Essene presence on the Masada, and Josephus tells us that Essenes fought actively in the war with Rome. The holy man Banus, of whom Josef speaks, was evidently a real person, but Nathaniel is my fiction. Likewise Jonatan, although the Scroll excavations reveal the existence of a scribe named Johanan ha-Taleh (John or Jonathan the Younger) who had exceedingly fine penmanship.

Eleazar ben Ya'ir, of course, was real, as were his ancestors. His personality and appearance are my own inventions; what we know historically is that he was a great warrior and leader, obviously possessing some kind of charisma in order to keep a refugee community together for three years, to hold off Silva's forces for nearly a year, and finally to invoke successfully the Kiddush ha-Shem.

Flavius Silva is real, though I have taken certain liberties with him. Silva served as a lieutenant with Titus and was probably a contemporary of that young man rather than of Vespasian, as I suggest. It also seems likely that his daring scheme for taking the Masada was the work of some historically anonymous engineer with the legion. In any event, Silva fades from history after his involvement with the Masada.

Most of the names used for Eleazar *chev'ra,* including that of the priest Aqavia, were taken from the shards found on Masada. Their characters, however, were taken from my imagination.

Johanan ben Zakkai and his circle of rabbis are historic and noted in the Talmud. Ben Zakkai's escape from Jerusalem is legendary and appears in historical sources pretty much as I have written it (though without Aliterus). The story of the woman eating her own baby during the siege of Jerusalem also appears in the Midrash, as well as in Josephus' history. The name given is one "Mary," who, unlike Hadassah, was articulate enough to explain her plight and to invite the intruders to join in her sad feast.

The massacre of the Jews in Caesarea took place the same day (Sabbath) as the Roman garrison was slaughtered by Menahem in Jerusalem in violation of the oath. Menahem's invasion of the Temple and killing of the High Priest are also recorded by Josephus. The epilepsy is my own invention.

The siege and capture of Jotapata, Jerusalem, and Masada are all graphically described by Josephus. In fact, Josephus has given us the only contemporary account we have of the events at Masada, including Eleazar's speech exhorting his followers to commit mass suicide. How did Josephus know these things? Part of his information probably came from the Roman commander, Flavius Silva, but it is possible that he also spoke to someone who had actually lived on the Masada, for he reports that an old woman escaped, "along with another who was related to Eleazar, in intelligence and education superior to most women, and five little children." Thanks to Josephus, we know the reaction of Silva and his legionaries on that silent morning when they bridged the gap between platform and ramparts, greeted only by the flames of the still raging conflagrations and a "dreadful solitude." Coming at last upon the rows and rows of dead bodies, the Romans "did not exult over them as enemies but wondered at the courage of their resolve and the way in which so many had shown . . . an utter contempt of death."

But what of Alexandra bat Harsom? Did she exist? There was a House of Harsom, which was one of the "great houses of Israel" cited in the Talmud. It appears that one Eleazar ben Harsom was so wealthy "he owned a thousand ships and a thousand cities" and served as High Priest, or at least as a high priest, for eleven years. But while I have made use of the name and its connotations of wealth and power, Alexandra and all her family are fictitious.

Still, in many ways the character of Alexandra was prompted by an intriguing passage that I came across in Josephus' *Autobiography:*

> After the siege of Jotapata, I was in the hands of the Romans and was kept under guard while receiving every attention. Vespasian showed in many ways the honor in which he held me, and it was by his command that I married one of the women captives, a virgin and native of Caesarea. She did not, however, remain long with me, for she left me on my obtaining my release and accompanying Vespasian to Alexandria.

A few words about sources and spellings: Obviously, *The Jewish War,* by Flavius Josephus, was constantly at my side, in both the Thackeray and the Whiston translations from the Greek. In the more than twelve years of thought and research given to this project I have also read and studied more histories, articles, scholarly papers, and works of fiction than I can possibly list here. My "bibles," throughout, however, were Yigael Yadin's own *Masada: Herod's Fortress and the Zealots' Last Stand*, as well as his *Message of the Scrolls; Judea Weeping*, by George C. Brauer, Jr., and Professor Solomon Zeitlin's three volume study of *The Rise and Fall of the Judean State*. Mention must also be given to the guide book, *This is Masada*, by Gaalyah Cornfield, which made the ascent to and descent from Masada with me many times, and to works dealing with the Talmud and the Midrash by H. L. Strack and J. Goldin.

As for spellings, I found that the spelling of proper names and places from the period often varied according to the translator. Thus, Joav might also be written Joab or Yoav or even Yoab. In most cases I have relied on the work of modern Israeli scholars such as Yadin, but in one or two instances I have created my own version of a name of the period for my own reasons. Josef, for example, seemed an apt compromise between Yosef and the latinized Joseph. I have also made use of alternate spellings in a few places to differentiate between similarly named characters (Simon, Shimon, and Shimeon, for example).

I was as careful as possible regarding anachronisms, but in some cases the use of a word or term not in currency during the first century seemed excusable because it was so well known. "Khirbet Qumran," for example, is the Arab name for that area near the Dead Sea where scrolls believed to be the work of the Essenes were discovered in 1947, and so I have used that name even though the Essenes themselves, or anyone else of the time, would hardly have referred to "Qumran." Similarly, the Feast of Lights was not known as "the Hanukkah" until much later, although the work *hanukkah*, meaning "rededication," was always used in connection with the holiday. And while many of the sayings of the sages were incorporated into the Talmud and Midrash at a much later period than the time of this novel, it certainly seemed possible that they were quoted long before they were written down.

Finally, *The Tenth Measure* is a work of fiction, a personal vision of an epic story, not only of a people—my people—but of the human spirit—as seen through the eyes of a figure whose position has been precarious throughout history: a woman and a Jew.

—BRENDA LESLEY SEGAL

ABOUT THE AUTHOR

Brenda Lesley Segal, who was born in Philadelphia and graduated from Beaver College, is married to an Israeli; they now live in Bucks County, Pennsylvania with their two children.

The author of one previous novel, ALIYAH: A LOVE STORY (written in association with Marianne Kanter), Brenda Segal has been working on THE TENTH MEASURE for more than twelve years. She says of the book: "What I envisioned was an epic, not only of a people—my people—but of the human spirit. In the end, it was not the struggle of Jew or Christian against Roman that mattered so much as the struggle of reason, kindness, courage, love and simple human decency against ignorance, cruelty. and brutalization of soul—as seen through the eyes of a figure whose position has been precarious throughout history, a woman and a Jew."

trees p.320

MS READ-a-thon—
a simple way to start youngsters reading

Boys and girls between 6 and 14 can join the MS READ-a-thon and help find a cure for Multiple Sclerosis by reading books. And they get two rewards — the enjoyment of reading, and the great feeling that comes from helping others.

Parents and educators: For complete information call your local MS chapter. Or mail the coupon below.

Kids can help, too!